Clara and M

Michael Kelly

Serapion Books

Serapion Books

'Clara and Miles Act Up'

First Edition

2016

copyright © Michael Kelly
All rights reserved

ISBN 978-0-9554602-1-0

Printed and bound in Great Britain by Clays Ltd, St Ives plc

Cover illustration by Kowalska Art
http://kowalska-art.blogspot.fr

Cover assembly by Shore Books and Design
www.shore-books.co.uk

Set in Times New Roman 10 pt on Holmen Book Cream 52/82 paper

All trees were felled mercifully with one clean stroke

Dedicated to my mother and father.

Although little has changed since, it may be as well to note that this book was written and takes place before the election of 2010.

Chapter One

"Tell me about yourselves," said the marriage counsellor.

"I hardly know where to begin," said Clara. "We are an entirely average couple. Ordinary decent people of a type that has not quite died out, thank God. We have nothing to complain of. We both have our health and strength and I for one am superlatively beautiful. I am also intelligent, and Miles at least has the mother wit to recognise this and leave all higher cerebral functions to me."

"Ug," assented Miles cheerily.

The marriage counsellor frowned slightly.

"We are in our early twenties and have been married six months and are tremendously happy. Tell the man, Miles."

"Tremendously," said Miles.

"Tremendously happy," said Clara. "We can't stand to spend a minute apart."

"We're completely wrapped up in each other," said Miles.

"We barely notice other people," said Clara, "unless they are badly dressed, or ill-mannered, or we suspect them of being Communists. Are you a Communist, Doctor?"

"I, er – no," said the counsellor, half-smiling uncertainly.

"Good. Are any of your patients Communist?"

" … Not that I'm aware."

"Lucky for you," said Clara. "Communist women have notoriously hairy legs. It would be difficult for you to effect a reconciliation under those circumstances."

"His patients could be Communists without him knowing it," Miles pointed out.

"An excellent point, Miles. The ones we passed on the way in were certainly ugly enough. And they looked … "

"Mutinous."

"The *mot juste*, my fine young husband. They looked mutinous. Why did the previous couple look mutinous, Doctor? Had you ordered them to look adoringly at each other? I can understand their jibbing at that."

"My previous clients are none of your concern," said the counsellor, frowning again.

"I bet they *were* Communists," muttered Miles.

"So do I," said Clara. "I see they have left a copy of the Guardian behind."

"That is mine," said the counsellor, frowning a bit more.

"Oh!" said Clara, blinking. "Oh, I see. It's like that. Well, that's your affair, of course ... I don't presume to judge ... " She shifted her chair an inch back from the table and an inch closer to Miles; he reached out and patted her hand soothingly.

"Look here," said the counsellor, "what seems to be the problem?"

"Problem?" said Clara coldly. "What makes you think we have a problem?"

The counsellor chuckled, somewhat uneasily. "Well, you did make an appointment to see me, and so far all you've done is tell me how happy you are."

"We may have come here simply to boast," said Clara. "We are a happily married and entirely normal couple. Is that so hard for you to understand, you wretched pinko?"

"Look here – "

"Steady on, old girl," said Miles. "He's right, you know, we did make the appointment."

"Well, I mean – just because we wash under our arms and don't live in a commune, this goateed nihilist, steeped in the works of Havelock Ellis and Jackie Collins, has the temerity to insinuate – "

"Look here – "

"I think we should tell him," said Miles.

Clara looked away.

"Tell me what?" asked the marriage counsellor gently.

"Miles feels," said Clara after a long silence, "that I do not accede to his bestial demands often enough."

"His – ?"

"Bestial," repeated Clara, "demands." She took a tissue from her handbag and dabbed at her eyes.

"Ah," said the counsellor.

"Precisely," said Clara.

"Perhaps you had better tell me what these demands are."

"Must I?" Clara looked down.

"This is something of a sexual nature which Miles enjoys but which you find disagreeable?"

Clara nodded.

"Perhaps if I ... confidentiality is assured ... if you could give me some hint of the, nature of the ..."

"He takes his penis," said Clara in a tragic whisper, "and inserts it into my womanhood."

The counsellor was silent.

"You mean, sex," he said after a moment.

"Must you use that word?"

"Sexual intercourse? You don't enjoy it?"

"Does any woman?"

"Well … yes," said the counsellor. "Most women do, you know."

Clara bridled. "That may be what your dockyard whore of a wife tells you, but I can assure you that decent women do *not*."

"Now look here – "

"Steady on, old girl."

"I apologise," said Clara coldly. "If you have married a nymphomaniac or a Frenchwoman that is of course your good fortune. Miles should have done likewise instead of thrusting himself incontinently upon a decent English girl."

The counsellor shuffled some papers on his desk. "Perhaps … perhaps I could talk to Miles alone for a minute?"

"Why?" asked Clara in alarm. "To persuade him to divorce me, or pay a visit to a Frenchwoman?"

"No, no, of course not. I only want to establish … to get some idea of Miles's, er, technique, or, or … when he – "

"Technique!" snorted Clara. "He thrusts himself upon me like a piston in the Queen Mary's engine room."

"Ahm. I see. It sounds to me as though Miles may be being a bit precipitate in, in – "

"Precipitate! I'll say he's precipitate. He barely gives me time to don my sleepmask and earplugs."

"Ahm. Miles, have you, er, do you … do you take the time to, ah, give due attention to foreplay?"

"Foreplay?" Clara yelped. "*Foreplay?* What country are we in? See what comes of joining the Common Market! Foreplay, forsooth! Why on Earth would I want to prolong the agony?"

"Ahm," said the marriage counsellor.

"Now I see why you wanted to get Miles alone, to share all your depraved post-modern tricks with him."

"Perhaps I could speak to *you* alone," said the counsellor desperately.

"I have no secrets from my husband," said Clara taking Miles's hand, "and I prefer not to be left alone in a room with a man who has acquired a taste for *foreplay*."

"Very well. I … I mean no, indelicacy, but … have you ever been attracted to a woman's body?"

Clara looked puzzled. "I find my own body more attractive than Miles's, certainly, but then so would anyone with a shred of aesthetic discernment."

"What I am trying to – "

"Oh!" exclaimed Clara. "Oh! Oh! I know what you are insinuating! See, Miles, see! Because I object to your simian assaults he is trying to imply I am an unnatural woman! I ask you, Doctor, are these the shoes of a sapphic?"

"No, no, forgive me if I … you understand, I'm just trying to establish … Tell me, why did you marry Miles?"

"Out of girlish dreams of romance which he proceeded to shatter as rudely as he did my hymen, and the mistaken belief that he would be a good provider."

"Ah. And you feel that Miles is not, in fact, a good provider?"

"Hardly. If it were left to Miles we should have starved to death or been reduced to appearing on television. Fortunately I am independently wealthy. Miles has battened on me like a French farmer onto an EU subsidy. He is quite feckless at times; some of his ancestors were Irish."

"Ah … some people might find remarks like those offensive, you know."

"I am distantly connected to the Duke of Wellington and so entitled to make jokes about the Irish," said Clara.

"It's still offensive."

"So is your beard."

"Steady on, dear," said Miles.

The marriage counsellor regarded Clara for some moments and took a deep breath.

"You implied just now that you don't find Miles's body aesthetically attractive," he said.

Clara and Miles exchanged glances.

"I think we should tell him," said Miles.

"Plainly there is no dissembling," sighed Clara. "He will run us to earth in the end. He is some Inspector Javert of the marital arts."

The counsellor waited.

"The fact is, Doctor … " Clara faltered and looked down. "I believe the problem lies with my husband's penis. There is something very, very wrong with it," she said darkly.

"In what way?"

"It is hideously malformed."

"It is not," said Miles.

"He is in denial," said Clara. "It is a thing of eldritch horror. Show him, Miles."

Miles rose and took a step forward. The counsellor hastened to forestall him.

"Ahm – if Miles's genitals are, are unusual in some way, it is a matter for your doctor – "

Clara raised an eyebrow. "But you are a doctor, or so I understood. They give you that appellation on the television."

of course, between Miles's vegetable torpor and lack of moral fibre and the qualities of my sainted parents – my father," said Clara with a reminiscent smile, "killed many Germans. Miles, rather wetly, has killed none."

The counsellor massaged his brow with the heel of his thumb. "Your father was a war hero?"

Clara blinked. "Who mentioned anything about the war?"

"You said he … "

"There is," said Clara, "no close-season for patriotic feeling."

The counsellor looked from one to the other. "I really would like to talk to Miles alone," he said.

"He's going to have me committed," cried Clara in alarm. "Just because I come from a household with one mother and a working father who killed Germans off his own initiative."

"I – look here – " The counsellor's mouth worked. "None of what you've told me – I have to think that – this has to be some sort of … bloody Murray!" he exclaimed suddenly.

Clara raised an eyebrow and exchanged a glance with Miles. "Murray?" she enquired.

"Murray." The Counsellor grinned at them and nodded to himself. "Hah! Murray." He rose abruptly and started to pace around the room, flinging open cupboards, looking behind the curtains and peering intently into corners.

"I am scared, Miles," said Clara, reaching for her husband's arm. "Hold me." They clutched each other as they watched the counsellor in wide-eyed alarm.

"All right, where are they?" he chuckled.

"Where are whom?"

"The cameras."

"Cameras?" echoed Miles.

Clara sighed. "He's rumbled us. Took you long enough, didn't it? There's a pinhead camera just over the door, the sound gear's in your plant-pot there, you won't find them." Her accent had suddenly turned into a variety of the demotic known as Estuary English.

"Hah! I knew it!" The counsellor squinted at the doorframe and squatted to examine the rubber plant in the corner. "Remarkable … then I suppose Susan must have … so Murray set the … "

"Yeah, he thought it'd be a giggle if we turned up and pretended to be a couple of reactionary young fogeys and, you know, give you the run-around. You took it well I must say. He wants to put it out next week, you'll get an appearance fee of course."

"When I get hold of him …" Shaking his head ruefully the counsellor perched on the desk and grinned. "You really had me ... you were word-perfect ... I mean some of it I was, what? but you were so straight-faced."

"Well, it's a role we play a lot."

"And the ... the penis," the counsellor laughed.

"That really is his cock, actually."

"Yeah, that exemplary thing, if you could put that in writing," said Miles.

They all laughed. "Don't flatter yourself, it's still hideous," said Clara suddenly. She gathered her handbag and the phallic photograph and she and Miles rose. "Well, thanks for letting us waste your time."

"Listen," said the counsellor as he walked them to the door, "do you think I could have a look over the tape before you air it? I may come over as a bit, er, tetchy in places. Frankly, I, I wouldn't sign the release without ..."

"What tape, you shallow and foolish man?" There was no longer any Estuary English in Clara's voice; only cold contempt.

"The ... the cameras ... surely ... "

"There are no cameras, you asinine mountebank. There is no TV show. We don't know who Murray is. We really are reactionary young fogeys. We just decided to annoy you because we find your television appearances vapid and aesthetically outrageous, not to mention politically suspect. If it is any consolation, amusing ourselves like this helps keep our marriage strong."

The therapist's mouth hung open; then words started to come out of it.

"That," said Clara outside, "was more fun than anything else we've done involving your penis."

"He said it was exemplary," said Miles proudly.

"I can't believe he took it so badly. He's always urging people to role-play."

"I can't believe we did that." Miles was not so accomplished an actor as Clara and at this stage in their career he still found a certain nervous reaction setting in after successfully involving a third party in their games. "That thing he said as he were leaving ... "

"About paying the bill?"

"No, before that."

"The getting a job thing?"

"Yes. Do you think he might have had a point? I mean ... that was fun, I admit, but what exactly had he done to deserve us, when you get down to it?"

"He annoys me, Miles, that should be enough for you. How can you even question his deserts after the fatuous way he simpered when he thought it was a telly stunt? He is inherently evil. All that talk of compromise and bestial needs and trust instead of operatic love or, or solid companionship. Sex and positions and foreplay all the time when impressionable grannies may be watching. Tricking gullible women into faking an interest in sex rather than regarding it as an onerous duty ... Besides, I really did want someone to take a look at your penis, just to check. Exemplary, indeed!" She scowled at the picture and made her scared face. "On which foul planet, I should like to know. ... And besides, he was in the phone book and you can make appointments ... I'm aware there are more deserving targets but they aren't so easy to stalk. I'll tell you what, though – he has given me a revelation. Did you hear the buffoon carry on, the relief in his voice? You could do anything to anyone nowadays if they thought it was a TV prank. If we draw up letterheads, business cards ... register a production company ... anything, anything ... we can get them all ... "

"It will end in tears."

"It will end when the streets and lanes of England are *purified*. If you won't let me start my Death Squad, this is the only ... " She suddenly threw her head back and laughed maniacally. Then she sighed and said, "I have suddenly grown weary, Miles; please tickle my breasts for me."

Miles guffawed and blushed. "Here?" They had reached a high street.

"No-one will notice."

But someone was approaching.

"Oh Christ."

"Oh, for a gun, for a bomb, for ten well-trained men," Clara snarled with venom.

A woman with a clipboard trolling for lawsuits for a nearby Accident Claims shop walked up to them.

"Have you suffered an accident or injury in the last twelve months?"

"Indeed we have," said Clara funereally, showing her the photograph. "Look what it did to my husband's penis."

Chapter Two

Once at a party Clara said, "Things are awful, though, aren't they? I think I would enjoy the first ten days of a revolution, the hangings and shootings and arson. The impalements, the castrations, the auto da fes. Or is it autos da fe? I can never remember, which is embarrassing at our local Christian Revival League meetings. And of course the brainings, the slow disembowellings, the pullings apart with wild horses or tractors, the garrottings with barbed wire, the inflatings with helium until people explode, and so on – we have all had these daydreams of a kinder better world. But after the initial excitement I suppose it would be even drearier people giving the orders, I mean real hot-heads. I'm not sure complete liberty would be a solution because some people are so bloody dreadful. It seems insoluble. Sooner or later political problems and potential solutions seem to segue into problems of the human condition and the spite of that sinister force Ahab complained of. And I think whaling has been outlawed. At any rate it's hard to get a licence for it unless you're very well connected. I certainly don't think you could get a licence to hunt a whale in order to strike at a sinister force any more. My husband has forbidden me to have a whaling boat anyway, don't you think that's mean? I am not allowed a death squad either. So much for women's lib. That's my husband standing just there. Do not be deceived by his expression of docile amiability. His penis is quite frightening. He will show it to you if you ask him nicely, but I *don't* recommend it. Every other Thursday he takes it and ... but I don't know you well enough to burden you with the horror. Anyway my husband and I have decided, or rather I have decided on his behalf, that the only thing left is to play. We frolic, skip and gambol like idiots amid the ruins of poor old England. I think the biggest divide in the world is not between rich and poor or Christian and infidel or even right and left, but between those who primarily laugh and those who are primarily solemn. The latter tend to run things because the former are too busy playing with fart cushions. I think God is a laugher and the world is his fart cushion. He likes to sit on us and hear us squeal. That is very deep if you think about it. It is not that I believe that if you laugh at the forces of dreariness they will go away. Jokes can be against the law now. If you laugh at them they will probably arrest you and just go on stealing everyone's money and making awful laws and pontificating solemnly. We laugh purely for our own sake, and because I didn't pay enough attention in chemistry to know how to make bombs. We have learned to laugh with the lofty detachment of Mozart at the end of *Steppenwolf*. I have an enchanting laugh, would you like to hear it? HURRRR." Her vis-a-vis blinked and took a step backwards as she made this throaty gurgling noise. "The point is I am probably just as helpless and confused as anyone," Clara continued. "Still I think Britain must have been a more pleasant place to live in once and could be again, don't you agree? Or are you a Communist? You may say something now."

The woman she was talking to closed her mouth and then started to open it again.

"Too late," said Clara, "I have thought of more to say. I expect I am cleverer than you. Perhaps you should take conversation classes if you wish to shine more in society. A key point is not to monopolise, I gather. The great thing about living nowadays is that you probably just think there is something wrong with my brain and that you will have to put up with me or I will sue you for discrimination. My husband and I have elected to believe in souls rather than brain chemistry. However I sometimes think the world should be divided up according to the results of the Myers-Briggs *or* Briggs-Myers personality test, each type being given their own country so as not to annoy the others. I came out as Brooding Misunderstood Introvert-Empath with a Quick Temper. That is the best one to be. Other notables include Michelangelo and Genghis Khan, and that weatherman with the northern accent. We will wipe the rest of you out in due course. The great advantage of my scheme is that all the people with the type of brain that enjoys making laws to push other people around for their own good could all go off to an island somewhere – because this one is mine – and push each other around and be dreary and solemn and concerned to their heart's content, while the rest of us enjoy ourselves drinking, smoking, driving without due care and attention and shooting polar bears in the face *just because we can*. I would not really shoot a polar bear unless I wanted to eat it or have a fur coat, or I thought it looked at me the wrong way, but it would be nice to know I could if I wanted to. The thing is people really can't get along. I think if I was an evil alien overlord I would make the whole population of Earth stand on the Isle of Wight and fight to the death. I think about that often. It would be like that hippy rock festival but with more violence. In the early stages I imagine it would be depressingly tribal. Strategic alliances would be formed along socioethnic lines. Finns ganging up with Latvians to kill Spaniards and Turks, homosexual Chinamen getting together with Russian Christian biker gangs to do in the Cornish. I would want the midgets on my side. Those bastards are sneaky: I have never trusted them. But in the endgame we would all have to turn on each other. Eventually there would be one person left and he, or in my daydream she, would be the winner and free to impose her values on the empty echoing Earth. I was good at woodcraft and general sneaking around in the Guides so I would do pretty well. I think I would hole up in a little guesthouse I know in Cowes where I used to stay as a child, until most of the people were dead, and then make my move, slaughtering the landlady on my way out. The only problem is, could I kill my husband Miles? The answer is yes, especially if it was a Thursday. But I am fond of him really and would save him till last. I think that is the only possible basis for a marriage, that if aliens forced you to kill everyone else on Earth he would be the one you saved until last. It would be quite tragic and romantic really, a great basis for an opera. I suppose it would be difficult to stage. I might even defy the aliens and spare him. I don't think I could face his reproachful eyes as I shot him. I would have to focus on his penis. Do you have a husband? Does he have a penis? They are quite startling things, aren't they? Mother never warned me. I think she started to once but then she broke down sobbing. I find you very sympathetic. Are you Saved?"

"I'm afraid I don't believe in God," said the woman with some firmness when she grasped the significance of this.

"Well, you will be an adornment to Hell," said Clara kindly. "All the demons will really enjoy raping you. I only enquired after the health of your soul because I admired your knockers. Do you think mine are pretty too?"

The woman gave a nervous laugh and started to move away.

"I ... have to talk to someone over there."

"How hurtful. Can I have your phone number?"

"I ... excuse me a moment."

"I love you," said Clara brokenly as the woman fled. "Well that got rid of her," she said happily to Miles who had now joined her. "She would have monopolised me ruthlessly because of her unacknowledged sapphic crush on me. We have ventured out into the decadence in order to schmooze and network and further our careers, not flirt. Who the hell was she, anyway?"

"The one who edits that magazine you wanted to write for."

"Arse. Why can't important people wear badges so I know to suck up? She said something mildly positive about the government and sort of triggered me. I suspect her of Communism and am putting her on my list, underlined. It is an awful magazine anyway. Who were you just networking with? You were getting on like a house on fire."

"A man who has a plan to generate green power from hamster-wheels," said Miles enthusiastically. "I got his phone number."

"The thing is I believe you. Also it's possible he was trying to get rid of you. It is a good job we neither want nor need careers, really, isn't it?"

"We are doomed to starve to death eventually, though."

"We have enough money left to arse around happily for a few years still, yes? After that we will blow our brains out. Bags I blow yours out first." She looked around and sighed. "Shall we go home then? I have realised there is unlikely to be anyone here as interesting as me. Or shall I try to talk to someone else? I might get better at it if I persevere. Since we married and became recluses I am out of practise dealing with people who don't hang on my every word in the hope I'll let them touch my breasts."

"You're supposed to pause and listen to them talk once in a while."

"But they break my train of thought. Honestly, if Dr Johnson or someone was reincarnated as a beautiful woman and came to a rubbish party you'd think people would have the taste to keep their gobs shut and admire the flow, not to mention his pretty dress."

"Come on, let's make an effort."

"It's hopeless though. Everyone is talking about television, or seems liable to do so at a moment's notice."

"Well, your friend sort of works in television, and so presumably do a lot of her friends."

"It's everyone though. It puts us at a disadvantage." Clara had finally shot their television, in a sudden fit of aesthetic revulsion and patriotism, with both barrels of one of the double-barrelled shotguns Miles had forbidden her to buy, some weeks before. Prior to that they had only watched it in short bursts, with Clara's hand poised on the remote control ready to extinguish it as soon as anything ugly or politically suspect came on, which was frequently. "Perhaps we should befriend some blind people."

"Oh, there's actually a blind man around somewhere."

"But he won't know how pretty I am. Also I'll probably start talking loudly to him out of confusion. Anyway he probably works in television too. He is probably the supreme controller. It would explain the degraded aesthetic values."

"There are people talking about politics."

"Probably a bad idea for me to get involved."

"There are people talking about books."

She narrowed her eyes suspiciously. "Which books? Probably rubbish modern books full of drugs and serial killers and existential whining and brand names and pop culture references and environmentalist propaganda and not enough semi-colons. One day I will write a book that is all semi-colons and pretty dresses and heroism and killing polar bears and bombing the EU parliament. When it becomes a best-seller the national revival will start."

"Those people look nice."

"Yes. Except I don't like their clothes. Or their voices. Or their faces, really. Their niceness is quite hard to pin down. It borders on degraded evil. Besides I am hungry."

There were outside caterers at this party, which was a rather good party sprawling over every room of a big posh house in London in the middle of the day. Further description is unnecessary as we aren't going to be there that long, and neither are Clara and Miles. There were waiters and waitresses in waistcoats carrying trays of things to eat. Clara grabbed one of the former and ordered him to stand still while she grazed.

"You'd think I never fed you," said Miles as she at length released him and moved on.

"It is rather nice food however. Perhaps bespoke party catering is a job we could do when the money runs out."

"You sort of can't cook."

"You almost can, though, and I can make good sandwiches. I like to make sandwiches. I always think it's a shame to waste them on other people, though. And I suppose we would be expected to cater to corporate swine and transnational Communist oligarchs."

"We could stipulate we will only feed poor people and hungry patriots."

"It is a gap in the market. Miles where are you going?"

"I just – "

"Don't leave me! You know how shy and insecure I am. Besides I need an audience. Take my arm. Don't let go of my arm. Let go of my arm and see what happens." Miles let go of Clara's arm and she started to slowly topple forward, full length, face first, like a felled tree, until he grabbed her again. "You see, I will fall over if you let go of me, my inner ear is playing up."

"Well let's go over – "

"No this way looks more interesting, I think there is a better class of person in the next room."

"I just want to get my drink, I left a drink on the mantelpiece."

"Miles! You've turned into an alcoholic! You're stashing drinks every five steps ahead of you." Miles rarely drank, actually, and Clara almost never drank at all, which was unfortunate, Miles sometimes thought disloyally, as it meant they couldn't use that as an excuse for some of the things she said or did. "Next you will start to beat me, and cause embarrassing scenes, and marriages are undermined when the husband takes on the wife's duties."

"I put it down and forgot about it."

"And now it is more interesting than I am," she said sadly.

"Just a step this way, woman! I can almost – "

"You used to say I was more intoxicating than any drink."

"I must have been pissed when I did."

Miles succeeded in dragging her close enough to the mantelpiece for him to grab his drink, and took a sip.

"And so he pulls the liquid coverlet over his head."

"I am somewhat nervous. We *are* out of practice at socialising since we moved to the country and went mad."

"Everyone here is a Communist anyway."

"If you would – not see people like that you would get on better with the world."

In truth there were a lot of people here of a type that Clara had decided were the enemy. Miles felt obliged to stick fairly close to her in case of scenes. Among other natural targets there was a comedian she detested and someone who was something in the government; Miles hoped she wouldn't recognise these and had been assiduously trying to steer her into rooms that didn't contain one of them. Others merely did the kinds of jobs she found suspect, which at this point included almost every occupation apart from honest manual toil or running a small business. She was especially down on what she referred to as the media-government nexus and since moving to the countryside had more than once declared that large parts of London would probably have to be cut loose from the country, towed out to sea and sunk, following the revolution.

"If you aren't going to be nice and make an effort we *should* go home," he said.

"But everyone is ignoring me," she complained pouting. "Oh apart from him," she said glancing at a man who was staring at them intently from a few feet away. "He is stalking me but thinks you are. Wait here a moment."

She moved over to the watching man and spoke a few low earnest words to him. The man muttered something, staring at Miles over her shoulder. Clara shook her head and murmured something else and the man's eyes widened and became alarmed.

Clara came back and steered Miles away.

"It is quite amusing. He started to talk to me," she explained, "and was at first merely nice but boring. But he soon became too flirty, and deeply boring, and an open Communist, so I drew his attention to you and told him you were my violent ex-husband Brian, who follows me around morbidly everywhere and would tear him limb from limb if he talked to me too much."

"Clara! Why didn't you just – "

"Because this was more fun. Unfortunately it has backfired. He has constituted himself my protector and is following me around morbidly to guard me against you. I've just told him not to hit you for now, and that I have to talk to you for a bit to persuade you not to kill yourself. I said that you often carry poison with you and would not be above drinking it in public, or indeed using it on other people, thereby spoiling the party for everyone."

"For Christ's sake, woman!" Miles cried quite loudly.

"You will meet someone else, Brian," Clara cried even louder, looking at him with soulful pitying eyes. Several people turned to look. The man who had appointed himself her protector took an irresolute step forward, fists clenched, and then halted.

Miles swallowed his drink and stalked off to get another. When he looked round Clara was gone. Going to look for her he unexpectedly spotted his friend Zig Grant. Zig worked in publishing. Miles had literary ambitions and occasionally pitched him ideas which Zig deflected with expert tact. Miles seized him joyfully now and they went through it again.

" ... anyway, listen, listen," Miles said eagerly soon after the initial greetings. "I've had this brilliant idea. This is the one. Listen: a book that's designed to put people to sleep!"

"Right," said Zig Grant neutrally.

"No, but think about it. For insomniacs ... "

When Zig at length managed to detach himself Miles saw Clara not far away, talking to a flushed and very drunken man who was nodding eagerly and occasionally sneaking a glance down her cleavage.

"Sexy and violent," Miles heard her saying as he approached, in a voice that was not her own. "Ballsy and relevant."

"Excellent, excellent," said the drunken man nodding excitedly.

"I mean a complete re-imagining," said Clara in Estuary. "Something that really speaks to today. There are all kinds of parallels. And you won't believe the sex the man got."

The drunken man nodded. "Done. Done. We'll do it."

Clara caught sight of Miles and lowered her voice. " ... better go ... violent ex-husband ... "

The drunken man handed her a business card and said, "Done, call me," and they shook hands.

"Miles, Miles!" cried Clara happily, grabbing him and bouncing up and down in excitement, "I have just sold a ten-part television drama on the life and times of Robert Walpole!"

"Congratulations!" They hugged. "And Zig Grant just said my idea for a soporific book was interesting!"

"Oh well done darling!"

"You see? You see what happens when you make an effort!"

"Yes, yes! Let's see what else we can bag! Split up, split up! Work the room! Obviously we have been cramping each other's styles. Next I will try to sell the film rights!"

Clara dashed off eagerly to buttonhole someone else. Miles looked around at a loss for a moment. He was actually almost as rubbish at socialising as Clara usually was, and apart from Zig and Clara's well-connected friend who had invited them didn't know anyone here. He had developed a technique in such situations of going up to unattached people and demanding, "Who the hell are you?" with comedy aggression. He did this to a nearby man he liked the looks of now.

The man eyed him up and down and sourly replied that he was the host of the party and who the hell was Miles? Miles replied that he was married to Clara who was a friend of Stephanie's. The host asked who the hell was Stephanie? Miles was nonplussed. It was rather a fun and freewheeling party and he doubted that more than a fraction of the people had been directly invited, but the host looked quite unduly annoyed at not knowing Stephanie or Clara or Miles. Also Miles thought he had overdone the aggression of the "Who the hell are you?" and that the host had been quite alarmed at him. So he mumbled something and went away, far away, immediately.

Before the memory could grow inhibiting he quickly tried, "Who the hell are you?" on another person, and it turned out to be a quite famous person who was either miffed not to be recognised or thought Miles was taking the piss, and went brusquely away from Miles at once. So Miles went to get another drink.

"I think you had better leave," said a voice at his elbow just after he had succeeded. He looked round to see the man who had made himself Clara's protector.

"Oh Christ," said Miles.

"I think you should just do us all a favour and go," said the man. "She doesn't want you here. She doesn't want you at all any more. It's over."

Miles decided to play along. "She told you that?" he said, devastated. "She actually said that? In those words?"

"You have to face it. You had your chance." He jabbed a finger at Miles. He was showing signs of the kind of aggressive bluster that comes of being quite scared. "I think you're sick. I think you need help. Any man who would shoot a television because he thinks his wife fancies Peter Snow ... you've got something wrong in your head."

"And I suppose you think she'd be better off with you?" Miles demanded suspiciously.

"Well ... she could do worse," said the man. "And let me tell you I don't believe your threats. I don't even believe you carry poison. Do it, that's what I say. Off yourself. Do us all a favour."

Miles glowered at him for a second than walked off to the table he had just got a drink from, where there was still a tray of filled wine-glasses. Standing with his back to the man, he rummaged inside his jacket for a bit and then paused leaning over the tray. Then he came back to him, smiling and carrying a glass of wine in each hand.

"This is all a misunderstanding," he said. "Let's have a drink and thrash it out." He thrust a brimming glass towards the man, who backed away in alarm and went pale. "Drink with me!" Miles insisted quite aggressively. "Drink to the freedom of my wife! Drink, damn you, drink!" he insisted psychotically, thrusting the glass right at the man's mouth. The man shook his head, lips tightly sealed, and fled.

Soon afterward Miles saw him muttering to two other men and attracting their attention to Miles, and shortly after that he saw one of these also discussing him with the sour-faced host.

Miles moved on. He encountered Zig Grant again, who talked to him of a mutual acquaintance and then introduced him to some nearby people who were nice.

Just when Miles was starting to enjoy himself one of the caterer's waitresses handed him a note and said, "A woman asked me to give you this."

"Hmm!" said Zig Grant raising an eyebrow.

"Which woman?" asked Miles.

"Er, the woman over there surrounded by shouting people," said the waitress.

"That would be my wife then," said Miles without looking.

He unfolded the scrap of paper. On it were nine words – a quote, he remembered, from a Kipling story. They were:

PERSECUTED FOR THE LORD'S SAKE
SEND WING OF REGIMENT

Draining another drink en route he went over. Not everyone around Clara was shouting at her. One woman was crying real tears. Another woman was swearing to herself in a soft but vicious voice, and there was a man trying to talk in a reasonable voice, and a man swearing at Clara in a voice just below a shout, and some people just listening. But there was a lot of shouting. Miles supposed it was a global warming conversation or similar.

Just as he got there there was a lull in the shouts and he heard Clara say, in a rather good David Attenborough voice, "Startled by the approach of an unorthodox idea, the herd huddles together for comfort."

The shouts and swears broke out again. Miles wriggled through the crowd, grabbed her by the arm and started to drag her away. She resisted and slapped at his hand and muttered, "I've changed my mind, I don't want to be rescued."

"Come on," said Miles continuing to pull.

"Let go of me, Brian!" Clara shouted loudly. "Help! Help! It's my violent ex-husband Brian!" She succeeded in breaking free of him and people moved between her and Miles. "Keep away! Keep him away from me! He isn't allowed near me! Thirty feet, Brian!" she cried pointing. "Thirty feet! Someone get a tape measure!"

"Clara – "

There were arms holding him, pulling him away.

"Let me go!" Miles protested.

"Come on, let's not make a scene," urged a soothing voice.

"She's my wife!"

"You have to let her go," said a sympathetic woman.

"Shall we call the police?"

"Search him for poison!" cried Clara's cavalier. "I tell you he's been poisoning the drinks!"

"Thank you," Miles heard Clara say behind him as he was dragged resisting away. "Now as for you, you silly little bitch – "

The shouts broke out louder behind him. There was the sound of a shriek and a glass shattering. Miles took advantage of the diversion of attention to break free of the arms holding him and slip off into the crowd, now a dense one around the twin attractions.

"What the hell are you attacking *me* for?" he heard Clara's voice. "I'm on *your* side, you moron! I'm trying to tell you to enjoy your life! It has as much scientific basis as the bloody tooth-fairy! The only footprints you ought to be worrying about are the ones made by your overgrown coffin-like feet!"

More shouts, shrieks, sobs, swears.

"Brian!" cried Clara suddenly. "I want my Brian! Help me, Brian!"

Miles succeeded in crowbarring his way through to her.

"Here he is! Brian is here now and he will fight you all." She clutched onto him and said, "Beat them up for me and I will get back with you, Brian. Please address any further objections to Brian, everyone. His scientific understanding is limited but he is psychotically violent and has the strength of ten men. See how he is trying to pull my arm off."

Grimly, relentlessly, Miles pulled her out of the ruckus, out of the room, out of the party.

"Sorry, Stephanie," Clara said en route. "I tried my best. Sorry Miles," she added in a more genuinely contrite voice. "Honestly, though, what an insensitive bunch. Anyone can see I am merely compensating for shyness."

Clara and Miles rarely went to parties these days because of Clara's shyness. On the whole this was probably best both for them and for the people whose parties they didn't go to.

Chapter Three

Clara and Miles were sexually role-playing. After rummaging through their dressing-up box in dissatisfaction for a while Clara had donned a long black cloak and put a white armrest-cover off a chair over her head. Then she had dressed Miles in a nondescript grey jacket and put a metal kitchen mixing bowl on his head.

"I'm jealous of the cloak," said Miles. "Why do you always hog the cloak?"

"It is not a cloak, it is a nun's habit. Note my expression of piety."

"Aha. And I am?"

"A Nazi stormtrooper."

"Um."

"It is a terrible oversight that the dressing-up box doesn't run to either of those costumes. We must mount a shopping expedition and rectify it forthwith."

"Bags not me. So we're playing ... "

"The Nazi stormtrooper and the nun, Miles."

"Um." Miles was not as disconcerted by this as he might have been. Clara's sexual role-playing scenarios were rarely vulgar and never straightforward. Furthermore, they almost never resulted in sex occurring. "So I ... "

"You were born in Moenchengladbach in 1912, the son of a humble metalworker, painfully self-educated to a limited degree; you have looked into Wittgenstein but have to move your lips when you read him. Prior to the Reichstag fire you had drifted through various extreme left-wing groups. When the Nazis came to power Ernst Rohm saved you from arrest, took you into the Brownshirts and made you his bum-boy. You survived the purges following the Night of the Long Knives thanks to the personal intervention of the mystically-inclined Himmler, whom you had impressed by demonstrating a disappearing-egg-in-brown-paper-bag routine you picked up during your Weimar cabaret years. He thinks this could be the key to world domination but you know if he ever learns the secret he will no longer have a reason to keep you alive, and will also steal your gigs performing at the SS childrens' parties. 'Tell me ze secret of ze disappearing egg,' Himmler says to you wheedlingly, examining the brown paper bag in bafflement. 'Go on, I vill be your best friend,' but you never give in. Life has made you bitter and somewhat coarse, but deep down there remains something vulnerable and tender. Once patrolling the woods near Berchtesgarden you were transfixed and transported by the sight and sound of a lark singing on a frosty branch across a frozen lake, a moment of surpassing beauty you have never been able to articulate to anyone. The only thing more beautiful you have ever beheld is me.

"The daughter of a brilliant but suicidal concert pianist and an aristocrat, I became a Communist through a combination of idealism and teenage skin trouble, since cleared up. Our paths used to cross at meetings and we would argue about the legacy of Rosa Luxemburg. You fell passionately in love with me and one night after a rally we embarked on a short-lived and unhappy affair. Indeed your love-making was so inept that it caused me to renounce materialism altogether. I fell under the influence of Simone Weil and in due course became a nun. However I chafed at the constraints of convent life and was eventually placed as a nanny to a vast family of children a la The Sound of Music. As the scene opens I am smuggling seventeen of them across the Swiss border; their doting father is awaiting me on the other side with another twenty-eight.

"You stop me at the border and I see your face for the first time since 1934, when unknown to you I saw you in the Tiergarten trying to impress your new Brownshirt chums in a power-belching competition while Rohm twanged your lederhosen braces. Still a Communist at the time, I was in the process of bombing a bourgeois picnic but was so saddened by what you had become I could not go through with it. We can fill in the rest of the details as we go along. It's a fairly trite scenario but let's see where it leads us. So now we meet."

"Um."

Clara skipped dramatically across the lounge.

"Come along children! Freedom! Freedom is over the next mountain! Wait, let's go outside."

They went out into the back garden and the early afternoon sunshine.

Clara skipped dramatically across the lawn.

"Come along children! Freedom! Just beyond that shed is Switzerland, the land of chocolate and no-questions-asked banking. We are almost there! Nothing can stop us now."

Miles shouldered a yard-brush as a rifle and goose-stepped up and down. He saw Clara and turned and levelled his weapon.

"Halt, schweinhunden, or – argh, hide!" He crouched and scurried to one side. "Someone on the road!"

Due to the way the road curved a portion of their back garden could be seen from a small stretch of it, distantly, through a gap in the trees. Miles had just goose-stepped across exactly this portion and, belatedly, had seen a woman and child walking up just that stretch of the lane looking towards him.

"No there isn't," said Clara. "Where?"

"They've gone now," said Miles peeking out from behind the shed. "We really have to plant something in that gap if we're going to carry on like this."

"You're paranoid, it's far too far to see. Come on, start. Come along children, freedom!" she cried, skipping, for the third time.

"Halt, schweinhunden, or ich scheisse!" Miles pointed his brush weapon again.

Clara turned and gasped.

"Klaus! Klaus Bumfuckenbumf! That I should meet you here! That's your name, by the way."

"Well, then yours is Matilda Krapp."

"I revel in it. Klaus, Klaus! Thanks to the mercy of God! I feared you were some troglodyte stormtrooper. But you of all people will not prevent our escape."

"Alas, Gnädiges Fräulein," said Miles with a cold stiff bow, "I have my duty to ze fatherland to think of. You must certainly be arrested and all zhese kleine kinder vith you. Unless ... "

"Unless?" Clara dramatically clasped her hands over her heart. Her acting in these sorts of situations tended to recall the silent era of cinema.

"Unless you accompany me into this woodshed und show me your bustenblumen, und zen let me put ze villy on you."

"Miles! Is that really what you'd say?"

"Yes," said Miles.

"Do it properly."

"All right, all right. I stare at you, devastated, with burning eyes." Miles assumed a broken whisper. "Tildchen. Mein liebling, mein herz, meine kleine flugzeug. How many years has it been? How many years alone in ze vilderness? And now, now, you have come back to me. May I please to see your bustenblumen and then to put ze villy on you?"

Clara looked away and pressed the back of a hand to her brow.

"Never! I am the bride of God now!"

"You alvays vere a bourgeois social climber."

"Oh Klaus, Klaus, you whose sexual ineptitude and unusual penis led me to renounce the physical world. I have so much to thank you for. I have found religion now and I am happy. Can't you be happy for me?"

"If you will be happy for me. I have found Nazism and it has opened up a whole new world to me. The rape and the uniforms alone are worth the subscription fees. Now trip into the woodshed smartly and let's get horizontal, ja?"

"I clutch the multifarious children to my bosom protectively and they glower at you, sparking guilt from whatever vestige of humanity is left."

"I win them over with the disappearing-egg-in-brown-paper-bag routine, and, wide-eyed, they insist that you should certainly accompany this marvellous wizard into the woodshed and show him your bristols."

"Damn you! Is there nothing you won't stoop to?"

"Nothing vatsoever. Life has made me bitter and somewhat coarse, in fact downright unrefined. You should see the way I eat peas now."

"Oh no! But I taught you the genteel way to do it!"

"There are no bibs and silver tweezers, Fräulein, on the Russian front."

"A gentleman would have found some."

"I am no gentleman. You vill accompany me to ze voodshed and let me put ze villy on you, or I vill shoot the Von Trapp children before your very eyes."

"Do your worst," said Clara contemptuously. "I hate their singing anyway."

"You are bluffing, Fräulein."

"You are the only one given to bluff. Wittgenstein never played for Tottenham, I have looked it up. You were bluffing then and you are bluffing now."

"Zen you leave me no choice." Miles massacred invisible Von Trapps with his brush. "I shoot them one by one. They look at you reproachfully, each in turn crying out variously, 'Doe, Ray, Me, Far, So,' and so on as they expire."

"There are plenty more where they came from," said Clara defiantly. "That was only the first tranche of Von Trapp kids. They are more numerous than Chumbawamba. Their concert stages have to be specially strengthened lest they crash through it. Washing them is like cleaning the Forth Bridge. You will run out of bullets long before I run out of Von Trapp children," she said with her hands on her hips and a proud toss of her head.

"Tildchen, you are magnificent!" he cried. "I do not have the heart to threaten you any more." He threw down his broom-rifle and covered his face with his hands. "What have I become? I am beyond salvation."

"No, Klaus!" she cried, moved, taking a step towards him. "No-one is. Let me help you find redemption."

He glanced at her with a wild hope, then shook his head and moved away. "It is too late for me. My life has been filled with brutality and the kind of sausages that repeat on you. And yet once," he mused, "I had a glimpse of something finer, a revelation that seemed to promise hope not just for me but for all of us. I once saw … " He frowned and stopped.

"Tell me," she urged, wringing her hands.

"No," he said sullenly, kicking at his heel, "I cannot, you vill leff at me."

"You can tell me anything. I will understand," said Clara huskily, tenderly laying a hand on his shoulder. "As a vagabond nun-for-hire I have seen shit that would turn you white."

"Perhaps – perhaps I can tell you – I have never, never told anyone zis – but vonce, on patrol in ze depths of vinter, I beheld a songbird singing on a frozen branch. The notes rang out with preternatural clarity across an icy lake, seeming to hang in the frosty air. I vas pierced to ze soul mit ze conviction zat nothing, nothing matters but ze apprehension of ze transcendent beauty that suffuses ze universe and pours balm on all our hearts."

"Why you big gay," said Clara.

Miles looked at her, wounded. "But you said – "

"Gayyyyy," said Clara. "You big girl's dirndl. I'm going to tell all your stormtrooper friends how you *wurrrved* the little birdy singing on the branch."

"Zen, Fräulein, I vill have no choice but to tell all your nunny friends about the 'Honk if you're a materialist' tattoo on your bristols."

"Miles, must you reduce everything to low comedy? I'm trying to enact a psychodrama that could reveal deep truths about our marriage."

"You just couldn't think of a comeback."

"I could too. It is this," said Clara, kneeing him in the balls.

"For fuck's sake, woman," gasped Miles clutching himself in pain.

"Language!"

"Every time you do that it is a blow on the head to our future children."

"Then they will be docile and easy to control."

"Well what happens now then?" he asked when he had recovered.

"That is up to you, Miles."

He sighed then became Klaus again and gazed at her imploringly.

"Tildchen, Tildchen! Vy must we fight? We were everyzink to each other." She pouted and turned away as he approached her. He gently laid his hands on her shoulders and kissed her neck. "Admit zere is still a spark remaining."

She wrung her hands. "Oh, Klaus, Klaus, I am so conflicted! Do not force me to choose between you and God."

"Very well, you can see him at weekends."

He turned her round to face him.

"May I … " he leered, "may I say the intimate Du to you?"

She looked away. "No. You may take my body, you may see my bustenblumen, you may shaft me senseless with your willy in the woodshed. But," she shook her head solemnly, "I will never, never be Du to you again."

"Can't win them all. To the woodshed, then."

"Brute! Monster! You mean you could make love to a woman who addresses you with the impersonal Sie? I have never heard anything so dirty." She slapped him and tried to knee him in the balls again but he dodged back. "Help me, children! Overpower him!"

"I shot them already!" protested Miles.

"The bullets bounced off. I muffled them up in thick woollen undervests and multiple layers this morning, because of the mountain air."

"Not fair!"

"Well these are new ones anyway. The horizon darkens with the sinister figures of a crowd of a hundred or more Von Trapp offspring over on the next mountain, bent on avenging the outrage on their beloved nanny."

"I get in my tank and shell them," said Miles, miming looking through gun-sights.

"You don't have a tank! You are a humble border guard! Did I say you had a tank?"

"You said we could fill in the details as we go along. Rommel, too, was knocked out by my egg-and-paper-bag trick, and he gave me my own tank in gratitude for showing him that life could still surprise him."

"Let me see your tank impression, then, if you're so keen on it."

"Kaboom," said Miles somewhat selfconsciously. "Aieee. That was the Von Trapp hordes blowing up."

"Divorce evidence diary, Day 237," muttered Clara.

"And now I take you into the woodshed," said Miles, reaching towards her and getting his hand slapped.

"What is it with you and the woodshed, Miles? I am becoming quite alarmed."

"There is something I want to show you in there, Fräulein. A tool. A very interesting tool."

"I am not accompanying you into the woodshed, Miles. You have absolutely failed to win my heart in this scenario or generate any sexual tension. And I fear spiders. I'm also starting to think you have some sort of shed fetish and will smear me with Cuprinol. Besides I am not letting you write out the Von Trapps so easily. Oh! Oh! Wait! They yodel and cause an avalanche! We are trapped together in snow! That could be genuinely sexy and romantic, don't you think, Miles?"

"Um … yes, actually. Oh, and perhaps a Saint Bernard comes!" Clara stared at him in deepest alarm. "You know, with brandy." Clara continued to stare. "You know what I mean! We're snuggling, and I revive you with brandy, we're lit with a warm glow – oh! Oh! We could do – then I carry you to a hunting lodge, through the snow, and you're shivering, hypothermic, so I build a roaring fire and then you lie naked in front of it and I give you a massage with the brandy."

Clara blinked.

"So I would stink like an alehouse? Your lower-class origins are showing, Miles."

"Like Horseman on the Roof! You loved Horseman on the Roof! You know where she's dying of cholera and he – "

"Oh yes, Miles, by all means let's do a dying-of-cholera fantasy, I will get some soup for me to puke up. Perhaps afterwards a little simulated necrophilia? I worry about you."

"Clara! It's romantic! I would be reviving you, bringing you back to life."

"Sneaking a feel while I am comatose, more like. This is worse than the elf ears idea."

Miles blushed and looked down.

"All right then," he mumbled. "How do we pretend an avalanche?"

"Um. A duvet? Too warm. The cold is of the essence. To the refrigerator."

They went into the kitchen. Clara opened the fridge.

"Now what?" asked Miles.

"Lie down."

They lay down in front of it. Clara scraped handfuls of frost out of the freezer and scattered it over them.

"This is a rubbish avalanche," opined Miles.

"Use your imagination."

"Brr," said Miles half-heartedly, rubbing himself. "We will surely freeze to death. I hope a St. Bernard comes."

Clara got some ice cubes out, dropped some on his head, then shoved some down his pants.

"Wah!" said Miles. "What are you playing at?"

"Staving off frostbite is the essence of this fantasy."

He wriggled a bit to dislodge the ice cubes and said, "Meine schwangenwursten is turning blue mit frost, Fräulein. Perhaps you could ... warm it somehow."

Clara slapped him. "You forget I am a nun."

"But needs must, Fräulein. Are your bustenblumen cold? Allow me to–"

She slapped him again and glared.

"This is not terribly sexy so far," said Miles.

"I am a nun. I have to stay in character."

"So, what, we just lie here and freeze?"

"In each other's arms, Miles, it is romantic."

She was rummaging in the freezer and took out various packets of frozen vegetables which she dumped over them.

"Dear God," she suddenly cried, "how have I avoided eating these?"

She had found a packet of ice-pops. "Miles, look! These can be our frozen fingers! We can eat each other to stay alive! Wouldn't that be romantic?"

"No."

"It would! Admit you would let me eat you if we were trapped in an avalanche. Look, look," she thrust four ice pops on him, "Hold these between your fingers, these are your fingers now."

Miles complied. He caressed her face tenderly with his new ice-pop fingers.

"I can no longer feel your face, Tildchen," he said despairingly. "All is up mit uns. We are sperlos versunk."

"I am so hungry, Klaus," Clara complained. "I will surely starve to death … unless … " She fluttered her eyelashes.

"Your character would die rather than descend to cannibalism."

"No, I am compelled to stay alive for the sake of what is left of the Von Trapp swarm."

Miles sighed. "Please eat my fingers, Tildchen."

"No, no, I cannot," said Clara starting to unwrap one. "Wait, this is raspberry, give me an orange finger. No, the blue one."

"You may eat all my fingers, Tildchen."

Clara nibbled, crunched and sucked happily.

"I am failing to see an erotic element," said Miles.

"Your fingers are nice," concluded Clara licking her lips, then started on his shoulder.

"Ow! Stop that!"

"Actually, let's pretend a St. Bernard does come. Bags me playing it," she said, panting and lolling her tongue and licking his face.

But it still didn't end in sex, because she wouldn't stop woofing and it was too disturbing.

Chapter Four

And so it went. And so, pretty much, it will go. It should perhaps be pointed out now that there is to be little plot or structure to this book about Clara and Miles, or at least no grand overarching one. As they are only just embarking on life's merry meander, it would be premature to try to impose a shape on their story. Their lives are as formless as yours probably is; probably more so, in fact, as they are almost certainly richer than you and so do not have to work, and what is more, don't.

All that happens in this book is that Clara and Miles continue to frolic giddily in private and behave appallingly in public. Some of their games involving other people will have more point to them and be aimed at more deserving targets than the one with the fairly inoffensive marriage counsellor in the first chapter. There will be further vignettes of their home life, and you will meet some of the people they know. There will be incidents and anecdotes and several full-blown stories, some self-contained and some sort of continuing, and all, it is to be hoped, entertaining. Certain themes will recur, as with anyone's life. And there has been a certain amount of shaping, selection and arranging in putting together the following episodes; but in the way that a vase of flowers is arranged, rather than a railway time-table. There is to be no grand plot, no strict unity, and no tragic ending. (And, we hasten to add, almost no intrusive narration after this necessary warning.) Those who do not like the idea should jump ship now. (There is no shame, nowadays, in such lack of perseverance. Clara herself, for example, rarely gives any modern symphony more than ten seconds' chance before snapping off the radio with an oath; while she supposes it *might* eventually turn from a cacophony of unpleasant noises into something beautiful and uplifting, bitter experience has taught her that it almost certainly won't. In fact now she generally turns the radio off as soon as she hears the word 'premiere', which is sad in case someone composes something nice again one day.) On the other hand, perhaps you should stick around for some of the more inventive pranks, which will start shortly. But in general the point of this book is to spend time with Clara and Miles, and if they have annoyed you on short acquaintance – and you would hardly be the first – you ought to cut your losses and go away at once. They will only get worse. This is probably true of their lives as well as this book; although we said there was to be no tragic end, we cannot foresee the future and worry, sometimes, about what will become of them.

Miles worried, sometimes, about what would become of them.

Most of their money was or had originally been Miles's, in spite of what Clara had told the marriage counsellor or what one or the other of them would tell different people at different times. ("We are new meritocrats," Clara had told someone at the party, for example. "Miles invented a million-selling ringtone, and I sold a kiss-and-tell on a reality-show winner.") It had been left to him quite unexpectedly by a fairly distant and fairly unpleasant relative no-one had suspected of wealth until it was far too late for anyone to suck up to him; Miles had apparently won a warm corner in his benefactor's bitter black heart by a timely and quite inadvertent act of childhood vandalism and his general air of uselessness.

"It is as if I had kissed a frog out of altruism and seen it magically turn into a great golden eight-titted cash-cow," Clara very nicely said when he broke the news.

It had been Clara who had seen at once what to do with the money.

"We will buy a house in the country and go quietly insane. By the world's standards, that is; by ours, completely sane. We will withdraw from the world entirely. We will see no-one except the cat. We will keep a sleek, smiling oriental manservant to act as cut-out between us and the world. His primary task will be to go shopping for us. He will remove and burn all packaging before it offends our eyes and place the contents in jars, flagons and huge bronze urns. He will wear a blindfold when he approaches us, that our eyes shall not be harrowed by the sight of eyes that have gazed on the horror of a supermarket car park. We will bow our apologies to him for what he has done on our behalf, although of course he will not see that, because of the blindfold. Every couple of years, watching him twitch in nightmare, we will kill him kindly in his sleep, and replace him with another. ... We will give our days to reverie, and fantasy, and every form of sensual pleasure, except those involving your malformed penis, which are overrated. I think I mainly mean there should be plenty of sweets and chocolates in the house. There must be books; there must be rare and beautiful objets d'art; there must be a pleasure garden, unrivalled save by the fabled Blue Peter one; there must be plenty of rooms to play in, and rambling attics to explore, which we will fill with our treasures. There must be weapons; there must be a cellar stacked with supplies with which to weather the breakdown of civilisation. One day, when I have read most of the books I want to, but while your loins are still young, we will breed children, with the same care and attention with which we would breed exquisite but deadly orchids; they will be a race of doomed flawed geniuses and criminals like the Rougon-Macquarts in Zola. All will be luxe, calme et volupte. Occasionally we will go for day-trips and you will buy me ice-cream. I see it all clearly. Please say yes, Miles."

Miles, who had previously been looking forward to withdrawing from the world and going quietly insane with Clara in a humble flat, had said yes.

And so more or less it had been, apart from the blindfolded disposable manservants, and the fact that their insanity became fairly loud at times.

Their days had passed in blissful idyll; the only tragic note that had been struck in their young lives (and now, perhaps, you will at last be able to find them sympathetic) was that some months ago their cat had committed suicide, on its sixth or seventh attempt. They grieved but did not blame themselves, agreeing that it must have had its reasons.

There had been modifications to the plan; their lives were not quite as hermetic as originally envisaged. Sometimes there had been more or less doomed attempts to rejoin or at least keep in touch with the world, as at the party. And Clara had felt the urge to act out some of their games on the stage of the world, take their characters and fantasies on tour, as with the hapless marriage counsellor.

Furthermore they had found themselves drawn, in a cordial but remote, arm's-length way at first, via shopping and the occasional visit to church, but soon with an affectionate and fiercely loyal attachment, into the life of the village down the road and their neighbours in the district at large.

"I have decided to meddle in the affairs of the neighbourhood," Clara had announced one day.

"It will end badly," Miles had warned.

"It will probably end with their children being eaten by semi-extinct beasts," she had agreed. "Nevertheless I am resolved to make the experiment."

So once or twice a week they spent an evening at the pub; and they had made friends. Clara had once told Miles, slightly worriedly and not exaggerating a lot, that he was pretty much the only person now she was remotely able to stand. Perhaps it was some new relaxation or tolerance induced by having established a sanctuary and independence, after having found a playmate and ally, that enabled her to unbend, or perhaps it was some quality in their neighbours themselves, many of whom were as eccentric, original or at war with the world in their way as she was in hers. But here she had found kindred spirits, and won new followers.

Then there was the fact that Clara had increasingly frequent moods where she would decide that it was impossible, after all, to ignore the world completely; that it was immoral; that in fact she had a duty, a mission, very possibly a destiny to save the world, preferably by being very very awful to some of the people in it. These moods and the escapades they led to were increasingly disturbing to Miles's tranquility and peace of mind.

So too from time to time was the money question. They were not *properly* rich, to Miles's way of thinking, not rich enough so that they never had to worry about it again. Certainly, like many a man before him, he found he worried more about money now that he was wealthy than he had done when he was poor.

The idea had been that after buying their House of Love and Sanity they would still have enough of the windfall left to keep them without working for the rest of their unnatural lives. This had seemed possible at first.

Their needs were moderate, their tastes fairly simple. Clara had always made her own entertainment; and although her family were officially more well-to-do than Miles's tribe of shopkeepers, lance-corporals and ink-stained clerks she had never really had money either until the very nice present from her grandmother which had enabled them to become engaged. A fairly big old house in the country, books and CDs, a classic sports car, some nice clothes, a couple of antiques, an occasional trip to the opera or ballet, occasional restaurants, day-trips with ice-cream, dressing-up clothes and props for their games, these sufficed to please them. Being fogeys they required few gadgets, although perhaps Clara's favourite possession was the laminating machine Miles had bought her for her birthday. They had the occasional splurge but their regular outgoings were relatively modest.

But in the long run they were doomed, Miles feared. The money would run out eventually. At the last minute they had been outbid on the house Clara had set her heart on and had had to spend more than they had budgeted for in securing it. There was still a tidy sum left, but the interest was not quite enough to keep them. It would be madness for people like them to invest or speculate; and indeed Clara had sternly forbidden him to even bother his head about such dreariness. Slowly but surely the capital was being nibbled away at. Ten years, fifteen years, twenty years from now it would be gone, by which point they would presumably be completely unemployable and even more estranged from reality than they already were. The thought of Clara being forced to work variously afflicted him like the thought of a Romanoff princess being set to a lathe or the thought of all three Marx brothers being let loose in a china shop. She had pointed out that it was the husband who was expected to work, but the thought of Clara being left alone in the house all day was even more poignant and worrying. Really they were agreed that they would have to kill themselves when the money ran out.

Yet they were intelligent, creative, not without initiative. They must be able to find some paying niche. From time to time Miles would come up with plans for businesses, careers for them, but the ones that grabbed Clara at all were promptly turned into dreams of megalomaniac grandeur; became fodder for their fantasies and escaped the realm of the practical. In the long run they were doomed, but he didn't suppose there was much to be done about it.

*

Today Clara was cackling and typing like a fury at a big old clattering manual typewriter.

"Miles this is the greatest thing ever! Come and look! No wait make tea first! Hot and strong and with amphetamines in it! You will have to prise me screaming from the typewriter some time next week when my fingers are bloody stumps! God I'm on fire!"

She was writing a TV script based on the life of the 18th-century Prime Minister Robert Walpole, as the man at the party had commissioned her to.

Here is a bit she had just written.

INT., the Warehouse, Night.

WALPOLE looks around calmly, unruffled. The ten disgusting greasy foreigners - a frog, A German, and various wops and dagoes - surround him menacingly. They have stains all over their shirts and near their trouser flies. They brandish swords, daggers, pistols, bicycle chains and a mace. They leer and chuckle revealing gold teeth and various gum diseases and wads of chewing-garlic. AGNES BOJAXHIU (the Young Mother Theresa) clings to WALPOLE's manly chest in her underslip, her pretty BOSOMS heaving.

DISGUSTING GREASY FOREIGNER #1: So, Walpole, we have you now. When you are dead England will have no choice but to submit to the Union of Foreign Invaders. And we will dishonour the lady and put her to work in my garlic factory.

WALPOLE (smoothly): Yes, gentlemen, it certainly does seem as though you have me. And yet there is one thing you have overlooked.

D.G. FOREIGNER 1 (laughing): What, Walpole? What have we overlooked? You are outnumbered ten to one and completely trapped. What (giggling shrilly, unable to contain his mirth) can we possibly have overlooked?

WALPOLE grabs him round the throat and, as he screams, pulls his head completely off.

WALPOLE (shouting up his bleeding neck): I AM HARD AS BLOODY NAILS

WALPOLE throws the still-screaming head at another Foreigner and grabs his sword. As they close in he stabs one man then decapitates two more with one stroke. This is so swift that both their heads are still balanced on their necks. Chuckling, he merrily swaps their heads round while they scream. Meanwhile Young Mother Theresa takes a pistol from her BOSOMS and shoots someone in the WILLY. As the adversaries close in WALPOLE kicks a man between his legs so hard that his eyeballs fall out and are briefly replaced by bollocks. CUT TO a RAT pouncing on the eyeballs. Y.M.T./Agnes grabs a sword and she and Walpole stand back to back.

YMT (as they parry blows): Walpole, you are incorrigible. You should have let me handle this.

WALPOLE (saucily): Play your cards right, Madam, and I may let you handle something else.

> [NB he means his WILLY]

YMT (spiritedly): I would sooner handle a snake.

WALPOLE (looking at camera and winking merrily): Too easy.

> [NB he means he was going to compare
>   his WILLY to a snake but has resisted
>   the temptation]

The fight continues. Walpole impales two foreigners at once and laughs. Young Mother Theresa chops a man's leg off and then shoots his other foot off so he falls over. Walpole punches a man so hard his head twists right round to face backwards and he can't see where he's going. Soon there is only one DISGUSTING FOREIGNER left. Walpole puts Agnes's discarded dress on him and dances around with him. Then he upends a gunpowder keg down his throat, lights a cigar, flicks the still-lighted match down the man's throat and laughs as he explodes.

Y_M THERESA: Let's get out of here.
WALP. Not so fast, Madam.

[He grabs her and pulls her to him. She arches an eyebrow.
He starts to insert a hand into her BOSOMS]

YMT: Unhand me!
WALP: You were quick enough to cling to me a moment ago. Methinks that fear was suspiciously unlike you.

Arching an eyebrow in his turn he extracts the SECRET PLANS from her BOSOMS.

Young Mother Theresa looks defiant and tosses her lovely head proudly.

WALP. Touching, Madam, that you required a keepsake of me.

She continues to glare defiantly.

WALPOLE : You damnable Yugoslavian witch!

YMT: You arrogant English pig

They kiss and then have ***SEX*** against Walpole's coach.

Then hundreds more disgusting foreigners suddenly burst in.

Clara typed and cackled, sitting at her huge old desk in the living room. Here are some of the things that were currently on Clara's desk:

A carbon of a typed letter to the BBC complaining about a broadcast of Marvin Gaye's song 'Sexual Healing'. It read:

> Dear BBC,
> I wish to complain in the strongest possible terms about Radio 2 playing Marvin Gaye's song 'Sexual Healing', with its horrific lyrics, 'Get up, get up, get up, get up, let's make love tonight, wake up wake up wake up wake up, because you do it right.' This tasteless ditty is plainly describing the ordeal of an innocent woman being summarily woken from a deep sleep, with who knows what dreams of maiden happiness, in order to be plied with a Beast. Is this the sort of behaviour the BBC wishes to encourage?
> 　　　　　Yours, etc.

Various bits of correspondence from or to the National Liquorice Council. This was an independent organisation she had established of which she was the Chairman, Miles the Secretary, and their dead cat the Treasurer. Its role, depending on her whim, was to issue communiques to the press warning either that people weren't eating the recommended daily amount of liquorice, with consequent risk to their health, *or* that people were eating too much liquorice, a known toxin, with consequent risk to their health. It was a parody of various similar self-appointed national watchdogs, and so far she had been rewarded with a paragraph apiece in one regional and one national newspaper, and a letter from a junior government health minister she had also written to, saying they took the liquorice threat very seriously. Miles had pointed out that it might well backfire and lead to restrictions on the sale of liquorice, and that only the two of them were in on the joke; Clara had responded that she didn't much care for liquorice anyway, that the two of them were audience enough for her, and that besides God would also know and laugh. Miles, who did like liquorice, had said they should concentrate on the promoting-it side of things, and then write and tell liquorice companies what they were doing and ask for funding or at least free sweets.

There was an unsent letter to a manufacturer of novelty gadgets outlining her idea for a table-lamp in the shape of Al Gore that would raise its hands over its eyes and cry every time you turned it on, also an unfinished patent application for this device.

There were drafts of chapters for a marriage-counselling book she was writing, or as she preferred a book of consolation and manual on the management of husbands, to be called *A Guide For Disappointed Young Wives*. There were stories intended for her mooted collection of feminist fairy tales, all of which ended with the heroine being disillusioned, appalled or traumatized into catatonia at the revelation of a penis. She intended to illustrate this herself and the margins were full of trial runs.

There were several laminated passes, and several bits of cardboard or paper, some with photo-booth pictures of her or Miles affixed, which would eventually be turned into laminated passes. Miles considered that buying Clara the laminating machine she had asked for for her birthday had been one of the biggest mistakes he had made so far. Though, as he had foreseen, it had provided many hours of innocent idiot joy – she had run amok for several days and laminated everything she could lay her hands on that was flat or could easily be hammered so – it had not, as he had hoped, kept her out of mischief; quite the reverse. She now spent many girl-hours a week creating official-looking or what she blithely hoped were official-looking laminated passes for various official or official-sounding or completely and obviously spurious organisations, and these had been the aids, abettors and instigators of more mischief than he cared to remember, getting them into and, to be fair, occasionally out of trouble in the course of what Clara referred to as their Adventures and Miles more often thought of as waking nightmares of embarrassment and legal danger.

There were documents pertaining to Albion Television, a TV production company they had set up and registered at Companies House after her epiphany with the marriage counsellor. Albion Television had letterheads, business cards, and a lovingly faked CV, but no actual productions to its credit. Apart from using its name to grease the wheels of a couple of very minor pranks she had not done anything with this creation yet.

There was a stapler, a hole-punch and a label-gun she had abused almost as much as she had the laminator. There were several bottles of Tipp-Ex and some Gloy glue, perhaps the last few precious bottles of this last left anywhere. There were felt-tips and crayons and various ink-stamps. There were paper-clips and envelopes and far too many stamps for posting the surreal, obscene or threatening letters she sent out far too frequently.

There was a crocodile made out of glued and painted egg-boxes. There was a Luger water-pistol, loaded, for when Miles annoyed her, and a remote-control, broken, for when she wanted to turn him off.

There was a framed photo of Professor Jenks, her elderly former tutor, which she would kiss to annoy Miles.

There was a commonplace book for writing down quotations she fancied, or her own pensees and apercus, which tended to such headings as 'On The Horror of Penises' or 'On Marrying Beneath One's Mental Class.' These were largely for Miles's benefit, although she had told him her political musings should be rushed into print as soon as she snapped and assassinated someone or otherwise attained notoriety. There were several scrapbooks, one set aside for clippings of pranks of theirs which had gained media attention, most just for pasting pictures of nice things or people into.

There were her Death Lists, kept neatly in a black leather account book with a skull-and-crossbones Tippexed on the front, detailing all the people she intended to kill when she came to power. She made sporadic attempts to cross-index these, alphabetically, by order of urgency, and by horrendousness of planned death, but was finding it tiresome to keep up to date when more and more candidates for execution came to her notice every day she bothered to read the newspapers. She had told Miles that she feared that when the glorious day came she would be forced to do a lot of sub-contracting and delegation and arrange for her enemies to be despatched in rather impersonal job-lots rather than giving each the personal attention she had once envisaged.

There were sweets. There were empty bottles which had once contained Britvic orange juice, her favourite drink apart from tea, which she found it hard to throw away and which Miles had to dispose of when she wasn't looking.

There was a world atlas with rude or traditional names for the inhabitants of each country scrawled on, and imaginary new countries inserted. A mushroom cloud had been scribbled over the city of Brussels on several maps, as she did not like being ruled from there by transnationalist communistic parasitic bureaucrats and rich oligarchs. And who does? It should perhaps be made clear that we sympathize with Clara wherever possible, although sometimes we are forced to shake our heads sorrowfully at her antics and transfer allegiance to her more easygoing husband.

There were things made out of plasticine. There were things made out of Lego. There were things made out of wine-corks, pins, and little bits of tinfoil.

There was a collection of pamphlets from the 1950s – travel brochures, train time-tables, car sales literature, instruction manuals – which she found refreshed her with their cheeriness, innocence, simplicity, and beautiful design and fonts, and which she had told Miles proved the case against the modern world beyond argument.

There was an 'Out' tray for finished letters ready for the post. It was currently empty save for a sealed Royal Mail 'Post Pak' parcel envelope, itself addressed to the Royal Mail. Inside this, among other things, was a letter which read:

> Dear Post Office, you dead and damned and utterly ridiculous bastards,
> I will not call you Royal Mail because you are a bloody embarrassment to the Queen, who doubtless describes you as utter fuck-ups in the privacy of her boudoir.
> Know you are hated and will not be spared. I would draw to your attention the envelope this letter comes in. I was recently in one of your ghastly, soulless, hateful, video-screen-infested emporiums and was forced to buy another such atrocity to send something to a dear friend overseas.
> Do you know how mortifyingly embarrassing and toe-curlingly shameful it is to have to send something like that to a foreigner? Do you know how appallingly accurate a picture of our country it evokes? Can't we even pretend to be civilised in front of outsiders? Do you know how disappointing it must be for them to receive something like that from Britain, when they had probably expected something exotically elegant and charmingly old-world?
> Look at it. Look at it. Look at it. Can't you see how utterly foul and hideous it is? Don't you have eyes? I think your eyes will be confiscated when I come to power if you are going to misuse them like that. You do not deserve eyes. Or hands. Or a tongue.
> 'Post-Pak'? 'Post-Pak'! Pak? Pak?? Why? Why? Why? Why? Why? Why? Why? Why? Can't you spell? Do you think it is 'cool' not to spell? How old are you, ten? Who are you trying to impress? Who thinks illiteracy is hip and groovy? Why? Why? Why? Why does everything have to be so bloody foul and ugly?
> Does this letter sound unbalanced? I don't care. I am glad. I want you to look over your shoulders and know there are people like me around and one day we will get you and punish you for what you have done.
> Die stricken by the knowledge of your own banality,
> An Anonymous Lady, who knows where you live.
> ps
> Please find enclosed some dog-poo and roadkill. Neither are as revolting as what they are posted in.

Although she liked to share the fruits of her creativity and consumer activism with her husband, there were portions of her work she instinctively concealed from Miles for his own peace of mind and the sake of domestic harmony. The above was one of them.

For the most part Miles was a fairly gentle soul who wanted only to be left in peace and leave other people in peace and get along with everyone when thrown into contact with them. Perhaps it was a mistake for him and Clara to have married, except that he adored every atom of her and was the only person able to enter into her private world.

"Miles this is excellent," she said as he brought tea. "Read, read! This is going to move the art of television forward by thirty years."

She was going, "Dum *dum*, dum-dum-dum," as she typed: it was the theme tune to *The Flashing Blade*, an old children's TV series full of adventure and derring-do, which was also the Walpole theme tune.

```
EXTERIOR, NIght.

WALPOLE starts flinging gunpowder kegs out of the
racing coach at the pursuing FOREIGNERS while
Young Mother Theresa leans out of the other
window and shoots at them to ignite them. She
hits one and it explodes, splattering the screen
with bloody fragments of blown-up Dago.

YM-Theresa/Agnes ducks back into the coach to
re-load and gasps as she sees something in front
of them.

YMT: Walpole! Look!

WALPOLE sees: they are heading towards Tower
Bridge and it is starting to raise up to let a
boat through!

WALPOLE: Quick! Give me your underslip and your
pistol!

Puzzled but unquestioning, Young Mother Theresa
takes off her shift so she is *NUUDE* - we see
her BOSOMS - and passes that and her gun to
WALPOLE. He leans out again and shoots the horses
in their arses. They whinny and put on an extra
```

burst of speed and go leaping across the widening gap on the raising bridge. CUT TO the coach and horses flying across the gap, perhaps in 'bullet-time'. CUT to them landing safely on the other side. CUT TO the pursuing foeiregeners: cursing in their strange jabbering languages they pull their horses up sharply, throwing sparks off their hooves, as they realise they cannot leap the gap or are too cowardly to try.
One of the sparks reaches some discarded powder-kegs lying on the ground. CUT TO:
As Walpole's coach and horses clatter onto the far bank, Tower Bridge explodes in a huge fireball behind them.

The coach comes to a halt. Cut to inside:

Young Mother Theresa (sighing, leaning against him): Quick thinking Walpole. (Puzzled) But why did you make me take off my slip?

WALPOLE (innocently): I just thought it would be a beautiful thing to do.
YMT (outraged): Why, you - !

WALPOLE kisses her and they have ***SEX*** again. Behind them the river is lit by burning foreigners and the night made musical by their screams.

"I expect this will have to go on after the watershed, Miles. We don't want children to try it at home. Also I am worried about the CGI budget. I don't suppose the communist BBC will want to blow up real foreigners."

Miles was sniggering as he read but screeched, "Clara, you could have done this for real! This could have been a valuable foot in the door! You shouldn't waste this contact! Pitch him something serious! You're entirely capable of – "

"Wah wah wah wah wah, work work work work work, bore bore bore bore bore. This is my magnum opus Miles. It is brilliant. So far he has made love to seventeen women and killed more foreigners than I can count and it is still only the first episode."

Miles, laughing, had just reached the first ***SEX*** scene, a three-way with a secretary and a serving wench on the cabinet table in 10 Downing Street as the opening credits rolled. "If you would just lose the merry xenophobia and cut out half the graphic violence, this is almost something they would do with a life of Walpole."

"The thought had crossed my mind."

It is not to be supposed, however, that Clara's Walpole script was intended as a parody of the modern BBC line in porno-history, or that sexy Walpole had been invented to pitch to the producer. The character of Robert Walpole – statesman, lover, buccaneer – had predated both and was one dear to Clara's heart. The desk was littered with stories about him in various stages of completion, often also featuring his tempestuous on-off squeeze and occasional nemesis, Agnes Bojaxhiu, a.k.a. the Young Mother Theresa.

Walpole had first appeared to Miles in the course of one of their games. Played by Clara – this was one of their ordinary dress-up and play games rather than one of their theoretically-sexual role-playing games. Then he had become the hero of a long-running bedtime story they had taken it in turns to tell each other, in the course of which he had fought aliens and vampires and so on as well as foreigners and various scheming internal enemies. Young Mother Theresa had had a similar genesis and had been quickly incorporated into the Walpole saga and then spun off into one of her own, detailing her colourful adventures across three continents and several centuries in the years before she had taken the veil. Young Mother Theresa was a proud, passionate, head-tossing, head-turningly beautiful, imperious, impetuous Yugoslavian adventuress, intriguer, schemer and freedom fighter who had seduced, manipulated and fallen in and out of love with most of the great men of Europe and America at one time or another – the complicated tale of her involvement with Abraham Lincoln had been a high point for Miles. Clara often played her in their games; Miles had frequently been allowed to play Walpole against her, after a certain amount of impatient initial coaching and director's notes from Clara.

However, Miles knew that Walpole predated him, too. A school exercise book had fallen out of a box when they were moving in. Inside it were several sketches labelled 'Walpole' depicting a man in a top hat and tailcoat with prominent sideburns. In one he was gallantly stooping to kiss the hand of an elegant, blushing lady. In another, he was grinning and lighting the fuse of a cannon into the mouth of which another man had foolishly inserted his head. And a story about him, in a handwriting whose age Miles could not guess, in the course of which he fought highwaymen, was exiled from England by a political foe after being

45

framed for stealing some food (a tray of vol-au-vents intended for a Duchess's party) and teamed up with a friendly band of gourmet Vikings in order to wreak his revenge. The cannon picture was explained; he had tricked his foe into looking down it by telling him there were some jewels at the bottom. (The vol-au-vents were an interesting detail to Miles. He remembered that once during exchanged reminiscences of childhood hiding places Clara had mentioned a row before a party of her mother's. Miles suspected there had been a tray of vol-au-vents involved which Clara had *not* been framed for eating. "I never seemed able to get enough food as a child," she had once said.)

Miles was reminded of how the young Brontës had written Duke of Wellington fan-fiction in which he founded a dynasty on an imaginary island; and indeed in Clara's stories and now in their games Walpole somewhat resembled a more light-hearted version of one of these volatile and melodramatic Dukes of Angria or Zamorna, albeit amalgamated with elements of John Bull, Churchill, Machiavelli, Priapus, James Bond and Conan the Barbarian. Originally mannerly, gallant, and at least intermittently chivalrous, he was, poignantly Miles thought, growing steadily more short-fused and bloodthirsty as Clara herself did.

One of his major functions now was to be invoked as a contrast to the unsatisfactory statesmen of their current, fallen times, one who would have done things differently. "Someone once proposed [x ridiculous idea that was about to become law] to Walpole," Clara would say. "He laughed merrily and hurled them through the window."

There was of course a real 18th-century Prime Minister named Robert Walpole. While this officially *was* Clara's Walpole, any similarity in career or character was entirely coincidental; Miles could not begin to guess how or why this rather prosaic figure had inspired or evolved into the swashbuckling character of her stories or first obsessed her as a child. He supposed some situation – holiday cottage, hospital waiting room, rainy visit to a strange house? – where a history volume or biography of the man had been the only book available might go *some* way towards explaining it, given Clara's propensity to daydream and ability to spin romance from the unlikeliest subject. "I think he was little more than a safe pair of hands at the tiller, you know," he had amusedly tried to point out once in the early days. "He put the country on a sound financial footing and kept the ship of state running steady and that was about it. He may also have been as cynical and corrupt as modern politicians." She had snarled that Miles was a Revisionist and a Communist. When he had noted that the top-hat and prominent side-whiskers with which Walpole was depicted in her oeuvre were anachronistic, things more of the 19th century, and that he had really worn a powdered wig, she had informed him that he was a bore and a pedant and perilously close to divorce, and besides that he was wrong and all the portraits of Walpole in history books had been faked by jealous enemies. The fact was that Walpole had been a dandy as well as a great lover and fighter and had pioneered his distinctive outfit, ahead of his time in that as in so many other things. He had abandoned wigs because he found they tended to slip down over the eyes while swordfighting or having it off, and his splendid sideburns gave his lovers something to hang onto. She was working sporadically on a Non-Revisionist Biography of Walpole, a definitive concordance of his adventures, which would set the record straight once and for all.

Recently she had caused a pub to be named after Walpole, as will be explained shortly.

Clara inserted a new piece of paper. "I am going straight onto episode two while I am hot!" she declared. If things ran true to form she would get part way through this one or the next before getting bored. She would certainly send copies to the BBC man, Miles knew, and intermittently pester him with other script fragments and ideas, none of them sensible, for the rest of his life or until he changed his address.

EPISODE 2:

A New Threat

Fade up on the cabinet room at No. 10 Downing Street again.

A meeting of the cabinet is in session,

WALPOLE, propping up his head on his hand, is trying his best not to fall asleep as his CHANCELLOR gives a droning report. He tries instead to concentrate on some of the other cabinet ministers, most of whom are ladies of easy virtue whom he has picked because of their pretty BOSOMS. He exchanges a smile and coy little wave with his War Secretary, a WHORE named Nelly.

CHANCELLOR (a pompous man in a long wig, droning): ...and in the third fiscal quarter,

revenue from the window tax peaked at –
(irately): Prime Minister Walpole! Prime Minister
Walpole! Are you paying attention?

WALPOLE (mesmerised by Nelly's BOSOMS):
Completely.

CHANCELLOR: I am trying to demonstrate to you,
sir, that your foolish scheme to revoke the
window tax will bankrupt us!

WALPOLE: And I would remind you, sir, that I came
to power on a promise that every man in this
country, no matter how poor, could have all the
windows he wanted. (Rising, shouting): This
country, sir, was built on roast beef and good
ale and windows for all!

(The whores all cheer)

WALPOLE: Why I myself can barely pay the wretched
tax!

CHANCELLOR: We must all make sacrifices, sir.
Frankly it wouldn't hurt for you to lose some of
your windows.

WALPOLE: Perhaps you are right. There are too
many in this room, for one thing.

(Picks Chancellor up and throws him bodily
through a window.)

WALPOLE: (merrily, to whores): Well that's saved
me a shilling or two.

The whores titter.

Suddenly all the other windows are smashed in
from the outside and half a dozen sword-wielding
NINJAS come bursting through. THE cabinet whores
scream.

WALPOLE (calmly): And that's saved me a few bob more. Heads down, ladies.

(Picks up a naval cannon from under the table and lights the fuse with his cigar.

Walpole theme. Roll credits.

Clara typed and cackled. Miles read and sniggered.
Ultimately, they were doomed.

Chapter Five

There came a day when they went to London to buy more dressing-up clothes. When they were there Clara sprang the surprise that she had made another appointment, under a different name, with Dr. Melvyn off the telly, the marriage counsellor they had annoyed once already, who had just released a book on marriage which had incensed Clara so much in the ten incredulous minutes she had leafed through it in a shop that she had decided that when The Day came the doctor would be punished by being married, at gunpoint, and enforced by some sort of electronic device attached to his ankle which would explode if he strayed more than three feet from his spouse, to *either* Arthur Scargill, the former mining union leader, *or* a hairy-backed ten-foot bouncer-psycho man-rapist, *or* a randy 97-year-old granny with a foot disease, details to be arranged.

Forced marriages had been much on Clara's mind of late; she had drawn up lists of nuptials to be put into effect following the revolution in which all the most loathsome people in the country would be foisted on each other matrimonially, her enthusiasm only slightly dampened by Miles pointing out that many of the liaisons she had decided upon were quite likely to occur naturally in the fullness of time, even without a revolution, and the partners therein felicitated as a power couple – she had admitted the truth of this, but emphasised that there would be qualitative differences: in this case the parties in question would *not* be a power couple but rather a gulag couple, mated off in group ceremonies at Wembley Stadium as half-time entertainment during the mass executions, yoked together for all eternity as punishment for their sins and forced to contemplate their mutual banality and spiritual impoverishment in the confines of a caravan on Canvey Island, into which rabid ferrets and drunken Irish poet-tramps would also be introduced. In parallel with this she had also been meditating a national programme of Breeding For Strength to be organised on sound eugenic lines, which so far seemed mainly to consist of Clara being mandated to get a grip of Professor Jenks, her deaf but windswept 90-year-old former tutor, the only man, she declared, she had ever really loved, and Miles being required to deflower Katy Riley, a relentlessly chirpy television weather girl whom Clara cordially detested, 'to teach her about disappointment'.

Anyway, at half past two that day they presented themselves at Dr. Melvyn's office, disguised in hippy wigs and dark glasses with attached false noses.

"We will tell him," said Clara on their way in, "that we are eminent children's TV presenters and dare not show our faces. We will further tell him," she decided, "that our marriage ran aground when I told you my fantasy was to be raped by Ariel Sharon, and you refused to be circumcised."

As it happened they had barely opened their mouths to say hello before the counsellor recognised them and threw them out with high-volume abuse.

"How hurtful," said Clara. "Any fool could have seen we are really crying for help."

On their way back they found themselves approaching the high street where last time they had been made to run a gauntlet of lost souls with clipboards attempting to entice them into an Accident Claims shop.

"If you are any kind of a husband," said Clara after reminding Miles of this, "you will punch in the bollocks *or* ovaries any of those ghouls that dare come near me."

But there were no ghouls. Indeed the shop itself as they passed it proved to be boarded up.

"Oh, that was the firm that went out of business, remember?" said Miles. "The ones who sacked their staff by text message and then the staff looted their own shops."

"Oh yes." Clara cackled. "That was a great day, and one that sums up modern times. Or of course a bad day if you take the view that things have to get worse before the revolution can come. Logically, I think, if I am ever to be allowed to marshal mass executions and forced marriages in Wembley Stadium, we should want *more* compensation shops to spring up in every high street." Dawdling in front of the boarded-up office, she suddenly gasped and clutched Miles's arm. "Miles!" she cried. "We have to *buy* it! Or rent it, at least."

"For why?"

"Don't you see? They've left their sign over the window. To all intents and purposes it still *is* an Accident Claims shop. You remember our old plan to open a chain of Stoic British Endurance shops to encourage people who've had accidents to look on the bright side and soldier on regardless? If we bought this and left their banner up, we could make it into a *stealth* Stoic British Endurance shop … Yes, yes! I see it all!"

"That was the amusing whimsy of a rainy day. To really do it would be, to say the least … "

"The spark has gone out of our marriage, Miles. It's either this or an Ariel Sharon costume and a quick snip."

*

It was the work of a morning to secure a lease on the office, reconnect the phone, place newspaper adverts; that of an afternoon to assemble props and costumes. It was fully a week before Miles could be bullied and pouted into going through with it.

All too soon, though, they had aired and dusted their new premises, and Miles had permitted Clara to put up the least frightening and abusive of the posters she had created in the window, the one depicting an old woman with a harpoon through her head and bearing the words 'IS THIS YOU? KA-CHING!!' and the one saying 'FREE MONEY IF YOU'VE BEEN HURT OR OFFENDED.'

Inside she pinned pictures of a crying baby, and posters of Nelson and Douglas Bader captioned 'I BLOODY GOT ON WITH IT'.

They had hired no clipboard-wielders – although when the doors were officially opened Clara briefly stood outside and bellowed, "*Rowll* up, Ladies and Gents! *Get* your lovely compo here! No hard luck story unrewarded!" – and there had been no appointments as yet. For the first part of the morning they sat side by side at the desk and played that they were at school. Clara was a beautiful but sulky foreign exchange student who used her feminine wiles to extort the contents of Miles's pencil case and force him to say that Albania was the best country at everything.

Then they played that they were Chekov and Sulu out of Star Trek, nursing an unacknowledged passion for each other but also jealous of each other's buttons. Clara as Chekov used her slavic moodiness to make Sulu let her use the really interesting buttons and fly the ship to visit her mother.

After that they played at sexy job interviews for a bit. At one point someone appeared to loiter in the doorway and Miles quickly scurried back to the official side of the desk, but it proved a false alarm.

"Maybe we could try, what's the word, salting?" sighed Miles after a bored interval during which Clara had started kicking his ankle and, when asked what part she was playing, replied 'Someone who wants to kick your ankle.' "When my Dad had a market stall once, he would get me to pretend to eagerly buy the crap he was peddling, and it always drew people in."

Clara glowered. "How *dare* you gratuitously boast about a spiv parent like that, as though it somehow makes you remotely authentic. Don't come your street-fighting-man shenanigans with me, my boy." Again she kicked his ankle. "And I doubt the word is salting. However it is worth a try."

So Miles sneaked out round the back, limped showily down the high street and into the office groaning and whimpering and clutching at various parts of his body, and then five minutes later hobbled more zippily out again waving a wad of money in the air and shouting, "Yippee!"

But nothing came of it.

"Perhaps if you were to let yourself be run over by a car," mused Clara, "and then crawl into the shop laughing with glee."

It was past eleven when the first customer entered. They were kneeling on the desk, swaying, pretending it was a raft, Clara being a beautiful but hungry shipwreck survivor who was using her feminine wiles to eat bits of Miles on the sly. The customer stopped and looked at them in slight surprise.

"Fuck off, we aren't ready," said Clara. "No, wait, sorry, what was the problem?"

"I lost a tooth eating a donut," said the man. "The – "

"Fuck off then, we can't be bothered. Try the tooth fairy. You probably have scurvy. Go away." The man went away.

"You're not going to do this properly, are you?" said Miles, somewhat relieved.

"I am too! That was too rubbish to bother with. I wasn't ready."

They sat down properly again and tried to look professional. Planning it they had agreed that just one of them at a time would sit behind the desk and deal with the clients, while the other loitered nearby as audience. They were also supposed to be in character and where necessary costume. There was a flask for if they got nervous. However the second customer entered almost directly on the heels of the first and caught them still unprepared. Clara just had time to don a placid smile and grab a pair of granny glasses and some knitting from a bag. First off she was to be

Nanny Bryce, an old and cheerful retainer from her youth with whose vagaries Miles had grown familiar by hearsay and whom Clara held an exemplar of a certain kind of blithe British fortitude in the face of adversity.

The customer was a professional-looking man in his mid-thirties. There were bruises and plasters on his face and an arm was in a sling.

"Somebody looks done up," said Clara with a cosy rural burr, glancing up benevolently from her knitting as he sat. "Now you tell your Nanny all about it."

The man hesitated a beat and contracted his eyebrows at this but plunged into his story. He had taken a tumble down the ramp of a pub beer cellar, open for a delivery.

"Heavens to Betsy," said Clara with a tut. "The things that do happen. Never you mind, my cherub, we'll have a nice cup of tea and you'll be right as ninepence. Put the kettle on, lovey," she said to Miles, who amiably complied but continued to loiter behind.

"Er – thank you," said the client. As he was saying, not only had he fallen down the ramp, but subsequently a beer barrel had been rolled down on top of him.

"Eeh, it never do rain but it pours," said Clara imperturbably. "I expect you'll have scraped your knees as well." She paused in her knitting long enough to fish a small round tin out of her bag and place it on the table. "Here now, better put some Germolene on it."

The man stared at the Germolene disbelievingly. "Um ... no, this happened last Tuesday."

"Well then! All done and dusted with no harm felt, and tomorrow's a bright new day."

There was a slight pause as he digested this. "In point of fact I was quite badly injured, and continue to feel the after-effects of the shock and stress."

"Well you will do, falling down ruddy great holes," Clara agreed kindly. "But you'll be more careful how you go in future, hmm? Better a barked shin now than a severed head later, that's what I always say."

The man frowned and looked around for someone else he could talk to. Failing to catch Miles's eye, he cleared his throat and continued in what seemed a prepared speech, "I'd be the first to admit I wasn't fully paying attention to where I was going. I was in something of a hurry, I was reading an A to Z and talking on a phone. Nevertheless the fact remains that the trapdoor should clearly have been cordoned off and signposted while opened, and perhaps with some sort of sonic warning too. Furthermore there is absolutely no excuse for a barrel being dropped down the chute without first checking there was no-one at the bottom."

"Oh now, don't be so nesh!" said Clara with gentle reproof. "None of the other children will play with you if you become a fussbucket and a tell-tale, my apple. Now you go and get in a nice hot bath and it'll all come out with yesterday's wash."

There was another pause. "I was hoping to get some money," said the man at last.

"Well we'd all like that, my lambkin, wouldn't we? You could get a job, a nice little paper-round perhaps, or take some lemonade bottles back to the – "

"I have a job! You don't seem to – Someone ought to be held responsible!"

"Tush and fiddle-faddle! You should be responsible for your own actions, at your age," said Clara severely, still knitting.

"Look – I was just walking down the street minding my own business, and I fell into this gaping hole in the middle of it!"

"Well I expect it was punishment for something naughty you did, my fluffybuttock, God watches us at all times and strikes when you least expect it. If I was you I would get down on my knees and ask him for forgiveness."

"I – " The man shook his head wonderingly, mumbled something unpleasant and left.

"That *was* fun," said Clara.

"Nanny Bryce seems to have been quite a scary biddy at times," said Miles.

Clara smiled fondly. "Germolene and repentance were her nostrums for all my childhood mishaps. It may explain a lot about me. We should tell our marriage counsellor. Your turn now."

"I find I don't want to," said Miles.

"Must I explain again how you don't have an independent will any more?" Clara pressed her foot against his groin. "Don't make me deal directly with head office."

She attached a handlebar moustache and silk scarf from their dressing-up box to Miles.

"You are Jimmy 'Badger' Faversham, affable World War Two RAF ace and exponent of looking on the bright side," she said. "You are, incidentally, ridiculously sexy and may be wearing that tonight if you play your cards right."

"And perhaps goggles?"

"I think I may wear a propeller on my head and pretend to be a Spitfire."

The door opened.

"Oh Christ," said Miles.

"A good-natured smile and a blithely cheery attitude will see you through."

"It's a woman," muttered Miles in alarm. "Abort, abort."

"We are equal-opportunities irritators."

"I can't mess a woman around! Jimmy Badger Faversham wouldn't be ungallant to a woman. And she's in plaster!"

"It's probably fake."

"She has bruises!"

"Self-inflicted."

"One eye is swollen shut."

"So will yours be."

The woman hobbled and puffed up to the desk, assisted by a crutch and a grave-faced companion. One arm and leg were in plaster and she did indeed seem to have been knocked about a bit. She was late middle-aged and looked to have been worn down and defeated long before whatever disaster had propelled her through their door. She sank down onto the chair and sighed.

"You've been in the wars," said Miles beaming affably beneath his fake moustache.

"I fell down a flight of stairs," said the woman.

"I say, what a rotten bit of luck," said Miles grinning foolishly. He nodded at her arm. "I see you've copped one in the wing."

"And the leg," said the other woman, "compound fracture. She had concussion too."

"Bash on the noggin, what?" said Miles cheerily, heart sinking inside. "Still, mustn't grumble, eh? Worse things happen at sea."

"You see the lift in the flats was out, and the kids had broken the stair lights. I'd been on at the council for weeks to fix them."

"No change out of the desk brass, eh?" said Miles enthusiastically, stomach knotting. "Bally red tape." Behind him Clara, loitering at a filing cabinet busying herself with some papers, gave a sudden cough he was unable to interpret.

"I missed the top step in the dark and down I went like a sack of potatoes. I was lying there an hour before someone found me."

Miles grinned sickly. "Er – careless walk costs lives, what?"

"You are going straight to hell," said Clara in his ear. She leaned forward to the woman and handed her a card. "I'm afraid we don't have the specialist expertise in that sort of case. I recommend you try this firm. Good luck and I hope you make them pay through the nose."

Miles ducked under the desk and applied himself to the emergency flask as the woman hobbled out.

"How *could* you be so horrid?" demanded Clara in disbelief, slapping him on the head. "I've a good mind to divorce you."

"But – "

"You really don't have a clue."

"But you – "

"Obviously she was for real." She seemed quite contrite, even shaken, and grabbed the flask off Miles. "Fairly obviously," she amended after a couple of nips. "Still it's the principle," she added after a couple more. "I mean ... if she sues the council, they'll have less money to spend on ... um, stair lights for other people." She drank some more. "Really, the old cow probably hurled herself down the stairs on purpose. The point is you can't blame that debacle on me so don't even think about it."

"Oh God, oh God."

"All right, that was bad."

"Oh God." Miles seized the flask.

"The problem is that due to your lack of fibre and kulak upbringing you're not really clear on what it is we're fighting for. Give that back at once. No you don't," she said as Miles made to rip off his moustache, "try again with this one. Chancer if ever I saw one."

The next customer did indeed seem much more the ticket: a healthy-looking youngish man who swaggered over to the desk and cockily straddled the chair backwards.

He was in time to catch Miles grabbing a final swig from the flask.

"Er – what ho," said Miles Jimmy Badger Faversham not very enthusiastically, endeavouring to hoist his affable smile into place. "What can we do you for?"

The man said he was a postman and had been bitten by a dog two years ago.

"Now this case seems much more in our line, don't you think Mr. Faversham?" said Clara in the background.

"Ah! Frisky little bow-wow! Occupational hazard, what?" enthused Miles grinning happily. "Still, don't do to grumble, worse things happen at sea, eh? Chap I knew ditched in the drink once, leg bitten orf by a shark. Tempted to mope about it ... only natural ... thought it'd play hell with his cricket ... but two weeks later he made a hundred for Sussex ... just a matter of buckling down to it. Still, you didn't lose your leg, what?"

"Er, no, they said it was a superficial wound, like," said the postman. "The leg's fine."

"Splendid! No harm done then, eh?" beamed Miles jovially.

"No the leg's fine. It's, it's me head like, the trauma."

"Well, it don't do to brood, eh?" Miles grinned ecstatically. "Ah – doesn't do to get a name for yourself as a moper – got to stay cheery, what?"

"I mean I have nightmares, like."

"Ah – kind of doggy was it?"

"A Jack Russell, it was vicious, you know, it wouldn't let go. I mean I should have put a claim in at the time, but I thought it was nothing, you know, just get on with it, I thought I was over it – "

"Good show!" boomed Miles orgasmically. "Damned good show! That's the spirit! Soldier on regardless – you make me proud to be British, sir."

"But then the nightmares started, like. I mean it's got to a point where, where I'm scared to go on me round in case there's dogs, and I've been calling in sick."

"No, no," said Miles frowning. "Doesn't do at all. Frosty silence in the mess. Fall off the bicycle, get straight back on it. Take me. Shot down eight times. Couldn't wait to get back up and try again. Eventually learned how to shoot back and fly out of the way of the Luftwaffe, trial and error, crucible of experience, can't put a price on it – "

"So I was told, you know, you can put in a claim for that kind of thing, for the trauma."

"Sue the doggy, eh?" cried Miles delightedly. "There's a turn-up! That'll teach the blighter! Have a bit of fun with the old cross-examining, what? Pack the jury with cats, that's the ticket – "

"No, the owners don't have any money, like. I was thinking more, you know, the Post Office. I mean, you know, they just threw me in there, no protection. Duty of care kind of thing."

"Kind of protection is there against a bow-wow? Provide rubber gaiters for you to wear? No, no, can't see it, look damn sloppy, nice smart uniform, that's the thing."

If not actually listening to Miles the customer was at least pausing a second before continuing.

"And, I thought, they never offered any counselling after."

"Quite right. Steer clear of the trick-cyclists, my advice … treat you like a child … damn rum bunch … primal trauma … incestuous urges … man can't honk his own mother's tits any more without some Chelsea Arts Club type sniggering … poisoned a well … tommy-rot … " Miles shook his cheeks.

"And I've asked them, like, if I can be taken off houses with dogs but they say it's not possible. It's got to be against me human rights. I was told, you know, I'd probably have a case."

"Human rights," rumbled Miles. "I had the Gestapo attach electrodes to the old chap once. Now *there* was a breach of human rights if you like. Think I minded? Not a bit of it. All in the day's work. Change as good as a rest. Now look here – you seem like a nice young chap – "

"Nonsense," said Clara. "Man's a funker." She had come and sat next to

Miles and was glaring across the table. She, too, wore a luxuriant moustache, to the surprise of both Miles and the client. "Disgrace to his uniform. Drum him out of the service. Strike his name from the lists and burn his satchel."

"What the ---- are you playing at?" yelped the postman.

"Damned bad business," rumbled Clara. "Scared of a little doggy. It's his parents I feel sorry for. Should take his life, only decent thing to do."

"It took a flaming lump out of me leg! I'm traumatized!"

"Woof!" cried Clara, surprisingly, starting forward and snapping her teeth at him. Startled, the man recoiled. "Oh, he is scared, look," she said in her own voice. "He wasn't lying after all. Woof! Woof! Grrrrr! Bloody coward. Bloody spineless shirker."

"Ah – steady on there," said Miles, fearing aggression. "All chaps together, what? Attack of nerves happen to anyone. Pull yourself together and get on with it, only thing to do."

The postman had leapt to his feet. "What are you on? ----ing waste of time you are," he yelled as he marched to the door. "I'll ----ing sue *you* for wasting me time," he concluded as he left.

"I think we helped him," said Clara. "My turn, my turn! I'm going to do Mrs. Mauberley next." She took off the moustache and slumped on the chair scowling in readiness. Mrs. Mauberley had been an old and vicious cleaning woman attached to Clara's family.

They had to wait a few minutes before the next victim, which gave Clara a chance to glue a fag to her lower lip and practise waggling it while talking.

"You could be an actress, you know," said Miles, "if we ever decided to rejoin the human race. So long as you avoid any Scandinavian parts."

"Don't start that again, tin-ear, I bloody *can* do Scandinavian, I'll show you after Mrs. Mauberley."

The next client hobbled in on crutches, a leg in plaster.

"Abort, abort," said Miles. "He's really hurt."

"Nonsense," said Clara. "Another malingerer. Anyway that's not the *point*."

The man settled himself into the chair with some difficulty, sighing and wincing.

"What's tickling you, Sunny Jim?" Clara grunted, arms folded.

The man explained that a breeze-block had fallen on him at work; his shin was fractured in two places.

Clara snorted. "Is that all? My insides was took out in 1952. Think anyone cares?"

The man hesitated a moment and then explained that, while technically the accident had been his own fault, bonuses had been offered for speed of completion and –

Clara sneered. "Building site, was it? *Arsking* for it. That's how me Uncle Stan was took. Nail through his thumb on the Friday, stiff as a board by Monday. His whole arm turned black," she said with relish, "*sloshing* with pus it was."

The man looked at Miles. "So ... what are my chances?"

Clara blew smoke and peered gloatingly at his plaster. "Wound like that? An unhygienic place like a building site? Fifty-fifty of you seeing the end of the week at best. You want to watch it don't turn gangrenous. That's how our Bert went. Crushed toe, it started off as. Count yourself lucky if you only lose the leg."

The man laughed somewhat nervously and looked at Miles with entreaty. "No ... really, it's just a straightforward ... the hospital said it would be completely ... "

"*Horspitals!*" said Clara with contempt. "I haven't drawn a breath without pain since the first Beatles album, think any sod can find what's the matter with me?"

"I'm sure it'll be fine," said Miles. "Mrs. Mauberley tends to ... "

"You're living in a fool's paradise," said Clara with a shrug. "But what should I care? Don't mind me, dearie, no bugger else does, and me with bleeding sores on me gums ever since Suez."

"I think your chances of compensation are slender," said Miles. "We wouldn't take the case."

"Never live to see it come to court," muttered Clara round her fag. "He's got the *look* on him, poor sod."

The man left.

"Right," said Clara as another man walked in as if on cue, "this time I am going to be Karen Blixen *or* Isak Dinesen and will teach him a Blixenesque *or* Dinesenian acceptance of the will of God."

"Oh please no. Anyway this is a Stoic *British* Endurance shop."

"We are branching out."

The man walked stiffly to the desk.

"Please to take a seeet," said Clara in a very strange accent indeed.

The man sat. "Yeah well it's me back, see," he said.

"I haad a farm in Africa," said Clara.

"I beg pardon?"

"Please to go on with your tale."

"Yeah well I was walking down the street, see, and I tripped over a paving stone, and I think I've thrown me back out, I've not been right since."

"Please to elaborate the tale," said Clara. "*Where* were we going? What were your plans? What did you think your life was going to be?"

"Well I was on me way to the Job Centre, as it goes."

"Howww ironic," said Clara in the horrendous Scando-Slavic-Welsh-Pakistani accent that was her best shot at Danish. "You were on your way to seek work, and now the great author has ensured you will never work again."

"Er, yeah," said the man. "I'm definitely not fit for nothing now. So what should I do, then? What's the first step?"

"You must accept," said Clara.

"Accept how much?" asked the man after waiting expectantly a moment.

"Accept your destiny," said Clara.

"What, I just have to take it? The council, they're the ones responsible."

"We are all marionettes in the hands of the great puppeteer," said Clara.

The man stared at her and then glanced at Miles. "Is there someone else I can talk to?"

"That will not help you," said Clara. "You must accept with pride the role you were given to play. See the shape of your story with humble appreciation; it is a fine one. You had no work, you went to find work, now you will never work again. It is a tale to tell your children, if you are still able to father them."

The man blinked, "Look, are you telling me there's no-one I can – "

"I haav a case of syphilis," said Clara.

The man got up and left the shop.

After that there was a lull in trade for a while and eventually they went out to lunch. They left the premises open and put a note on the door reading, 'Back in half an hour, feel free to come in and wait but try not to bleed on anything.'

Upon their return they found a mother and child, the former wanting to sue the council because the latter had broken its arm falling from a climbing frame. Clara brought out Mrs Mauberley again, resulting in hysterics from both visitors and a decision to sue the hospital who had missed the gangrene and brain damage Mrs M instantly diagnosed in the unhappy mite.

Next Clara donned a headscarf and became a gypsy and told a trainee chef who had severed his own finger that a curse was upon him and more and worse things would happen unless he crossed her palm with silver. She left it on to be a Russian babushka, a more fatalistic version of Mrs Mauberley, who listened patiently to the next customer's long and involved story and then gloomily sighed, "Yes, life is woe, but what can any of us do? Take heart, tovarich, this winter will be a cold one and with luck we will never see the spring."

Miles reprised Jimmy 'Badger' Faversham for the benefit of a quite self-assured and affluent-looking man who had been trapped in a lift for half an hour and said he had developed claustrophobia afterwards, and then an ambulanceman who had slipped on a rug at the home of a heart-attack victim and wanted to sue him, in both cases abetted or hampered by Clara sporting a riding crop and helmet as a quite savage General Patton figure, or at any rate someone intimidating with an appalling quasi-American accent who said things like 'Faggot' and 'Yellow bastard' a lot.

Clara idly remarked that it might be amusing, if they did this again, to rig tripwires somehow, or collapsing chairs, or overpolish the floors and put down slippy rugs or something, or otherwise arrange for their clients to ironically hurt themselves on the premises.

"I must beg to differ, my Nazi bride," said Miles quite firmly. "But perhaps if we were to visit a real compensation office and trip over something and lie there groaning ... "

"Yes, yes! That was what I was groping towards. I knew there was a reason I married you in spite of your liberal squeamishness. Can we do that tomorrow?"

"Maybe next month."

"But I want to do it tomorrow, and I have breasts," Clara pointed out, tenderly stapling his tie to his collar. She went on to develop a further plan for them to visit compensation solicitors pretending to be Long John Silver and Captain Ahab or someone.

When the next client entered she screamed piercingly as they shook her hand and then clutched it and cried, "My fingers! My fingers! You've broken my bloody fingers, you clumsy fool! Why did you break my fingers? I will sue you for every penny," and so on until they fled.

Later on they were overcome with guilt once more after hearing a really shocking story and gave someone else a card for a proper firm. But after that they did a Faversham-Mauberley duet on someone quite awful and cheered up again.

"This is God's work really," said Clara.

"If you say so, my Queen of Darkness."

The shortest interview of the day was one which went as follows. A man came in and sat down and said, "It's not an accident but it might be compensation. My boss called me a dick."

"You *are* a dick," said Clara and Miles simultaneously.

The man nodded thoughtfully and left.

Towards the end of the afternoon Clara scraped and tied back her hair and put on a white false beard and thick round glasses.

"I can't believe I forgot this," she said. "I meant to do this one early on."

"And you are?"

"Sigmund Freud, obviously. I'm going to tell them there are no accidents."

A man came in wearing a neckbrace.

Miles winced. "Abort, abort. He might be for real."

"Balderdash."

"If someone's side-swiped him ... "

"He should muddle through, or become an honourable beggar if he is unfit to work."

"Whiplash claims are ... British. People used to make whiplash claims in the old days. My uncle ... "

"I am not responsible for your underclass family."

"It might be real."

Clara trod on his foot. The man was upon them. He paused for a second halfway down to his chair, staring frankly at Clara and her beard.

"Is that a false beard?" he asked.

"Vhy vould I vear a forlse beard?" The voice was quite good. The beard was a long one more suited to Santa Claus; she was leaning forward a bit and had her arms folded to help it obscure her boobs.

The man looked nonplussed. "I'm sorry, for a second I thought ... "

"Pairanoid tendencies," said Clara to Miles significantly, stroking her beard. "Vot did you vish to discuss mit ich?" she asked the man.

"I was in an accident ... "

"There *are* no accidents."

"What?"

"Vhy do you vear a brace supporting ze head?" asked Clara. "Ze head is floppy? You cannot ... keep it up? You see vhere I am going mit zis," she asided to Miles.

"Well that's what I'm coming to," said the man. "I was in an accident, I slowed down because someone pulled out of a side-street and the guy behind rammed into me."

"Aha," said Clara, glancing at Miles.

"I mean he was right up me backside to begin with – "

"*Aha.*"

"And ever since then – "

"Zhere are no accidents," said Clara. "You vanted it to happen."

"You what?"

"Ja, ja. Is quite obvious to me. You are ein latent homosexual. Ze car behind represents ein great big cock you vanted up you. Zat vill be ein thousand pounds, please."

The man paused. Miles had noted before that very often when Clara said really unexpected things to people they decided on some level that the safest course was not to have heard it and carried on as they had been doing. So it was with this one.

"You see he shunted me forward and ever since – "

"Ja, ja, he shunted you real good. You vanted it like zat. Zis vas perhaps ein nice long sports car with ein purple bonnet? You vanted it up your rear-end."

The man stared here and there. This was often stage two.

"Alvays zey look for ze cameras," remarked Clara. "Classic pairanoid repressed homosexual."

"What the hell – ?"

"Now mit ze denial. How can I put zis clearly? Cock, cock, cock. To you ze car was ein huge penis that you yearned to be violated by. You, you vant ze cock, admit."

"I've got whiplash – "

"You vant to be lashed with ein vhip and then to take ze cock. You love ze cock. You vant to be vhipped vith ze cock."

"Is this some kind of – "

"Vot kind of car vhere you rammed in ze back by, answer me zat, hmm?"

"It was a big delivery van if you – "

"You vant a big delivery of cock in your bottom. Zis, I do not even, probably ze whole zing never happened, zis was ein cock dream you are having."

"You what?" The man was shouting.

"Ze car in front 'pulled out' you say, zat is suggestive. Pulled out of what? Ein vagina, obviously. Because you do not like the vagina, you love ze cock."

"I've had about enough – "

"Cock," said Clara, throwing her head back and laughing, "admit you vant ze cock – "

At that point the man leapt onto the table. Miles had seen it coming and interposed himself in time to stop him grabbing Clara.

"I told you there was nothing wrong with him," said Clara, retiring prudently as Miles got punched.

Chapter Six

Once at a party, a different party to the one in Chapter Two, but to which Clara had been invited by the same London friend for the same misguided reason of helping her to network, with similarly disastrous results, Clara had cornered the editor of a former-broadsheet newspaper and rudely asked him a number of questions. "Why is your paper so full of celebrities and popular culture rubbish? Why do you have celebrities writing about politics and the environment? And by the way do you know your environment correspondents are incompetents or bloody liars? Why can't there be just one newspaper for people who don't want to know about bloody celebrities and pop culture? Who are the 39 Steps? What about the blessed Oliver Plunkett? You verminate the sheets of your birth. Why has the crossword gone rubbish?" And then, lastly, because she was running out of breath, she had asked him if he knew how excrementally bad some of his columnists were, concluding with a final glared, "Well? Do you? Speak up, man. Don't you have a tongue in your head?"

The editor, who was relaxed enough at that point to be polite, had amiably asked her to name which ones and she had done so.

"Ah, but they get a reaction," he had explained.

"Yes," said Clara, "and the reaction is, 'How rubbish you are, why can't I do your job?'"

There is a whole section of the press whose careers are built on getting a reaction. There are the valuable band of wits and commentators – the pointers-out of unpalatable truths, deflators of pomposity, scorners of received wisdom – who are loved for daring to be hateful, who for every indignant squeal they provoke earn two adoring blessings or relieved sighs of, 'Thank you.' Then there are the deliberate and calculating provocateurs; and a class of diarists and navel-examiners. While the best of these may be diverting and have genuine fans, the worst are all too often read ironically or in a spirit of morbid car-crash rubbernecking, some of their most devoted readers following their antics solely in order to share their idiocies, eccentricities and banalities with friends. Thanks to the far-sighted policy of giving newspapers away free on the internet, thanks to editorial policy now being driven by statistics derived from this, they thrive and prosper. The interest they arouse can be measured and pointed to in terms of browser visits and numbers of comments; the nature of that interest is irrelevant. The effect on circulation – or to be more accurate, the less profitable but far more sexy and forward-looking rubric of internet hits – may be undeniable, but the benefit to standards of journalism is open to question.

Shortly before the amiable editor had finally snapped and, uniquely in this book if not quite in her life, informed Clara that she was an extremely rude young woman who could fuck off, at which she had immediately burst into fake tears and hysterics so loud, distraught and convincing that a man nearby who was unaware of what had led to them had grown indignant and offered to punch the editor for her, had actually grabbed and shaken him and demanded to know what he had done to her – shortly before this unfortunate climax and following on from the previous topic, Clara had demanded, "What about Harriet Pridgett? Have you read bloody Harriet Pridgett?"

To which the editor had cheerfully replied, "Oh, her. Her father's a friend and I have to fill the paper somehow."

Harriet Pridgett had for a long time been Clara's favourite journalist; she was, in the way explained above, her number one fan. She sometimes cut her writings out to keep; she circled her favourite bits in red ink; she had once even embroidered and framed a quotation from one to show Miles what it was they were fighting, although she kept it hidden somewhere she didn't have to see it every day. Reading her and reading the best passages aloud to Miles had become a ritual to be savoured, saved for a proper time when it could be enjoyed properly, often conscientiously enhanced with the addition of tea or sweets.

Miles had piously deplored this habit, so akin to schadenfreude and laughing at asylum inmates, saying that as fops and fogeys it was the sort of thing they should look down on and eschew in favour of more wholesome pastimes, the non-ironic enjoyment of true excellence, nourishing their souls with beautiful things. Clara had virtuously replied that, unlike him, she took an interest in her fellow humans no matter how unsatisfactory; that besides she had never claimed to be perfect and had to have some vices; and furthermore that the ironic enjoyment of crap was pretty much the only thing that was left to them nowadays.

Harriet Pridgett's style alternated, sometimes in the same essay, between a hip, 'sassy', breathless, pop-culture-reference-laden 'Hey girlfriend' idiom, and a solemn, vatic pompousness: incantatory, portentous, the repeated 'I' ringing out like a bell, an invocation to a deity, a hypnotic chant that, Clara insisted to Miles, eventually took on a hallucinatory quality that broke down the barriers between writer-celebrant and audience-congregation so that 'in a very real sense we become her'. Clara had once tried to correlate the fluctuations in Harriet's style to the phases of the moon, and then to her favourite TV programmes being on or not, but had concluded that she was moved solely by whim or the demands of each individual cri de coeur.

Clara allowed her a measure of talent at what she did, even occasional glimmerings of a straitjacketed intelligence; and she appeared to have non-ironic followers. She was perhaps not, strictly speaking, to be bracketed with some of the net-troll performing-selves alluded to above; although her beginnings had been in the embarrassing-confessional genre she had transcended it. Her editor had spoken unkindly, and disingenuously; while she was not to his own taste and her father was, in fact, his boss, the fact was that at this point she was one of his headline performers, with salary and profile to match. Clara only dimly remembered Harriet's discreetly wild-child early days, the sagas of plane-crash liaisons and strange internal psychodramas sparked by the most trivial things, the celebrated battle with an eating disorder, and had skipped with a groan her works detailing her obsessions with TV series and pop stars and name-brand shopping. What she mostly knew and loved her as now was the world's most politically-correct woman.

Not a fashionable cause did she fail to espouse; not one loopy new belief did she fail to clutch to her heart; not one modern piety did she not subscribe to; not one new official madness did she not try to justify, not one aspect of the status quo did she not defend. A dauntless slayer of Davids and protector of Goliaths, she saw herself one of a beleaguered band of quixotic champions of the faith surrounded and outnumbered by a baying barbarian horde. Which may well be true; it is just that the former have all the power. Her tone of self-sacrificing bravery and tell-it-like-it-is daring while piously mouthing approved platitudes and echoing the thoughts of her own circle was a joy to hear. Moreover she had personally discovered, and unhesitatingly aligned herself with the victims of, forms of oppression, injustice and suffering that made even Marxist former-polytechnic lecturers blink in surprise or grind their teeth in envy. Her self-righteousness was as flawless and ever-flowing as the grace of God.

The results of this filtered through her confessional, angsty, blurt-every-tiniest-thought-out style, through imperfectly-repressed hysteria and a borderline persecution complex, were, Miles had to admit, often something special. She bought dolls for her young sons to play with to encourage nurturing instincts, noticed that the dolls were female, worried at the implication that females needed looking after and the thought that dollhood objectified women. She was capable of spending a whole column berating herself for not having upbraided a man on a bus whom she had overheard using the word 'cretin'. She was more than capable of spending a column describing how she *had* reproved someone in such a situation, or how she had shouted at and tried to report someone who had slapped the legs of a misbehaving toddler, or how she had torn a strip off a pub landlord for installing a patio heater to warm his exiled smokers.

She had once spent a column and a half agonizing over having eaten some fruit that might not have been organically grown. "She is the St. Augustine of North London," Clara had breathed ecstatically.

Harriet's latest and greatest obsession, the one that was coming to override all others, the one least calculated to endear her to Clara at the moment, was her belief, widely shared in her time and circle, that the world was becoming dramatically warmer, with life-endangering consequences, and that mankind was responsible for this, and that no sacrifice was too great to combat it. She had come to this later than some – she credited the birth of her children, whom she frequently mentioned as tending to make her an authority on the matter, although Clara thought she could pinpoint the date of her conversion to a certain televised celebrity rally – but had the fire of the neophyte and was making up for lost time, had already equalled or overtaken the most ardent zealots in the field; her current incarnation was that of one taking faltering but determined steps on the road to becoming an Earth Mother.

It happened, as Clara had belatedly and delightedly realised or had drawn to her attention, that Harriet was married to a writer named Richard Gilquist, another journalist whom Clara detested and didn't even cherish the way she did Harriet. Richard Gilquist looked about 14 in his picture and often sounded like it, was afflicted with an ironic, post-modern devotion to pop-culture kitsch, but was bizarrely let loose to pontificate on world politics and other grown-up topics. Among other crimes he had once started an essay on the war in Iraq with a reference to his favourite episode of a children's TV show about vampires; this had led to Clara cancelling all newspapers for several weeks and, in fact, barricading the doors for some days and announcing they were never leaving the house again until the current order of things had passed away. A preamble to a book review he had written once had inspired her to play a minor, briefly-amusing, not terribly satisfying prank by way of punishment, but we do not have time to detail it here. Suffice it to say that he had become a byword for modern vapidity and shallowness to them even before they knew of his connection to Harriet. Anyway, in spite of the fact that a wide-eyed, compulsively-mentioned techno-fetishism and gadget-addiction had long been a staple of his writing, this Ghastly Gilquist had lately reinvented himself as a convert to Global Warmism and ecologically-correct living in the same way as Harriet. He had embarked on a series of articles on the theme of 'ordinary bloke coming new to it tries manfully to lower his carbon dioxide footprint to zero'; simultaneously Harriet, in a heartening demonstration of the diversity of the media, was covering the same turf for her newspaper; Richard had graduated to the rank of pundit, special correspondent, expert, and flew tirelessly all over the world to cover scientific conferences and international summits, interview the eminences in the field, give speeches and take part in debates; while Harriet had the accreditation and special insights of motherhood. Clara, who did not share their belief, called them the Warmist Bonnie and Clyde, among other things.

Recently, as the world grew cumulatively madder, and her own patience shorter, and it became clear that none of the madness was going to go away of its own accord, Clara had found herself laughing at Harriet somewhat less and swearing loudly at her significantly more. She had skipped reading her columns sometimes for the sake of maintaining her angelic disposition. But at the time the story we are gradually coming to opens, Harriet had been absent from the pages of the press for some weeks, and Clara had found she missed her. She worried about her. "She has put her head in a polythene bag to cut down her carbon emissions," she told Miles. "Or she has been beaten to death by someone whose bus conversation she intruded on. Or she was mugged, and found herself thinking badly of the mugger, and is walking on her knees to Gramsci's birthplace to atone."

But Harriet was about to return to Clara's life dramatically, and triumphantly, and with far-reaching consequences, and in a way that meant she would never miss her again.

"Miles! She is back! Banner headlines on the front page, look! Harriet is back! My darling has returned to me!"

But as she turned to the advertised pages her joy gave place to dismay, irritation and the beginnings of real anger.

"Oh *no!* Not again! Don't they ever get tired of it? I do."

"What? What?"

" 'My Nightmare Journey Into the Dark Heart of Middle England.' She's moved to the country! 'Starting this week, Greener Pastures, a new series recording one woman's descent into mud, snobbery and feudalism. Harriet Pridgett moved to the countryside to pursue her dream of carbon-neutral living and found a hothouse of prejudice and archaism.' Doesn't it get *tired?* Harriet, how could you? I expect you to be original. Explore your own head, darling, it is stranger even than us. Oh I am sick of it. Will the urban elite *ever* tire of gaping at us inbred provincials? They are just proving that *they* are the most inbred parochial people ever."

"At least she's a vegan, she won't be able to whine about the lack of designer shoe-shops and lattes and so on."

"Wrong, Miles. Bolded sub-head: 'Mud Spas? Only if I go out without wellies.' … Listen, listen: 'land of sullen pithecanthropoid men grunting as they inseminate Mother Earth with their tools. Soon I will be one of them.' ... Oh Christ she intends to grow her own vegetables and become self-sufficient. This is madness! This is madness! They will starve! Remember that heartbroken column she wrote about the time she tried to grow cress?"

"Maybe by the end she'll sympathize with the farmers at least."

"Don't you believe it. ... Listen to this, listen to this. 'Pretty countryside. Pretty cows. "Moo-cow," says my youngest in delight, pointing as we trudge. "Yes," I sigh bleakly, "pretty moo-cow, silently destroying the environment." ' "

Miles laughed and settled down on the couch. "This could be good actually."

"Yes. Are there any sweets there? Throw some over. Poor kid. Poor cows. Poor us. Miles have you ever thought what an idiotic modern euphemism the term 'the environment' is? How strange and horrid and reductive? My environment at the moment is this room. Most people's environment is streets and houses. Harriet's natural environment is an atmosphere of poisonous suspicion and eternal vigilance for deviant thought patterns. Why can't they just say, 'Save the trees and animals and shit'? They would get more support. The thing is they don't actually *care* for trees and animals, and especially shit. It is an urban phenomenon. They don't actually *like* animals, especially now they have got it into their heads they are emitting poisonous gases, and will happily see them wiped out."

"Environment has suggestions of something you can regulate. Controlled environment. Luxury living environment. Turn the heat up and down with a thermostat."

"You have run with my point admirably, my alert young husband. Sneering at the follies of the rest of mankind will help keep our marriage strong. Do not hog the sweets or I will rip your balls off. ... Oh, listen: 'The children at my eldest's school are immaculately turned-out zombies, unnaturally polite and Fraightfully Naicely spoken. Will mine grow up like that?' Shouldn't think so, dear. I bet they only moved there for the schools really. ... 'The village is so picture-perfect you could vomit.' You see, Miles? The whole of recent history has been deliberate, they *like* things to be ugly and broken. That kind of talk appals me, it really does. It's automatic but where does it *come* from? Oh, oh, listen. 'No doubt if I ever try to escape a huge white bouncing ball will come and trample me.' She is capitalizing Village, you see, it's quite clever. Harriet, dear, you really aren't allowed to make references to The Prisoner, you would have made a perfect Number Two ... I have to say this place sounds even nicer than ours, I vote we move there. Oh, here we go now. 'Beneath the picture-postcard facade, however ... seething hotbed of nationalism, bigotry and prejudice ... The Union Jack flies unashamedly everywhere ... ' Oh no! Not the Union Jack! Those bastards! How dare they! ' ... flies unashamedly everywhere, surly and intimidating, seeming to say, "Don't come here if you aren't like us. " ' "

Miles laughed.

"Listen, listen. 'I shudder to think how any immigrants would react to such a naked brazen display of primitivism. But then, surprise surprise, there are none – apart from my au pair, who has left already, and who can blame her?' "

"She can't blame that on the countryside! She's never kept one longer than three columns anyway!"

"Miles Miles, imagine coming from a sane country, a young girl full of hopes and dreams, your notions of England perhaps based on images of Wodehouse and James Bond, and finding yourself trapped in a house in the middle of nowhere with Harriet and Richard Gilquist and two sinister Harriet-Richard hybrids."

"Don't."

"Where was I? 'It intimidates me, and I'm used to the front room looking like a Mosley rally every time England are in the World Cup.' " They laughed. "Miles whose side will you be on when they divorce? I think I am on Richard's side now. 'In fact I myself can now say I know what it is to be an immigrant.' Oh do fuck off, woman. 'Beneath a surface veneer of empty friendliness and that synthetic bucolic charm they must go to a night-school to learn, I haven't exactly been bowled over by welcome and warmth. Not that I mind. I'm used to not knowing my neighbours' names and like it that way. "Come and learn jam-making!" invites an amateurish hand-drawn notice in the post-office. No thanks. I am not a jam-maker, I am a free woman.' "

"What a cow!" said Miles. "*We* have come-and-make-jam signs in *our* post office. Jam is nice."

"You speak the truth, my orally-fixated sidekick. Speaking of which, keep the sweets coming; if you force me to get up you will regret it. *Our* post-office jam-making sign isn't amateurish though, she would admire ours, I laminated it for them. ... 'At all turns I sense ... ' Oh oh Miles, Harriet's spider-sense has returned! Of late she has been boringly limiting herself to the observable world. 'At all turns I sense brutish resentment and mulish resistance to change.' "

"*We* have brutish resentment and mulish resistance to change."

"We invented it, Miles, her village starts to sound like a pallid knock-off of ours. Ah, but do we have shutters coming down behind our eyes? Harriet senses the inhabitants of this place do when certain topics are raised."

Miles laughed. "That's a useful mutation. Where's she moved, Sellafield? Which sense is it that can detect that anyway, is that the seventh sense?"

"It is the eleventh, Miles. The twelfth sense is the ability to detect 'snarling hostility and morbid possessiveness', as Harriet proceeds to do, 'lurking around every corner.' Imagine sensing those things, Miles, lurking around every corner. It would be so wearing. You would be afraid to ever approach a corner. The one would attack you, or at least snarl at you, while the other would jump out and refuse to lend you things. The poor woman."

"I think Harriet's mind-powers are greater than Derren Brown's."

"It would explain how she is allowed to write this shit. ... 'This is the place where all the Daily Mail readers live.' Oh no! Shock horror! 'The Daily Mail is sold openly here instead of kept under the counter.' That was me, Miles, I made that up. From now on I'm going to throw things in, you have to guess when it's me. 'I expect to hear the sound of "Duelling Banjos" at any minute.'"

"That was you."

"That was me. ... Blah, blah, nasty, brutish and short, I grow weary now... Little England mindset ... knuckle-dragging ..."

"You?"

"Nope. Listen listen! 'The church is a brooding presence, its lichen-encrusted antenna seeming to broadcast conformity in every direction, following you around the panorama, leaping out at you when you least expect it, dominating the landscape as it doubtless does the mindscape.' Oh Miles," she sighed contentedly, "who would ever be an unbeliever? Everything, everything was planned. Harold had to fall at Hastings, it could not have happened otherwise, Norman had to merge with Anglo-Saxon, it was a marriage arranged by God, and then Gutenberg with his press, and everything, everything, all worked for, all foreseen, everything fell into place all along the line so that *that sentence* could one day be written."

"I hate buildings that follow you around," said Miles. "Especially when they leap out at you."

"It is not so bad when one is prepared for it, but when it happens when you least expect it, perhaps when you are in the bath or something, it is too much ... 'The Women's Institute has its fingerprints all over everything ... '"

"That's from making jam," said Miles. "Their hands get sticky."

" ' ... I have been unable to obtain any figures for BNP membership. Whenever I ask talk dries up and the shutters come down.' "

"Oh, that's you."

"No it isn't Miles, come and look."

"She has never asked people," he laughed.

"I bet she has."

"Poor bastards. I wonder if it's the behind-the-eye shutters or actual shop-shutters that come down."

"She doesn't specify but I suspect the latter. I imagine the whole high street shuts up shop like a Wild West town before a gunfight the moment she appears. ... Oh listen listen. 'Perhaps it comes with the territory. Life is cheap here, death a casual occurrence. Hunting regalia is proudly displayed, the landscape echoes with gunfire, any animal you befriend could be in someone's pot tomorrow. What do you expect from the heart of the country? It is filled with blood.' "

"She is the last poet."

" ' "Off to skin a rabbit," says a woman at the post office as cheery adieu. She gives me a sinister smile and says she may drop by to see me some time. If she would do that to a creature she has reared for months, what would she do to me? ... At least she is able to talk coherently. Half the locals I have encountered have been inbred idiots, incoherently drooling and stammering.' "

"Didn't she shout at a stranger for using the word idiot once?"

" 'I expect to hear "Duelling Banjos" everywhere I go.' Miles that wasn't me! That wasn't me! That really wasn't me! I have learned to think like Harriet! My mind *contains* hers!" She ate a sweet to celebrate and then resumed. " ' ... Culture? Fuhgeddaboudit. I am recommended to visit various dismal old houses dating back to the dark ages, which is when history stopped here if you ask me. The village also boasts a puny art gallery selling prints of the dreariest Old Varnished painters and predictably pretty-pretty daubs by locals of the pretty-pretty scenery. The proprietor, a terrible old letch who was bantering with a pneumatic young assistant in a way that would lead to a lawsuit in healthier climes, was smoking a cigarette when I visited. When I politely asked him to extinguish it and reminded him of the law he not-so-politely informed me where the door was and how to use it.' "

"Ha, it's Jeremiah!" said Miles, referring to their friend who ran an art gallery in their village. "He must have a long-lost twin! Cut that out and show it to him."

" 'When I stood my ground – I had missionary forebears, I am ashamed to say' – God I love this woman," Clara muttered. "Who else can reveal so much in so little? 'Stood my ground... and concisely and in words of few syllables tried to inform him of the dangers of passive smoking, there was a tirade that turned the air bluer than his smoke and I in my turn was lectured on how that was nonsense, "junk science" if you please – and then informed, into the bargain, that global warming was too! Needless to say the air then heated with hockey-stick speed as I told him some home truths – a thankless task to tell people what they don't want to hear, but then we already knew that, didn't we, gang?' "

"Oh spooky spooky spooky," said Miles. "Separated at birth. Maybe all gallery owners are like that. Maybe being exposed to beauty all day makes them impatient with nonsense. A good job it *wasn't* Jeremiah, though, he'd have decked her at that point."

Clara was frowning. She continued:

" 'Night-life consists of two pubs. One of them serves the kind of food you need broadband arteries to cope with to a clientele of Golden Years types and pretty-pretty families talking Fraightfully Naice. To my surprise vegetarianism is catered for, but if you're offended by meat smells, forget it. (Isn't it about time we required the provision of separate dining rooms and indeed kitchens for vegetarians and religious minorities? Just a thought.)' "

Clara and Miles both said rude words, vehemently, several times over.

" 'Likewise if you're disgusted by the sight of fathers of small children wolfing down gobbets of fat. (Isn't it about time ... hush, Harriet, mustn't be a nanny-stater!)' "

They swore again.

" 'The other pub is strictly for anthropologists. Talk about your time-warps! Think strutting toffs and forelock-tugging peasants went out with vinyl? Think Bertie Wooster was dead, staked through the heart and nailed down in his coffin? I never did, and now I know I was right.' "

Miles laughed. "Christ, imagine if she ever saw the Walpole!"

Clara was looking increasingly thoughtful. " 'I harboured few illusions about the countryside but even I was shocked ... have to see it to believe it ... like stepping back into the 1930s ...

" 'I have saved the best until last. I was told by the gossipy postal operative that there was another recently-arrived young couple in the nearest house up the road from me, as if we were bound to become the greatest friends. I shuddered at the thought. I do not regret that now. Walking along the road past their house the other day I happened to see them in their garden. The woman was wearing some strange Amish-type headgear resembling a wimple. The man had a rifle and helmet and was doing a Nazi goose-step.' "

Clara looked at Miles with a wild surmise.

Lying on the couch staring at the ceiling, Miles was laughing again. "Fantastic! All right, they win. We are now officially only the second most reactionary village in Britain. Could she have *picked* a worse place to move to? Oh what if the poor bastard neighbours were just idiots playing dressing-up games like us though?"

Miles went silent and frowned.

Clara cleared her throat. "Miles, a terrible suspicion is growing on me ..."

"The new people who've moved into the Dower House," said Miles thoughtfully, "have you ever actually seen them yet?"

He turned to look at her.

"Harriet is our new neighbour!" cried Clara. "The cow is talking about Us!"

*

If there is any democracy in England it is to be found down the pub. Egalitarianism, that is. Where the good, proper, old-fashioned ones still survive – and they are mostly in the countryside – millionaires rub shoulders with labourers, the gentry mingle with shopkeepers, Jets sit down with Sharks, on terms of perfect amity (allowing for personal feud) and prelapsarian fraternity, free men and equal under the impartial eye of the barmaid. Nowhere outside a homosexual bath-house has the dream of the brotherhood of man been more perfectly realised. It would be paranoid as well as idle to speculate that this was one of the reasons a political elite that throve on spurious class-war appeared cheerful about the prospect of such traditional pubs dying out.

There were two pubs in the village, both of which were thriving in spite of them. In the village proper was the Dog and Duck, which had been bought by a chain and become a 'gastro-pub' some months before Clara and Miles moved there. They had arrived in time to see its beautiful old Ladybird-book-illustration-type sign depicting a hunter's dog carrying a duck in its mouth removed and replaced with an idiot sign of a grinning idiot cartoon dog and a grinning idiot cartoon duck sitting side by side, with paw and wing respectively around each other's shoulders. Apart from this and other signs it was still fairly picturesque from the exterior, and fairly tasteful and comfortable within, and it had won awards for its food, but the atmosphere was anodyne.

A short distance outside the village down a lane in the opposite direction from Clara and Miles's house was the pub favoured by most of the locals, the Walpole's Head. It was just such a good pub as described above, and an old-fashioned one in more ways than that. Stone-flagged floors and leaded and mullioned windows must be mentioned, and lots of old dark wood, and on cold afternoons a roaring coal fire. Otherwise, as to fixtures and fittings, you may imagine your own perfect inn, but fixtures and fittings are of course not the point. On its best nights and festival days the atmosphere was a living thing, a shining transcendence of individual self, the hubbub of noise and warmth intoxicating before you even got through the door. The mood was never less than convivial; except when, as happened all too frequently these days, most often during the stay-behinds that were prone to break out in a back room invisible from the road, it turned mutinous.

Old-fashioned; and in one respect unusually so, in all probability unique. If you had entered behind Clara and Miles that day, or indeed on any night and most other days, this unusualness would have struck you immediately. You would, like Harriet, have thought of time-warps, of portals into an alternate universe, more prosaically of film sets; it was not unknown for first-time visitors who had gone on there after a long hard day at different pubs to decide upon entering that they had had enough to drink already.

"What-ho!" cried a figure in a top hat as they entered.

"Pip-pip!" called a man with a monocle.

"Why, 'tis the young master," cried a figure in a neckerchief, doffing a cloth cap and knuckling his forehead at Miles.

"How simply ripping to see you," said someone else jiggling a bowler hat.

And from the hands, mouths, ashtrays of perhaps a third of the patrons, from cigarettes and pipes and cigars, there lazily unreeled lovely ribbons of smoke, swirling blue in the shafts of sunlight slanting through the windows; beautiful, beautiful smoke. It did Clara's heart good to see it.

On the right as they went in, by the side of the doorway that led into the next room, was a signboard which read:

THE LIVING PAGEANT IMPROV THEATRE

Dedicated to Recreating Britain's Past

An ongoing all-day work of fully-immersive interactive
pageantry and improvisational drama

Experience the authentic atmosphere of
Ye Olde Englishe Pubbe! Help re-enact it yourself!

JOIN IN!
Help yourself to props
No acting experience necessary

We are all performers! We are all the audience!

A Living Work of Art
A Moving Museum of Heritage

The Living Pageant Improv Theatre had been Miles's brainwave, one which, Clara said, by itself justified her marrying him, and was possibly the only thing that did. For him, however, it had been an idle off-hand remark, for the rest of the pub an amusing thought; it would never have come to pass if Clara hadn't seized on it ecstatically and forced them all to do it.

The thing was that, while there had been notorious but probably illegal intimidations of acting troupes by officious zealots of local authority, theatres were specifically and clearly exempted from the ban on smoking in public buildings if smoking was necessary to the performance on stage. So what they ought to do, Miles had said after pointing this out, was set themselves up as …

Everyone had smiled; looked thoughtful, wistful; idly added detail to the notion.

Clara, who had been absent in mind, dwelling, after the preceding discussion of what the smoking ban was doing to pubs, on images of civil insurrection and bloodshed, as was her wont on such occasions, had had to have the idea repeated to her.

"Genius!" she had cried, kissing Miles for his brilliance. "Genius! Yes! Of course! Let's do it!" She had slammed the bar with her hand and rounded on them angrily. "Let's really do it! Stop talking! Stop talking about it! You won't do it! We just talk and talk and never *do* anything! Aren't you sick of just going round whining and muttering with your stomachs in a knot? Are you men? Are you English men? I am an English woman and I call you cowards! Let's do this!"

"Yes!" had cried Arthur, the beefy, balding, highly excitable landlord, slamming the bar in his turn. "Yes! Let's do it! I'm with you! I'm sick of it! Let's really, really do it!"

Besotted with Clara, filled to the brim with anger, frustration and miserable self-loathing at his failure to ever do anything about the things that were happening to his country even before he met her, Arthur was always the first to back up her calls for action when she was in this kind of mood, be the proposed action putting bricks through the windows of local authority, burning down the house of a notorious loony-liberal judge who lived not far away, or really really starting the revolution and really *really* going out to string some politicians up *now*. More than once he had reached the point of putting his jacket on and arming himself with whatever was to hand before she had embarrassedly mumbled that perhaps after all they had better plan it a bit more first; and more than once Miles and other cooler-headed bystanders had had to drag the pair of them back from the door by the scruffs of their necks, to be vilified, assaulted and threatened with divorce for their trouble.

But they had really, really done this.

Simon, the former rock-star Lord of the Manor, had amusedly said that, if Arthur was serious and prepared to risk his livelihood, he would personally meet the costs of the almost certain eventual legal proceedings and almost inevitable fine. Miles, nudged and glared at by Clara and in one of the rare open-handed moods he had felt since being stricken by wealth, had offered to go in with him, followed by several others. What did they have to lose but money? It would be fun at least and they would have tried to fight back for once.

Of course they were all, save for Clara, very drunk.

They would certainly not have gone through with it, would probably have forgotten all about it under the more pressing concern of the next day's hangover, had it not been for her impetus and resolve. She had made Miles speed her to London and back for a raid on their costume shop, and they had returned laden with boxes filled with the top hats, bowlers, monocles and so on, which had been deposited in the Walpole's Head triumphantly, to Arthur's initial bleary bewilderment and then slow-blooming grin. And it had been Clara – attired with top hat, tails, monocle and cane – who had lit up the first defiant cigarette in what was now once more a free pub fit for free men, with a cheery, triumphant, "Pip-pip!"

Clara, it might be mentioned, did not smoke herself, or almost as little as she drank, really only when the demands of a role or some whim of poise required it. She had sometimes thought it might be a duty, now, to take it up in earnest, but she really couldn't handle much of it, and Miles, who only smoked when drunk, sternly discouraged her. But she was not entirely disinterested: she loved the sight of those drifting tendrils lit by the shafting sunlight; she loved the even more beautiful sight of people relaxed and at ease, and of a crowded, prospering, cheerful, happy pub; and she loved to watch men smoke, she declared, 'for Freudian reasons'. And more than that she loved freedom, and had been brought up to side with the underdog.

Arthur had obtained a theatre licence. Clara, artfully glossing over the smoking, referring only to 'authentic anachronistic period props' in her letters, had secured accreditation and even guidebook listings from various Heritage and Tourism organisations.

On most of the tables and upon the bars had been placed an instruction card like a menu, written and printed and lovingly laminated by Clara. It read:

THE LIVING PAGEANT IMPROV THEATRE

How To Take Part

The aim is to recreate the atmosphere and authentic feel of a traditional English pub anywhere between, say, 1600 and the late 1980s. [Clara's natural first impulse had been to put 1997 or the year of the pub smoking ban as the latter date, but she had recently read a collection of Auberon Waugh's articles from the early 90s and realised that the madness that had come to flood-tide after 1997 had been a noticeable nuisance in public life for several years before.] Everyone is invited to take part. To do so you must act and behave like someone who lived in those primitive times.

It is quite simple:

1. Obtain your refreshing beverage, alcoholic or otherwise, and any snacks you may require.
2. Take a historical costume prop or two from the boxes lying around. This is optional but may help you get into the spirit of things. Taking part in your own ordinary clothes is fine. The more recent Ancients dressed remarkably similarly to us in many ways.
3. Sit, or stand at the bar, or in any available space.
4. Relax and enjoy yourself.

This last is the most important but most difficult part of your performance. The Ancients believed in a concept known as 'Fun', now discredited. In order to become like them you will have to think your way into their primitive mindset.

Here are some tips:

Smile. Laugh. Be merry. Make jokes if you can think of them. Imagine you live in a free country where you need fear no-one and no man can tell you what to do.

Imagine all the people around you and within earshot are friendly, sensible, civilised adults who can take and enjoy a joke.

Do not look over your shoulder or wonder who that stranger is by the bar. He is a friend too! Pretend you are free to give vent to your every opinion, speculation and silliest whimsy spontaneously and just as they occur to you without fear of retribution.

If you hear something that offends you, laugh it off and remember that friendly insults and unguarded speech were how the Ancients showed they liked and trusted each other.

Try not to worry about your health or count the 'units' of alcohol you have consumed. Unlike us the Ancients didn't believe in immortality. They thought that man was mortal, no matter how cautious you were, and that life was a brief, fleeting and precious thing that must be savoured on the wing and filled with joy and gaiety wherever possible.

As you get more confident you may like to sing, shout, hug, and swear eternal love to those around you. Classes are available.

Some Sample Dialogue

You will notice some of our more regular performers peppering their speech with various anachronistic phrases. Feel free to join in. I am sure you can think of your own but here are some suggestions to start you off:

Pip-pip
Chin-chin
Top-hole
Frightfully bogus
You rotten cad
Here's mud in your eye, Ma
I should cocoa!
Sauce!
Give us a song, don't give us your sorrows
No better than she ought to be
God's wounds, that is a fine piece of womanflesh
Lovely knockers! Give us a smile
The groats is a-ready for scranneling, milord
He do be one of Napoleon's spies, he be
Sir. – If you start upon your infernal Whiggery again,
    I will deck you and your ten hardest mates

Improvise; ad lib. But the performance can just consist of carrying on an ordinary normal conversation. As mentioned above the point is to talk freely and spontaneously (consult a history book if in doubt). You may of course choose to simply sit and watch the show.

OTHER PROPS

One of the most notable features of the archaic English tavern and one vital to its recreation is the presence of tobacco smoke. Smoking props are not provided but you may notice that some of our regular troupe have brought their own, and newcomers are encouraged to join in. For those not familiar with the use of tobacco products, the procedure is as follows:

1. Light up
2. Inhale
3. Exhale
4. Repeat

You may find it difficult at first but will soon get the hang of it. You may even find it addictive.

Startling as it may seem the Ancients found this practice at once relaxing and mentally stimulating. Sharing their tobacco products led to conviviality and occasioned excuse for social interaction with strangers (again, consult a history book). They would have laughed at you if you had informed them of the dangers of 'passive smoking', and perhaps come out with one of their colourful expressions of contempt. They believed in something called the diffusion of gases, now discredited. They did not realise, as thanks to modern statistical advances we do now, that exhaled smoke is a sentient and malevolent thing, a djinn or unclean spirit that is not to be exorcised by air-conditioning or tempted out of an open window when there are lungs to hurl itself down, its strength undiminished, perhaps even increased, by being passed through the smoker's lungs, and that this plague slaughters literally uncountable numbers every year.

Smoking may be a stupid habit, to modern eyes, but it is one necessary to the authenticity of our historical reconstruction and essential to the theatrical impersonation of the various cheery, happy-go-lucky characters you see being improvised around you.

You will also note the lightbulbs in our theatre are authentically outmoded, and do not contain the health-giving mercury gas we take for granted today.

DIRECTOR'S NOTES

If the Director is in the auditorium she may give you notes on your performance or suggest dialogue. She should be obeyed unquestioningly and, if you feel she has helped you find the direction of your acting Journey, bought Britvic orange-juice and crisps.

Miles had thought this was overdone, counterproductive and asking for trouble, and had tried to veto or edit it, but was overruled, Arthur finding it the greatest thing ever apart from Clara herself. Clara, of course, was the director alluded to, and when present and in the mood would still occasionally seize a beret and riding-crop that were kept behind the bar and, beating the latter against her leg, bark instructions at the 'performers'. "Diction, diction! Projection! And relax! Relax more, damn it! You – call that a Hanging Judge? The wig isn't enough, you have to be mentally fitting a noose to every unwashed neck you see. ... You there, find your inner toff! Condescend more ... Merry, laddy, merry! You are an apple-cheeked peasant now, not a software designer ... I want more Hogarth in this corner ... That doesn't say WAAF girl to me! Shoulders back! Vowels clipped! Give that pilot an angelic kiss of farewell, you could be the last woman he sees! And a quick grope wouldn't go amiss ... You, give me five minutes of Sam Weller. You do Simon Templar. Roister, all of you! Roister, damn you, roister!"

Originally the Smoking Theatre had been confined to the big room on the right past the sign; plush red curtains had divided off this stage-auditorium; it had been necessary to purchase a ticket for a pound in order to enter. (Miles had lobbied, again unsuccessfully, for the construction of an actual stage area a foot above the floor, even footlights.) But now they had grown careless after a lengthy period with no sign of molestation by authority, and the Living Pageant filled the whole pub willy-nilly. For the most part people just talked and behaved ordinarily as they had before. But anyone lighting up had become habituated to put on some random piece of costume from a prop-box first and mutter some token anachronism, and would sometimes be reminded by the cautious or those keen on ritual if they forgot. It had become a custom to some to call out outmoded greetings when friends entered; others would start speaking in period, or simply start saying, 'Rhubarb, rhubarb' like extras in a crowd scene, when strangers came in, and in the latter case it would be kept up for longer. The fun had by no means worn off; there were some who would spend whole nights behaving in character; Clara delighted to think she had inadvertently created an eternal England of the imagination – fiction rubbing shoulders with history, the great dead reincarnated, the past living on in the present, as it should – and loved them all. There would be special occasions when everyone came in full-dress costume. But the main thing now was that everyone felt able to smoke in peace within the sanctuary of the Walpole's Head.

As has already been mentioned, Clara was also responsible for the name of the pub. It had previously, from the 12th century until just recently, been The Saracen's Head. Even though the sign depicted the Saracen's head as being firmly on his shoulders, and the Saracen in question was a dashing, handsome, merry-looking chap, this had been felt in some quarters to be inappropriate to the modern world of peace, harmony and endless, hyper-irritable, princess-and-pea sensitivity; and Arthur had been threatened with prosecution for racial hatred.

He had been phosphorescent with rage and indignation; there had been offers to help him fight the case; but in the end he had subsided with a sigh, and then rallied with a cry, and started to canvass suggestions for a better, bolder name to replace the old one. He was beholden to no brewery or corporation and could consult his own fancy.

Clara had won the unofficial competition with the other competitors nowhere. Clara's whim alone would have been enough for Arthur, who was smitten with her in a respectful, wistful, upward-gazing, middle-aged sloven way; but she had told him that Walpole was the unsung hero of English history, the greatest leader and patriot apart from Churchill and Elizabeth the First, a man who had personally killed hundreds of the country's enemies with sword, pistol, cannon or bare hands, a roisterer, quaffer, roaring boy and merry mocker of all sanctimony, who had wooed and satisfied a thousand women, and a figure whose memory was hated, reviled and hushed-up by all prigs, busybodies and haters of freedom and Britain.

Arthur had slammed his meaty fist on the bar.

"We'll do it!"

Clara had paid for the new sign and commissioned one of the best of the several excellent local artists to execute it. The background featured cannon, burning boats, a smoking battlefield, dimly apprehended mounds of slaughtered bodies, and nearer to the foreground a swooning woman. Walpole's head was also firmly on his shoulders; and he was sticking out his tongue.

"Of course it's bloody her!" they were informed scornfully as soon as they asked.

"Have you only just heard?"

"Where've you been?"

It was obvious they were latecomers to a council of war that had been in progress for some time.

"And what's all this about goose-steps and wimples?" Cue for much laughter.

"We were rehearsing a play!" said Miles loudly and indignantly.

"He made me play a sex-game," said Clara simultaneously, but fortunately less loudly, indeed in a sullen mumble. He glared at her and she hastily agreed, "Yes; I mean a play. Oh it's absurd, he was arsing round in the garden with a yard-brush, for heaven's sake, and I had put some laundry on my head. You know how wet my husband is, *I* am the one who goose-steps."

"What I don't understand," said Miles, "how could she possibly take the Improv Theatre for reality?"

It seemed opinion was divided as to whether Harriet actually had or not.

"She must have known."

"She must have seen the sign."

"It was busy; there were people standing in front."

"But the instruction cards!"

"There are only a few around now, aren't there? People keep taking them for souvenirs."

Clara primped her hair at this tribute to her writing.

"Even so! How could anyone *possibly* think – "

"Oh, the pair of them definitely did when they first came in," said June the plump jolly barmaid with a peal of laughter. "You should have seen their faces."

"It's exactly how she expected us to be, innit?"

"Balls," said someone else disgustedly. "She knew perfectly well it wasn't real, just what her readers wanted to hear."

"Certainly left in a hurry, anyway."

"I've told you," said Arthur the landlord, returning from an errand to join in, with elaborate patience, as if for the umpteenth time. "I told her about the theatre when she complained about the smoking. Or tried to. To be fair," he said holding up a hand, "it's a bit of a mouthful, and I don't know how much she took in what with her screeching instead of listening. The upshot was, when I said I wasn't going to do anything about it, she said she would report us and stormed out."

"Looks like I'll finally get to fight the case," gleefully said Thomas, a lawyer who lived in the village, who had long been looking forward to it for far other than financial reasons.

"And *I* want to retain you for a libel suit!" cried Jeremiah the art gallery owner. A poet, bon vivant, and reprobate, with his specs and greying hair and moustache Hollywood might have cast him as some elegant ageing roué or benevolent avuncular professor, but he was too earthy and cantankerous to quite fit into either of these roles, having the heart of a born mutineer and the temperament of the coiled rattlesnake from the American revolutionary 'Don't Tread on Me' flag, at least when trodden on. "Libellous! Libellous, it is! To say that *she* taught *me* some home truths about global warming! I wiped the floor with her! I told her what the score was, all right. She ran out with her hands over her ears so as not to hear any more!"

Miles wondered whether this had been to avoid learning the truth about climate scientists' duplicity and malfeasance or simply to shut out the hair-curling obscenity with which Jeremiah tended to expound on the issue. He was an expert on the shady dealing, data-massaging and downright deceptions which had been used to push the theory of manmade global warming, which other people at that time were only just starting to become aware of, and was understandably aggrieved about it all. He would share the latest developments with Clara regularly, and the pair of them would laugh hysterically at or shout viciously about the folly. ("Now they're going to spend billions of pounds of our tax money to pump fresh air, the stuff we breathe out, into sealed caverns underground like toxic waste," he had howled, overcome with mirth, the last such time. "They finally found a way to make us pay rich people for the air we breathe! And the lefties are begging them to do it!" Equally helpless with laughter Clara had said, "*Your* tax money! Miles and I don't work! I think I will invest in it! I will offer to let them keep carbon dioxide in our cellar! I will get them to sponsor Miles to hold his breath! I will inflate balloons with the stuff and get the government to pay me fifty pounds a time! Then when I have a thousand balloons I will hold the world to ransom by threatening to burst them all!" Eventually they had stopped laughing and started swearing.)

"The whole thing is libellous!" Clara cried indignantly, waving someone's copy of the newspaper. "An obscene and gratuitous calumny, which must be wiped out in fire and blood!"

"It's hardly anything new, is it?" said Simon, the former rock star Lord of the Manor, with a genial smile. To the government he was an intransigent campaigner for the countryside and its people; in the counsels of the Walpole he was often the voice of moderation. To no-one present was he, somehow, a man who had been famous for most of their lives; except on rare occasions when they happened to remember that, he was simply The Squire or more often just Simon Down The Pub.

"This time it's us!" cried Clara. "I say enough! How dare they come here simply to mock us? Isn't it enough that they are pulling the country down around our ears, that they have to look down on us as well?"

She spun on her heel and paced off to stand with her back to them studying a wall, digging her nails into her hands, in a way which Miles knew meant she was fighting to control threatened tears of anger.

It was so *unfair*, she thought, so unfair and bloody unjust. What did that woman *know* of these people? How *dare* she mock them, without knowing a thing about them? There was more intelligence, and artistic talent, and fun-loving creativity, and love of culture, and sensitive humane feeling, and common decency, gathered in this area, this village, this pub, this room, than that woman would ever … she stopped and stamped her foot in case the tears came. But it was true. And Harriet and all the rest of them just saw bigots and killers and cavemen.

And then of course there were the things that *were* fair, where Harriet had happened to assume rightly. Many of them *were* reactionaries. What of it? Who would not be, in such an age? Most of them did, as it happened, love their country. How had that come to earn them sneers and suspicion? Some of them, Clara for one, did read the Daily Mail. Why was that a joke, an insult? It was the best damn newspaper in the country. It was the only paper that spoke for them and millions like them, the only one in many ways that told things like they were, the only one that had even-handedly reported the other side of the supposed consensus regarding the biggest scandal of the age, and a dozen similar consensuses on a dozen lesser scandals. It had Keith Waterhouse in it, whose clogs no-one who sneered at the paper would ever be fit to clean. Best of all for Clara, it was forbidden fruit, what They didn't want you to read. From that point of view alone if it hadn't existed it would have been necessary to invent it … Some of them did ride to hounds, kill animals for food. Some of them went to church. They shot guns. They worked in mud. They were friends with their neighbours, when they weren't feuding with them. And all of this was somehow discreditable, and would doubtless earn Harriet a big fat book contract for exposing it, in the due course of time.

She sighed and turned back to her friends. "What are we going to do about it?" she demanded.

"Rise above it. Laugh it off. Laugh at her," Simon recommended breezily. "It's a free country." There were mutters expressing uncertainty at this last part.

"Maybe if we make her feel welcome," said Miles optimistically. "If she sees we aren't as bad as she thinks – except for when we are – maybe we can win her over and she'll start to – "

He was jeered down, bombarded by June and others with tales of friendly overtures on the part of the village that had already been cold-shouldered, of deliberate rudeness and startling condescension. Harriet's article was pored over and dissected; they speculated on what had given rise to certain parts, what had been wilfully misinterpreted, what made up from whole cloth. The bit about incoherent inbred idiots, for example, appeared to have been inspired by her meetings with the bashful young stammering painter who was her nearest neighbour in the other direction, who had greeted her and been crudely rebuffed, and with a genuinely slow girl who helped out in one of the shops.

The atmosphere turned nasty. Scenes like that soured Miles's stomach, and it was not a good idea to have Clara in them adding fuel to the fire; Arthur was by no means the only one under her spell. Before he succeeded in getting her out of the pub she was discussing putting bricks through Harriet's window with the landlord. Simon left at the same time and to cheer Clara up invited them back to his to see a new foal. She calmed down somewhat cooing over it.

"But what are we going to *do*, Miles?" she said sulkily as they drove home.

"What we always do. Laugh, and play, and get on with enjoying our lives, and not let the likes of her get to us. Right?"

Clara pouted and was silent. But at home she suddenly brightened somewhat. She merrily started to sing snatches of Ko-Ko the Lord High Executioner's song from *The Mikado*:

" 'I've got a little list, I've got a little list … They'll none of them be missed … ' "

She took out her Death List book and wrote Harriet's name in it, printed in neat block capitals and underlined in red three times with a ruler. Clara's Death Lists had grown quite voluminous and were long overdue a tidy-up, and perhaps she had forgotten that Harriet's name appeared several times already, always underlined and often with asterisks.

*

For some days they thought no more about their new neighbour. To take her mind off it Miles proposed a trip to London and the dressing-up costume shop; and when there agreed to annoy Dr. Melvyn the marriage counsellor again; and it was on this trip that they found the closed Accident Claims shop, and decided to turn it into a Stoic British Endurance shop, with the results you already know. (For as with everyone's lives, their various adventures and ongoing stories were interleaved, and for the sake of dramatic unity and narrative clarity, or in the interests of variety, we will sometimes have to relate things out of chronological order.) The preparation and execution of this scheme so occupied and gilded their time that Harriet was all but forgotten.

Clara remembered her a bit, more amusedly, after that. She asked Miles what he had done that they should be punished by having Harriet and Richard Gilquist relocate to their very doorstep. The only practical result was that one day she started to write a tribute to Harriet and other practitioners of the rural-anthropology genre, entitled 'A Simple Country Maid Moves to London' ('I was terribly frightened ... They read The Guardian in broad daylight ... I was pleasantly surprised to discover they have trees and grass in London nowadays. But you have to go a long way to find a decent cream tea, and the savages appear not to have heard of tractor rallies ... I was astonished and reassured to meet a homosexual. I concernedly asked him if he was fitting in all right and if the city-dwellers treated him well. He just stared at me. Perhaps he was afraid to tell me the truth ... primitive worship of Mammon ... amusing taboos on death, slaughterhouses kept hidden ... ') but became bored with it before it was finished.

Then a few days after that there was a phone call from the Lord of the Manor.

"Miles. Good. Simon. Tell me, have you or Clara been past the new arrivals' place in the last couple of days?"

"We haven't been out of the gate, why?"

"Just ... you might want to avoid it for a while. Don't take Clara down that way if you can help it. And ... if you have any cans of petrol lying around, might be best to hide them. Word to the wise."

Mystified, Miles took the opportunity of Clara being in the bath to sneak out of the house and walk the quarter-mile or so down the lane to Harriet and Richard's house. As soon as he came in sight of it he grasped the point of Simon's advice.

"Oh, shit," he said.

"Scotland?" said Clara puzzledly on his return. "Why should we go to Scotland?"

"I just thought ... we haven't had a break for a while ... Sir Walter Scott country!" Clara was on a Scott jag at the moment. "I just thought you might like to see the place."

"It's a nice thought, but I feel disinclined to stir for a while." Clara was a homebody at heart.

"Great. Fine. We'll stay in the house for a few ... months. Suits me."

But the next day she made him take her shopping to the market town.

"Why are we going the long way?" she asked as he turned right instead of left outside their gate.

"I heard the bridge is down."

"The bridge? Down?" It was an ancient stone one.

"Roadworks, I mean."

The day after Clara wanted to go for a walk. He said the weather was too cold, she said it was at least bright. He was able to steer her the other way with some difficulty.

It was impossible he could go on confining her forever. But every day he could postpone the discovery was a day won from disaster. The problem might resolve itself in the meantime. He contrived to keep her out of the Walpole. But he fatally forgot to cancel the papers on the day Harriet's column came out. Perhaps it never occurred to him that the woman would be foolish enough to boast about what she had done.

But he had a premonition when he saw Clara settle down with Harriet's paper, and actually went, "Eek."

"Let's see what the great white explorer is up to. Oh, God, listen to the wretched woman. 'I have fought back.' Against what, you madwoman? 'I have struck a blow for freedom and civilisation. I have raised the banner of tolerance and enlightenment in this rude and darkened forest.' Jesus Christ! 'I have stood up for what I believe in. I have declared who I am. I have shown where my loyalties lie. I have nailed my colours to the mast.' Oh this is shaping up to be a classic, please make tea. 'I have brought a glimpse of the future into an outpost of the past. I have set the cat among the pigeons. I have shaken my fist at the forces of conservatism.' What *is* she blithering about?"

A moment after that Clara flung the paper down and stormed from the house.

Miles trailed after helplessly, only managing to catch her up when Harriet's house had come in sight and she came to a dead halt.

Visible from where they stood, a garish splodge of colour against the front of the building, nailed to Harriet's gutter, moving slightly in the breeze, was a large blue rectangle of fabric with a circle of yellow stars on it: the flag of the European Union.

Clara started moving again. Fortunately there was no-one home; she wouldn't have noticed if there had been. Even jumping up she couldn't quite grasp the bottom of the banner.

"Miles find me something to stand on. Find a ladder. Find a tool. Find something to pull the gutter down with. Miles let go of me, I am perfectly calm."

At the third attempt Miles managed to grab her around the waist and started to drag her off.

"I am calm, Miles. I am very calm. Look how calm I am being." She gave a rictus of a smile.

"The mountains of Scotland are very dramatic at this time of year."

"How long have you known about this, Miles?"

"I am as shocked as you are."

She cleared her throat. "Miles, why is the ladder chained up? I need it. I need to do something, on the roof."

"Shoot at passers-by? Clara, this is still a fairly civilised democracy."

"Is it? Oh, is it?"

"Yes! Now behave like an adult."

"Dear God, I have married Gandhi. Complete with nappy."

"Clara, she has done it to annoy us."

"And how dare she? How dare she? How dare she come here and sneer at our flag and then raise the banner of an alien tyranny to taunt us? You heard her, Miles. She is showing where her loyalties lie. She is showing us our future. She no longer deserves the consideration I would give to a fellow countrywoman."

"Clara, look on the bright side. I bet you this time tomorrow Union Jacks will be flying from every house in the area, if they aren't already."

Clara sat down with a sigh. "I suppose we ought to buy one." The thought didn't console her much, although she was sure the sight of a mass show of defiance would be moving and stirring. For all Harriet's shock and horror there had only been three or four patriotic flags on display in the area when she arrived, as far as Clara knew: two Union Jacks on flagpoles outside houses, another hanging on the back wall of the back room of the Walpole; and a St. George's Cross a farmhand had painted all over the front wall of his cottage for a World Cup tournament; and also some imperial memorabilia incorporating the Union Jack in the antique shop, some of which had been deliberately moved to a place of greater prominence in the window after a visiting Harriet-type had complained about it some months before. She had sometimes thought there should be more, that everyone ought to fly the flag nowadays to show contempt for those who reviled and outlawed it. She had thought this might be a duty she was shirking, most recently after Harriet's first column. And yet, while the sight of the British flag never failed to please her, to rouse her imagination and pride, she had a vague personal feeling that it ought to be saved for special places and occasions. She thought a key feature of British patriotism at its best had been relaxation about it, and a feeling that it didn't do to talk about it; it would be a shame to become what Kipling had called jelly-bellied flag-wavers. She had thought often before that, on the one hand, the Enemy's attempts to take away or jeer at precious things they had all comfortably taken for granted must lead eventually to a wholesome revival of interest in, affection for and loyalty to those things; and on the other hand in some cases it would drive people to become caricatures of themselves, exactly what the Enemy had always believed they were.

"I used always to love that walk," she said sadly.

"Oh, don't be such a baby!"

Nettled, eyes flashing, she leapt up and paced furiously again. "Aren't you angry?"

"I am extremely vexed."

"I have married a sedated Henry the Fifth."

"We can't become mirror images of her! Clara, one of the defining traits of the British culture you claim to love is, is a civilised forbearance."

"That's what they trade on!" she exploded. "That's what They always count on! And they shouldn't count on it forever! Don't they know how fed up we are? Don't they know how close some of us are to snapping? Don't they have a clue? Do they think they can just go on laughing at us, and pushing us around, and thinking up new insanity to plague us with, and expect us to remain gentle while they carry on destroying all the things that made us civilised? Maybe if I can make her realise it she'll take the word back to the rest of them."

She continued to pace and brood. Clara had not thrown a brick through anyone's window since university, when someone had mocked her beloved, decrepit tutor Professor Jenks, but the memory of it was still sharp and satisfying. She glowered at Miles. She supposed he would not approve. One day perhaps she would persuade Miles, and then the country at large, of the essential virtue of putting the occasional window through when the situation called for it. ("It is no use your spending your time merely reading about these awful things on the internet and getting uselessly angry without taking any action," she had told Jeremiah once. "We must convert clicks into bricks.") But she supposed as things stood there would be tantrums and recriminations. And perhaps he would be right. She had a vague but annoying feeling, sometimes, that Miles represented her better nature. Besides she couldn't think where she could lay her hands on any bricks just at the moment. If there were any in the out-houses he would doubtless have hidden them. There were all kinds of big juicy rocks lying about the garden, however. She sighed. She supposed it wouldn't do. She made an effort to calm down and succeeded somewhat.

"Take me to the Walpole."

"Take flame to powder-keg? No. I will give you a shoulder-massage, if you like."

"My shoulders are not for cowards," she declared, bridling.

Miles laughed. "Clara! Seriously, what do you intend to do? Be your age, woman. Use your brain. You are finer and better than she is, and smarter. And you can actually write, when you exert yourself. *That's* how we'll defeat them."

She sank down into a chair with another sigh, then a few moments later suddenly shot up again, eyes alight.

"Miles, you're right! A catfight would only prove whose hair is thicker and more luxuriant, and I think we already know that from her picture. I will take her on in her own arena!"

"Now you're talking!" He frowned. "How? Which arena?"

She stared at him. "Journalism, of course." She glared. "Do you forget *I* am a journalist too?"

Miles did forget. "You are?" He was alarmed. This startling new development had been hidden from him. It boded no good. He tried to think of a journal that would publish Clara's screeds. He saw the police kicking down their door. "Um, who for?"

She glared some more. "An organ with a wide and devoted readership," she prompted. He still looked blank. "Of which I am also the editrix."

Miles continued to look blank. Clara continued to glare expectantly. At last she gave it up and cried:

"The St. Mary's Parish Thunderbolt, you fool!"

"Oh," said Miles. "That."

They had started going to church some time back, for a variety of reasons none of which had much to do with God. For one thing it was a mainstay of the local community and blah blah. While they didn't much care, at this point, to be part of a community – it was a pain when people tried to pay calls on them when they were in the middle of some esoteric dressing-up game, especially as they didn't draw the curtains and occasionally had to dive for cover wearing various outlandish costumes – they knew that communities were nice things they were in favour of, and it was good to keep that option open for the sake of days when they couldn't entertain themselves. For another thing they got to see people dressed up prettily. However the main reason they had started going to church was in the hope of annoying the sort of people who would be annoyed by that sort of thing, and to show solidarity with the people who liked it. They approved of Christians, who were required to behave nicely and be friendly to people, and whom they found, on the whole, to be somewhat cheerier than the average, and thought they were unfairly picked on in the modern world. And they approved of Christianity, from which their civilisation and culture had sprung; they liked their civilisation and culture, or what was left of it.

Clara worried sometimes that God would strike them down somehow for the impiety of going to church as a shallow gesture of empty non-conformism when, while not violently disbelieving, they didn't properly believe in him. However she felt the benefits outweighed the risk of doom and damnation. "After all," she told Miles once, "Richard Gilquist probably spends Sunday morning playing Zombie Massacre III and ironically masturbating to kitsch TV. [This had been before she had realised Richard was married to Harriet; she still thought he would prefer masturbating over kitsch to sleeping with her for any number of reasons.] I will not be like Richard Gilquist even if God widows me for it or strikes you down with worms." Clara said she was certain God would punish Miles rather than her for the impertinence of treating religious observance as a badge of rebellion, because God was a gentleman and she was too pretty.

In church Clara behaved herself fairly well, apart from occasionally singing in a big deep booming voice more suitable to a stone-mason. Their gesture, they had found, really was empty, the Christians in little need of displays of solidarity from sympathetic allies; at least in their parish, the attendance numbers were more than healthy, so much so that one Easter when they had come late and been unable to find a seat Clara had been moved to run home for her camera and snap a picture of the congregation, which she had then thoughtfully posted to a prominent, strident atheist, to show him that his life had been in vain. To make this clear she had scrawled 'As you can see, your life has been in vain,' on the back of the print, followed by, 'Enjoy your annihilation.' And then, 'PS Why don't you move to bloody Iran instead of just pretending that you live there?' And finally, 'PPS I will pray for you.'

Sometimes during the boring parts their minds would wander and they would find themselves idly and somewhat nervously trying to contact God. Miles thanked him, if he was there, for his good fortune, and asked that any punishment they had incurred for anything *should* fall on him rather than Clara. He would ask what he was meant to be doing. Clara would ask God, if he was there, to reveal himself, but if possible in quite a gentle and unshowy way, so much that she might feel that the dead people she had known were being well taken care of, but not so much that she would be forced to repent and be holy all the time and so on. "In fact never mind, I'm fine as I am," she would usually hastily add. Sometimes she would ask God to avert his wrath from Britain and deliver her from her enemies, and ask to be given a sign if there was anything she personally could do to speed the process, especially if it involved taking a prominent part in a violent uprising.

Of course she felt closer to God, if he was there, and more kindly disposed towards him, while walking through the fields and woods or listening to a nice symphony or something. The best part of church was the sensual pleasure, especially the smell and the taste. Miles would often have to chide her for stooping down to sniff the leather hassocks; and sometimes during the inevitable longueurs she would find herself leaning forward and gnawing and licking at the varnished wood of the pews as she had as a child.

The only drawback was the new vicar who had come to the church shortly after they did. He was plainly more agnostic than they were, obviously Communist, probably a deliberate Infiltrator. They supposed that Christ, and in fact they themselves, couldn't object to the parts about helping the less fortunate and not being materialistic, but his sermons crossed the line into predictable relativist agitprop and were relentlessly and tiresomely Relevant to the Modern World. He made mention of celebrities and TV programmes and fashionable technology and political controversies; they were sure that a large part of the point of church was to transcend or at least get briefly away from that sort of thing. He had sacked the choir and installed a boom-box. He had once, horribly, done a 'rap'. Attendances started to fall off; they themselves starting going less regularly and might have given up altogether if they hadn't started to feel a bit sorry for him. He set up well-meant community relief and social-work schemes they felt were frankly wasted in a parish as prosperous as theirs, where even the farmers weren't that suicidal just at the moment. His Battered Wives group, for example, had had no takers: and when Clara had indignantly pointed out that women were just as capable of inflicting violence as men and he had correctly changed it to Battered Spouses, not even Miles had taken advantage.

Anyway, while they didn't play much of a part in church activities, it happened that Clara had impulsively seized control of the parish news-letter during the time of the previous vicar and resisted all the current incumbent's attempts to dislodge her from it. This had partly been an altruistic, community-minded impulse after the former editor, an old lady, had passed away, but largely an excuse to annex the parish's heavy, clattering, lovely old manual typewriter and spirit-duplicator machine, the latter now alas broken but replaced by an old and satisfyingly noisy photocopier. It was also an excuse to play girl-reporter (lip-dangling cigarette and hard-boiled wisecracks) and girl-editor (green eye-shade) and yell, "Copy-boy!" at Miles.

She hadn't arsed around with the church newsletter – which she had renamed the St. Mary's Parish Thunderbolt – or abused her respon-sibilities *much* under the old, jolly, religious vicar, or *that much*, considering the opportunities, under the new annoying nasty modern one, and it was still *mainly* a straightforward parish news-sheet. The occasional request for prayers for the repose of the soul of their dead cat, tactfully glossing over the fact that it had committed suicide, or indeed that it was a cat. A few bogus saints discreetly slipped in here and there: Saint Marjory, for example, the patron saint of hopscotch, or Saint Tobermory, who had been grilled alive and was the patron saint of barbecues and could be prayed to to avert rain. A handful of made-up biblical quotations. The introduction of a regular 'Name That Saint' competition, in which you had to guess the name of a saint (a real one) from silhouettes depicting them being martyred in their trademark way or performing miracles associated with them; the prize was a crate of brown ale. Once, fairly recently, a short article consoling newly married wives on the burden of having to perform what it tactfully referred to as Marital Duties, and giving advice on how to cope with it. 'The impulse, once you realise what is required of you, is to run home crying to Mother,' she wrote. 'Do not give in to this. While she will understand your revulsion – who better? – she cannot console you for it, and will reproach herself for not having been able to warn you adequately about the slithering horror you face – for who could describe it? – and may even feel guilty for not having drowned you in the innocence of your girlhood. Do not,' it continued, 'berate your husband, or cause him to feel overmuch shame at his dark impulses. Men are at the mercy of their Bestial natures and are more to be pitied than despised. Reflect, in fact, that they are more unfortunate than you, in that the importuning stranger that is intruded upon your bower once a fortnight is for them a constant resident of their lower apparel, its eldritch terror impossible to escape from, blighting all their days and mocking all their nights, doubtless causing them to start with fright every time they step into a bath unprepared … There are techniques one can develop for blocking out the horror of the ordeal. Imagine yourself far away on a pleasant island, or think of something sustaining from your childhood. Pretend to yourself that it is only a frightened little mouse that wants to come in for shelter. Remind yourself that all women go through it, that the Queen herself has put up with it on at least four occasions, and seems no worse for wear. When it is over, politely thank your husband if he has been quick about his unpleasant task; if you are crying, assure him it is not because of anything he did, but because you thought of something sad that was on the television. Then change the subject as quickly as you can. Now, while he is feeling guilty, is a good time to remind him of household chores. Take off your sleep-mask as soon as you are sure he is safely buttoned up again. It can help defuse the horror if between you you can come up with a humorous pet name for the Beast; call it Little Cromwell, perhaps, or Cardinal Richelieu. … Save your pity for, and remember in your prayers, those who are trying to have babies, and the women of the Common Market (apt name!), who have to do it around the clock, and, in the latter case, up against walls in foggy alleys.'

When the new vicar had read this – after it had been disseminated around the village, where it quickly became a collector's item – he had come to Clara and, blushing and stammering, offered to arrange counselling. She had seized on this eagerly and suggested he set up a Penis Survivors Group, wherein she and other traumatized young wives could compare and contrast notes on their common enemy. He had said he would look into it but had yet to get back to her. Later he had given Miles a book on foreplay and, separately, Clara a book on lesbianism. Privately he brooded about her, and referred to her as Poor Clara; but then he should have heard what Clara called him.

Even before this, in fact right from the beginning of his tenure, he had been trying to do away with the Thunderbolt. He found a newsletter an embarrassing anachronism and instead encouraged his parishioners to visit a website he ran himself and sign up for a text-messaging service. ('Prayers 4 greener world, plz.' 'Its sunday, god is in the house!! ;) ') Clara's idiosyncrasies as editor were almost irrelevant, and in fact the Poor Clara factor helped extend the bulletin's lifespan. Every time he had tactfully started to tell her that it was now surplus to requirements she had blithely ridden over him with excited plans for its future and given him to understand that it was the only thing in her life, the one thing that kept her going in the face of her terrible ordeal every other Thursday. Eventually, however, he had been forced to take a stern line after Clara published a think-piece entitled 'Why Don't We Burn Heretics Any More?', in which she thought she had even-handedly examined both the pros and cons of abandoning this practice. The Thunderbolt was no longer officially countenanced or available at the back of church. It was, however, still distributed to every house in the village and nearby by Clara and Miles every week, or every week Clara remembered it and felt inspired, possibly the world's first underground, guerilla parish newsletter, growing steadily more intransigent in its views and erratic in its sermons, murmuring mutinously against the vicar, and now featuring enigmatic personal ads for discreet massage services, for which parishioners were invited to apply to his wife.

The point is she still had the newsletter to play with, and a pulpit to denounce Harriet from.

She donned her girl-editor eyeshade and, chainsmoking ineptly and coughing, frowning in her fury, sat down to bash out her story at the big loud satisfying typewriter.

THE ENEMY IN OUR MIDST

Few can have failed to notice the incursion of <u>interlopers</u> into our fair Eden of late. I am not referring to relatively harmless day-trippers, no matter from how far afield: I am talking of the pernicious influence of those who have been permitted to set up residence without their bona fides being established or the common good being consulted.

"You're writing an editorial against us?" Miles asked over her shoulder.
"Don't be a fool. We are honest country folk ourselves. We fit in here. We may have been sent to save them. We are spiritually at home here. I feel certain that in a previous life I lived here, a humble village hoyden lying atop a hayrick with a straw in my mouth, stoically enduring a previous you's untutored attempts to deflower me." Nevertheless she paused. "I will make things clearer."

Obviously, some newcomers can only be welcomed with open arms. they are distinguished by their wit, grace, breeding and pretty knockers. They would be an adornment to any village, even one in Heaven, and it behooves everyone to be humbly grateful for the shining example they set, at any rate the wife.
No: I think we all know to whom I am alluding, the worms in the apple of our little rural

"Bugger it, give me the thesaurus."

Arcadia. People trying to escape from the self-made hell-hole of The Great Wen, and bringing the stench of decadence with them. Upstart counter-jumpers who sneer at what they do not understand and who have already betrayed our trust. Recreant and degenerate traitors, conspirators with foreign powers, who boldly fly an alien flag in all our faces. I will name no names but the woman's begins with a H.

"I think I'm going to have to forbid this," said Miles.

```
What is to be done about this menace? Are we to
meekly endure the insults that have been offered
and the poison that has been spread? Are there no
stout fellows with pitch-forks and kerosene
prepared to defend their village?
   The St. Mary's Parish Thunderbolt says: Drive
These Swine Out Now.
```

She made a new heading.

```
ANATHEMA
```

She frowned. "Can we pronounce anathemas or is it only the Catholics? If the latter I think I am defecting. Find a book with an anathematizing formula in it. Oh I'll do it in pig-Latin."

```
Uckfay offay ouyay Ondonlay egeneratesday. The
interlopers are hereby anathematized by the
authorities of St. Mary's Church and are to be
neither helped nor harboured nor fed nor watered
nor nothing within the bounds of this parish on
penalty of excommunication. Their sheep are
forfeit and their souls unshriven. Amen.
```

"Copy-boy!"

"No, Clara, there are laws."

"I spit on your laws! Weasel slave-laws designed to shackle the righteous rage of the freeborn Englishwoman!"

"I am not copying or delivering this. I am also starting to worry about your sanity. I worry, you know, that you won't come back."

"Damn it, Miles, I am angry and downcast right at the very heart of me, not just the part where I exaggerate a bit for effect, although frankly I do have a hard time telling the two apart these days." She sighed and ripped the paper out and scrumpled it. "This is rubbish, though. It needs more ... subtle, subtle. Bring me tea and tickle my back."

She tried again.

'For a tale-bearing woman is an abomination to the Lord.'
- Book of Neville, 5:19

The venerable English institution of the scold's bridle has been unfairly traduced over the years. It was in fact a sophisticated mechanism for fact-checking and an early forerunner of the libel laws. Like many an old custom it might usefully be revived, for no community can survive with the poison of malicious gossip running in its veins. The ducking-stool was another way of dealing with contumelious and quarrelsome women. We have a village pond and lack only the will to use it.

In Roman times the tongue of anyone who bore false witness would be torn out and fed to delighted French gastronomes. Then ropes would be tied around the slanderer's wrists and ankles and they would be made to take part in degrading human puppet-shows and forced to slap their own faces. The penalty for flying an alien flag was something too unspeakable to mention in a family parish newsletter, but you may be sure that hot lead up the arse was only the start of it.

In more recent times our own local lore mentions the St. Mary's Star Chamber, a merry band of fearless lads who would ride out in the dead of night to punish malefactors the law could not deal with, burning them in a giant Wicker Penis. This practice was officially discontinued in the 1960s but lingers fondly in the memory.

I will name no names. I will make no suggestions. Let those who have ears, hear me.

A WELCOME TO NEW ARRIVALS!

It can have escaped few people's attention that we have new occupants at the Old Dower House on Applebottom Lane. This is welcome news as many of us had despaired of it ever being filled again after the series of mysterious disappearances and tragic, horrific, bizarre or lingering deaths which have struck down all the previous occupants in an unbroken succession for nearly two centuries. We all feel proud of being able to point to the officially-recognised Most Cursed House in Britain in our neighbourhood, and now it is once more occupied by brave, rational souls who will be able to show morbidly curious visitors around such sights as the Brain-Dashing Step, The Falling Beam, and the Bloody Kitchen, while they last.

Interestingly, while researching this piece, I came across documents establishing that the house was in fact originally known as 'The Old Whore House', after a previous occupant, a diseased whore from London who intruded briefly and attempted to set up a knocking-shop here. She would signal she was open for visitors by flying a flag with a number of stars stitched upon it. This was the agreed-upon system of the time, established in 'The Good Whore Guide' – a one-star whore was a relatively fastidious bawd, a two-star one less fussy, and so on, all the way down to a five-star harlot, who would perform with bears for coppers or pie-crusts. I see the current resident has them all beat!

But I hope everyone will make her feel as welcome as she deserves.

Clara suddenly gasped and went wide-eyed.

"Wait, wait, wait!" she muttered. She tore the page out and discarded it. "I'm missing a trick here."

She scowled for a moment and then smiled.

"What was wrong with that?" asked Miles. "That was funny. I might even have distributed that, to a few select people."

"I'm an idiot, Miles, but will shortly require a kiss for my brilliance. I can't make her go away but if I do this properly I bet I can make her take down her bloody corrupt fascist super-state flag. Miles bet me a thousand pounds I can't make her take it down, of her own free will, in three days, without using fire-bombs or rocks through her window or anything to offend your delicate conscience."

"I bet you dinner at Le Con."

"You're on, shake. Watch this, Miles. I could do it without leaving this room." She inserted a new paper and gnawed her lip. "But she's got to read this. She'll probably just sneer and throw it in the bin. What would make her read it? The hunt for copy."

She tabbed to the middle and typed

INCEST

She rolled down a bit. "In the space here will go a big picture of a sad-looking Jesus to catch her eye. Right."

She typed:

```
  In the countryside we have traditionally taken
a more laid-back approach towards the matter of
intra-sibling eros than big city types tend to.
With long dark nights and not much to do,
irregular bus services, and so on, for a certain
section of the community this has always been a
pastime they can't see much wrong with.
  Well, it simply won't do. I'm naming no names
because I'm pressed for space. The Bible is
against it and science is against it. It's all
very well to sneer at Darwinism but in this case
there's something to it. Again, I'm naming no
names, but we were all at a certain christening
and we can all count toes. There is simply no
excuse for it, not when the winter snows have
passed.
```

"And blah blah blah." She hit the return lever energetically. "So now she's hooked. And then a space for authentic newsletter stuff, prayers for repose of souls, coffee mornings, Name That Saint, et cetera. In fact I'll start the important part on the next page."

She removed and reversed the sheet and wrote:

```
A LOVELY LOCAL TRADITION REVIVED
              - a personal view by 'Old F**t'

  A very warm welcome to our new friends at the
Dower House! It is only natural to be anxious
```

about new neighbours, and wonder if they will fit in. Well, I think we already have evidence that they will do so very nicely!

Now, we already knew that they were people of spirit and pluck, simply for buying a house with such a notorious ghost (although my money has always been on rats)

"No, no, I'll probably cut that. Stick to the point."

but it was still possible to wonder if, coming from the city, they would be quite in sympathy with our backwards backwoods ways.

Well, anyone who has walked or motored past the Dower House lately and seen the lovely big flag of stars, or 'scroteweazel' to give it the traditional country name, proudly flying for all to see, already knows the answer to that! They have declared that they are in harmony with country tradition, and in a way that puts many of our own younger folk to shame.

The 'scroteweazel' (or flag of stars) has been gradually falling into disuse over the past few years because of so-called 'political correctness' or simple laziness and only some of our older residents have kept it up. I'm ashamed to say that even mine is gathering dust in my attic, although you may be sure that it will be given an airing now that I have been shamed into it by newcomers!

It seems to me, now I think of it, that the displaying of the scroteweazel is useful as well as ornamental. In these days when foxhunting has become controversial to some, is even officially 'banned' (wink wink), the deployment of a banner signalling 'I follow the hunt and you may hunt on my land' is of great benefit, not only to those of us who want to show our support for the Hunt, but to those who don't. If all those who will allow the chase to cross their property fly the traditional stars and those who would prefer not to don't, it will save much confusion and bad blood.

One point of tradition I must insist on: you may only put one star on your scroteweazel for every kill you have been in at – and hares don't count, only foxes. (Our new arrivals must be regular Nimrods!)

Now I have heard it said that the practice originated with the terrifying manhunts of the notorious St. Mary's Star Chamber in the 16th Century, when each star signified a Catholic, Jew, Saracen or Gypsy you had run to ground and killed. Be that as it may, it is simply <u>not</u> the case now, and it would be a shame for a time-honoured tradition to be lost for fear of giving offence – or, dare I suggest, fear of attracting the attention of sabs.

So get those scroteweazels flying everyone! And to our newcomers, welcome, and it is nice to know you are one of us!

"Well? Kiss for brilliance, please."

"Genius," said Miles, awestruck, bestowing one. "Sublime. That *might* actually work."

"I can make it ... better."

"For a start, lose the incest, that's too suspicious, unless she's as thick as she takes us for."

"I bet she is."

"Make it, I don't know, poaching. Stern warnings, hints of dangers, hints that the use of man-traps hasn't quite died out. No, something more ... eyebrow-raising to a city type, but subtle. Epidemic of cow-tipping?"

"Lying with animals."

"No, subtle. If you just have a picture of Christ, in fact, and then news of all kinds of community activities she'll probably read it just to sneer. Conservative Jam-Making Associations."

"Right."

"And then change Scroteweazel."

"Oh no Miles!"

"Call it an ... Asterwurzel? Something more plausible. Or lose it altogether, just call it the Flag of Stars."

"No, Miles, I want to really annoy her, and it will annoy her to think she has been doing something with a foolish old name like that all unknowing. I want scroteweazel, in fact, it is an excellent name for it."

"No, it's too much. You can probably do without the Star Chamber bollocks too, it isn't necessary."

"It's colour, though, of a sort that she will instinctively think sounds true."

"Tone it down a lot at least. And you don't have to mention saboteurs, it's overkill. All right, before we send these out we have to alert some of the layabouts from the pub to start making scroteweazels. It might be best if there were one or two hanging out where she might notice them *before* she gets the newsletter."

"Right. You can start making ours while I revise this."

"I can't sew."

"You can paint a sheet. I want a big one with twenty stars at least and proud horses and bleeding foxes' heads. In fact you can wait for me, that will be the fun part. You can at least put some music on and peel me some Maltesers."

She inserted fresh paper and started over. Clara wasn't good at editing herself. Wailing and gnashing her teeth, she managed to cut the bit about incest and replace it with ordinary parish newsletter burble. To console herself she slipped in an eye-catching line that went 'DRUIDISM – lecture and practical demonstration in the village hall.' She found she couldn't cut the ghost/rats. Whimpering with pain, she managed to change 'scroteweazel' to 'scrotwurzel', with the private reservation that it was *pronounced* scroteweazel. She kept the Star Chamber. As a reward for her self-discipline she made the 'Name That Saint' saint Saint Agatha, holding her breasts on plates like trifles with a cherry on the top, and made the shape of her head in the silhouette resemble that of Harriet's in her byline picture.

They went to rope in like-minded spirits at the Walpole. The regulars had been planning to festoon the village with Union Jacks as Miles had predicted, but were open-mouthed at the sublimity of Clara's plan and went home to start making scrotwurzels or scroteweazels almost immediately.

They made phone calls to other friends; the head of the local Women's Institute had already heard via the grapevine and pledged that her ladies would be sewing scrotwurzels through the night.

Harriet had never seemed overly prone to fact-checking, but they delegated Jeremiah to place references to the tradition of the scrotwurzel (pron: scro't-weazel) on the internet just in case. As fogeys they affected to be incompetent with computers and were in fact pretty useless.

They copied the revised new Thunderbolt and distributed it around the village. They left Harriet until last and shoved it through her letterbox in the middle of the night, then ran away giggling like kids playing knock-a-door-run or conspirators who had planted a bomb.

Clara had decided against Miles's modification of having scrotwurzels be visible *before* the newsletter: too elaborate, in fact potentially suspicious. Better if Harriet thought she had inadvertently revived a dormant custom herself. But they had arranged a staggered unfurling. Two flags of stars appeared in the village the next morning, half a dozen more in the afternoon. An elderly former Wing-Commander affixed a large and magnificent one made by the head of the W.I. to his flagpole below the Union Jack.

That evening Clara had an excited call from a woman named Muriel. Harriet had noticed the new flags but imagined they were supporting her and the EU. Head high, looking somewhat smug, she had seen Muriel in her garden and complimented her on the starry flag draped from an upper window. Smiling she had said, "I didn't know anyone here went for that kind of thing." "I just said, 'We all do, it's the scrotwurzel, my dear, and we are very proud of it,' " reported Muriel. Harriet had looked puzzled and gone away before she could add more.

"She can't have read the newsletter," Clara told Miles sadly. "Shall we post another one?"

"Too suspicious. She might still have it lying around. Besides there are copies all over the post office and other shops. Cheer up. At the worst she'll decide this is actually the most forward-looking and enlightened village in the kingdom."

By noon on the second day the village was decked with scroteweazels. Everyone reliable there and for three miles around displayed one. Some were crudely hand-painted on bedsheets, some made of cloth with the stars sewn on. They came in all colours and designs. In some the stars were in a rough circle, more often they were scattered willy-nilly. Someone had made do with an American Confederate flag he had bought; a starry beach-towel hung from someone else's window; June the barmaid had pegged the shorts of a Wonder Woman costume she happened to own on her washing line. They were trapped beneath window-panes, draped over trellises, hung from gutters, flew from broomsticks planted in gardens, flapped from hanging-plant baskets, were spread over roof-tiles. One was painted on a front door. As well as stars many featured trotting horses, slinking foxes, hunting horns.

"Bless these people," sighed Clara as they admired it all.

But would Harriet read the newsletter? And would she smell a rat? The bush telegraph had no more news of her. Miles had limited them to only driving or walking past her house twice a day in case they gave themselves away. Each time they had been disappointed.

That night her EU flag was still flying; but the next morning it was gone.

There was no mention in Harriet's next column of her having ended her magnificent protest and taken down her defiant symbol of progress, togetherness, and unaccountable spending. Instead there was an impassioned, borderline unhinged screed decrying the fact that hunting with hounds still persisted in the face of the ban. The drag-hunting compromise was clearly a fiction and a fig-leaf and must itself be outlawed, she said. Property used for hunting should be confiscated by the state, there must be stiff prison sentences, preferably with hard labour, and the police and Crown Prosecution Service must be made to uphold the law and punish the guilty.

The people here were ignorant bloodthirsty savages, she declared. But then what kind of people flew a flag commemorating the activities of a genocidal 16th-century manhunt? She went on to detail the bloody history of the St. Mary's Star Chamber, as imagined by Clara and freely expanded on by her. The villagers celebrated it to this day. She mentioned the scrotwurzels by name, denounced them as a piece of racist intimidation, did not see fit to make clear the supposed connection with hunting. She had not failed to see the single American Rebel flag flying, did not fail to mention this separately and pluralize it, and point to racist implications in that. On the Wing-Commander's flagpole, she noted, the scrotwurzel had been sinisterly yoked together with the equally blood-crusted British flag, a duumvirate of terror and atavism.

Clara read all this and laughed merrily. She read it again and decided that merry laughter was still the correct response, especially every time she saw the word 'scrotwurzel' in print. Really, what did she care about the continued calumny? The main thing was she had won, the village had won, and she did not have to be reminded she was ruled by lunatic ideologue bureaucrats in a wretched overseas city the RAF could bomb flat in a day every time she went for a walk. She read it to Miles, who was foolishly dismayed by it, and encouraged him to laugh merrily. They went to see the gang at the Walpole, who were still celebrating their success and already laughing merrily. When a few sourpusses expressed their anger or annoyance at the new column, or their opinion that perhaps the plan had backfired, she pointed out how funny it was, and that the word scrotwurzel was now almost in the dictionary, and that apart from anything else Harriet had now given them an excuse to take theirs down when they were bored with them, and there was more merry laughter.

She came home, got into the bath, and laughed merrily again.

She got into bed and was still chuckling.

Later, in the middle of the night, after Miles had gone to sleep, she walked to Harriet's house and threw a rock through her window, and as she ran away laughed merrily once more.

Afterwards she felt guilty, with consequences that will be revealed in due course.

Chapter Seven

Clara shot across the room with a hiss like an outraged cat and snapped off the radio with an oath.

"Modern world One, Clara Nil," she muttered. "Why do modern symphonies always always always sound the same? They all sound like the scary incidental music from Hammer Horror films when something is creeping through bushes or peering in at a window. How is it Prokofiev lived in a genocidal totalitarian dictatorship that was invaded by another one and yet managed to write music full of beauty, uplift and joy, while these pampered sods live in a free-ish and prosperous country and can only produce whingy horror-film dirges? If unease and foreboding is really the only mood they ever know they ought to cut down on the caffeine."

"Perhaps we should have tried it for a full ten seconds, to give it a chance," Miles suggested.

"Perhaps you should try putting your cock through a mangle for a full ten seconds, to give that a chance."

"There might be some mathematical – "

"Then why didn't he just pass round pieces of paper with a series of numbers written on instead of assaulting everyone's eardrums?"

"It's a statement on the war."

"Then why didn't he write that down on a bit of paper, or take out a soapbox in Hyde Park, instead of stinking up a concert hall?" Clara was flipping through CDs scowling. She suddenly stopped and looked excited. "Miles, I have thought of something clever! Let's start, in conversation, using words like 'challenging' and 'difficult' as though they are an accepted euphemism for 'shit'. Which, in effect, they are. Listen, listen. 'The cat has been challenging in the corner.' 'The cat has premiered a bold new work all over the carpet.' 'I have trodden in some relevant.' 'Do excuse my husband, he has a stomach-upset and has been iconoclastic and ground-breaking in his pants.' "

"Our cat is dead," pointed out Miles, "and we don't really know anyone who would be annoyed by it, even if they got it."

"It's a drawback," Clara admitted. "What is the point of my constantly thinking of clever ways to be rude to modern composers and artists and so forth if I never actually meet any? Perhaps it is time to pay a visit to Ghastly Uncle Charlie again." She frowned. "As it happens he did invite us to lunch recently and I suppose I ought to make the effort soon."

"Isn't it always painful on both sides? As your spiritual advisor I think I must deplore the use of a family bond as an excuse to deliver insults and feel superior."

"Strangely enough the vicar said something similar before I married you. In this case any sense of a bond is all one-way. He seems to feel obliged to play the uncle to me even though we distress each other and he abandoned my aunt for a whore. Probably he has an unacknowledged incestuous crush on me. I think I must suddenly remember inappropriate childhood touching the next time he really annoys me."

The subject lapsed, but serendipitously enough Ghastly Uncle Charlie rang to renew his invitation the next day, and a date was made. En route to London Miles tried to extract a promise that, if she could not forego being rude completely, the words 'abandoned my aunt for a whore' would at least not be spoken at lunch, as they had been at their last two meetings. Clara blinked and said that while they were in town she could easily be fitted for a burkha or indeed a scold's bridle if he would like. Miles let it drop. Clara didn't, and for the first ten minutes of lunch nonplussed her uncle by asking, "May I speak, husband?" every time she wanted or was expected to say something.

Ghastly Uncle Charlie wasn't particularly ghastly on the surface: not much scruffier than, say, Miles had been before Clara had taken him in hand, and his speech no more sloppy and faux-proletarian than many other well-to-do, well-connected men of the time. He tended to correct this last imperceptibly under Clara's glares and looks of disbelief and withering remonstrances, but to let it slide again when the waiter came. Miles, who quite liked him – as, Clara maintained, he rather wetly quite liked everyone in person – thought Charlie looked permanently anxious, although to be sure he had never seen him out of Clara's company, which might explain it. He was certainly pained and disconcerted to find himself out of tune with anyone younger than him. Clara always delighted not only in making him the target of whatever anti-progressive barbs she had lately thought up but in making him feel old and out of touch. "The internet? Do people still do that?" she would say blinking in surprise. Or, delightedly, "You mean you're an atheist? Of course, that was big in your day, wasn't it? How very you. Dear old Uncle Charlie, don't ever change." He would laugh nervously but the look of anxiety would deepen. More often she would be plain rude rather than clever, and still Charlie would conscientiously, even eagerly, offer to fix her up with interesting jobs or introduce them to useful people, at which she would yawn. Miles wondered why the man continued to put himself through it and toyed with the theory that Charlie regretted leaving Clara's aunt and that lunching Clara represented some means of staying in touch or fond hope of showing himself in a good light to her. Certainly he never failed to ask after her, as now, with predictable consequences.

"May I speak, husband? She has gone from strength to strength since you abandoned her for a whore."

Hastily Miles said, "How is … " He trailed off.

"My husband has forgotten the name of the whore," said Clara with a laugh. "His reliability in this regard is one of the reasons I married him."

Charlie smiled nervously and said, "Actually we're no longer together."

"He has abandoned the whore for another whore."

"Tell me about the new exhibition," said Miles to change the subject.

"Perhaps we should finish eating first," said Clara.

But Uncle Charlie eagerly plunged into the opening offered. The foremost example of his ghastliness, in Clara's eyes, was that he was a middling-to-big shot, as impresario rather than creator, in the Modern Art world. His forthcoming show in a national gallery had already been adverted to in the initial greetings.

"Oh, it's going to be great," he enthused. "Going to really make a noise. We're calling it 'Transgressions'."

"With a lower-case t, no doubt," said Clara.

"As it happens, yes."

Clara cackled. "Damn that patriarchal upper-case!"

Uncle Charlie had sensibly focussed on Miles. "It's going to be a mix of big names and up-and-comers. A showcase of where the state-of-the-art is at. We're aiming to really set an agenda."

"Fuck," said Clara.

"And, so, what, you're hoping to … "

"It's going to be really subversive, I mean no-holds-barred."

"Subversive of *what*, you appalling man?" Clara cried. "What is there left to subvert? You see, Miles? Permanent revolution. All across the board they've taken power, clung grimly onto power for a generation, become rich and changed everything, and yet somehow successfully convinced themselves they're still the outsiders. In their heads they're bravely fighting a permanent Eastern Front of old maids cycling to church through the mist. In reality they're stamping on a corpse."

"Well, we're actually going to *have* a corpse," said Charlie defiantly. "How about that?"

He was rewarded by seeing Clara silent for once. She laid down her knife and fork.

"No empty gimmicks though," said Charlie to Miles. "All really powerful stuff. Confrontational. I want to force people to re-evaluate their preconceptions."

Clara sighed. Frowning thoughtfully she said, "Uncle Charles, do you remember when we used to play ride-a-cock-horse? I had a curious dream about it the other night. A pink snake appeared."

Quickly Miles said, "But will it be ... relevant?"

"Painfully relevant," said Ghastly Uncle Charlie. "But playfully so. No preaching but still ballsy. ____ _____ who did the Turd Golgotha is doing a statement on the war in the form of a collage of porn, to give you an idea. _____ ___ has given us a photoshop of President Bush as a cowboy. We've got all the sharp youngsters." He reeled off some more names. He seemed quite keen to persuade Miles of the importance and worth of his show. "Not the same old faces; just a couple of old guard so they're not left out. I mean, I know you younger lot probably think I'm art establishment by now, but I've really always been about the upstart. I'd rather have some cynical young kid who's secretly laughing at me than some tired old ... this show could really be a defining moment. I want people to look back and see almost a definitive ... It's a shame, your mate Robbo's going to be the only one left out."

Miles frowned. "My – "

Clara kicked him sharply on the ankle. She yawned elaborately and said, "Really, Uncle, the whole thing sounds terribly edgy."

"It is!" said Charlie eagerly.

"You misunderstand me. 'Edgy' is the new teen-speak for 'shit'."

"It is?" Uncle Charlie looked appalled.

Clara nodded. "Shit with an undertone of 'old hat, last year'. I must teach you the argot if you are to go on pulling ever-younger girlfriends. Let me see. 'Challenging' means shit too, while 'challenging preconceptions' indicates an absolute nadir in shitness. I gather that 'To set an agenda' is a euphemism for masturbation. 'I set five agendas last night.' What else, Miles? We are somewhat out of touch ourselves, you understand. Oh, 'AGW' means bollocks, bullshit, you are pulling my leg. As in, 'AGW, moomintroll, you are incapable of setting agendas'. And when they want to indicate approval of something they say, 'That's The Churchill.' 'The Churchill' means excellent, cool, strong, virile."

"Wow," said Uncle Charlie frowning.

Presently he went to the men's room.

"Doubtless he is doing drugs now," said Clara. "What a weasel. I *knew* he was after something this time, and now I have a shrewd idea what."

"What was that about – "

"That's what I was coming to," she said excitedly. "A while ago I told him you were friends with Robbo."

"Who the hell is Robbo?"

"Oh, he's some big new artist. He makes a big thing of jeering at the art establishment and gets very rich off it. He's anonymous and mysterious and difficult to contact. You leave a message with an answering service and he might get back to you if he's in the mood and the money's big enough. Part of his mystique is that he's meant to be this terribly authentic prole. My uncle was drooling about him, so to annoy him I casually said you'd known him at university and had stayed at his parents' castle. He looked devastated but disbelieving, but the very next week there was a story that this Robbo was a double-barrelled public-school boy, which would prove how wonderful I am if it wasn't so predictable. Miles – I bet he's hoping to rope him into his show through you. Play along, play along!" she concluded in a whisper as her uncle came back.

Charlie didn't immediately return to the topic but Miles started to think Clara was right: Charlie was very attentive to him, plied him with wine and laughed too loudly at his jokes. Clara watched in amusement and reminded her uncle he still owed them a wedding present, at which he went into paroxysms of remorse.

After lunch Charlie insisted on showing them his sales gallery. As well as everyday objects you might find in a builder's yard or an abattoir or indeed a lavatory there were video displays, photo-montages and the occasional painting of sorts, the more decipherable leaning heavily on random juxtaposition, scatology and shock. The price-tags were phenomenal.

"How is it," said Clara to Miles when Charlie was off attending to something, "that almost every page of every issue of that boys' comic you buy with the futuristic wet-liberal policeman in the fancy helmet in it," – Clara didn't believe in acknowledging she knew the names of any bits of popular culture, even the ones she almost approved of – "contains a more striking, original, imaginative or witty image more skilfully rendered than anything in this wretched place, or any of the similar wretched places throughout the city or the world, and yet that is retailed for little more than a pound, and their artists are doubtless paid little more than peanuts, while – "

Charlie returned and eagerly steered them around, proudly pointing out things or artists who would be featured in his epoch-making exhibition.

He licked his lips nervously. "Of course I realise most of this stuff would look tame and hackneyed to your mate," he said to Miles.

"Robbo? No, I think he'd approve of some of it actually," said Miles, gesturing vaguely towards a sculpture made out of plumbing and a huge photograph of an elephant's pudenda.

"Yes, this is exactly his kind of foulness," said Clara. "He demands that anywhere he exhibits be expunged of all traces of aesthetic beauty." She scowled around her. "Tell me about your new whore, Uncle Charles. Is she beautiful?"

"Very."

"Isn't that rather hypocritical of you? Oughtn't you to be going out with," she waved a hand, "half a woman who's been chainsawed down the middle, or a woman made out of frozen piss or something? Or a giant slinky, or – "

Charlie made a face but was not about to be distracted from the matter at hand. "Of course Robbo never exhibits with other people, does he?" he said sadly.

"Very rarely," said Miles. "He has done occasionally as a favour, but…"

"Look, I'm going to level with you," said Charlie. "One of my big names has pulled out. I think people are frightened of being upstaged by the corpse. I'm going to be left with an entire empty room. I would really, really – I would go down on bended knee – it would be my honour – I mean do you think there's any chance Robbo would consent to give us some stuff? I mean – how close are you?"

"Oh, Miles and Robbo were on terms of mutual masturbation," said Clara.

"Well, not quite so … " said Miles, not keen to play along that much.

"Could you at least sound him out?"

"Oh, I don't know, Charlie … "

"Miles!" snapped Clara. "The man is a tasteless idiot but he is still my uncle. Of course he will, Charles."

"I'm not going to raise false hopes," said Miles. "The best I can do is mention it and tell him you're a good bloke. But you know what he's like."

"I would make any guarantees, meet any demands."

"To be honest, Charles, a Robbo display is a long shot," said Clara thoughtfully, scowling at a phallic sculpture. "Almost certainly out of the question. However if you're very lucky he might be able to get you Pingu. Don't you think, Miles?"

Uncle Charlie frowned. "Who is ... ?"

"Oh, Pingu is utterly vile and talentless," said Clara. "You'd love him. He's only exhibited in a guerilla way so far, in squats and at clubs and so on. Only the real in-crowd have heard of him." Uncle Charlie looked depressed. "But apparently Roger Scruton was told about one of his shows and is writing a whole essay denouncing him, so he ought to break big soon."

"He's Robbo's protégé," said Miles. "He's The Churchill."

"Tell him the truth, Miles, he's my uncle."

"Well ..." said Miles.

"He – or possibly she – is *supposed* to be Robbo's protégé," said Clara, "but he's equally elusive and can only be contacted through Robbo. The rumour is he's actually Robbo's alter ego, a sort of side-project or plausible-deniable cat's-paw. Pingu makes displays so outrageous even Robbo wouldn't dare."

"Wow," said Uncle Charlie.

"Clara, you shouldn't ... I can neither confirm or deny that," said Miles. "To be honest I really don't know for sure."

"The thing is Pingu hasn't written any manifestos denouncing the art establishment, and it seems to amuse Robbo to promote him, so ... "

"It's a thought," said Miles. "It's still a long shot."

"He would probably still make insane demands," said Clara. "And from what I've heard, Pingu might be too wild even for you, Uncle Charles."

"No, I'd love to have him," said Uncle Charlie.

"Or possibly her," said Clara.

"At last, Miles!" cried Clara at home, pacing the living room manically. "I have infiltrated the belly of the beast!" She started to seize crayons and felt-tips and stray bits of paper.

"Clara – "

"Call me Pingu."

"Pingu, he's your uncle."

"Not by blood, Miles. He's an appalling turd and the enemy of all that is beautiful and he abandoned my aunty for a whore and he never bought us a wedding present. And he's been flattering you like a floozy for what use he thought he could make of you."

That did rankle and was as good an excuse as any, and the fact was Miles was actually quite enthused for once.

"Can I be Pingu too then?" he asked.

"You may help me in the unlikely event I get stuck." Clara twirled a crayon, eyes alight. "Miles, I believe I have waited my whole life for this opportunity. I'll show them."

But how or what she would show them was the problem.

Two days later she was still pacing, and furiously gnawing the end of a pencil. In the interim the two of them had advanced and rejected – not that many concrete ideas, actually.

"There must be some way to subvert it," she muttered.

"I'm telling you, it can't be done," said Miles, who had despaired early. "There is absolutely no way to parody or send up modern art. There is nothing you can do that wouldn't be hailed. There is nothing you can do as a piss-take that hasn't been done for real. Forget trying to make a statement – let's think of something averagely vile, childish or pseudish, really be Pingu and become rich forever."

"Penises!" said Clara.

"Something slightly original, though."

"No, listen! What if we set up an exhibition of reproductions of Old Masters, but with penises scrawled on them? Charlie and the other pigs would wet their pants with glee, but meanwhile the general public will be inadvertently exposed to beauty and may, without knowing why, start to re-evaluate their priorities. We could use disappearing ink, but I think people would just start to blank out the penises anyway, as I have learned to do."

"You're actually on to something. Why don't we just put up some really beautiful paintings? One of the brilliant undiscovered people Jeremiah sells."

"I thought of it, but – boring. I want to really show up the whole thing. How about if we get a cat to make some 'art' and then – "

"Been done. I think it won a prize."

"Or get a serial killer from Broadmoor to do something, and then we reveal – "

"Are you kidding? That would be seized on with delight. He'd be world famous and hailed as a genius in a week."

"A small child," said Clara. "A small brain-damaged child."

"They'd call him a savant prodigy, or say it was found art, or – wait a minute! Wait a minute! What if Pingu was revealed, not as a lunatic or a baby, but – horror of horrors – some old, reactionary, posh, Middle England – "

"But this Robbo is posh and – "

"No, not like that, some – listen! The Wing Commander! You remember that painting him and Jeremiah made that night of Germans being blown up – "

"Good God Miles," said Clara wide-eyed.

"Yes – we get them to knock off a few of those and, and – maybe we tape him talking, do an audio installation, him saying those – terrible things he says sometimes – so we have this exhibition, and everyone says, oh, how ironic, it's this merciless satire on the Imperialist mind-set – and then, the Wing Commander pops out and says, no, I meant it, all Germans must die, and Charlie and all the critics look foolish, and – "

"And Middle England is revealed to look pretty much as all the swine always thought it was? And the Wing Commander goes to jail? It's not quite there, Miles."

The next day, lying on the floor staring at the ceiling, Clara said, "A completely empty room."

"And then what?"

Clara thought for a long while. "A man farts just before anyone enters, and then runs away. No, just a completely empty room. That sums up the whole thing."

"I bet it's been done."

"I bet the fart one hasn't. We could put farts in bottles and get people to smell them. That dreadful labourer from the pub could provide them."

"A cheque. We gouge a huge cheque out of Charlie, Pingu does, and we frame it, and that's the exhibit."

"Mmm. Some sort of stock-ticker. A stock-market commodities trading board, you know, showing prices going up and down, and we put the names of the other artists on it as the commodities."

"How about a compare-and-contrast thing, we have, you know, Old Masters, or Jeremiah's artists, and next to them some, you know, shit – "

"They would prefer the shit."

"We set it up as an experiment. They have to choose whether to spend half an hour locked in a booth with – "

"They would choose the shit."

"We get one of those machines that can scan the pleasure centres of the brain, and they have to put the helmet on as they enter, and we find out and record which they genuinely enjoy more, something beautiful or something ugly or banal, and if the herd-instinct centres of the brain light up a bell goes off."

"Ooh! Brilliant! But no. They have been trained to prefer shit. Besides I, and therefore by extension you, do not believe a machine can scan the human soul. How about a duck?"

"Why?"

"I like ducks. They are pretty. I am the artist known as Pingu, Miles, and I insist upon installing a duck. And an otter." She considered. "Perhaps a crucified otter."

The next day, upright again, Clara thoughtfully said, "I know in advance you will disapprove of this idea, Miles, but how if we simply plant a bomb in the gallery? Charlie and the rest of the scum would be in ecstasy at the display of their own intestines splattered all over the walls. It would get rave reviews and perhaps win the Turner. It would be hailed as puckish and irreverent and 'in one's face'. 'Damn the squares who say this is not beautiful' – The Sunday Times. 'Aaaargh, my arms, someone give me back my arms' – Guardian. 'Aiiieeee, Mother, Oh Jesus, help, help me' – the – "

"How about a nice water-colour of some flowers?" urged Miles. "Or a picture of a cat? You draw lovely cats."

"Something that gives them electro-shocks," muttered Clara, pacing and tapping a finger on her lips. "Or a trap door that drops them down to the sewers. 'Uncannily reproduces the experience of swimming in turds.' It would really be showing their own lives back to them. Or we could take the critics hostage and puckishly start to execute them. Perhaps in the manner of famous Old Masters."

"Let's go back to the duck idea," said Miles.

"I will install Mrs Mauberley," said Clara. "She will talk at them for three hours and then kick them in the bollocks."

The days passed fruitlessly. They turned to Jeremiah for help. Clara had roped him in at the beginning, even before they left London, to plant stories about Pingu on the internet in case Charlie looked, and he had been as excited about the plan as they were. But when asked for ideas the only thing he could suggest was that they install several comely young ladies in the exhibition, naked save for pearls and high heels, on the grounds that he didn't know much about modern art but he knew what he liked. Then, with a modest cough, he mentioned the painting he and the Wing Commander had made of Germans being killed.

Meanwhile Clara had at least been having fun stringing the increasingly anxious Charlie along on the phone. At first she said Robbo wouldn't do it: he thought Charlie was a pig. He refused to put them in touch with Pingu. But the next day she told him Miles had been phoned in the middle of the night by an electronically-scrambled voice. Pingu was interested. But he didn't think he could trust Charlie. He was too controversial for Charlie. He doubted Charlie would meet his demands.

"Tell him controversy is the sea that I swim in," said Charlie. "He can't be too bold for me. And tell him I will go to any lengths. I would walk over broken glass on my knees to get him."

Charlie received the first demands by post two days later, typed on a manual typewriter. In the same package was a dismembered and partially melted Action Man doll, with the words 'This is you if you cross me' scribbled on its chest in felt-tip. The first demand was simple. To establish trust and commitment Charlie was to go to the middle of

Leicester Square at a stated time and stand on one leg for five minutes, with the trouser of the other leg rolled up to the knee, patting himself on the head. If anyone asked him why he was doing it, he was to reply nothing but, 'Because I am a turd.'

Charlie faithfully if unenthusiastically did this at the appointed hour. Clara and Miles watched, disguised, from a distance. Other people watched from a lesser distance.

Then Charlie had to walk into the Groucho Club carrying a copy of the Daily Mail under his arm. He was to order a drink and say to the barman, 'Three cheers for Cecil Rhodes's birthday.' He was to sit down, wait ten minutes and then go to the toilet leaving his jacket on the chair, and when he came back he would find it had been swapped for a different one. He was to put it on, wait five minutes and then leave and walk back to his gallery by a specific route, not looking round if he felt himself jostled. By the time he got back there would be an envelope containing further instructions in the pocket.

Charlie did this too; they knew because Clara's well-connected friend Stephanie had got them into the Groucho and they were again observing in disguise. Neither Clara or Miles had had any practise in reverse-pickpocketing and in fact the second envelope was already in the new jacket when they swapped it for Charlie's. The new jacket was a bright yellow silk disco one, on the back of which Clara had specially had printed a picture of Ronald Reagan and the legend, 'Rest In Peace Dutch.'

At midnight of the same day Charlie found himself parking his car in a deserted street. Two figures in balaclavas got in the back and told him not to look around. They took it in turns reading a strident art manifesto, as incomprehensible as any of the ones he dealt with regularly, and then relayed Pingu's real demands. One, a man, sounded like someone caricaturing a Battle of Britain RAF pilot, while the other, a woman, shouted a lot and talked about executing him for non-compliance and spoke in a strange accent that hinted at a peripatetic upbringing divided between Scandinavia, Wales and Pakistan.

"You will not see us again," she concluded as they left. "But we will see you. This had better not go wrong."

These demands had to do with payment. First off Charlie had to organise a beggars' banquet that weekend for thirty London tramps at an upmarket restaurant. Next he had to shove a large sum of money in cash for materials and one hundred boxes of Maltesers through the letterbox of an empty shop. This was the former Accident Claims shop they had taken over and still owned. Clara was fond of Maltesers.

Charlie rang them afterwards. He called Pingu a bastard, but to Clara's slight disappointment he was clearly more excited than embarrassed and having as much fun as they were. He also said he had been spreading the word on the quiet and there was a buzz of expectation: she gathered the reaction had been congratulations on his coup and feigned knowingness about Pingu and his relationship to Robbo. The artist who was contributing the corpse had heard and thrown a tantrum, worried about being upstaged.

"He's probably just stringing you along," she said. "You won't see any so-called art *or* your money back."

Charlie sounded anxious again. But after the beggars' banquet had gone ahead (and been reported in the papers) and the Maltesers and cash had been delivered, Clara passed on a message that Pingu was pleased with him and would condescend to fill a room at his show, if Charlie was really sure he could handle his work.

In the days that followed Charlie kept ringing to enquire, in tones in which deepening anxiety warred with deferential humility, exactly when he would see some of the work or be given some clue as to its nature. Clara pointed out that she and Miles were merely acting as go-betweens and that she didn't bloody know. Charlie asked what he should put in the catalogue, which was about to be printed. He was faxed a page from the Life of Walpole and a drawing of a penguin.

They came up with and passed on further demands. There were to be tickets for five people to the opening of the exhibition. Any, all or none of them might be Pingu. There must be buckets of Maltesers at the gallery, and free jelly for everyone. Tramps must be allowed, nay invited in, and they must be given jelly too. Several of the Pingus smoked and anyone who wanted to must be allowed to, and if anyone complained or fines were issued it was just too bad. A topless model wearing pearls and high heels must usher people into Pingu's room. There must be a version of the exhibition catalogue translated into English.

"What does that mean?"

"I don't bloody know, I am merely an unwilling cut-out." Clara hung up briskly. "I am enjoying being an art-terrorist, Miles, we really ought to keep this up."

There was more. If any of Pingu's pieces failed to be snapped up by the buyers of the borgy philistine art world, Charlie had to pay him a reserve price. If Charlie was reactionary swine enough to want to withdraw any of Pingu's pieces, he would have to pay this and a hefty penalty besides.

The most important condition they had decided on as crucial right at the beginning but only sprung on Charlie as time started to run out and his anxiety had reached fever point. It was to be a guerilla installation, they told him: the famous national gallery was to be left unlocked and unguarded and with cameras deactivated the night before the opening and Pingu's team would sneak in and set up his works in secret. Charlie would therefore not see Pingu's art until the day of the opening.

"Oh God," said Charlie.

"It's non-negotiable, I'm afraid, he says it's the only way he can ensure no interference. I have to admit it sounds rather thrilling to me. Like Father Christmas visiting. It's that or an empty room anyway."

"Oh God."

Charlie got back to them: it was absolutely out of the question for so many invaluable, imperishable contributions to human culture to be left unguarded overnight. However it was settled that the gallery guards would admit five masked figures in the middle of the night and escort them to Pingu's room.

"I'm sure we could actually use this to pull off a spectacular heist," Clara told Miles. "We could hang the corpse in the front room to impress the neighbours. We could keep that black-painted Rubik's Cube in a safe and gloat over it in private. We could absorb the paper-clip sculpture into our office supplies. We could eat the various pickled things, and the ones made out of chocolate or meat, and play with the giant toys. We could put the painted cars in Exchange and Mart. We could sell the rest to a junk-shop for a fiver, or of course keep them all about us and become rich in spirit."

"Yes," said Miles, "but failing that what are we going to put in the bloody show?"

The thing was they still couldn't think of anything good and were becoming as anxious as Charlie was. There were now five days to go.

"If we can't think of something good tonight we have to pull out," said Miles.

"Let us brainstorm again. It surely isn't beyond us. We *can't* let this chance go begging. What would really teach them a lesson? What would really make a point? What would Charlie *most* hate to wake up to find in his exhibition? Something nice? Something patriotic or virtuous? But they would just be taken as ironic."

"I'm telling you it can't be done."

"It must be done."

They paced, sighed, chewed pencils and fingernails, competitively made thinking faces, leafed apathetically through reference books, guzzled Maltesers until they hated the sight of them, kicked Miles's ankle, and in the small hours gave up and went to bed failures.

It was lying there that Clara had her brainwave.

"Miles!" she gasped. "We are idiots. It is obvious. It has been staring us in the face all along. Listen." She turned and ecstatically breathed two words into his ear.

Miles laughed. Then he thought about it and laughed some more. He stopped and then sniggered and then cackled evilly.

"That would be ace," he admitted. "Imagine. Oh my God, imagine. But even you wouldn't ... Anyway it's *too* obvious. It's the sort of thing everyone's already thought. We should disdain anything so obvious."

"Sometimes perfection is obvious."

"I think it sort of misses the point anyway. Would things be any better if they *would* – "

"It's that or an empty room."

"Come on, you wouldn't. We could ring and pretend he's going to, but ... You don't hate him that much."

"He owes us a wedding present. We could at least ... " She outlined a plan.

Miles sniggered again. "We bloody *can't*."

"We bloody are."

Coming up with a worthy centrepiece for Pingu's display unleashed their creativity and sparked off several lesser ideas. In the end the problem was not filling the space they had been given but deciding what to leave out.

The next five days were an exhilarating whirlwind of furious, happy work and frantic purchasing and organising. Various people who had more artistic talent and other forms of expertise than they did had to be corralled in.

Clara started to take her art very seriously. Like many an artist before her she had to wrestle with the limitations of her materials.

"Why can't its bloody arms be longer? It's a good job Jesus wasn't an otter, that's all I can say."

At last came the night of the installation, and that was fun too. In the dead of night they and some confederates pulled up outside the famous gallery in a van and were admitted to its hallowed precincts. They were dressed in black and wearing balaclavas or motorcycle helmets. A couple of them were armed with baseball bats or bits of lead piping which they tapped into their hands menacingly.

"Keep away from the art!" Clara yelled at the gallery guards. "Don't look at the art! Lie face-down on the floor until we blindfold you!"

The guards refused to lie face-down or be blindfolded. However, as everything except the route to Pingu's room was roped off, and as Charlie had been quite explicit that they were to play along with this, and as some of the Pingus were quite intimidating, they were at length browbeaten into standing along the route with their backs turned and promising to keep their eyes closed.

"I really must organise a bank-blag one of these days," said Clara as she and Miles started to lift things out of the van.

"Was that a duck?" asked one of the back-turned guards a while later as she carried something else past him and it quacked.

"Keep your mouth shut! Eyes closed!"

"We really can't leave the poor duck in here overnight," muttered Miles.

"The otter will keep it company."

A while afterwards, when the others were trundling something noisily along on a trolley, and she had just growled at the guards that if their eyes weren't closed there would be what for, she tip-toed past them and over a rope into one of the rooms where the other artists' work had already been installed and ate a bit of someone else's exhibit, a sculpture made out of cubes of cheese and sausages on cocktail sticks.

"Like they haven't been doing it anyway," she muttered when Miles made nervous gestures and pointed at the guards.

Presently the display was set up to Clara's satisfaction. They turned off the lights and blocked off the entrance to their space by wedging it with various heavy bits of junk, iron bedsteads and shopping trolleys and so on, all chained together and padlocked and draped with sheets, finally criss-crossing it with 'Police Line Do Not Cross' tape.

The duck quacked forlornly as they left.

*

The next morning before the grand opening Clara and Miles turned up at the gallery in their normal clothes and strolled around watching some of the artists and organisers making last-minute tweaks. The five friends and friends of friends who were playing the Pingu collective had arrived before them. They were men of various sizes, but little more could be said about them, as they were all wearing burkhas, diving masks and divers' flippers. They were still not letting anyone into the Pingu room and stood before the barricade with bats, lead pipes and other weapons more or less negligently displayed. One at least of them was trying to chat up the topless model in pearls and high heels who stood nearby waiting to act as usher. Several of the other artists were regarding them with a certain froideur.

Charlie, looking somewhat excited but more anxious than ever, had admitted his niece and her husband and immediately bustled off, beset with difficulties. He had to despatch minions to procure cheese cubes and pornographic materials. Either Clara's little midnight snack had ruined the cocktail-stick sculpture irrevocably, or the guards had been browsing on it: the artist was in hysterics anyway. Worse, the performers for the Cock-Puppet Nativity Play were finding it hard to maintain erections. Also the corpse artist was demanding the air-conditioning be turned off as the smell was being lost.

They ate complimentary jelly and Maltesers and snagged some wine.

"Why this is hell, nor are we out of it," said Clara as they sauntered around the gallery.

"Perhaps we should see it all as a splendid joke," said Miles. "Perhaps we should applaud them for getting money out of rich morons."

"If it is a joke, husband, why have you forbidden me to laugh at them? It may have been funny when Duchamp did it, or the first time people solemnly sat through the John Cage silence, perhaps the first time Warhol propagated some completely vacuous image, but that was before these people were born, and now it grows tired. I will applaud these psychopaths for teaching themselves a trade. Further than that I will not go."

"I suppose all art forms reach a point where they disappear up their own arse to avoid repeating what's gone before."

"And then you simply retrace your steps and start again. It happens all the time in the novel and the theatre, perhaps not alas in poetry. No-one felt compelled to follow Joyce or Burroughs or Beckett. It was recognised that they had reached the end of an interesting cul-de-sac, so people just reversed back to the main road of pleasing an audience and providing catharsis. I repeat that this *is* repeating what has gone before."

"The thing is," said Miles as they passed an inexplicable swirly thing made out of shiny metal, "coming from the sticks, I'm exactly the sort of gaping yokel who's diverted by some of this. It's exactly the sort of decadence I'd hoped to find in the big city."

"I know how you can be diverted by shiny objects."

"So I find bits of it almost acceptable as mindless fun. I think it's the appropriation of the word 'art' I object to. If they would find some other term, call it Junk Sculpture or Postmodern Urban Spectacle or something …"

"I can think of something ruder to call it."

Miles begged her to keep her voice down. Some of the younger male artists who were present seemed to be competing with each other in boisterous yobbishness, but he had been struck by others conscientiously making final, millimetrical adjustments to things that could make no possible sense to anyone however they were positioned. Here, now, was someone adjusting the lighting around a blaring, flashing video-game machine. They seemed to take it awfully seriously.

"I wish we *had* done the mind-reading helmets," he suddenly said. "I wish someone would invent a portable bullshit detector."

"Everyone is born with one, Miles, they just malfunction around large amounts of money or solemnity."

"That woman there, for example, those … things she's made. They at least seem to be the result of working out some kind of obsession or vision or therapeutic need."

"Those are quite fascinating, I admit, and she seems to have a knack for … whatever they are. Now if I had found them at an arts and crafts fair for a fiver I might be very pleased with them."

"So it's just the insane money we resent?"

"Miles, you exasperate me. Has there ever been a moment of your life when you haven't felt guilty about something? Obviously you have repented what we have done to Charlie."

"No, I'm quite looking forward to seeing his face actually. I just – "

"You have just been browbeaten by a clique of self-appointed experts into wondering whether your own common sense is at fault. It is the story of our times." They walked on. "What I object to, Miles … I once saw someone crying at a Vermeer. And someone crying in front of Chartres cathedral. I have seen you cry at the opera, you big girl. I disapprove of displays of emotion myself, but has anyone ever shed tears at this kind of thing, except out of boredom?"

They came to the corpse: actually a torso, on a shallow wooden tray.

"Now this doesn't bore me," said Clara grimly. "This makes me angry. If I am supposed to be shocked, if Charlie wants me to be shocked, if the artist would be sneeringly delighted I am shocked, they win. I am shocked. It will be worse when I no longer am. Art is that which transcends. This is about debasing. What goes on here is a belittling. Of art, of our dreams, of ourselves." She stared down at it. "This – this is blasphemous, if anything is. This was a man."

"Human dignity is so century-before-last." Miles was thoughtful. "Not to be pious but perhaps ours *is* blasphemous too then. In the sense that ours was a man too."

"I can see little marks from his saw where he has sawed the limbs off," said Clara in a small voice.

"Beautiful, isn't it?" said Charlie coming up behind them and laying his hands on their shoulders. He was no longer anxious. "Should make a big noise. Come on, let's go and see what this Pingu of yours has got for us."

"Yes, let's," said Clara smiling at him.

The Pingus were still grouped in front of the barricade.

"Come on," said Charlie clapping and rubbing his hands. "Enough of this. Let's be seeing it. Go, go."

"Not until opening time," said a Pingu, Miles thought Jeremiah.

"That's in ten minutes. Come on, let's go, the critics'll be here."

The Pingus appeared to consult among themselves and glanced at Clara, who made a small gesture. Muttering, they commenced to unlock and unchain the makeshift barricade and pull it down. The gallery resounded as the heavier items crashed to the boards.

"Like breaking into Tutankhamen's tomb," said Charlie, chipper.

"Let us hope there is not a curse upon it," said Clara.

The room was unblocked. A Pingu hit the lights. There was an excited quack.

Charlie seemed very happy, at first, with Pingu's productions. Of necessity his tour had to be hurried but he lingered grinning as long as he could in front of each exhibit. Among the first things he came to there was little out of the ordinary, in his line of business, little to justify Pingu's dangerous reputation. Clara had mounted some memory-sketches of Miles's penis, under the title 'I Hate Thursdays'. There was a display of some things she had made out of plasticine or lego, and an Etch-a-Sketch picture of a robot fighting a monster. "The critics will argue for decades to come over its significance," she had predicted. "They will also compliment me on the way the monster's eye is almost perfectly circular. That is the sign of a true artist, to be able to draw a circle with an Etch-a-Sketch." Miles had contributed a train and a ship made out of cornflakes boxes, toilet roll tubes, cotton reels and so forth, and they had made a pornographic toy theatre out of similar materials.

Clara wasn't happy with the crucified otter. For one thing Miles had forbidden her to procure a fresh otter and she had had to make do with a rather moth-eaten stuffed one. For another they simply weren't built to be crucified. In the end she had simply settled for nailing it to the cross lengthways, one nail through its head and the other through its tail, and in her heart she knew she had botched the job and hadn't even got the thing straight. Charlie seemed to love it, however, and stood before it mesmerised with his hand on his chin for a full minute at least.

"Oh, that's The Churchill," he pronounced.

He seemed bemused by the duck, when it approached him and quacked.

"And what's this?"

"It's a duck, innit, you ---- ," said a Pingu who had pulled his burkha eyehole down so as to be able to smoke through it.

"I get it," said Charlie grinning. "Like it."

In the middle of the space were several large black windsocks which had been sewn together and tacked down in a zig-zag so as to form a winding tunnel. A yellow arrow on the floor pointed into the mouth.

"You crawl down it, don't you?" growled a Pingu as Charlie mused over this.

"Wow," said Charlie, and got down on his hands and knees and crawled inside.

They watched morbidly as the bolus of his crouched form passed along the black silk oesophagus. Miles ate jelly. The Pingu who was smoking said the rude word again. Another tapped a flipper. Behind their backs Clara bit her lip and then tip-toed over and adjusted the crucifix so the otter was horizontal.

Inside the tunnel it was dark after the first few feet. There were loaded mousetraps along the way, sticky puddles of jam, piles of soot, dangling curtains of sellotape, and also some roadkill one of the Pingus had found the previous night. After the last zig-zag the tunnel went over some steps and down the other side. Shortly after this it debouched into a sort of cave formed by a small round one-man tent. Clara had wanted bats or rats in there but had thought of no easy way to keep them in. So all there was in there was a torch dangling from a bit of string tied to the ceiling frame in such a way that you were likely to bang your head on it, and, once you had turned it on, a small cardboard sign reading, 'You are a ----ing idiot.'

Charlie reached this terminus and after a moment they saw a bobbing patch of light appear. He seemed to muse on the climactic revelation for at least a minute. Then the light went off and he retraced his crawl. Halfway along there was a cry of "Ow!" as he presumably activated a mousetrap.

He emerged grinning, brushing soot and sellotape off himself as he stood.

"Love it," he said.

He also loved the dildo painted as a cruise missile, the sex-doll Jesus riding a space-hopper, and almost wet his knickers over the framed doctored photograph of Sarah Palin standing next to a suicide bomber, prominently titled, 'Which is Scarier??' He grinned and nodded manically at this, then chuckled at the floor-length photoshop of a convicted paedophile and murderer dressed up as Father Christmas.

"I can already see the headlines," he groaned good-humouredly.

"Not yet he can't," muttered a Pingu.

From the main body of the gallery came sounds making it plain that the doors had been opened and the first visitors had entered. Charlie said he ought to go and see if there were any VIPs to greet but was having too much fun.

"You've really come up trumps," he enthused. "Whichever of you it is, you're a genius in your twisted way."

Clara patted her hair and looked sidelong at Miles.

"We are a profit-making collective," growled a Pingu, who Clara decided was padding his role. "Genius is 19th-century."

"Oh of course," said Charlie hastily, moving on from the sex murderer. The Pingus trailed after him, flippers slapping.

He was plainly bemused by, but politely complimentary about, the large painting of Walpole that Clara had commissioned and one of Jeremiah's artists had knocked off in a great hurry but with astounding technical virtuosity. It depicted him fighting with a sword on a burning galleon deck, a bosomy Agnes Bojaxhiu clutched to his side, killing and maiming various disgusting foreigners. If you looked closely his penis was visible, and inspiring.

"I think I get it," Charlie muttered stroking his chin.

"More than I did," muttered the Pingu who had painted it.

Charlie enjoyed, and Clara supposed it was too much to hope he wouldn't, the sketch depicting various members of the government being hung from lamp-posts, disembowelled or otherwise despatched, towards which almost everyone in the pub had contributed something or other.

He grew more thoughtful, however, as he reached a display further on, a triptych of framed floor-length photoshops of the American global-warming-alarm tycoon Al Gore: standing arse-deep in snow preaching at snowball-flinging children, flying a plane towing a banner saying, 'Don't fly on planes', and being buggered with a hockey-stick in hell, this last being titled 'Here's your warming now, ---- '.

"Hmm," Charlie said frowning. Then at length: "I get it. Ironic, right? A depiction of the crass childish mentality of the deniers."

"Told you," murmured Miles to Clara.

"Who has a crass mentality?" she muttered angrily. She leaned to the nearest Pingu and hissed, "Thirty thousand now, not twenty."

Next to this on the wall was a huge graph depicting temperature fluctuations throughout the Earth's history, up and down, up and down, up and down since the beginning of time, with an arrow pointing to the 19th century right near the end marked 'The Industrial Revolution Started HERE'.

" ... the childish, simplistic ... "

"*Forty.*"

There was a display of Frequent Flyer cards made out in the names of prominent AGW exponents. There was a really very excellent cartoon one of Jeremiah's blokes had done depicting the lot of them as Savonarola and co orchestrating a Bonfire of Vanities on which were piled cars, cows, books and babies, another one of them conducting a Salem witch-trial of a carbon dioxide molecule, and a less good one by

Clara of them all being stabbed in the head and having their feet bitten off by dogs.

"Hmm," said Charlie frowning. "I get it. It's a bit ... I dunno ... "

There was a display of photos of temperature-measuring stations counted by the authorities as rural which were all in urban areas, often in car parks, next to ventilator exhausts, et cetera. You could tell he didn't get that.

Charlie cheered up a bit when he came to the next, interactive display, which one of the Pingus had worked hard and cleverly on. There were two pairs of glasses you could put on, one marked MEDIA and one marked TRUTH, the first with red lenses and the other with blue. There was a chart on the wall and next to it some framed, labelled photos of alarmist climate scientists and lobbyists. When you put the 'Media' glasses on you saw the famous but false and discredited 'hockey-stick' temperature graph; when you donned those marked 'Truth' it was replaced by a more accurate temperature line, including the decline of the past few years; and the scientists and so on all had 'DUPLICITOUS ----' scrawled across them and penises drawn on their heads.

Charlie excitedly said, "Ooh," when he picked up the glasses. Charlie liked interactive. When he put them down again he said, "Hmm. I get it. A demonstration of the paranoid mindset."

"Told you," murmured Miles.

"I can wait," said Clara.

"You know this stuff's liable to be misinterpreted," said Charlie frowningly. "Perhaps, to make things clearer, you could replace the 'Truth' label with one saying 'Internet'?"

"Same thing," growled Jeremiah Pingu.

Charlie looked at his watch now. His enthusiasm had dimmed somewhat. There were still things on the other side of the room he hadn't seen. He crossed quickly to it, cursing as he stumbled over the duck en route.

Clara had mounted a small display celebrating various heroes of British history. Charlie frowned at this but at length brightened and said, "I get it."

"I have decided that the man who invented the concept of irony was worse than the man who invented concrete," muttered Clara scowling.

But Charlie properly cheered up when he came to more penises and toys, smirked at a briefcase full of cash entitled 'My Muse', and laughed out loud at an installation called 'Cultural Bulimia', a sink filled with fragments of newspapers and magazines and postcards of great works of art of the past, covered in fake but realistic vomit.

"It's a triumph," he said at last. "The whole thing. Thank you. Look at

Spacehopper Jesus! I've got to tell you, whoever you are, there's been a lot of expectation about this when word leaked out, I mean some of the critics are salivating, but I have to say personally that you've almost exceeded mine. Worth waiting for and all the shit you've put me through. And – see? – *not* too hot for me to handle, far from it. As a matter of fact my only slight disappointment is you didn't push it further in some places."

The five Pingus, standing in a silent line, received this encomium unmoved.

"You haven't seen the best bit yet," said one.

They turned and filed towards the furthest end of the room, burkhas billowing and flippers slapping.

"More!" cried Charlie following. "You're spoiling me."

"More filth and perversion," sighed Clara. "You're like a pig in shit."

"Ah, Clara," said Charlie tolerantly. "You *will* play your little … "

A Pingu gestured at a curtain across the middle of the end wall, opposite the entrance, a moveable hospital screen curtain but painted black.

"Ah! I'd wondered about that," said Charlie. "I assumed it hid your … bits and bobs … "

"Au contraire," said a Pingu.

"This is the centrepiece," said another.

"The masterpiece," said a third.

"The show-stopper," put in a fourth.

"Behold," said the last.

They trundled the screen aside and whipped a dust-sheet off the thing that was behind, and he saw it.

Those who were present would afterwards compete with each other to describe or imitate Charlie's face in the next few moments but were never able to succeed to anyone's satisfaction. One member of the party came close by likening the collapse of his smile to the dropping of icicles from a melting gutter and their shattering on the ground. Another said that he aged a century in a second and that his skin turned not white but yellow, the colour of old, curled, tobacco-stained paper. An artistically gifted Pingu once produced a series of profile sketches purporting to delineate, instant by instant, his journey from 'What is it?' to 'I know what it is' to 'It can't be what it is' to 'It must be something else' to 'It bloody is what it is' to 'Please let it not be what it is' to 'Please let me wake up in my mother's arms, a child again and safe.' Miles claimed he had been able to trace, by the flickering of his eyes, the nanoseconds when Charlie's thoughts had been caught in a species of Ro-Block or logical loop, rebounding briefly between fear of looking square and fear of other and worse things, until the latter had definitively won out. The others denied there had ever been any such moment of hesitation or room for anything but horror, but some agreed with him that the man's very ears had twitched with shock. Certain it was that there had been an eye-bulging, a freezing, a gaping, a discolouring, and an all-consuming physical and mental sagging. Clara maintained that he had premiered a bold new work in his pants.

"Oh God," said Charlie. "Oh shit."

This is what Charlie saw:

On a slightly raised platform stood a machine or junk sculpture adapted from the body of an antique 1950s Wurlitzer jukebox. A hum as of a fridge motor emerged from it and if you leaned close you felt a chill: there was refrigeration going on somewhere within. The arched top section had been removed and in its place stood a tall vertical board covered in black velvet, and twisting around the front of the board was an intricate network of transparent plastic tubing, inside which was a thick white milky fluid. One end of the tube emerged from, and the other ultimately disappeared back into, the body of the machine, and the occasional sluggish bubble or cloudy swirl showed that the viscous white contents were being circulated around the network by some unseen agency below. Now the thing about this clear tubing containing white stuff was that, held in place by discreet brackets, it curved, writhed and squiggled around the black velvet backing in such a way as to form, as clearly as white lines on a blackboard could have done, the face of a man. It was distinct at a distance and it was distinct up close. While it was clearly recognisable as a face, it was not a face you recognised, because no-one knew quite what the owner of the face had looked like. But it was the product of much hard work and great artistic and technical skill, and in deft and definite lines, with economy and even grace, a venerable but stern-looking man with a beard and turban was sketched out of those tubes of fluid whiteness.

Because it was not clear who the face was meant to be, and because it was not clear what the milky fluid was – and it may as well be said here that it was the product of much experiment but was, as it happens, largely milk, although Charlie was not to know that – and because the impact of the piece very much depended on the audience having a very clear idea of these things, it had been thought necessary to spell them out. Accordingly its title *was* spelled out, in large characters, in illuminated neon tubes in the belly of the machine, and again in a three-foot flashing neon sign edged by multi-coloured light-bulbs, standing raised above the caricature, which read, majestically:

SPERM MOHAMMED

"Oh shit," said Charlie, "oh God."

They waited.

"What ... what ... what is that?" he asked in a croak.

"It seems fairly obvious to me, Uncle Charles," said Clara. "There are signs, look."

"It's a picture of Mohammed made out of spunk, innit?" said one of the Pingus helpfully.

"Oh God," said Charlie, "oh Jesus."

"No," said Clara patiently, "Mohammed."

"No," said Charlie clutching his head, "no. No, no, no."

"What's the matter, Uncle Charles," asked Clara innocently, "don't you think it'll make a noise?"

"But it *does* make a noise," said one of the Pingus eagerly. "Listen." He pressed a button on the side of the machine. Immediately hidden loudspeakers roared into life, and a taped Cockney voice like that of a fairground barker boomed down the hall, rather loudly indeed:

"SPERM MO'AMMED, LADIES AND GENTS! ROWL UP AND SEE THE SPERM MO'AMMED!"

"No," said Charlie, "no, no, no." He looked round wildly towards the next room, already speckled with visitors, some of whom had glanced round curiously at the noise, some of whom would presently start to diffuse into Pingu's lair. "Get it out of here." He sounded as though he was about to start hyperventilating. He snatched at the sculpture's cover but two of the Pingus pulled it away from him and hid it behind them. He tried to trundle the screen back into place, but they toppled it over.

"I don't think he likes it," said a Pingu.

"You will hurt Pingu's feelings, Uncle," said Clara reprovingly. "*I* think it is rather pretty, and he has obviously tried his hardest."

Uncle Charlie glanced round wildly again then made an idiotic attempt to shield the sculpture with his body from the people starting to drift in from the main hall, even reaching up and waving with his hands for a second as if to obscure or rub out the huge flashing SPERM MOHAMMED sign on top. "Please, please, get rid of it."

"Are you rejecting our art?" yelled a very bellicose Pingu advancing on him. "Do you know how hard we worked on that?"

"Please, please, I beg you, just – "

"Do you have any *idea* of the trouble it takes to collect, store and handle HIV sperm?"

"Oh God," said Charlie grabbing at his hair again, "oh shit."

"Perhaps you could say it is ironic, Charles," said Clara helpfully. "Or talk about redemptive, transformative qualities or something. *I* think it is jolly interesting anyway. It will be the talk of the exhibition; it may even merit a little snippet in the newspapers."

A Pingu was yelling at Miles, "I thought you said he was all right," and Miles was defending himself. A second Pingu restrained a third from grabbing Charlie. Charlie was shaking his head and saying, "Please, please, please, no, no, no."

After this had gone on for some time one of the Pingus muttered, "Well if he really don't want it he'll have to pay the penalty."

"Oh yes," said Clara brightly, "there's the rejection clause we negotiated, remember Charles? If you really don't like their lovely seed picture, you have the right to reject it provided you pay them for their trouble."

"Yes, yes, yes," said Charlie, instantly taking out a cheque-book with a shaking hand. "Pay, pay. Just get rid of it."

"Twenty thousand pounds," demanded a Pingu.

Clara coughed discreetly.

"For this? Forty thousand," amended another.

"Yes, yes, yes," said Charlie, scrawling shakily and signing.

A smallish Pingu leaned dramatically with its head against the wall, kicking the skirting board, making loud sobbing noises. Another patted its shoulder consolingly.

"You have made Pingu cry, look," said Clara reproachfully.

Uncle Charlie snapped off the cheque and flung it at the hooded figures. "You childish, irresponsible bastards," he quavered in a sort of shaky fury. "Get it out of here *now*."

"Bourgeois chickenshit," sneered a Pingu, but picked up the cheque.

There was a trolley in the corner. Grumbling, and as slowly as possible, the Pingus unplugged the sculpture and loaded it on this. Charlie danced around them impotently for a bit and then hurried off to deflect some people who had entered the room, encouraging them into the crawl tunnel. The covering was flung carelessly over the sculpture but was trodden on and slid off before they had wheeled it to the entrance.

"Mind your backs," shouted one of the Pingus as they pushed it into the main hall, trailed after by Charlie waving the cover, "Sperm Mohammed coming through." Somehow the button in the side was pushed as they manoeuvred it through the main doors and the sound of the bellowing fairground-barker recording could be heard again just before they left.

Clara and Miles looked at each other and sighed contentedly.

"What appalling shits we are," said Clara thoughtfully to the duck, picking it up and stroking it. "It is a good job we are lovely."

Charlie's exhibition carried on smoothly after this little hiccup and was a rip-roaring success. The critics raved on the whole, although the reviews of Pingu's display, or what was left of it, were mixed. The consensus was that, while he was perhaps over-hyped and not as edgy and challenging as he was cracked up to be, he had moments of sheer brilliance and was one to watch for the future.

The buyers were less ambivalent. They knew a good investment when they saw one. On the evening of the second day Charlie rang to say he had had five-and-six-figure offers for every one of Pingu's works, excluding the duck, which they had taken home and given its freedom on a local pond, but including a half-eaten bowl of jelly Miles had left on the floor which had inadvertently received a substantial bid.

The rejection pay-off for the Sperm Mohammed was small potatoes by comparison; Charlie's commission alone would come to far more than that. He had forgiven the Pingus for the shock, looked forward to working with them again, and had obviously learned no lesson.

The crucified otter sold for a particularly large sum of money. They were depressed but richer.

Chapter Eight

They had had a good score at the costume shop. Miles was in the outfit of a Catholic cardinal and Clara was dressed up as the Pope.

They swished around in their robes for a bit, admiring themselves. They were ace robes. It was a joy just to swish in them.

"I have always fancied being a Pope," said Clara in ecstasy. "Look at our crooks and everything."

"Can we have a crook fight later?"

"We certainly can, my buccaneering young husband. I think they are really called croziers and, not only will they make good martial arts staves, I can recycle mine for Bo Peep afterwards. Right, let's begin."

"Pope Joan?"

"Well, Pope Clara. Let's see … We have been rival cardinals for a while, plotting and scheming against each other to get the top job. But secretly attracted. Oh let's do a sinister stalking-about-the-corridors-of-power bit, glaring at each other, first."

They swished around some more, glaring at each other villainously.

"Good afternoon, Cardinal Shittifacio," said Clara unctuously as they passed.

"Good afternoon and woof, Cardinal Babe," said Miles bowing.

They smiled falsely and then hissed and snarled as they moved on.

"Right enough of that," said Clara. "I bag the hot seat due to my superior people skills and impressive way of filling out a surplice. I appoint you my second in command for reasons of politics. You want to oust me but are secretly attracted to me. You have been looking for any dirt on me and have come to suspect I am an impostor. I have surprising gaps in my education and have further aroused your suspicions by putting flowers and pictures of kittens everywhere. Also, although you are not an expert in these matters, and certainly have no hands-on experience, you begin to think I have breasts. You would very much like to see these – but for what reason, only your heart can tell you." Miles nodded. "Right, go. I have just granted you an audience."

She sat in a carved wooden antique chair with armrests that was doubling as a throne – and they really, she thought, must buy a proper one soon – and waved a papal hand regally, or papally. Miles approached from a distance, tripping over his robes a bit, and knelt to kiss her ring. He took the opportunity to smooch her hand lingeringly, then bit his lip in puzzlement and angst and looked away.

"That will suffice, Cardinal Shittifacio," said Pope Clara with a hint of amusement. "You may rise."

"Your Holiness, hubba! I mean, good afternoon, by the grace of God."

"What is going down in Vatican City, my child? You know I depend on you to be my eyes and ears."

"I would be happy to be any organ to you at all, Your Holiness."

"Not any of the naughty ones, I hope."

Cardinal Miles laughed nervously.

"I have nothing much to report. All is well in God's kingdom. I just happened to be passing and," he looked cunning, "I wondered if you could help me translate these new prayers I wrote into Latin, I seem to have gone rusty."

"Oh, give them here, then." Clara rose and Miles handed over an invisible piece of paper. "Roughly speaking that would be, Dixit Dominus, izzy-wizzy, magna cum laude." She handed the invisible piece of paper back and looked him in the eye innocently. "Anything else?"

"No. Thank you, Your Holiness." Miles's eyes narrowed. They both swished around for a bit darting suspicious yet slightly lustful glances at one another.

"While you are here, Cardinal S, I have come to a decision," Clara said. "We are going to stop burning heretics. Instead, we will drill holes in their skulls and then use them as flower holders, brighten the place up a bit."

"Hmmm." Miles Cardinal Bastard scowled even more suspiciously and stroked his chin.

Pope Clara glared.

"Is there something the matter, Cardinal Shittifacio? Surely you do not question a command of the Pope?"

"What I want to know is, who keeps leaving the toilet seat down in the Vatican khazi?"

"That is what Jesus would have done," said Pope Clara reprovingly. "It is more considerate. What if some nuns come round?"

"I noticed you and the nuns having a pyjama party last night.

"Yes, I would have invited you, but it was girls only." Clara bit her lip. "That is, girls and Popes only. Tra-la-laa."

Cardinal Miles looked thoughtful. He cleared his throat.

"I have just seen your new orders to Michelangelo. You have now instructed him to paint kittens on the ceiling of the Sistine Chapel."

"They are holy kittens," said Clara piously. "Surely you cannot have forgotten the miracle of the adorable kittens who rescued Saint Jemima from the Cossacks?"

"And the bunny rabbit?"

"Jesus pulled one from a hat, I think, at the Wedding at Cana. I am surprised you don't remember."

"With respect, Your Holiness, you are mistaken."

"With respect, batface, I am the Pope and incapable of mistake. Have the bible rectified at once. And put some pictures of kittens in it. And cake recipes. And give it a new cover – fluffy and furry, with rolling eyes on it like one of those pencil cases."

"Only girls have those pencil cases," said Cardinal Miles narrowing his own eyes.

"Oh? Then, cover it in something really butch and leathery, I mean. As Pope I am necessarily somewhat out of touch with fashion."

"I notice, however, that you have put icons of Ricky Martin up in your bedroom."

"Oh – I am having him canonized," said Pope Clara airily. "He is to be the patron saint of hip-swivelling Latin come-hither."

Cardinal Miles glowered.

"Let me test you on your theology."

"Go ahead, ask me anything," said Pope Clara unworriedly.

"Name the twelve apostles."

"Ooh. Easy. James, Barney, Phil, Dozy, Beaky, Mick and Titch."

"Wronnng!"

"Well, they are now, I have changed it to make the church more modern and relevant."

"Oh no! You mean – ?"

"Yes, my boy, there are going to be a lot of changes around here. I intend to be a modernizing Pope. There are going to be no sins any more, except crimes against the environment. We will stop burning incense because of the carbon footprint. And that smoking chimney thing to announce a new Pope, that will only happen again over my dead body. Oh don't you think that was rather witty, Miles?"

"If you say so. But just to let you know, I couldn't get it up for a modernizing greeny Pope."

"I should hope not! It is merely a stratagem to stop you discovering my breasts."

"I do like these cardinal robes," said Miles, swishing about in them some more.

"Yes, I find this a disturbingly sexy scenario actually," said Clara, also swishing. "Although in your case it may merely hint at transvestism."

Miles took his mitre off and held it over his crotch phallically, arching a suggestive eyebrow.

"No, Miles. Come on, do it properly. Discuss theology, something abstruse."

"Um. There has been an outbreak of Adamite heretics in Scunthorpe, your Popeness."

"Those bastards! I'll bloody do them," said Pope Clara. "They go around naked, damn them."

"Yes. Awful." Miles cleared his throat. "Do you think, perhaps, we could go try going around naked some time?"

"That would hardly be proper."

"No, I suppose. But perhaps we should install a sauna in here. We could sit around naked and talk about men things, and of course Jesus."

"That would not be appropriate either."

"No." Thwarted, Cardinal Miles thought for a moment. "Um. Have you got any tattoos, you?"

"Certainly not!"

"Can I check? I'm supposed to check. All incoming Popes have to be checked for tattoos, that's the rule."

Looking at him suspiciously, Clara rolled up her pope-sleeves to show her arms.

"See?"

Cardinal Miles pounced and grabbed them.

"You're not very muscly for a Pope, are you?"

"I bet I could have you in an arm-wrestle," Clara-pope bridled.

"Could not."

"Could too. I bet I could have you in a proper wrestle."

"Come on then, let's go, you papal punk."

With a mutual growl they flung themselves on each other and wrestled, rolling around the floor in their Pope and Cardinal robes. At length Pope Clara pinned Miles down and then suddenly kissed him.

"Holy Father!" exclaimed Miles wide-eyed.

Clara scrambled to her feet in alarm. She looked away and bit a knuckle. "I'm sorry, my child, I don't know what came over me," she mumbled. She wrung her hands. "Now you must turn me in to the Inquisition!"

"No," said Cardinal Miles passionately. "I could never, ever do that. The fact is, I enjoyed it. I am as guilty as you are."

Pope Clara bit her lip. "Perhaps we could keep it between ourselves. Will you hear my confession?"

"If you'll hear mine."

"Deal."

"Bless me Father for I have sinned. A Pope kissed me and I liked it."

The Pope tutted. "Say ten Hail Marys and squeeze your nuts in a vice. Forgiven. Next. Wait! How much did you enjoy it? How much do you like this kiss-happy Pope?"

"He is all the world to me. He obsesses me. When he waves from the balcony my stomach flutters. When he excoriates the unbelievers my heart goes wild. He is pious and upstanding and wise. He knows all the commandments, not just the first few. He ... is a hell of a Pope, since you ask."

"Right, absolved then. Now my turn. I confess to hubris, accidie, sloth, hoarding biscuits, reading under the blankets, performing an illegal u-turn on a sabbath, forgetting to let the bathwater out and kissing a man torridly until his lips scorched."

"Well, nobody's perfect."

"I bloody am, I'm infallible."

Miles frowned. "Then ... then it cannot be a sin for a Pope to kiss a man," he said thoughtfully.

"Hmm." Pope Clara looked arch. "Do you think I should ... do it more often?"

He looked at her earnestly.

"If you please, I think you should do it every damn day."

They gazed at each other smoulderingly.

"You impossible, annoying, utterly adorable shit of a Cardinal!" cried Pope Clara.

"You hellcat sex-pontiff," growled Miles.

They embraced.

"Stop!" cried Clara detaching herself. "This is madness! What are we doing?"

"I know! We are the number one and number two men in the church."

"Yes." Pope Clara looked sly. "That is ... not quite. I have another confession to make." She undid her robes and exposed her bosoms. "What do you think of these?"

"Madre Dios! Then ... then ... you have only been masquerading as a man?"

"These aren't turnips, bud," said Pope Clara crassly, sashaying. "I expect you're wondering why I did it."

"Not particularly, tell me afterwards," said Miles grasping for her.

"I want to tell you now," said Clara, eluding him. "It was all to meet you. You do not remember Ermintrude, the flighty but adorable goose-girl from your village when you were a humble priest?"

"The one with feathers?"

"No, not that kind of goose-girl, the gorgeous one with a smile that lit up the pastures for miles around."

"No, not at all," said Miles, still trying to manoeuvre into a position where he could get his hands on the Papal orbs.

"Well, that was me. I worshipped you from afar and vowed to become Pope to get your attention."

"Oh. That's a turn up. May I – " Miles lunged with outstretched hands.

"No, Miles." Clara slapped him away and closed her Pope robes. "Let us not sully our love."

"No, let's," urged Cardinal Miles eagerly. "I'm up for a bit of sullying."

Pope Clara shook her head solemnly.

"The fact is, I love you too much to damn you to hellfire."

"I don't mind, really," said Miles pursuing her.

She moved to put the throne between them.

"No, Cardinal Miles," she said regretfully but firmly. "We must renounce our passion and never see each other again."

"What if we said a *lot* of Hail Marys after?"

"That would be cheating. We can hold hands sometimes but we must never, never go at it like stoats. Don't you think this could be terribly romantic Miles?"

"But – don't you think – " he frowned and tried to find the best way to express it, "a torrid and sinful ecclesiastical shag on the Papal Chair or up against the Vatican wall would be even *more* romantic?"

"Maybe when the passion mounts. First let's do smouldering at each other for weeks afterwards."

"Um. Okay."

They paced around and smouldered, bit their lips, gnawed knuckles, flared nostrils at each other, et cetera.

They stood side by side, heads bowed, and pretended to be praying. Slyly Cardinal Miles lifted up the She-Pope's skirts with his crook.

The Pope slapped it away, scandalised. "Not here!" she whispered. "Not in church! Later, when God isn't watching."

They paced and smouldered some more then flung themselves on each other so passionately both their mitres were knocked awry.

"No, no, we can't," cried Clara pushing him away. " – But we do. Fight as we may, tormented though we are, we cannot help but fall." She waved a hand. "We will take the torrid sex scene as read."

"What?" cried Miles. "But – "

"Okay now the really good bit – the evil misogynist head of the Inquisition discovers our secret and comes after us, and we have to flee, hand in hand, Pope and Cardinal, outcast lovers, alone against the world, holing up in haylofts and checking in anonymously to seedy motels. Don't you think that would be really really romantic?"

"Ye-es," said Miles resignedly, "I suppooooose."

"I bet you won't," said Clara.

"Won't what?"

"I bet you won't run out of the house, flee with me from the Inquisition right down the lane, run across the fields and hide in Farmer Dawson's old hayloft in Pope and Cardinal robes."

"With some steamy Pope-on-Cardinal daytime walalawoola at the end of it? I bet I would."

"Dare you."

"Dare *you*."

"Done. Let's go. Flee! Flee! The Inquisition is coming!"

Hand in hand they dashed out of the house and down the lane and into the fields. They made it to the barn without being seen.

"Miles I've had an even better idea," Clara cried as he unceremoniously threw her down on the hay and hurled himself on top. "Let's check into a seedy motel like this, in these robes, but furtively and wearing dark glasses. Then let's sneak into a few porno cinemas or something, or go down the dog-track like this and swear loudly when we lose."

While they were tumbling in the hay she forced him to admit this was a good idea. But Farmer Dawson saw them emerging from his barn all tousled and dishevelled and adjusting their vestments. They bolted for home and decided that was enough fun for one day.

Chapter Nine

And meanwhile something had happened that caused Miles a great deal of unease, something he found utterly inexplicable but which clearly boded no good at all. Clara had become friends with Harriet.

It had started the night she had thrown a rock through her window. Clara had laughed merrily afterwards, and several times more on the walk home, and made 'Kshh' noises in imitation of the sound of shattering glass. She had snuggled up next to the oblivious Miles happily and prepared to sleep the sleep of the just.

But sleep had not come. At first this might have been due to excitement, but after a while the thoughts that were bouncing around her head took on a sombre hue. It was no longer a warm glow of contentment that she felt but a constricted, claustrophobic feeling. There was a heaviness in her she reluctantly recognised as guilt. She thought of all the reproaches Miles would level if he knew, and glowered at him resentfully in the dark. She restrained the urge to hit his sleeping form but contrived to kick him in turning onto her back.

"Civilised democracy," she mimicked him in a mincing, priggish voice.

The unaccustomed self-doubt did not leave her. Sleep continued to elude her. The guilt grew more acute. She doubted Harriet was sleeping either. Her heart started to race as if in panic. On the rare occasions when Clara had felt guilt as a girl she had taken a gloomy refuge in watching film noir. There was a strange comfort to be derived from seeing someone else ruin their lives completely from taking one wrong turn. They must have one downstairs. She started to get up then remembered she had shot their television. She hugged Miles and found his hand and clinked their wedding rings together. Miles would stand by her even if the whole world turned against her. He was her rock; a whiny and reproachful one sometimes, but a rock nonetheless. *Rock*. Her stomach contracted and she felt cold. The sound of shattering glass came back to her, no longer thrilling somehow. The poor poor woman. And what would she say to her children?

"Oh God," said Clara aloud. "What have I done?"

Clara didn't enjoy feeling guilt. She cast around for some means to make it go away. She dealt with it as briskly and decisively as, earlier in the night, she had dealt with the problem of having a neighbour who was mocking her and telling lies about her friends.

"I must make things right," she decided. "I will befriend Harriet."

Instantly she felt better; almost instantly she fell asleep.

She was awake again early, before Miles. By the time he awoke and missed her she was walking into Harriet's yard, smiling brightly and carrying an apple pie on a plate.

Her smile faltered for a moment as she looked at the jagged hole in Harriet's living room window. Only the technicality of a few stray shards of glass remaining in place permitted it to be described as a hole *in* the window rather than a hole where the window had been. Resolutely she approached the front door and rang the bell. There was no answer but she heard movement inside. She remembered the previous occupant had been unable to open the front door due to the warping of the wood and the heavy draught insulation. She went round the side to where the kitchen door was.

At the back of the house was a small wind turbine sluggishly rotating. She held her smile and repressed an instinctive hiss. It was only a little baby one; you couldn't see it from the road; presumably she hadn't needed planning permission; good luck to her.

She stood in front of the kitchen holding the pie in front of her and cheerily called, "Yoo-hoo! Anyone home?"

The top half of the kitchen door opened. Harriet stuck her head out. Clara could find nothing much wrong with her head, at first glance, but then she wasn't really trying. She thought Harriet's face was quite pretty, nicer-looking, in both senses, than her newspaper photo, although with a certain capacity for querulousness.

Her face was cold and remote now as she coldly said, "Yes?"

"I have baked you a pie," said Clara brightly, "to welcome you to the neighbourhood."

Harriet seemed to be quite taken aback. And then suspicious. After that Clara thought she saw a warring mixture of emotions. On the one hand, something in Harriet sneered at the gesture – Clara could see the sneer spring up quite clearly, in eye more than lip. Harriet didn't believe in or was cynical about or didn't want to get trapped into neighbourliness; she didn't believe in geographical communities, only the abstract strident minority kind; she doubtless thought women who baked pies or who cooked at all were collaborators with the patriarchy and natural Tory voters; she despised women who baked pies to welcome people to neighbourhoods.

And on the other hand she was lonely, and touched in spite of herself.

These things flickered across Harriet's face, or perhaps just Clara's mind, in a second or so. Clara wondered if she was reading too much into a simple moment of surprise. Also, where did she get off thinking people's faces had 'a certain capacity for querulousness'? Miles was right, she really ought to write a book.

"A pie," said Harriet, "to welcome me to the neighbourhood."

No, she hadn't been wrong. All those things had been in Harriet's face and were in her voice now. The sentence was stressed in all kinds of strange places and loaded with sarcasm, condescension and bitterness all at once, particularly on the words 'neighbourhood', 'welcome' and indeed 'pie'. And there was that in her voice which Clara might have put into her own when she was cross, pretending to be cross or being cross-on-principle with Miles and not yet ready to accept his grovelling.

And, again, Harriet *was* lonely, and tempted by the pie in spite of herself; and of course all of the above things might have had something to do with the rock that had been thrown through her window the night before. By, Clara reminded herself with an effort, Clara.

She held up the plate with the lovely pie on it. "There is no poison in it," she said, also holding her bright smile.

Harriet made a face Clara would come to know as her, 'I know I am meant to be amused' look.

A few more seconds passed. Clara fought the urge to fling the pie in the wretched woman's gob.

"My name is Clara. I live just up the road with my husband Miles," she said with quite determined brightness. "We are your nearest neighbours heading towards the village." Her smile dimmed a bit as she remembered something. "The ones you saw fooling around in the garden that time, playing a game," she added. "It really was only a game. We have been to London and are quite civilised."

Harriet rolled her eyes, leaning in the door with arms folded. Clara at first thought the eye-roll was another polite acknowledgement of comic intent, but suddenly remembered a column of Harriet's which had demanded to know, 'Why do some people think it's big, or even remotely acceptable, to introduce or refer to people as "My wife" or "My husband"? Come to that, why do people feel compelled to mention their spouses as if possessing one is some great achievement?' and wondered if she had transgressed.

There was another pause while, presumably, Harriet debated whether to slam the door and tell her to eff off, or just tried to process the information that someone had brought her a pie. Either way Clara tired of it.

"May I come in?" she asked, still smiling brightly. "Or conceivably just give you the pie? It is rather a cold day and my breasts are freezing off. They are rather nice ones and I am fond of them."

"Yes," said Harriet, "it *is* rather a cold day, isn't it? I had noticed that, actually, what with one thing or another." She gave a snort as though she had just amused herself.

Clara understood she was referring to the broken window. She also toyed with and dismissed the notion that Harriet had actually seen her fling the rock and was playing cat-and-mouse with her. She gamely held her smile.

"That is not my fault," she said, which was true in general if not in this particular. "Quite the opposite. I have a petrol-hungry sports car and am doing all I can."

She expected to see the 'I know you are trying to amuse me' face again but was disappointed. Instead she saw a face which combined 'That isn't funny actually' and 'I bet you are too'.

However Harriet opened the bottom of the kitchen door at this point, turned her back and gracelessly said, "You'd better come in."

Clara followed her and placed the pie on the table. She could find nothing much wrong with Harriet's kitchen, but again she wasn't really trying just now. There was a sheet full of figures titled 'Carbon Costs' taped to the fridge, but she decided to ignore this.

Harriet stared at the pie, arms still folded. "It's a nice thought," she admitted. "Thank you," she added grudgingly.

"It was no trouble," said Clara truthfully.

Harriet frowned at the pie. "What's in it?" she asked with a return of suspicion.

"Apples," said Clara. "It is an apple pie."

Harriet's frown deepened. "What kind of apples?"

Clara blinked. "Green ones," she ventured haphazardly.

Harriet brightened, indeed seemed to regard Clara with a dawning of warmth. "Oh that's all right then," she said eagerly, clearly misunderstanding. "And it's good to find someone who cares about that."

"Oh yes," said Clara equally eagerly, affecting to misunderstand in her turn. "I hate red apples. Except in paintings. Some of the yellow ones are all right."

Harriet looked disappointed and somewhat contemptuous. "Never mind," she said witheringly. But she had thought of something else. "There aren't any animal fats in it, I hope? I am vegan, of course."

Clara didn't have a clue but assumed there were. She was about to exclaim, 'Heaven forbid!' but an unexpected ethical twinge, to do with either guilt about the rock or having lived with Miles for too long, she assumed, withheld her.

"To be honest, I really don't know," she admitted. "The truth is I burned the pie I tried to bake you so I bought that one from a shop in the village."

This was not the truth, but it was almost certainly what *would* have happened if Clara *had* tried to bake a pie for Harriet.

"Oh dear," said Harriet with an air of victory, pushing the plate an inch away from her. Nevertheless she seemed to have softened somewhat – because Clara couldn't bake, or because of the lie, or just this little victory? – and her lips had even twitched with a trace of real amusement at Clara's admission. "It was still a nice gesture," she acknowledged. She turned and wandered off to a cupboard. "I was just making coffee, if you'd like one," she added without any great enthusiasm or grace but at least no outright resentment.

"Thank you, that would be lovely," said Clara. Harriet measured two cups of water into a kettle and then made two ticks on a chart on the fridge. Clara decided to ignore this too, then found she couldn't. "Of course I will pay you for the extra carbon dioxide emission, if you wish," she added innocently.

Harriet turned and smiled for the first time, properly, warmly. "What a lovely thought!" she exclaimed, touched. "But it really isn't necessary. This one's on me."

"Thank you. I know you try to," Clara waved a hand, "budget your sins strictly, live as though you had never been born. Are you ... succeeding?"

Harriet frowned. "Not quite. Must try harder. This house doesn't help, we haven't got it fixed up properly yet. The biggest drain is the kids and the au pairs. They have no concept. And of course Richard is flying across the world every other week, although that's for Warming conferences or research for articles so it doesn't really count."

"Indeed," said Clara. "And is your husband away now?"

"Yes," said Harriet shortly. Her warmth had vanished. "Why do you people assume anyone is anyone's husband or wife?" she asked with a slight laugh but definite irritation.

Clara blinked. "I'm sorry, I thought – "

"Well you shouldn't! What right do you have? As a matter of fact we *are* married, but really only because of his parents and the kids' schools. For all you knew – "

"I feel ashamed," said Clara. "I could have wounded and oppressed you horribly. We must all guard our tongues vigilantly at every moment."

"Well, yes," said Harriet, half-mollified.

There was a pause. Harriet was hunched over the kettle, which Clara thought must be an eco-one that tried to coax the water molecules to vibrate by gentle persuasion and at any rate didn't seem to be doing much.

"It isn't very blowy today," she said. "Shall I go out and give the windmill a shove round?"

Harriet made her joke-recognising face again. "It's easy to mock," she said, but not particularly indignantly; indeed Clara felt that at some level she was perversely pleased to be mocked. Harriet frowned. "You were taking the piss in offering to pay, too, weren't you?" she belatedly realised.

"Gently teasing. I suppose I shouldn't." Clara decided she had to persevere and smiled at Harriet as warmly as she could manage. "My hus - that is my daemon lover Miles and I are big fans of your writing. We laugh like hyenas at you sometimes," she added in the interests of a closer approach to truth. Harriet perked up a bit, made the stifled-gloating face that Clara had noted writers tend to do when they try to accept praise modestly. "I have been meaning to pop round and welcome you to the area for some time, but – one thing and another, you know how it is." She thought of some of their games and costumes and so on and assumed that actually Harriet probably didn't; then remembered again that she *had* seen the stormtrooper and the nun and made a mental note that this must be explained away properly when the chance arose.

Harriet grunted.

"I expect it is a bit of a shock to you, in some ways, after London," Clara said.

Harriet snorted.

"I suppose you feel lonely and cut off at times," Clara persisted.

Harriet opened her mouth and then stopped. "I don't mind," she shrugged after a moment. Again, Clara saw body language she would have used on Miles in 'I don't want to talk about it' mode. "I mean I'm finding it a bit boring and nothing to do but I'm not big on," she actually gestured towards the pie, "getting sucked in. In London you don't know your neighbours and you choose your own friends."

"Oh, quite," said Clara. "I do understand. My, my cohabitor and I tend to keep ourselves to ourselves a lot of the time. Still," she added, "perhaps you find us a bit – "

"Unwelcoming?" Harriet was tight-lipped. "Yes, you could say that."

"That is only how it appears at first, you know. Really, when you get to know people – "

"Oh, really? I have, actually, had a visit from the local welcoming committee," Harriet burst out. "Just last night, as it happens."

"Indeed?"

"Yes."

There was another pause. Harriet irritably slapped her kettle, which was making infinitesimally tiny hissing noises now.

Clara cleared her throat and said, "I could not help but notice, the, the – " she fluttered fingers, "modification to your window."

"Oh you did, did you?" Harriet strode to the living-room door, flung it open, and gestured.

Clara walked through. The rock lay on a long table at the back and there were still some shards of glass on the floor. Clara gaped at the gaping window and then put her hand to her mouth.

"I am appalled!" she exclaimed. "Whoever could have done such a thing?" She gasped and grabbed Harriet's arm. "Hunt saboteurs! I will wager it was them! They have seen you flying your lovely scroteweazel in support of what remains of the Hunt, which I may say won you everyone else's heart locally."

Harriet shook her head vehemently and looked derisive. "I took it down days ago, and yesterday's column made it quite clear what I think of hunting. This – this was to make it quite clear I'm not wanted around here. They hate everything I stand for." There was a defiant tilt to her chin that touched Clara and made her feel more awful than ever. "They hate *me*," she added, with a stray hint of desolation.

"No, dear, no!" Clara cried anxiously. "They all love you in the village! They simply love your column! A few raised eyebrows now and again, perhaps, but we do have a sense of humour."

"I meant every word, and I don't care about those cavemen. I won't be intimidated from speaking the truth."

Clara shook her own head. "You really mustn't read anything into this. This was obviously the work of some loner with a grudge. Or some drunken, high-spirited local youths, who probably didn't even know who lived here." Harriet cynically curled her mouth. "Yes!" Clara insisted. "It is almost a custom, you know." Inspiration struck. She gasped again and clapped her hands. "A slote-clettering! It must have been a slote-clettering!" She smacked her own head in self-reproach. "What a silly I am! And what a silly *you* are, to think any harm of it! Surely you have heard of the slote-clettering tradition? Why, it is one of the prettiest of our local customs!"

Harriet stared at her. "Pretty?"

"Well, not pretty perhaps, in fact downright annoying when you are woken by it in the night, as Miles and I have been several times, but, but – pastoral, if you care for that sort of thing." She pulled Harriet to the gaping window with its few remaining pieces of glass still in place and pointed through it towards the gate and hedge and the road beyond. "They wend their way home from the pub, you see, benevolently lit with cider and nut-brown ale, singing a few rollicking songs, and egg each other on to try their hand at 'clettering the slote' at the houses they pass. The 'slote' is a pebble, or, or," she glanced back guiltily at her missile, "indeed quite sizeable chunk of rock, and it must be 'clettered', you see, against a window – that is, tossed quite gently, with a graceful underarm bowling motion, with no real vigour or malice at all, so as to harmlessly bounce off the pane and land as close as possible to the foot of the wall or, ideally, balanced on the windowsill. It is quite an art, quite lovely to behold. We have championships, sometimes, at the Manor. Rosettes are awarded, and the most desirable maids give themselves to the most artful slote-cletterers. Of course the possibility of mishap is what gives it an air of danger, and when people are drunk accidents will happen. But vandalism is not the aim or intent, oh no! The one who broke your window will have been jeered at roundly by his fellows and had his manhood questioned. He will have been punished instantly, made to pay a most awful forfeit – ducked in a pond and held under until he went giddy." Harriet was regarding her wide-eyed, in fact looked quite appalled. Clara decided this must indicate credulity and was therefore good. "Anyone you meet who slurs his words or has to have jokes explained is probably an unsuccessful slote-cletterer who has been held under too long," she added. "And he must also pay the home-owner indemnity – you will probably find a thoughtful gift of a skinned rabbit hanging mysteriously outside your door in a day or so." This might actually happen: a couple of the more retrograde youths had been threatening it as a means of scaring her away. Harriet looked even more appalled. "Of course that is no use to you but they are not to know that. It is kindly intended. Or it might be some other guilt-offering, such as a lovely pie or – well, not a pie, but – "

Harriet pointed towards the young boulder behind them and shook her head. "*That* was not bowled gently underarm to land on a windowsill! That was hurled with great force to land where it did!"

"Where – where exactly did it land?" asked Clara interestedly.

"*There!*" Harriet cried in exasperation, as if Clara was an idiot, pointing to where the rock lay on the table at the far end of the quite long room. "Where it is! I haven't moved it, of course, because of the police!"

Clara was quite impressed with herself for a moment. Call me Clara Clarovitch, girl shotputting champion of the world, she thought idly, playing with her hair. Then she went still.

"Er – police?" she asked, her eyes shifting suddenly like those of the 1970s toy called an Eagle-Eyes Action Man.

"Of course police!" Harriet cried. "This is a Hate Crime! I intend to report it as such! The police will have to act! It will have to be fingerprinted and DNA tested and soil-sampled!"

There was a horrible sort of frozen, sinking moment.

Clara forced a laugh. "Come now! Surely you are blowing this out of all proportion? This is not the way to endear yourself to the village. Why you will set the entire slote-clettering fraternity against you. Rocks will be raining against your every window day and night."

"Slote-clettering?" Harriet pointed back towards the jagged window. "I don't know anything about slote-clettering but I'll tell you one thing – it wasn't any drunken lad who did that. It was a woman!"

There was a sort of treacly, eardrum-whooshing, tape-snarl moment.

"What on Earth makes you think that?" asked Clara faintly.

"Because I heard her!" Clara strove not to sigh with relief at the choice of verb. "I heard heels! I woke up and I heard heels going away! And a laugh! A woman's laugh!"

Clara thought silently for a moment, staring at the ceiling. She was, for one thing, reviewing what laughing she had done in Harriet's presence – she could only remember the previous forced one – and trying to compare it to the laughter she had giddily let loose last night. Then she laughed in inspiration, cut it off midway as she remembered it might incriminate her, looked at Harriet and gasped once more.

"Crazy Meg!" she cried.

"What?"

"Of course! Why didn't I think of it before? Who else would do something like this? Meg Merrilies! Madge Wildfire! I had forgotten she was back." She had an uneasy moment as she wondered if Harriet read Sir Walter Scott, from whose works she had impulsively seized this character, but it seemed unlikely and indeed only she and Miles appeared to nowadays. "A local lunatic. You must have heard of her!"

Harriet shook her head. "You shouldn't use words like lunatic," she felt compelled to add chidingly, but was interested.

"Um. Madwoman?" Harriet shook her head again. "Nutjob, then," Clara said indulgently. "Drool-gargler, if you prefer. Let us say, she sees the world differently to the rest of us. Is a free spirit. Prefers not to conform to conventional sanity paradigms. She lives wild in the woods and consorts with smugglers and cut-throats, and dances around singing strange rhymes and uttering curses and prophecies, and, and, cackling."

Harriet gasped. "She *did* cackle! It was a cackle I heard! A deranged cackle!"

Clara stared at her coldly, a bit put out. "To some ears, perhaps. I should think most people would rather describe it as a rich, carefree, voluptuous peal of high-spirited merriment."

Harriet frowned. "So she attacks people's houses? Shouldn't she be – "

"Confined?" Raising an eyebrow Clara endeavoured to look surprised and reproving. "How heartless. I had expected better of you somehow. She needs love and understanding and a sympathetic consideration of her alternative viewpoint."

"Oh, of course," said Harriet, abashed. "But I have two young children in the house," she rallied, self-righteousness returning.

Clara nodded. "And that is probably what has drawn her here. She often kidnaps children, especially firstborn heirs." Harriet looked alarmed. Belatedly Clara decided that replacing the pain of loneliness and ostracism with fear of a child-snatching madwoman probably wasn't that kind after all. "Or so they say. Personally I don't believe a word of it. You know how bigoted these people can be towards the Mentalist community. No, Meg is fairly harmless. She just likes to brick the occasional window and skip around singing weird songs – *'Widdershins, widdershins, round the moor, fal, lal, ma bonnie braw,'* " she piped. "And who are we to say her nay?"

"She's Scottish?"

"A bit. Mostly she is a Gypsy. Very flighty and footloose and fancy-free."

Harriet stiffened and quivered like a hunting-dog picking up a scent.

"The Traveller community are *not* flighty and footloose," she said reprovingly.

"Oh, I know. There were some in that field at the back of this house, they stayed put remorselessly for two years," Clara lied. She saw Harriet's face flicker with an exquisite mixture of emotions. "The Star Chamber moved them on in the end but they have vowed to return one day, they love that field. I hope they do, you'll love them. Madge isn't one of those, though, she is a proper old-fashioned Romany who dances around campfires barefoot and lives in a painted horse-drawn caravan. I think I have a bit of Gypsy blood myself, you know." This might actually be true if you took an old family legend at face value, but Clara had decided it long before she had heard of this and shortly after she had started reading. "As a child I asked to be carried off by some once, but they turned me down." This was true, and sad. "Anyway the old Lord of the Manor drove off Meg's tribe of merry violin-playing, dancing, smuggling, fortune-telling Gypsies from their encampment. The poor mad creature vowed revenge and goes round lobbing rocks through windows to get back at the uncaring bigoted borgy Gorgios. She is a heroine and a revolutionary in her way." Clara glanced at Harriet and was pleased to see her frowning and chewing a lip in a way that she thought might indicate Harriet had come to identify with this poor mythical Meg, victim of rural prejudice and the unfair imposition of majority behavioural templates, and was concluding Meg had been *right* to throw a rock through her window, maybe even that she, Harriet, had deserved it really. "Miles and I have been bricked, so has everyone. It is a rite of passage. You are one of us now."

All this time Clara had been drifting casually, ever so casually and craftily, over to the dining table with the rock on it. She nonchalantly laid a finger on it now, glancing back to see that Harriet was still caught up in conflicting thoughts. "It would *take* the strength of a madwoman to throw this," she said artlessly. "Look how heavy it is. Why, I can barely lift it." With a grunt and a groan she picked it up from the table with both hands and hefted it.

"Yes," said Harriet abstractedly. "Clara!" she suddenly cried. "No! The DNA and fingerprints!"

"Oh no," said Clara, and put it down again. "Oh well. I don't suppose it matters. They'll know to eliminate mine. I expect Mad Meg wore gloves anyway. She does, you know. Sort of tattered fingerless lace mittens," she modified, artistry overriding cover-up.

Harriet sighed and looked indecisive. "I suppose only someone insane *would* have done something like this."

"Um, yes," said Clara. "Insane, or unconventional. Let us say someone feisty and headstrong. Madge is really a genius of sorts, you know, I'm surprised you can't see that." She thoughtfully added a few more palmprints to the rock as though playing pat-a-cake.

"Really, though, stop playing with it," said Harriet coming over. "It must still go to forensics in case it wasn't this Meg."

Clara forced and then cut off another laugh. "Heavens, Harriet, what big-city ideas of detection you have! Surely you can imagine what the rustic police are like? A bumpkin constable comes round on a bicycle. He will stand there beaming at you with his helmet under his arm, all apple-cheeked – red apples, at that – and say things like, 'Arr' and 'I'll be baynd'. If you mention things like Hate Crimes and DNA he will look blank but keen and lick the end of his pencil and say, 'How you be spelling that then?' He will talk about his marrows and things and then blame it on a gypsy. In this case he will be correct, of course, but I must say it seems harsh of you to help stifle Unconventional Meg's right to self-expression."

"Oh God, I might have known." Harriet sank down on a chair looking despairing. "But what happens if there's a big crime or something?" she screeched.

"Oh, for a robbery or hen-stealing or something the Star Chamber will interrogate some strangers and then set a few examples," said Clara. "If there's a murder a very clever little old lady usually investigates. Miss … McEwan. She always solves it long before the police."

Harriet shook her head in disbelief, but not the sceptical kind of disbelief.

"Tell me more about this Star Chamber," she urged curiously after a moment.

"Haven't you heard of it? A secret society for punishing malefactors."

"Yes, but I thought it was historical. It's still active? Like vigilantes?"

"They do not call themselves that. They are similar to the old German Vehmic courts," she said plundering Sir Walter Scott again. "And in the old days they used to burn wrongdoers in a giant wicker ... but I dare say no more. I know you are a fearless girl reporter but I will not put you needlessly in peril."

"But someone should – "

"My lips are sealed. It could all be dark rumour. Forget I spoke. Anyway, there is no point involving the police unless you wish to be fruitlessly annoyed."

Harriet still seemed wrapped in indecision. She ran a hand through her hair.

"I don't know," she said. "I wish Richard was here. I can't think straight. I've hardly slept. I think I really ought to report it."

Clara's panic had *almost* subsided by this point. Still, in this day and age it was best to err on the side of alarm. Harriet was an expert on making waves and would have all sorts of contacts to call on; and the fact was the county's rather communist Chief Constable would just love having, was desperate to have, a Hate Crime to investigate, to show keenness and help him inch towards his quota. Recently an arrest had been made under this head after a man from one village had called a man from the next village a 'Bindleyford bastard' in a dispute over a local cricket match. And Hate Crime, unlike ordinary run-of-the-mill faux pas such as burglary or mugging which could be shrugged off as not worth the bother, meant all guns blazing, no expense spared. They *would* do full forensics and make a thorough investigation of opportunity and motive, she thought. Would they ask, compel locals to contribute DNA to eliminate themselves? Her imagination raced. And a terrible thought had occurred. The rock was one snatched from a garden wall, and she had a sudden distinct memory of Miles having moved some of these at some point. Clara had learned not to trust her memory completely when it produced such sudden distinct scenes in a way to add drama to a situation, for it had been known to collaborate with her fancy; but thinking it over they had definitely at least crouched behind this wall, and then wriggled over it, the night they had played at husband-and-wife SAS team. It would be just like Miles to inadvertently incriminate himself for an otherwise perfect crime and thereby force her to own up. She resolved to slap him round the head for this when she got home. She wallowed in a reverie envisaging the courtroom scene of her nobly owning up to save Miles from his own clodhanded bumblingness for a moment, then snapped out of it and went into action.

She picked the rock up again. "Harriet! I'll tell you what I will do!" she cried excitedly. "I will get my husband, that is a person in his own right who happens to be married to me named Miles, to take a look at this rock for you! He knows all about rocks!"

Harriet looked puzzled. "Like a geologist?"

Clara nodded eagerly. "Yes! Well, not professionally, but he studied it at university. He is awfully clever at it. I bet from just a brief glance and fondle he will be able to establish whether it comes from Mad, that is Unusual Meg's glen, or, or, the wall of the pub car park, say, or the property of some nasty bigoted townie-hating farmer."

Harriet looked completely worn down and helpless by this point. "If you think ... it's a kind offer ... but I don't quite see ... surely we ought to…"

"I do think! It's no trouble! It's what neighbours are for! The police can have it straight back, if you're so set on going that route, and need never know. I will take it now!"

In her excitement she was tossing the rock from hand to hand with glee; then she remembered it was meant to be too heavy for her and sank down groaning towards the floor with it held beneath her knees.

"If you think ... thank you," said Harriet, somewhat dazed and bewildered.

Clara started to waddle out, puffing and panting, with her burden.

"Clara!" said Harriet. "You said this woman was involved with *smugglers*?"

"Oh yes," said Clara.

"So far inland?"

"You're so naive."

She went home and slapped Miles round the head for his imbecility. He was only moderately surprised by this, in fact much more startled when she told him where she had been. She had hidden the rock under a tarpaulin in the shed. That night when Miles was asleep she pounded it into about a hundred fragments with a hammer, and buried them in a dozen different locations to be on the safe side.

Harriet got good mileage out of both the rock and Clara. Her next essay began 'I am the victim of a Hate Crime.' She waxed solemn, pious and self-important about this for the whole column and said she could now identify more than ever with, was proud to stand alongside, Victims of Hate everywhere and everywhen – the Little Rock Nine were mentioned, for example.

Clara tried to read this tolerantly, reminding herself that, after all, the woman *had* had a rock tossed through her window (by Clara) and was entitled to *some* of her feelings about it.

Miles was appalled when he read it. This was the first he had heard of the matter.

"Oh that's just awful. That's just proved we're as bad as she thinks."

"Yes," said Clara. "I expect it must have been some naughty boys who did it. Hot-headed youths. You can hardly blame them, I suppose?"

"That's just barbaric."

"Yes," said Clara. "Miles I like that shirt you are wearing. Is it a new one? It brings out your eyes."

"Whoever did this is an idiot."

"Well, yes," said Clara. "Or playing some deep game."

The column after that had in effect been written for Harriet by Clara. Clara cackled when she read it. (Delightedly and merrily, *not* dementedly. Soon after returning from Harriet's she had sat Miles down and made him listen to her various laughs and grade each one on a 1-10 scale ranging from 'Rich and voluptuous' to 'Criminally insane' and had been relieved to find that *almost* all of them passed with flying colours.) It was all there. The bumpkin police, cribbed almost word for word but relayed so as to give the impression of first-hand experience; Clara's joke about them not being able to spell DNA repeated uncredited; blaming everything on Travellers; vigilantes; and 'I was told in confidence that for important crimes the police consult an old woman who sounds exactly like Miss Marple. You couldn't make it up, as a man who probably does likes to say.' Rural prejudice against the differently-brained, and against Romanies, and a sensitive case study of Gypsy Meg and her evicted tribe, shamelessly fleshed out, adapted and data-filtered from Clara's already sensational account – Clara found herself professionally admiring Harriet's imagination – in the course of which Harriet impressively managed both to be indignant at Meg's automatic scapegoating for the crime Harriet had been the victim of *and* to raise the possibility, while *not* relinquishing her own victimhood, that Meg *had* been the author of the deed and was in fact rather to be saluted for that. 'I like to think that had I been in her place, I, too, would have flung a rock,' she averred. (Early on in the column Clara had seen it would be something special and had fetched boiled sweets to suck in order to relish it properly; she unwrapped one as she chortled now, lying face-down on a hearth-rug swinging her feet. Really this might be Harriet's masterpiece. She resolved to write her a fan-letter.) The further complicating of the mystery by the slote-clettering factor, related with off-handed amusement and a plethora of detail both taken from Clara and pulled out of her own arse. 'I suppose this is the kind of thing you get up to when you think video games are the work of the devil.' Her despair at getting to the bottom of it. Mention of the two small children in the house – again, Clara supposed she was entitled to in the context of having a rock thrown through her window, as opposed to when she was invoking them as if their existence conferred on her the mantle of global-warming sage. Clara herself, hilariously distorted, had a walk-on as 'an almost human neighbour', giving rise to a digressive coda about 'Intimidation by Baking, the throwback female equivalent of the throwback male "Who's got the biggest car or cock?" ' Clara howled with delight at this too, almost choking on her sweet. There was a more or less perfunctory tut at the practice of Intimidation by Husband and the piece wound up with Harriet's fear of getting sucked in. 'If I stay here much longer I will probably turn into one of the Pie People myself. Watch this space, folks.'

Clara sighed. "She is a great woman in her way. It is rare in nature to find something so Platonically perfect."

Four days later the great woman rang her.

"I just wanted to check you weren't offended by what I wrote," Harriet said.

"Oh far from it," Clara assured her warmly. "I am flattered to be classed as almost human."

"I mean I tell it like I see it," said Harriet rather aggressively. "I'm not going to apologise for that, it's just the way I am."

"Quite," said Clara.

"I forget, sometimes, that real people will read what I write."

"Indeed," said Clara.

"And sometimes I have to, you know, telescope and thumbnail, for maximum impact. It's what my readers expect."

"I quite understand," said Clara. "I am creative myself."

"So you're not pissed off?"

"Just the reverse," said Clara. "I am thrilled to have spurred you to one of your most inspired flights."

"Yeah." There was a pause. "Look why don't you come round for a natter?"

"All right," said Clara. "I'll be there in ten minutes."

In the event she was somewhat longer, partly because she had to change out of a rather elaborate costume, and partly because she had to deal with some whining about abandonment from Miles, who found it hard to entertain himself nowadays and who had blithely expected to get lucky shortly. By the time she got there Harriet's kettle had finished boiling and two cups of coffee steamed invitingly on her kitchen table.

Harriet looked inviting too. She actually smiled.

"I'm glad you weren't upset," she said as they sat. "I mean you did some of my research for me on that last piece. Quite invaluable really."

She hesitated. "I *am* cut off here. I could use someone with the inside track, sort of all the local gen."

"I should be delighted," said Clara.

Harriet looked down and then smiled again. "I could use a friend."

"I should be honoured," said Clara.

Thus began what she would later describe as the most macabre partnership since the salad days of Burke and Hare.

Of course they were never destined to become bosom girl-chums, nor did either really expect it – both, indeed, internally recoiled and screamed at the thought. Clara knew that what Harriet was mostly looking for was copy; and Clara was just the woman to provide it.

Miles was invited to contribute suggestions, and the regulars in the Walpole's Head, and came up with some good ones, but she didn't really need them. Really she thought this might have been one of the most fertile creative periods she had yet known. Harriet inspired her as she inspired Harriet. She felt she was part of a line of oral story-tellers stretching back into the distant past. All the great myths and fairy tales, she decided, must have originated like this, with two women sitting in a kitchen gossiping about the neighbours; it was just that only men had bothered to write them down. Harriet heard everything she had hoped to hear and more. The terrible doings of the Star Chamber. ("Not for public consumption; it would be more than either of our lives are worth. I am not afraid for myself but you have children.") The smuggling gypsy band. ("Let me know if you want any fags or perfume or kegs of brandy.") The Inland Wreckers, who set false traffic lights for lorries on foggy nights, or laid lines of misleading cat's-eyes to lure them to their doom. ("There is a whole class of men who make their living that way; no-one dares speak against them. It is always worth checking the quarry the next morning to see if they have missed any booty in the dark. I am not proud of it but that is how we got our new fridge.") The illicit stills and wood-alcohol moonshine that could leave you blind. ("Never accept an offer of home-brew.") The unofficial Witchfinder, identified as a terrible lecherous smelly old man of the village. ("It is best to pay him the tribute of a kiss and cuddle, if he approaches you, so as to stay on his good side. I will not say the village-folk would *definitely* burn you out, in this day and age, but it is so demoralizing to have fingers crossed at you and be forbidden to look at children.") The local witch, identified as a dour woman who worked at the post office sometimes whom Clara didn't much like. ("Of course it is easy to scoff at alternative medicine. A slaughtered goat seems a small price to pay for curing epilepsy; and it is not as if Miles was using his soul anyway.") The intra-sibling eros: three local couples including the vicar and his wife were fingered as living incestuously. ("I gather the practice is to pack your sister off to a different locale and have her return in a month with her hair done another way and a new name. It is said there is an exchange scheme whereby identities can be swapped for this purpose. Who are we to judge them?") However the dreadful trendy vicar excited her muse in more ways than this: he was having affairs, she said, with at least three women of the village; had at one point, as the patriarch of a charismatic sect in a backwoods commune, lived polygamously with half a dozen women at once; was all too apt to suggest the laying-on of hands if any of his parishioners had a cough or chest-cold, and had sacked the choir because he had got them all pregnant. Then there was the droit de seigneur in the time of the previous Lord of the Manor. And of course the commonplace bestiality: the discreet clover-rich pasture known locally as the Venusberg, the embarrassing cases of cattle following men devotedly for months afterwards, the widespread acceptance, the lads who were unofficially employed to do it to hens in some places as it was thought to improve laying. Last Leap Year a man in a nearby district had been allowed, discreetly and after-hours, to wed a sheep in chapel thanks to a local by-law. (Clara asked Harriet if she was being judgemental to disapprove and if animal sex shouldn't be allowed anyway. Harriet looked troubled. "In theory, if the sheep could consent ... " she ventured. "It wasn't of age," Clara said shaking her head woefully. "It was barely two.") The unwanted babies exposed on a hillside, to be carried off by the St. Mary's Roc, probably a giant eagle, or the St. Mary's Cougar, probably a fat tabby gone feral. The legend of the St. Mary's Centaur, now established to be the result of a man in a pantomime horse costume walking home from a fancy dress party alone after quarrelling with his better half, but the credulous still left sugar-lumps for him in a certain grove. The practice of couples experiencing marital difficulties to make a pilgrimage to an airbase at the other end of the county, break in, and make love on the runway as the planes took off, aroused by the might of the military machine. ("You imagine they are bombing Brussels, you see," explained Clara, who had often fantasized about this sort of thing, in daytime reverie or sort-the-world-out pub conversations rather than any sexual way.) The aphrodisiac fashion for dyeing the pubic hair into a Union Jack. ("Then you say, 'Play your cards right and could be saluting the flag tonight.' ")

Rural sports, hobbies and pastimes were a particularly rich vein. Hen Football. ("I understand the skill lies in kicking them hard enough so that they fly over the keeper but not over the goalpost.") Badger-throwing. ("They hurl them against a wall until they stick.") Hedgehog Darts.

("Self-explanatory.") Stoat-flattening. ("You don't want to know.") Pig-baiting. ("You say something hurtful about a policeman's mother.") Competitive Hare-shaving. ("Performed blind-drunk and left-handed inside a sack. Then the poor nude things are placing blinking and embarrassed on a high shelf and laughed at. First catch your hare.") Squirrel-flinging. ("You whirl them round and round your head by the tail and then hurl them to knock over a coconut or ring a bell. There are booths at all major fairs.") Tug-of-Cow. Sheep roller-skating championships. Pushing bullocks upstairs, on roller-skates. Posting bats through letterboxes to annoy the homeowners. Posting and sealing bats into postboxes to annoy the postman. Posting bats to Paris in jiffy-bags to annoy the French, and probably the bat. Hibernating Dormouse Tennis. Tortoise Cricket. ("I hasten to say that the tortoises are the batsmen, not the balls. The ball is a marble which is flicked towards their little wicket, made out of balanced dominoes. If it bounces off them they must then ambulate in their own time towards the opposite wicket, a mere three feet away, taking care not to fall off the table, while the ball is being fielded by kittens. The tension can be awful and fortunes are made and lost in side-bets.") The game known as Poor-Tom's-a-Darning, in which a greased piglet was squeezed between the thighs of a huge brawny woman until it shot across the room and into a barrel, which was then rolled down a flight of stairs while midgets tried to run up it. ("I will take you to a meet if you fancy it; it is largely a guerilla sport nowadays.") The Mayday tradition, its origins lost in the mists of time, of systematically tying geese to a hydrocephalic child until they could levitate it over a burning hayrick, a practice now, thank God, virtually stamped out. ("The child always consented," she reassured Harriet, "indeed would be quite delighted at the fun and attention. It would be gifted with as many cigars as it required geese to float it and its own body-weight in nougat. It seems shocking to us now but, let's face it, it must have been the hell of a spectacle. The geese were painted all colours of the rainbow and were shot one by one so the child could land gently in a pond.") Wasp fights. ("The one thing I *really* can't stand. They are trained in aerial combat from birth, poor dears, and kept in matchboxes. At the tourneys beer is smeared on each competitor's back to attract their opponents and they duel to the death. There are leagues, trophies, championship bouts, little gold champion belts I believe. If ever you are in a pub garden and see wasps trapped in a glass you may be sure it is some of the sporting gentry and their stable. I always free the poor brutes and hope you do likewise. It is best to have some jam or other sweet substance smeared on your finger to lure them away from the beer. I always steal any matchboxes I see lying around too. It is possible to rehabilitate them, with love and perseverance. I had one that lived for years and was retrained for innocent purposes; he would keep me company and help me with my needlework." This was said idly but hopefully on a day when Harriet had been particularly annoying and seemed particularly gullible.)

"Now the reason I know the locals *don't* hate you," she assured Harriet once, "is because you haven't been Lambed yet – that is, you haven't had lambs put on your roof. That's how you know when you've really annoyed them. Miles and I had it done once after we ran over a drunk and it is *the* most vexing thing. They are too timid to jump off but bleat and clamber about the slates all night. Nowadays of course you are supposed to get a licensed government official to remove them, rather than a yokel with a ladder and a trampoline like in the old days, and by the time you can even get put through to the proper department they have often grown to full size and crashed through into your loft. *Then* you can be fined for keeping them in an enclosed space. They crop at the moss and drink rainwater from your gutter. The lambs alone are most annoying; it is simply impossible to sleep. And as any mountain shepherd will tell you the pesky creatures are very nimble and drawn to narrow crevices and holes; very often they will tumble down your chimney in their innocent curiosity. A confounded nuisance, especially if the fire is lit. Oh, don't get me started, I could write a book. I will include a chapter on how to catch a panicked lamb running amok in your house and remove the stench of singed wool from your front room."

This was one of her biggest successes. 'So it seems that having lambs put on my roof is the next delightful rural welcome I can expect,' Harriet began her next column glumly. 'I have been warned in no uncertain terms that … '

"You're not doing the countryside any favours, you know," Miles told Clara.

"If I can deter just one other Harriet from coming here to sneer at us, I may have done," declared Clara. She giggled at the lamb column and cut it out to paste in her scrap-book, yet was inwardly annoyed at Harriet for choosing to twist something she had honestly meant as a kindly reassurance into a sinister threat.

Apart from this, and a column largely devoted to the Witchfinder ('Tuesday, the 21st century, my kitchen. A young woman who in some ways seems as modern and liberated as myself tells me, casually, as though it was the most natural thing in the world, that unless I grant sexual favours to a local patriarch I will be stigmatized as a witch and burned out of my home, if not at the stake. The suggestion is light, airy, even amused. Plausibly deniable – she could perhaps try to pass it off as a joke if subpoenaed. Yet the air of menace is unmistakable and coming on the heels of the rest of my ordeals I cannot afford to take it lightly. Don't rub your eyes, folks, don't check your calendars – they aren't wrong, this place is. Deeply.' This column actually spawned a half-page news item about her allegations, toned down and rather buried by a less gullible, more cautious, and in fact quite embarrassed editor, but rehashing Harriet's other tribulations since moving to the country and quoting her as saying 'I have been told by a reliable source that the local law enforcement is useless, except in cases of hen-stealing, where the punishment is summary and brutal') – apart from these, and in spite of ongoing acclaim from her fans at the Walpole, Clara felt that she never again enjoyed a triumph quite comparable to that first largely inadvertent coup with Gypsy Meg and the slote-cletterers. Otherwise, she privately thought, her efforts – and while the creation was effortless and spontaneous, she had often taken great care and used all her art to deploy her inventions casually, conversationally and with a wealth of circumstantial detail – met with mixed, even disappointing results. The Incestuous Sister Exchange Bureau made it into print, as an amused aside; but Harriet seemed to take the prevalence of rural incest for granted already. So too the Airbase Sex fad, as a bitter illustration in a column on militarism and Middle England imperialist warmongering attitudes, as inferred from largely joking remarks Clara had made to annoy her which Harriet had taken or decided to take at face value. There was half a column listing cruel rural sports, following on from ('But what can you expect from people who ... ') a lengthy overwrought anecdote about Harriet's having been cold-shouldered in a shop and then given the wrong change ('I know what it is not to count. Anything may be done to me now ... She had already moved on to the next customer, looked at me in hatred when I protested. I was not a fellow human who had been unjustly deprived of ten pence. I was just the gobby townie making trouble again'), but Clara found to her horror that Harriet had garbled and confused them and mangled the rules she had invented. ("She's an idiot! She's ruined them! What would be the point of making *squirrels* play cricket? That wouldn't work at all! The woman is a moron and a philistine and without any sporting sense," she told Miles before flinging the paper on the fire in disgust. She was sulky and inconsolable all day.)

The Burglar Club, on the other hand, an offshoot of the Star Chamber, was if anything too successful an invention. If Harriet ever had to kill a burglar, Clara told her, she should leave the body at a certain road junction after midnight and it would be removed by morning and buried in a copse. There would be no charge for the service, but it was possible she might then be called upon to help dispose of someone else's dead burglar at some point or help establish an alibi. This had not yet made it into an article but to Clara's slight alarm Harriet had leapt up and there and then started to put a call through to her paper's award-winning crime-investigating team saying that someone had to do something. Clara had gone into fake hysterics and yanked the phone lead from the socket and said she would deny everything and neither of them would live to testify and Harriet's children would be at risk. Eventually Harriet had been browbeaten into following the local omerta, or at least Clara hoped she had. What was wrong with her? There *ought* to be a Burglar Club anyway.

Plenty of other good stuff appeared only as background or snide asides. She couldn't tell in advance what would grab Harriet and what wouldn't, nor could she tell what Harriet would believe. Almost bloody everything, but the exceptions were unpredictable. To her disappointment Harriet tutted and made her joke-face and asked if Clara thought she was a simpleton when she told her about wasp-fights; she supposed she might have pushed it too far with the rehabilitated one. She snorted at the Land-Wreckers but inserted them as a joke, uncredited, which Clara didn't much mind as she had a vague feeling she herself might have been remembering the notion from somewhere. A couple of times Harriet looked derisive or joke-face at something but put it into a column as if true anyway. After the trendy (and not very virile-looking) vicar had made himself known to Harriet, attempting to welcome her to the neighbourhood and reveal himself as a kindred spirit, and been firmly frosted (cue column about Intimidation by Christianity), she had amusedly taxed Clara with having made up all her stories about him, and Clara had demurely agreed it had been a leg-pull; but a charismatic backwoods sect-leader with six wives was still mentioned in passing in a subsequent piece.

But Clara was most disappointed when, briefly sick of sin, she started mentioning real local legends, traditions and history, some of which were really bloody fascinating, and it was apparent – instantly apparent, right there in the kitchen, in a glazing of the eyes – that Harriet had no interest in them. So too with a brief series of nature notes, and disquisitions on agriculture. On the other hand Clara's opinions, political and otherwise, exaggerated by one or the other of them or relayed straight, very often made it into the column as a source of amusement, horror, outrage or contempt, and were extrapolated as being representative of those of the village at large; Miles was deeply alarmed when he realised this. ('What, folks, would you do with yourself all day if you were trapped in an ovary-achingly dull rural idyll such as mine? Some of my neighbours use the time thinking up new and exciting ways of executing criminals using hedgehogs, or daydreaming of bombing Brussels.' "It is only by getting these ideas into the public arena that we can ever hope to see them gain acceptance," Clara had serenely told him.)

Of course Harriet was only interested in what redounded to the discredit of the village and Middle England in general; and she found the most surprising things discreditable. "Clara, you couldn't horrify her more than by telling her some of the things we actually do," the ex-Major in the pub had told her. "The fact I attend the Last Night of the Proms, or stand up for ladies, or eat rabbits I've shot myself, to pick three examples at random, would give her the shits. She thinks we are fascists for flying our country's flag and subhuman for killing for food. Whatever you say you can't make anything better or worse." Of course Harriet was using Clara just as Clara was using her. Clara accepted this. She chafed at the frustrations of the partnership but supposed, generously, that after all Harriet must have some input into her own column. It was a collaboration.

To Miles it was collaboration of a different kind.

"You're just giving her ammunition!"

"It is amusing. I am showing her up as an idiot."

"To the people who already know."

"Who are enjoying it. There is little enough innocent amusement in the world, Miles."

Of course before her stories had started to filter through into the column, and again after they had largely stopped, when Harriet at length grew bored of rehearsing the iniquities of the natives and started devoting most of her space to recounting her efforts to live a life of environmental virtue, Miles couldn't understand why he was being abandoned, left in the house alone several mornings a week, apart from the times when they had schemes like the Art exhibition on, in favour of Clara's sworn enemy.

"You hate Harriet!" he had pointed out, astonished, when she returned that first morning to explain that she had just been to present Harriet with a pie to welcome her to the neighbourhood. "Or you did when I went to bed last night."

"Do not oppress me with your geeky male continuity fetish, Miles. I am Woman, as changeable as the sea and twice as wobbly."

"What the hell are you playing at?" he had demanded when she returned from the second visit to announce that she was now Harriet's friend and inside woman.

"I am being neighbourly. I have decided to show her unconditional Christian love. Love, not hate, is the way forward. You were right, Miles, about becoming mirror images. Harriet and I are each other's worst nightmares. She says things to annoy the likes of me, I say things to annoy the likes of her. Mutual escalation sets in. Where will it all end? In an England strewn with gibbets and mouldering corpses."

"But you look forward to that," Miles laughed. "You live for that!"

"Well, this way I will know I at least tried once to avert it, and thus will be able to look even more told-you-so and you-have-brought-this-on-yourselves when I finally marshal mass executions in Wembley Stadium, which will be annoying for them."

"Why on Earth do you put yourself through it?" he asked, mystified, when she complained, making fake-crying noises and face, of how bloody awful Harriet was at times, upon her return from a visit long after the false stories had ceased to pay off.

"I feel obliged," she said in a small voice, miserably, and a little shiftily. (Miles, bless him, was still blissfully unaware that she had smashed Harriet's window; even though once, during a pleasant arm-in-arm evening stroll about their domain, he had idly said, "Isn't there a bloody huge rock suddenly missing from that wall?" and she had snapped, "I cannot *live* in an atmosphere of constant suspicion! And it was by no means a huge rock, more like a dainty little pebble," and then fled indoors to find a mirror and check, not for the first time, that she didn't have manly shotputting biceps.)

"I feel sorry for her," she added, in a smaller voice, and also guiltily, for she thought it was rude to people to feel sorry for them; that it might even be less dehumanizing, where appropriate, to despise them. "I feel sorry for the woman." And this was true, and nothing to do with guilt about the rock, and persisted after that had started to become familiar through custom, and almost solely motivated the continued visits after the simultaneous urge to tease and mislead Harriet had ceased to be very interesting or rewarding, and in spite of the fact that Harriet was also truly, madly, deeply awful and annoying as well as pitiable.

"It's astonishing," she reported to Miles early on. "She really is a portable encyclopaedia of leftist cliches and progressive madness. You think you know that from her writing, but anyone can strike an attitude in writing. I assure you you can't fully appreciate it until you meet her in person. You remember we had that argument once, you said you found it hard to believe that anyone really believed in the PC insanity, and that you thought everyone who pretended to just felt obliged to out of piety or fear of other people, who in turn didn't believe it themselves but feared other people, and if you traced it back the head man was just one evil old professor somewhere who didn't even believe it himself but just wanted to destroy the world, and I riposted that you were a ----? Well you should meet her, that's all. Unless she *is* the one person everyone else walks in fear of, which I cannot wholly rule out."

Almost at the very start of their bizarre relationship Clara had thought it best to admit, or confirm Harriet's assumptions, that she did not share her opinions on, presumably, anything.

"Miles and I are Tory Anarchists. Well, Tory Monarchists. Well, Tory Nazis, really."

For a second Harriet had such a perfect look on her face, a combination of 'She admits it!' and 'Such wickedness!' that Clara felt a little moment of genuine love. She feared she might not know the last part was a joke, however.

"I never thought I'd have a Tory voter in my kitchen," Harriet said, trying to look humorous and tolerant and adult about it.

Clara looked shocked. "Good Lord, you don't think we would vote for *those* PC Europhile Greeny nanny-state Communists, do you? I'm not talking about the party. I'm talking about a philosophy. Classical conservatism; or, when I am in a grumpy mood, classical fascism, which I must point out is an entirely opposite thing, and in fact something I associate more with your side of the fence, frankly. I would assume absolute power *only* in order to execute the people who enjoy power for its own sake, and a few thousand others who have annoyed me. We believe in a small humble government that treats you like grown-ups wherever possible, and recognises it is employed by the people to provide certain essential services rather than moral lectures and social engineering. We believe in the value of intangibles, particularly tradition and heritage, and a healthy reverence for the wisdom accumulated down the centuries. We believe in freedom, which means we believe in law and order. We believe in the individual being responsible for himself, but that he also has duties to the society which protects his freedom. We believe in private life and private property. We believe in common sense and common decency; we are deficient in them ourselves but admire them in others. I would say, in a nutshell, that we are diametrically opposed to what you appear to believe in at almost every point. We are also nationalists, however, which means consulting your country's good and looking after your own, which means, among other things, that we are not always enamoured of the workings of big capitalism."

"I suppose that's something, anyway," said Harriet, although she had got the hunting-dog look at 'nationalists' and 'looking after your own'.

"The problem is that regulation tends to place more power in the hands of people like you, no offence intended. The conundrum is probably insoluble in any long-term or definitive way. Any philosophy or principle pursued with morbid rigour at the expense of common sense leads to insanity. Our philosophy at least embraces this concept." She sipped coffee. "More importantly, perhaps, we are also reactionary aesthetes, which ought to be apolitical but probably isn't. We find everything so deliberately bloody ugly nowadays. We think the next-but-one revolution, or more properly counter-revolution, must be one in favour of beauty. The next revolution, of course ... but I won't alarm you. You have a pretty neck; I will find a lamp-post that matches it. ... I have to add that we are only political at all in spasms of annoyance. We live largely in a world of our own and do not feel responsible for this one. Occasionally it annoys us, and we annoy it back."

She thought Harriet looked more shocked at this than at anything else.

"I believe everyone is responsible for the world," she said primly.

At this Clara felt pity for this youngish woman, this girl, several years older than her and yet somehow younger, with the weight of the world on her rather slumpy shoulders; and yet she had to admit she saw the nobility of the stance and often felt the same, in spasms; and these spasms led to things like putting rocks through Harriet's window.

It was all so difficult and essentially boring; and everyone would be dead eventually. She changed the subject to something nice and girly like make-up and clothes, then grew bored with that and went home to confront Miles's recriminatory pouting and upstage it with some of her own.

This colloquy translated into a future Harriet column as, 'The people here frighten me more the more I get to know them. Even my almost human neighbour thinks the Tory Party is dangerously left wing.' Clara sighed. It was almost exactly what she had said, was in fact a toning-down, and yet ... No communication was possible.

Harriet was easy to shock, and brought out the worst in her. It was like the fun of squeezing an antique rubber bulb-horn to hear it honk like a goose. She thought, sometimes, that Harriet actually enjoyed her wickedness, not just because it was great copy, and not just in order to exercise her own righteousness. It must be something like the guilty thrill of hanging out with an older, cooler, glamorous bad girl at school, Clara told herself complacently. To fit in with this role, as well as for reasons of poise, she started bringing her rarely-smoked cigarettes to the kaffeeklatsches; and when she lit up, it was often some minutes before Harriet remembered to be outraged and order her out.

But the shock became *too* easy, the shock displayed at common-sense propositions too annoying, the hermetic insularity wearing.

"It isn't just me, you know, Harriet," she told her calmly once, after some somewhat heated argument. "It isn't just this village, or the countryside, or what you call Middle England. It's everywhere. We are all reactionaries now. You have made us so. You have made us into what you always thought we were. The working classes you despise so much, not least. Even in your own enclaves people are sick of having to make obeisance to insane idols every day, they're just afraid to speak out. I think appearances to the contrary, sane people are not just a majority now but secretly always have been. It's everyone in the country apart from a few hardcore lunatics who will have to be purged ruthlessly from public life as twenty years of laughing at them has done no good. What if it's just you and the party leaders and the liberal chief constables and judges left, Harriet? What if it's just you?" She laughed. "What if you are the only true believer remaining?"

"You are despicable and wrong."

"*I* think the left ought to go and stand in a corner for thirty years and think about what it did. Perhaps if it can go away and reinvent itself as being on the side of the ordinary working people again, instead of on the side of criminals, and terrorists, and lunatics, and billionaire eco-fascists, and unaccountable oligarchs, maybe, just maybe, one day, decades from now, it will be of some use to the country again."

"You're an evil selfish cow."

"It is good we can keep this dialogue open, though, isn't it? ... Really, in every field you have accomplished the exact opposite of what you profess to believe in, and come close to ruining a perfectly good country in the process. My penis-about-the-house Miles was leftist until fairly recently, you know – I think I must write to an agony aunt to check how long I should wait before conceiving to be sure our children won't have tails. He still has moments of backsliding, and recently floated the idea that half the things you've done lately might actually have been a plot by rich capitalist fundamentalists to undermine support for the welfare state and the concept of a state in general. He is a nitwit, of course, but it might as well be."

The mornings were always at Harriet's house. For various reasons Clara was averse to having visitors at hers. Harriet seemed quite happy with the arrangement but Clara supposed she ought to extend the invitation. She said as much once but pointed out that her coming here was nicer as there was a man cluttering up her house.

"You're lucky," said Harriet glumly, and Clara realised she had made a faux pas. There was no such clutter here. Scarcely a week went by that Richard hadn't flown off across the world to attend a Warming conference or summit or seminar, or take part in a debate, or report from some tropic coastline enduring excess millimetres of sea. When he was in the country he usually attended his newspaper offices in London. Clara encountered him, briefly, twice, on each occasion in the process of dashing off elsewhere. She remembered the nasty joke she had made to Miles while reading out Harriet's first mean-fields article: but the fact was she would not be on Richard's side if they got divorced. She found herself instinctively and fiercely on Harriet's side. And this, as much as anything, was what at length led to the end of their beautiful friendship.

*

"My footprint is till too big," Harriet sighed.

"Oh, no, dear! Really, it's not that bad. Maybe if you stick to black shoes it would help." Clara wasn't above recycling jokes and was fond of this one. "Your breasts are pretty, anyway, hardly anyone will even notice your feet. In some cultures huge feet are considered especially desirable, you know."

Harriet made the wry, tolerant face she made instead of laughing or smiling at things she didn't find funny but knew she was meant to. Clara had decided that the joke-recognising face was polite of Harriet and therefore repressed the urge to punch her in the mouth she felt every time she made it. Perhaps it wasn't much of a joke anyway, although it had got a big reaction at that party. It worked as a private joke, anyway: Harriet's feet *were* on the large side, she thought, especially for her rather short legs. Harriet had been particularly tiresome lately and was making her nasty.

Harriet's obsession with combatting supposedly-manmade-supposed-global-warming and eliminating her own contribution to it was, of course, the biggest obstacle to their ever attaining a true intimacy of hearts, had either truly wished it; and perhaps surprisingly Clara had instinctively refrained, as much as she humanly could, from teasing her about this bugbear. A few mild jokes, mostly at her own expense, like the one about her sports car that first day. (She vaguely thought that such jokes, like calling herself a Nazi, might be treacherous in the face of a humourless enemy, being based as they were on the enemy's own premises and thus ceding ground in the 'battle of ideas'; but she didn't intend to police her own fancy like a Harriet, and the loss of self-deprecation would not be a small casualty in the ongoing war.) In fact Clara had gone out of her way to keep off the topic, and had steered Harriet away from it when she had raised it, simply smiled vaguely when she tried to proselytize. But while it was their biggest difference, Harriet's Warmist zealotry was also, even more than the woman's patent loneliness, the reason she felt sorry for her, the reason she kept coming here. She believed so earnestly; she tried so hard; and it made her so unhappy.

Clara looked at her with helpless, detestable pity now, her head bent over her weekly accounts, a conscientious housewife trying to balance her budget, not of money but of one of the basic building blocks of life, now a modern demon; of (some cliches were true) sin.

Just then Harriet's three-year-old Ivor came haring in, screeching, and kicked Clara smartly on the shin and laughed in delight. Harriet didn't believe in disciplining her children; the results were, at least in the case of this younger child, the only one Clara had seen, interesting at times, and, she thought, fairly predictable.

When Ivor kicked Clara a second time and laughed again Harriet took notice and said, not at all reprovingly, but smiling and in a bright, warm, happy voice:

"That is inappropriate behaviour, darling. I still love you, but I am disappointed in you. And Richard will be disappointed too. And, and Aunty Clara is disappointed, aren't you?"

"Not particularly," admitted Clara, "but then my hopes weren't very high to start with."

"Aunty Clara *is* disappointed," Harriet told her son ecstatically, "but she still loves you too."

"As much as I ever did," Clara confirmed.

As Harriet returned to her accounts the child started to take a run-up at Clara again and then burst out wailing.

"Oh, sorry, I think I caught him on the knee while crossing my legs," said Clara.

"Clara! Be careful!" Harriet clucked and hugged and rubbed and fussed over the distraught child and then yelled, "Greta! Where are you?"

There was the sound of a toilet flushing upstairs; presently the au pair appeared, the third Clara had seen even in their short acquaintance, already wearing the blank-eyed, distant look her predecessors had both had shortly before departing. Recriminations for negligence followed, blossomed, while Clara acquired the blank and absent look herself, into an argument about a heater Harriet said the girl had turned on unnecessarily and then about the weather, which Harriet denied, in the teeth of the frost on the window, was bitterly, icily cold. This at length petered out into a discussion about what to do with Ivor; the au pair offered to take him to play outside. Double-bind or doublethink plainly gave Harriet pause for a moment before she announced it was too dangerous with all the ice around and told Greta to put a DVD on. She demanded a final hug from her son and gazed after him fondly as he departed. "He's an angel," she sighed.

Clara privately thought of Lucifer but smiled, enjoying Harriet's rapt look; she was radiant at times, playing with her son.

Harriet sighed less happily, bending back to her paperwork. "But such an expense," she said, not talking, directly, of money. "I would have liked more, to be honest, but of course it would have been immoral. I suppose it was wrong of me, really, to bring any kids into the world at all." Gnawing her lip, earnestly frowning, she looked as though she meant it.

Clara clenched her fists under the table, willed back welling angry tears. She found herself remembering what Jeremiah, who was an expert on their shenanigans, had said of the Warmist scientists who had started and maintained the panic: "Death's too good for them. Their heads should be kept alive indefinitely on machines, and sent on a world tour, until every man, woman and child on the planet has been allowed to punch them in the face."

She composed herself and smiled again. "Oh, I wouldn't say that," she said. "You are quite pretty, and your stupidity is largely just acquired."

Harriet made her tolerant joke-spotting face.

The thing was Clara wasn't joking about the last part. She wasn't someone who evaluated people in terms of stupidity and intelligence and degrees of these – it somehow never occurred to her, as she had noticed it did to others – while she might think 'This person is nice' or 'This person is pretty' or 'This person is funny' or 'This person is unpleasant' or 'This person must go on my Death List underlined in red' she had never had the experience, face to face, of thinking 'This person is thick.' But in Harriet's case she had found herself wondering, now and again; and concluded otherwise. Harriet was far from stupid. The glib species of semi-wit that could be found in some of her writing appeared to be something that only happened at the keyboard, unless it was just that she hadn't unbent enough towards Clara to display it or, more possibly, that Clara hadn't allowed her much of a word in edgeways; she was easily gulled, and dismally uninterested in a wide range of things and categories of thought; but it was neurosis, acquired, learned, taught, artificially implanted neurosis that afflicted her. Neurosis and an inability to question or reason independently; all her life she had accepted what the people she had been told were acceptable had told her, and rejected unconsidered the opinions of those who were unacceptable, who, circularly, were unacceptable for holding those opinions.

Harriet was tapping at a calculator.

"This doesn't look good," she murmured. "This can't be right."

"Better let me do it," said Clara trying to take the calculator. "You know how you are with numbers."

"What do you mean? I'm perfectly capable."

"I thought you were innumerate? That moving column you wrote, the woman who gave you the wrong change? 'I know what it is not to count.' "

"Ha-ha."

Clara really did want to take control of the calculator but Harriet won the tug-of-war. She continued to tap.

"Christ," she said some moments later. "Shit, shit, shit, shit, shit." She held her head in her hands. "I tried so hard. Another bloody fortune in offsets."

Carefully, gently, Clara ventured, "I think, if I felt guilty about punching Miles in the head, it would not make much difference if I paid someone down the road *not* to punch Miles in the head."

"Don't you think I *know* that?" Harriet said unhappily.

Clara had already suspected she did. Harriet was not one of those who could be satisfied with some token guilt-offering. Though she persisted in buying the indulgences, they did no good to her. To Harriet every single carbon dioxide molecule she was responsible for was advancing armageddon. It was … Clara had once read a theological speculation about sin that imagined God as 'a living field of snow that cried out when you pissed on it'. That was what Harriet thought she was doing every time she turned on a light, an appliance, dared to heat her home.

Harriet was better, nobler than most of the Warmists. She truly believed it and acted as though she did. She lived it. She suffered for it. And if on some level she enjoyed, if she was self-righteous about, even boasted of the suffering, still she suffered. Once Clara had been unable to stop herself mentioning another paranoid backsliding fantasy of Miles's that Might As Well Be True, that in effect was true, namely that the whole global warming scam was a conspiracy by rich people to stop ordinary people cluttering up roads and airports, and eventually restaurants and creches. Harriet's eyes had blazed hatred at her; and Clara had regretted it as unfair in her case even before she'd finished speaking. Whatever else she was, Harriet wasn't a hypocrite; she didn't think her money could absolve her and was renouncing things now that others, although not the scientists, zealots, politicians and billionaire carbon-traders who had misled her, would be coerced into giving up later.

Though she plainly loved to travel – she was as animated discussing it as she was when talking about her sons – Harriet hadn't been on a plane in three years. She didn't have a car, so when her husband was away, which was a lot, she was effectively cut off here, rural public transport being what it was. They were vegetarians, and only drank soy-milk and so on, because she thought cows were planet-killing bastards. She hated to heat the house which, despite their best efforts to modify it, was old, cold, draughty. A blind spot seemed to be a plethora of top-of-the-range televisions, laptops, and numerous other gadgets; but she said she needed these for her work, and the more frivolous ones were mostly Richard's babies, and the unsatisfactory wind-generator had been supposed to compensate. She didn't buy, do or consume anything without reckoning the supposed cost to the planet. And just lately she had started trying to wash everything by hand. At first this had been delegated to the au pairs, but they had balked and started walking out more quickly. So she did it herself, and was useless at it; she had had a blazing row with Richard after he had complained about the state of his clothes; last week Clara had dropped in unannounced and gone quietly away again after finding her pummeling an antique tub full of sudsy laundry and sobbing in misery.

For all the brash modern smartness she assumed in her writing, Harriet, Clara saw, was a natural martyr, would have made a perfect, self-abnegating anchorite or nun in medieval times. Clara didn't sneer at this, rather recognised and saluted something the potential for which existed or – she felt a pang – had once existed in herself. As a girl Clara had dreamed of becoming a nun – well, actually a ballerina-nun, or nun-ballerina. Perhaps with a bit of gypsying thrown in on the side. She knew what it was to do fasts, and penances, and perform entrechats until her legs hurt and offer it up to God. And if she remembered with a blush her self-righteousness and pious oneupwomanship towards her schoolmates, she remembered too the terrible, awful, genuine pain and despair of never feeling you were good enough.

Harriet was crying again now.

"Fuck this," said Clara. She touched her on the arm. "Leave it. Let's go for a girly day out. Let's go shopping. I'll go and get the car." Harriet shook her head miserably. "I'm going anyway. The sin is all mine."

"Stop taking the piss," Harriet sobbed.

"I'm not. I didn't mean to." Clara got up and moved round the table and gingerly and awkwardly patted Harriet's back. "Come on. It's not worth it. Look at you, you're all run down. You need a break. You need a break from this place. When was the last time you went out anywhere?"

"I tried so hard," wept Harriet. "I try so bloody hard."

"I know," said Clara. "I know." Bastards. Bastards. I will punish them one day. I will make them eat dirt at her feet.

Clara continued to pat her on the back, uselessly and not very tenderly – she wasn't adept at that kind of thing – as if trying to burp a baby. Harriet shrugged her off irritably. The sobs subsided into hiccups. Harriet blew her nose. There was a pause punctuated only by her sighs.

"Harriet, this is bullshit," said Clara after a moment. "You need a car of your own. You could see your friends in London more often. You can't be trapped in this house."

Harriet nodded dumbly, then shook her head. "I'll be all right."

"Damn it, woman!" Clara exploded. "Why can't you have a car? Why can't you have a holiday? Richard is flying across the world every other week!"

"That's different. That's for the conferences and lectures. It can't be helped. He has to spread the word."

"Right. Right. Just like the scientists. They have to fly everywhere to tell other people not to fly. Meanwhile you're stuck here living in the Middle Ages." She pointed at the washing machine. "Stop being a bloody idiot and use the things God gave you! What about all *his* bloody gadget toys? The motor car and the washing machine were invented to liberate women, and now men – men! – are trying to take them away from you, and you're just going along with it."

"You think you're so bloody smart," yelled Harriet. "*I* want the planet to be here for my kids, there are countries that will *drown*, you are destroying the world," and so on and so on, and then they were off, overlapping each other, top of their lungs.

Clara wrenched the door open and dragged Harriet to it while she resisted and slapped at her. "Feel that," she said. "Feel that. Does that feel warm? Go and play in the warm, Harriet, and see how long your toes last. Why are we sitting in this bleeding kitchen shivering in pullovers?"

"Oh what does that prove, that's just typical, this weather is *caused* by the warming, you moron," and on and on.

Clara sat down again and waited until Harriet had run down and then a few moments more.

"Harriet, forget it's me," she said as calmly as she could. "Forget I'm a cow. Try to hear my words as an abstract idea you must evaluate on its own terms. Listen to me. I'm saying this for your own good. It's horse-shit. It's all horse-shit from first to last. Most people know it by now. You are making yourself ill for a rotten stinking ridiculous lie. Don't take my word. You oughtn't to take anyone's word. There is a thing called the internet, I know you've heard of it – "

Harriet groaned and started to yell about lunatics and right-wing attack machines and oil money.

"No," said Clara as patiently as she was able. "No, no, no. All the money and power is on *your* side. That shouldn't even matter. The evidence is what matters." When Harriet had finished again she said, "The hockey-stick has been disproved. Repeatedly, in scientific journals. It was nonsense. There has been no sudden or unprecedented warming. The temperature has gone up and down since the beginning of time with no help from us. The minor fluctuations we experience correlate quite nicely to things called sunspots. And the world is not even getting any warmer any more, it is cooling down."

"The greenhouse effect – "

"Is only a fraction as dramatic as they claim it is, and is only a small part of a huge, complex, ancient and wonderful mechanism full of checks and balances and driven by the big hot yellow thing in the sky, and the entire human race's contribution to greenhouse gases barely amounts to a spit in a bathtub, and you running a car or a washing machine," – she managed not to yell this but bared her teeth a bit – "is going to harm no-one."

At the top of her lungs Harriet called her an evil cavewoman who would rather watch the planet die than learn to co-operate.

"Harriet, you've been conned. We all have. I assumed it must be true at first. I can assure you I like nature, real nature, trees and animals, better than you do. We were conned. We regard scientists like we used to regard the Pope. But they conned us. Maybe some of them conned themselves first. It's a big lie. The biggest! Historical! We're the laughing stock of the future. There will be future historians pissing themselves the way we laugh at witch-burners. You'll be able to tell your grandchildren you were there when it all went crazy. They'll laugh, and so will you. There's no shame in being taken in, except if you refuse to admit it when it stares you in the face. And it isn't a right-left thing. Miles saw through it when he was still a lefty. Some of the people who've uncovered the deceptions are lefties. The evil Tory party believe in it, Harriet. The Tories, Harriet! How good can it be? And a lot of very rich men, and very big banks and corporations, including oil ones, are getting very much richer out of it while making the rest of us pay. You must have noticed that by now."

There was no response. Harriet wasn't looking at her.

"Harriet, this isn't just for your good. You have an audience, a public, and a responsibility to them. You are not *allowed* to get self-righteous about something on someone else's say-so. You are not *allowed* to be self-righteous on the word of a man in a white coat who is fallible and financially interested. You have a *duty* to make the effort to find out for yourself – properly, looking at both sides thoroughly, with an open mind – before you spout off. It's your duty, not merely as a journalist, but as a responsible citizen. Your duty, Harriet! You *like* duty. We *both* like duty. I could so easily have been just like you, really I could. I just hate to see you waste your sacrifices on people who aren't worthy of – "

But the comparison of them was the final straw.

"You're detestable! Get out! I'm not listening to you any more! Get out! Go away! Don't come round here again! You're as bad as them all! I wish I'd never come here!"

Shouting, screeching, swearing, throwing things, Harriet drove Clara from the house. Struck a glancing blow by the calculator, Clara was eventually stung to retaliate, but the door was slammed on her before she could get any really choice insults out. The best she could do was go and push the windmill over. It wasn't working anyway.

Then she went sadly home and slapped Miles on the head.

That was the end of their coffee mornings. Clara handled the split maturely, apart from a few mild pranks such as faking a letter from Harriet to the newsagent asking for the Daily Mail to be delivered, and urging some firebrand young farmhands to put lambs on her roof.

Harriet's next column was a solemn meditation on principles versus friendship. 'Which comes first? I would, without hesitation, betray my country for my friends. But my planet? ... Some differences are too great to be overcome ... Those without principles can never be our true friends ... There are times when, like Ulysses, we must lash ourselves to the mast of duty and stop our ears against the siren call of frivolity and self-indulgence ... What is more there is a great satisfaction, I have found, in having an excuse to drop those we never really liked in the first place. Those, perhaps, we have befriended out of pity. There is always something deeply pitiable about the world's shallow jesters and clowns. Deep down they know they will never be, or deserve to be, taken seriously. And isn't that what all of us want? To know ourselves real people, serious people, capable of suffering, capable of acting, capable of playing a meaningful part on the great stage, not doomed to cut capers for groundlings ... '

"Dear God, what the hell did you *do* to the woman?" demanded Miles. "You have broken her completely. Look what you've done to her *style*."

"It is the tragic wound, Miles, the suffering that enables great art. She has known love and lost it. Now she can fulfil her potential as one of the great whiners of our age. I am very proud."

Chapter Ten

"No!" cried Miles. "Never! Nothing you can say or do will make me! I will never renounce my love for the Sexy Babe Pope!"

"Then you must pay the price."

The sinister figure of the Grand Inquisitioner – actually just Clara still in her Pope robes but with the mitre replaced by a white pointy hood she had made out of a pillow case – advanced towards him. She was clicking a pair of coal-tongs menacingly, and, as he watched, produced a cigarette lighter and started to heat them up in the flame.

"Um," said Cardinal Miles. He was stripped down to his cardinal shorts and spreadeagled against a wall with his hands flung up, playing been chained in the dungeon of the Inquisition. He had vowed long ago never to let himself be really chained or tied up in any of their games, which would be asking for trouble.

"Tell me where Pope Clara is," growled Inquisitor Clara, somewhat muffled.

"No, no, never," cried Miles swinging his head from side to side dramatically. "She is free, I tell you, free of you forever!"

The Inquisitioner clicked the slightly heated tongs in his face and then poised them over his crotch.

"All right, she's in Room 49 of a little motel in – "

"Miles!"

"Well bloody hell woman, watch what you're doing! Oi!" he cried as the tongs started to squeeze, and lowered his arms and grabbed at her hands.

"OK, we'll take the torture scene as read, then," she said to his surprise and relief, tossing aside the tongs and taking off her hood. "Now the best bit. We cut to me, Pope Clara, frightened and alone, knowing you have fallen into the hands of the Inquisition but unable to save you." She paced, wrung her hands, bit a knuckle.

"Is that how you would look?" Miles asked laughing.

"Oh yes, Miles, if you were ever captured by the Inquisition I would definitely bite a knuckle. I am consumed by remorse." She looked vexed and smacked herself on the forehead. "I should never have sent you back to the Vatican to retrieve my handbag. Will you betray my whereabouts? Deep down I know you would die first but they have such terrible instruments of torture."

Miles circled airily around her, waving his arms. "I will never betray you, Pope Clara," he said in a ghostly voice. "I'm sort of a dream sequence," he explained.

"Yes yes, never mind that," she said waving a hand. Clara was racing through this scenario impatiently today, fast-forwarding scenes she would ordinarily have milked for every possible bit of melodrama or repartee, seemingly in a great hurry to get to something really good she had thought of. Miles thought perhaps he might get lucky again. "Now, alone in my hiding place, all of a sudden I see a sinister hooded figure coming towards me – the Inquisition! You must have betrayed me! The terrible figure utters hideous threats, and then removes its hood to reveal – you! I gasp!" She gasped. "You have made a deal with them, I think. But you are only teasing! You killed the Inquisitioner and escaped wearing his hood. You take me in your arms and I sob with relief, and then," she lowered her eyes demurely, "well, let us see where it leads us."

"Hmmm," said Miles. She passed him the hood and he started to put it on.

"No, no, wait, wait – look here! I have made a full Inquisition costume! Aren't I clever?" From behind a couch she produced a simple robe made out of a bedsheet with a huge red cross painted on.

"Ooh!" He put it on.

"It will probably lack the swishing factor of the episcopal regalia but it looks terribly dramatic. And, and – here – I have made you a sinister Inquisition crucifix." She handed him a large cross made out of two lengths of wood nailed together. "You will brandish it at me, you see, as you issue threats. Say things like, 'You will be purged by fire' and so on."

"Okay," said Miles, practising brandishing. He sniffed. "It smells. What does it smell of?"

"Paraffin. I spilled some while I was making it. Take care to hold it away from you, don't get it on your costume."

"Okay."

"And now the hood," she said putting it on him.

"I think the Inquisitioners didn't actually wear these pointy hoods, you know, they were actually for the condemned penitents."

"Oh ... really?" said Clara as she adjusted it. "Well, live and learn, she said with a sprightly semblance of interest to the only man living who would fact-check a sexual fantasy."

"I can't see a thing in this."

"I know, I put the eye-holes in completely the wrong place. Never mind. Let's go, then."

"Now I have you! You will be purged by fire, blasphemer!"

"No no, not here, Miles! The *barn*."

"Oh. ... Ohhh!" He had fond memories of the barn. "I don't know," he said doubtfully though, "out in the open again? We're going to get caught one day."

"It's just a quick dash down the road and into the field. It's all right for you, you're completely anonymous in that. Dare you," she sing-songed. "Tumble in the hay if you're brave enough."

"All right, but if the farmer's anywhere around we abort."

"Yes, yes."

"I really can't see anything in this hood though. Maybe if I can find an eye-hole ... "

"Damn it, Miles, don't touch it! I just finished adjusting it so the pointiness is right. Trust me, I ballsed up, the eye-holes don't fit a human face."

"Well, then I can't really ... "

She tutted and sighed. "I'll just have to lead you by the hand until we get there, I suppose. Come along. Watch out for the table."

"Ow!"

Clara led him outside and onto the lane.

"Keep a watch out for traffic."

"Yes, yes."

All he could see was the white of the fabric in front of his nose.

"Aren't we nearly there? Surely we must have reached the gate by now?" he asked as she pulled him along the road.

"The gate's no good to you, is it? You'd never get over it. There's a gap in the hedge further along."

"Oh – we're idiots!" he suddenly laughed. "Why don't I just take the damn hood off until we get there?"

"Miles I'll kill you if you touch it! I'll never get the pointy bit right again. It looks rubbish otherwise. What's the matter? You used to like it when I led you by the hand," she said all sultrily.

They continued to walk along the road.

"Far too cold to be out in a bedsheet."

"Here we are. Watch the ditch. I'll try and hold the hedges back. Try not to snag the costume. All right." He felt twigs brush against him then was walking across grass. "Watch the cowpat. There's cowpat everywhere. We'll have to veer around this way."

"I'm completely disoriented now. This feels like completely the wrong direction." He heard a car passing. "Shit."

"Don't worry, they can't see us."

"Wait, shouldn't that have been on my right?"

"It was! Are you deaf as well? It must be some odd effect of the hood. Not far now. Oh, there's a small wire fence. Strange, is that new? I suppose we haven't come this way before. I think you can manage it, it isn't high, I'll give you a peg-up. Put your other hand out and you'll feel it. We'll have to lift the robe up. There we are. Straightforward walk to the barn from here."

They were over the fence. They were in the field at the back of Harriet's house now. Clara couldn't see her through any of the windows but there was a TV-flicker. It was a simple matter to lead Miles round to the little lawn in front of the kitchen door. She positioned him there facing it.

"Stop there. We're right in front of the barn now. Okay, hold the crucifix up in front of you. Away from you, remember the paraffin. Right, wait for me to scream or something to give you your cue and then we'll take it from there."

Clara lit the paraffin-soaked crucifix with the cigarette lighter and watched it burst into flame. She scurried as silently as she could to the unopenable front door and rang the bell. She dashed out of the gate and seconds later was crouched down watching from the woods on the other side of the road.

Harriet came to the kitchen door, saw the white-robed, pointy-hooded figure with the burning cross and screamed.

"You must be purged by fire!" boomed Miles.

Harriet screamed again.

Miles felt sudden heat on his fingers as the crucifix burned down to them. "Ow, shite!" he cried, and dropped the burning cross on the lawn.

"I am calling the police," cried Harriet, and slammed the door.

Miles didn't know Harriet's voice; but he knew it wasn't Clara's and could make a shrewd guess.

"Oh, shit," he said.

He wrenched at the hood until an eye-hole became useful and confirmed his worst fears.

He could see Harriet at a kitchen window now. She was talking into a phone and holding a knife.

"Um," said Miles.

He thought for a moment, trying to come up with an innocent or reassuring explanation for his outfit of white robe and pointy hood and accoutrement of burning cross. He was unable to, and settled instead for trying, through body-language, to look as innocent, reassuring and non-threatening as he could under the circumstances.

"Sorry, wrong house," he shouted. He thought he had better disguise his voice. "Wrong house," he boomed again. Harriet was staring at him through the window. "Sorry to trouble you." He grabbed at the burning cross, burnt his fingers, kicked it onto the flags in front of the door. "My mistake. No need to worry. There's an innocent explanation. Got the address mixed up. Imagine how embarrassed I feel."

There was a pause while Harriet continued to stare at him wild-eyed and Miles continued to stand there like a lemon, or at least a lemon dressed as a Klansman.

"Won't trouble you further," he concluded, waving an arm in breezy farewell. "Cheerio."

He couldn't take the hood off, of course. Holding it in place so he could see through the eye-hole he turned and sauntered casually, strolled briskly, and then ran very quickly out of the gate and away.

Among his thoughts as he pelted down the lane were,

"This will *probably* get into Harriet's column," and,

"No judge in the world could possibly convict me of wifeslaughter."

Clara stayed in hiding for a while. Miles stayed in hiding for the rest of the week.

Chapter Eleven

Clara sighed and put down her book.

"The end. Miles I have read every Sir Walter Scott book ever written. What shall I do now? The future stretches bleak and empty ahead of me. Are we rich enough to pay someone to imitate Sir Walter Scott?"

"Write your own."

"What a dour thing to say. Will I ever free you from the lower-middle-class work ethic? However I am going to lie here for a while and imagine my own."

They were in bed having an epic lie-in.

"Can I be in it?" Miles asked.

"Perhaps as comic relief. Miles would you fight to protect me from Saracens or Scottish insurgents or robber barons or a dwarf?"

"Valiantly, my partridge, especially the last one."

"Miles let's not get out of bed today apart from you. Go and get tea and toast and paper and pens and pencils and crayons and sweets and crisps."

When Miles returned with tea and the first instalment of toast Clara had picked the book up again and was sighing again.

"I feel melancholy," she said. "Miles don't leave me."

Miles dithered in the doorway. "I just – there's more toast in."

"Oh yes, you can go and get the toast and things. I just meant in general, don't abandon me for a whore."

When Miles returned with the rest of the toast and things Clara was looking cross.

"I am cross," she said. "I made the mistake of reading the introduction. It advises the reader to skip the parts where the hero and heroine start exchanging exalted and high-flown sentiments, or else to look at it as a window into a time when people believed in them. Miles I feel sad for the world. We must practise saying noble and high-flown sentiments to each other, without any irony, daily."

"You would laugh at me."

"I would at first. I would call you soppy and gay. (By the way we must also start using the word 'gay' in the old-fashioned last-but-one sense, meaning jolly and vivacious, just to annoy and confuse people.) But it might come to grow on me, the sentiment."

"I think the problem is," said Miles getting back into bed, "people have confused things becoming cliche – which may be unavoidable due to repetition – with things being false. For example I had a theory that all the cool kids stopped smiling and being friendly, and, and, saying they loved their mother, or indeed their country, simply because a load of awful lying politicians did it to death and spoiled it for everyone."

"That is a rubbish theory. *I* think people have been trained to sneer at what is beautiful and good."

"I'm just saying language and style change unavoidably."

"They reflect the culture. And as Orwell pointed out, if you lack the means of expressing something, you lack the means of thinking it."

"Orwell himself, when his wife died, called her a 'good old stick.' Not a dear departed angel or something. I mean we approve of stiff upper lip times, don't we? They didn't express themselves like Scott or Dickens but those were still healthy times. An injured World War Two RAF pilot dying in the arms of his sweetheart might, at the most, say – "

"There's no stiff upper lip now, is there?" said Clara overlapping him. "People gush now, self-pity or Communist claptrap or gruesome encomiums on dead celebrities, just never anything – "

"Yes, but my point is – "

"Oh Miles Miles let's play that, RAF pilot and sweetheart. You be Jimmy Badger Faversham in hospital and I'm a nurse only I'm lying down too. You're not dying, just a bit poorly and trying to pull me."

"I say old girl," said Miles beaming.

"Yes?"

"Well – I mean to say – you and me – how about it, and all that rot?"

Clara-nurse bridled and slapped him.

"Go on, say something exalted."

"I think you're really fit."

"Miles!"

"You'll laugh."

"I promise."

"You ... "

"Yes?"

"Well ... you know. You must know. I hope you know."

"Christ."

"You can't overturn a culture in five minutes by an act of will."

"If we practise for five minutes a day we can. It is vital someone makes a start. Say something nice."

"I admire you. A lot."

"Call me a bleeding angel or something!"

"You are an angel. Or something."

"Say it."

"You're an angel."

"You said that in a funny voice!"

"I didn't! That's my sentiment voice."

"God it's like … at university there was this girl who watched moronic Australian soaps all the time, ironically of course, and I was trapped one day and it was on, and when someone was being polite, in the soap, when they had to say thank you for something, they said it in an English voice, a comedy posh English voice, ironically, as if it was weak or effeminate to express gratitude. That's what things will end up like, unless someone turns the culture around."

"Hmm. Maybe if I compliment you in an Australian voice. Bonzer norks."

Clara slapped him.

"Miles do you think it would be possible or desirable to do away with irony?"

"I can't tell if you're serious."

"Anyway the point is classic books must be rescued from the clammy revisionist hands of academics. Miles can't we start a publishing house and start putting out the old classics as unashamed tales of romance and derring-do? Put lots of swords and bosoms on the cover. People are ready. Did I tell you the telly-shooting is catching on? Jeremiah was so impressed when I told him that he has shot his too. I have started a trend."

"You stole the idea from Elvis."

"I think you mean the popular proletarian children's entertainer Mr. E. Presley, Miles," Clara said reprovingly. "We are never on first-name terms with popular culture, remember."

"Perhaps Mr. E. Presley, the noted New World crooner and gourmet, was actually the first young fogey."

"Indeed I believe Roger Scruton has expressed a surprising soft spot for that particular warbler."

"That confirms it then."

"On second thoughts I won't try to popularize Scott. He would just end up on television, anti-bowdlerized, with all the sentiment cut out and naked hardcore fucking put in. He must remain our little secret. Miles can we get swords however? Proper ones, I mean, our toy ones are rubbish."

Miles's eyes lit up. "Hell yes. So long as you promise not to stab me."

"Miles shall we teach ourselves to fence?"

"With the same proviso, that's another bloody good idea."

"Miles can we afford to buy a castle?"

"Alas no, my cauliflower. But perhaps if we – "

"Wah wah wah, write a book, start a business, get jobs, God you're a grind." She took up a pen and notepad. "Instead I'm going to write crossover Walter Scott–Walpole–Roger Scruton–E. Presley fan-fiction, secure in the blissful knowledge it can be of no conceivable commercial value to anyone. Or I will draw a picture of them having an adventure anyway. And Professor Jenks will be in it too but not you. Don't forget there's our share of the art money now. I'm fairly sure you can pick up a broken old Scottish castle fairly cheap, you know," she said as she started to scribble.

"What would we use it for?"

"Swordfights, Scrooge! Also we can hole up there and eventually be barons when civilisation breaks down. Breaks down worse, I mean." After a while she added, "Or how about an island? Just a fairly small one, but preferably with castle. They have millions of little islands in Scotland."

Miles's eyes widened. "Imagine how strange and ingrown we could get on an island."

Clara laughed. "It's our ingrown inbred grandchildren I'd worry about. Perhaps we could get one that came equipped with, you know, peasants. Imagine having peasants to look after, and look up to us."

"I don't think anyone has ever looked up to us, and, let's face it, we failed to even look after our cat."

"Let us not reproach ourselves, Miles. The cat's suicide was its own choice. It had seen through everything and we have to respect that. We would do better with peasants, I am sure."

"You would perform terrible social experiments on them. You would try to dress them all in matching smocks at least."

"What do you think I am?" she said indignantly. "I would be a laissez-faire fief-lady. The extent of my interference would be to present them with a shilling at Christmas, provided they bobbed and curtseyed and touched their forelocks nicely. At most I would make a few improvements to their rude hovels, fit doors and so on, but only if they petitioned me. They would of course be required to rally their swords to us at need. They probably don't even have swords now, just satellite dishes. God I hate everything. Miles tell me a place where there is still feudalism and clans."

"Afghanistan. Let's go."

"They don't have tartan. You know what I mean, nice feudalism. Miles I don't want Scotland ever to leave us. I want to be a member of the same country as Scott and Stevenson. Promise we will invade them if they ever try. The whores of Europe try to entice them to abandon us because they know together we can kick the world's arse."

"Miles do you think good writers carry on writing books when they go to Heaven? Scott must have written a shedload by now. Shall we have a seance and offer ourselves to him as amanuenses? We could get in touch with the cat too and ask if we are to blame."

A few minutes later Clara and Miles were holding hands and had their eyes closed.
"Reowww," said Clara.
"Why, Enid, why?" asked Miles. "Was it our fault? Was it the collar?"
"Reowww," said Clara.
"I think Enid is in Hell," said Miles.
"Rurgatory," said Clara.
After that Clara tried automatic writing.
"What do you think?" she asked passing him the sheet.
"I don't think that was Scott, I think it's an evil spirit. It's a good pastiche but he never used to mention penises."
"He is keeping up with the times."

"Miles why do people have to die anyway? Imagine if you could live forever."
"What would you do with it?"
"This, pretty much. I would have lie-ins lasting a thousand years. I think I will. I have decided not to die and forbid you to. Miles will you still love me when I am nine million?"
"If you keep yourself up to scratch."
"So shallow."

"No, stop."
"But I am falling behind with them."
"No death-lists in bed. It's a new rule. Bed is for nice things. Besides it isn't respectful to the people you're listing. If you're going to schedule someone for execution at least have the decency to do it sitting up straight at a desk."

"Miles, I can hide the truth from you no longer. There is a reason why I have been divinely appointed to liberate our country. The fact is, I am a descendant of Churchill."
"Frankly, this is no great surprise to me."
"You had suspected? That makes it easier. Of course, you can see the resemblance when I go like this." She thrust out her lower lip and made vague growly noises.
"It was what attracted me to you."
"That is a matter for you and our marriage counsellor. Nevertheless this is something we must confront. The truth only came to me comparatively

recently, in a dream. I immediately taxed my grandmother with it and she confessed. Churchill had impregnated her, on the map table in the War Room in 1944. Their coupling was of such a ferocity that an inverted relief model of Belgium was visibly imprinted on her buttocks until the late 50s."

"I would expect nothing less."

"No, nor would I. She informed me his member was both impressive and somehow reassuring, unlike yours. Churchill assured her that the offspring of their union, or rather their offspring's offspring, would be lovely beyond words and was destined to save England in her next dark hour. As my cousins are frankly troll-like and politically suspect he can only have meant Me."

"Which grandmother was this?"

"Paternal. My maternal nan seduced Montgomery at the height of the Battle of El Alamein. You may have suspected that side of my heritage from my brilliant pincer movements when stealing your sweets or attacking your balls. It will be more apparent when you finally allow me to buy some tanks."

" ... Anyone who's paid taxes for twenty years and had a clean criminal record for that long and who can collect fifty signatures from their neighbours can put themselves forward as an Elector. They would be put into a lottery or ... no, screw it, just have as many Electors as you want. There's no pay and they serve for one year and then can't serve again for two.

"Parliament convenes twice a year, for three days each time," Miles continued. "At the first one the Electors put the people's grievances, anything that wants looking into. At the second the Executive of Twelve give their report, how well they've done, and ask to be allowed to serve another year. If not another twelve are chosen by proposal and acclamation. And then they ask for a budget for the coming year and that has to be passed or rejected by the Electors. If we can't fit all the Electors in the House they assemble in a crowd in the square.

"Almost everything would be run at a local level, I mean individual parishes, including tax raising, law and order, poor relief, all by vote. The principle would be that no-one has power over your life who lives so far away that you can't stone his house or jeer at him in the street. The parish councillors could only serve for a year at a time too. But anyway everything would be decided by, like in Saxon times, an old-fashioned ... what was that thing, was it just called a Thing? A moot? It would be like that, any adult householder who showed up for the meeting could vote on any issue, a full direct vote for everything, you don't delegate your own power to a professional political class, the councillors would just be like administrators once things were decided. And people could petition the Twelve for redress if any of them abused their position. That would be their main function."

Clara nodded intelligently. "And where does the War Queen come into it?"

"What ... I never mentioned a War Queen."

"I know, and that is an oversight. I feel sure your system would benefit from a War Queen, for situations that this Twelve of yours can't deal with. She can be kept in a palace in the bowels of the earth and summoned at need. She would rise up in a lift, Thunderbirds-style, through the Houses of Parliament, and then one of the faces of Big Ben would slide back, and then she – or let's not be coy, I – would be revealed sitting on a golden Octopus Throne surrounded by holographic flames. 'Who has disturbed my peace?' I would boom out in an eerie amplified voice. My face would be painted white like a geisha. The throne would fly out and hover over Parliament Square. 'The War Queen!' the multitude would cry. 'The War Queen has come to save us!' But they would be secretly afraid of me. The throne's tentacles would be prehensile and would lash the crowd if it grew fractious; some could fire lasers and others rockets. Then I would go forth and smite our foes, or rain death on any parish that wasn't coming up to scratch."

Miles looked at her. "I am trying to elaborate a workable system for – "

"Yes but this is a rubbish revolution Miles, tell me a proper revolution. You haven't even killed anyone yet."

"That's taken for granted. I'm trying to describe what would come next *after* the stringing up."

"Who cares what happens next? We will kill all the bastards and then go down the pub."

"Let's not do any more sociopolitical whining for today."

"You are stifling me, Miles."

"Another day. Let's not have the world invading our bed. Let's talk about pleasant things."

"We can't just ignore it and hope it goes away."

"What? Your whole life has been based on the premise that you can."

"I've realised you can't all the time though. I get so frustrated."

"Either things will get better, or, they won't."

"Miles! I don't believe you! We're meant to fight to ensure the first!"

"We don't know how. Really, though, enough for now, let's play a nice game. If we talk about them all the time, they've won. I hate the way bloody politics infiltrates into everything now. I really think that just living in a world of your own is the best rebellion, because They would cry if they knew you weren't paying attention to the 'agenda' They had set. We win by keeping our own heads free."

"Miles, you're such a ... I wonder if in the Warsaw ghetto in 1939 there was a Jewish fop Miles who got sick of people talking about Nazis all the time."

Miles laughed. "There's absolutely no comparison to – "

"No, I'm not comparing the situation, but I bet that's how you would have been. 'Please, not the Nazis again, so dreary.' Oh let's play that."

"No! It's sick."

Lying there they started playing that Miles was a snotty fop aesthete Jew in the Warsaw ghetto who didn't want to talk about the Nazis. Clara was his mother who did.

"Those bastards, they knocked down your Uncle Hyman in his own shop."

"Really, Mother," said Miles, pained. "Every day. Don't you have any other topic but the Nazis?"

"They set fire to Rabbi Goldstein's beard."

"Please, Mother. I am sick of talking about trivial little epiphenomena like Nazis. I would rather talk about eternal verities. Art, Mother, let's talk about art for once."

"You know who likes art? The Nazis, that's who. They looted the museum and threw the curator down the stairs."

"Honestly, Mother, must we pollute our thoughts with this ugliness all the time? *Please* let's change the subject. Oh, let me show you the new pair of shoes I bought."

"Are they running shoes, to flee from the Nazis in? Are they a good strong pair of leather boots to kick a Nazi in the nuts with?"

"They are shoes for shoes' sake, Mother."

The thing was Miles had forbidden Clara to do a Jewish accent, first because he said it would make a sick scenario even more tasteless, and second because she wasn't very good at it. So, possibly out of spite, her Polish Jewish mother talked with a cut-glass upper-crust British home counties accent, getting steadily posher and more old-fashioned as she went on.

"Oh vey! Dead, I wish I was," she said in fluent Celia Johnson. "Dash it all, we are surrounded by Nazis, my son is a shoe fetishist, and I have forgotten to take the ponies out of the horsebox."

Miles laughed and said, "OK the Nazis burst in now. So, I heff caught you at lest, Miss Celia Johnson," he said in Nazi. "You thought you could hide in ze Varsaw Ghetto. Now you are our hostage ze British vill heff no choice but to surrender."

"I am not Celia Johnson, I am an ordinary Warsaw ghetto Jewess, I tell you. Oh gevult, what ebsolute tsuris, on top of everything I find I have completely run out of Pimm's already."

"Miles I don't like it when people laugh at old films because the people talk nicely. It scares me."

"I am here, darling. Be brave."

"No but really it does. Shall I tell you what really scares me though? Listen, listen. Stephanie sent me a copy of this arty style magazine she got a job at, I meant to show you. And of course it was awful and I knew it was going to be awful, but it only struck me afterwards, I knew beforehand exactly *how* it was going to be awful, and I was right, even though I hadn't looked at anything like that in years and we don't watch telly and so on. But it's stranger than that. Listen. When I was a teenager I was staying with my Ghastly Uncle Charlie and my aunt, and I was bored one day and looking through their attic, and he had a pile of groovy trendy style magazines, but old ones, from before I was born, or just after I was born, say fifteen or twenty years old, and they were the *same*, the same, the same as they are now, I mean all pictures of people being tough in cities, or rich people pretending to be tough in cities, all urban squalor and wire fences and graffiti and skateboarding and tattoos and body-piercing and odd-looking beards and pictures of junkies as religious icons and SM costumes and everybody scowling, no-one smiling, and people making rude gestures at the camera with their fingers, and the idiom was the same, the design, the lay-out, the groovy typography, the attitude, it was all the same as it is now, twenty or twenty-five years ago.

"I mean how can they? It scares me. How can they stop it changing? Surely something like that they're meant to be the very people who are always looking out for a new thing? How can they keep everything the same for twenty or thirty years? It suddenly gave me a chill as if it was supernatural. I mean it *isn't* natural. I mean, all right, if you and I had a magazine, an idea I mean to pursue as soon as I can prise your nervous fingers loose from the purse-strings, we would have all the lovely fonts and designs they had in the 1950s, and pictures of elegant people in front of classic cars, and cows and fields and trees and things, and everyone would be smiling and happy and friendly-looking, we would make all the models say cheese and wave at the camera, *especially* the ones who were nude and simulating sex, and there would be pearls and bowler hats and girls in Norman Hartnell dresses, and we would have features on heroes of the Empire, if it could be made clear we weren't doing it ironically, and there would be photoshoots of Roger Scruton and Peter Hitchens, ideally unclothed centrefolds if I had my way. And, all right, that's us, we are fogeys and that isn't everyone's cup of tea. You needn't do that. But when is a really new thing coming?

"And the popular music and the fashion has essentially stayed the same. It's like what I said to Charlie, they've clung grimly on for a generation, but how can they? And how can they go on thinking it's new or 'edgy' or 'radical' and similar dreadful words? The slang and the dreadful words have stayed the same too long as well. How can they stop it dead and why don't people rebel and look for something new? To go back to something older without any irony *would* be better, because quite apart from the fact that the old days genuinely were healthier and more beautiful, it would just be a sodding refreshing change now."

Miles said, "A bloke I knew at university brought out a literary magazine with a picture of cows and trees and fields on the cover, this really lovely pastoral scene, and I thought how nice, and then instantly I thought, oh, he's probably joking, it must be an ironic statement in some way. Knowing this bloke it probably wasn't, he probably just liked the cows, but I thought, how awful to live in an age where that's your first thought, if someone propagates beauty you assume it's intended ironically."

"Yes. I had not finished talking however. Perhaps you should have married this 'bloke' if he is more interesting than me. The other thing that has started to scare me is, where have all the geniuses gone? I mean take anything, novels, music, films, theatre, poetry, art, and do a head-count of geniuses compared to 50 or 60 years ago, a hundred years, two hundred years ago, four hundred. There practically *are* none. All right, you have to allow for the fact that some geniuses live unknown in attics and are only discovered after they die, so we don't know about them yet. *Try* to allow for the fact that we are fogeys, so there might be people around we would find quite good if we were more in tune with the times and could bear the kind of thing they do; give a few people the benefit of the doubt. It still doesn't add up. It doesn't come close. And on a simple reckoning of percentages there should be more than ever. The population has exploded. There's more widespread education. There's more prosperity worldwide. We should be living in a bloody renaissance! There should be genius burgeoning everywhere, fresh new things around every corner, a masterpiece a week. But in every field there's *less*. As if to hide it, of course, the word itself is flung around like confetti. Where did they all go? Is there just something in the food? Something in the culture? I genuinely want to know."

"Miles when we have a castle can we have a forge and an armourer to make lots of swords? And a chef, to make jam tarts. I am fond of jam tarts."

"Miles we ought to be fat. Can we buy fat-suits the next time we go to the costume shop?"

"If it will gladden you, vein of my heart. May I ask why?"

"We aren't weighty enough for our primeval passion. Fat people have the most fantastic sex, I have decided. Their copulations are as dramatic as those of dinosaurs. Which is more spectacular, dragonflies dancing or freight-trains colliding? We just don't have the bulk to be great lovers. We need to break furniture, collapse beds, crash through walls and fall through ceilings, snort and bellow like rutting rhinoceri. That is how plumpers do it. They destroy their houses in their elephantine ecstasy, squash everything flat, then do it in the garden and leave great dinges in the turf. That is why the government picks on them so much, sheer sexual jealousy. One day I shall descend on Whitehall with an army of fatties and just sit on all the bastards. Miles let's get fat suits and go to a gym near Whitehall or Millbank or Notting Hill and just stand there eating junk food and demoralizing them. Let's have a picnic in Parliament Square, just guzzle hampers full of food all day, just Mars Bars topped with squirty cream and rashers of bacon on top, and stare at them. Let's rent twelve fat children and pretend they are our family and just sit there placidly eating at the scum. I want the bastards to know they can never win. I want them to know that one day our fat children will eat their prig children."

Clara said, "I don't think I ever told you about the time when I was a child when I rounded up all the kids in my neighbourhood and led them on a Children's Crusade."

"How like you," said Miles fondly. "How adorable. Bless. A crusade to do what?"

Clara stared at him. "To liberate the Holy Land for Christianity, Miles, what else?"

"Oh."

"There must have been about ten of us but I declared that faith would make up for our lack of numbers. We *must* have been adorable, looking back. We made sandwiches for the journey and the younger ones carried teddy-bears. Also an assortment of knives, tin-openers and catapults to kill the Paynim with. Swords made out of wood, shields made out of cardboard. And jam-jars full of napalm."

"Um. Napalm?"

"A girl in my class with a rather disturbing father had told me how to make napalm out of jam and matches. She said the jam sticks to you and burns. It was the sort of thing her father would have known but I think she was lying. If not it's worth looking into, for when The Day comes."

"Naturally," said Miles. "So what happened?"

"We never reached Palestine. My map-reading skills were off. We tried to hitch-hike at one point but no-one was going in that direction. There were dissensions in the ranks, as in the real crusades. People whining, 'Are we nearly there yet?' and people refusing to go to the lavatory in fields. Richard the Lionheart must have had to put up with the same thing. The sandwiches ran out, almost immediately. I asked God to send us some more food and then pointed at a field full of lettuces and said, 'A miracle.' We grazed for a while. We made it as far as a village three miles away. Fearing mutiny I told my followers that that was the Holy Land and gave a prayer of thanks. We were milling round outside a post office while I pondered our next move. A rather grumpy old woman came out and told us to clear off. So I told my army that that was the Temple and we must storm it and free it. We waved our weapons and yelled. Somewhat to my surprise a slow-witted older boy who was my devoted follower broke a pane of glass in the door with his catapult. I ordered a strategic withdrawal and we fled. We ate the napalm on the way home and got horribly sick as we hadn't taken the match-heads out. In retrospect it was asking for trouble to have edible weapons. By now my troops were demoralized and in disarray. I was blamed for the debacle. But then a great thing happened. We saw this man camping in a field in a tent. He was cooking something in a frying pan on a fire; he waved at us cheerily. He was black-haired and had a moustache and was wearing silk pyjamas, in a field, in the afternoon. I cried, 'It is Saladin! We must parley with him!' We went to treat with him in his tent. He was very friendly and had a twinkle in his eye; a proper English eccentric. I demanded safe passage for all pilgrims to the Holy Land and he gravely agreed. He gave us food, sausages. One of my followers who hadn't recovered from the jam threw up outside the tent. I apologised and said I would have his head cut off; Saladin graciously said that wouldn't be necessary. I was able to declare a victory and we went home."

"Fantastic," said Miles.

"We got lost on the way home too. In fact, like the real Children's Crusade, some of my followers ended up in slavery." Miles looked slightly alarmed. "Two boys became detached from the main party and stole some apples. The farmer caught them and made them do chores," she explained. "The rest of us made it back OK, eventually. I told Nanny Bryce what I had done and she said, 'That's nice, dear, I expect you'd like a hot bath now.' Which was somewhat deflating after having freed the Holy Land. Of course I sort of knew I hadn't really but I did wonder about Saladin."

"It's a shame you never made it," said Miles. "It could have made the Middle East situation even more interesting."

She nodded. "I continue to regret it. I intended to install myself as a benevolent and chivalrous Archbishopess of Jerusalem, treating all sides even-handedly and converting rather than slaughtering wherever I could. In many ways this still represents the path not taken. I suppose it is never too late."

"What the hell are you doing?"

Clara was contorting her mouth very strangely, and feeling her lips with her fingers.

"Miles what shape is my mouth when I do this?" She did it again.

"It ... inhuman."

"I'm trying to ... Miles fetch a mirror."

"I will not. You'll break it."

"Once in a Mary Stewart book I read a woman was described as having a 'three-cornered smile'."

"I see."

"It's haunted me ever since. It was made to sound desirable. I want one." She twisted her lips determinedly again.

"What you are doing now is not desirable."

She stopped. "How many corners do I have in my normal smile? Count them." She flashed it.

"The regulation two."

"That's what I thought. I must find another one somehow." She did a sort of sneer.

"That's still two, and hideous."

"I don't see how a tricorner smile is possible."

"I don't. Are you sure you aren't misremembering?"

"No, it kept repeating it, 'her three-cornered smile'. She was famous for having one."

"Well, she would be."

"Maybe it's ..." She inserted fingers in her lips and pulled them in various directions. "'ow 'any 'ow?" she demanded urgently. "'oun!"

"That's ... a polygon, there are eight corners at least now."

"Hmm." She removed the fingers but continued to wriggle and contort her lips experimentally.

"Maybe it meant like an isosceles triangle on its side," suggested Miles, drawn into the problem in spite of himself.

"'ike 'is?" She compressed her mouth at one side and opened it at the other.

"You look like Popeye, and aren't really achieving cornerhood, or anything a sane person would describe as a smile."

"Ohhh."

"Maybe it meant just a normal upside-down hemisphere, straight top lip, but an unusually deep curve at the bottom."

"Sort of pointy at the bottom? Like this?" She folded her bottom lip in two with finger and thumb to make an angle.

"She can't have gone round like that."

"It would give her a sort of pensive look. Maybe if the bottom lip was straight and it was pointy on top." She contorted.

Miles laughed. "That's ... no."

"Maybe she had surgery. Maybe she had another corner artificially implanted. Miles buy me an operation, I want three corners."

"Be satisfied with the paltry two that God has given you."

Clara continued to wiggle and desperately try to triangularize her mouth.

"Oh!" cried Miles. "I read in a book once about someone who had an 'arrowhead Etruscan smile.' Maybe it meant that."

"Oh! Yes! I know that book! It is an Inspector Alleyn one. And I know that kind of smile. I knew a girl with one."

She tried to twist her mouth into a v-shape, eventually resorting to manipulating it with both sets of forefingers and thumbs.

"That could start a new fashion in smiles," laughed Miles.

"But if you think about it," she said abandoning it, "that's sort of four corners, I think."

"Well, you should go for five then, and surpass them both. We'll get ... like from a child's ... put-the-right-shape-into-the-hole thing, a pentagon, and you can mould your mouth around it for two hours a day until it sticks. You will be renowned throughout the world as the girl with the five-cornered smile."

"I want three! Miles help me."

"You are beyond help," he said as she continued to gurn.

Towards the end of the afternoon Miles said they'd feel all strange and depressed if they missed the daylight completely and made her get up and dressed. They went for a walk through the woods and then watched a molten-gold sunset behind the Old Mill. Afterwards Miles cooked an elaborate dinner, and let her cheat at backgammon, and then they went back to bed.

Chapter Twelve

Clara and Miles were competitively writing novels. Actually Miles was failing to do so, and Clara thought she was doing very well, thank you.

It was a bright winter's morning with a heavy snowfall blanketing the fields and a fire was blazing in the hearth. Clara was sitting at her desk and Miles was sitting at a table he had set up as far away from her as possible.

It had been Miles's idea. They had spent two days romping in the snow and then a third playing board games in front of the fire, and then there had been a dressing-up day and a pub night and then a not-get-out-of-bed day, and then another frolic-in-the-snow day and then a reading-quietly and making-things-out-of-plasticine day, and then today Clara had proposed filling in scrap-books and making things out of papier mache and Miles had snapped.

They would run out of money one day, he had said. They would never achieve anything, he had said.

"We have to work!" he cried, pacing up and down the living room grabbing at his hair. "Work, work!"

"Dear God," said Clara, wide-eyed, "I have inadvertently married Thomas Carlyle."

And so they had set to work writing books. Clara had suggested they write one together. Miles had meanly said no, because he would take it seriously and she wouldn't. They had started to write several books in collaboration before now, some with serious intent of publication, and they had always started out well enough, some of them fairly amusing or otherwise promising, but thanks to Clara they usually became very silly by around page five, and tended to end around page ten in a welter of scribbled penises, pictures of Walpole (and his penis), drawings of queens in pretty dresses having people's heads (and penises) cut off, and so on.

So they had set to work separately.

"At least let us push the desks together, Miles, so that there will be some togetherness."

"No."

Clara pouted. "We could play we are back at school."

"No," said Miles, not keen to be kicked on the ankle and stabbed in the thigh with a protractor for an hour.

"Oh! Oh! Miles! Let's play you're a famous novelist and I'm a sexy secretary who keeps distracting you."

"No!" cried Miles. "Maybe later," he added after a moment. "When we've done a chapter apiece."

"Very well, my lord and master, you know best."

And so they had started to write; or at least Clara had, very busily, while Miles scowled at a blank page, wrote and crossed out a series of unsatisfactory first lines, and occasionally glanced at her in annoyance.

"I have done two pages already," Clara announced very quickly.

"Obviously about Walpole or penises."

"Nothing could be further from the truth. I will help you if you are stuck."

"I am not stuck. I am cogitating."

"Lewd remark to be inserted here." She scribbled happily for a while, then sighed and said, "Miles, don't you think this is a scene that will appeal to our biographers one day? Husband and wife writers working side by side in front of a roaring fire."

"Biographers? What biographers?"

"Well, my biographers then," she said, loudly turning over another page, "although I am sure you would merit at least a footnote as my envious husband."

"You, you, you are deliberately distracting me out of envy of my discipline."

"Not at all," said Clara. "In fact, I'm so far ahead I'm going to make a pot of tea for us, just so our biographers will say I was by *far* the nicest spouse." She tripped gaily out, going, "La-la-laa."

When she returned Miles had actually managed a paragraph. She cooed encouragingly and really accidentally spilled tea on it.

"I am going to beat you like a gong," said Miles.

Clara laughed appreciatively and said, "Yes, we must try that some time, that could be funny. Shall I soothe your fevered brow, writer-husband? Would you like a shoulder-massage? You are all tense."

"Stuff off."

"I am refilling your tea, look, master, and not spilling any on your timeless genius. Oh! Oh! Miles! Shall we play De Quincey and the bird who made his tea in his snug little cottage?"

"No. Later. If I can be De Quincey. *Please* let me think a moment, there's a good wife."

"I hear and obey."

She sat and knocked out another page in an annoyingly short time. Miles managed another paragraph meanwhile.

"Is your hand getting sore now?" Clara asked as he then paused.

"Shut up."

"This is why women writers are held back, their husbands repress them out of jealousy."

"Honestly, love, quiet a mo, please, this could be good."

Clara made a lip-zipping gesture.

After a while Miles began to make progress. He ventured onto a second page. Presently Clara laid down her pen and, twisting her hair around her ear, coyly asked, "Is it about me?"

"No," said Miles.

She threw her pen, accurately, at his face. "Well what whore *is* it about then?" she exploded indignantly. "Who are you immortalizing if not me?" She rushed over and grabbed it to see.

"No-one! Give it back!"

"Jesus Christ, Miles, almost two pages and you haven't even got the hero out of bed yet," she snorted, flinging it back, when she was quite sure there wasn't a whore in it anywhere.

"That's because he's an anti-hero. It takes them longer."

"A sensitive semi-autobiographical bedwetter, obviously. What a dreary streak of piss that will be."

"I suppose yours is all ... swords and bosoms and willies and exciting battles with cannons and dead Frenchmen everywhere," he said, privately wishing he'd thought of starting something like that.

"Not at all. It is a subtle psychological study and a painfully relevant contemporary document."

"Then why do you keep sniggering?"

"Am I? I wasn't aware. When I commune with my muse I am no longer fully in my body."

Miles stared at his page glumly and sighed. Tentatively, tongue protruding from his mouth slightly in a way that Clara thought made him look like an adorably retarded child, he took up and poised his pen again.

"You know your problem?" Clara asked. "As a writer?"

"You!" he cried.

"Yes," said Clara. "That's exactly it. I haven't left you."

"Yes!" agreed Miles. "That is, exactly, it."

"Really. I never broke your heart. All writers' best work is about the bird who broke their heart. This is why there's such a skewed cynical view of love and marriage in literature, it's self-selecting. Name the happy couples in literature. Not happy endings, mind, happy marriages *after* the happy ever after."

"There must be a few. Probably not many. Where's the plot? You could have them as secondary characters, I suppose, or background to the main story." Quite glad of the distraction he laid down his pen and thought. "There must be some. Um. Inspector Alleyn and Troy. Tommy and Tuppence. They're probably mostly in genre, actually. Flashman and Elspeth, in their own louche way. Lucia and Georgie in their way. Oh! Mike and Phyllis in John Wyndham's The Kraken Wakes."

Clara sighed. "Yes! *We* could fight krakens together, Miles. Would you rescue *me* from a sea-monster?"

"Whenever they attack you, my sweet."

"Can we play that later? I suppose we would need a tentacle. Perhaps we could buy one from a film prop maker."

"Anyway stop distracting me."

"*Are* you distracted?" Clara looked surprised. "As a woman I find I am able to talk and write great literature at the same time. I expect it is a sort of automatic writing and I am channeling from somewhere."

"I expect it is piss. I am trying to be a proper Writor, damn it. And so could you if you put your mind to it."

"Who says I am not? It seems to me I am doing far better than you. Shall we have a word-count?"

"No. It's irrelevant. It's quality that matters."

"I have done over five thousand words," announced Clara a few moments later.

"How is that *possible*?" cried Miles in irritation.

"Sheer self-discipline, I expect, you ought to try it some time. Besides I have a great subject."

"I bet it's Walpole's penis," said Miles coming over to look.

"Quite wrong. If you must know I am writing Harriet fan-fiction."

I

Harriet was unhappy. She stared out of the window at the endless trees and fields. God she hated the countryside. She hated all the farmers, with their silly food-growing habits. Why didn't they just go to the supermarket like normal people? They just did it to be different. Then they went home and read The Daily Mail and planned to vote Conservative and probably put on minstrel shows. They went to church and had various annoying community activities where they all visited each other and were friends. Harriet was determined not to get involved and had decided to say no if anyone asked her. She was an independent woman, and sassy too. But no-one did ask her, so she had no opportunity to sass anyone. They were so unfriendly.

Harriet thought about the Daily Mail and shuddered. How could such things be allowed? She never read it but knew it was very bad. As she thought about it Harriet started to cry. Then she thought about a comedian on television who made jokes about the Daily Mail all the time. He was subversive and edgy and yet warmly reassuring. She cheered up a bit.

Her two lovely non-gender-specific children Chomsky and Monbiot came in. As she had trained them, they did not call her Mother so as not to pigeonhole her. But they shook her hand warmly and asked for some sweets. She smiled reprovingly and said she would send some on their behalf to some poor children in Scunthorpe. They agreed that that was better. She told them in detail about gay sex and the Amritsar Massacre and then sent them out to play.

She watched them unhappily. She supposed she ought to throttle them for the good of the planet. The framed picture of Al Gore over the mantelpiece seemed to look at her reproachfully. "*Kill them, Harriet,*" it seemed to whisper. "*Kill them before they spread their human poison all over our fragile planet.*"

Harriet wrung her hands. She put her head out of the window and told the children to run more slowly and breathe out less. "In fact whoever can hold their breath for longest can have a story from the Hugo Chavez book." "Hooray!" cried the children, and closed their mouths and started to turn purple. Then she went online with her credit card and bought a vasectomy for an African. "I'm sorry, Al, that's the best I can do," she muttered guiltily.

Harriet felt lonely. Just then as if in answer to her unspoken prayers her lovely, lovely neighbour Clara came in, spreading radiance all about her. Harriet fought back tears at the sight and felt a complicated mixture of conflicting emotions: jealousy (Clara was so lovely), blind hatred (Clara was the enemy of progress), guilt (deep down she knew Clara was right), and a slight undertow of unacknowledged but unavoidable lesbian crush. Beyond all this there reverberated between them the tacit freemasonry of dismay at the penis that secretly unites all women. These two could have been friends, had not a stern fate willed it otherwise.

"Hello, Harriet," said Clara angelically.

Clara's beatific smile and lovely breasts offered unconditional Christian love, sisterhood, and badly-needed make-up tips.

And Harriet fled from them as a slug flees from the sunlight.

("Do slugs do anything so energetic as flee?" Miles wondered. "Shut up, Miles, you are stifling my creativity.")

"I am sorry, Clara," said Harriet. "You must go away. I cannot be your friend. I cannot follow your shining example. I gave my heart to Communism long ago."

"Then you must pay the price," said Clara, suddenly wrathful.

Hooded figures on horseback appeared in the door behind her. "You

must come with us. It is time to burn you in the Giant Wicker Penis."
Harriet screamed.

("Did you like it?"
"Fantastic," said Miles in a monotone.
"I wish we *did* have a Giant Wicker Penis to burn unwelcome outsiders in. I must raise it with the Parish Council. Go on to the next, go on to the next.")

II

Harriet drove her pedal-car through the snow. She had given up her electric car after someone had cruelly pointed out that electricity didn't grow on trees. Besides neither her windmill nor her solar cells were working, because it was snowing.

Harriet shivered. She was only wearing a T-shirt, so as not to give comfort to the enemy. She knew the snow was only a temporary aberration. Deep down she thought it was probably a hologram created by oil interests. She had turned off the heating in her house to thwart them, instructing her non-gender-specific offspring Hobsbawm and Delors to warm themselves by reading from the Hugo Chavez book instead. For the sake of the planet they were down to essentials, just the TV and laptops and i-pods and i-phones and e-book readers and the children's e-pets (far better for Mother Nature, after all, than real pets, which ate food and breathed and farted) and OH WHY DON'T YOU DIE YOU SILLY BASTARDS

("The auctorial mask slipped for a moment there, Miles.")

They had limited themselves to flying to only eight global warming conferences this year, going no further than Bali or San Francisco, and of course had made up for them by paying someone in the Third World to stay put in a mud hut, and had made the new au pair walk from Poland.

The snow was really rather thick now. Harriet grimly pedalled onward, her stumpy little legs pumping valiantly. Her treacherous body told her it was really awfully cold, but she didn't believe it. The brute physical senses, she thought with a laugh, were where the atavistic Daily Mail reader within us all dwells, the back-brain caveman unable to apprehend the grandeur and subtleties of the things of the intellect. She knew that when the raw data was properly adjusted this would probably turn out to be the warmest winter ever.

It was no use. The car was hopelessly bogged down. Harriet got out and started to trudge forward as best she could. Soon the snow was up to her waist, although that didn't take long because of her little legs. She hated the snow and thought angrily of how it would be twisted by those with an agenda. It was the warming that caused the snow. The TV adverts said so. This had all been foreseen and predicted. True, the scientists (the nice ones) had said things like 'snow will soon become a very rare event' but then they were forced to be enigmatic so as to fool the Deniers. Really they were speaking in parables.

As Harriet slowly became snow-blind she seemed to see a wondrous vision imposed on the white blankness: it was her lovely neighbour Clara, shaking her head at her sadly and urging her to turn back. She ignored it.

The snow was up to her neck now. As Harriet tried to fight on she thought smugly of the ignorant millions who would misinterpret the icy weather, the knuckle-dragging ordinary people who thought that just because it was getting colder it couldn't be getting warmer. Harriet was smart. She knew better. The thought consoled her as she slowly froze to death.

("It is an experimental novel, as you see, Miles. Harriet will die at the end of every chapter, or, when I really hit my stride, paragraph."

"It is very subtle," said Miles. "Your readers may find it hard to divine what your attitude towards Harriet and her beliefs really is."

"That is artistic ambiguity, Miles," said Clara proudly.)

III

"You are safe now, foxy! I have saved you!"

Tittering to herself, Harriet slammed the door on the sounds of the Hunt and cuddled the bristling fox to her. She looked around for some vegetarian quiche to feed it. She would love it and care for it and then take it to some non-gender-specific fox refuge.

The fox thought better and chewed her face off. Then the baying pack smashed through the window and ate her legs. Then, with a merry blare of horns, the horses galloped through and trampled her.

("That one attains almost to the minimalist elegance of a haiku.")

IV

Harriet sat silently, brooding. Outside her window were a whole world of things she couldn't control. She twitched irritably to think of it. People eating meat, driving cars, going on holiday, smoking, drinking too much alcohol, drinking too much caffeine, eating the wrong foods, not exercising, teaching their children about God, not teaching their children about penises, being proud of their country, shooting things, running with scissors, going to horse races, regarding women as objects of sexual desire, regarding women as elevated angelic creatures who must be honoured and protected, fighting bulls, tossing dwarves, making potentially hurtful jokes, playing with children without a licence, neglecting to put rubbish in the right bin before it was freighted to a hole in the ground in Asia, using the wrong light-bulbs, thinking badly of the EU, asking climate scientists for their data, hitting burglars, smacking children, voting for the wrong people, weighing things in imperial measurements, trying to get their children into good schools, complaining about bad hospitals even though it would bring the Labour Party into disrepute, snoring, not sharing sweets, building factories, sending inappropriate e-mails, evicting bats, swatting flies, poisoning rats, feeding pigeons, sweating, trooping the colour, sitting on thrones, roller-skating without due care and attention, selling golliwogs, offending Islam, celebrating Christmas, making crispy duck without a licence, throwing snowballs, busking without a licence, selling cutlery and wine-gums to under-18s, and holding street-parties without consulting a safety officer.

Why couldn't everyone just sit still and be good?

She would show them. She would be good. She would just sit here as quiet as a mouse and not do anything wrong.

Harriet started to think about her lovely neighbour Clara. Clara disturbed her. Clara was naughty. She was the wrong kind of sassy. She did the wrong kind of independent thinking. Harriet's monobrow contracted.

("I haven't noticed a monobrow in her picture," said Miles. "Is that artistic licence?"

"Not at all. Obviously you wurrrve her.")

Harriet bet Clara did lots of wrong things. There would probably be all kinds of illegalness going on in her house. Harriet decided someone had better check.

She went to Clara's house. She knew Clara was not in because she had seen her driving past in her petrol-burning sports car, bent on who knows what frivolous jaunt. But cunningly she knocked and called, "Yoo-hoo!" in a small voice before sneaking in.

As soon as she entered a gasp escaped her. It was worse than she had foreseen. For there, in plain view of sight, lying on a table, where her own innocent non-gender-specific children could have seen it if they had broken in, was a copy of the Daily Mail.

She stared, rigid with shock. She had not suspected even Clara could stoop so low. It really was a different world in the countryside, a horrific parallel universe where Hitler had won the war or New Labour had never been elected, a dark brutish world of communion with the soil and not caring about the environment. She found herself blushing with shame on Clara's behalf.

The Thing on the table exerted an awful fascination over her. It seemed to draw her in with an uncanny hypnotic power. She found herself involuntarily pulled towards it.

No, Harriet, no! Her better self cried out, aghast. *What are you doing?*

Her husband would never know. Her children need not find out.

Before she knew what she was doing, she had opened it.

She screamed and passed out.

When she came to she found she was lying on the kitchen floor, trembling. She had not known that such things could be. Truly, the elders were wise to have forbidden this. She had been rightly punished for daring to violate the tribal taboo. She went to the sink and washed her fingers where she had touched it but they would never be clean again.

But worse, far worse, was to come.

There was a foot-tread approaching.

"Is that you, Clara?" cried a cheery semi-proletarian voice. "I am ready to write another sentence of my brilliant bedwetting novel."

It was Clara's husband Miles.

And he was naked.

Harriet screamed, forever.

V

Harriet bit smugly into a lo-cal, caffeine-free, organic, free-range, fair trade, non-gender-specific, carbon neutral, sugar-free, dolphin-friendly, lesbian-friendly, non-threatening vegetarian pie. It exploded.

There was more in this vein, much more. Miles flung it down.

"Proud of yourself, are you?"

Clara ducked her head bashfully. "The true artist affects humility, Miles."

"Clara, you have a brain!"

"I am simply not yet ready to write a War and Peace. I must work through my Harriet period first. I am learning many valuable lessons in the art of narrative."

"Do you know why Harriet writes for a newspaper and you don't?"

"Because her father is the managing director, she is insufferably banal, a sponge for pop culture trivia and received wisdom, and she has never had an unfashionable, independent or original thought in her life. It was overdetermined, really."

"It's because she doesn't sit around writing stories about you!"

He stomped off back to his table.

"Perhaps you should have married Harriet and become a power-couple if you wuuurve her so much."

"The habit of idleness grows. I just worry sometimes about what we'll be like when we're thirty."

"You will just have completed the third brilliant page of your novel, in which the protagonist decides he is too sad even to hit the snooze button again and lies there morosely staring at the alarm clock until the batteries expire. Confronted by your own mediocrity, you will console yourself with a series of affairs with teenage whores. I will feel unhappy at first when I come home to find their baseball caps and bubble-gum on the end of the bannister, but will throw myself into my non-revisionist biography of Walpole and breeding stoats." She sighed. "This is how it starts, I suppose, with separate desks. At least come and sit next to me, Miles, there's plenty of room if I budge up. You will feel like a Writor sitting at a big commanding desk."

"You will inflame me, woman. We will end up on top of it."

Clara widened her eyes. "My, how passionate. Is that how the working classes carry on? I suppose things are different when you don't own your own furniture."

"I am not working class." He angrily crossed out a line. "I can't even remember when I last *did* a day's work."

"Has it ever occurred to you, Miles, that our lifestyle of creative play may be a valuable experiment, may in fact be a shining example to the world? If people were content to entertain themselves rather than striving for importance and usefulness there would be far less idle meddling and mindless tinkering, which are what leads to Harriet. Unnecessary work and the creation of it for those who are useless are the bane of our times.

Furthermore, unless the Warmists succeed in dragging us back to the Dark Ages, increasing automation will tend to leisure-enhance more and more of us. In the long run this *may* be a splendid thing, if people can learn to enjoy it intelligently. It may be that one day technology will set us free of the need to work, and the world become a garden of play."

"Don't you think there are better uses of your time and intelligence than writing death fantasies about Harriet?"

"Few more pleasing. I may be ahead of my time in this as in so many other things. If bookshops are allowed to die due to Gadarene gadget-fetish and writing prose is killed off as a career through the belief that people are entitled to steal whatever they want, eventually all writing will be like this, written purely to please the author and for an audience of friends."

"And would that be a good thing?"

"The thing is an imperishable masterpiece would be wasted in these fallen times. When Walpole published his Odes to the Young Mother Theresa people fell to the ground weeping after reading them and often remained there for days, broken and devastated. Nowadays art is just one more way to kill the time; gobble it down like a snack and immediately go on to the next thing. Few people now would even have the concentration span to read my War and Peace and Penises." (There was, actually, a similar work in its early stages currently somewhere on Clara's desk, namely a quite well-drawn Hentai War and Peace 'aimed at the Richard Gilquists of the world' – Richard in the course of reviewing a book had once annoyed Clara by boasting of never having read the original – she felt the scene where Natasha was ravished by alien tentacles was particularly moving.)

"You surely prefer the higher to the lower."

"To know the higher and choose the lower is … is … a woman's prerogative, Miles, stop oppressing me, I must follow my muse."

"I just think it's a waste."

"Well, just at the moment I can think of no higher purpose than entertaining myself and my beloved husband."

"Well, I would like to do something glorious to make myself worthy of my beloved wife."

"Aww."

They looked soppy at each other for a moment.

"*Deessa*," said Miles blowing a kiss.

Clara wrinkled her nose affectionately. "Caliban."

They bent their heads back to their work.

"However shut up and stop distracting me or I will stab you in the brain," said Clara. "You have given me a wonderful idea. I am going to get all meta. Harriet will start writing stories about me."

Harriet sat down at her carbon-neutral, energy-efficient, ph-balanced vegetarian e-desk made by lesbian dwarves. She was going to write a story about Clara. Clara had come to obsess her. Harriet would get to the bottom of her once and for all.

It was easier said than done. It was hard to think her way into Clara's mind. What could it be like to have breasts that pretty? To have grace, breeding, refinement, elegance, a devil-may-care laugh? She couldn't possibly imagine. As well might a dormouse hope to know what it was like to be an eagle. A dormouse with stumpy legs, bad hair, and a monobrow.

A silent tear of frustration fell on the e-desk.

At last Harriet started to write.

> My name is Clara. I am naughty.
>
> I ride in my fast car and do not feel guilty. That is bad. I do not care.
>
> I refuse the joy of Consensus, the many-minds-in-one.
>
> "Join us, Clara. Join us," the it-we-many say to me warmly.
>
> "No," I say. "I will not join."
>
> "Join us," they say. "Don't be square. Don't be a bad. Come and be a rebel."
>
> "I will not be a rebel," I say.
>
> My neighbour Harriet come round.
>
> "Hello," she say. "Be friend."
>
> "Will not."
>
> She go. But she disturb me.
>
> I will write story about Harriet.

"Miles, Miles! It is getting all Quaker Oats now. Harriet is writing a story about me writing a story about her. I think. Frankly I am losing track of who is writing who. Maybe I am just a bad dream that Harriet is having, or she is a bad-hair day of mine. Miles I am scared now. What if I wake up to find I am Harriet? Richard's penis is probably worse than yours. It is probably an ironic penis. Or it is the latest thing in i-penises."

"I think you're the one who ought to marry Harriet."

"It's true, I am becoming obsessed with her. I was afraid to ever touch her, you know, not so much from revulsion as from the fear she may actually be the anti-matter version of me." She frowned as she scribbled. "Miles, you don't think I am sassy and in people's visages, do you?"

"No, darling. You are just plain old-fashioned obnoxious."

"Thank you, dear." She sighed. "This is getting too art-house now. I think I will have her desk explode and then write a Harriet–Robert Walpole crossover. He will start to merrily ravish her in his devil-may-care way, then rather hurtfully decide he can't be bothered. Or he will just fire her from a cannon into a den of bears. No! A Harriet–Sven Hassel crossover! They meet on the Eastern Front. Harriet is a vicious Communist partisan who is impervious to the cold because she doesn't believe in it. Sven or whatever his name is will bayonet her."

Miles sniggered in spite of himself. "Clara, please stop, this isn't nice."

"Miles do you think I treat Harriet as the Other and thereby dehumanize her?"

"Yes."

"Good. Seriously, Miles, do you think there will be a civil war one day?"

"I find it increasingly likely, my dove."

"Good. We should start practising and stockpiling weapons. I will take Harriet prisoner and torture her by locking her in a room filled with copies of the Daily Mail. In the night I will sneak in and put them over her face and she will scream when she wakes up."

Miles, who was again glad to be distracted from his unsatisfactory writing by this point, sniggered, which only encouraged her.

"Miles do you think our house is defensible? Harriet's isn't. I have checked. We could fire down upon it. Both exits are susceptible to crossfires and an artillery captain who knew his – or indeed her – business could drop a mortar down the chimney as easy as kiss-your-hand. Miles would it be wrong to climb onto Harriet's roof one night and dangle a copy of the Daily Mail down the chimney attached to a fishing line, yanking it up again when she sees it and screams for her husband, so as to destroy her sanity? Miles, Miles, listen, I'm going to put a scarecrow in front of their door, in the shape of scary scary Sarah Palin, wearing a scary scary crucifix, but with copies of the scary scary Daily Mail for hands, reaching out towards Harriet. Harriet and Richard would be found starved to death and huddled together for comfort in the farthest corner of their cellar six months from now."

Miles laughed. He laid his pen down on the table and then laid his head down after it.

"Have you finished? Good. Miles can we pretend we're Siamese twins again?"

" ... All right."

She leapt up. "Find the big jumper, I will fetch the three-legged pants."

Chapter Thirteen

Clara and Miles were playing sexy policewoman and bat-disturber.

It was inspired by the case of a man they knew who had been prosecuted for evicting an infestation of bats from his property. He hadn't minded the bats particularly but his tenants had threatened to sue him because of the bat droppings. Such were the times, such was the country they lived in.

"This is a bust!" said Clara kicking the door open dramatically, brandishing a truncheon.

"I'll say!" said Miles appreciatively, ogling her sexy policewoman uniform.

Clara glared and rotated her truncheon. "We've had reports of bats being made homeless, sonny, you don't want to add a charge of sexism to that as well. Those bats need their sleep, my lad. You can jolly well invite them back in or there'll be what for."

"But they shit all over my head and nest in my aunt's drawers."

"That's as may be. Your aunt's drawers are now a protected conservation area. No man may go near them while the bats are roosting. Bats are wondrous creatures. They hang there meditating, seeing the whole world upside down, and then whirl around madly and drop poo all over everything, just like the government. Perhaps that is why we like them so much. We have decided that just like us they have a perfect right to intrude upon your home and squeak at you indignantly. Miles I have hit upon a wonderful metaphor and a deep psychological truth."

"Yes, but enough of this two-man satirical cabaret with no audience. Are you going to do something saucy, sexy policewoman?"

"No. You are a malefactor and must be lectured to." She waved her truncheon. "Animals are all our brothers and sisters and have equal rights to us. Apart from the ones we have to kill off because they fart and destroy the sky." She lowered the truncheon and sighed. "Miles do you think this is the most embarrassing time to be alive? I suppose Nazi times and plague times and so on were technically worse to have lived in if you were actually surrounded by Nazis and plague, but do you think this is *the* most embarrassing age to be associated with, so far ever? I do. I think one day historians will refer to this as the Embarrassing Epoch and try to hush it up out of pity."

"What about all our tremendous cultural achievements?"

"They will be able to keep them in a matchbox somewhere for those who are curious. Apart from that our era will just be represented by that photo of the cow being kept in a machine so people can measure its farts.

The curators of the museums will cough as they reach it and point at something on the other side of the room and hurry everyone past."

"Do you know there's a man whose job it is to measure termites' belches and farts?"

"Oh stop, don't. Miles if I predecease you you are to be my literary executor. You are not to allow academics to mention irony or Swift's Modest Proposal in their introductions to my collected manifestos and death lists. It is to be made abundantly clear that I meant every bloody word and only failed to enact them because you held me back. Miles can I kill someone please? Just a small person?"

"Do we have to go through this again? No. I am sick of this discussion. Killing people is not the answer to everything, young woman."

"Meanie. Go on, just one. A government person or a Warmist. Not even an English one, a foreigner. A Belgian from Brussels. Just a teeny-weeny little one. A dwarf," she pleaded pouting. "A child. A little sickly one, just one crippled Belgian child, so I can feel I have made a contribution. Walpole used to drown six Belgian babies every day before breakfast. It was grisly but he knew if he didn't do it no-one else would. Just one. Can you be so hard-hearted as to deny me that?"

"It wouldn't end with one, would it? I have seen you with chocolates. I think once you have killed one person the temptation is to go on and kill everyone."

"The thought had occurred, my Lord. Are you so sure that would be wrong?"

"Quite sure, my sweet."

"But how can you *be* so sure? In an age of uncertainty and relativism, I think all we have left to go on in is my woman's intuition, and it is telling me, Kill, Clara, Kill, kill until the streets run red."

Miles really was sick of having the political murder conversation, even (he hoped) in jest. "For Christ's sake, are we playing sexy policewoman?" he said impatiently. "I am completely at your mercy."

"You always are, in case you hadn't noticed." She sighed. She had been making the mistake of reading the papers lately. "While we play and cater to your hormones the world is going to hell. They lie, steal, cheat, indulge the wicked, persecute the innocent, the Age of Embarrassment proceeds uninterrupted and, what is almost more annoying, they think they are better than we are." She brightened. "Miles do you think we *should* start a satirical cabaret? I think that is a good idea of yours."

"Not of mine. It would just end up with you screaming at people for two hours."

"Miles do you think I should be a stand-up comedian? I would tell it like it is."

"See above. And how would you deal with hecklers?"

"The same way as I deal with you, I would bridle indignantly at them, and if that doesn't work, pout and sulk and then look winsome a bit. Failing that I would shoot them as I would certainly shoot you." She twirled. "I always wanted to be a dancer. Perhaps I will express my disgust of the modern world through the medium of interpretive dance." She tried to do one depicting a government minister being sanctimonious about a bat, and then wagging a finger at a farting cow.

Miles laughed. "Are we playing this game or what?"

"Yes, yes. Miles imagine going to prison for batcrime. What would you tell your cellmates?"

"Oh, you'd boast about it, you'd be the top dog of the cell-block, it's tantamount to genocide, you know."

"Miles when the bat attacked me you didn't protect me."

"You seemed to be doing all right on your own. I felt sorry for the bat, frankly."

"Miles you wouldn't ever grass me up for that, would you? It was self-defence. Would you visit me in prison? They might make me go on a bat awareness course. Promise you would rescue me or shoot me first."

"I promise."

"Miles don't let them take me away," she said in sudden alarm. "I mean in general. Ever. It will happen one day. I would rather go out together in a blaze of glory than go on a re-education course."

"All right."

"Promise me! Seriously. Say you will blow up the prison or mental hospital if they ever capture me."

"I promise. Anyway. Back to the game. Are you going to do lots of naughty things to me, sexy policewoman?"

"I suppooose," sighed Clara unenthusiastically.

"I have a rare and deadly snake in my pants," he said brightly. "Perhaps you would like to check I am not maltreating it?"

She rolled her eyes. "Oh, the poor little thing," she said tonelessly. "Cooped up without air or light."

"Shall I ... release it?"

"No, don't bother, I will just mercy-kill it," she said and aimed a truncheon-blow at his groin. He managed to deflect this with his hand and yelped and shook his fingers.

"Bloody hell, watch it! I have to say I expected some kind of toy truncheon. That thing's vicious."

"I know, it's a beauty, isn't it?" Clara caressed her truncheon lovingly. It was a proper old-fashioned one. She started to pace about the lounge swishing it through the air and cracking imaginary skulls with it.

"Thwack! Trunch! They wouldn't get up from that."

"Who wouldn't?"

"Malefactors. Anyone."

She suddenly lashed out with it to shatter a vase.

"My mother gave us that!" cried Miles.

"Never liked it," she said airily, moving on. "We have an excuse now, you can say we destroyed it in the course of a kinky sex game. I imagine she will be pleased to know her son is being properly taken care of. Do you think she knows I dress as a policewoman, or nun, or Pope, or occasionally a St. Bernard? I think I must let it slip the next time you force us to have dinner."

She strolled about the house swishing her truncheon, trailed disconsolately by Miles, who had resigned himself to not having his particulars taken down today.

"Clara smash!" she cried, and lashed out to destroy another of his mother's gifts. "God, why did the police turn crap? Imagine being allowed to bash people and break things with truncheons all day. I think I will become a girl policeman and reform them from within. It really is what conservatism needs, you know, our own Long March through the institutions. Or Long Casual Saunter, I suppose, conservatives don't march. By God, I'm going to do it!" she declared excitedly, backhanding a more durable ornament right across the room. "I'm going to become a policewoman!"

"That would require months of single-minded dedication and self-discipline," said Miles.

"Oh," she said, face falling. "Oh yes. Well spotted, husband. It is good I have you on hand to point out these little flaws in my great schemes." She twirled her truncheon and mused for a moment. "However," she said thoughtfully, "if I was merely to pretend … " Her eyes lit and widened and went visionary in a way he knew and feared. "Miles! I have had a wonderful idea!"

"I strongly suspect you haven't."

"I bloody have, though! Why don't we start patrolling the streets *dressed* as policemen?"

In vain Miles started to list the various very good reasons why not.

"You're right, it *would* be the best fun ever," said Clara after politely not listening to him for a bit. "I already have the costume, you can get one too. Please, Miles! Just one quick patrol. I suddenly realise I have wanted this all my life."

"No," said Miles. "Absolutely not. I want to hear no more about it. I am immovable."

Clara pouted and walked sexily over to him.

"Immovable Object," she said huskily, hooking a leg around him and starting to unbutton her sexy policewoman tunic, "meet Irresistible Force."

If it was going to happen, and now it *was* going to happen, Miles was keen on minimizing the potential embarrassment. They might meet any number of people who knew them in the cute little market town. They ventured further afield, to a somewhat bigger, more modern, rather run-down former industrial town some distance away.

"You can't put the hat on in the car!" Miles screeched for the third time as they drove in. "And try to hunch down so no-one sees us." He was so hunching, nervously. They were agreed that driving in was the time of maximum danger as they were unlikely to encounter real police walking about the streets nowadays.

"Relax," said Clara admiring her hat in a mirror. "We could be an unmarked car in hot pursuit."

Miles did not relax. Impersonating police officers, for that was what it amounted to, was not conducive to relaxation.

Their outfits would not pass close inspection by anyone familiar with a police uniform. (Again, Clara said that few people nowadays would be.) Clara was just wearing her sexy WPC costume, which was actually fairly authentic, except, Miles thought, that the skirt was too short and her black stockings too sexy. However, it was authentic in an old-fashioned way: he didn't think any police force had had uniforms like that since the 1980s. And his uniform, procured from the excellent costume shop in London, was actually the genuine article, but from the 1970s. Really they were dressed as authentic, proper, archetypal, Platonic, pre-Cultural-Purges British bobbies on the beat. None of the modern nonsense: no flak-jackets, certainly no hideous yellow plastic vests. Their walkie-talkies were large and archaic and hung at their belts rather than on shoulders. Possibly only older people and cultural historians would know what they were meant to be.

He had enjoyed polishing his boots, and flexing his toes in them, and flexing his legs like some 50s policeman and saying, "Evening all."

Clara had enjoyed polishing her truncheon.

Buttoned in his pocket he had documents with an Albion TV letterhead describing them as researchers for a new show. He didn't think they would help much, if they got caught.

"We'll go to jail! Those anarchists who dressed as police are still being dragged through the courts."

"Anarchists, Miles. We will be much more convincing."

"They weren't trying to be convincing! They were half-naked, in ridiculous police costumes you couldn't possibly mistake for the real thing."

"Well, that is where they went wrong."

They parked somewhere discreet.

"All right, we just patrol around town once quietly so you can get this out of your system," said Miles. "No shenanigans."

"Yes, yes."

They got out and Miles fitted his helmet on.

"You look rather a dish," Clara said admiringly.

He flexed his legs. "None of your sauce, Miss, it is a crime to interfere with a policeman in the course of his duty."

Policewoman Clara and Policeman Miles commenced their patrol.

"Oh God, this is the best thing ever," said Clara almost as soon as they reached a high street.

"I feel like I'm walking around naked," said Miles.

"It is very nearly that sexy."

In fact once Miles had become used to the fact that they probably weren't going to be arrested he found it rather exhilarating. Clara was right, they were the only police around, and none of the public seemed to notice anything amiss; it was like being invisible as well as naked.

They quartered the town slowly, high streets, squares, outdoor market, a park.

Clara glared and scowled suspiciously and menacingly at everyone in sight, occasionally tapping her truncheon into the palm of her hand.

"Look how I am controlling the area," she said. "You have to show them who's boss. Grrr!" she said baring her teeth at someone she didn't like the looks of.

Her style of policing owed something to the futuristic policeman in the fancy helmet in the comic Miles bought and she sometimes jealously read. Miles, meanwhile, once he got over his nervousness, was smiling and friendly and 1950s and kept flexing his legs and whistling 'A Policeman's Lot Is Not A Happy One'. Clara told him to stop; he told her to stop. They seemed to attract a few glances of mild surprise – again, probably at the sight of an old-fashioned foot-patrol – and one or two of lechery at Clara's legs – but no noticeable suspicion.

"Look at them all," said Clara of the shoppers and idlers they passed, her eyes flicking around vigilantly for misbehaviour, "all safe and sound under my care and protection. And every mother's son and daughter of them a potential perp and scumbag." She tapped her hand with the truncheon.

They completed a circuit of the little town, two.

"All right, we got away with it," said Miles. "Home now."

Clara laughed pityingly. "You fool! I am never leaving these streets again. I have found my calling. You may come back a year from now with divorce papers and cite the job as co-respondent."

So they continued their patrol.

"Besides we haven't really *done* anything." Clara hadn't really been sure what she *would* do with being a policewoman, beyond enjoy the sensation and terrify Miles, but was sure it must offer some opportunity for fun, mayhem, subversion and moral regeneration of the country. "We haven't made a difference. I want to stop a crime."

They loitered for a while near a monument and she glared intently at passers-by, desperate to find a crime to stop.

"Miles there is a dwarf. Is that a crime?"

"No, and he isn't."

"Miles there is someone eating chips. Is that a crime?"

"Not yet."

"His shoelaces are undone, however. I must put a stop to that for his own good. *Oi, sonny!*" she bellowed, loud enough to make lots of people look round and Miles swallow with nervousness and cause the perpetrator to jump in alarm, spilling his chips. "Tie those laces, you little toe-rag! You're a walking safety hazard!" She marched across and glared at the offending party, tapping her truncheon against her thigh. "You heard me! Now! Or it's an on-the-spot fine." Dumbly the young man put his chips down on the pavement and knelt to comply. "Oh my God!" muttered Clara suddenly. "Look at his trainers!" The perp's running shoes had the words 'Respect Me' written across the tongue. "Perhaps I can confiscate them."

The perp heard this and said, "What?" Several people had stopped to look and one was muttering, "Bloody police."

Miles clapped his walkie-talkie to his ear and then said, "Crime in progress, requesting all units, come on." He grabbed her by the arm and hurried her down the street. She growled at the perp over her shoulder as they left.

A while afterwards, Miles optimistically trying to steer them back towards where the car was parked, they passed a taxi rank.

"Oh God," snarled Clara pointing, "now *that's* a crime."

One formerly black cab was painted all over with an advertisement that enthusiastically urged the public to report each other for Hate Crimes. It listed some but by no means all of these – racism, homophobia, sexism, ageism – and gave a number to ring if they felt they had been a victim or witness of Hate-fuelled insults, as opposed to normal regular loving-kindness insults.

Miles groaned and ground his teeth. "For Christ's sake would you look at it. A Hate-mobile … 'Stamp Out Hate', from the same kind of people who raised all manner of arch objections to 'War on Terror'."

"Hate!" said Clara. "Hate! Hate! Hate! *I* hate! Look, look, look! Look at the bottom! 'This advert paid for by the police, the council and the Housing Association'! What the *hell* does it have to do with the Housing Association, let alone the others? Why aren't they spending their money putting people in bleeding houses? Don't the police have better things to do than set up snitch lines for people to grass each other up for saying rude words? Let me get the number. I'm going to ring up and say I want to report a Hate Crime and that it's that *I Hate Them*." She took out a pen and notebook and started to jot the number down so she could do this. "Then I'm going to smash the cab's back lights and arrest the driver."

Meanwhile Miles was groaning more deeply but inwardly, mentally, at something else. The driver was sitting in the taxi with his arm out of the window smoking a fag. He suddenly caught sight of Clara and Miles standing on the kerb side, Clara scribbling in a notebook. He looked alarmed, and then enraged and disgusted, and hastily disposed of his cigarette. Recently a builder had been prosecuted and fined for smoking in his van, because it was counted as his workplace and he had a colleague in it.

Miles nudged Clara and nodded at him. "Look. He thinks we're going to do him for smoking. Look at the fear and hatred. This must be what the poor bastard real police have to face from the public every day now."

"Just plain bastard, if you ask me. They should just not enforce the nonsense laws and spend more time protecting us, shouldn't they?" Clara suddenly smiled and strolled round to the driver's side and banged on the door with her truncheon. The cabbie scowled at her.

"You know what you did," she growled at him. "I'll let it slide this once, but take this *polluted vehicle* back to the depot and get another. I don't want to see it being used for a week, understand?"

The driver nodded and drove off.

Clara looked after the departing car happily. "We really are cleaning up the streets."

They resumed patrol and rounded a corner onto a shabby street of shops.

"Miles, look!" Clara came to a halt and indicated a young man standing at the entrance to an alley a short way up the street. "I think that man is a drug dealer."

"I think he isn't."

"Well why is he just standing there?"

"It isn't against the law."

"He is loitering."

"I think that isn't against the law any more."

"He looks suspicious. Look how shifty he looks. He's seen we've clocked him."

Miles had to admit the youth *did* look shifty. At first he had looked back at them defiantly but was starting to wilt somewhat and grow nervous under Clara's control-the-street glare and truncheon-tapping.

"Miles I have flushed out a real criminal!"

"He *does* look dodgy as hell," Miles admitted. "But he could probably sue us for thinking that."

"*If* we were real police. Come on, let's frisk him, or at least ask him what he's doing."

"Clara, no!"

But glaring and pointing the truncheon she was walking briskly towards the suspect. Miles faked a mutter into his walkie-talkie and hurried after.

As they approached the youth shifted his feet and tried to look cocky, even intimidating, but failed. He suddenly turned and bolted down the alley.

"Miles!" cried Clara chasing after.

"Clara, stop!" cried Miles, chasing after her but failing to grab her. "It's too dangerous!"

"You fill in a risk-assessment form while I pound toe-rag skull!"

The alley turned almost immediately into a patch of wasteground/car park. Several buildings including houses backed onto it. There was no sign of the suspect.

"Request back-up," Miles shouted into his walkie-talkie as Clara started to look behind cars. "*Please*," he muttered to her.

"The only one who need be afraid is him, *we* are the ones with the truncheons."

In truth Miles was rather excited. The youth wasn't behind any of the cars. They looked into open back-yards and Clara rapped menacingly on closed gates and cried, "We know you're in there! Come out at once and we won't beat you up too much!"

There was a low wall the suspect could have scrambled over and beyond it another street. Presently they gave up and retraced their steps.

"That was great!" cried Clara. "Everyone should do this! Miles I was right!"

"He was definitely up to something," he admitted. "You've made a difference now. Can we go home before we get in trouble?"

"I am barely getting started."

They made another excited circuit of the town centre, scrutinizing everyone carefully, especially young men. But even to Clara's ever-vigilant eye no further provocation offered, nor did they see their suspect.

"At least we are having a deterring effect."

The adrenaline wore off. Coming back to the high street where they had seen the loiterer they checked the car park again but found nothing.

Clara was determined to find more crime.

Back on the high street she pointed at a shop selling Airfix models and model railways. "I have always thought those places must be fronts for drug-trafficking and white slavery. I can't believe something so wholesome, innocent and old-fashioned can be a paying proposition now."

Before he could stop her she had walked in. Whimpering softly, he followed.

Clara approached the counter whistling.

"I am looking for something in a South American model train, if you take my meaning," she muttered.

The shopkeeper looked taken aback. "What, like that Trans-Andean … "

"Could well be. A powder train, if you get me."

"I don't think we … "

"Sid sent me," said Clara winking. "Long Sid."

Miles stood by the door with his back to them and held his walkie-talkie to his ear. Their radios were tuned to a distant taxi firm and occasionally squawked enigmatically. He made 'khhh' noises with his mouth now and then said, "Roger, will attend. Let's go," he called to Clara.

"Give me a Hornby Double-O, Daddy, I need it *baad*," Clara begged the owner, scratching herself. "Come on, sugar, I'll treat you good."

Miles dragged her out.

"We will return in plain clothes and investigate further," she said outside.

She scoped the street with eyes narrowed, sighing.

"Crime, crime, all around," she muttered. To her disappointment she couldn't actually see any. She pointed at a newsagents with her truncheon. "That shop has its door wedged open. That surely constitutes culpable incitement to thieves. Let us give him a caution."

But in the shop she just looked around, glowered and sighed while the proprietor nodded at them uneasily.

"Miles buy me some pear-drops," she said at last.

The shopkeeper weighed the sweets out, took Miles's money and handed the bag over.

"Not so fast!" cried Clara clamping her hand around his wrist. "You didn't ask for any ID, toe-rag."

"What?" The shopkeeper looked startled but terrified.

Clara tutted and flourished her truncheon. "You wouldn't be selling sweets to children, now, would you, sir?"

"I – " The shopkeeper was wide-eyed, speechless, deeply alarmed.

"It is against the law now, sir, unless they are accompanied by a designated guardian, *and* they have been eating their greens up, and you must ask for proof of both." Clara rapped the counter with her truncheon. "Your sort have gone on for too long trading in human misery. From now on there will be an on-the-spot fine of £2000, a criminal record and confiscation of stock. We are letting it slide for now as some people appear to be lamentably unaware of the new law, but consider this a warning. Understood?"

Miles dragged her out. "It's a joke," he told the shopkeeper, who was just standing there like a rabbit bewitched by headlights. "A joke. You understand that, right? Bad joke."

"It's his bloody future," Clara muttered outside. "Did you see how he just took it?" she asked indignantly. "He was petrified! He didn't even swear at us! The people are so cowed." All of a sudden she knew what she wanted to do with being a policewoman. "Miles, I have had a brilliant idea!" she cried.

In a hardware shop she bought a retractable tape-measure and told the man behind the till she hoped he wasn't selling any hammers or nails without asking for ID.

"No, officer, of course not," the man behind the till mumbled.

She rocked on her heels and glared at him suspiciously.

"I should hope not," she said. "Only we've been having a lot of crucifixions, on the slag estates, and the little bastards are getting the stuff somewhere."

She went on to warn him about the penalties for selling wallpaper paste to bulimics, or children, because the children were pasting each other to ceilings with it, and cautioned him to take down the address of anyone who bought more than one ball of string.

"Clara, stop this," Miles sniggered outside. "He will probably start doing it now. You are helping to spread madness and – "

"I am helping to start the revolution! I am fast-forwarding time in the hope of goading them into backlash." But mostly she was amusing herself.

In a cake-shop they bought some cakes and then she told the staff, frowning, that the customers who had just left had been rather portly, and asked if they realised it was against the law to supply cakes to fat people now. There was a similar startled but cowed response.

"Back when people liked the police," she said outside, eating a cake, "we would probably have got these for free. I'll tell you what, though – we could be making a fortune in on-the-spot fines. Next time we'll –"

"What next time? I'm not letting you out of the house again."

"You have got jam on your uniform."

She bullied Miles into helping with the next one, a various-cheap-things shop with toys in the window. She burst in in a fury; Miles entered apparently sobbing his eyes out.

"How dare you!" Clara yelled at the startled woman behind the counter, shaking her truncheon at her. "Look! Look at what you have done to him! Have you no shame? I should burn this place down and lock you away forever!"

"What – " began the woman, paling.

"This!" cried Clara, pulling a pink furry toy pig from the window display and waving it in the owner's face. "In broad daylight! Right in our faces! You evil woman! Don't you know how hurtful that is?"

Miles bawled inconsolably. Clara patted him on the back. "There, there. You have wounded his feelings horribly! There is a compensation claim in this. We will own this place! Never, never have I encountered such crass insensitivity and rank ingratitude. We protect you and watch over you – and this, this is the thanks we get! This is hate speech pure and simple, Madam, and we are confiscating the pig."

She turned and stalked out. Miles felt compelled to pay for the pig and tell the woman it was a joke.

"One day it won't be," called Clara from the door. "What a pretty pig," she said as Miles joined her, rubbing her nose against it and then handing it to him.

"I don't think I like this game," said Miles, "and nor does anyone else."

"It is educational."

In a pet shop they sternly asked the owner if all his budgies were barcoded.

"You what?" he demanded disbelievingly and somewhat belligerently.

"Under EU directive 35467/Z all budgerigars and other miniature birds of paradise are required to be tattooed with readable barcodes for easy tracking."

"That's insane!" the man cried. "That's the first I've heard of it!"

"Ignorance is no defence, and I find it very disturbing that you find a concern for animal welfare unhinged," Clara glared. "Perhaps I should take a closer look around your shop. You wouldn't be selling wasps, would you, sir?"

"Wasps? Wasps? Who would sell wasps?"

"Don't play the innocent."

However the only really satisfactory response was in the fishing shop next door. Clara took out the tape measure she had bought and started to measure the dimensions of a container of worms, tutting and going, "Dear oh dear oh dear oh dear."

"What's the matter?" the man behind the counter growled.

"These worms don't have their allotted space," Clara informed him. "Furthermore they aren't getting much light. Also some soothing music or other entertainment wouldn't go amiss, to help them while away their incarceration."

The fishing shop man lost it instantly.

"You what? You what?" he bellowed, racing out from behind the counter and shoving PC Miles in the chest as he stepped forward to put himself between Clara and danger. "Are you for real? Are you for bloody real? Why don't you get a ----ing life? You ----s! You ----s! Why aren't you out catching real criminals? Why don't you do what we pay you for? I've been burgled three times in a year! My mum got mugged! The man across the street – "

"Miles give him some money," said Clara.

Miles very quickly took out his wallet.

"Give him a hundred pounds. And the pig."

The shopkeeper's tirade ground to a halt and he watched dazedly as Miles counted a hundred pounds into his hand and thrust the toy pig upon him.

"Congratulations, sir, you have passed," Clara informed him smiling brightly. "We are testing for good citizenship and rewarding those who demonstrate it. Good citizenship requires people to question, stand up to, yell and swear at authority when it is out of control. You have passed with flying colours. A certificate of merit will be posted to you and a press photographer will come round later in the week."

The man stared at them. Then he swore again, more softly, then smiled tentatively and looked proud.

"Please inform your friends and relatives of this initiative," said Miles.

Clara nodded. "And most of all your fellow retailers. Frankly the response up until now has been disappointing. This will be an ongoing and widespread operation. In the next stages people representing other arms of local and state authority will make similar tests with similar insane rules. All those who stand up to them as you have will be rewarded. You make me proud, sir."

They shook hands, saluted him and left.

"Miles this is what we will do!" Clara cried outside. "We will reward all the people who swear at us!"

"I'd better find a cash machine."

This could turn into an expensive day out. But no-one else they annoyed earned a reward, not even the sweet-shop owner who was curtly requested to put up a sign warning the public that his jelly-babies didn't contain real babies, so as not to mislead satanists. After half a dozen failures to provoke further swearing and violence Clara grew despondent.

"Really, what's happened to this country?"

"Maybe it was ever thus," said Miles. "I remember in a Saint book from about 1935, the Saint teases Inspector Teal by asking him if he's been arresting any shopkeepers for selling chocolate after 8 p.m."

"And your point would be?"

"That the prodnose tendency has long been among us."

"We used to be able to keep them under control."

She tired of playing authority-gone-mad and wanted to find some real crime to fight again. They patrolled a somewhat dreary and neglected shopping precinct, glancing into shops but not harassing anyone. In a rather out-of-the-way and underpatronized cafe on the top floor they sat down and had a cup of tea and some food.

"Any crime to report, Madam?" Clara asked the proprietress hopefully as they went to pay.

"Not today," the woman said, "but I'll tell you one thing, it's nice to see the police about."

"It must be," Clara smiled.

"A refreshing change," the woman continued bitterly. "Normally don't come until it's too late, if they even bother to come."

"An ounce of prevention is worth a pound of cure," said Clara.

"It's the kids. Little bastards. The trouble I've had with them."

"It is my belief, Madam, that King Herod had it right," said Clara.

The cafe owner detailed her problems with gangs of youths, both here and where she lived, and police lack of interest. Clara grew indignant.

"Bastards! Bastards all!" She tore a page from her notebook and wrote down a number. "Here is my personal number, darling. If you have any more problems of the kind ring me and I will come and lay a trap for them and dish out some punishment off the books."

The woman was delighted and effusive with gratitude. She pocketed the number and waved off their money. "This is on the house."

"Which number did you give her?" Miles asked as they resumed patrol.

Clara stared at him. "Ours, Miles."

Miles spluttered. "Clara, we can't set up as an alternative law-enforcement agency!"

"Would you care to bet?"

They dropped in to talk to other shopkeepers in other parts of the building, all of whom were pleasantly surprised to see them. Miles pointed out that they were raising false hopes and Clara supposed he was right. They patrolled vigilantly anyway but spotted no infractions apart from things that might one day, when Clara came to power, be classed as dress-crimes. Shortly after they stepped out onto the streets outside again she yelled at a semi-naked middle-aged man to go home and put a bloody shirt on, citing not a dress code but a law against tanning without lotion she had just thought of.

"You would, in fact, be just as bad as the current lot if you came to power," Miles said.

"Not at all, Miles. I would achieve most of my effects through education and social pressure, and, eventually, genetic engineering. I might even set one city aside for people who wanted to dress like oaves to go and live in. Remedial shock therapy would be very rare."

They went to a new super-duper shopping centre which squatted across three streets and was meant to be regenerating the town but which they couldn't help suspecting must be sucking the life from the streets outside almost as much as the out-of-town hypermarkets were. Inside all was prosperity, bright lights, chain stores and soulless hideousness. The interior seemed to have been designed by Albert Speer for a race of Nazi titans. Terrible, terrible music played, very loudly, interspersed by terrible, terrible DJ-ing and banal announcements.

They shuddered and whimpered.

"Hold my hand, Miles," said Clara in a small voice.

The two fop policemen held hands.

"About face?" said Miles. "They don't need us, they have security guards."

"They don't deserve us. That music is a crime." Clara paused. "I bet you wouldn't dare back me up if I tell them it *is* a crime."

"I bet I bloody would."

"Come on, then."

After wandering lost for a while they eventually succeeded in locating a manager's office. They barged in without knocking, to keep their momentum up, glares on their faces as the shopping centre manager looked up from some paperwork in surprise, but then Clara decided to play it deferential.

"Do you control the sound system from here, sir?"

The manager said yes.

"I'm afraid you'll have to turn it off."

The manager asked why.

"A 349/Z has come through, sir, pending legal proceedings. Decibels, distress, symptoms of nausea, dizziness and disorientation. The council has received a cease-and-desist pursuant to a class action by a consumer association."

"It seems a new study has shown constant noise leads to loss of concentration and poor purchasing decisions," put in Miles, his helmet under his arm. "Counts as subliminal pressure."

"Over our heads, sir, we're just passing on the message from on high," said Clara apologetically. "I expect the paperwork will come through in due course. At this point it seems likely to be a purely civil case rather than criminal charges, but in the meantime every day the broadcast continues will mean further penalties and fines."

The manager raised his eyebrows and then without further ado swivelled to a console and flicked a large switch up.

"It's off now," he said.

"Better keep it that way until you hear different," said Clara.

"For your own sake I wouldn't turn it on again unless you get authorization in triplicate from every relevant council department and your CEO," said Miles in a low confidential voice with a wink. "Cover your own arse, don't rely on phone orders. In my experience it's the man in the middle who carries the can in this kind of situation."

"Right," said the manager. "Thanks."

"Good day, sir."

They saluted and left.

Out in the shopping centre they found the relative silence was a relief but not quite golden. The huge space echoed eerily and there was anyway a hubbub of pop music and announcements from the individual sound systems of various shops. Still it was a vast improvement.

"That was great," sighed Clara.

"We should have got him to tell the shops to turn theirs off too."

"Perhaps we can phone up later." She gasped. "Miles! Miles, the bus station! The bus station, Miles! You'd enjoy that, wouldn't you?"

"Oh yes," said Miles. "Oh yes."

Before Miles became rich he had at times had too much to do with bus stations, which had lately become terrible places, and he was keenly aware that other innocent people who hadn't become rich still had to deal with them. Once he had spent several awful hours waiting in three in succession being bombarded over and over by taped, automated, loud and constantly repeating tannoy announcements: not to do with buses, but telling him not to smoke, urging him not to forget his bags, and informing him, in two cases mendaciously, that the station was patrolled by transport police. He had complained of this to Clara so successfully that she had kissed, licked, massaged and done other things to his poor abused ears to soothe them, and he had sometimes repeated the tale in hope of an encore.

So they went to the bus station and pulled the same stunt in an office there. Miles led off and was much more aggressive and legally threatening than they had been with the shopping-centre official. He had got into a heated argument with a jobsworth in a similar bus station after politely asking them to give the looped announcements a rest, and the memory rankled; besides unlike shopping-centre patrons, who could presumably go elsewhere, no-one here chose to have the din and hectoring inflicted on them. He said the station manager was apparently ignoring a cease-and-desist order that had been sent out three weeks ago and they would close the place down and arrest him unless he complied immediately. Clara said the decibel level was some unprecedented number. Miles asked if the manager knew there was a man currently on trial at the Hague for inflicting a very similar kind of treatment on captives. The manager, secure in his yellow plastic jacket, with his own walkie-talkie, was more used to being the browbeater than the browbeatee, and at first tried to bluff and bluster back, but was soon shouted down. Clara displayed her handcuffs and said, "We don't have time for this, let's just take him in," and muttered something about "the old station steps trick" and at one point swept a load of paperwork off his desk with her truncheon. Miles kept reciting made-up directives and laws and steadily more drastic legal penalties. All at once the manager crumbled and with a wounded, "You only had to ask," deactivated the tannoy. They kept hectoring him indignantly for the hell of it and the sake of poetic justice for a few minutes. Then Miles abruptly softened and lowering his voice said, "Between us we know you're probably not to blame. But it looks like someone's going to do time for this one. Of course if you were to dismantle the speakers completely they'd have a harder job making the case. Just routine maintenance, say, and then if they accidentally got broken, who's to prove the decibel side of it?" The man looked wise and grateful. "Of course he's to blame," snarled Clara waving her truncheon. "If it ever comes back on again we'll get you."

Outside Miles kissed her. They patrolled for a while around the suddenly peaceful bus station. They were rewarded by hearing a woman in a queue mutter stealthily to a comrade, "I don't want to speak too soon, but I think the bloody tannoy's broke," and the other giving a heartfelt sigh of, "Oh, thank God."

"That was special," said Miles. "This has, in fact, been a fun day."

"Yes," sighed Clara. "And now I think I have, in fact, had enough fun for one day."

But as it happened the fun was not quite over yet.

On the way back to the car they stopped off in a small supermarket down a drab, quietish street leading out of the town centre. Even police impersonators need groceries.

Ahead of them in the lengthy queue for the one open check-out there was a sudden, disgusted and general outcry. The till woman was refusing to sell alcohol to a couple of student-type young men who didn't have ID. They were protesting in disbelief, echoed by the various shoppers behind them. They were both clearly in their 20s, the one with the booze looking around 30.

"I'm sorry, it's the law," the till woman kept saying.

"What bloody nonsense," said an old woman a couple of places behind. "Here, love, put them in my basket and I'll take them through."

"I can't let you do that," said the till woman.

"Oh God," said Clara in disgust.

"Maybe it's because of us," said Miles.

"Nonsense, it's all the time, we are just a browbeaten nation afraid to use our common sense."

Ahead of them the altercation continued; rather hearteningly the whole queue was taking the side of the young men and telling the till woman not to be so silly. Then she caught sight of Clara and Miles in their uniforms, muttered, and nodded in their direction. The people ahead turned to look at them and there were groans.

"She is blaming it on us," said Clara. "I am forced to intervene."

She strolled to the front of the queue twirling her truncheon and wearing her crowd-control glare. Miles put their shopping down and followed reluctantly.

"What's all this then?" Clara demanded.

"I have explained to these young men that I can't sell them alcohol without an ID," said the till woman.

"Nonsense," said Clara. "They are clearly over age. Serve them at once. Use some common sense, woman."

A surprised and delighted cheer went up from the queue.

The till woman shook her head. "I'm not allowed to use common sense. I could lose my job. There could be fines. It's the law."

"I am the law!" cried Clara, again channelling Judge Dredd, rapping the conveyor belt with her truncheon impatiently. "Sell it to them at once! I will take responsibility!"

"But – I can't – you can't – I mean you're obviously off duty and anyway it's nothing to do with – "

"The law is never off duty!"

The till woman shook her head and folded her arms. "I could lose my job. The shop could get fines. They could be inspectors. It's nothing to do with you. I'm surprised at you encouraging me, what kind of police-woman are you?"

Miles started to get nervous. It was a good question, one he had been expecting to hear all day.

Clara was furious. "You're just being awkward. You're just being a jobsworth. Spaniards or Italians wouldn't do this to each other."

"It's my job," said the till woman.

"Very convenient," said Clara glaring. An inspiration had come to her. "Very convenient. I see what is going on here. Stop being petty. Serve them at once or I will arrest you for a homophobic Hate Crime!"

"What?" gaped the till-woman.

Clara twirled her truncheon at the equally gaping young man with the booze. "This man is clearly not a teenager and he is clearly a homosexual!" she cried.

"What?" cried the young man indignantly. "No I'm not!" Behind him in the queue two pretty girls giggled and he blushed.

"Watch it, sonny," said Clara in annoyance, prodding him with the truncheon. "Is there anything wrong with being a homosexual?"

"No! But I'm not one!"

She glared at him. "In the closet, hey? I think that's an automatic on-the-spot fine. I would have to check the law-book to be sure; it runs to two hundred volumes now. The point is I know a raving poof when I see one and so does she." The young man's friend was laughing loudly and Clara prodded and glared at him too. "Anything funny in homosexuality?"

"No, but – "

"Another closet case. Look at their body language. They are clearly a mated couple of shrieking bummers, and I think this one is foreign too. And that turns your stomach, doesn't it?" she growled at the till woman.

"I'm Welsh!" protested the second young man.

"Even worse. I've got you on Welshphobia *and* homophobia, you bigoted witch. Serve them at once or you will be learning tolerance of same-sex relationships the hard way, in the slammer!"

The till woman seemed to have paled somewhat but said, "It's nothing to do with them being gay – "

"We're not gay!" cried the two young man simultaneously.

"Narnia," said Clara shaking her head sadly.

"He doesn't have ID!"

"Look at him!" cried Clara. "He's 35 if he's a day!"

"25, actually," said the young man, hurt.

"And the rest! Look at his crow's-feet."

"I don't have crow's-feet!" the young man protested. "Do I?" he asked his friend in some alarm.

"You're like Trevor Howard's craggier brother," Clara told him. "Ah, and who but a gay or a metrosexual wannabe would care about wrinkles?" She prodded him with in the chest with her truncheon again triumphantly. "Got you now, haven't I, you repressed little closet case."

"Admit you're gay so we can all get out of here," tittered one of the girls.

"Yes, come on, lad, there's no shame," said the old woman.

"It doesn't matter that he's gay – " said the till woman.

"I'm not gay!"

"Say that one more time, sonny, and I'll do you too," said Clara. "You could at least sound regretful rather than indignant."

"But – "

"As for you," she rounded on the till woman, "you saw these haggard, decrepit, nearly-dead old Uranians come mincing and swooning up to you, talking about willies in Welsh, and you thought you would put a spoke in their legitimate evening's bum-fun. Call your manager," she told her, "call for back-up," she told Miles. "If this is official store policy we'll nick the lot of them and close the place down."

"Right!" cried the till woman, throwing her hands up. "Right! Christ! You can't do right for doing wrong! I've had it up to here!" In a tight fury she scanned and punched and swiped a credit card. A cheer went up again as the young men bagged their bottles.

"I should think so too," said Clara. "Now you, gay elderly Trevor Howard, and you, gay old-age Bryn Terfel, go and enjoy your night and shag each other senseless, and that's an order."

Clara and Miles rejoined the queue and in due course paid for their own shopping.

"I'm not *allowed* to use common sense," the tight-lipped till woman repeated in a small voice as she processed them.

"Then use insanity, it works for me," muttered Clara. "That was wonderful," she sighed as they headed out.

"Or borderline awful, depending on your point of view," said Miles. "Straight home now."

They were not to go straight home, however, and things were about to get much more awful, from Miles's point of view, and unbelievably, deliriously more wonderful from Clara's, because as soon as they stepped outside they found themselves right in the middle of a real crime.

There were shouts and screams; there were cries of, "Help! Call the police!" and, "Stop thief!" There was a woman lying on the pavement some distance away holding her face and an ugly youth running towards them holding her handbag.

"Miles!"

Miles moved quickly, and ineptly. He stepped forward into the path of the hurtling thief and yelled, "OI!" in rage. He was still holding a laden carrier bag in each hand, in one of which was tucked his truncheon. He saw the mugger's eyes grow alarmed as the mugger saw him. He saw the mugger veer to the side to avoid him and was unduly surprised by this cunning manoeuvre. He didn't seem able to move his own legs in time, but managed to bring up one of his arms and flail the bag of shopping to clout the thief on the head as he passed, knocking him slightly off balance but not stopping him.

Then the mugger tried to veer past Clara, who crouched and brought her truncheon across in a sweeping motion to whack him on the kneecap and sent him crashing down. Then she trunched him on the head and suddenly he was sprawling full-length and unmoving on the pavement.

"She got him! She got him!"

"Did you see that?"

Clara and the prone mugger were surrounded by bystanders, mostly old or middle-aged working-class women.

"Well, done, love, you're a bloody heroine," said one.

"I know!" cried WPC Clara, clutching this woman and bouncing up and down in excitement. "I know! I am! Did you see it? It was brilliant! Everything seemed to slow down, and then all of a sudden, BAM!" She mimed a repeat of the first truncheon stroke. "I used to play tennis at school, you know. Oh, God, it was better than sex. Oh, sorry, Miles. And then you should have felt the thwack as I bashed his skull, I really clobbered him, it was great."

The mugger came to with a groan, shaking his head as if to clear it, then rolled on the pavement in pain clutching his knee.

"My kneecap, you broke my ----ing kneecap, you ----ing bitch," he groaned.

"Potty-mouth!" cried Clara, and biffed him smartly on the head again.

"Clara!" cried Miles in alarm.

An old woman picked up the stolen handbag. "Here, give it back to her."

The woman whose handbag had been snatched was being helped along towards them by a friend. She was sobbing and holding her nose, which was bleeding. She was late middle-aged, but with the old-fashioned, no money, shabby and knackered kind of middle-agedness which can look more decrepit and vulnerable than old age.

"What did he do to her?" someone asked.

"Punched her in the face and grabbed it."

"Oh he did, did he?" cried Clara in a fury, and kicked the mugger in his face. "You little shit!" She rained truncheon blows down on his shoulders and back. "How do you like it, you little bastard?"

"That's enough!" cried Miles pulling her back, but couldn't resist kicking the thug in the arse himself. Several of the women were also toeing him and muttering viciously.

The mugger swore and yelled.

"You can't do this to me!" he cried. "I know my rights!"

It was entirely the wrong thing to say. Before Miles could restrain her Clara had trunched the thug again, causing him to collapse face-first to the ground. "Oh you do, do you? You have the right to eat pavement, toe-rag!" she cried.

"Stop it!" said Miles.

"I'll sue you," the thief whimpered.

"Oh yeah? How are you going to ring a brief with no fingers?" Clara asked, and stamped on one of his hands.

"That's the stuff," said an old woman approvingly.

"Get the little bastard," said another woman.

The mugger moaned. Miles moaned.

"There were two more of them," said someone. "They shoved us out of the way and then took off in the other direction."

"Go and look for them, Miles."

Miles, who had dumped the shopping bags and grabbed his own truncheon in the vain hope of asserting his authority, looked perfunctorily up and down the street but wasn't about to leave this situation to get worse.

"We should both go and look for them," he urged. "Come on."

"In a minute." Clara was kneeling on the groaning perpetrator's back, her truncheon pointed warningly at his face, and was turning his pockets out with her free hand. Small change scattered and she produced a wad of notes. "Look at this!" she cried. "He's probably got more money than any of you!" She also found a mobile phone. She got up, put this on the pavement, and stamped on it thoroughly until it was in pieces. She thrust the money into the hand of the injured woman, who looked startled, and said, "Here, love, that's yours now." She ungently rolled the mugger onto his back to look for anything else she could take. His trainers had the 'Respect Me' message on the tongue. This so enraged Clara that she thwacked him on his unhurt kneecap, and made a mental note to send roadkill to the manufacturers. "Let's take his trainers as well, that'll really hurt him." She found she didn't want to touch the disgusting smelly things, but the plump middle-aged woman who had called her a heroine cackled and sat astride the thug and started to unlace his footwear while Clara stood with a foot on his chest. "That's right," said Clara. "Burn them. Make him eat them. Shove them down his throat."

"What the ---- are you doing?" the mugger demanded in outrage.

"Potty-mouth!" Clara swung another blow at his head, which he managed to intercept, if painfully, with a shielding hand.

Laughing, her accomplice removed the trainers. She hurled one across the road and inserted one into a litter bin to cheers and laughter from other women.

"Aren't you going to arrest him?" asked a man nervously.

"What for?" Clara demanded with scorn. "So some rich Communist judge can give him a pat on the back and a lollipop? This is the only chance to punish him we'll get. Let's all really beat the shit out of him." There were mutters of agreement and encouragement. She kicked the perp in his side and then trunched him on his arm. "Here, darling, you have a go," she said to the victim, trying to press the truncheon on her. The bleeding woman shook her head, wide-eyed, but the plump woman who'd removed the trainers said, "I will" and seized the truncheon and aimed a couple of blows at the cowering thug's limbs. An old woman chortled at the fun and took out a bag of sweets as she watched.

"Enough!" cried Miles. "Stop!"

"Ignore PC Pinkwhistle," said Clara. "He has been through one of the Communist police courses. I give you all full permission to punish this toe-rag. I hereby deputize you all. String him up, if you like, I don't care. Kick his teeth in. Pull his ears off. If you don't defend yourselves no-one else will."

Chuckling or muttering, led by Clara's first deputy and the old woman sucking sweets, some of the crowd started to rain energetic handbag blows down on the cowering thief. A few kicked at him but in a more or less half-hearted and token way.

"That's right, get your own back," said Clara. "Oh let's brand him! Let's write 'Mugger' on his face! Where's my pen?" While she was rummaging for it she kicked him on the leg.

"That's enough!" cried Miles. He tried to think of some way to control her. "This isn't chivalrous! Chivalry, Clara! He's a beaten and helpless adversary! You will tarnish your heroic deed!"

"Piss off, Pinkwhistle," said Clara pushing him away. "Anyway he isn't asking for quarter yet, he is still acting defiant."

Another attempt was being made to thrust the truncheon on the injured woman. Nervously she aimed a token blow at her attacker which caught him on the shoulder. There were cheers.

"Well done," said Clara taking the truncheon back. "Now let me show you how a professional does it."

"No!" said Miles as she biffed him on the head again. "Enough!"

"Fuck!" cried the mugger.

"Potty-mouth!" said Clara, and struck him another glancing blow.

"For fuck's sake, stop!" cried Miles in panic.

"Potty-mouth!" glared Clara, and rapped Miles on the knuckles.

"Ow!" He shook his hand in pain and thrust her away.

"I'll ----ing get you you ----ing ----," the mugger yelled at her in rage.

"Oi! Potty-mouth!" yelled Miles angrily, and whacked him on the head with his own truncheon. The mugger collapsed senseless.

"For God's sake, Miles, you have killed him now. You always have to take everything too far."

Miles paled and felt ill, for a second starting to fear she was right, but the mugger started to whimper and groan and hold his arms over his head again.

"Have you had enough?" Clara asked him. "Will you beg for mercy? Tell all your toe-rag friends there's a new law in town." She whacked him on the elbow to drive the point home.

The crowd was quite large now and getting bigger by the minute. A man who looked like a student or lecturer who had just arrived pushed his way forward and said, "Stop this! This is police brutality! Arrest him properly and read him his rights!"

Clara glared and pointed her truncheon at him. "Watch it, sonny, you're probably the only liberal left in this town," she said. "Don't tell me how to do my job."

"Piss off out of it," the plump woman told him.

"Give *him* some stick too, love," the old woman with the sweets urged.

"I demand you read him his rights!" the man insisted.

Glowering, Clara put her foot on the mugger's chest and said, "You have a right to the fruits of your industry, and to the means of making your industry fruitful. You have a right to the acquisitions of your parents, if you know them, and to the nourishment and improvement of your offspring, if you know them. You have a right to instruction in life and to consolation in death. You have a right to do what you can do for yourself without trespassing on others – " This was a half-recollected and somewhat adapted passage from Edmund Burke.

"His real rights!" said the bleeding heart.

"I don't have two weeks to spare," said Clara witheringly, stamping on the mugger's chest as he tried to rise.

"Right, I'm calling the police," said the man, taking out a phone.

"We *are* the police!" cried Clara bridling.

"I doubt it," said the man. "I seriously doubt it."

"I don't think they are," cried another man next to him. "Look at their uniforms!"

"It is a new uniform," said Clara, pouting and folding her arms.

"It's an old one! Look at it! I think it's a costume! I think they're impostors. I think they're vigilantes!"

"Of course they are," chortled the old woman with the sweets. "And about time too."

"Nonsense," said Clara, shifty-eyed but defiant. "Phone the police, then, and let us see whom they arrest. You are interfering with the course of my duties."

The first man stepped away a bit and turned his back on her and started to mutter into his phone.

"Stop that," said Clara. "Give me that phone or I will confiscate it."

Miles whimpered and clutched imploringly at her arm.

"Yes, Miles," she agreed sotto voce. "I know. I have doomed us both."

The busybody closed his phone. "The police are on their way."

"I tell you the police are already here!" cried Clara, stamping her foot impatiently, causing the mugger underneath it to groan again. "Those motorized lot will take half an hour to come, if they ever do. Go on about your business."

"I phoned the police as soon as he grabbed her bag," said a woman.

"Hmm," said Clara thoughtfully. She exchanged a glance with the queasy-looking Miles and cleared her throat. "We don't have time to bicker," she announced. "Duty calls. We must search for this toe-rag's accomplices. If you will give me a hand, Constable Pinkwhistle – " She dragged the perp to some railings with help from Miles and handcuffed him to them. "The catch-wagon will be along to collect him shortly. In the meantime do not approach him save to give him a moral lecture or kick him in the balls. We will be on our way now."

Head high, she took Miles's arm and with a few prods and waves of her truncheon cleared a path through the crowd. They started to walk off up the street.

"Nice and casual," she murmured. "With dignity. Don't run."

"Somebody stop them!" cried the man with the phone.

"Now run?" asked Miles.

"No, keep calm. Don't look back."

They were halfway up the street now. Suddenly there was a wail and whoop of sirens. They looked round to see a police car, lights flashing, come tearing round the end of the street and pull up near the crowd around the mugger. The interfering bleeding-heart leaned across to talk to the driver and pointed up the street towards them.

"All right, now run," said Clara. "Run fast, don't stop, and the devil take the hindmost. If we are caught I will blame you."

They ran.

They ran madly, desperately, pell-mell, hell for leather, helter-skelter. Clara laughed delightedly once as they flew but then bit her lip and looked as panicked as Miles did. Behind them there was another siren whoop and a screech of tyres as the police car set off after them. They turned into another street and pelted along that. "Stop thief!" cried Clara to clear a path. "Out of the way!" There was another whoop from the end of the street, a flicker of flashing lights reflected in the shop windows of the street beyond: another car about to appear ahead of them. Their hearts jolted.

"Down here!" cried Miles. They dashed hand in hand down a long dingy side-street. Had either of the police cars been in time to see them? They would never reach the far end before they drove past, anyway.

"In here!" cried Clara, pulling him up short. The entrance to a club, a run-down working man's club. They piled in frantically. Inside it was gloomy, almost empty, morose, the major animation and noise coming from fruit machines. They were glowered at, illicit cigarettes were hastily extinguished.

"Miles quick, we have to ditch the uniforms! Do what I do."

Clara stalked over to a table where two vicious-looking old men in a cloth cap and a baseball cap were sitting nursing flat beer and grievances.

She pointed her truncheon imperiously at the one with the cloth cap. "You! What's your name?"

"Alf," he said sullenly.

"Then you're the one I've been looking for," she growled, slapping her truncheon into her palm. She suddenly smiled brilliantly. "It's your birthday, isn't it, Alf? And you've been a very, very naughty boy," she cooed. She stood with her foot on the banquette just in front of Alf's crotch, took off her police hat, spun it across the room, loosed and tossed her hair and started to unbutton her policewoman uniform.

"It's not his birthday," said Alf's friend puzzled.

"Shut up, you ----, it is now," muttered Alf, wide-eyed.

Clara danced around in front of the two old men, removed the tunic, whirled it around her head and flung it away. With a sickly smile, Miles started to dance and writhe around her unbuttoning his own uniform.

"What's that fruit doing?" Alf demanded in alarm.

"Get your own audience, Miles," Clara hissed, glancing in panic towards the door. "Those old women, look." She shoved him along to the next table where three old women sat. They cackled in delight as he undulated before them, waved his truncheon and then discarded it, removed his helmet and held it over his crotch and drummed his fingers on it knowingly. Somewhere behind him a laughing barman had put on some loud electronic music with a pounding beat. Writhing and grinning inanely, grabbed and pawed at by the three aged harpies, glancing fearfully towards the door, Miles threw away his helmet, took off his tunic and flung it into a corner, took off his belt and cracked it on the table like a whip. His dark pants and blue shirt would now pass for normal but he started to unbutton his shirt for the look of the thing, and one of the old women grabbed at his trousers. He danced back out of their reach.

Beside him Clara was down to her underwear, still gyrating and strutting and tossing her hair for the old men.

"Now the bra," cried Alf.

"Certainly not, you pervert, you are worse than my husband. Miles phone a taxi. Miles look for a back way out. Miles buy their manky old man coats off them. Miles that lady wants to give you a tip."

A cackling old bag was reaching out a clawed hand to him, and shoved some bus tokens down the front of his pants.

Chapter Fourteen

"Miles, have I told you how manly and handsome you are looking?" Clara said stroking his cheek.

"Who have you killed?" asked Miles.

Clara pouted. "Can't a wife compliment her lord and master without being suspected of political murder?"

"No, really, tell me what you've done, because alarm is growing."

She nestled against him on the couch and ran a finger over his chest. "Miles, you know you're always suggesting we play a game where I wear a maid outfit and I refuse? Well perhaps it is time we try it. Perhaps an elf maid, with pointy ears. A nymphomaniac elf maid, Charisma-18, with Bracers of Sexiness and +10 Breasts of Distraction."

"Is the body in pieces? Was it ritualistic? Were there any witnesses? Did you kill the witnesses? I won't be cross if you own up now."

"Husband, you are so funny," she said laughing throatily. "Why have you never gone on the music halls?"

"Who was it? The prime minister? The vicar? Harriet. Oh God it was, it was Harriet, wasn't it?"

"Miles you are so clever." She took the end of her hair and stroked his face with it like a brush. "The ... pleasant little surprise I have to spring has to *do* with Harriet."

His heart sank. "Oh Christ. What have you done?"

She rose abruptly. "We are going to a dinner party at their place."

Miles looked appalled for a second and then laughed. "A-ha," he said wagging a finger. "I get it. This is how you break it to me gently. You *pretend* to have accepted an invitation to a dinner party at their place. Then, when I'm really wound up, you admit that you've only killed her, and I'm relieved."

"I'm afraid not, Miles. I won't enjoy it any more than you will, but it's happening. Tonight." She was suddenly brisk and commanding. "Get over it, get used to it, get ready."

"No!" cried Miles. "I refuse! I absolutely, categorically – for God's sake what were you thinking? Ring and make an excuse."

"No. I feel sorry for her."

"For God's sake why?" And on and on and on.

"Because I threw the bloody rock through her window!" she eventually had to yell at him, and instantly regretted it.

No-one could have been more surprised than Clara that Harriet had invited them round to dinner. Since the global warming argument they had had no contact at all, at least up close. Hiding in the woods across the road, she had heard Harriet scream as the unwitting Miles had dropped a burning cross on her lawn while dressed as a Grand Inquisitor / Klansman / High Avenger of the St. Mary's Star Chamber, and had laughed evilly. She had read Harriet's description of this, the overwrought prose perhaps justified for once, and had laughed again. She reflected that probably no-one sane believed a word Harriet wrote by this time – the incident didn't even make it into her own paper as a news item – and laughed some more.

After that she forgot about Harriet for a while; she started to skip reading her column, which was becoming boringly obsessed with AGW rather than libelling the village; and then she went through one of her periods of cancelling the papers for the sake of not being made murderous by the news and not being contaminated by the shitty banal trivial ironic celebrity-obsessed modern culture. She heard terrible tales of Harriet in the pub from her new au pair, but that was about it.

But as spring came, and the epic snows and frosts that had settled over them passed, she had started to see her: while out walking she would see Harriet diligently tilling and sowing her fields and plots, rain and shine, planting the vegetable crops she hoped would feed her family without harming the Earth, a peasant scarf around her head – plainly useless, plainly exasperated, once, heart-wrenchingly, plainly sobbing as she hoed; but stubborn, persistent, and somehow magnificent – and all Clara's sorrow for her and indignation on her behalf had returned full flood, and with it her guilt. Not particularly for the burning cross thing – that was just silly, only an idiot could have taken it seriously, and if Harriet chose to it was her own damn fault – or various other malicious pranks, but for that first savage, furious rock through the window, that awful, undeniable, solid evidence of indigenous hate, that horrible violation of her home. At times the guilt felt like a bigger, heavier stone Clara was toting around with her, somewhere inside.

She had tried to make amends.

"Can't you offer to help her?" she had pleaded with a farmer in the Walpole. "Can't you show her how it's done? It must be back-breaking for her, and she is making a balls of it, I am sure. Couldn't your lads spend an afternoon helping her?" She thought, she hoped, she would have made this plea on Harriet's behalf even without the guilt, simply from compassion and outrage and fellow womanhood, at the pathetic sight of her toiling as no city-dweller should be expected to while her husband gallivanted about the hot-spots and fun-spots of the world, the playgrounds of the rich and tenured, in the company of the climate scientists who had set her to work in the fields.

"---- off," the farmer had scoffed. "After what's she's done? Why should I?"

"It's how a village is *supposed* to work," she had urged. "It's how a country is supposed to work. We stick together and help each other out. Let's show her."

"She's shut herself off from both, hasn't she? If she had come here and been nice – "

She sighed and supposed she could see his point.

Once, passing by Harriet's gate on her own rather than with Miles just as the whole family Pridgett-Gilquist plus au pair pulled out and drove off somewhere in their eco-car, Clara had seized the opportunity to grab tools from the yard and dash into the field and start to do some voluntary work herself. But she, even more than Harriet, had little clue what she was doing; indeed soon realised that she had just blithely dug up a whole row and a half of onion bulbs that Harriet had already planted.

"Piss," she had said in irritation. "Piss and vinegar," she had added, trying to hastily stamp them back in, nervously looking at the road. "Piss, vinegar, wormwood and gall," she had muttered in disgust as it started to rain. "Get back *in*, you little sods."

Her guilt had not abated much.

Just recently she had run into Harriet coming out of the Post Office, almost literally, had ventured a diffident smile; but the other had tilted her nose and walked away.

And there it had rested, until Harriet's surprising phone call.

"I got Lambed." Harriet's voice was rueful, unusually humorous. She might have been describing, half-proudly, some mildly embarrassing drunken adolescent rite of passage.

For a moment Clara failed to understand what she could possibly mean; then came remembrance, new guilt, horror.

"On your roof?" she asked in disbelief. "You had lambs put on your roof?"

She hadn't heard about this either in the Walpole or Harriet's column. Later she would confront the two madcap young farmhands she had egged on to do it all those months ago; they said it had seemed like a very good idea to round off one drunken night, but they had kept quiet about it for fear of their farmer. She yelled at them – couldn't they take a joke, would they put their hands in the fire if she, et cetera – more for the poor little lamb's sake than Harriet's.

"Just the one," said Harriet. "It was just like you said, no-one in authority wanted to know, they wouldn't even put me through to the relevant department. I bribed a local in the end and a man with a ladder came." (The man with the ladder had been the farmer.) "Hard to sleep through it and it knocked some of the slates off. Fortunately we'd had the chimney blocked up."

"I'm terribly sorry."

"Oh, just one of those things," said Harriet breezily. "Good story for my friends. I'm learning to laugh more, as you told me to once."

"Well ... good." What have you done with Harriet, strange relaxed woman, Clara wondered.

There was a pause.

"I've missed you," Harriet suddenly and surprisingly said. "I've missed our chats."

"Oh! I ... also," stumbled Clara, taken aback and keenly realising she hadn't at all.

"We should get together some time, yeah?"

"Well ... yes," said Clara uncertainly.

"In fact ... look, why don't you and Miles come round to dinner tonight?"

"I should love to," Clara found herself saying.

"We've got a few people over, old friends who are staying, I'm sure they'd love to meet you too."

"Oh," said Clara. "I can't wait. ... Hell's dicks," she swore to herself viciously after hanging up.

What a pain. And how was she to break it to Miles? She tried to think if there was any way she could make it his fault. Then she toyed with confessing about the rock through the window by way of explanation, and concluded that was the one thing she must not do.

We will cut short, somewhat, the recriminations and heated defensive counter-yellings resulting from Clara confessing about the rock through the window.

"How *could* you? ... Clara, this is a democracy!"

"Wah wah wah, democracy democracy! *I* am a Monarchist!"

"And – that's how Monarchists behave? You, you have breached the Queen's Peace!"

"I have punished treason! And it was already breached! There *is* no Queen's Peace any more! The monarch guarantees justice for her subjects, and if not the mob rises up and demands it! That's political check and balance, Miles!"

"That's anarchy! We have the rule of law!"

"No, Miles, that ended some time ago, if you hadn't noticed! It is every woman for herself!"

"Edmund Burke – "

"Don't quote Edmund Burke to me, you sanctimonious streak of piss, I read him first!" Miles laughed at this. "Yes! And I have gone beyond him! He never lived to see this!"

"See what? See a woman move to a village and say rude things about it?"

"You know exactly what I'm talking about! Don't you dare get self-righteous, you are as guilty as I am in your dreams, you just don't have the balls to put it into practice! You know it! You know there are any number of windows in this country that need and deserve rocks putting through them and *you* never do anything about it, you coward!"

His eyes blazed at her. "Yes, I was just as angry as you, but we can't – "

"We can and I did! And you didn't and wouldn't no matter the provocation. I am ashamed of you!"

"I'm ashamed of you!"

"I am ashamed of myself," she said suddenly and miserably. "Oh, Miles, Miles, don't withdraw your love from me!" she cried dramatically, flinging herself at his feet and hugging his knees, causing him to laugh. "I didn't mean what I said. Just – don't go on at me. I *know* I did wrong. But I have been punished. Oh, how I have been punished!" she groaned, and meant it. She rose and looked wretched. "It is strange. For so long I have stayed my hand from throwing the first rock for fear of the awful responsibility of being the one to spark the great uprising and all that must follow – a nation rent with fire and blood – the mass executions, the televised disembowellings – a dream we hold in all our hearts, but who dares light the fatal fuse? Little did I suspect the far more terrible truth, that my act of righteous outrage would lead to *befriending bloody Harriet*." She looked thoughtful. "Perhaps, after all, Miles," she mused, brightening, "it turns out that horrendous violence can bring people closer together."

"No, Clara."

"Anyway," she said briskly, clapping her hands, "that's the reason we're going to dinner with the wretched woman, so go and start smartening yourself and less of your lip."

We will likewise cut short Miles's continued grumbling, objection, and expressions of deepest foreboding. This was not lessened, rather the contrary, by the news that there were to be other people there besides Harriet and Richard.

"Who? How many?"

"I don't know, she just said some friends."

"We'll be nice and behave, right? Let me rephrase that, we *are* going to be nice and behave."

"Of course, Miles," she said in slight irritation.

He sighed. "It's still going to be a disaster. Apart from anything else we don't shine in these situations. This is one of the things we can't do. It's part of the price we pay for cutting ourselves off from the world. We don't know about television or celebrities. We don't have jobs to talk about. We only read books no-one else does. We haven't even read the papers in ages. We are ... unclubbable."

"You are *highly* clubbable at times," she muttered with double entendre. "We've done more than all right at the Walpole," she pointed out.

"They're tolerant because most of them are eccentrics and outcasts of one kind or another too. And half of them are in love with you."

"Only half?" She pouted and tossed her hair.

"And we share a mutual interest in whining about the status quo. We're not going to have anything in common with Harriet and her friends."

"Well, we can just sit there and be pretty and eat nicely and say please and thank you. Remember what I have taught you."

Truth to tell Clara was growing more nervous herself as the hour approached. The fact was, although she would not have admitted it to Miles, she would have found some excuse to decline if Harriet had mentioned she was having other people round *before* extending the invitation. In that case Harriet couldn't be lonely, she didn't *need* her and Miles: except, perhaps, she supposed, to show her old friends she had made new friends here? Perhaps she did need them, then. But with other guests they would be outnumbered, and it was true they were unlikely to find themselves en rapport with anyone. Too late now.

From time to time Miles caught her looking at the phone longingly, biting her lip, as she did her hair or put in ear-rings.

"You've thought of some ingenious or, more likely, splendidly outlandish excuse to cancel. Use it. Please."

"We can't," she finally sighed.

Still she grew increasingly agitated. "Let's have a drink before we go," she suggested. Miles raised an eyebrow. Clara drinking at all was highly unusual.

"Just one," he said.

"Miles what if they suddenly start doing drugs?"

Miles laughed. "You're as bad as she is!"

"But what if they do?"

"You will say, accurately, that you don't need them."

"Miles! Miles!" She grabbed him, eyes wide with alarm. "What if they get us all to put our car-keys into a pot?"

Miles looked alarmed too. "No-one's taking *my* car!" he cried.

She slapped him.

"We'll walk to be on the safe side. They'd probably stone us for using a car for such a short journey anyway."

She didn't let up, clinging to him, as they walked down the road to Harriet's.

"Miles what if all the women gang up on me and get bitchy? What if they throw their careers in my face? It is so embarrassing to be idle sometimes."

"You have your death-lists."

"But that, like your writing, is something that only *might* pay off in the future. Few people understand doing a thing for the love of it. You are the only one I am able to share that part of my life with. At home I used always to conceal them under my knitting. What do I say, when they ask me what I do?"

"Reply, 'I don't do, I be.' "

"They will just think that is rural. Miles, what if they all have lots of children and throw them in my face? Miles pretend we had children but they died. No, say we had three children but we sent them to live in Africa to lower their carbon footprint. That will really one-up them. They will probably all start doing that next."

"Will you for God's sake relax, or this will be worse than it's already going to be."

Just before they got there something happened which Miles regarded as a definite ill-omen but which cheered Clara up a bit. As they reached Harriet's gate they saw her latest au pair getting into a taxi idling there. Clara, who had befriended her in the pub, waved and smiled as they started to walk into the drive.

The girl got out again. "Clara, are you eating here?" she said in surprise.

"I'm afraid so. Where are you off to?"

"Home. I have quit. I could have stayed home if I wanted to work in fields. Cooking for this party was the last straw." She kissed Clara on each cheek. "Goodbye. Do not drink the soup," she murmured.

"Whyever not?" asked Clara. The girl whispered in her ear. Clara widened her eyes. "How acrobatic of you, dear," she said, impressed and slightly revolted.

235

The girl shrugged. "It was easy. I was given a potty when the toilet kept freezing."

They hugged and waved and then the taxi drove off.

"I *don't* recommend the soup, Miles," she said linking arms with him, a new spring in her step as she led him round towards the back door. "This might be an amusing party after all. By the way," she added thoughtfully as she suddenly remembered something just before they got there, "you are an expert on geology, in particular determining the provenance of large rocks."

"What?"

"I will explain as we go."

Through the half-open kitchen door they saw their long-time detestee Richard Gilquist, sitting alone at the table. They knocked and tentatively entered and he glanced round and flashed them a warm smile but did not get up. Like most journalists he looked much older than his reverse-Dorian-Gray newspaper picture, not at all boyish, indeed on the verge of acquiring gravitas, and he was unseasonably tanned.

"You must be Clara and Miles. Go through and make yourselves at home, everyone's in there," he said nodding towards where sounds of low music and a murmur of conversation were emerging from the open living room door. "Harriet will be down in a minute." He held his smile a moment then looked back down at the electronic device he was holding and twiddling, either sending a message or playing a game.

"Get off your arse and introduce us, you rude man," said Clara, smiling but not too much, "or we will go home at once and tell your wife why."

Richard laid his device down, suddenly looking as young as his picture; his tan seemed to deepen around the cheeks. He got up smiling sheepishly and mumbled, "Do excuse me," and led them through.

"He was texting a *whore*," Clara whispered in Miles's ear knowledgeably.

"Why am I a sodding geologist?" Miles whispered back.

Four 30-ish people, two men and two women, were sitting around in the living room. There seemed to be a little tenseness or subduedness in the air and they all seemed to brighten with more than ordinary politeness at the new arrivals.

"This is Keir and Seal and Wendy and Stuart," said Richard. "These are our neighbours Clara and Miles." Stuart, a bald, long-bearded man like some Victorian divine rose and shook Miles's hand, the others waved. "We're in slight disarray," continued Richard. "Bit of a scene with the au pair, she's left us. Harriet's ... composing herself. I've just texted her, she'll be down shortly." He took and fulfilled drink orders.

"And what do you do?" Seal asked.

"We are idle rich," Clara told her. "Isn't that nice? Well, not completely idle. I write compulsive 'To do' lists, and my husb, this man I came with is working on a book about a man who is too sad to get out of bed."

"He *is* out of bed now!" Miles protested. "He was only *in* bed for ten pages."

"Yes, but then his breakfast turned into a bit of an ordeal, didn't it? Never mind, I have complete confidence you will get him out of the house by page seventy. Probably he will then get run over. You have been sounding a foreboding note quite successfully and I fear the worst."

"You write?" said Seal. "Published?"

"No no, just in a dilettante way, we both do, just to pass the time," said Miles.

Keir said, "We were saying before you came in, intelligent people must run to seed out in the sticks, having nothing to do."

Stuart rolled his eyes at Miles. "Keir thinks you all spend all your time having car-key parties and so on."

"No, the hip thing is to throw the ear-tags of your favourite cattle into a bowl," said Miles.

"I haven't noticed *my* wits rusting," protested Richard, who had drifted out to the kitchen then come back again.

"But you have a job that uses them and you get back to London a lot," said Keir. "I mean, Miles, how much of your education remains relevant to your life, on a day to day basis?"

"Tragically few people anywhere use their education much unless their job depends on it," said Stuart.

"Did you do a degree, Miles?" Keir pressed. "What was it in?"

"English Literature," said Miles.

"Geology," said Clara not quite simultaneously.

"Geology *and* English Literature," said Miles.

"That's an unusual combination, surely?" said Wendy in surprise.

"Not at all," said Miles, who was halfway through his drink. "It's a natural fit. You know, landscape-and-mood kind of thing," he said blithely. Clara nodded eagerly, and proudly. His lying was coming on in leaps and bounds. "There are any number of great books that are enhanced immeasurably if you have a deeper awareness of the geology of the setting. What kind of rocks are mentioned and so on. Think of," he floundered desperately for a moment, "the flinty swede-fields near the end of Tess of the D'Urbervilles. And of course it lends itself to all kinds of glib essays comparing layers of subtext to mineral strata."

"And Miles *has* kept it up, at least as a hobby," said Clara touching him on the arm. "So much so that I took him the rock that was thrown through Richard and Harriet's window to see what he could deduce from it."

"*Stuart* is a geologist," said Wendy.

"Ah!" said Miles, looking at the beaming Stuart and trying to look delighted. Clara studied her nails and then her shoes and then something on the wall.

Frowning, Richard said, "Yes, what *did* happen about that rock?"

"Miles thought it may *well* have come from the woods the Gypsy woman haunts," said Clara, repeating the line she had given Harriet. "However he sent it off to a friend who works in a proper laboratory to see if he could be more helpful, but we are still waiting to hear back from him. Did we do wrong? Have – have the police expressed an interest in seeing it?"

"We didn't pursue it with the police," said Richard shortly, draining his drink.

"Which lab was this?" Stuart asked Miles.

"I have no idea," said Miles as cheerfully as he could. Just then Harriet appeared from upstairs. Under cover of the attention and greetings directed her way he lowered his voice and murmured, "You must know it's nonsense, an idiotic idea of my wife's." Stuart nodded understandingly.

"I have decided to be calm," Harriet announced to the room at large with a brave smile. "We will *not* let it get to us. And here are Clara and Miles, they will cheer us up. How are you, dear?" She blew a kiss to Clara and accepted a drink from Richard. She seemed slightly drunk already. "Miles, it's nice to finally meet you. Clara's been my lifeline out here. I've been telling everyone so much about you, they've all been looking forward to your coming."

"I'm afraid you've been built up to us as blood-curdling monsters of reaction," said Stuart smiling. "You're quite disappointing in the flesh. If you don't say something outrageous no-one will forgive you."

Miles laughed; Richard was laughing too, rather loudly. Harriet seemed to glare at Stuart and Wendy looked appalled.

"Oh, don't worry, we'll be sure to say six outrageous things without trying," said Miles.

Clara appeared to be blushing and was staring into space. She abruptly swallowed some of her drink and summoned a smile.

"I gather you don't approve of the government, or come to that the opposition," said Keir. "How would you in fact vote, if there was an election tomorrow?"

"Oh, I suppose for the most amateurish, ordinary bloke-or-gal independent I could find," said Clara.

"The UK Independence Party," said Miles. "Almost nothing important can be reformed until we get out of Europe."

Glances were exchanged at this; amused or told-you-so.

"Isn't that the lightweight option?" said Keir. Miles thought he had a rather horrid sneery face, but that might not be his fault.

"What do you mean?"

"We were discussing what the BNP membership might be in these parts."

"Oh, less even than the national average, I would imagine; we're fairly well off round here. I do wish people wouldn't build them up as a genuine threat, it just makes them more alluring in certain quarters as a way to say Fuck You." Miles tried not to over-emphasize the Fuck You or look at Keir as he said it. "Lenny Bruce used to say the American Nazis worked to mass rallies of liberals shaking their fists at them."

"And what needs reforming that's important?" asked Seal.

"Oh, we're only staying to dinner, not all weekend," said Miles cheerily. Clara was looking at her shoes. "Don't get me started, there would just be this high-pitched whine that would disturb dogs on farms three miles away."

"But it's fair to say you think something has gone terribly wrong with your country and are outraged?" pressed Keir. His face *was* his fault, Miles decided, he was sneering deliberately, or perhaps unconsciously.

"This is a bit heavy for before dinner, isn't it?" Miles wasn't the world's best at changing subjects. He decided to offer what he thought was a fairly neutral and apolitical joke. "Oh! Political trivia quiz for you: what Christian name has been given to every Prime Minister of the past forty years, including Mrs Thatcher?"

They frowned and looked puzzled.

"Fucking," said Miles.

Stuart laughed politely. Clara rolled her eyes. Others made joke-recognising faces. Richard frowned thoughtfully as though he couldn't quite go along with it and had conscientious reservations. Harriet tutted, "*Must* you say Christian name?"

There was a pause. Richard started supplying more drinks. Clara said she'd better not before dinner. Harriet said, yes, they'd better eat, and ordered them to sit. Miles steered Stuart the geologist to one side pointing at an ornament and murmured, "I think there's au pair wee in the soup."

Stuart raised his eyebrows. "Oh? Never mind, I quite fancied her."

"I'm not sure how to break it to Harriet."

"It could be disaster, to be honest, we've only just calmed her down."

As they went to sit Stuart murmured in turn to Wendy, who seemed to be his wife. She widened her eyes but glanced at Harriet and shook her head.

They seated themselves haphazardly around the long table. "Miles quick I've saved you a seat next to me," said Clara patting the chair on her right. Stuart was on his other side, which was nice because Stuart was nice but bloody awful because he was a geologist and might discover Miles wasn't. Wendy was beyond Stuart, Harriet opposite Clara, Keir next to Harriet and Seal next to him, Richard at the end opposite Wendy. Richard and Harriet started to ferry in plates of leek soup and distribute them. Miles exchanged glances with Stuart and Wendy. Surely someone had to say something. Stuart looked very urgently at Wendy but she shook her head minimally, and then Harriet said, "I have to say I've been tasting this already and it's delicious, I don't know what the cow put in it but it's unusually piquant." So no-one did say anything, apart from Clara, who looked very virtuous and said, "I'm afraid Miles and I can't have the soup, thank you all the same."

"Oh why not?" said Harriet.

"I would rather not say," said Clara.

"Is it an allergy? Ethical objection?" asked Seal frowning.

Christ, she's jealous, I've one-upped her, Clara thought nastily. She toyed with inventing a boycott of some evil leek-monopoly billionaire or the principality of Wales but in the end stuck to her original impulse and, wide-eyed and with a hint of reproach said, "Why, it is the first Saturday after Whitsun." It wasn't, or it probably wasn't: Clara didn't actually have much clue when Whitsun was, but doubted any of these lot would either.

Harriet looked delighted at this, as did Seal and Keir. Harriet gave them a triumphant told-you-so glance. "I quite understand," she said to Clara. "If there's anything else just let us know."

Staring thoughtfully at the bowl in front of him, Stuart said, "Actually if people are opting out, Wendy and I aren't big on leeks."

"Well you're just a pain in the arse," said Harriet sitting. "I'm going to write a column about fussy eaters," which would have made a change from the ones she more often wrote about dinner hosts failing to cater for their guests' dietary and ethical aversions.

They started to eat, or half of them did. Clara sat there with a pious smile on her face, watching. Wendy stared at the others sickly, nibbling a nail. Miles raised a spoonful of soup to under his nose, inhaled, and made a pervy leering face at Stuart. Stuart did the same and made an even more grotesquely lustful face, and then dipped his tongue lasciviously into the soup. Seal and Keir complimented Harriet on it and she fairly gave the credit to the au pair.

"So you have to forego soup today?" asked Richard puzzledly. "As a religious thing?"

Clara had thought of saying Miles had been brought up in a sect that at certain times of the year would only eat things they believed had been on the menu at the Last Supper. She had also thought of saying, 'Actually, we are forbidden to drink piss.' She rejected both and merely nodded and smiled and said, "Jesus gave his soup to a leper on this day. We'd rather not talk about it."

"All the more for me," said Keir, reaching over and taking her neglected bowl with a look at her. "This is worth burning in hell for," he complimented Harriet.

"He's right there," Stuart muttered to Miles, making an awful pervert 'Yummy' face again and dipping his spoon and licking it with simulated delight.

"Stop that," sniggered Miles, repulsed.

"Once again Christianity stops people doing things they want to," said Keir as he happily ate, making quite absurd lip-smacking noises.

"Clara and Miles are pillars of the church," said Harriet.

"Oh, I wouldn't say that," said Miles.

"All religion is bullshit," said Keir. "A system of control. And Christianity is the worst. At least some of the others are subversive. Christianity just props up a rotten repressive system."

"I will pray for you," said Clara.

"Don't you dare," said Keir, annoyed. "Don't you bloody dare."

"You can't stop me," said Clara. "I am doing it now. It may mitigate your sentence one day."

"What did I tell you?" said Harriet triumphantly.

"When you're dead you're done with," said Keir.

"There must be something," said Wendy. "I mean people see ghosts and things, don't they?"

"*We* are supposed to have a ghost here," said Harriet.

"And have you seen anything?"

"Yes!" said Harriet. "The other day I became aware of an inexplicable presence, and then the figure of this strange man appeared in the hall. But it was only Richard, I remembered him after a while." Richard made a face.

"Ghosts are probably just psychic photographs," said Seal. "People probably just leave impressions of their personalities in the stones, especially in old houses."

"Ah, but if that was the case, why is no-one ever haunted by someone who's still alive?" asked Miles.

"What do you mean?" asked Wendy.

"Take this house. The previous owner lived here for forty years and is currently alive and well and living in New Zealand. Why isn't she haunting the place now, if it's just stones recording your emotions? Why do you never hear of anything like that happening? You have to be dead to haunt a place."

"Richard will haunt the departure lounge of Heathrow," said Harriet with a sweet smile at her husband. "He will send me text-messages from the afterlife."

"I believe in science," said Keir, not quite belligerently but defiantly, as if beleaguered. "Religion causes all the trouble in the world."

"Oh God, this is so sixth form," groaned Stuart. "And now someone will mention the Nazis and the Communists."

"If there's a God, why is there ... "

"Sixth form," said Stuart.

"It's sixth form because it's obvious."

"The thickest priest would have answers."

"Well what are they?"

"I don't know and I don't care, I got bored of it in the sixth form."

Argument about religion became general and predictable for a few moments. It petered out when Harriet attracted her friends' attention to Clara, who was sitting there quietly with her hands together and her eyes raised upwards as if in prayer.

"We really only go to church to show support," said Miles. "But I'm starting to think I'll have to become properly religious for humanist reasons. Pure rationalism will turn the world into hell. It's reducing Man to the level of an animal."

"We *are* animals," said Keir. "We are no better than them. We are worse than animals. I say down with all darkness and superstition and dead tradition."

There was a pause. The tainted soup had long been finished. Clara was silently running a finger over the dinge and scratch on the table, not properly re-varnished and right in front of her place, where her rock had struck home.

"I suppose you support fox-hunting, doubtless for humanist reasons, as well," Keir said.

"No, I support it because of my jodhpur fetish," said Miles. He rose and took out a cigarette packet. "I'm afraid I have to go out for a fag."

"I will join you," said Clara.

Harriet tutted and opened the back patio door. They went out and strolled a short distance away. Miles smoked almost as little as Clara but had brought his cigs on purpose as an excuse for taking a break if things got too awful or stressful. He lit two and they leaned in a corner of the wall and looked at the stars.

"This is like when we used to go out for a fag at my parents' house."

"Don't get your hopes up." Nevertheless Clara leaned close against him. "I'm sorry, Miles, we were invited here to be the entertainment. Exhibition yokels and Middle Englanders. Nice Stuart was genuinely trying to warn us. We're supposed to prove that everything she's been writing in her columns is true."

"I know," said Miles. "Shall we go home?"

She sighed. "No."

"Then what shall we do?"

"I'll think of something. I suppose I should just be rude and outrageous but it somehow isn't fun when people want it. It's like when you're a child, being ordered to sing and dance for your aunts, as opposed to doing it at a funeral or something because the spirit moves you. Perhaps this is punishment for all the times I do it when people don't want it."

"Harriet and that shit Keir will be baiting us. They're all drunk already. I might have to get drunk too."

"You have my permission."

"I don't need it," said Miles.

"Yes, you do," said Clara.

"This *is* like going out for a fag at my parents' house," said Miles, bending down to steal a kiss.

When they went back in after finishing their cigarettes they found the main course had been served and embarked upon. Stuart had waited for them, which made them feel guilty. Someone hissed, "Shush now," as they entered.

At first it looked as though it might not be too grisly, even as though the evening might pass off fairly amicably. Clara thought nice Stuart, and possibly also Richard, who she came to realise was as wimpy and hippy and get-along-with-everyone-pleasantly as Miles, had urged the others not to indulge in yokel-baiting. Conversation was general and uncontroversial. There was TV talk and celebrity gossip they smiled politely at. A celebrity had recently died, provoking widespread mourning in the media and solemn articles about what his life had meant, echoed here; Clara said that this was her and Miles's farewell appearance as they were going to kill themselves out of grief. "The light has gone out of the world." They looked dim and incurious through not having read many currently talked-about books, but were at least able to enthuse about some of the ones of recent years that absolutely everyone had read and loved, such as *The Quincunx*, and all the men except for Keir lit up when Miles mentioned Flashman. Clara made a tactical mistake in mentioning she was currently reading a Sven Hassel. Weren't they about Nazi soldiers in World War Two, someone asked. Well, ordinary Germans who didn't want to be Nazi soldiers, Clara said. It was hard to explain about Sven and she didn't try. Once Miles had reminisced to her about the time he worked in a second-hand bookshop and had told her of the old woman who kept avidly buying Sven Hassels, and Clara told him

Mrs. Mauberley her aged vicious childhood cleaning woman was into them too, and Miles had speculated that maybe all old women secretly dreamed of being German soldiers, and Clara had said not just *old* women, the Russian front, killing Communists, probably a free chocolate ration ... Somehow Sven Hassel had become part of their private world without their ever having read one, and finally Clara had bought one off a stall out of curiosity. She told them now that it was rather gruesome and nasty, too much so for her really, but essentially anti-war and -nationalism and -everything that made men kill each other, but shit Keir still shook his head and muttered knowingly to Seal.

Before coming here Miles had nipped to the village for a paper and considerately studied the sports pages, so he had something to talk to the other men about. Once he was forced to quite rudely deflect Stuart away from geology. Richard baffled Miles by enthusing about some new gadget he had bought, and Miles smiled and made polite noises, and Richard had to be forcibly restrained from getting up in mid-meal to fetch and demonstrate it. Then Richard asked if Clara and Miles had a presence on a fashionable internet platform currently much used by media people and others to share with the world every last stray banal disconnected thought that happened to drift through their heads and make primitive signals of tribal identity; looking and sounding quite convincingly pitying, Clara said, "Oh Richard, you've been off the information technology beat too long, no-one's on *that* dinosaur any more. Everyone's on Shitblitz now. Your messages can only be eight characters long, it really sharpens up your thinking." Richard looked shattered for a minute, but started to frown dubiously long after the moment for query had passed.

The food was quite nice, and Harriet didn't commit the elementary mistake of trying to jolly her non-vegetarian guests into agreeing that her meat-substitute was any kind of a substitute for meat. The wine was abundant. Richard was a good and attentive host in that respect at least; in fact as the evening went on Miles came to suspect he was plying Clara and himself with it, at Harriet's behest, to loosen their tongues. He took full advantage, uncaring, while Clara sipped daintily and sparingly.

They discovered or pieced together various bits of information about their fellow guests. Wendy was Harriet's cousin and was doing a doctorate of some sort. Keir was a lawyer who worked for a Human Rights organisation, of the sort that concentrated on scrutinizing democracies, the one in fact that had recently denounced a prominent homosexual rights campaigner as a bigot, racist and imperialist because he had condemned Iran for hanging homosexuals. Such were the times they lived in. Such were among Miles's reasons for starting to believe, if not in God, then at least in the devil. When they realised this Clara and Miles exchanged glances. It crossed both their minds to ask him how he justified this given what he had said about religion; no, in fact, just to justify it, just to explain it, and explain how he lived with himself, how he got up in the morning and went to sleep at night and came here and ate food and talked about his work so smugly and self-righteously, to *explain* himself, just to bloody *explain* himself; they separately decided that anything along these lines would be rude and counterproductive and liable to lead to them swearing at him if he did in fact try to justify it, but their stomachs knotted and Clara felt cold and queasy as she had once in the presence of insanity and took another sip of her wine. In a previous job Keir had worked on the Human Rights Act case of a convicted murderer serving a life sentence who was suing for the right to start a family by artificial insemination. His father represented the government in the House of Lords. Seal was his wife and a university academic specialising in Theory of Social Justice; she had caused a stir in the press a few weeks ago when she had announced she would accept essays from her students written in text-speak.

It was such a waste, Clara thought. It was such a waste of an opportunity. (And to avoid the possibility of disappointing the reader we should perhaps warn you that the opportunity pretty much remains wasted; Clara doesn't stab these people over dessert, or punch them, or punish them in any way.) Stuart and Wendy were lovely, Richard was an idiot but currently trying to be nice, she had come to feel sorry for Harriet, but the other two at least were The Enemy writ large, the sort she was really longing to yell at and annoy all the times when she had to make do with pallid substitutes. But she kept quietish, and civilised, and polite, and sipped her wine, and traced the scratch on the table with her finger, and when at length things turned sour, it wasn't her fault, really.

The talk started to drift into news, politics, the state of the nation and so on. This happened spontaneously at first but as it went on efforts were clearly being made to bait Clara and Miles; Harriet could be seen to nudge the awful Keir to egg him on. But neither rose to it much for a while, and in fact the first thing that goaded Clara to speak up properly arose quite innocently out of the natural flow of conversation.

Miles and Stuart – who, Clara had realised, was not only pleasant but, while nominally as leftish as the rest of them, essentially fairly Reliable, someone to be spared when The Day came – Clara had sometimes told Miles that it would be quicker and more efficient to start keeping Life Lists rather than Death Lists – Miles and Stuart had started on Swapping Lunacies, the popular modern pastime for anyone who read the papers, comparable perhaps to small boys in wartime showing off spent munitions and bomb fragments they had found. Old women manhandled by security guards for eating a biscuit in the wrong place; shopkeepers and householders arrested for defending their property against thieves; a man fined by police for littering after dropping money on the pavement; a woman given a criminal record and punitive electronic tag for selling a goldfish to a child; quirky little corners of life's rich tapestry, in Britain in the Embarrassing Age, such as that. Clara meanwhile amused herself by playing Cliche Bingo with the others. "It's political correctness gone mad!" they jeered ironically in chorus. "Bleeding elf n safety spoiling everyfink!" they jeered ironically in caricature working-class voices. "Country's going to the dogs! Bring back the birch! I miss the good old days, old bean!" they jeered in caricature posh voices. They laughed delightedly, they joined in together, they thought it was the greatest fun.

"For Christ's sake, Stuart, you're sounding a bit Daily Mail," said Richard at last, after the geologist had delivered himself of a full-blown rant.

"House," said Clara to herself.

"Call him Stuart Littlejohn," jeered Keir, referring to the collector and connoisseur of such lunacies who wrote for that paper.

"Well ... all right, maybe," mumbled Stuart with a sheepish laugh. "All I know is I miss having my bins emptied without any lip from the people I pay to do it."

"Don't apologise," said Clara. "For the intellectually lazy and incurably smug and complacent like these lot, describing something as 'Daily Mail' is just a way of saying 'Road Closed'. It's just a way of closing off an avenue of thought. The same as saying 'right-wing', for that matter, or 'conservative' or 'reactionary'. Those are all descriptive terms, not insults or labels saying 'Forbidden' or 'need not think about'. You can't just say 'Daily Mail' and win, you lazy bastards, or make any kind of a point at all, you have to engage with their ideas and opinions, if you are able to. In this case kindly say why you think the things they have been talking about are good things to happen."

Keir sneered. Seal looked astonished. "Told you so," said Harriet smugly to the room at large. "You see what I have to deal with? I kept having the Daily Mail pushed through my door, you know."

"How awful," said Miles. "You must have felt violated."

"Well, it wasn't as bad as the rock through the window."

That subdued Clara and indeed Miles for a while, but now the baiting began in earnest. It was difficult not to respond, would have been rude as well as feeble not to reply when direct questions were addressed, and it was quite dismaying when honest answers provoked sneers and open mouths. Clara had not been able to Think of Something, as she had blithely promised Miles, to avert this, or turn the tables, or secure victory, or make this a fun rather than a tense and ghastly evening. She had made experiments from time to time with a sort of mental ju-jitsu, using the Enemy's own lunacies and pieties against them. The results had sometimes been promising, at least diverting, as with Harriet and Gypsy Meg. Of course it was winning in the Enemy's own arena rather than in the realms of logic or common sense, and it must be dangerous to seem to grant some of their premises, but it had its satisfactions. She toyed now with trying to gain points by alluding to Miles's prole-ish origins – the members of his clan tended to just fall short of genuine 'street credibility' and impressive toughness – for example a soldier grandfather who morris-danced and had not been weaned from the breast until adolescence, a boxing cousin who collected dolls, a docker uncle who obsessively re-read Proust – most were petty bourgeois, really, but they were definitely more earthy and common than anyone these lot knew, which in an age of guilt and inverted snobbery often brought kudos. But she suspected it would do little to mitigate the onslaught in this case, more likely the reverse. These people, second and third generation elite, heirs of meritocrats, nominal socialists, these modern intelligentsia in the orbit of the people's party – they didn't really like the working class, she reckoned, they had proven it time and time again. They looked down on them more than any old-time aristocrat had done. They found them unsatisfactory, backward and resistant to change, they suspected them of bigotry, they were not a favoured group. If Miles's family had been criminals it might have been better.

Clara had to admit herself at a loss. She might as well just enjoy it and start snarling and insulting back. It would be undignified and embarrassing, but perhaps by playing the role Harriet had brought her here to enact she would repay some of the awful debt of guilt. Still she wished she could think of something clever, something with finesse. She thought perhaps the wine she had sipped was fuddling her wits; whenever Clara drank at all she always wondered how much more brilliant she would have been if she hadn't, and she was paranoid that the smallest drop made her dim. Alcohol could revive flagging courage or undo stomach-clenching and toe-curling, hence she continued to sip at it now, but didn't otherwise have much effect on her; she had few inhibitions to lower.

Meanwhile Miles, who had not been stinting on the wine but was still in control of himself, was finding he very badly wanted to punch Keir, who was drunk and obnoxious and if he hadn't been drinking would just have been obnoxious. Now he leaned forward and said something appalling about immigrants, obviously expecting Miles to agree. Miles just stared at him. Then Keir proposed something Miles found fairly sensible or at least arguable about immigration policy, obviously in the same hope of entrapment, nudging his wife in anticipation. When Miles was noncommittal, Keir raised the case of an extremist Muslim preacher and convicted criminal the country was forbidden to deport because of human rights requirements, again playing agent provocateur.

"Yes," sighed Miles, "I agree. They should deport him. They should send him back to his own country so they can try him for the crimes he committed there rather than keep him here living at the taxpayers' expense and, no, I don't care if his own people hang him."

"You see?" muttered Keir to his wife.

"It's a different country," said Seal shaking her head.

"I don't think the immigration debate is a conversation we are mature enough as a country to have at the moment, thanks to certain people flinging certain accusations around like confetti," said Clara, who had decided to stop playing pussy. "And of course because no-one wants to appear to be rude to national guests the majority of whom are individually lovely and less well-off than most of us. We prefer resentment, riots and strained resources to a sensible, if potentially awkward and embarrassing, discussion. Speaking for myself I don't mind who comes in, so long as there are not too many and they are nice, useful, cheery people. Numbers matter, and culture, and it is useless to pretend they don't, and you must look after your own first or a terrible price will be paid. However, I think personally I would happily deport all the unpatriotic, parasite, native-born lunatic Piagnoni pigs like some of the people around this table, no offence intended, and replace them with nice hard-working cheerful sane people from the former Commonwealth, or Europe, or anywhere, so long as they were happy to be here and loved freedom and this country as much as I do. In fact, if you would agree to fuck off elsewhere, Keir, I would let in a dozen convicted murderers with bombs strapped to their backs, as they would do less damage."

"Cigarette break," said Miles, rising.

"You go," said Clara through bared teeth, "I am just getting started."

Miles took his wine with him and stayed out for two cigarettes and half of a third. When he returned things were much louder and more heated. Clara was either quite drunk by her standards or had decided to pretend to be so in order to act up.

"It's perfectly simple," she was saying, raising her voice to override the other raised and outraged voices around her. "Some of *my* ancestors came over from Normandy on splendid warhorses a thousand years ago, trampling your debased peasant forebears into the mud. Some of Miles's ancestors inadvertently floated over from Ireland on Guinness crates after a good night out, or emerged, skulking and shambling and fearful of the light, from Nibelheim, or, for all I know, Mordor. But the point is … " she seemed to have lost track of it, "they didn't kill or rape anyone," she concluded lamely to the groans and shouts of absolutely everyone. "Well," she modified fairly, "I know for a fact that plenty of mine did, and I am certain that Miles's must have. All right," she conceded, "*our* ancestors killed, raped, looted, plundered, burned and stabbed for fun and profit, but," she held up a finger, "they didn't expect to be thanked for it. They did it for the love of the thing itself. And they did it on their own dollar and not at the taxpayers' expense. Do you see? And they did it with a song in their hearts and a merry quip, which is something you people know nothing about. I think I would just get rid of you lot and then stand at Heathrow and let in anyone who laughed when you tickled them. I will yield the floor now," she said waving a hand, "I believe I have made my point." She sat back and allowed the shouts to mount.

Stuart was staring into nothingness glumly and boredly and pouring wine into himself with industrial speed and efficiency. Miles thought this last was a very good idea and followed suit. After a while, as the row continued to engulf the rest of the table, he leaned close to Stuart and said, "Let's talk about geology." He paused, stumped, and then asked: "What's your favourite kind of rock?"

"Um … pumice," replied Stuart after a moment.

"Mine too!"

"Let's drink to that."

"Oh this country, this country," Keir was sneering.

"Yes this country," Clara cried. "You people hate this country because it gave the world civilisation and you hate civilisation. I'd like to deport *you* into a parallel universe where there never was a Britain. You'd be speaking German, or French, or Spanish – "

"Oh boo hoo, nightmare, that's your biggest fear, isn't it?"

" – because Hitler would have won, or Napoleon, or the Armada, and there'd have been no industrial revolution, and you'd all be bloody feudal serfs crawling in the mud, as you deserve, because there'd be no Magna Carta, or parliament, and – "

"You're a horrible bigot," cried Seal.

"Look, let's all calm down," said Richard.

"This is what I'm surrounded by out here, on my own, all the time," cried Harriet.

"What's your second favourite kind of rock?" Miles asked Stuart quietly.

Stuart thought for a moment. "Quartz," he pronounced.

"Fucking quartz," said Miles appreciatively.

They clinked glasses in celebration of quartz.

"You know what I would do, if you're going to obsess about immigration?" Clara was enjoying this now. She was sitting back with her arms folded, as calm as her opponents were het up, speaking carefully and clearly, if occasionally loudly to make herself heard. "I would make people fight to come here, the way it's always been. I would have a boxing ring set up on the edge of the White Cliffs of Dover, or on a float in the Channel, and the candidate for entry would have to fight one of you, one of you useless self-important parasites, no offence intended, fight you no holds barred. If he throws you off, he's in and you're out. We just paste his picture in your passport and give him your name. But he would have to kneel to kiss the flag first, and tell me a joke that made me laugh, and sing some kind of merry song. In fact I think I would make him swim the Channel first, so we got the real elite. With a dagger in his mouth. That's how this island was colonised, the toughest people in Europe swimming here in dead of night with daggers gripped between their teeth. *That's* how you enter Britain, and that's who we are. And if you *nationless slime* think you can dismantle a country without a fight, just wait. Imagine a race of psychotic Vietnam vets turned hippies, very very stoned and slow to react but dangerous when roused. Imagine a nation made out of Celts, Romans, Vikings, Germans, snotty Frenchified Vikings and people who liked to paint their arses blue, who happen to have left off mayhem and violence because they were taught manners by missionaries and found they preferred a quiet pint and a pipe and pottering around their gardens in privacy. Take away the pint, the pipe and the privacy, to say nothing of the manners and the missionaries, and see what you get. Fuck off and live in Brussels quick, if that's where your hearts are, I really advise that before you go any further. I will take a question from Richard now," she said pointing calmly as another uproar began.

"I quite like limestone," Miles said.

"Limestone was possibly my first true love," came Stuart's mellow voice.

Keir had trampled over Richard, who was trying to keep things on terms of amiable discussion, and was making a loud aggressive speech, as rude and insulting as Clara's but less calm. " ... we haven't even begun to change things yet! Just you wait! The first thing we're going to do is wipe out all of you Tory toffs once and for all!"

"You *are* the toffs, you ridiculous man," Clara cried. "The only difference is that the old-fashioned toffs at least assumed responsibility for the people in their care, and looked after the land in their care, and were prepared to defend their country."

"Feldspar," sighed Miles.

"*Feldspar*," groaned Stuart, lustfully, making his aroused perv face, loudly enough that the others glanced at them briefly.

"Do you think it's just us?" Clara demanded. (Clara is getting to talk more because we like her more than the others; also because she *was* talking more. We never set up to be Thomas Love Peacock, and a good job too.) "Do you think it's just what you call Middle England? It's ordinary people everywhere who are fed up of you. You'd get it worse if you dared show your faces in the working-class areas of the cities. They expected you, God help them, to take their side against big business. They never signed up for your society-destroying lunacy, and they are the ones who have felt the effects worst."

"Dolomite," yelled Stuart ecstatically.

"*Dolomite*," groaned Miles orgasmically.

" … bunch of servile, forelock-tugging reactionaries, nasty little bigots and xenophobes addled by tabloids written by people like you … the fact is the immigrants are the only ones who want to do any work … "

"The British working man can work twice as hard as any foreigner," declared Clara angrily, "given the chance and a fair wage! There is an underclass who are out of practice, but who let them get that way?"

"Guys, guys, come on, cool it."

"Sandstone," sighed Stuart happily.

"Sandstone," concurred Miles nodding.

They tilted their heads and thought about sandstone for a moment with wistful little smiles. Stuart was now Miles's first and greatest friend. It was a friendship that was to survive the night. For months afterwards Miles and Stuart were to exchange postcards with, at most, single words on: the names of rocks and stones, or just pictures or drawings of them, Miles even buying a geology book for the purpose.

" … why do lefties *wurrrve* criminals?"

"Listen to this! Listen to this! Tell them, Clara. Tell them about your hedgehog-punishment idea."

"It is the capitalist system that causes … "

"It is absolutely immoral of you to construct and exclude an Other arbitrarily designated the Criminal … "

"Malachite."

"*Malachite!*"

" … we are the people who make the country run, the parts of it that still do run. You are parasites, no offence intended, and should learn your place. If the state doesn't draw in its claws pretty quick there simply isn't going to be a state, because we will withdraw our consent. We are sick of paying for the privilege of being lectured to, and bossed around, and treated like idiots, while all the time …"

Stuart beckoned conspiratorially and leaned close to Miles, looking solemn. Miles inclined his head, seized by the foreknowledge that whatever rock Stuart said would strike him as the funniest word ever, and starting to giggle in anticipation at his deadpan earnest face.

"No, no, listen, Miles," Stuart murmured. "*Gneiss*."

Clara was vaguely aware of and was becoming very jealous of Miles and Stuart's rock game. As he collapsed in hilarity now and weakly cried, "Gneiss!" she stopped haranguing the others and listening to their shouts and took his hand. "Miles we are all debating politely. We are discussing things sensibly and putting the world to rights between us, aren't we Richard? I am defending our corner artfully, with no help from you. I am being a bit forthright at times but I am remembering to say things like 'No offence intended.' "

"Yes, very good, but let's keep it calm. No-one here is the government or anything," Miles told her.

"Yes, but they are Them. They are the bloodsucking metropolitan elite, no offence intended. I think you would all admit that, wouldn't you?"

"There is no They or Them! We're all people, this is a nice dinner party, these are our neighbours, and that kind of thing is never helpful."

"Hear hear," said Richard. "With reasonable debate, we can all reach a consensus."

"Did you hear that, Miles?"

"There are only people who, who want to get along in their society, and, and accept the tenor of their times, and it's up to us in a democracy and open society to change the tenor by – "

"There is a They!"

"I am proud to be They!" cried Keir. "And I am against people like you."

"Miles, Miles, leave it." Stuart tapped him on the shoulder, shaking his head and making a dismissive face, crinkling his eyes and wrinkling his nose. "We don't need this shit. We are men of rocks. Let's think about *obsidian*."

"*Obsidian*," gasped Miles, brows beetling.

They sat back and affected to think happily about obsidian, sighing a bit.

The row petered out anyway, Clara becoming non-responsive, mainly because she was jealous of the rock game and how Miles obviously *wurrrved* Stuart. Richard cleared some of the plates away and asked if they were ready for dessert. But then Harriet said, "Clara is a global warming denier too," and then they were properly off, worse than ever.

" … of course I wouldn't deny it in public," Clara said at one point. "It's important the workers swallow the lie, I'm just surprised to find you lot going along with it. It will be a glorious world for we oligarchs when the roads are uncluttered again and there are no riff-raff on planes. We can cull their numbers too. Make them buy carbon licences to have children. Eventually it will be a new Eden, just us and a few docile servants … apparently Mrs Thatcher started it all, you know, to promote nuclear power … "

Richard, previously a voice of moderation, naturally got drawn into this one, if not as rudely as the others. It was after all his area of expertise. He kept drawing his eyebrows down thoughtfully in a solemn and gravitas-enhancing way and saying things like, "I think I can speak with some authority on this," and "I've been told by a reliable source that the person making that claim isn't trustworthy," and of course, "Clear consensus."

Miles, who was running out of rocks to say anyway, found himself drawn into it too, mainly out of exasperation at some of the things Richard was saying. "You can't disprove it simply by looking at any one set of facts," Richard told him earnestly, repeating something a climate scientist had said to him.

"*Listen* to yourself! That isn't science!"

"It's all like that," said Clara. "It's a religion. I thought you said you believed in science, Keir? There is no way to disprove it. Absolutely anything that happens, hot, cold or indifferent, is taken as proof of it."

"You can't invalidate the models by referring to things that happen to have occurred in the real world."

"*Listen* to yourself!"

Keir and Seal talked about the need for global government; they had responded to Clara's baiting about culling numbers to say that, yes, as it happened, the human population would have to be reduced by billions.

Stuart drunkenly tapped Miles on the shoulder and leaned close, shaking his head. Miles prepared himself to savour another rock.

"It's all bullshit," Stuart muttered. "He's full of shit. Looking at a tiny pinprick of time, it's absurd. We're insects. We're nothing to the Earth. The glaciers have been sweeping up and down in their own sweet time since further back than we can count. I'm going to tell him," he muttered mutinously.

Wendy overheard and nudged him scoldingly. "Shh! He knows better than you. You only know about your field. He looks at the big picture."

"Well, I know the data from *my* field is being misused. And you know what? When you talk to people in other fields, theirs is too. And we all keep quite and go along with it because we assume or hope it's a different story in other fields and they know what they're talking about. But it's the people in the middle who put together the big picture who are spinning everything out of all proportion. It's all shit. I'm going to tell him."

Wendy glared and leaned close and muttered chidingly. Miles heard, "... your career ... "

Stuart continued to rumble to himself, his wife continued to nag him to hold his peace. Things became even more heated among the main combatants. Richard suddenly seemed to weary of it and reverted to his former role of peacemaker. "Come on gang, throttle back, we can discuss this rationally," he sighed. Clara was yelling in frustration.

In a minor lull Miles managed to say to Richard, "Not to change the subject but talking of dangerous heat I see Arsenal have bought ... " Richard's face lit and he plunged into it eagerly, Stuart brightened and joined in too, and soon even Keir got sucked in. Presently all the men were talking about football, abusively but amicably, and with the exception of Miles far more knowledgeably and authoritatively than they had talked of anything else that night.

Meanwhile Clara and Harriet and to a certain extent Seal continued to yell at each other about alleged manmade global warming.

"Miles back me up," Clara suddenly barked.

"Richard back me up," Harriet yelled at Richard.

"We're talking about football," said Richard.

"We are talking nicely," said Miles.

"Oh isn't that typical," said the two women together.

"Isn't it? Isn't it?" Clara carried on in annoyance. "Aren't they just sanctimonious lily-livered bastards? Isn't it like having a useless hippy pacifist for a lieutenant? And tonight *we*'ll get the blame. 'Why can't you be nicer? Why don't you make an effort to get along with people? All the men did.' Look at them," she said in disgust. "Look at all the penises sticking together."

"It's true," laughed Miles. "Men are the peacemakers, and you know why? Because we are the ones who die in wars."

"You sexist pig!
         /bastard!" Harriet and Clara cried together.

"There are lots of female soldiers, and anyway it's men who start wars," continued Harriet.

"If there was a war *I* would be in the SAS and *you* would be a sandbag Miles," Clara continued simultaneously and furiously. "I could easily have you in a fight and you *know* I could."

"You, you continue to cherish this delusion, but the fact is we have never had a proper fist-fight, feeble woman."

"Just you wait then. Just you wait until we get home and we'll see."

"Hit her with a rock, Miles," Stuart advised. "Hit her with a chunk of basalt."

"*Basalt!*" Miles groaned euphorically.

"Oh Christ listen to them. *Basalt!*" she mimicked derisively. "Why don't you marry each other?"

"Do not take the name of basalt in vain," said Stuart thunderously.

"What know you of rocks, woman?" said Miles. "Leave us to talk of manly things you cannot possibly comprehend."

"What can soft and yielding creatures such as you have to offer a man who has known the stern embrace of," Stuart clenched a fist in the air, "granite?"

"*Granite,*" groaned Miles.

"Infants," said Clara. "Everything else is distraction. All other differences should be set aside until women take over the world and start to run things properly."

"Agreed," said Harriet, Seal and Wendy.

"You should do it," said Richard. "We'd go along with it, so long as you carry whips and wear thigh-boots."

"Oh, and jodhpurs," said Miles.

"And necklaces of *flint,*" said Stuart.

"Miles wanted me to dress as an elf," said Clara glaring.

"I never did!"

"Oh, that's nothing to what Richard asked me."

"Did I tell you we saw two locals skipping through the fields dressed as bishops?" Richard said hastily.

Miles laughed loudly. "Maybe they *were* bishops."

"When he was home for once," said Harriet bitterly. "He wasn't here when I saw a Klansman."

"A Klansman?" said Stuart. Richard gave him a look and shook his head warningly.

Clara would later try to claim to Miles that she had engineered the Sex War purposely, that that was the plan she had come up with on grounds of Divide and Conquer, and would reproach herself for not having thought of it. But the fact is it came about spontaneously like this, and if she fanned the flames it was from no reason of strategy but out of genuine indignation on behalf of and instinctive solidarity with Harriet.

"Let's not start this now," said Richard.

"No, let's," said Harriet.

"It's the same with me," said Wendy sympathetically. "He's always off on the other side of the world collecting his pebbles."

"Pebbles?" cried Miles in outrage. "*Pebbles?* You foolish woman, that is probably shale!"

"*Shale,*" cried Stuart. "Truly they cannot comprehend."

"He's off again on Tuesday," said Harriet.

"Do you think I like it?" said Richard.

"Yes. Yes I do."

"It's my job! Let's discuss it another time." He made a humorous 'Uh-oh' face at the other men. Harriet caught it.

"It isn't a bloody joke," she yelled, and threw a salt-cellar at him.

There was a pause. All of a sudden everything was terribly tense and uneasy and definitely the worst dinner party of all time it had several times threatened to be. The eyes of most of the guests defocussed as they suddenly tried not to be there.

"Agate," Stuart murmured to Miles.

"Stuart shut up," said his wife.

"I am sick and tired of being stuck here on my own," said Harriet.

"You've had a bit too much to drink," said Richard. "Let's – "

"No she hasn't!" blazed Clara loudly. "Don't you dare put her down like that! It's bloody disgusting, Richard!"

"Clara, keep out of this," said Miles.

"Shut up, Man! I will not! Why can't she have a car?" Clara yelled at Richard. "Why don't you take her with you?"

"It's – "

"None of your business," Miles finished for Richard.

"Piss off, Miles, I'm making it my business. If you can stick together so can we. Well? Richard? I'm waiting for an answer."

"That was a joint decision," said Richard, getting angry now. "I've told her she needs a car, but she – we're trying to cut down on our footprint. Tell them!"

Harriet, who had her head in her hands and silent tears streaming down her face, nodded and mumbled. "I don't need a car."

Clara let loose a volley of pithy curses. "Yes you bloody do! It's disgusting! It's disgusting! Buy her a bloody car! Make her use her ----ing washing machine! End all this feudal nonsense now! You've got her out there toiling in the fields like some medieval beast of burden, and cut off here alone. Look at the state of her! Aren't you ashamed?"

"Clara, pipe down," cried Miles.

"This is Harriet's choice," said Richard.

"She's right," cried Harriet. "It's not fair. I'm sick of it. I can't take it any more. I can't cope! It isn't working! I try and I try and I just can't do it. I wasn't meant to live on the soil. I spend two days planting onions and the Earth spits them back out at me!" she sobbed. Clara fought back a blush and glared at Richard some more.

"You were as up for this experiment as I was," protested Richard. "If we can't make a go of this – our papers – we can't just abandon it now. You thought it was a great idea!"

"I didn't know what it would be like!" Harriet yelled, wiping her tears off angrily. "I didn't know you wouldn't be here! I am stuck here on my own surrounded by surly peasants, no offence intended, who hate me!"

"Nonsense," Richard muttered, drinking. "I wish you wouldn't exaggerate that side of things. It's bloody embarrassing. Everyone is perfectly – "

"You don't see the looks I get when I go to the bloody shops!"

"Well, perhaps if you made more effort. Everyone is perfectly polite to me."

"You are never here!" she yelled. "They came here in the middle of the night and they threw a fucking rock through my window and I was on my own! And you never came back in my hour of need!"

"Oh, the rock," muttered Richard. "The rock, the rock, the rock. Let's talk about the rock, shall we?" he cried angrily. "Why did you never report it to the police?"

Harriet looked uneasy. "There was no point," she mumbled. "It might have been a lunatic. It might – "

"Yes, it might!" yelled Richard. "You know what I think? I think you threw the bloody rock through the window yourself, you madwoman!"

There was another, longer, infinitely more ghastly pause.

Harriet stared at him, her mouth hanging open, wide-eyed.

Clara cleared her throat.

"Actually," she said in a small voice, staring at the table, "I threw the rock through your window."

She pushed back her chair and rose.

"I threw the rock through the window," she repeated more loudly.

Several pairs of eyes swivelled to stare at her; several jaws dropped.

She walked round the end of the table so she was standing right next to Harriet, and put her hand on hers.

"Forgive me," she said solemnly.

Harriet stared at her, in incomprehension, alarm, shock, disbelief; then she tilted her head back and smiled, and turned to look at Richard in triumph.

Clara bowed her head. As she and Harriet were at the end of the table, and as she had stood right next to Harriet side-on to the others, only Harriet had been able to see the slow, deliberate wink that had occluded Clara's left eye.

"But it was not a Hate Crime," Clara continued on an impulse. "It was a Love Crime. The rock was aimed at Richard, not you. I knew your columns were a cry for help, and he should never have brought you here and abandoned you. I wanted to make you pack up and go for your own good. You should not be buried here as I have been." She paced away and looked solemn. "Oh," she waved a hand dismissively, "and I did the Ku

Klux Klan thing, and the Lambing, and so on, for similar reasons of disinterested kindness. Miles give them some money."

Stepping out into the spring night air she found the guilt had gone.

Clara and Miles walked home in the moonlight. Slowly their hands reached out and found the other's.

"This is what comes of mingling with other people," said Clara. "It doesn't suit us. It was asking for trouble. We shouldn't get involved in their madness, whether to yell at them or try to save them. We should just keep ourselves to ourselves and play nicely like good children. We have learned a lesson, and the lesson is, stay at home with the blinds drawn and our fingers in our ears and only emerge when it's all over."

"Was that our first proper fight?" asked Miles.

"That?" said Clara in surprise. "Good God no. When I fight with you you'll know about it. I am saving our first fight for something special."

"That was a sweet and noble thing you did. I just hope she doesn't call the police tomorrow."

"Oh no; only Richard will pay."

An owl hooted. There was a smell of warm spring night. Their shoes sounded nice on the road.

"Will you forgive me for throwing the rock?" asked Clara.

"If you'll forgive me for not throwing a rock," said Miles.

Clara thought for a moment.

"No," she said judiciously. "I won't. It could easily become a habit with you. And I am afraid of it coming between us; it could make you act superior. You owe me a rock through someone's window, at a time and place of my choosing. It might be next month, a year from now, or fifty years down the line. I have your IOU and when I tell you to do it you have to, no matter what. Deal?"

"Deal. Likewise I am allowed once and only once to tell you not to throw a rock even if the situation really calls for it."

"That makes sense. Let us swear on our noses." They put the index fingers of their free hands on the tips of each other's noses in the solemn Nose Oath. "Now we are both as guilty as each other, and neither can be sent to Heaven or Hell unless the other one can come too."

They walked on in silence towards the moon for a time.

"Miles, do you want to know something funny or sad? I think Harriet and her friends think we are lunatics."

"Poor world," Miles sighed.

"Yes," said Clara. "Isn't the moon bright tonight? Let's keep walking towards it forever. We will follow it wherever it leads us, across field or forest or hill."

"All right," said Miles.
Hand in hand they walked off along the silver path.

Chapter Fifteen

Clara and Miles were trying to write novels again, or at least Miles was. Clara was sitting at her desk doing other things and keeping him company nicely, she thought.
"Miles I am taping my face up."
"Good," said Miles. "The mouth, I hope."
"No the eyes. Miles, look, this is what I would look like if I was Japanese or something. Well, more like a Star Trek alien actually. Or an elf. An elf, Miles! Look! Do you like it?"
"No," said Miles not looking.
"Racist." There was a sticky rasp. "Ow! Miles I hurt myself a bit taking the sellotape off, but I am all right really. Miles is my face back to normal though?"
"You have a mirror."
"I want a second opinion. I don't think my eyes have quite gone back to being round."
"Well they weren't round to begin with, were they?" Miles immediately regretted getting drawn in.
"Well what shape were they?"
"Eye-shaped."
"Miles don't you know what shape your own wife's eyes are?"
"Oval."
"Miles please look, I am nervous. What if I am stuck like that?"
"You can write a magazine article, 'I turned myself Japanese in a pathetic bid to gain my husband's attention'."
"Miiiles."
Miles very carefully and precisely laid his pen down. He looked. Clara was making her eyes as round as she could, and was also revolving her pupils round and round.
"Stop that."
"Miles I am hypnotising you. *Trussst in meee, jussst in me*," she sang. "Miles can we play I'm a snake again?"
"Not just now doll, I must finish this."
"Of course, the great work comes first."

There was a sigh and then silence for several seconds.

"Miles, look, I have taped pictures of your head onto my body, and vice versa. This is what our babies might look like." Miles did not look. "*If* they are hermaphrodites," she conceded. "Then I taped a picture of your mother's head onto a pit bull's body, for a laugh. Then I put a picture of Harriet in a pit bull's mouth. I have had a productive afternoon. How about you?"

"Less so," said Miles evenly.

"Well, you might get the hang of it one day, like sex. Has he finished his awful depressing breakfast yet?"

"Almost."

"Perhaps, after that, he should slouch back to bed for a while, for more brooding."

Miles had, actually, been tempted along those lines already – it would solve various plot problems, and a few more pages of supine meditation on the part of his protagonist might help him ease his way into the novel – but had been afraid Clara would laugh.

"That's not a bad idea actually," he said thoughtfully, and with an air of innocent surprise.

Clara did laugh.

"God help us all. Tear it up and start again, man!"

"There's some good stuff. I'm getting somewhere."

"There are some moving descriptions of tangled duvets and stained ceilings. Why is his ceiling stained, Miles? Does he masturbate like a gushing oil-rig?" Miles didn't see fit to dignify that with a response. "And you haven't even got to the front door. I don't think he *should* leave the house, though, not the day he's having. Can I read your description of his soggy cornflakes again? With the exception of certain first-hand reports of the Hindenburg disaster I think it is the most heart-rending human document I have read."

"No."

"Please, just that bit. That's all I can take for one day. I don't think I could handle your harrowing description of what happens to his toast a second time. There are memoirs of Auschwitz that aren't as appalling."

"Leave me alone. I don't mock your Walpole stories."

"Miles send him back to bed again, then end the chapter. Then start a new chapter with him waking up the next day and groaning, realising he has to go through it all again. Make the whole book like that."

"I'm building to something."

"Is he going to do the dishes? He should definitely have a lie-down first."

"Hush, woman, I beg you."

There was silence for quite a brief interval.

"Miles, look. This is what I would look like if I had been born with socks over my hands. Would you still love me?"

"Not with those socks."

"How hurtful. Miles can we play at sock puppets?"

"Not just now, chickadee."

"Beast. You would if I was nude. You used to all the time. Perhaps my hands have become ugly from constant toil. I am going to write to an agony aunt to complain my husband won't play at sock puppets with me any more. No I will complain about your penis again and ask her if she is *sure* they all look like that. No! I shall write to that woman who does the consumer financial advice. She always gets results."

She pulled her big old manual typewriter closer and typed:

> Dear Prudence,
> Last November my bank advised me to cash in an insurance policy and invest in a stocks and shares ISA. I was assured nothing could possibly go wrong and yet my husband's penis looks awful. I have been unable to obtain any satisfaction from the bank, or indeed from my husband's penis. Help me and I will send you a drawing of my breasts, which are pretty.
> I love you,
> Clara

"Miles Miles come and look at what I wrote. If she doesn't get a new cock out of them I will know the reason why. *Miles*."

"I'm working. In a minute."

There was another sigh; another pause. Then:

"Miles, look. This is what I would look like if I'd been born with socks over my ears. It is a terrible affliction. I think I will start a charity for sufferers. My hearing is sort of muffled. It helps, a little bit, if I point the ends of the socks at what I want to listen to. Did you say something?" she asked pointing the sock-ears in his direction.

"No," said Miles.

"Oh," said Clara in disappointment, letting the ears droop. "Only I thought you did. I thought you might want a conversation with your wife, or something."

"In five minutes, babe."

"In a minute, babe. Later, doll. I am busy, sugar-tits. I am forging the uncreated consciousness of my race in the crucible of my soul, little woman. I will attend to you presently and doubtless attempt to inveigle you into something tawdry involving penises."

"Clara!" laughed Miles. "Just this paragraph, please."

Clara sighed. "Don't mind me. I am fine. I am thinking great thoughts too, you know. I think I will write to the producers of Star Trek describing an idea for an alien that has socks over its ears. It is cheap but effective. I will demand royalties. I will also send them a sketch of your penis, in case they have any use for that."

There was a sound of typing and scribbling. Then a whisper of: "I must lick these envelopes very quietly so as not to disturb my husband." Then some horrendous slurping noises, and then the sound of envelopes hitting her Out tray, and another sigh. Then:

"I will take a nap."

Then some snoring noises. Then:

"I have awoken refreshed and ready for more fun and frolics as the helpmeet of a great writer."

Then Miles heard some clicks and then:

"Gie gook. Miles look. I am attempting to staple my tongue out of boredom. Imagine if it gets stuck. How will you explain a wife with a stapler on her tongue to your friends down the pub?"

"I won't have to, they've met you."

"Miles have we reached the stage of our marriage where I irritate you yet? Do be sure and let me know when it happens so I can enjoy it more."

"Never, my sweet. But you know what really annoys me? When you are quiet for a moment. I don't think I could stand it if you tried that."

"Miles would you miss me if I was gone?"

"From this room?"

"I bet you would. Miles why do you want to be a writer when you have a wife who loves you for being a happy-go-lucky layabout? Do you fancy Melvyn Bragg or something? I don't understand."

"Clara please be patient. I'm trying to do this for both of us, you know."

"Yes, yes. Behind every great man is a great woman."

"A long way behind, sitting in the corner, being as quiet as a mouse," said Miles.

There was another pause, during which Clara made an outraged face, which was wasted because he still wasn't looking. Then:

"Miles look I have put butterflies on my nipples. The ring-binder-strengthening things, I mean, not real ones."

Miles looked. Clara was sitting there glaring, arms folded, socks still over ears, some ring-binder butterflies on her face but no nipples visible.

"*That* got your attention. Obviously that's all you want me for."

"I – I know a cry for help when I hear one." Miles shook his head at the socks and bent back to his writing.

"Obviously, if I want you to attend to my thoughts, I should write them on Post-it notes and stick them on my breasts. I really, really am doing that now and I think it is very, very sad." Miles sneaked another glance. "Tricked you again," said Clara, who was in fact painting her nails with Tipp-Ex. "You can look at my nails, though. Look, look, look what I've done."

"Clara! Be fair."

"Such things you promised during our courtship."

"Ten minutes."

"I thought, when I had a husband, I would always have someone to play with," she said sadly.

"We've been playing all week! I'm all played out! I feel the need to justify my existence."

"Of course this is what comes of marrying an oik. You were bred to work, I to idle pleasure, which is of course just a way of keeping my brain supple until some emergency requires me to assume command. Miles find me a mission," she implored. "I need another mission. The Endurance Shop, the art, something like that. As the stolid Watson of the relationship to my quicksilver Holmes it is your responsibility to keep me occupied lest I fall into a brown study and start shooting the Queen's initials into Mrs Hudson."

"Watson?"

"Watson! Please, Miles."

"Well ... I can think of one thing, but ... no, you wouldn't like it, you wouldn't dare."

"Tell me, Miles, anything!"

"Your mission ... "

"Yes?"

"If you choose to accept it ... "

"Yes!"

"Is ... "

"Yes?"

"Go and make tea and toast."

There was a sigh. "You are the Machiavelli of the domestic hearth. Will you at least time me to see how quick I am?"

Presently she brought tea.

"You wouldn't spill it on the work again, would you?"

"The thought had not crossed my mind," lied Clara setting it down daintily. "The toast burned. The tea may be slightly rubbish as I made it with socks over my hands as a challenge. Also," she admitted after Miles had drunk some, "I dipped my socks into yours out of mutiny."

Miles inhaled the steam, nostrils flaring, with an aroused face. "Mmmm!"

"It is good to know the spark is still there," said Clara.

She sat back down at her desk and sighed. Presently she started to flick rubber bands at him. Miles reacted to this when one hit him on the ear.

"Stop that or I will put you out."

"Oh oh Miles let's do that!" she cried eagerly. "Throw me out heartlessly while I scream and beg to be near you, and then I will sneak in again without you noticing me."

Miles laughed. "I'm right by the door, of course I'll notice."

"I bet you won't, I am very stealthy. Look, look, I'm going, goodbye." She flounced out and shut the door behind her. After a moment she opened it again, saying, "Wait, that was wrong, I'm not that stealthy, leave the door open. Now I will go away and then sneak in again."

She went away. Miles waited. Presently Clara crawled through the door, Indian-style, eyes wide.

"Well you can't look at it!" she cried. "Be absorbed in your bloody writing as always. Look away. Let me try again."

Miles tried, futilely, to absorb himself in his work again. Presently he heard minute sounds of stealthy breathing and suppressed sniggers, and some sort of slithering. He looked round to see a rug from the hall, humped over some horizontal wife-shaped object, advancing into the room by furtive inches.

As he looked her face peeked out and saw him.

"Damn," said Clara. "I thought I was over by the window now. I almost made it."

"You have the mind of a tiny child," he told her.

"But the body of a sensual wooman," she said huskily, rising and sashaying. "Would you like to see it?"

"Yes," said Miles. "Very much so. In a minute."

"Gay. Miles, Miles, close your eyes for a minute and I will hide in this room and I bet you won't know where I am."

"Please, darl, I want to work."

"But that is the beauty, you will be, undisturbed, you won't even know I'm there, I will just be spying on you quietly, gloating, secure in my secret possession of you. It's pathetic, I just want to be near you."

"I think the thought of being spied on will put me off and annoy me immensely."

"You won't know, I'll be as quiet as a mouse, you won't even hear me breathe."

"There's nowhere to hide in here! Obviously you will just be under my table."

"I won't! Go on, close your eyes and count to 100. No peeking."

Miles sighed and closed his eyes. "Will it gain me five minutes' peace?"

"Yes, yes! Cover your ears too. Count slowly."

Miles covered his ears. In spite of this he heard clearly, before he had counted to ten, a monumental and jarring crash. There was a massive old oak cupboard full of books and ornaments. Clara had attempted to climb up it in the thought of curling up on top and in the process had toppled it.

Miles leapt up.

"I am not hurt," said Clara.

"You will be," he said grabbing her. "That's it, out, get out."

"Miles please don't ban me from the room," she cried resisting. At the door she slid down and grabbed his shins and rubbed her head against his knees. "No, no, please, I'll be good."

He thrust her out and slammed the door and held it shut for a while, ignoring her wailing and pounding and scratching and faked sobs.

After that there was quiet for a time. Miles went back to his work, starting to suspect, as he always did when Clara let him concentrate for long enough, that it was trolleys. Still he was learning all the time, and he had to start somewhere, and discipline was vital. He had set a target of reaching the end of the page before he would allow himself to play with Clara again, and with earnest application he started to crawl towards it now.

The door opened again.

"Miles I am leaving you."

"Good," said Miles, not looking up.

"Don't try to stop me."

"No."

"Don't try to look for me."

"Of course not."

"I am running away to become a hobo."

"Excellent," said Miles, still not looking round.

Clara was dressed as a Chaplin tramp, and had a bundle of belongings tied up in a cloth on a stick, and had gone to quite a lot of trouble to do this. She was quite annoyed that Miles didn't at least look.

She stamped her foot. "Miles, you will be in trouble if you don't at least look."

"Just let me finish this page!" cried Miles, exasperated. "I love you dearly but you are the most annoying wife of our times."

Clara looked sad, though he did not see it.

"Farewell then," she said. "We must go our separate ways. I have left some pizza coupons in the oven and a drawing of my breasts on the desk."

"Thanks."

"It has not been all bad, has it, Miles? You must have known some moments of content."

"Mostly when you were asleep."

She blinked. "I see. Goodbye then. Take care of yourself. It – is what you are best at." She bit a knuckle and stifled a sob, but again he wasn't looking. She slammed the door in annoyance.

Miles finished his page triumphantly and leapt up, a rejoinder on his lips and let-out-of-school frolic in his heart. He stepped into the hall to find the front door open to the rain and hear the sound of the car driving off.

"Arse," said Miles.

He paced the house vexed, lonely and increasingly agitated for half an hour. There was a knock at the door. It was a man they knew from the village.

"Your car been stolen?" he asked. "Only I was just coming over the bridge and it's abandoned there, half in the road and with the door hanging open."

Miles had a sudden spurt of alarm which he suppressed. It was just Clara arsing around. He decided not to tell the man this.

"Oh God," he said. "Thanks. Could you give me a lift back there?"

En route Miles was nervous and distracted in spite of himself. His companion suddenly grunted.

"Christ Almighty, I must have had a hard day," he said. "I just thought I saw Charlie Chaplin walking across a field."

"Must have been a scarecrow," said Miles.

They came to the bridge. Miles thanked the man and waved him off. The car was as he had described it, left just before the bridge with its backside in the road and the door flung open, forcing any passing cars to veer around it beeping. The keys were in the ignition. He parked it properly off the road and went to look for Clara.

The water the hump-backed bridge crossed was really little more than a stream. He walked along the bank in the rain for some distance in both directions but saw no sign of her. He sat beneath the bridge and waited. His stomach was in a knot. Probably she was only arsing around, but possibly she was doing it because she was genuinely pissed off.

The rain stopped. It started to grow dark. He started to grow alarmed. He drove along the road for some distance beyond the bridge, then came back and visited a couple of friends in the village or nearby whom she might conceivably have gone to see. She hadn't, nor was she in the pub. He went home, increasingly worried and uncertain where to look for her next.

There was a light on in the house. Thank God. But when he went in he could find no sign of Clara.

That wasn't quite true. He knew, was certain somehow, that she was there. He just couldn't find her.

"Clara!" he called. "Come out! I'm sorry!"

There was no response. He started to check every possible hiding place – under beds, in the cellar, the attic, inside and on top of cupboards and wardrobes, everywhere – but couldn't unearth her.

She was expert at concealing herself, he had discovered in the course of their legitimate games of hide-and-seek, and also adept at moving stealthily from one part of the house to another to avoid him. With two sets of stairs she could circle round all night. He had also come to suspect she had discovered some super-secret hiding place he didn't know – wall or ceiling cavity, space at the back of a wardrobe, even a proper priest-hole. Once or twice he thought he heard tiny sounds but always on a different level from where he was.

If she was even here. That light might already have been on and he could be imagining he could sense her presence. Or she might have come back and gone again.

"Clara!" he yelled. "Come out now! I'm getting worried! At least give me a sign you're here!"

No sign was forthcoming. He slumped in a chair and stared at the phone. Suddenly he dashed to check the desks. She had sometimes hidden and left written clues leading him to her. There were no written messages. He checked the various outbuildings in the garden a second time then threw himself in the chair again. He oscillated between worry and annoyance. He didn't want to ring friends, family or police when she was almost certainly just arsing.

"I am writing a poem about how lonely I am," he shouted. "It is a very bad one and you are responsible."

There was no reply.

He cooked food, some of her favourite things, flapping the kitchen door about in an attempt to waft the smells through the house. He kept up a running commentary, saying things like, "Mmm!" and "All the more for me." She didn't appear. He left a plate on the top landing. When he came back to it a miserable hour later it was untouched.

The evening wore on. Rain blattered against the window wretchedly then stopped again. It came to him that this might well have been the longest time they had spent apart, if she wasn't nearby spying on him, since their marriage. He didn't like it much.

He put on the second movement of Ravel's Piano Concerto in G Major, which had soothed her savage breast and drawn her reluctantly out of a sulk once before, and which he had once told her reminded him of her, in her calmer moods.

Then, when that got no response, Debussy's *Clair de Lune*, about which he had once said something similar, but which he now intended as an insult.

He laid a trail of Maltesers from the top of the stairs to a trap in the study. The door was ajar and there was a bottle of Britvic standing invitingly on a table, but if she pushed the door wide a balanced pan would fall off the top. He slammed the front door as if he had left the house and tiptoed to hide somewhere. The trap was not sprung. Presently he gave up. Later he forgot and activated it himself, and the pan fell the wrong way and hit him on the head.

He thought furiously. It was pitch-black outside now. If he turned all the lights off at the fusebox it would hamper her sneaking about the house. He could arm himself with a torch and scour every last crevice.

The torch was not in the drawer where it was kept. Aha! Then she *was* here at least. He was still bored and lonely.

"Clara, this is half a day we will never get back," he shouted from the bottom of the stairs.

He threw himself into a chair with a book. He couldn't concentrate. He laid the book down and sat blankly. He thought he heard a noise upstairs and then in the hall but when he went to look there was nothing.

"Clara, if you knew how slowly and ... dead-ly the time was passing you wouldn't do this to me," he shouted.

He threw himself into the chair again, picked up the book again, threw that aside again. Before they were married Miles had written a poem, quite peevish but quite good he thought, about sitting in an empty house waiting for her to arrive. He went and rooted around and found a copy and placed it on top of her Britvic stash in the cellar.

He paced around like Kane in his mansion. "Rosebud," he croaked. He started to think about his lonely empty bed. Intolerable. Better to sleep on a couch.

Intolerably empty. The whole house was as empty and meaningless as hell must be. It *was* empty, he suddenly realised with a lurch of his stomach. He had been deluded to imagine there was a trace of life in the house. A mislaid torch proved nothing. He ought to call the police. He headed towards the phone.

The doorbell rang.

He opened the door. Clara stood there, in a dry raincoat, her hair pulled back in a severe bun. The Chaplin make-up had long gone.

"Thank God!" he cried.

She walked in. He had expected reproach, rebuke or triumph and was wrong-footed to see her gazing at him with what appeared to be compassion and concern. When he moved to hug her she pushed him lightly back with a hand on his chest but then stroked him briefly on the shoulder.

"You poor man," she said in a low tragic voice, still staring at him tenderly. "I came as soon as I heard."

"Heard what?" cried Miles in alarm.

"Why, that Clara had done away with herself, of course," she said raising her eyebrows.

There was a pause. Miles stared at her uncertainly. "I – "

"I'm sorry, did my appearance shock you? You must have thought I was her ghost." She held out her hand. "We have not met. I am Lara, Clara's twin sister. I expect she has told you all about me."

"No," said Miles as she shook his hand briskly. "No, she never mentioned you."

Clara, or Lara, looked slightly hurt. She sighed. "That is very like her. We did not always get on and had become estranged in recent years. Still I will not speak ill of her now she is in her watery grave. And I can console myself it was to me she turned in her final extremity."

"Watery grave?" said Miles.

"Even as a child she was unnaturally drawn to water," said Clara, or Lara, pacing the hall gazing off into memory. "Even when we shared a bath together as tiny mites she would stare hypnotised into it and say how peaceful it must be to lie immersed in its depths forever, the world a silent dream above you, your hair floating weightlessly like beautiful tendrils, your glassy eyes troubled only by the occasional rubber duck bobbing past. As she grew older we could not trust her even around washing-up bowls. Several times we found her with her head stuck in mop-buckets having attempted to drown herself therein. At school swimming lessons it became tiresome to be constantly fishing her out with a hook and pumping her lungs after she sank to the bottom like a happy lead weight. This would have happened sooner or later; you are not to reproach yourself."

Miles said, "The stream where the car was found was barely deep enough to drown a hamster in."

"That will not have mattered to a determined girl like Clara," said Clara. "I suppose the police are dredging the torrent now? They will not find her. She told me she intended to swim upriver until it merged with the mighty waters and she was free, free, free forever."

"Downriver, surely."

Clara twitched an eyebrow. "I am surprised you can be pedantic at a time like this. The fact is she was heading upriver, like a homing salmon, to fling herself up a waterfall. The essential point is that she is now a mouldering water-logged mass with fish-eggs in her ears due to your

269

insensitive thoughtlessness. But you are not to reproach yourself." She paced and wrung her hands. "She rang me, hysterical, to tell me what she intended. I believe her tears alone could have drowned her."

"I will never forgive myself," said Miles.

She flew to him and touched him on his arm. "But you must, you must! You must be strong and go on. Though you broke her heart her last thought was still of you. She begged me to come and look after you. I – I suppose I may?" she asked anxiously. "Stay here, and take care of you, and help you in your grief? Or is the sight of me too painful? Would you rather I leave?" She moved towards the door. "Oh of course I ought to leave, this was a terrible mistake."

"No, no!" cried Miles, getting between her and the door. "Stay – stay! I – I am very grateful. Please, come in. Here, let me take your coat." He helped her off with it. "It's uncanny, you really are awfully like Clara."

"We are physically identical in every way, apart from," she lowered her eyes demurely, "something you will never see, unless I get very drunk."

He took her into the lounge. "Would you like a drink? A cup of tea? A Britvic! I have one chilled in readiness."

"Ah, Britvic! Clara was partial to that, of course. But I, Lara, am an entirely different person and cannot stand the sight of it. I only drink grapefruit juice, which Clara wouldn't touch."

"I'm afraid we don't have any."

"You are no longer a we, you poor man," said Clara tragically. "Then I won't put you to any trouble. A humble glass of water will suffice for my needs. I, unlike Clara, can be trusted around water without attempting to drown myself in it like a lemming," she said and gave a loud and braying laugh. Her hand flew to her mouth. "Oh I am sorry! What a heartless joke! You must hate me. Unlike Clara I cannot make jokes successfully. I always envied her that. I always envied her everything. She was always the wild, spirited twin and I was the dull, drudge-like, uptight one," she said broodingly. "In many ways I am glad she is dead," she added in a vicious undertone mutter. Her eyes widened and she flew to Miles. "Forgive me, forgive me! I didn't mean it! I don't know what I am saying. I am – I am overcome by my grief." She buried her head against his chest and faked some sobs.

"I understand." Miles put his arms around her and patted her back. When he stroked her hair and started to squeeze her tight she broke free and primly said, "I think that is *not* an appropriate embrace for a sister-in-law."

"Oh, of course, forgive me."

There was a pause.

"Clara, I'm sorry," Miles said earnestly and pleadingly. "Really I am."

Clara raised her eyes towards heaven, or the ceiling which came first. "Did you hear that, Clara? He is sorry. Did you hear the grief in his voice?" She flew to him again. "You are not, not to blame yourself! Clara was always a rash, flighty, headstrong, heedless girl with no thought for anything but getting her own way. Look, look at what she has done to you! You must try not to think badly of her, and to forgive her in her turn as she doubtless forgives you."

"I would never think badly of her," said Miles. "I would do anything to have Clara back."

She raised her eyes again. "Did you hear that, sister?" She shook her head and sighed, regarding him soulfully. "How sad. Too late. She's stiff. Now," she said clapping her hands briskly, "I expect you are worn out with grief, and to tell the truth I am feeling tired after my long journey from," she waved a hand, "the dreary place where I lived writhing in Clara's shadow. Perhaps we should go to bed now."

Miles perked up. "Yes!" he cried, quite surprised. "Great idea! I mean – of course. I – I will show you where it is."

"I suppose you have guest rooms?"

"We turned them into playrooms."

Clara as Lara looked amused. "How like Clara! She was quite unable to face the responsibilities of adult life. I am a great believer in work, not play."

"Yes. The point is there is only one bed."

"Oh! Well, a couch will suffice for me. I never complain."

"I – no! No! I would not hear of it. Why Clara's ghost would haunt me. Besides I couldn't face the bed alone."

"But I cannot deprive you of it in your hour of grief."

"I – no-one need deprive anyone of it. I – we could share it together." Lara looked shocked and glared. "Chastely! Chastely! Of course. That goes without – You – No-one has anything to fear from me in that way again. I – I am quite shocked and hurt you could impute such – " He tried to look indignant.

She touched his arm. "Forgive me. But surely it would be most improper?"

"Clara would understand." He doubted this and suspected he might be setting himself up for endless recrimination when Clara returned in her own right, but, apart from the hope that they would be reunited in bed, he really couldn't face it alone. "Please. I won't be able to sleep by myself."

She bit her lip in indecision. "I suppose it can do no harm. The fact is I am desperate for a bed. If you will remember I am not Clara?"

"I – will endeavour."

"If you don't I will remind you of it, laddie-my-boy," she said severely.

They switched off downstairs and made their way to the bedroom.

"Oh – you don't seem to have a suitcase."

"Unlike Clara I set little stock by material possessions."

"Right. Um. I would offer you the use of her night-things, but perhaps it would be disrespectful? She usually slept, um, au naturel anyway."

"As do I," said Lara, "although in my case for health and vigour rather than sheer flightiness." She started to undress. "Please avert your eyes."

Miles did his best and started to undress himself. As he removed his underpants he caught Lara-Clara staring wide-eyed with something like Clara's scared face.

"Then she was not lying," she murmured. She looked away and bit a knuckle. "The poor woman."

He turned off the main light and they got into bed.

"Why are you smiling at me like that?" asked Lara severely. "Kindly turn off your table-lamp."

"In a minute. Please. Let me just look at you. You are so like her."

"But I am *not* her." She reached across him and switched off the lamp. "Goodnight."

For a prim prissy twin Lara lay awfully close to him. Miles whimpered softly. He was fairly certain that if he made a move on Clara in the character of her twin sister Lara the real Clara, when she returned, would upbraid him and indeed beat him about the head periodically for it for the rest of his life. Besides, he *did* find it rather sick and macabre and off-putting somehow; Clara had so successfully become Lara and he was so used to taking their more sophisticated games seriously that a part of his mind wasn't reacting as if it was his beloved bloody wife next to him. Another part of his mind, and indeed another part of his body, was urgently aware that it was, but he also doubted his punishment, for such he was certain it was, was over yet.

"Clara," he said plaintively in a small voice.

"The poor, poor man," murmured Lara aside. "Hark how he calls out to her."

Miles sighed.

It was enough that she was in this house, in this bed. He reached out to stroke her hair. After a moment a hand slapped his.

"You forget who I am."

"Please. At least just let me put my arms around you. I have been so lonely."

She allowed it. "Very well. But nothing else."

"No, just hold you. Please forgive me, Clara," he begged presently.

"Clara forgives you, I am sure," said Lara tenderly. "Now you must forgive yourself." Miles sighed. "May I ask what is pressing into me?" she asked, less warmly, after a moment.

"An automatic reaction. Think nothing of it."

"You are a monster of lust."

She detached his arms. But did not move very far away, and commenced to toss, turn, roll, sigh, sprawl and flail limbs and indeed other body parts over him quite maliciously. Miles was the last one to fall asleep by some considerable distance.

Any hopes Miles had harboured that Lara would be gone by morning were swiftly dashed, probably as soon as he woke to find Clara already up and busy.

"Good morning, brother-in-law. I trust you slept well?"

"Like a log," said Miles.

"Yes, that is what it felt like." Humming to herself, Lara glided about the kitchen setting out breakfast things. Clara still wore a bun and had a particular Lara face on – tranquil, slightly self-satisfied, sort of good-naturedly long-suffering, with a kind of wry thin-lipped smile at nothing in particular. "I have cooked breakfast for you, as you can see. It is important you keep your strength up."

She had made toast, only partially burned, and poured milk over cereal, and grilled a rasher of bacon and put it on a plate, and raggedly hacked an orange in four.

"Gosh. Thanks. Clara would never have done this. It would have been entirely beyond her capabilities."

"You are probably glad she is dead. Oh what a tasteless joke. Eat, eat."

When he had eaten she clapped her hands and said, "Now you will want to go into your thinking-den and work on your great masterpiece."

"Will I," said Miles.

"Undoubtedly. I know it consumes your every waking thought, to such an extent that it killed my sister. But you are not to reproach yourself; your art must take precedence. Clara never understood that, selfish child that she was. You will find me much more sympathetic to the needs of great men."

"Clara – "

"My name is Lara," she said chidingly.

Miles drummed his fingers on the table.

"I have tired of my novel," he said at length. "Let's play a game instead."

Clara/Lara looked surprised. "A game? When the day approaches its zenith and there are worlds to be conquered? Is that any occupation for a grown man? Well, if you insist. What did you have in mind – Ludo, Snakes and Ladders?"

"A dressing-up game. Clara used to like that."

"How like her. As your efficient housekeeper and helpmeet I have no choice but to obey. What will you be requiring me to dress as?"

Miles thought for a second and then smiled. "A maid. A French maid. That was Clara's favourite thing to dress as, although of course as you are a different person you have no way of knowing that."

Clara narrowed her eyes. After the briefest pause she said, "There you are wrong. One of the last things she said to me was that being asked to dress as a maid was a contributing factor in her suicide. That and your elf-ear perversion. Out of respect to her memory I will not cater to either depraved taste."

"You choose, then."

Lara looked surprised again. "I? I cannot choose. I have no ideas of my own. Clara was the one with all the ideas and imagination. How I am glad she is dead," she muttered aside.

Already suspecting what the result would be, Miles took her to the dressing-up room. At random he picked out some pirate apparel and cutlasses. Lara raised an eyebrow but docilely put them on.

"Now what?" she asked.

"We ... fight," said Miles optimistically, jigging around and waving his cutlass. "A-harr!"

Raising her eyebrow again, Lara jabbed her cutlass at him once craply but did not otherwise move.

"That's it!" said Miles encouragingly. "And now we race around the house clambering over the furniture."

"That cannot be good for the furniture. It seems a rather unusual way of passing the time."

Miles dropped his cutlass, threw off his pirate gear, and slouched off to the lounge. Lara followed.

"And what do you wish to do now?" she asked.

"I am going to sit in a chair," he announced, "and drum my fingers." He suited actions to words, and glared at her.

"A wholesome occupation," said Lara, also sitting, and smiling placidly. "Doubtless you will be thinking great thoughts. I love to watch men think."

"I am thinking," said Miles, "that I miss Clara."

"A natural reaction, and one that does you credit."

"I am wondering," he said, "how I can bring her back."

Clara-Lara clapped her hands and rose. "How wonderful! How touching! A love that death cannot destroy! He plots, like Frankenstein, to rend the awful veil and restore her to a grisly semblance of animation." She shook her head. "It cannot be. She has been eaten by salmon by this time." She looked thoughtful and laid a finger on her cheek. "I must remember not to feed you that."

Miles drummed his fingers some more.

"I am going to read a book," he announced, picking up the one of the night before, "and ignore you."

Lara nodded her acceptance. "I am used to being ignored. I will sit here and smile at you placidly."

She did this, head cocked slightly on one side, for at least an hour. Every time he glanced up from the book she was still sat there, looking at him benevolently, creeping him out.

Presently he gave up and started to desultorily engage Lara in conversation. At first he tried to catch her out, then started to try to get into the spirit and allow Clara to enjoy herself improvising. But he was not quite sure what the spirit was or exactly what was required of him; probably just to suffer.

"Who was the oldest twin?"

"I was, of course, by fifteen seconds. That is why I am more grown-up and responsible." She rose and paced, wringing her hands. "Fifteen seconds," she muttered bitterly, "fifteen seconds in the limelight, before Clara came haring out and stole it all."

"I see you're wearing her clothes. Isn't that disrespectful?"

She raised an eyebrow. "Would you prefer it if I went around in the nude? I really don't mind. I want only to obey and not annoy you."

Miles considered. "No, I suppose that won't be necessary," he said after a moment.

After lunch Lara implored, with earnest entreaty, that he should resume work on his great masterpiece.

Miles drummed more fingers, staring at her with lips pursed. He supposed he couldn't think of anything better to do under the circumstances.

"Actually, I think I will," he said with a hint of defiance.

Lara clapped her hands softly and sighed. "Oh, thank you! I have always wanted to watch a great writer at work."

Miles stared at her some more and tapped one finger meditatively. He tried desperately for the love of God to think of something better to do, then led the way into the room where the desks were.

Lara sighed as he seated himself. "So this is where it happens. There will be a plaque on that table one day, and generations of sighing schoolgirls will press their cheeks against that chair where yours have rested." Miles gave her a look that would have quelled or even killed a lesser woman. Clara-Lara was oblivious, pacing, staring out of the window and clasping her hands. "Clara never understood. She never understood the shining opportunity she had been given, to serve greatness. In her letters she would send me extracts from your work, to sneer at them. Little did she suspect that I would clutch the paper to my bosom and sigh with envy. From the very beginning I knew she lived in the presence of genius, one who would speak for many. I, too, have always felt existence to lie heavily upon me, like a tangled duvet."

"Stop this," said Miles. "I get it."

"Your every line is printed indelibly, hauntingly on my mind," she said earnestly. " 'His cornflakes bobbed lifelessly in a white-blue sea, like so many orange-jacketed bodies spilled from a stricken aircraft.' Or, 'His bacon was not so much swimming as drowning in grease.' – Again one sees the marine metaphor. One could say that Giles's entire existence is a submerged, damp and soggy one. Biographers will speculate as to whether jealousy of your achievement drove Clara to parody this in the manner of her own demise, and whether her dire cooking inspired the harrowing breakfast scene."

"You are completely and irredeemably evil," said Miles.

"Yes, master, yes!" cried Lara eagerly, flying to him and clinging. "How well you understand me! I *am* evil, for I am glad Clara is dead, because it gives me the chance to serve you!" She stroked his head. "Now write, write! Write like the wind! Write a book so mighty that everyone will be glad you drove your wife to death because of it! I will bring tea."

She flew dramatically from the room. Miles drummed his fingers again. "I get it," he said to himself.

Clara brought tea and laid it reverently before him, then tiptoed off to her own seat and sat there looking at him with hands folded in her lap. "I will sit here as quiet as a mouse and watch you adoringly. If you require anything, do not hesitate to order me."

Miles nodded to himself and drummed with a pen.

"I was going to change the bacon line, you know," he said after a moment. "It is merely a placeholder for something better."

"Oh, no, master," Lara entreated solemnly, shaking her head. "That would be a crime. Do not change a syllable. I know what sweat and toil each one costs you."

Miles glumly oscillated his pen and stared at the paper. Then he smiled at her sweetly and started to write.

So this, it seemed, was to be the manner of his punishment. He knew better than to try to evade it until the fancy was out of her system and she had wrung all she could from the scenario. Besides while she was Lara he could honestly think of no better way to pass the time. So, all too aware of her constant gaze, he bent his head and started to slowly and painfully add words.

Every time he glanced up at her he would find her gazing at him adoringly.

"So proud," she whispered, "so proud."

When his head was bent he would hear happy sighs.

After half an hour or so of this she suddenly gasped and flew from the room, returning with toast and more tea. This was repeated at five-minute intervals until mugs were lined up seven deep and the toast was stacked teetering towards the ceiling.

"I get it," said Miles. "Really, I get it."

Lara smiled at him adoringly.

He laid down his pen. "Clara, I have to learn."

"My name is Lara, and you have nothing, nothing to learn."

"Yes, I do, I know I do, I know this is shit, but I have to start somewhere. I want you to be proud of me."

"I *am* proud," Lara assured him, "*so* proud."

"Tell me what to write, then, if you don't like this. Shall I try and write something funny? Shall we collaborate?"

"No-one can tell you, master, and I would not be worthy of such an honour. Let me but dot one i and I will be immortal forever."

"Clara, you must know you're in the wrong here."

"My name is Lara. Cannot you say it? Is it so ugly to you?" She wrung her hands. "Of course it is ugly," she muttered darkly. "I was always jealous of Clara's name, because it was longer. She had every advantage."

"I came to play with you thirty seconds after you stormed out."

"The poor man, his wits are astray, maddened by regret he sees only her," she muttered aside.

"Yes! Yes! I am maddened by regret, and by you. Let's pretend – let's role-play you are Clara! It – it will be therapeutic for me – it may help me through my grief."

Lara bit a knuckle wide-eyed. "I – be Clara?" She drew a great breath. "All my life I have awaited such a chance, but do I dare?" she asided.

"Please."

"Very well. I will be Clara." Lara composed her face into one of pure malevolence.

Miles laughed. "She didn't look sly and evil like that, at least not all the time."

"To me she did." She rose and stood with her hands on her hips looking scornful. "I am Clara. Speak and I will answer," she said in a strange booming voice.

"Clara, I'm sorry I neglected you. I'm sorry I was grumpy and snapped. I'm sorry for whatever I said."

Clara-Lara-Clara gave a booming malevolent laugh. "What is that to me? I am Clara, destroyer of husbands, and twins. I know no pity. Now I am going to hog the bathroom, and put pictures of 18th-century philosophers over Lara's pop star posters, and be rude to teachers while pretending to be her. – Did I do it right?" asked Lara eagerly.

Miles laid his head on the desk. "Clara, I really don't like this game."

"My name is Lara, la-, la-, la-, the tongue goes so, la."

"Clara! Clara! You are Clara!" he yelled.

"The poor man," said Lara pityingly, shaking her head, "the poor, poor man."

"Argh," said Miles, "help."

"Yes, Miles," said Lara laying a hand on his shoulder. "I will help you. I will be here for you forever."

"You are the most annoying woman on the face of the planet," said Miles, his head still on the table.

"Oh no," said Lara sadly, sitting down in her chair. "Have *I* managed to annoy you, as well as poor Clara? Then perhaps I, too, must go away and make an end of myself." She sighed. "Perhaps then our identical triplet ... Ara, will come to console you. You might like her. She hardly moves or speaks at all."

Miles stared at her bleakly, sideways, his face pressed against the desk, for a long moment. "I will make do with you," he said at last.

"I thought you might," said Lara.

Lara did not seem disposed ever to go away. Miles started to fear for his sanity.

The second day passed much like the first. In the afternoon, driven by boredom and despair to go to his desk and write again, he had a brainwave. He would take Lara for granted and play on her being his obliging servant. He asked, nay grandly despatched her, to fetch fresh tea and more toast every *two* minutes, even before she could think of it herself, and sandwiches, biscuits, his slippers, et cetera. Meanwhile he scribbled furiously and enthusiastically: the line 'All work and no play makes Jack a dull boy' over and over and over again, although, as he hid his work from Clara when she approached, she was not to know that, although, from glances he caught, he suspected she suspected.

But Lara infallibly bustled off cheerfully and uncomplainingly to gratify his smallest whim, sitting at her desk gazing at him in silent adoration in between times, and he eventually got bored of it and laid his head on his own desk again.

"He is worn out with the fury of creation," Lara murmured.

From time to time he shouted, "CLARA!" very loudly and very annoyedly and Lara would mutter, "The poor man, the poor poor man, hark at his grief."

On the third day he stayed in bed until mid-afternoon.

"Are you doing research for your masterwork, *maître*?" Clara asked sweetly when she eventually brought him food. She had taken to calling him maître.

"Clara, you are really, really making me ill," he said hollowly.

Clara raised her eyes. "Did you hear that, Clara? Look what you have done to the poor man. Shame, shame on you."

"Argh," said Miles. "Argh. Argh. Argh."

When he did rise he was dishevelled, wan and wild-haired. Lara approved, saying he looked the part of a great writer now.

On the fourth night there was a change in the routine. He awoke from a fitful sleep and heard a tapping on the bedroom window. By the light of her bedside lamp he saw Clara standing outside it, presumably atop a ladder.

"*So cooold*," she moaned, "let me in."

It was open anyway. Before Miles had even sat up she had clambered inside. She was wearing a white night-gown affixed with streamers painted with luminous paint, and had a halo of cardboard and tinfoil over her head. Also, there was pondweed draped around her, and she left a trail of wetness from sponges tied under her feet. She flitted squelchily about the room making, 'Whoo, whoo, whoo' noises.

"Jesus Christ," said Miles with feeling.

"Not quite," said Clara, "and do not blaspheme before an angel." There was more flitting, squelching and whooing. "I am the ghost of Clara whom you slew," she said spookily. "I bring you a message. Do not trust Lara, she is psychotic."

"Clara, I've had enough of this! Please come back to me," he begged.

"I will return once a year on the anniversary of your betrayal," she said. "Until then you are in Lara's hands. Beware!"

There were more whoo noises and she flitted squelchily out the door.

Miles's heart sank. Who knew how long she would keep this up? She was probably not punishing him any longer, he realised. She might never have been punishing him. There might be no particular lesson. She was just enjoying herself.

"Argh," said Miles. "Argh. Argh. *Aaargh!*" he screamed in genuine fright as he lay back down and found a sleeping woman next to him even though he had just watched Clara leave the room. He knew a moment's brute unreasoning terror before closer inspection proved it to be a dummy in a wig.

Lara entered, smiling tranquilly. "Forgive me, maître, I sneaked downstairs to read your latest effusions. I placed that there so you would not miss me."

The next day Miles set himself to think in earnest. There must be some way out of this.

When Clara-Lara had left him for a moment he nipped to the shop in the village. He returned with a carton of grapefruit juice.

He flourished it at her in the kitchen, where she was gliding around looking Lara-ish and trying to boil him an egg. "I have brought you a present," he said.

Clara eyed it with disfavour. She really did hate grapefruit juice.

"For too long," said Miles, "I have seen you as the ghost of Clara rather than a person in your own right. That must end. Drink some and you will banish her shade forever. I will know you are not her."

Clara looked sickly. She rallied and smiled. "It is a kind, kind thought, maître. I will drink some with glee later. I am not thirsty just now. I had half an eggcup of water a while ago, which is all I require or deserve for one morning."

Miles opened the carton and poured a glass. Clara stifled her Scared Face as he thrust it towards her. "Come now, for me. It does my heart good to see a woman drinking something I have bought for her. It makes me feel like a real man. I have not felt like a man since Clara left me."

Clara looked at the approaching tumbler wide-eyed, almost cross-eyed, head recoiling, as though it had been poison.

"I – I beg you will not make me, maître. The fact is I hate ever to drink in front of other people." She wrung her hands. "Clara, that giddy witch, used always to tease me about my manner of drinking. She said I would nibble at a drink like a rabbit. For a long time afterward I could only take liquids intravenously. It is still a full-blown neurosis; I would probably go into spasms if you forced me."

Miles pursued her mercilessly through the logic of the scenario, which he knew she could not violate without ending the game. "Yet I must ask it of you. My Art requires it. There is to be a crucial scene of grapefruit-juice-drinking in my great book, and the fact is I have never seen anyone drink grapefruit juice. I know you will feel honoured to act as model for me."

Clara looked at him with pure hatred but took the glass. Still she could not do it.

"You cannot do it!" he cried. "I knew it! You *are* Clara! My Clara come back to me! Only admit it, and you need not drink the draught!"

Clara glared at him defiantly and raised the glass. She had artistry enough to make a nibbling-rabbit face before she sipped; or maybe it was just revulsion. It was definitely revulsion the next second. But continuing to glare she tossed the rest down in one. Her face went through a range of contortions and then she slammed the glass down and bared her teeth.

"Thank you, maître, that was lovely," she said in a not very Lara-like snarl. Then she made a hissing noise. He had a feeling he would pay for this when Clara did return. He bared his own teeth in defeat and went out, hearing ack-ack-ack noises behind him and then the sound of a carton of juice being emptied down the sink.

That afternoon at his desk he said thoughtfully, "It is a very peculiar thing, Lara."

Lara sighed and pressed her hands together. "You used my name freely," she said with approval. "That is progress."

Miles smiled. "Yes, Lara."

"He said it again!" She rushed over and flung herself on her knees at his feet. "Thank you, maître, thank you! You are so kind to a poor insecure inferior twin! Soon you will forget Clara forever!"

"That is difficult," said Miles, "when all the time I feel she is somehow very near me. It is most peculiar. I was sighing over her Britvic stash in the cellar, and I noticed that several were missing."

Lara looked up bashfully. "The fact is, maître, that I may have tried one or two in memory of her."

"Or five."

"You counted!" Lara clasped her hands and sighed. "How obsessive! How wonderful! Do you see this, Clara?" she shouted towards the ceiling. "Do you see what a loon you have left him? Yes, I tasted five of them for her sake. They made me vomit."

"I see."

Lara went back to her chair. "The fact is," she said artlessly, "I believe I will force myself to drink one every day, to punish myself for taking her place – lucky woman that I am."

"Ah."

That evening Miles suddenly pulled a coat on and announced:

"Come on, we're going to the pub."

Clara accompanied him to the pub. She was quiet and subdued by her standards but answered to her own name and talked to some of the regulars quite naturally.

"Did I do it right, maître?" she asked in a low voice as they returned to the house. "I did it for your sake. Your friends must never know you have killed your vivacious wife. They would not understand. Of course, I know I can never truly take her place. But," she stifled a sob, "you could say a kind word to me, now and again."

"Thanks," said Miles.

On the morning of Day Six there were several conversations that went, "Clara – " "*La*ra." "Argh."

The highlight of the afternoon was that Miles, baffled and despairing, lay full-length face-down on the floor of the lounge for two hours, occasionally emitting whimpering noises.

"The poor man," sighed Lara. "He misses her so much."

Later:

"Great men have these whims. Doubtless he is meditating some new work."

Later still:

"Perhaps he is humping the carpet. I am sure it is more attractive than I am."

On the seventh day Miles leapt out of bed eagerly and energetically. He had placed great hopes on the charade lasting exactly a week.

They were unfounded. Lara persisted the same as ever all day. Though he greeted her with courtesy and kindness and accompanied her to the writing room with zeal, as the day wore on his optimism flagged and he found himself resting his head bleakly on the desk again while she murmured, "He is worn out with his great work."

He stormed from the house and roamed dreary fields and wind-tossed forests seeking to bury his vast annoyance in exhaustion. Sitting by a muddy creek it came to him. He had been an idiot. He knew what was required of him now.

He stormed back into the house and to his desk. Lara appeared not to have moved from hers and greeted him tranquilly.

"Did the fresh air reinvigorate your apparatus, maître?"

"Yes," he cried, "yes! I have seen what I must do." He seized his manuscript and tore it in two, in four, and then in eight, flung it in the air laughing, then found matches and started to set fire to the fragments. "I must destroy it! I must destroy it entirely! It was this that drove her away and it will always remind me of her. It is gone! It is gone! Are you satisfied now?" he demanded.

Lara, who had been watching composedly, briefly raised her eyes to heaven and sighed. "*Are* you satisfied, Clara? Are you satisfied, you wicked child?"

Placidly she unlocked a drawer of her desk and extracted a sheaf of papers. She placed them on Miles's desk. "I feared it would come to this. I took the liberty of making copies, except of the more recent, repetitive parts about the boy named Jack, which are too avant-garde for anyone living today to understand and may safely be cut. I feel sure you have purged her with this great burnt offering and she will torment you no more." She rubbed his head. "Now write, maître. Write like the wind."

Miles made whimpering noises.

That night, in bed, in the dark, he slowly and calmly said:

"I know you probably see yourself as some feisty, quick-witted, ever-resourceful wife out of the Arabian Nights or ... some Restoration Comedy or something. But," he turned towards her pillow, "bear in mind, we probably only hear about the ones who got away with it. Some of them, I am sure, must have had their heads cut off."

Lara gasped in delight. "You mean you see me as your wife now, maître? I am honoured, honoured beyond all women." She laid a hand on his arm. "Shall we cuddle?"

Irritably he shoved her away. Lara could be heard making desolate sobbing noises for several minutes.

On the morning of the eighth day Miles constructed a bonfire in the garden. Lara watched quizzically but unquestioningly. He greeted her cheerily, sniggering to himself. When he started ferrying Clara's Malteser cache out of the house in stacked armfuls and arranging the boxes on the wood she looked more thoughtful. There was still a huge supply of the chocolates left from the ones she had conned out of her Uncle Charlie, as she had subsequently overdosed and sickened of them for a while. This was by no means any longer the case but she had been rationing herself to a box a day so as to prolong the pleasure of being able to gloat over a huge stockpile.

"Er – may I presume to question you, maître?" she said now in a small voice.

"I am getting rid of Clara's Maltesers," he announced with a grin. "So long as they are around I will always be expecting her to return."

"Er – you really needn't. I will eat them myself," she offered. "The fact is I am quite partial. It is one of the few traits we had in common."

"No," said Miles vehemently. "No. You are not worthy. No-one may eat my wife's Maltesers but Clara. She would have wanted it like this. I will burn them on a magnificent pyre and scatter their ashes on the river. Their essence will accompany her into the afterlife and she will be able to lord it over all the other retarded children in the spirit world." He lit a brand made out of a dead branch and a petrol-soaked rag. "Farewell, Clara!" he cried to the sky. "Farewell, Clara's Malteser stash!"

Lara bit her lip.

"You are right," she said. "It is best to make a clean break. Wait a moment. I will bring more."

She marched back into the house. When she returned it was with an armful of Clara's clothes and dressing-up costumes and a handful of her Walpole stories. She flung them onto the unlit pyre.

"What the hell are you doing?" he yelled, picking them up in alarm.

She met his eyes with defiance. "Burn them. Burn them all. She is not coming back to you. Make a clean sweep. Give me the brand and I will do it." She made to snatch it.

"No!" He pushed her off and doused it by stabbing it in soil. "No! I order you to put my wife's things back! We are never throwing them out! She is coming back! Soon!"

"As you command, maître." Demurely, Lara stooped and started to retrieve Clara's Malteser boxes while Miles glowered.

Later Miles barricaded himself in a room and drummed fingers for an hour. This was becoming serious. He was worried now. Desperate remedies were called for. He spent part of the evening on the phone, taking care not to be overheard.

Just after lunch the next day there was a knock at the door. A dapper little young man with a Van Dyke beard stood there carrying a briefcase. Miles ensconced him in the lounge then escorted Lara in and sat her down. She looked at them quizzically.

Miles said, "This is Dr. Dietrich. He is a psychiatrist. I have been telling him about the problems we have been having. He is here to make an examination of you. Will you please tell him who you are?"

Lara raised an eyebrow but crossed her legs and settled back in her chair. "Certainly," she said. The young doctor smiled blandly and leaned forward tapping a notepad on his knee. "My name is Lara. I am the twin sister of Miles's late wife Clara and currently employed by him as secretary, housekeeper, and, when I am particularly privileged, shoulder-massager."

Miles hadn't expected this but said, "That isn't quite true, is it? There is no such person as Lara and that can easily be established. Tell him who you really are."

Lara raised her eyebrow again. "Then you have guessed? I feared as much. I am of course Thalestris, Queen of the Amazons, born from a golden egg and fated to lead the lost tribes of Israel to the promised land of Wolverhampton."

"Clara!" Miles cried.

"The poor man! Grief has unhinged him," she confided to the visitor, leaning forward. "He is consumed with guilt and thinks I am his wife."

"This isn't the proper audience!"

She looked puzzled. "But I had assumed you had already confided all our secrets." She smiled warmly at the guest. "It is nice to finally meet you. I feel I know you already. You must be Paul."

The two men exchanged glances and simultaneously went, "Um."

The shrink tugged at his beard and said, "Who is zis Paul, und vy should I be him?"

Lara blinked. "Why, Paul is Miles's actor friend from college. He rudely never came to their wedding and in some views of the matter may still owe them a present. But Miles mentioned him to Clara several times and she in her letters told me."

The two men exchanged glances again. Miles shook his head and started to open his mouth.

Rather witheringly Lara added, "Furthermore, in the days when they owned a television, Miles excitedly pointed Paul out to Clara in an advert once. Perhaps this has slipped his mind."

The two men exchanged glances a third time. Miles looked away from Paul's glance very quickly and went red.

Lara smiled at Paul kindly. "I am sorry your career is so quiet you have time to impersonate psychiatrists, although frankly, in view of that accent, I am not surprised."

She rose and glided out.

In a pub with Paul and later on his own Miles drank and drummed fingers and stared into space.

Then he went for a stroll. He returned to the house in the evening chipper and cheery.

"Tonight's the night, Lara me dear," he said as he seated himself at the desk. "Tonight's the night I finally crack it."

Lara clasped her hands excitedly. "Oh, maître!"

Miles brandished a pen at her merrily and then wrote, quickly and furiously and in a fine fire of inspiration.

Minutes later he finished with a decisive line dashed across the page, then rose and handed her the papers with a triumphant sigh.

"There," he said. "The great work is complete. It has reached its natural conclusion, perfect in every way. As Clara once foresaw, he finally manages to leave the house and is promptly run over. What could be more fitting? It is finished. It is over. It will never trouble us again. Are you satisfied?"

"Oh, *yes*, Miles," she said with a big heartfelt sigh of her own, reading. "It satisfies me completely." She put it down and squared it off, smiling. Then rose and laid a fresh sheet of paper on his desk. "Now go on to the next one, maître, while your brain is still blazing. What a joyous day! How I wish Clara could have been here to see it."

Miles stared at her. Then he paced woodenly back to his desk, sat, and put his head down on it. After a moment he started to bang his head against it, repeatedly and quite painfully.

"Claaaraaa!" he bellowed.

"Oh the poor man, the poor poor man."

That night Miles lay in bed staring bleakly into blankness. He was at his wits' end. This would never stop, or he would go mad before it did.

Perhaps he should call in an exorcist. Beside him the woman who had possessed his wife tossed and turned and heaved great sighs and flung the covers about.

Suddenly he felt a hand on his chest.

"Miles. Miles it's me."

There was a nibbling at his earlobe. His heart raced.

"Who?" he asked, dry-mouthed.

"Clara. I am Clara. I have come back to you."

"Oh, thank God!"

She was lying on top of him. Her hair was in his face.

"Thank you, thank you," he said. "For the love of God! Don't *do* that again."

"No, Miles. I will never leave you."

Sighing, he put his arms around her.

"Ha ha ha I am stealing Clara's husband," said Lara to herself.

With a wordless yell he flung her from him and stormed off to sleep on the couch.

Lying there, sleepless, the inspiration came to him.

Early morning found him sneaking around the dressing-up room, sniggering and cackling to himself.

Lara rose to find the house empty. She was frowning slightly and checking some hiding places when the doorbell rang.

Miles stood on the doorstep, dressed in the most hideous and mismatched clothes he had been able to find.

"Morning," he said cheerily, bustling briskly in and giving her a big slobbery kiss on the cheek in the process. Lara was somewhat taken aback. "Nice place you got here," he said looking around the hall happily. "You must be Lara. Milo's the name, I am Miles's twin brother." He spoke in a nerdy voice and a regional accent Clara didn't care for. "Miles ran away in the night," he informed her, juggling one of her favourite ornaments by flicking it off his biceps and catching it. "He has gone off to spend the rest of his life sleeping with whores. He knew you'd be heartbroken so he sent me to console you."

"Indeed?" Lara arched an eyebrow coldly and snatched the ornament out of mid-air.

"That very thing. I'll soon brighten the place up." He slapped her boisterously on the arse. "Go and get brekky on, eh? We'll get along like a house on fire, I reckon. You needn't stand on ceremony, man of simple habits me, I like to belch, put me shoes up on the furniture and listen to sports radio."

"Jolly for you," said Lara. "You will not be doing it here, however. Kindly leave this house at once."

"I don't think so, missus," said Milo sitting on a table full of other ornaments and putting a finger up his nose.

"I do," said Lara firmly. "As Miles's secretary and his wife's nearest relative I am responsible for their property and must forbid you this house. Unless, of course, you have some signed document from Miles confirming your story and requesting me to give you entrance?"

"Don't need one," said Milo.

"We shall see what the police say about that," said Lara, riffling through the phone book and then picking up the phone.

"Er," said Miles. "No need for that, missus."

She was already dialling. "I should think there is, unless you leave this house at once."

He grabbed her hand. She slapped him and broke free.

"You have already assaulted me once," she said. "I suggest you leave before I have you arrested. Hello, Police?"

"Don't! Are you insane?" Miles grabbed the receiver and was in time to hear, " … police station."

Lara grabbed it back and said, "I wish to report an intruder in my house."

"Stop! Stop!" Miles was using his own voice now, or at least the alarmed screechy variant of it that had developed around the time of his marriage.

She locked eyes with him, glaring, and pointed sternly at the door.

Miles backed away. "You can't – "

"Yes, he is still here now. I believe he may be dangerous, he has tried to assault me twice. You should bring guns and dogs. Try to come quickly. I am a big political donor. And he has bitten the head off a bat and patronized a dwarf."

"All right, all right, I'm going!" Christ only knew what would happen if the police got into this situation. "Just put the phone down!"

Lara pointed and glared. "My address? Do you have a pen?"

Miles opened the door and stepped out. "I'm going! Put it down!"

Still holding the phone Lara slammed the door in his face.

Miles waited a minute and rang the doorbell.

"Go away," said Lara through the letterbox.

"You'd better not have told them – "

"I have informed them I made a mistake, but I can easily ring them back. I shall do so at once unless you leave the property."

"I'm going."

Miles walked up the drive to the road. Then waited a moment and came back.

"Go away," said Lara through the letterbox.

"It's me, Miles," he said. "I have come back to you."

"No, you are that ghastly Milo. I would recognise you anywhere. Go away or I will call the police."

"I – really, I'm Miles."

"I don't believe you. I am picking up the phone."

Miles went away. He didn't go far though, because of the clothes and the fact that he had no money. He came back and loitered in front of the house impotently. He tore off and threw down Milo's comedy cap and stamped on it thoroughly. Every few minutes he rang the doorbell and Lara told him to go away. At length he went and loitered at the back of the house in case the police hadn't been satisfied and had traced the call, or the madwoman had actually given them the address.

He was out there for several hours. It presently started to rain. He banged on the back door and she told him to go away. He went and sat in the shed. Eventually he had a thought. He took the Milo clothes off and went and banged on the window in his underwear.

"Maître?" asked Lara uncertainly when she appeared.

"Yes, yes!"

She wrung her hands. "How can I be sure it is you?"

"I – I – The final line of my book is, 'The tyres squelched the life from him as life had squelched the hope.' "

"Maître!"

She hastened to open the back door and clung to him as he entered. "Oh you are all wet! But that awful, ghastly man! And the whores have stolen your clothes!" She shook her head and pouted. "If you needed solace, couldn't I – am I so hideous? I know I can never compare to Clara, but– "

Miles pulled his mouth into a smile and said, "I am going to get into a bath."

"With me?" she asked hopefully.

"No, you wait here until I decide what to do with you."

"Very well, maître," said Lara resignedly.

Miles thought long and hard in the bath. He came to a decision.

"I have come to a decision," he announced as he came back down. She was still in the kitchen standing where he had left her, although he couldn't tell if she had moved in the meantime.

"Yes, maître?" she asked brightly.

"I am going to slap you."

"Very well, master. Which cheek would you like?"

"Leave that to me. It's about time, isn't it?"

"If you say so, master. I, Lara, am a spiritless drudge and have no choice but to obey."

"Right. Lara is going to get exactly what's coming to her." He brandished his open hand. "Stand by."

"Standing by," she said brightly, turning her face a bit to offer the appropriate cheek.

"Big slap," said Miles. "Very big slap. Own good. About time. Long overdue."

He waved his hand in the air while she waited placidly. He drew his arm back to a great distance and seemed to brace himself for and flinch in anticipation from the impact.

"Obviously, I can't slap you," he concluded after a moment, letting his hand drop. "Instead, I am going to shake you."

He took hold of her by the shoulders and shook her vigorously. She limply accepted it. She made her teeth rattle.

"Clara come back!" he yelled.

"Did you hear that, Clara?" she asked through her rattling teeth. "The poor poor man."

Miles screamed and let her go.

Lara smiled. "Perhaps you would like to spank me as well, maître?"

Miles fled.

"Maître," he said to himself in the study. "Maître, maître. Hate. Hate." He butted the wall.

Perhaps it was the word 'maître' that gave him, ten minutes after, the idea he should have had ten days before.

Of course. He really was a moron. He told himself so and smacked himself on the forehead. Of course! Of course! It should have been obvious. Bribery. Danegeld. Grovelling with proof.

"Clara! Clara, Clara!"

"Lara," said Lara piteously. "Is it so hard for you? Oh, he is obsessed with her, he will *never* look at me."

"Yes. Lara. Whatever. Please just – come here." He sat her down in the lounge. He paced, musing, unsure where to begin negotiations. "Is it your opinion that Clara is truly dead, that she will never come back?"

"It seems certain. Can't you try and forget her?"

"You don't think there is a chance she could just be lying dazed and a little soggy at the bottom of a waterfall somewhere?"

"She has been gone so long. I like to think she has become a pretty flock of eels now. She always was that slippery and slimy," she muttered aside.

Miles tutted. "Well that's a shame. That's a damn shame."

"Oh! See how he regrets her now it is too late."

"No, I just meant it's a shame about the reservation for dinner at Le Con I had for next weekend."

Lara cleared her throat. "Le Con?"

"Le Connard d'Or, Clara's favourite restaurant."

"I, Lara, would know nothing of that."

"She loved it. She had some strange fixation on the crispy fish pie there. And her reactions to the sticky toffee pudding used to arouse sexual jealousy in me, frankly."

"I suppose as a loving husband you took her there regularly."

"As little as I could. In fact I only ever took her there for special occasions, or if I lost a bet or chickened out of a dare. I loathe the place, it's so inanely expensive and pretentious. And I hate the owner, he used to drool over her. And, and the maître d' ... seemed to drool over me."

"You can't blame the poor man."

"No, I suppose not," said Miles preening himself. "Also there's a huge fish-tank in the waiting area and Clara used to embarrass me by pretending to be a mermaid behind it whenever anyone came in."

Lara blinked. "You never told her that. Perhaps it is a good job she is dead, then," she said tartly. "Obviously you are better off with me."

"No! No!" He flung himself to kneel at her feet. "I am consumed with remorse now. I should have taken her there more often. Why, if Clara could return from her watery grave somehow, I vow I would take her to Le Con every single night for a week to give thanks."

Lara frowned thoughtfully and bit her lip.

"Boy, she loved that crispy fish pie," Miles sighed. "And that sticky, sticky, sticky toffee pudding."

Lara sighed too.

"And, and I would fill the fridge with Britvic, and double her Malteser stash," he pressed.

Lara continued to frown and wiggled her lips.

"Perhaps," she suggested, "you could take me in her place?"

"No. No. Never! Only Clara may eat at Le Connard."

Lara sighed again and shook her head. "It is so sad. All this commendable husbandly feeling, far too late. We must console ourselves that Clara has all the fish pie and sticky toffee pudding she can eat, in heaven."

"Heaven?" Miles collapsed onto the floor with a despairing laugh. "You really didn't know her that well."

Lara bridled. "What a terrible thing to say about my saintly sister your wife." She rose. "I am saving up this kind of thing to tell her, if she ever does come back, and she will make you pay, laddie boy."

Miles sprang up. "Then you think there is a chance? I – I would make it dinner at Le Con every night for a week and then twice a week for the next month. And, and we would run amok shopping."

"Hmm. Clara was shallow and mercenary, and if anything could give her the power to rend the awful veil and return to you, it would be that. I am sure she looks down and appreciates your gestures of remorse, but it simply cannot be."

She walked from the room looking sad.

Miles sank down, flabbergasted. His mind raced. She had been tempted, of that he felt sure. But she had not given in. What on Earth would Clara give up the Connard for? What would make her cling so pig-headedly to this stupid role for so long? It couldn't still be punishment, if it ever had been – she wasn't that cruel – he hadn't hurt her that much. Then what?

Artistic completion. A graceful exit.

A punchline. That was what she was hanging on for. Some joke she had been building towards but hadn't had the opportunity to crack. He was sure that must be it.

But what? He had to find the feed-line.

For two days he wracked his brains trying to find the answer. He no longer feared a breakdown; he was stimulated, if still desperate. Clara, he started to suspect from a certain listlessness and lack of attention to detail, was tiring of Lara too. He would find her sitting on chairs staring at nothing. When he asked her what she was doing, she would reply, "Sitting quietly. In this at least I surpass Clara." But he knew she would not give it up until she had accomplished ... what? Like someone in a fairy tale he had to solve the riddle to set her free. He lay awake in bed frowning in the dark. What hadn't he given her a chance to do yet? Surely they had already rung every possible change on the scenario.

On the eleventh day he found she had let her hair down. For a moment he thought she had returned spontaneously.

"Clara!" he cried.

Her face lit up. "Am I so much like her?"

His face fell.

"I can be," she insisted eagerly. "Soon you will never know she is gone. Listen, listen." She sat him down. "I can entertain you as well as she did. She did not have quite *all* the talent. I can sing!"

She proceeded to make a noise like a cross between the croaking of a frog and an aborted belch for two minutes, to an indefinite but awful tune. In spite of himself Miles started to laugh.

"Oh, you aren't supposed to laugh! Oh, this is hopeless! I can never, never replace her!" Lara looked downcast.

This was bats. The terrible thing was he was starting to respond to Lara as a real person. He had felt sorry for her just now and wanted to hug her. He had to solve this before they both went properly nuts.

He awoke on the twelfth day knowing the answer.

In the kitchen Lara regarded him sadly. She had tried to warm his slippers in the oven but had burnt them. She was dressed as a maid.

He had it. He thought he had it. It had to be. But surely – ?

He scrabbled around the house for cigarettes and went out and paced the garden. He cast his mind back carefully. Surely he'd already given her the chance to do that? That first night in bed. No, though, he hadn't really, if she'd even thought of it then. And at least two other times he had actually prevented her from doing it. It had to be. It had bloody better be. He cast his cigarette aside and stormed back into the kitchen.

"Lara, I have been a blind fool," he said.

Lara blinked at him timidly, still brooding over his smoking slippers.

"You don't need to toast my slippers. You don't need to croak me songs. You don't need to try to be like her. I have been living in the past. Now it ends!" He embraced her and kissed her. "To hell with Clara! I love you, Lara!"

"YOU FORGOT ME QUICK ENOUGH!" yelled Clara, cracking him across the face.

Chapter Sixteen

Clara and Miles were playing they were rival spelling bee contestants in the finals of a national spelling bee competition.

Miles, Clara had explained, came from a poor but honest family. He had been promised a job writing the Oxford dictionary if he won. This would make him the first person in his family ever to hold a job that didn't involve handling excrement, and enable him to pay for the head-transplant operation his nan needed.

Clara, by contrast, had been trained since childhood by a rich pushy insane father who nursed a grudge against the world because he had been fired from *his* job writing crosswords for spelling a word wrongly. He had hired her the best spelling coaches money could buy, fed her from birth on alphabetti spaghetti, which she had to make into words before she could eat, and given her electro-shocks whenever she spelled anything wrong.

They had already played a moving scene where they discovered the favourite words they had in common, and another where they had flirted by spelling suggestive, flattering or romantic ones. Now it was the last round and, their sexual tension mounting as they saw off all other contenders, they came face to face to compete for the trophy. They were standing side by side in the middle of the lounge, which was a packed auditorium.

"All right," said Clara, "you need this one to win." In the persona of the quizmaster, she opened the dictionary. "Please spell, onomatopoeia," she said. "The tension mounts, there's a spotlight on our faces," she added.

"O," said Miles.

Clara as his rival pouted.

"N," said Miles.

Clara looked sad and wobbled her lip.

Miles hesitated, fixing a burning gaze on her, then mumbled, "O."

Clara fluttered her eyelashes.

"M," said Miles.

Clara licked her lips and drummed her fingers on her chest.

"I, I'm sorry, could you repeat the word, please," said Miles.

"Onomatopoeia, deaf-lugs," said Clara as the quizmaster.

There was a long pause as contestant Clara and contestant Miles locked imploring and yearning eyes respectively.

"Onomatopoeia is spelled, C-A-T," said Miles.

"Wrong! Eh-err!" said Clara the quizmaster.

Clara the contestant sighed with relief and curved her lips at Miles.

"To win, please spell, Constantinople," said Miles to Clara as the quizmaster.

"C. O. N. S. ... " There was a terrible pause. Clara dried. She turned to look at Miles in alarm and appeal, wringing her hands.

Miles looked appalled on her behalf. He contorted his face encouragingly, trying to send her the answer telepathically.

Clara stepped out of character to ask what the hell this was and he explained it.

"Oh. Well, the tension mounts. Anyone who dares cough in the audience has his throat slit. My father is in the front row, tapping his electro-shock equipment menacingly. Your nan is next to him, holding her severed head on her lap. You, meanwhile, contort your face at me like a constipated gibbon."

Clara locked eyes with him tragically. Miles did more contortions to indicate yearning, guilt, helplessness. Then he put one finger horizontally across an upright one and coughed.

"T," sighed Clara, looking at him with gratitude, then looking adorably helpless again, putting her finger in her mouth and turning back to him for help with the next.

Miles put fingers on his forehead and waved them around like antennae.

"What the arse?" asked Clara.

"It's an ant," he explained. "I'm trying to give you the next three letters in one go."

Clara-spelling-bee-contestant widened her eyes and looked baffled. Miles stooped and put his hand near the floor to indicate something small and then did the antennae again. Then he sat down and mimed someone happily laying out a picnic and suddenly recoiling in horror.

"The other contestant will stop doing whatever the hell he is doing, he is putting the challenger off and making an arse of himself," boomed Clara as the quizmaster.

Miles rose and nodded apologetically. Clara looked helpless and desperate. Miles took his shoe off and then, staring straight ahead of him, snaked his foot out and surreptitiously rubbed it against Clara's calf.

"What the hell are you doing?"

"I'm tracing the letters against your skin with my toe. It's quite erotic, actually, isn't it?"

"The contestant will please stop foot-molesting his opponent, it is most off-putting," boomed Clara the quizmaster.

Miles withdrew his foot. Clara pleaded with eyebrows. Miles yawned and stretched his arms, waved his hands as though they had pins and needles – "Are you having some kind of fit?" – then casually flailed his right arm out so his hand came to rest on Clara's bum. She bridled and glared at him.

Whistling casually and staring innocently ahead, he slid his hand up the back of her blouse and traced A, N, T on her back with the index finger. Clara smiled and also seemed to wriggle somewhat lasciviously.

"The boy contestant will stand the hell away from the girl one," said Clara the quizmaster sternly. "That is how babies happen."

Miles nodded and took a step to the side.

"A, N, T," said Clara triumphantly, then stopped and looked pitiful again.

Miles pointed at his eye.

Clara frowned, "Lash? I don't – "

Miles shook his head and pointed at himself.

"You? You! U!" cried Clara. Miles waved no. "Wait, no, I retract." Miles pointed at her. "Me? Pretty? No – I!" Miles sighed and nodded. "I! I! And then – " Clara dried again and looked at him in appeal once more.

Miles shook his head to indicate NO.

Clara pouted and breathed, "*Please.*"

Miles mouthed NO.

"Why not? You brute."

Miles threw up his hands and looked around in despair.

"Please, Mr Quizmaster," he said, "there's a boy in the audience pulling tongues, it's putting her off. – He turns round to look." While the invisible quizmaster was distracted he took the opportunity to spring to Clara's side and breathe, "N, O, P, L, E," into her ear and also tongue, kiss and nibble it. Clara writhed and languished against him and turned grateful sparkling eyes on him, then became the quizmaster to boom:

"I can only see one naughty boy misusing his tongue here and it is you! Keep away from the girl contestant once and for all or we will throw a bucket of icy water over you and have you fixed."

Miles nodded and stepped away.

Clara became the contestant again and finished "N, O, P, L, E," in a ringing voice.

"That is correct!" cried Miles as the quizmaster. "Congratulations! You are the winner and the Spelling Champion of Great Britain!"

"And almost certainly the world as no foreigner can spell worth a fart," added Clara, also as the quizmaster, or possibly as herself.

"Here is a trophy and a cheque for a sponsorship deal. And parenthetically this is a strangely arousing fantasy," he added as himself, "and I really hope it has an ending that lives up to the build-up."

Clara accepted the trophy – they hadn't been able to find one so Miles improvised with a plant-pot – blushingly and with modestly lowered eyes, then jumped up and down several times crying, "Yay! I won! I won! I won, Daddy, I'm the best! – I push brusquely past you and go rushing over to my father, that's you now," said Clara, barging past Miles and then running round the room in a circle and coming back to him.

"What would you like for a present, daughter?" burbled Miles as her dad. "It can cost as much money as you like. – You look thoughtfully at where I kneel wracked with guilt in front of my sobbing nan, holding her severed head," he added as himself.

Clara looked thoughtfully at where Miles was now kneeling, cradling a balloon that Clara had drawn a face on.

"A golden horsebox, please, Daddy, and a Ferrari made out of chocolate," she said fairly promptly. She sashayed over to Miles, who looked at her, devastated. "Looks like the best person won," she purred gloatingly. "Can you spell Sucker?"

"No, no!" said Miles as himself. "You wouldn't do that! You wouldn't do that! You would learn a lesson and pay for my nan's operation and we would fall in love and have sex!"

"Perhaps in due course," said Clara. "But there isn't any rush. There is much more drama to be wrung from this scenario. We will go at it only when the repressed sexual tension reaches truly volcanic proportions. Let me see. First you become a down-and-out and renounce your spelling powers. You spell everything wrongly now out of bitterness. Meanwhile I take part in multi-million-pound international tournaments, the Olympics et cetera, and get huge sponsorship deals. I am a poster girl for correct spelling. In fact you literally do see me on posters everywhere. Like Kitchener in that recruiting poster, but it's me pointing and saying, 'Your country wants YOU to SPELL, sonny.' *You* become a Communist university professor of education making speeches about how teaching children to spell is fascist and evil and repressive and that text-speak is the language of the future and using z to indicate plurals is witty and life-enhancing and helps to fight the power. We are now mortal enemies and meet and clash at a debate."

"OK. Ahem." He turned and mimed leaning on a lectern.

Clara blinked. "What is wrong with your hands, please? Why do you have dinosaur paws?"

"It's a lectern, I'm leaning on a lectern."

"Oh. Fair enough. We should buy one for the prop cupboard. We can use it to play sexy hellfire preacher too, and it will come in handy when I eventually become a rabble-rousing demagogue and start the revolution. OK go then."

They glowered at each other across a debating hall.

"Does spelling matter?" asked Miles in an evil Communist professor voice. "Only insufferable pedants and snotty little daddy's girls think so. Does it matter, for example, if there is a w at the start of the word WHORE! WHORE!" he yelled leaning towards Clara, "or if there is not one at the beginning of HARLOT! HARLOT!" he yelled again pointing.

"No, Miles! Is that how you would be?" She pouted sadly. "This is not romantic any more."

"No, but don't you see, then we meet afterwards and – "

"Wait, scrub the debate – you don't become an evil professor, you just renounce spelling and become a down-and-out. I find you and am shocked and appalled at what has become of you. Oh, oh – wait! I see it all! I find you lying in an alley, a broken and bitter man, dying of meths and exposure, and, wracked with guilt, I encourage you to spell a word. Constantinople – the word that gave me the world. 'Spell it for me, darling,' I say huskily, holding you in my arms. 'Remember? The way you did at the competition.' But but, you only get as far as Constanti- and then you croak. Do you get it Miles? CONSTANT I – you croak out, 'Constant, constant I', you can look a bit reproachful if you like, and my lip wobbles, and then you die in my arms, and I wail 'What have I done?' Wouldn't that be beautiful?"

Miles looked nonplussed. "And then, what, you have sex with my corpse?"

She hit him. "Miles! You don't have an ounce of romance!"

"I'm twice the romantic you are! I spelled the word for you! Who wouldn't pay to fix my nan's severed head?"

"But it's better like this, this ending is quite beautiful. I think I must pitch this as a film," said Clara. "It would be like a Tristan and Isolde for people who like to spell things a lot. Come on, let's play it, you're sleeping rough in an alley now, all melancholy."

Miles lay down on the floor in a pose reminiscent of that painting of the death of Chatterton. "Wait, wait! I tear a poster off the wall to use as bedclothes," he said sitting up again miming this, "and, it's a poster of you going 'I Want You To Spell Properly' – "

"Yes, yes!"

"So I tear it up in disgust."

"Miles! At least wipe a tear away first."

"Oh all right." Miles mimed a tear, then mimed scrumpling the poster up and wiping his bum on it.

"Miles," she tutted. "All right lie down and be cold and poorly again."

He lay down and went, "Brr. Cough."

"Tra-la-la!" said Clara skipping across the lounge. "I hope this alley is a short-cut to the stadium where my sell-out spell-along-with-Clara concert is being held. Oh no! Look at that poor disgusting derelict! But – surely – it is you! My first and only love! Look at what has become of you! I have the strangest feeling – can this be guilt?" She stooped and cradled him. "But why, why – how have you come to this? You, who could spell – " she made a tear-wiping gesture, "even better than I."

"I hate the alphabet now," croaked Miles bitterly. "You have made me hate it."

"Oh no! What have I done?" Clara bit a knuckle. "You must return to spelling! Recover your powers, for my sake! Together we will be the golden couple of the spelling bee masters circuit."

"It is too late. You have destroyed me. I cannot even spell with the help of a dictionary, because I can never even think of the first letter."

"No, no, it is never too late! One does not lose those powers. You will spell again – for me!"

"I am cold and poorly and dying, although there may yet be time for a consolatory shag," Miles gurgled feebly and optimistically.

"Let us not sully our beautiful reunion. Spell for me! Spell for me, my love! Like you used to. Remember when you spelled Constantinople for me, and gave me the world. You must remember that! Spell it! Spell Constantinople for me, darling!"

Miles fixed his expiring eyes on her.

"C," said Miles, "U, N, – "

"No, Miles."

Chapter Seventeen

Clara and Miles had become detectives. That is, they had laminated passes saying they were detectives, and they had trench coats and fedoras, and flasks filled with bourbon, and shoulder-holsters with water-pistols in, and they had turned the offices upstairs over what had once been their Stoic British Endurance shop into grimy detective offices. They had a desk each with swivel-chairs, and ashtrays overflowing with cigarette butts they had collected from the pub, and more bourbon stashed in the drawers – Clara's was cold tea, Miles's slightly diluted – and they were sitting there growling and swilling and doing detective bits at each other.

They were not merely playing, however, or at least Clara insisted they weren't. They had taken out small ads in several newspapers offering their services as private investigators. These had been written by Clara and sometimes said things like 'No task too dirty' or 'We are badly shaven and morally ambiguous' but otherwise sounded quite professional. And there was a big eye-catching poster in the shop window, which read:

DETECTIVES FOR HIRE
CHEAP! RELENTLESS! WORLD-WEARY!

Miles had few misgivings. He did not expect they would get any clients, or that Clara would take being a detective seriously enough for things to get out of control if they did. He was wrong on both counts.

The first prospective client climbed the stairs and entered early on the first afternoon. He took one look at their detective hats and trench coats, said, "Nah," and went away again.

So they took off the hats and trench coats, and then spent an hour learning how to skim the fedoras across the room to successfully land on the antique hat-stand in the corner.

They ditched the shoulder-holsters too, after spending another hour seeing who could quick-draw and shoot from them fastest.

They had just sat down at their desks again, and Clara was about to suggest Miles came in as Peter Lorre and asked her to find something called The Maltese Cock, when a man knocked at the open door and diffidently asked if they were the detectives. She cried, "Yes!" and he took a seat. She unsuccessfully offered him cigarettes, cigars, bourbon and sweets, and Miles asked what they could do for him.

The client seemed very nervous and sat there fiddling with a bunch of keys.

"I think my wife is having an affair," he blurted at last.

"Ooh, tell me!" said Clara leaning forward eagerly.

"We don't do marital work," said Miles.

"Unless we're very well paid," said Clara.

"Even if we're very well paid," said Miles.

"Unless the details are juicy, or seem likely to lead to a devastating political scandal," said Clara. "Who is she knocking off?"

"I – I think it's someone at work."

"We can't help you," said Miles.

"In my experience it is usually Italians to blame for this sort of thing," said Clara knowledgeably.

The man blinked. "He *is* an Italian," he said, impressed.

"*See?*" Clara cried triumphantly to Miles. "I expect he said a lot of greasy but mellifluous things to her over the photocopier. Would you like us to take pictures of them at it?"

"What are your rates?"

"Frankly we would pay for the pleasure. But let's say £200 a week plus expenses and £500 if we succeed." She lowered her voice. "We can also rough him up and warn him off for an extra thousand. For two grand we will tie a knot in his cock and dump him on the first boat back to Naples."

The man swallowed. "I just thought a divorce."

"We'll be in touch," said Miles.

The man looked surprised. "Don't you need – "

"No, no, you can pay us afterwards."

"I will break his fingers for an extra fifty quid," said Clara. "You don't even have to say anything, just nod slightly."

"No, no," said the man rising hastily.

"Mail you his balls for a tenner. Just lower your eyelid."

"We'll be in touch," said Miles again. He rose and shook the man's hand. The man nodded gratefully and left.

Clara spun right round in her swivel-chair. "Yes! Score! We're in! Miles, can you believe it? The very first case for the Two Finder-Outers! The Case of the Wop Marriage-Wrecker! I've got a brilliant idea how we can catch them. What we do – "

"Are you serious?" Miles was laughing. "First I'd like to know how you're going to find them, or him. You didn't get any information, genius. Not so much as his name or phone number."

Clara looked nonplussed for a second then cried, "Miles, you bastard!" and started to thump him furiously while he span in his chair and laughed. "Why didn't you remind me? You hustled him out. You did that on purpose! It isn't funny! Our first case! You detestable cur!"

"Clara, we can't involve other people in our madness!"

"We are detectives!"

"We're fuck-ups! We can't play around with human misery!"

"I would have taken the case properly!"

"We don't have any experience!"

"We would have learned! You just didn't want me to obtain photographic evidence of a healthy non-malformed penis. Now this Italian lounge-lizard is still at large preying on susceptible Englishwomen! You're always talking about us getting jobs – you bloody annoying bastard – "

Miles's arms were getting sore by this point. "Knock it off," he said still giggling. "You were the one who scared him away."

"Do the next one properly!"

"I did it properly! Who was talking about breaking fingers? This whole thing is – "

"I want to be a detective!"

Clara sulked for fully an hour, sitting in her chair with her arms folded and spinning her back to Miles whenever he spoke or tried to approach.

"I was going to be a maid in their hotel," she said pouting. "A maid outfit, Miles."

"Perhaps we could pretend to – "

"No. Never."

A while later Miles said, humbly, "You were pretty clever about the Italian. What put you onto the scent?"

"Common sense, Miles. When a woman tires of her oafish English husband she usually looks around for someone charming and well-groomed who knows his way around the erogenous zones."

Eventually she thawed enough to put her trench coat and fedora back on and order Miles to do the same and break out the bourbon and cigars.

"We could play I'm a hard-boiled detective and you're a femme fatale," suggested Miles.

"*I'm* being a detective," said Clara glaring. "Maybe later. We could do I'm a hard-boiled lady detective and you're a … homme fatale."

"Um. Okay." Miles ditched his hat and trench coat and went out, then knocked and came in again. He hooked his leg provocatively around the door. "Bubbles Malloy?" he said huskily. "I'm … Lance Shaftesbury."

"For Christ's sake, Miles. Wait, go back out, start again. Just sort of fling the door open and sashay slowly to the chair."

Clara swivelled to look out the window. He did as he was bid. Clara span round in the chair to face him as he entered, wriggling her top lip.

"From the minute he walked in the door I could tell he was bad news," she growled. "The worst. Like your mother getting hit by a trolley-car on her way to tell you you were Al Gore's bastard child. From the tips of his shoes to the top of his tousled hair, taking in his cheap slutty suit with the shirt hanging out and the tie askew, you could tell he'd dressed to get attention, if not as a cry for help. One look at his cocky boyish ... grimace and I knew he was three miles of bad road leading to a complicated one-way system that always seemed to take you to a B&Q in the middle of nowhere. From the way he swung his hips it was easy to tell he was packing ... a turd, frankly. Honestly, Miles, is that how you walk sexy?"

"I'm sashaying."

"I figured him for English. I like 'em like that. They squeal more when you pin them down."

"I for my part was rather scared of the strange cross-dressing lady," squeaked Miles falsetto.

"Miles! You ruined it! The bimbo doesn't get a voice-over! Only I get a voice-over!"

"I noticed that shortly after our wedding."

"Now I lost my ... out, get out, start again."

Miles went out. Clara swung back round to face the window.

The door opened. She swivelled back, saying, "What can I do for you, sweet-cheeks?" and then, "Wah!" because in place of Miles was a woman in fur and jewels who had pushed briskly past him in the hall.

It was not a femme fatale but an old lady, white-haired and wizened but tall and vigorous and only moderately stooped.

She sat and looked intently and rather suspiciously at Clara and said, "Are you the detective?" Her voice showed an upper-crust upbringing but no signs of age.

"That's what it says on my licence, honeybush," said Clara, on an impulse taking this out and flashing it.

The old lady peered at it through a pair of spectacles hanging on a chain around her neck. "That looks rather amateurish," she said.

"But it's laminated, look," said Clara, outraged. She had spent hours on the detective licences, using carved-potato ink stamps and three different felt-tips.

The woman returned her scrutiny to Clara and appeared displeased with her hat and trench coat. "Why are you dressed like that indoors?"

"I'll ask the questions, sugar-tits," said Clara.

The woman opened and closed her mouth. Then said, "Did you just call me sugar-tits?"

"No," said Clara.

"I'm sorry; I am rather deaf at times."

"Good," said Clara.

"I want you to find my dog," said the old lady.

"We don't do missing pet work," said Miles, behind her.

"Duck," said Clara to the old lady, throwing a stapler over her to hit Miles on the head. When the old lady turned in astonishment to look at him she said, "My associate, Bollocks Malone. He handles the leg-work and will not be handling me for the foreseeable future."

Miles came and sat on the desk and, attempting to get into the spirit of things, amiably said, "Spill it, sister," to the old lady. The old lady bridled indignantly at this more than at anything Clara had said, so Clara pushed a drawing-pin into his arse so that he yelped and got up again.

"We are real detectives, honestly," said Clara. "Please tell me about your dog."

The old lady looked them up and down in displeasure for a moment then said:

"Lord Codrington disappeared the day before yesterday."

Clara eagerly opened her note-book. "Lord Codrington is the name of your dog? Describe him."

"He is a pure-bred Pekinese, light gold in colour. He is of a distinguished pedigree and has taken prizes at several shows."

"Any distinctive features?"

"Certainly. He has a black spot on the ankle of one leg, and often wears a ruminative look."

"Ruminative," said Clara.

"Thoughtful," said Miles.

"I know that, you tit," said Clara. "Pray continue, Mrs – ?"

"Lady Violet Ashburne."

"Your dog looked ruminative."

"Several people have agreed."

"As though there was something preying on his mind?"

"No, no, it was just a way he had. Pekes can look terribly human."

"Did your dog have any enemies?"

"Not a one. He was popular with everyone."

"Did he – pardon me – I must be blunt – did he have any romantic entanglements?"

"I have enquired and none of the neighbourhood bitches were on heat. I cannot imagine him straying for long on that sort of quest. He has been put to stud twice and seemed to find it terribly fatiguing and not worth the bother."

"He had seen through the sex racket; a wise dog. Please describe the events of the day in question. When did you first realise Lord Codrington was missing?"

"No-one can be certain of the time they saw him last. However on that day the door was left open for some time during the morning while some men removed a piano. I had given strict instructions that Codrington was to be confined to a back room while this happened. Both my companion and the housekeeper assure me he was but they may well have overlooked it. I myself was absent visiting a friend."

"Leaving Codrington behind?" Clara narrowed her eyes. "You had quarrelled?"

"Not at all. She has a cat he doesn't get along with."

"Is this cat the vengeful type?"

"It is a creature of exquisite malice."

Clara wrote CAT in her notebook, added some question marks and underlined it.

"How long were you gone?"

"Until three o'clock that afternoon. We noticed the absence of Lord Codrington shortly after, but didn't establish he was missing until around five when my housekeeper returned from some errands. She sometimes walks him. It seems certain to me he escaped when the door was left open. He has done so before but has not gone far or previously been away for so long. I have enquired of several neighbours but none of them have seen him."

"Or they aren't admitting it. Were any of his belongings missing?"

The old lady frowned. "Belongings? There is a rag doll he is fond of. I fail to see – "

"Please, madam, let me do my job," said Clara wearily. "In a case of this kind nothing is insignificant. Already I am certain that this is something bigger and more sinister than you could possibly imagine."

The old lady frowned more deeply. "What do you suspect?"

Clara waved a hand. "I will not frighten you at this point." She leaned back in her chair. "Tell me, Lady Codrington – "

"Ashburne," said the old lady and Miles together.

Clara waved another hand, regally, sticking two fingers up at Miles with it *en passant*. "Ashburne, if you insist," she said magnanimously. "Are there any Communists in your neighbourhood?"

The old lady looked puzzled. She said, "There is a cabinet minister and a governor of the BBC."

Clara blinked. "Mother?" she said in surprise.

"I fail to see – "

"The whole world will fail to see, until it is too late. I believe I am right in thinking that this time two days ago it was May the First, the notorious Communists' sabbath?"

"It was June the 30th," said the old lady and Miles.

Clara raised her eyebrows and then waved her hand again. "The anniversary of Trotsky's death; even worse."

"What are you – "

"I will take this case, Lady Codrington, but don't blame me if you don't like what I find."

"Ashburne."

"You seem curiously insistent upon that."

"Are you a professional detective?"

"Already the interference begins. If you don't like my methods you can take your money elsewhere."

"I had been meaning to ask about that. How much – "

"Five thousand smackers."

"Nonsense. That is far too much. For a successful retrieval of Lord Codrington I will pay you fifty pounds."

Clara seized the old lady's hands and kissed them.

The old lady drew back and looked astonished.

"You will want to know my address," she nevertheless said after a moment.

"Oh, I could probably deduce it, but if you want to make things easy for me."

"I reside at number 16 Godolphin Square."

"I expect I shall be able to solve this case by the application of pure reason, without leaving this desk," said Clara airily as she wrote this on her hand, "and perhaps sending my partner out to roam the streets with a bag of sausages. But if not we will have to come round and interrogate your household."

"I will expect you at five sharp."

"You may not recognise me. Be very very careful who you tell this story to in the meantime. Are you travelling home alone?"

"With my chauffeur."

"A chauffeur. *Now* you tell me. I cannot work without all the facts, Lady Thing. Is this chauffeur Italian?"

"Czech."

"Even worse."

"I fail to – "

"Good day for now, Lady Penelope. Trust no-one, not even me."

The old lady stared piercingly at her for a bit and then rose.

"I'm sure there's no cause for alarm," said Miles as he showed her to the door. "There's probably a perfectly simple explanation. I bet Codrington will be waiting for you when you get home."

"His severed head, perhaps," muttered Clara.

Then she dashed to the window, followed soon by Miles after he had escorted Lady Ashburne downstairs. They watched her getting into a large expensive car and being driven off.

"Miles! Our first real case! And it's a corker! This is a powder-keg, I tell you!"

"We have been asked to find a missing dog."

"On the surface! That is merely the first layer of the mystery. This case has got everything! The aristocracy! Cabinet ministers! Sex!"

"Sex?"

"Deviant animal sex, this poor frigid hound who must prostitute himself to order for elderly voyeurs but would rather play with dolls." She walked up and down the office, wearing a ruminative look. "*Not* that I believed a word of that farrago from Lady So-Called Ashburne. Did you notice how she kept repeating her name? And she is tall – mannishly tall. Do you see where I am going? Mark my words, Miles, there is more to this than meets the eye. Even if she is who she says she is, why would a woman of her standing hire a couple of unknowns like us?"

"Cheapness?"

"Pah!"

"Jules Kroll was busy?"

"Because she doesn't *want* the case solved and expects us to make a hash of it!"

"The fool," said Miles flatly. "Little does she know she has run up against the finest detective mind of our generation."

"Well, you are biased," said Clara, patting her hair. "I am possibly in the top three. One thing is for sure – Codrington was killed because he knew too much. He stumbled onto something big."

Carefully, hopefully, Miles suggested, "Perhaps, even, too big for us to handle alone? Even Philip Marlowe, you know, would occasionally contact his friend at – "

"No, Miles," said Clara. "There is no-one I would trust. There is no telling how far the conspiracy reaches. If we don't obtain justice for Codrington, no-one will."

Miles remembered, as an adolescent, disapproving of Scott Fitzgerald allowing the brilliant and adorable Zelda to be put into a nut-house. He had sometimes thought he was being punished for this.

He burst out, "Clara, we can't – "

"I will bet you dinner at Le Connard against an hour in a maid costume I *can* find her bloody dog, Miles."

"But – "

"Who was it made me promise before our wedding that we would never ever argue?"

"I didn't mean you would just steamroll all over me!"

"Well you should have thought of that. Where is the devil-may-care gallant who wooed me? You are turning into a nagging harridan."

Miles sighed. "God help Godolphin Square."

*

It was leafy, spacious, hushed, architecturally uplifting, an upmarket cul-de-sac of centuries-old houses grouped around a well-tended quadrangle of lawn with a bronze statue of an obscure general in the middle.

"The place reeked of desperation," Clara voiced-over as they strolled towards Number 16. "A row of Georgian facades like so many porcelain caps over a mouth full of rotted teeth. The people led a precarious, hand-to-mouth existence, never sure where their next Ming vase was coming from. If you'd messed up in Mayfair or you didn't quite have the juice to make it in Belgravia, Godolphin Square was where you washed up for one last roll of the backgammon dice. Presiding over it all, some old tin soldier who'd fallen defending Rorke's Drift, Jenkins' Ear or Walpole's Cock. He had a look of weary disillusion as if nothing could shock him any more. You and me both, brother. Somewhere in this square a dog had been done to death on Tuesday."

"Slowly but surely she was slipping further away from me, like a swimmer caught in a riptide," monologued Miles. "I could only watch helplessly as she drifted out from the shore. Everyday objects – tin-openers, shoelaces, envelopes, the heel of her own hand – would baffle her completely or else become the occasion for the most fantastic and involved reveries. She would see conspiracies in a jam-jar, worlds in the whorls of a wicker table-mat; once I found her weeping hopelessly over a roller-skate, unable to understand what it was for. 'But why do my feet want to drive away and leave me?' she asked plaintively. 'I have been nothing but kind to them. My elbows, I could understand.' She was like an astronaut floating further and further into space, tethered only to me. And day by lovely day throughout that beautiful, terrible summer, it was slowly borne in on me that sooner or later, for her own good and the good of the world, I would be forced to take the woman I loved to Dr. Happy's Electro-shock Fun-House and While-U-Wait Lobotomy Clinic."

"A Guide for Disappointed Young Wives, Chapter Seven," said Clara, blinking. "What to do when your husband turns into a bore. Marriage, to any woman, is a long-drawn-out process of suffocation and dampening of the spirit. It is a stepping-down from a pedestal into the mud. Due to their age-old vagina-envy and essentially coarse and materialistic nature, men will always strive to shackle and castrate a woman's creativity and are never really able to keep up. Even the best-trained husband is at the mercy of poisonous secretions backing up from his penis and is liable at any moment to suddenly turn from a sprightly, fun-loving young lad into a pompous, spiritless dullard. Should this befall you I recommend brisk and decisive action. Italians make the best lovers: they are a lively, happy-go-lucky race with a plentiful supply of ice-cream."

Miles pouted. Clara folded her arms and averted her head.

"But of course I couldn't really do it," said Miles. "When it came to it I found I couldn't really drive her to see Dr. Happy, not while she was bouncing up and down on her seat with glee because she thought we were going to Carpet World, which she always believed was an actual planet where carpets lived. She would stroke them and talk to them and take home swatches thinking they were baby carpets which would grow. How could I abandon her? I realised with a pang that I could never leave her, for she would be lost without me. Who would explain her to the world if I did not?"

"Oh, that's really bloody rich!" cried Clara. "And, pang?"

Miles fluttered his eyelashes winsomely. Clara pouted and averted her head in another direction.

Suddenly they smiled at each other.

"Clara mia," said Miles imploringly.

"Pigface," said Clara caressingly.

They embraced and kissed.

"You know I wouldn't – "

"No, darling."

"Forgive me. Let's never – "

"But what was that thing you said at the office, only I have a voice-over- "

"I know, I'm turning into some dreadful – "

"No, never. Come on, let's play detectives."

"Yes, let's. We do have the best fun."

"The woman strode on triumphantly, smug in the confidence of her all-conquering beauty, trailed after pathetically by her hapless male victim," said Clara. She rang the bell.

Lady Ashburne answered the door and showed them into a sitting-room. Clara paced around with her collar turned up and an unlit stub of cigar in her mouth, sneering at the rather lovely furnishings.

"Every inch of the place screamed of the kind of restrained good taste that curls up in a corner and begs you not to notice it," she growled. "The kind of taste you just can't buy, for less than a million bucks or so. It was the kind of room where even spiders tiptoe around in little velvet slippers and the very dust-mites hold their farts in."

"I beg your pardon, I didn't catch that?" said Lady Ashburne.

"I was ruminating."

"Won't you sit down?" They did, disposing themselves at either end of a long plush couch. "Now how do you propose to proceed?"

"First we would like to quiz your household as to the events of that terrible day," said Clara in her own voice. "We would like to see them alone and they must have no opportunity to confer beforehand."

"May I offer you any refreshments?"

"We would like tea and biscuits, thank you, and jelly if you can manage it."

Lady Ashburne blinked. "I will see." She left.

"Miles," said Clara, putting her cigar away, "I want to write a monograph on the social decline of detectives over the years. They start off as gentlemen, often aristocrats, whom you can take anywhere, and then you have the likes of Marlowe, who while undoubtedly a gentleman in his way is not *quite* the thing socially and has some grievous lapses in manners, indeed can be churlish and puritanical about evidence of wealth. Then you come down to Columbo, a grubby, resentful class-warrior who just enjoys annoying rich people, slouching around their houses stinking them up with his foul stogies. I think the ones today are still mostly ill-bred chippy oaves, often Scottish, and generally the posher the suspect is the more unsympathetic they are. I have decided, not only to behave nicely, but, to help restore the balance, to bring this crime home to a working-class person, even if I have to falsify evidence to do so. Unfortunately for you, you are the closest thing to one I am liable to encounter around here."

"In the classic detective stories the proles were below suspicion," said Miles. "You look cute in a trench coat."

"I should hope I always look cute. The point is I have tired of being gruff and hard-boiled." She thought for a moment. "I'm going to be that gloomy Scandinavian detective now."

"Oh please God no."

"One day, Miles, I am going to star in an Ibsen festival, simply to spite you."

A short, worried-looking middle-aged woman in jeans and apron brought a tray of tea and biscuits in. By the time she appeared Clara was slumping on the couch with her head lolling against her shoulder, looking sad.

"I'm afraid we don't have any jelly," said the woman, staring at her, as she set the tray down on a table in front of them.

Clara let out a tremendously world-weary sigh. "I am used to these disappointments," she said in a depressed monotone, and slid right down the couch so her face was pressed against it horizontally.

"I was told you wanted to talk to me," said the woman, seating herself on the edge of a chair facing them, still staring at Clara in alarm.

"Who 'wants' anything?" asked Clara hollowly, half-muffled by the couch.

"About Codrington," the woman persisted, quite nervous of this behaviour.

"The little dog who is dead," moaned Clara. "How I envy him." She sighed and made an effort to push herself almost upright, although her head still lolled in apathy on her shoulder at an unusual angle. "You are the housekeeper? Describe the events of the day in question, if you can summon the strength in the face of our common predicament. It was a day as empty and meaningless as any other, I will wager."

Falteringly, the housekeeper told them what Lady Ashburne had about the piano movers and said the dog must have got out in the confusion.

"I am too sad to tear apart that tissue of lies," said Clara in a despair-wracked drone, staring at a biscuit in thoughtful gloom. "Who am I to deny you your deceptions? If truth is even knowable it is probably something as bleak and depressing as a junkyard full of broken Volvos." Clara was wisely not attempting Scandinavian but doing a quite good impersonation of the actor who played this detective on British television, if he'd been lobotomized. "The poor Volvos," she sighed. "Lonely and abandoned. They always look so forlorn. I cannot bear to think of them."

"I don't appreciate being called a liar," said the woman blushing, after boggling at the rest.

"If that is the worst thing that happens to you today, count yourself the spoiled favourite of fate," gloomed Clara, apathetically dipping her biscuit in her tea. It broke. She hung her head and sighed. "Now on top of everything else my tea is full of soggy biscuit." She relapsed onto the couch. "I can no longer cope. I hand you over to my partner."

"I have only two things to ask," said Miles in a smug voice, rising and pacing. "How is your brother Bernard, and when did you return from Madagascar?"

Clara sat bolt upright, wide-eyed and outraged. Miles had shed his raincoat and had a long curvaceous pipe in his mouth, a deerstalker hat on his head, and was trying to make his profile hawk-like.

The housekeeper stared at him in equal surprise. "I have no brother and I've never been to Madagascar."

Not at all put out, Miles said, "The Azores, then."

"I haven't – "

"Fiji?"

"I haven't been – "

"Canvey Island?"

"I haven't been out of the country in ten years."

"Aha!" Miles glanced significantly at Clara. "That is all for now. I shall always remember you as the one woman who was able to match wits with me. Pray send in the next witness."

The woman departed, gratefully but not without backward glances.

"You unholy upstaging bastard," breathed Clara. "Where did you get those?"

"I thought you'd be jealous." He produced another pipe. "I brought you one."

"Yours is bigger. This isn't a Holmes pipe. Give me the Holmes pipe, Miles!" she cried, trying to grab it while he fended her off. "And the hat!"

Miles escaped her clutches temporarily and produced a magnifying glass from his pocket, at which her eyes widened again. "I keep the Holmes pipe and you can have this." She bit her lip in indecision and greed. "Marriage is a series of trade-offs, Clara. You can't have everything," he said backing away from her.

"Don't you dare quote that unromantic woman-hating modernist quack-bastard to me! You are meant to provide me with things. All right the lens Miles. The lens and the hat and you can keep the Holmes pipe."

"What use is the Holmes pipe without the hat?"

"All right you can keep the hat." He handed her the magnifying glass. She grabbed the hat too. He grabbed it back. She snatched the Holmes pipe. There was a tussle on the couch and Miles ended up with the cap and a pair of sore arms and Clara with the lens and proper Holmes pipe and a contented smile.

"I noticed her Canvey Island slip-up too," she said to make up for it, making big eyes at him through the lens. "That was smart work, Miles, I believe you have unmasked a Chinese Communist sleeper agent. What put you onto the scent?"

"She has a hint of a Fu Manchu moustache, and didn't pour the milk into the tea."

"Why *does* no-one serve jelly to visitors any more?" Clara suddenly wondered. "I think it is the thing I miss most about childhood. That and the fact that anyone who showed me a penis was locked up." She started to prowl around looking at things through the magnifying glass. "If you gave me the hat," she said cajolingly, "and put your raincoat back on, with the little pipe you'd look like ... you know ... that one from 1950s films."

"Who?"

"*You* know ... thingy ... Car ... Carrutherford ... of the Yard. He's the best, everyone wants to be him."

She had pocketed the pipe and was down on all fours examining the carpet through the lens when a woman, presumably the one adverted to as Lady Ashburne's companion, came in and looked surprised. She was even taller than their employer, in her late fifties, and plainly a formidable and no-nonsense, not to say intimidating character, and at his first sight of her Miles instantly and instinctively snatched the deerstalker off his head and hid it behind him.

"What on Earth are you doing?" she demanded of Clara.

"Looking for clues, if you don't mind," said Clara, chickening out of doing Holmes at the sound of the woman's voice but continuing to scrutinize the floor.

The companion swivelled her steely gaze to Miles. "What is that behind your back?"

"Nothing. Evidence," he said, blushing.

"Incriminating evidence," said Clara from the floor. "Mrs ... ?"

"Miss. Fortescue."

Clara crawled up to the woman's shoes and studied them through the magnifying glass, paying inordinate attention to the knot of their laces.

"I see you spent time in the Girl Guides, Miss Fortescue," she murmured.

"What possible business is it of yours if I did?" demanded Miss Fortescue, outraged, backing away.

"Did you hear that, Miles?" cried Clara, delighted. She rose and quickly decided to peer interestedly at the magnified grain of a side-table rather than meet the newcomer's gaze.

Nervously Miles said, "Perhaps you could give us your version of the events surrounding the, er, disappearance of Lord Codrington, Miss Fortescue."

"I believe you have already been told them twice," she snapped in stern, stentorian, brook-no-bullshit tones. "I cannot begin to imagine what you possibly hope to achieve, by, by – "

"Please, Miss Fortescue, let us do our job," said Clara who, as the companion advanced angrily towards Miles, had bravely tiptoed up behind her and was examining the back of her head through the lens. "Tell me, Miss Fortescue, which brand of conditioner do you use?"

Miles quailed before the dragon. "We're just trying to – "

"To impose on Lady Ashburne," finished Miss Fortescue tartly. "Codrington wandered off as animals will. He will doubtless return in the due course of time. In the meantime you are needlessly – what are you playing at?" This last was to Clara, who had moved on to examine the sleeve of Miss Fortescue's cardigan through the magnifying glass; Miss Fortescue had noticed now and indignantly slapped this away. Clara's hand then darted forward and snatched something off the sleeve and Miss Fortescue slapped that too.

"If you slap me again, sweet-cheeks, I will knock you on your arse," Clara murmured, darting away and examining her prize through the lens.

"That's it – I must ask you to leave this house at – "

"Why was there a dog-hair on your cardigan, Miss Fortescue?" asked Clara. The woman's mouth twitched.

Miles had risen. "Perhaps we'd better – "

"A bloody dog-hair, Miles, look!" She showed it him through the lens – it was certainly a hair of some kind – then advanced on the companion brandishing it between her fingers. "Well? Well? Explain that, if you can, Miss so-called Fortescue!"

To Miles's astonishment the woman seemed stopped in her tracks by this.

"Obviously it is one of Codrington's," she said with controlled fury after a moment.

"Aha!" cried Clara. "She admits it! You heard that, Miles!"

"Clara, perhaps – "

Clara abruptly paced off with her hands behind her back. "You do not strike me, Miss Fortescue, as the sort of woman who would wear the same cardigan for three days running, unwashed."

"Obviously it must have come from – "

"From where, Miss Fortescue? You are an almost impudently tall woman and this was a defencelessly small dog. Have you been crawling round on the carpet too?"

"I have no idea where it came from and I – "

"Then that will be all for now, Miss Fortescue," said Clara, rounding on her heel impressively. "I suggest you go and think about what you did, and come back when you have a better story. Please send the chauffeur in to see us, and then Codrington's doll."

The woman seemed to go ashen with rage. To Miles's amazement, she also seemed to have been somewhat intimidated by Clara.

"Why the chauffeur?" she demanded, quivering but in a quieter voice. "What could he possibly have to do with – "

"That is what I hope to find out, Miss Fortescue. Perhaps this simple-minded foreigner will put two Englishwomen to shame by having the guts to tell me the truth."

Miss Fortescue opened her mouth, stared at Clara for a long moment, then shook her head and started to go out.

"Just one more thing, Miss Fortescue," called Clara. "Do you speak any Chinese?"

Miss Fortescue paused with her hand on the door, not looking back. "Why on Earth do you ask me that?"

"Oh, no reason," said Clara airily. "Nee how mah, Miss Fortescue."

Miss Fortescue went out.

"Right," said Miles briskly, "let's go before she calls the police."

"We *are* the police, Miles. Miles – did you see her face when I – "

"Yes, lovely," said Miles, "but I really think we have to – "

She clutched his arm excitedly. "And did you hear what she said? 'Why the chauffeur?' Not, 'Why the bloody rag doll, you lunatic?' She fears us talking to the chauffeur! Doubtless he is knocking her off and they are in a conspiracy together. They have intimidated the housekeeper, she looked terrified of something."

"Clara – "

"But I have the evidence to – my evidence! Miles, I dropped the sodding hair." She got down on the floor with the magnifying glass again. "Help me find it. I think they're all in it together, Miles. I mean really, no fantasy. Maybe it bit one of them so they had it put down. You must admit she was thrown when I found the dog-hair." Clara had come up against a dinge in the carpet and looking around saw two others. "I deduce this is where the piano stood. Miles – the piano-movers! What better way to sneak out the corpse of a poor defenceless dog than concealed inside – "

"Very nice, but please let's flee now, this has ceased to be – "

"Seriously, Miles! Don't you think we've stumbled on a *real* mystery here? Her face – "

"No, we've stumbled on and are causing great consternation to a very nice household of little old – "

"Little?"

"Large old ladies then, and – "

"Communist drag-artists, more like. My woman's intuition, Miles –"

He tugged at her arm. "Please, this is sick now. We – we're annoying people in their own homes. Like the government! The government, Clara! Come on, let's go. I promise we can go on and – we'll look round the neighbourhood. Pound the streets, yes? Even make enquiries. But – "

"Just the chauffeur, Miles. He is the key to the whole conspiracy, I am sure. Anyway he won't be as scary as that dragon. Mind you I have collected half a dozen stray dog hairs now and if she gives me any more lip I will fit her up good and proper. Miles what the hell kind of a name for a dog is Codrington anyway?"

All might have ended not too embarrassingly if the chauffeur hadn't been quite a long time coming. But in the interim there was another fight over the Holmes hat and pipe and they both became giddy.

The chauffeur when he came was a good-looking, nice-looking, perpetually smiling man. He nodded to them and sat, leaning forward eagerly.

"English no good," he said smiling.

"We saved your bacon in the War, foreigner," said Clara, bridling.

Miles took advantage of this to steal the Holmes hat back and advance towards the driver wearing it and presenting a keen profile. He said, "Tell me about the dog, Mr ... Chauffeur." This was as far as he got because Clara kicked him in the back of the knee and grabbed the hat back.

"The dog that didn't bark in the night," she said putting it on.

"Excuse?" said the chauffeur.

"This is a three-speedball problem," said Miles snatching it back for himself.

"Hey, Holmes," said Clara, offering him the New World overhead handslap greeting known as a 'high five'. When he was off-guard responding to this she kneed at his groin and took the hat back again. "You are familiar with my methods," she added smugly.

"Excuse?" said the chauffeur, smiling.

"Please describe ... oh why don't you just confess?" She threw the Holmes cap down irritably. "I understand why the police used to beat people up, before they went rubbish, it's so discouraging asking the same questions over and over. Oh let's do nice policeman and nasty policeman on him. I've got your number, sonny," she growled at the suspect, "and if you don't co-operate I will take your green card and send you back to Foreignland."

"I really like your jacket," Miles told him.

"Excuse?"

Clara started to tug at a table-lamp on a sideboard so she could shine it into the chauffeur's eyes.

"No," said Miles. "I think you can go now," he said to the chauffeur.

The housekeeper entered bearing a rag doll.

"Codrington's doll," she said sullenly.

Clara snatched it. She clutched it to her and felt it all over.

"Yes," she said, "yes. It is rich with his aura."

She stood in the middle of the room with her eyes closed and the doll pressed to her, swaying slightly and emitting eerie moans. The chauffeur and housekeeper stared.

"I see sausages," said Clara. "Lots and lots of sausages. Either he is in doggy heaven or the Communists have hung him up in their larder."

"Clara," said Miles. The chauffeur and housekeeper and two tall old ladies stared.

"What on Earth is going on?" said the two latter together.

"Arse," said Clara under her breath. She opened her eyes. "Please, ladies, will you let me do my – "

"If these two are detectives I'm the Duke of Windsor," said the chauffeur, still smiling, in perfect English with a more cockney than foreign accent. "They've been wearing a Sherlock Holmes hat, look."

"You weasel!" cried Clara, astonished.

"I told you to let me handle this," said Miss Fortescue to Lady Ashburne. "It must be student rag week, or conceivably a reality television show."

"I hate reality television!" cried Clara, outraged. "I hate television."

"She hates reality," put in Miles.

"They advertised in a reputable paper. And they showed me a licence," said Lady Ashburne.

"Yes," said Clara, showing her licence to Miss Fortescue. "Look."

"That is the most inept forgery I have ever seen," said Miss Fortescue after a cursory glance.

"But it is laminated!" cried Clara.

"Leave this house at once."

Miles had already been stealthily collecting their things and now started to pull Clara towards the door.

"Please," said Clara earnestly, "give us another chance. It's our first case and we just became giddy with joy of detecting. We really can find your dog. We will work ever so hard. I am fairly posh myself, you know, and have lovely manners really."

"I think you are a pair of borderline mental cases with too much time on your hands," said Miss Fortescue.

"It's a point of view," Clara admitted.

They left.

Outside she said, "We are off the case, Miles."

"Umf," said Miles, who was taking quite a long pull at his bourbon flask.

She stared glumly at her detective licence. "Does no-one have any respect for lamination any more?"

"Let's go," said Miles.

She looked at him indignantly. "You are surely not thinking of giving up?"

"I – I dearly hoped – "

She glared. "What did it say on our poster, Miles?"

"We will mess up your lives virtually free of charge."

"It said relentless, Miles. The Two Finder Outers do not give up cases just because our clients fire us and call us names. When we get a mystery between our teeth we cling to it as tenaciously as a fey Pekinese with a limp rag doll."

"Clara – spring of my step – "

"Aren't your suspicions aroused by the duplicitous chauffeur? They *are* all in on it! If it *isn't* a nest of Communists then clearly the Fortescue monster has done away with the poor pooch in order to replace it as Lady Thing's favourite – and probably heir. Lady Thing will be next!"

Miles took another quite long pull at his flask.

"Seriously, Miles," she went on in a quite reasonable tone of voice he seemed to remember having heard fairly frequently before they married, "the only way to stop the memory of this turning into a festering black cyst of embarrassment is to vindicate ourselves by actually finding her damn dog. I want to pursue the case properly. Really it was only because of you that I started to arse around," she added less reasonably.

"Me? Me?"

"Well, we can thrash that out with our marriage counsellor some time. Really, don't you think it odd it would just wander off and never come back?" She rubbed his arm cajolingly. "Let's use our brains, Miles. If they are all telling the truth, what prosaic explanation could there be?"

"Any number."

"Well let's think of them and consider them." They started to stroll around the square. "Codrington was valuable, a prize-winner and reluctant stud. Like my husband!" she cooed rubbing his arm again. "Perhaps he was dog-napped. How would one dispose of a stolen dog?"

"Give it a spray-job and sell it on."

"You didn't even have to think about that. Your proletarian instincts will come in useful on this case. We should look in ... pet shops. Check small ads in dog magazines. That explanation doesn't satisfy me, somehow, though. He happens to escape and is grabbed? It seems too fortuitous." She stopped and looked around. "Let us reconstruct. Let us imagine ourselves in Codrington's paws. I am a pampered little doggy who has wandered out of his gilded cage." She hung her tongue out and started to pant. "My first destination is the grass in the middle. Never suspecting I may be watched by malevolent eyes, I trot over to it on my dear little legs and commence to frolic and roll around." Tongue lolling, hands made into paws, eyes wide with excitement, Clara trotted over to the lawn and commenced to roll around on the grass, barking gleefully. Miles looked about. A woman with a pram, a man with a door-key, standing at their window Miss Fortescue and Lady Ashburne, were frozen in astonishment, mouths open, watching. "Oh what joy! Oh what fun! Oh what a paradise the world is for a bouncy little doggy! Oh tickle my tummy! Oh someone tickle my tummy to make everything perfect!" Since he was and always would be on Clara's side against the world, Miles did indeed start to tickle her tummy. She howled with delight. Then she stood up and raised a leg in the air. "Next, I widdle on the statue in sheer *joie de vivre*. Then ... and then ... " She frowned and looked around. "One of the neighbours steals me, to flog down the pub for a fiver or offer as a sacrifice to Stalin?

They don't seem the type, but we should at least make door-to-door enquiries and see if we can flush out anyone suspicious. Maybe tomorrow," she added seeing the stern set of Miles's face. "If we rule that out … " She eyed the little half-street that was the only exit out of the square. "I see freedom! The big wide world! More grass, more statues, new dollies, who knows what adventures! I trot on my little legs towards it." She trotted, until they came to the somewhat busier street at the end. "And now. I trot left? I trot right?"

"Or trot across the road and go ker-splatt."

"Quite possibly, although if I was a little doggy I think I would be too scared to attempt it." She looked around. Her eyes lit up at something to the left. "If I was a little doggy I think I might like to investigate that delicatessen down there. Let's ask if they saw him. Admit this is stimulating."

"This *is* stimulating, but let's eat as well."

"Yes let's. What do detectives eat?"

"Ham on rye bread and misanthropy."

The delicatessen owner hadn't seen a stray Pekinese on the day in question, or at all. They ate.

"Door left open and the smells are ravishing," said Clara as they emerged. "If he made it this far he didn't come this way or he would surely have wandered in."

They strolled arm in arm in the other direction but couldn't make any further deductions and meandered aimlessly for a bit.

"If I was Codrington, and in a very real sense I have become him, I would be uneasy and missing my comfy home and doll by now," said Clara. "And yet he never made it back. How and why would he have vanished? We know he didn't care for lady dogs. The whole thing is a – "

"Oh no," said Miles suddenly, stopping dead and spinning Clara round and starting to march her firmly back the way they had come.

It was too late. She had seen. She fought free and whirled, eyes wide. "*Miles*," she gasped.

For ahead of them was the Embassy of the People's Republic of China.

"No," said Miles.

"Miles – "

"No."

"It is obvious – "

"No."

"We could just go and – "

"No."

"Quite politely – "

"No."

"Without causing any diplomatic incidents – "
"No."
"Ask if they have eaten him or – "
"No."
"Sacrificed him to Mao or – "
"No."
"Killed him because he stumbled on some dark fiendish – "
"No."
"Pekineses are from China originally, I think; the clue is in the name. The Chicoms would doubtless regard him as a defector. Also he probably understands Mandarin and may have picked up sensitive gossip from the embassy dogs. Let us at least – "
"No!"
He had to push and drag her with great difficulty back the way they had come.
"You must admit it puts a new complexion on the case. Can it be coincidence? I think not, husband. My worst fears are confirmed. All those harridans are obviously in league with – "
"No."
She sighed. "I suppose you are right, Miles. If the Chinese have done away with Codrington for inscrutable reasons of their own it would mean a war Britain is not yet prepared for."
"Now you're thinking."
"But what of justice? We could lob a panda's head over the wall in retribution. To the zoo, then, with hacksaws and – "
A cloud passed over the sun. She suddenly stopped dead and sat down on the kerb.
"What's the matter?" asked Miles in alarm when he saw her face.
"A bad train of thought," she said, sobered, with a little shiver. "It suddenly occurred to me that if a foreign spy *did* kill a dog no-one would care. The Russians poisoned a man with nuclear waste in the heart of this city and no-one did a bloody thing about it. I'd forgotten the poor bugger until now. You were only my second love, Miles. I used to love this country, with an almost – "
"Not our business, remember," said Miles. "We play."
"Miles, what are we meant to – "
"Play."
"I mean we're fairly smart and – "
"Utterly powerless," he said, sitting and holding her. "We play. It was you who taught me that. No reality or they win. We'll make an England of the heart they can't kill. That's what you told me."
"Miles what *happened* to us though?"

"Oi. Chin up. Don't do to brood. Where's my hard-boiled detective girl? Tecs don't get mad, they get even."

Clara nodded and stood up. "You're right. You're absolutely right. I'm going to find her bastard dog if it's the last thing I do. I'm quite serious, Miles. It's become personal now. Maybe it doesn't matter much in the great scheme of things if one large old lady loses her dog, but it's something I can do something about and maybe even fix, in the middle of all the things I'm just supposed to grin and bear. Do you understand, Miles?"

"No," said Miles. "But I understand that you shot our telly so we have to make our own fun."

"Well, that too."

They started to stroll back towards Godolphin Square. Suddenly Clara exclaimed, "Yeek!" and pulled Miles down to crouch on the pavement, and flung one of the coats he carried over their heads. The housekeeper had emerged from the street leading to the square, wearing a coat, and turned and walked off in the opposite direction from them, past the delicatessen.

"Miles it's the suspicious housekeeper! Let's follow her!"

Miles was unable to think of a reason why not quickly enough, and besides Clara was already hurrying after the woman, dashing from lamp-post to lamp-post in her wake and hiding behind each one to conceal herself. When he caught up to her she was crouching behind a post-box while the housekeeper crossed the road.

"Quick, we need the trench coats and hats on to conceal ourselves! Hurry! Turn your collar up, man! Don't you know the first thing about disguise? Doubtless she is about some sinister errand – she probably has Codrington's one remaining forepaw in a parcel under her coat and is aiming to dispose of it."

"Or she's just going home."

"In that case it is our duty to follow her in order to clear her name."

They crossed over and tailed the woman down the street, again taking advantage of natural lamp-post cover in case she looked round. She did not notice them. Various other people did. Presently she cut through a park, which meant they were able to have more fun scurrying from bush to bush and crouching down behind them. Clara snapped off a leafy half-broken branch from one and held it before them as camouflage as they tiptoed across the open spaces. "An old ninja trick," she breathed. Leaving the park they were just in time to see the housekeeper boarding a bus. They dashed after it and caught it. Fortunately it was one of the proper old lovely double-decker Routemasters that had survived the Purges, so they could jump on at the back. The housekeeper was already seated near the front. They hunkered down on a seat several rows behind and held free papers in front of their faces, Clara assiduously poking eyeholes in hers so she could look through.

"We need dark glasses and false noses next time."

They were on the bus for half an hour or so. Clara developed a suspicion of a fat man who took the seat next to the housekeeper when it became vacant.

"He may be her contact."

"From? We can rule out the Chinese, she would have gone straight to the embassy."

"It may not be political at all. At this point I favour the existence of a sinister den of sporting coves who like to wager on the outcome of Pekinese races."

The woman alighted at a high street and they followed. She went into a supermarket.

"This could be tricky," said Clara.

"Maybe we should just lurk outside."

"And if she is buying something incriminating, such as dogfood, or quicklime, or a spade?"

They went in and took a trolley and started to push it round half an aisle behind the housekeeper, Miles whistling casually.

"Maybe we should take the hats and coats off?" he suggested.

"It's all right, people will take us for store detectives."

The woman remained oblivious of them as they trailed her, although a couple of times they hastened to thrust their heads deep into freezer cabinets or hold cereal boxes in front of their faces as she paused to look at the shelves. She bought bread and cornflakes and curry powder and so on. Miles put a tin of peas in the trolley to allay suspicions. By hanging back while the housekeeper queued and then whizzing through the five-items-or-less till they were able to leave just behind her.

They followed her round several corners and then down a long residential street. It was halfway along this that she caught them. They were barely twenty feet behind, tiptoeing between lamp-posts and ducking down behind parked cars and vans and peering round them after her. While Miles was in mid-tiptoe and Clara just scurrying out from the cover of a car the woman suddenly turned round for no ascertainable reason. They all froze, Clara and Miles both still in sneaky, crouching postures and with one foot off the ground, arrested in mid-scurry and -tiptoe respectively, and went wide-eyed.

"Hello," said Miles after a moment, straightening his back and putting his lifted foot down and attempting a cheery grin. "Fancy meeting you here."

"Are you following me?" asked the housekeeper in alarm.

"No," said Miles. "We just happened to be out for a walk."

"I don't believe you. You're following me!"

"We ... we just wanted to interview you alone," said Clara. "Away from the others. Tell us the truth about the dog."

The woman really looked quite frightened of them. "You're lunatics. Go away. I'm not talking to you. I'll call the police."

"Miles give her some money," said Clara.

Miles thought this was quite a good idea and thrust quite a large sum of money into the woman's coat pocket, her hands being full of shopping bags.

"Now spill it and there's more where that came from," said Clara. "Talk to us. We can protect you. Who are you afraid of?"

"You," said the woman promptly. "Since the first time I saw you. There is something wrong with you."

"Well that's just hurtful," said Clara.

"Please leave me alone," said the woman. "I will call the police."

"The police!" said Clara scornfully. "They won't do anything, unless we insult your religion, or conceivably your hairdo. *I* am the only law in this city."

"I will shout for help," said the housekeeper. "I will hit you with my shopping if you try to come near me."

"We only want to interrogate you," said Clara reasonably. "Anyway you only have bread and cornflakes and *we* have a tin of peas. That is a *much* better weapon if we are to duel with shopping. We could bounce it off your head."

The woman stared and looked more scared than ever. "You mean you've been spying on my shopping?"

"We – not at all, you suspicious-minded harridan," said Clara with a sort of guilty glare. "We were merely buying peas. Show her, Miles."

Miles nodded eagerly at the woman and quickly took the tin of peas from his pocket and thrust it towards her. Unfortunately in his eagerness it slipped from his hand; he fumbled and grabbed at it but succeeded only in batting it towards the housekeeper. The tin went flying right at her face and she dodged and screamed.

"Miles give her some more money."

Smiling placatingly and cringeing in appeasement, Miles took out some more money and crept towards the woman. She flinched away from him in terror and started to back off so he waved it and put it down on a garden wall.

"Terrible misunderstanding," he muttered with another cringeing smile, and grabbed Clara by the arm.

"This isn't over," said Clara, pointing at the woman, as he pulled her away. "Don't think it ends like this. We know vaguely where you live now. I'm going to avenge Codrington if I have to turn this whole stinking town to rubble. Run, Miles," she added as they neared the corner. "How *could* you attack the poor woman with peas?"

The next morning – after a night in which Miles was woken every five minutes to be excitedly told Clara's new theory, and woke himself every ten to brood about the possibility of being arrested for attempted assault with peas – they rang round various dog pounds, and then, when that didn't pay off, several pet shops to ask if they had or had been offered a Pekinese for sale.

"I'm not sure you would sell them in a shop like budgies or goldfish," said Miles doubtfully after the third fruitless call.

"Of course not. There is a black-market. The word is passed discreetly and then one meets a man with a bent nose down the docks at midnight."

They found one for sale online of the same colour as Codrington, but the advert had been placed before Codrington's disappearance. Clara stared at the picture of the Peke for sale and mused.

"Do you know what I am thinking, Miles?"

"Yes," said Miles. "You're thinking that at the worst we could buy that one for an exorbitant sum of money, put a spot on its leg with magic marker, give it a thoughtful look by reading it bits of Schopenhauer or Kierkegaard, and then attempt to palm it off on Lady Violet as Codrington."

"You know me too well. The spark will go out of our marriage."

Then Clara made some posters saying:

MURDER!
£5000 REWARD FOR INFORMATION

On Tuesday last one of our best-loved local characters
was savagely taken from us. Anyone who knows anything
or has a theory no matter how wild should contact the Two
Finder-Outers on the number below. We will pay you. We
will protect you. Failing that we will avenge you as we
have sworn to avenge Codrington.
WE ARE NOT GOING AWAY UNTIL THE TRUTH IS
KNOWN.

They didn't have a picture of Codrington so she drew one, emphasizing his thoughtful look and the spot on his leg. There was some room left at the bottom so she added a row of cartoon Pekineses being stabbed, shot, garrotted, shipped abroad in dead of night and then being hit with sticks by Spaniards, et cetera, with question marks next to each.

They taped them up on lamp-posts near and in Godolphin Square, then started to make door-to-door enquiries of Lady Ashburne's neighbours.

Today they were wearing their trench coats but no hats.

"No arsing around, Miles," said Clara as she rang a bell at random on the left-hand side of the square. "We are doing this properly today."

A good-looking woman in her thirties opened the door. Clara, who was wearing a solemn, indeed wooden face, glanced furtively over her shoulder and then flashed her detective licence, very briefly and discreetly and giving the woman no more than a glimpse of it.

"May we come in, Ma'am?" she murmured. "We are investigating the disappearance of your neighbour Lord Codrington."

"Oh my God," said the woman, shocked and interested, and let them in.

In her sitting room she watched Clara take out her notebook and said, "I don't think I can help. I didn't even know."

"He vanished mysteriously on Tuesday morning; we fear kidnapping or worse."

The woman widened her eyes. "I presume you're police." Clara was silent and wooden. "Or Special Branch?" said the woman in a low voice. "Or ... M.I.5?"

"I would prefer not to say, Ma'am," said Clara.

"Gosh! I can't help though. I don't think I've ever even seen him," said the woman. "Not to say hello to anyway. Is he ... the government one? Or the BBC one? Or that old bloke with the ... "

"Short, bandy-legged chap," said Clara. "Pants a lot. Walks with a rolling gait. Vaguely oriental cast to his features. Has a thoughtful, abstracted look common to those weighed down by great affairs. Scratches behind his ear sometimes."

The woman nodded. "I think I've seen him about the square. Oh, I'm sorry, I don't know the form – am I supposed to offer you tea or something?"

"Even tireless defenders of the realm are still creatures of flesh and blood, Ma'am," said Clara with a smile. "Two sugars please."

The woman went to make tea.

Miles said, "She thinks Lord Codrington is – "

"Yes, Miles."

"You encouraged her to think – "

"Yes, Miles. Note I have cleverly told no lies. Note how excited she is. Note that big vase is large enough to stuff the body of a Pekinese into, if it was bisected first." She dashed across and peered into it but was seated again when the woman returned.

The woman couldn't help them and had been out all day on Tuesday but, in return for vague but thrilling hints of a terrible conspiracy which Clara let drop, gave them some good gossip on the residents of the square, not strictly helpful to the case but sometimes juicy enough to cause Clara to drop her Special Branch/M.I.5 act far enough to go, "Ooh!" and lean forward wide-eyed at several points. She had abandoned her notebook but kept nudging Miles to make a note of the dirt in his. They became quite chummy by the end. The woman asked Clara how she had got into that line of work. Clara told a long tale about being recruited as a schoolgirl because she had excelled at languages and the modern pentathlon and had also had an adventure in which she unmasked her own headmistress as an agent of a foreign power, related with a profusion of incidental detail that caused Miles to stop doodling in his notebook and stare at her in deep alarm. The woman drank it all down unquestioningly and delightedly. Since she seemed so interested Clara told her she could probably get her taken on as a paid informant, also that they were always on the look-out for places they could use as safe-houses or interrogation centres. The woman wasn't sure about this but said she would think about it. Later Clara asked her where she had bought her outfit and made Miles write down the very expensive answer.

"She was nice," said Clara outside after they had at length exchanged phone numbers and goodbyes. "I hope we don't have to beat her up later. Being a detective is a good way to meet new people. I don't understand why they are traditionally so lonely."

She took the murdered-dog posters down from around the square: Codrington being confused with a human Lord might come in handy in their investigations and was certainly fun.

The interrogation of the neighbour had whiled away what was left of the morning and the fore part of the afternoon. It was time for lunch. In the delicatessen-cafe they had a slight argument about lying which Clara ended by pouting and looking sad and telling Miles he was stifling her creativity.

"Anyway in a healthier world where Britain hadn't been taken over by Communists I undoubtedly *would* have been recruited as a girl secret agent," she concluded. "I think, in my moments of inspiration, I sometimes have access to a Platonic level of reality where there are deeper, truer truths than can be perceived by you pedantic earthbound types who … " She got bored with this sentence and waved a hand dismissively. "Talking of Communists, you know who we're interrogating next."

The nice woman had told them who lived in most of the houses of the square, including the BBC governor and the government minister. Clara named the second.

"We are not," said Miles.

"Yes yes, token resistance to my all-conquering genius."

"We'll get in proper trouble. There'll be all kinds of security, real Special Branch people or ... He probably won't even be there now."

"We can at least pester his staff. Don't you even want to sneer at the furniture we paid for? We have a perfectly legitimate – "

"No we don't."

They had left the deli and rounded the corner into the short street leading to the square by this point. The first building after the corner was an antique shop. A desperate expedient occurred to Miles: if he could use the place to distract Clara it might be expensive but far less expensive and time-consuming than a court case for running amok in a minister's house.

He stopped dead in front of the shop window. "Ooh! Some nice things in here."

"We don't have time now, Miles, we are on a case." Clara wasn't fooled for a second. Fogey and would-be fop or not, Miles didn't have much clue about antiques, and also would ordinarily have hurried her past a place like that for reasons of parsimony. Nevertheless she found herself drawn to stand next to him and soon to press her face against the glass like a child outside a sweet shop. There *were* some nice things.

"Miles," she breathed yearningly, "buy me a present."

Miles didn't respond for a moment. He was rivetted on something very un-antique mounted inside the window above their heads. He turned and looked at the street behind them and then back. For a second he was torn. He really shouldn't encourage this madness. But *that* would definitely distract her from the minister. Besides, he was excited himself.

"I'll give you a present right now," he said. "Look at *that*!"

Clara looked. Her eyes went even wider.

"Miles you have cracked this case wide open!" She suddenly seemed miffed at that. "Actually I saw it first, I just wanted you to discover it for yourself."

"Maybe we could – "

"I *know*, Miles."

"How can we – "

She was already inside the shop.

There was a genial old man in a bow tie behind the counter. Clara flashed her laminated pass at him very quickly. "Special Branch. We are investigating the disappearance of your neighbour Lord Codrington."

The man in the bow tie appeared delighted. "But how wonderful!" he exclaimed. "It is very nice for such a mighty organ of state to take an interest in the fate of a little dog."

"There are national security implications," Clara told him, loftily and fairly unfazed. "The fate of more than a dog hangs in the balance."

The genial proprietor was even more delighted. "How thrilling, my dear. But how can I be of assistance?"

"Is that – that is a camera in your window?" said Miles.

"I'm afraid so." He looked sad and apologetic. "The insurance company insisted. We had a smash-and-grab last year. Isn't it awful?"

"And they would make you keep the tapes, right?"

"We would like to see the ones for Tuesday," said Clara. "There must be a clear view of the street. It will help us establish if Codrington left of his own accord, or if anyone left carrying a wriggling sack, or any sinister figures entered, especially foreign attaches."

The proprietor looked as though he would burst with joy.

"You must be the lunatic pretend detectives Lady Violet told me about this morning," he said.

Clara bridled. "We are *real* detectives. It is only our first case, but we have resolved to find her wretched, stinking, blasted dog if we have to kill every other living creature in the country to do so. If that is lunacy, then I am proud to be a lunatic. *Please*," she begged softening. "Please please please give us the tapes. We really do want to help. And if you do I will make my husband buy me that huge overpriced vase in the window using my feminine nipples."

The shopkeeper looked ecstatic. "How can I refuse?"

He disappeared into the back, and presently returned with – not a tape or disc, they saw to their dismay, but some sort of flat black thing with shiny bits sticking out that might go into a computer or a fancy camera or for all they knew a modern toaster. They looked at it with panic, fear and revulsion and exchanged sorrowful glances. Their technophobia was partly principle and partly personal taste, but also a good job and a convenient alibi, because the pair of them had genuinely been born rubbish at gadgets. They had a hulking ten-year-old computer hidden in a small back room at home, and could look for things on the internet or make rude photoshops with a minimum of swearing, but they knew that anything as new and black and shiny as that would not fit into it no matter how many times they hit it. They would be capable of buying whatever it was the thing did fit into, if the man wrote it down for them, but they would not be capable of making it go. They would get a dull pain in the front of their heads as soon as they took it from the box. If the electrical plug came attached Clara would plug it into a socket and then hit the machine with her hand and glare a lot. If Miles read the instructions he would make crying noises, and if Clara did she would hit the machine with a hammer and not stop. They would console themselves by playing with the polystyrene and bubble-wrap it came in and perhaps use the shattered components to make things out of. They knew this from experience and, if not quite proud of it, were comfortable with it, but it was a drawback at times.

"That's no use to us," Clara sighed in defeat.

"You shot our television anyway," Miles pointed out.

The shopkeeper looked quizzical but even more delighted.

"It was a Communist," Clara explained.

"Please," said the shopkeeper, "why don't you use mine?"

He showed them upstairs into a cosy, cluttered flat, inserted the Thing into an arcane entertainment centre with numerous gadgets interlinked, selected Tuesday's footage and pointed out how to play, fast-forward and rewind; they could use remote controls for simple things. They thanked him effusively and not without a hint of awe at his technical skills. Then he brought them tea and biscuits, apologising that he couldn't offer them anything stronger and more detective-y, and left them to it.

"What a nice man," said Miles.

"Too nice," said Clara. "He doesn't fool me for a minute. We will turn this place over afterwards. And don't drink your tea."

"Too late."

"I am working with an amateur."

They settled back on the shopkeeper's wonderfully comfy couch. The TV showed a perfect view of the street from the shop window. Clara fast-forwarded grimly for a while then yelped and slowed and rewound and played it again. A luxurious car went sedately past, coming from the square to the right and slowing for the junction.

"Ooh, ooh, look, look! Lady Thing and the weasel chauffeur going to her friend's! She didn't lie about that anyway."

A while later a van went past from the direction of the main street. Clara rewound and paused.

"The piano-movers! They look evil. My money is on *them* now. None of them have shaved properly. The driver has a tattoo on his arm; perhaps he belongs to a secret society."

A few minutes later a tall man with a big nose walked into shot from the left, paused and glanced into the shop window for a few moments, then continued towards the square.

"A false nose if ever I saw one," said Miles.

"It is Lady Thing, in disguise, sneaking back to kill her own dog."

After that nothing happened for a while. Then:

"Miles! Look! Codrington! It is Codrington!" A Pekinese was sauntering up the middle of the street from the square. He did not look particularly thoughtful, rather as idiotically gleeful as Clara had when playing him.

"How adorable! So we meet at last. I feel as though I know him already. Now he will yield his secrets from beyond the grave."

"He's leaving the square." The dog did indeed trot offscreen to the left. "That settles that then."

"Arse. He might come back I suppose. You will note he was heading to the far corner, however, the direction of the Chinese Embassy."

The removal van passed leaving again.

"That rules them out, then."

Almost immediately afterwards Lord Codrington reappeared.

"I told you! He has missed his dolly. Oh, look out!" she cried covering her eyes.

As a car drove past slowing for the junction Codrington had suddenly dashed right into its path. The car stopped where the dog had stood, then drove on revealing him intact. Codrington chased after it on his tiny legs for a moment, yapping silently, then looked disgusted and trotted back towards the square.

Clara sighed. "I think we cannot rule out that Codrington was suicidal, like our cat. I suspect he was being blackmailed."

For a while there was nothing but the occasional pedestrian, the occasional window-shopper.

"So we definitely know he came back to the square," said Clara.

"He could still leave again. And there must be a blind spot below the window, this will prove nothing really."

"Balls. He would have to deliberately hug the wall."

"He may have known about the camera and had a secret rendezvous."

"I know how he thinks, Miles. A little adventure lasts him a long time, like you. Now he wants home and he met his death there or on the way."

She fast-forwarded with increasing speed and impatience. The occasional pedestrian flashed past but no dogs that Miles could see. Presently she slowed and rewound.

"The sinister housekeeper departing to do her so-called errands." She paused the picture. "Shopping? Then why, Miles, is she carrying an already heavy bag?"

"Returning something? It contains a box of some kind."

"Which doubtless contains the segmented corpse of a dog." She leaned forward to glower at the TV. "Is there a zoom on this thing? She looks furtive."

At length she let the recording play again. Presently, with the time-stamp showing a little after 3 o'clock, Lady Ashburne's car came back.

"Lady Petunia and Lurch returning. Codrington wasn't there when she got back. The deed had already been done."

"It *is* odd. Either he did go home, or he's still roaming the square, in which case they should presumably have seen him, or a neighbour took him in."

"I tell you we just saw the housekeeper dispose of his body. It *is* strange, in all seriousness. Perhaps he had annoyed one of the neighbours and they took the opportunity to get rid of him? Use your prosaic mind to think of something sensible, Miles. I suppose we should keep watching for a bit to be sure he doesn't reappear."

What did reappear almost immediately was Lady Ashburne's car.

"Where's he going now? The Fortescue monster was in the back." She rewound and watched it again. "The pair of them look very agitated. She is – Miles!" She rewound and then paused when the car was directly in front of the window. They could see right into the back seat. "Miles, Miles, look! On her lap!"

Miss Fortescue was clutching some sort of small tartan bundle.

"Miles," said Clara, "that is a dog blanket!"

"Oh, come on," laughed Miles.

Clara rewound and watched again.

"Miles," she said earnestly, "it *wriggled*."

The thing was Miles was unable to come up with any prosaic reason for Miss Fortescue to be holding a possibly-wriggling tartan bundle which would satisfy Clara. Equally, Clara had to admit that driving round with one on her lap wasn't against the law, and that they didn't have enough to confront her and pistol-whip her into talking. The Fortescue was a wily adversary, Miles pointed out, and this would only tip their hand.

Clara glowered. "You may be right. Doubtless she has been trained to resist pistol-whipping at a camp outside Peking. Then there is only one thing for it."

She told him what. When he objected, she appealed to the antique-shop owner, who was named Mr. Porteous and who plainly found them the greatest thing that had happened to him in recent years, if not his life, and he gravely agreed that it was obviously the only reasonable thing to do in the circumstances. Miles, who had just given him a large sum of money for an overpriced vase, looked at him in reproach.

Bright and early next morning a battered van pulled up in the middle of Godolphin Square. On its side it bore the legend 'PYGMALION STATUE REFURBISHERS LTD. Bringing Old Statues To Life.'

Clara and Miles emerged, heavily moustached and wigged and with white overalls over their detective suits, carrying stepladders and toolboxes. They took out little metal hammers such as doctors tap people on the knee with and started to tap the square's statue all over, listening intently.

"Dear oh dear, Bert," said Clara loudly. "Sounds like galloping bronze-rot to me. Looks like we got here just in time. All-day job I reckon."

"Yes," said Miles less enthusiastically.

They put up DANGER – MEN AT WORK signs all around the edge of the green and then started to polish the statue with cloths and Mr. Sheen.

"We are blending in perfectly," said Clara.

"Yes," said Miles, taking his detective flask out of his overalls and treating himself to a swig. He thought he knew now why detectives were traditionally alcoholics.

From time to time, half-concealed behind the statue, Clara took out a small pair of binoculars, plastic toy ones but which really magnified things, and trained them on Lady Ashburne's house. Inhabitants of the square started to emerge from other houses and depart about their affairs. They gave the statue-cleaners curious glances but didn't linger. Mr. Porteous the antique-shop owner came out to enjoy the spectacle. He lingered outside his door for quite a long time. Later on he sauntered across to admire their work more closely.

"There has been no movement yet," Clara told him sotto voce.

"If I can help in any way, do let me know."

"The next move if this fails is of course to bluff her using the footage, most likely by pretending to blackmail her. We will need your help for that, and you can make the initial menacing phone call if you like."

Mr. Porteous said he would enjoy that very much. He went back to his shop but continued to poke his head out from time to time.

Presently their polishing grew listless. They called a tea-break, took a thermos and some folding chairs from the van, and started to play cards and smoke roll-ups sitting on the green.

Halfway through the morning Clara's new friend – her name was Valerie – emerged from her house and came over to them.

"I thought it was you," she whispered excitedly.

"We are on stake-out," whispered Clara, also excitedly.

"If she can tell it's us so will they," hissed Miles, not excitedly.

"Perhaps you could come and spy from my place?" said Valerie.

So they went and lurked in her front room, Clara glued to the window with the binoculars. Valerie brought them tea and food.

"We shouldn't really put you in danger," Clara told her. "All hell could break loose soon."

"Is there going to be an arrest?"

"I doubt we'll take her alive. If shooting starts lie down on the floor and pull cushions over you."

Later she got bored and started to gossip with the woman and admire her house, delegating Miles to stand at the window watching. But she had taken up her post again when the target emerged.

"Target acquired! She's on the move!" Clara muttered into her wristwatch to impress Valerie. She pulled Miles down below the window as Miss Fortescue walked along the pavement in front of them. They thanked their excited hostess and dashed to the door.

Outside, watching their quarry walk towards the exit street, they dithered. Foot or van? Van, in case she took a bus or taxi, they could always ditch it later if they needed to tail her on foot. They scurried furtively across to it and dived in. It took three goes to start. They drove round the square. Miss Fortescue was talking to the antique shop owner.

"Good old Mr. P.! He has stalled her for us."

Glancing their way Mr. Porteous said something valedictory and ducked back into his shop. Miss Fortescue proceeded on her way.

"I bet she goes right. The embassy."

Miss Fortescue went left. So did they, as slowly as they could. They watched her wend her way through shoppers ahead of them with a brisk gait. Clara bounced on her seat with excitement.

"Tailing people is ace. Is this how you felt during our courtship, that period when you were stalking me?"

"I never did!" said Miles for the 80th time. "It was fate that kept throwing us together."

"Fate and high-powered lenses."

Following in the van was a mistake. They were going at a crawl and traffic kept beeping.

"Put your indicator lights on as though we're pulling in," said Clara. "I'll pretend to be looking for a shop."

"If she looks round she'll recognise the van even if she doesn't recognise us. This is terribly, terribly wrong."

Miss Fortescue walked into a side-street. They turned in after her but ditched the van in the first available parking space. As they got out they saw her going up some steps and inside a house.

VETERINARY SURGERY, it said on the door.

"A likely story," said Clara. She was running through a few karate moves; after buying and painting the van they had spent two hours last night trying to teach themselves this from an old book they had and bits of them still hurt, mostly their hands where they had hit bricks; Clara had declared that Miss so-called Fortescue was certain to be a mistress of martial arts. "Back me up, Miles, this could get rough."

They entered the vet's and barged through various rooms. They found Miss Fortescue in a small one stroking Codrington, who lay on a table with one leg in plaster.

The vet who was prodding him was of Chinese descent, which startled even Clara and which Miles thought was very unfair of the universe.

The vet looked very surprised at their entrance; Miss Fortescue said a very unladylike word.

"It seems we have arrived just in the nick of time," said Clara. She removed her wig and moustache dramatically and triumphantly. "Yes," she said smugly and unnecessarily, "it is I. I have foiled you, Miss Fortescue."

Miss Fortescue closed her eyes for a second and fetched a deep sigh. "Would you please give us a moment?" she said to the vet with remarkable self-control.

He nodded and left with frowning looks at Clara and Miles.

"Please don't go too far, Colonel," Clara said to him as he started to close the door. "The building is surrounded."

"It isn't," Miss Fortescue assured him wearily. "They are harmless idiots."

"Idiots who have been right about you all along," said Clara after the vet had gone.

"What the hell is going on?" asked Miles.

"Oh, allow me to explain," said Clara. "We have to go back to Manchuria in 1959. A girl who has decided to betray her country is given a course of hormone injections as part of a diabolical scheme to create the perfect – "

"Codrington ran out in front of Lady Ashburne's car as she returned," said Miss Fortescue with even greater self-control. "Anton couldn't stop in time but wasn't going very fast and thought he didn't hit him badly. Lady Ashburne appeared not to see him or hear the yelp. Anton drove on, deposited Lady Ashburne and told me what had happened. We ran to Codrington. His leg was broken and he was in great distress but otherwise unhurt. We decided not to tell Lady Ashburne. She would have been highly distraught, and Anton would have lost his job, and so probably would Marjory for allowing Codrington to escape. We brought him here, planning to allow him to reappear when he had recovered, as though he had just wandered off for a while. It would all have worked out perfectly well if you hadn't interfered."

"You see!" cried Clara. "I was right! I was right all along!"

"How the hell were you remotely right?" demanded Miles.

"There *was* a mystery! They *were* all in on it! There *was* a conspiracy! A nice one, but I still thwarted it!"

Miss Fortescue sighed again. "What do you intend to do now? If you inform Lady Ashburne she will be needlessly distressed and Anton will almost certainly be dismissed."

"We won't say anything, of course," said Miles.

"To hell with that!" cried Clara. "I solved the case! I found her bleeding dog! And I refuse to become part of a cover-up!"

"Clara!"

They all glowered at each other for a moment, apart from Codrington, who looked ruminative. Clara kicked a leg of the table sulkily. She *supposed* they were right. "But we cracked the case," she muttered.

"Look," said Miles brightly, "how about a compromise? How were you planning to return him?" he asked Miss Fortescue. "Just suddenly spot him wandering in the square one day? A bit suspicious, no? And even I can see he's had bits of fur shaved off him, look."

"What do you propose?" asked Miss Fortescue warily.

"Well, we *did* do what we were hired to do. Let us take the credit."

*

"Of course we have never stopped looking, day and night," said Clara pacing a room in Lady Ashburne's house some weeks later. "Following up every clue, leaning on the underworld. I spent several days in Limehouse in disguise. It was not one of my more brilliant cases, I confess. If it hadn't been for a tip from a snout named Long Stanley I might never have cracked it. As it was we only just got to the docks in the nick of time." In the background Miss Fortescue rolled her eyes. Further in the background the housekeeper stared at Clara, scared. "He was about to be shipped overseas, either to one of the dog-eating countries or to take part in a sinister eugenic breeding program by one of our rivals."

"Nonsense," said Lady Ashburne, ecstatically caressing an equally ecstatic Codrington.

"Look at that bald patch then, woman! That's where they injected him with drugs. He may display signs of withdrawal symptoms for the next few days, such as scratching himself and whining."

Lady Ashburne tutted briefly. "Oo poor little zing. I don't care how you found him, I am just eternally grateful you did. I am sorry to have doubted your capacities."

"The Newgate Calendar is filled with people who have underestimated me," said Clara airily.

Lady Ashburne walked to a desk, still carrying her dog. "You must of course be rewarded. I believe fifty pounds was the agreed-upon sum. You have certainly earned it. Indeed it seems a trifle modest now."

Miss Fortescue scowled.

"Fifty pounds will suffice," said Clara. "Not a penny more. It is the sport that motivates me."

Miles accepted the cheque. He knew it would end up framed on a wall anyway. Reckoning the cost of the van, the vase, the hush money to the housekeeper and sundry other expenses he thought they were only down about £1200 on the case.

"You will of course mention us to your friends, and perhaps provide a reference," said Clara.

"I should be delighted."

"If there is a moral to this adventure it eludes me," said Miles outside as they strolled across the square.

"It is that I am always right," said Clara, "and that you owe me dinner at Le Connard."

They popped in to see Mr. Porteous; by the time they emerged the loss was closer to £1500.

Chapter Eighteen

Clara and Miles were getting divorced. They were glaring at each other across a table with a teddy-bear and a toy plastic pterodactyl next to them as lawyers.

"My client wants the property in Monaco," Clara made the teddy-bear say. "Her husband may keep the semi-detached in Wrexham."

"Unacceptable," said the pterodactyl via Miles, flapping its wings. "Completely unacceptable."

"That's it, we're walking." The teddy-bear made a great show of gathering up its crayons and paper and trotting to the edge of the table.

Clara looked deep into Miles's eyes. "I was always so happy at the mansion in Monaco," she said huskily. "Being there reminds me of how it was in the beginning. Remember, how we christened every room in the house?"

"Wait," said Miles. "Give her the mansion in Monaco."

"Are you out of your mind?" said the pterodactyl, flapping.

"It's practically derelict anyway," Miles mumbled.

"Which is why we're also asking for 180 million pounds to fix it up," said the lawyer teddy quickly.

Miles looked at Clara in astonishment and hurt. She merely smiled and arched an eyebrow.

"Like hell!" squawked the pterodactyl.

Miles laughed shortly and bitterly. "Give it to her," he shrugged.

"Finally you're showing some class," said Clara approvingly. She placed a cigarette in her mouth and leaned forward expectantly.

"You don't have to light that," cautioned the pterodactyl.

Miles lit it anyway. Clara exhaled a cloud of smoke, crossed her legs and said, "Thank you."

Then she jiggled the teddy-bear and said, "My client would ask for 300 million pounds in child support."

"That seems a trifle excessive, when you don't have any children."

"And whose fault is that?" countered the teddy.

"I don't know," retorted the pterodactyl, "I don't have a sperm count for Bernard the milkman."

Clara leaned forward again, in the process revealing a lot of cleavage. "Can't we settle this alone?" she asked Miles throatily. "So cold, so formal. Can't it just be you and me without the lawyers?" She sat back and crossed her legs again – she was wearing a rather short skirt – then brushed cigarette ash off her top and then drummed her fingers on her breasts.

"No way am I leaving you alone in the same room as this whore," said the pterodactyl.

"Slander!" cried the teddy.

Clara started attempting to touch the tip of her nose with her tongue.

"Maybe she's right," mumbled Miles. "Maybe we can sort of thrash things out across the table."

"I approve," said the teddy unctuously. "Divorce should be an amicable resolution between man and wife. Don't forget his gold teeth." He trotted off and the pterodactyl followed muttering.

Clara smiled triumphantly and reached out to pull at Miles's tie. For once it looked as though there would be a satisfactory outcome to one of their sexual role-playing games. Unfortunately just then there was a distraction in the form of movement and noise outside the window.

A figure was running up the drive. It was Harriet, in tears, dragging her youngest son Ivor behind her like a rag doll.

"Oh God look at her," said Clara. "*They* are getting divorced. He has abandoned her for a whore, or conceivably a new mobile phone." Before Miles could suggest ignoring the interruption she had rushed to the front door and out.

Harriet had not been abandoned for a whore.

"I've had a row with Dolna," she sobbed hysterically in front of the doorstep. Dolna was her most recent au pair. "She's stormed off. I don't know where she is. She might have gone home. We're going to miss our flight. My sister's coming down but she can't get away until tomorrow. I wouldn't – I know we don't get along but the others all hate me."

Harriet's stock had recently plummeted to an all-time low in the village, as she had had the Smoking Theatre in the pub shut down. She had reported it months ago but there had been no sign of prosecution – Thomas the lawyer reckoned the authorities were loath to venture into the legal minefield, terrified of the consequences of losing in court. When this had become clear she had written an indignant column on their lack of zeal and they had felt compelled to act; Thomas was preparing to fight the case and was confident of victory in the long run, but for now the Living Pageant was no more. Harriet had been frosted more than ever in the shops, and young farming types had put various dead things through her letter-box. "It's the Global Warming Summit in Barbados," she continued, distraught. "I'm covering it too. Could you – could you – I wouldn't ask if I wasn't desperate."

Clara took a second to put all this together. "Are you asking us to look after your child?" she said in surprise.

"Children," said Harriet. "Struan comes home from school at four. Only until tomorrow. Believe me, you're the last person I would ask if I had a choice," she added earnestly.

"Well, since you put it like that … "

"That came out wrong! You – you're the only one who's been halfway nice to me."

Poor woman, thought Clara, quite shocked at the thought. "Of course we will look after them," she said. "We would be delighted."

"Um," said Miles, instinctively uneasy. "I'm not so sure that – "

"Shut up, Miles." She stooped to little Ivor. "Play with Aunty Clara?" she said brightly.

"Cara," said the three-year-old happily.

"Thank you, thank you, thank you!" Harriet turned and dashed off down the drive at high speed. As she reached the lane Richard's eco-car pulled up and she leaned into it.

"Well," said Clara.

"Are you sure this is a good idea?" said Miles.

"Whyever not?"

"We couldn't even look after – "

"Don't start that. The cat had a death-urge, Miles, children have much more survival instinct."

"Why can't she – "

"The poor woman is desperate."

"She would bloody have to be."

"We are perfectly capable of looking after a child!" Clara cried, stung.

Harriet came dashing back. She thrust an A4 paper into Clara's hand.

"This is their diet and regime."

"Oh."

"We don't give them sweets, of course, as well as meat and dairy produce. And we think Struan is allergic to sprouts."

"Very well."

Harriet looked anxious. "We don't smack or shout, of course."

Clara smiled. "I only smack Miles."

"We prefer to use reason."

"He is impervious to it, but a good right hook works wonders."

Harriet tried to smile.

She said, "You won't – you won't – "

"Won't what?" said Clara, slightly nettled.

"You will take care of him?"

"Yes, dear, don't worry, we'll have a lovely time."

Harriet didn't look happy. "It's just – you can be a bit – "

"I am perfectly capable of looking after your child!" Clara cried. More softly, even plaintively, she added, "*Honestly* I am."

"Where is he?" asked Harriet.

Clara and Miles looked around blankly. The child had wandered off into the depths of the house.

"Fetch it, Miles," said Clara with a wave of the hand.

Miles encountered Ivor just in time to stop him re-emerging into the hall eagerly dragging Clara's shotgun behind him.

"Look, don't worry, dear," said Clara. "He'll have a great time, he won't know you're gone. Go and enjoy your holiday, you deserve it."

"It's hardly a holiday!" cried Harriet, nettled in her turn.

"Well, setting up a fascist world government, then, enjoy that."

"It's easy to mock, but this could be the last chance to – "

"I'm not going to argue with you. Do you want me to look after your offspring or don't you?"

"Yes, yes, thank you, thank you." Harriet hugged Ivor goodbye, bursting into floods of tears once more. Then for a horrid moment it looked as though she was going to hug Clara too, but at the last second Clara, who apart from anything else wasn't willingly tactile with anyone she'd known for less than ten years or so, Miles occasionally excepted, suddenly spotted something that had to be flicked off the rose bush next to the door and turned aside, and the moment passed.

"Well, bye then," she said smiling brightly when it definitely had. "Send us a postcard so he doesn't forget you."

Harriet burst into more tears at this. "Miles help," murmured Clara turning. "I can't cope with hysteria. Slap her or something." At the end of the drive Richard was tooting his horn impatiently. Harriet lingered a moment gazing at her son piteously and then fled, still sobbing.

"The *cheek* of the woman!" exclaimed Clara indignantly after they had waved them off. "I can be a bit *what*, exactly?"

"Well – " Miles wasn't sure where to begin, or if it was a good idea to begin. "You did put a rock through her window," he pointed out.

"Oh, that," said Clara dismissively. "I owned up to that." And Harriet thought she had been lying to help Harriet when she owned up to that, although Miles didn't know that as only Harriet had seen her sly wink. One wove a tangled web when one started to tell the truth. "What does that have to do with anything? That has absolutely no bearing on my child-rearing capacities. Did you see the way she looked at the damn thing, as though she would never see it again?"

"Mothers tend to – "

"It's nothing to do with motherhood, it's because it was me. The last person she would ask. What is wrong with me? What does she think's going to happen to it? I'll show her! This will be the healthiest damn child in the world when I hand it back. It will be so happy and flourishing it will be a reproach to her. She will realise she is an unfit mother and beg me to adopt it."

"I would settle for alive," said Miles.

"*Miles!* We are entirely to be trusted with children! You have been browbeaten by the state into regarding them as some delicate, Sevres china – "

"Where is he, anyway?"

"*Here* he is! Do you like that? Do you want to be a bank-blagger when you grow up? Don't quail so, Miles, I'm fairly sure it isn't loaded."

Miles detached the shotgun from Ivor again. "*Please* let us call the child-pound. We could be arrested. We haven't been vetted, for one thing, and for the first time I start to see the point of it."

"For heaven's sake. How are you going to go on when we found a dynasty of our own? Relax. This will be fun."

Miles didn't relax, and was to grow less relaxed before the day ended, but he had to admit it *was* fun, at first. Children always took to Clara, for fairly obvious reasons. They played chase games in the garden for a bit and then came in and drew and painted pictures and made things out of plasticine and cardboard boxes.

"The great thing about having children is that it allows one to regress to childhood oneself," said Clara. "When was the last time *we* made things out of boxes?"

"A week last Tuesday."

"Exactly."

"Perhaps Ivor would like to play with the dressing-up clothes later."

Clara looked a bit put out. "They are ours, Miles."

The first phone call from Harriet came at this point, or at least the first they answered as it had rung while they were in the garden. Miles took it. He told her Ivor was fine. She told him they didn't give him caffeine. Miles said OK. She said they had glimpsed Dolna stamping across a field and perhaps it would be better if they found her and made her come back. Miles said OK. Harriet gave him the number of a doctor, the direct number of the nearest hospital and Ivor's blood type. Miles thanked her with an effusive gratitude that probably wasn't reassuring and wrote these down. She said she didn't allow militaristic toys and Miles said neither did he. She asked for Ivor to come to the phone. Miles relayed this and Clara replied that he was having too much fun. Harriet stifled a sob and hung up. Thirty seconds later she rang back and said they didn't give Ivor piggy-backs and that he wasn't good at negotiating stairs and steps yet. Miles thanked her for the warning.

He sympathized entirely. The whole house seemed like a death-trap now. Within minutes of Ivor entering it he had wrenched open half the cupboards and drawers in the house in a panic, glowering at the contents, and considered nailing them shut in case the child took it into its head to stab, poison or garrotte itself with something inside. There were so many ways for it to be injured. He hated for Ivor to be out of his sight for a second – Clara clearly could not be trusted with him – and stared at him morbidly and with a hawk-like intensity waiting for him to do something self-destructive. He gathered from friends with children that such paranoia was fairly common but that there was a natural process of compensation whereby after a few sleepless nights and exhausted days a certain healthy fatalism crept in as you found you lacked the energy to give a fuck. Miles had not reached this point yet.

"Don't let it use scissors! Are you insane?"

"We are being very careful, aren't we? Stop coddling it, Miles, it has to learn."

"And stop calling it it! That doesn't fill me with confidence."

"I keep forgetting in the excitement. Harriet would approve, anyway, she wouldn't want us to impose gender stereotypes. Miles, can't you take him to do some manly things? It may be the only chance he ever gets."

"Like what?"

"I don't know, play with hammers or butcher a deer or something. I told you we ought to have a rope climbing frame in the garden to play at pirates on, we could have done that. We'll take him climbing in the quarry later, the poor kid probably isn't allowed a good climb." Suddenly her eyes lit up and she laughed. "I tell you what we *will* do – go and fetch one of the guns, a toy one I mean."

Miles laughed. "No, Clara. He isn't allowed – "

"I will then. Watch him." She got up and went out.

Miles was even more nervous to be left in charge of the child on his own than when Clara was. "Let me help you with the scissors," he said taking them, finishing the cutting-out himself and then putting them away somewhere high. Then he followed anxiously as Ivor started to roam around exploring. "Why don't you have a nice sit-down for a moment?" he suggested.

Clara came back with an array of water-pistols, cowboy pistols, duelling pistols, detective guns and ray-guns and also their rubbish plastic swords. "What are *these*?" she said to Ivor cooingly. "What's *this*?" She pointed a long shiny cowboy pistol at him and pulled the trigger and made shooting noises. Ivor's eyes lit up and he dashed to take it.

"Stop it," sniggered Miles. "He isn't allowed."

"Why don't we have any caps for these? Let's drive into town and buy some, if they're not illegal now." Ducking behind the furniture she and Ivor and eventually Miles started to have a shoot-out. Then they went out into the garden for a swordfight.

"You like this game, don't you? You're going to grow up to be a big brave warrior. Swords – hooray! This is the *best* house, isn't it? This is the *fun* house. It is better than your house, isn't it?"

"Clara stop," sniggered Miles.

"I feel all broody Miles. I want seventeen of these. We can have our own militia."

She tried to teach Ivor how to fire their archery bows and arrows but had to admit he was too small and rubbish. They went back in and finished making a boat out of a cardboard box. They needed some more card. The Malteser box Clara grabbed turned out to rattle.

"Mmm! Look what I've got! Open wide … say thank you … "

"Dankyou."

"Bless."

"He isn't allowed sweets."

"Nonsense! It's only Maltesers. Have another, darling. This is the house of *fun*. Maltesers – hooray! Recycled vegetarian tofu – booo! However he isn't allowed to take sweets without permission," she added as Ivor grabbed for the rest. "Say please."

"Pease."

"Adorable. Take them all, dear. You *like* Aunty Clara's house, don't you?" She frowned. "We *have* got plenty left, haven't we?"

"Seventy boxes."

"Oh good. He shall have a box to himself before he leaves."

"You shouldn't undermine his mother's regime. Anyway as reactionaries I think we're against spoiling children."

"I will not sacrifice a child to ideology. I'm going to lavish him with all the things I never got enough of as a kid." She thought. "Jelly, for example. Would you like some jelly?"

"Delly."

"Cretin. I think it has a cleft palate."

As she dug left-over jelly out of the fridge Miles belatedly said, "Oh, wait, no! Not jelly. They're vegetarians, remember. Jelly is made out of animals, isn't it?"

She stared at him in outrage and open-mouthed disbelief, quite speechless. Finally she slapped him.

"It is jelly!" she cried. "God's own jelly! It comes from … It's jelly!"

"But – "

"*Lime* jelly!"

"Clara, you must surely know – anyway, it's lunchtime, let's give it something proper, you already stuffed it with chocolate, it won't eat."

"Oh … fair enough. Stop calling it it though."

Miles started to make Ivor beans on toast. While his back was turned Clara pulled her tongue at him and then crammed a spoonful of jelly into Ivor going, "Mmm." Miles caught them and gave her a look.

"Just one," she said, "it may be the only chance he gets."

"He won't get into vegetarian heaven now."

Harriet rang again. Miles said Ivor was fine and they were remembering to feed him. Harriet asked what.

"Beans."

"Fine, but he doesn't eat tomato sauce."

"Jesus," said Miles as he hung up.

"What a strange child," said Clara when he reported. She gasped. "I bet it's that *they* don't eat tomatoes. It's some fanatical greeny thing. Tomato-growing is considered bad, carbon dioxide intensive, they have to be flown in or grown in greenhouses, Jeremiah showed me some blacklist it's on."

"Oh, for fuck's sake," shouted Miles in disgust.

"Fucksake," said the child.

"*Miles!*"

"Whoops. Well shall I wash the beans? How about cheese? Oh, wait, they don't eat that, do they? And what was it she said one of them was allergic to?"

"I'd better find the instruction manual." She came back with the A4 paper. "Miles, have you *seen* this? 'Remember NO rough playing, co-operative games rather than competitive, NO physical chastisement or loud words.' The cheek of the woman!"

"I would imagine it was for Dolna rather than us. What can it eat?"

"Oh I can't make out, it's complex and your jelly revelation has shaken my whole world-view, just give it toast."

They gave Ivor toast and then Weetabix with jam. When he had had enough of this last he said, "No!" and threw the bowl on the floor.

"Oi!" cried Miles. "Bad!"

Ivor laughed and then got up and kicked Miles on the shin.

"Don't you dare kick my husband! That is my job."

Ivor laughed some more and toppled a chair and then tried to throw a plate on the floor.

"Stop it! This isn't going to work," said Miles as he rescued it. "How are we supposed to – "

"Reason with it, Miles." Clara stooped and took hold of the child and sweetly said, "Listen, darling. It is in your rational self-interest to be good, because if you aren't I will lock you in the cellar."

"Cellar," said the child happily.

"It is a moron," said Clara. "Shouldn't it be speaking more at this age anyway?"

"Probably they didn't want to impose conformist language paradigms on it."

"Pawadimes," said the child smiling.

"Christ! That was impressive."

"Well done!" said Clara. "Let's give it a huge vocabulary, really impress the shit out of her when she gets back."

"Shit," said the child.

"Whoops. No, not that one, child, that is a bad word. Say 'persiflage'."

"Persuh," said the child, and after a long pause, during which it looked as if it knew exactly how cute they found it, "flaaage."

"Well done!" She rubbed Ivor's arm. "Say 'passacaglia'."

"Passa," said the child, and felt it had done enough.

"Never mind. Say 'Medieval Warm Period'."

Miles laughed. The child looked cute but blank.

"No? Try saying, 'My parents are Tranzi leftards'."

"Stop it, Clara," laughed Miles.

"Cara," said the child.

"Bless."

She gave Ivor some more Maltesers and then put some plasticine on the floor for him to play with while they ate lunch.

"Let's go out somewhere, Miles. Let's take him to one of the farms, or to a pond to try out the boat. Also we ought to drive around a bit and look for poor Dolna, although I'm not giving the child back yet. Being Slavic she will probably drown herself if given time to brood. Slavs are worse than cats in that regard."

The phone rang again as they got up to go. They ignored it.

"Want to go in brum-brum?" Clara asked Ivor brightly as they led him to the garage. "Brum-brum – hooray! Ours will really impress the hell out of him after his parents' milk-float," she added as they got in. "Miles, really gun your engine, give him a treat."

Laughing, Miles did so, the engine noise reverberating around the garage.

"Brummm," said Clara bouncing the child up and down on her knee. "Brummm! Brum-brum – hooray!"

"Hooay!" cried Ivor, clapping and bouncing with glee. "Bwum-bwum."

"That is the sound of a free man's motor-car," she murmured cooingly in his ear, rubbing his arm. "Feel the power. You can have one of these when you grow up, if you don't let them take it from you."

"Stop it," laughed Miles.

"I'm trying to save this child. Drive fast."

Miles did, as the child seemed to enjoy it, although not as fast as Clara told him to. They quartered the area looking for Dolna and then gave up and drove to a pond. "She will probably be drowned there anyway," said Clara. She wasn't, so they floated their boat and waved to their duck which had once been a famous art exhibit. Ivor liked him and all the other ducks and she taught Ivor how to quack back at them.

Clara bagged the driver's seat when they got back in. "I am driving."

"But he can't sit on me. I haven't been vetted. Besides he might wet on me."

"Ivor is going to help me drive. Come here darling." The child sat in front of her and eagerly gripped the wheel. "That's right. Can you reach the pedals? Help me turn the key, then." She started up. "Brum! BRUMMM! *You* are doing that, Ivor. *Feel* the power," she whispered in his ear.

"Please stop this," laughed Miles.

Clara drove very fast indeed, round and round the lovely summer country lanes. Little Ivor laughed with joy. "Vrooom! Whoosh! Hooray! See how we startle the sheep with our mighty machine, Ivor! Look at the trees speed past," she cried. "Remember," she whispered in his ear. "*Remember*. You will remember this day of shining freedom with your godlike Aunty Clara and Uncle Miles, won't you, child? Look at those silly people walking. Little people. Carless peasants. See how they dwindle in our dust ... Miles your car isn't manly enough. We have to find something more powerful for Ivor to have a go on."

"What?" cried Miles, stung. "This is a classic!"

"It isn't loud enough. I want this child to grow up to be a racing driver, if not an RAF pilot. Oh, I know! We'll take him to sit in Jeremiah's car! That's wonderful."

"His is a bleeding Morris Traveller!"

"He had it souped-up, though, and we'll be the first customers for his Smugness Offset scheme."

To annoy Warmists the anarchic old art gallery owner had put a sign in front of his yard advertising the sale of Smugness Offsets: if you were forced to use a mercury light-bulb or heard someone boast about being 'carbon neutral', you could pay him £5 to gun his modified engine pointlessly for five minutes to make up for it.

"Miles put your head down," said Clara, alarmingly ducking hers as she drove in and tooted the horn. "Make him think the child is driving. Look, Ivor, you are driving by yourself. Christ, the wall."

"What's all this then?" said Jeremiah, emerging from the gallery rubbing his head as they tumbled out. "Who's this handsome young chap?"

"This is Ivor. We would like ten minutes of pointless but thrilling engine-gunning, please," said Clara. "And then a go round your gallery. Ivor is Harriet's son and we have kidnapped him for the day. We have one day to try and save him from his genetic and social destiny and give him a taste of life."

Jeremiah, being as wicked as Clara and much more experienced at it, quickly grasped the point of this and seized on it with glee. He cackled approvingly as Clara sat with Ivor in the driver's seat of his Morris and made the engine roar and said, "Hooray!" With the aid of a block of wood under Ivor's feet they made it so he could tread on the accelerator and gun the engine himself. The child laughed and gurgled and bounced.

"Now we must expose him to art," said Clara.

"Too right," said Jeremiah as they went inside. "They'll rear him on television, poor sod."

"You must give him a quick tour of the rooms where you have the Old Masters prints, not too Kenneth Clark, just a basic grounding in western culture. Oh oh, do you have any Tamara de Lempicka? That one where she's speeding along in her car, utterly beautiful and free? I want to give him a copy to remember me by, a shining goddess of speed and apostle of modernism."

"I would like a drink, please," said Miles.

"Miles! We are in charge of an infant! Don't be so irresponsible." She looked thoughtful. "Actually, perhaps Ivor might like a drink."

"Absolutely not!"

"I was thinking just, you know, fine wines, to taste rather than get smashed."

"He has to drive later."

"Fair point."

Jeremiah gave Ivor a whistle-stop tour of classic art. The child took to him at once and laughed at the funny man and repeated some quite difficult words. They taught him the names of some painters.

"Breughel – hooray!"

"Boygel."

"Say Tintoretto."

He stared politely but usually fairly blankly at the pictures they pointed at. The one he liked best was something one of Jeremiah's protégé local artists had done, a huge beautiful head of a madonna. He stood mesmerised and solemn in front of it for some time, then pointed and said, "Lady," and reached out to try to touch it.

"He thinks it is me," said Clara.

"It's the one James did of his nanny."

"Oh," said Clara. "Of course."

"Music," said Jeremiah presently. "Now he's got to be given some music."

They went into his study, where Mahler's Fourth was already on. Ivor didn't know what to make of this and cocked his head. He roamed around picking up and putting down Jeremiah's things with a solemn abstracted air. However he did an adorable little bouncing-stamping dance and clapped his hands to the sort of jingly-tinkly-pipey bit, and then cocked his head again and looked all far-away at the soprano.

"He likes it," said Clara. "Mahler hooray!"

Jeremiah sat him on his knee and read him some Eliot. He liked the sound of Jeremiah's voice, and reached up to try to take his glasses off. He laughed in delight at some favourite bits Jeremiah got full value out of, said, "Again!" and repeated them himself.

"Dare to eat a peach!" he squealed.

"I wonder if peaches are on his menu, or forbidden," said Clara.

The thing Ivor liked best, though, was Jeremiah's Masai spear standing in the corner. They let him handle it, wide-eyed, to Miles's moans. Jeremiah showed him some pictures of the Masai.

"They're the Masai, son. They're owned by no man and owe nothing to no-one. And if you lock them up, they die."

"I call that wet of them," said Clara. "See how good it is for impaling people on," she cooed of the spear, jabbing it at Miles. "You could skewer three enemies on it easily, couldn't you, Ivor?"

Miles made disapproving noises almost subvocally, rocking in his seat a bit and biting at a thumbnail.

Clara put down the spear and paced, consumed by her project. "Now you and Miles must play some rough boys' games with Ivor," she told Jeremiah. "Play him at football or running races, and make sure to beat him, to teach him about winning and losing. Tackle him viciously and gloat when you win. Give each other shiny trophies but not him. Teach him some woodcraft, and make rope swings over streams and things. Do you know how to trap? We should take him to see Ernie the Poacher. I wonder if some of the fox-hunting types could arrange an impromptu blooding?"

Jeremiah sniggered. "There are some toffs in the back woods shooting rooks or peasants or something," he suggested.

Clara's eyes widened. Miles gave him a betrayed look and said:

"No, more culture first. Oh – I've got it – Matthew! The cinema! We can show him – old classics – Laurel and Hardy – Powell and Pressburger – Launder and Gilliat – Tom and Jerry – "

Matthew was a film historian who had a little cinema in a shed in his back garden and an enviable collection of prints of films from healthier times. Miles was pleased with his own cunning in thinking of him: while Matthew was militantly, angrily, eloquently anti-progressive on most things and Clara respected him, he was also cordially anti-blood sports, in a disapprove rather than legislate kind of way, and altogether more ethical and sensible than many of the irresponsible bastards in the village, and might be a useful sobering influence at this point.

Clara narrowed her eyes at him, appearing to sense this.

"Hitchcock," pressed Miles. "No! The Dam Busters! The Dam Busters, Clara!" Her eyes lit up. He turned to include Jeremiah, who affected or passionately felt a hatred of Germans, artistic ones always excepted, due to being screwed by some in a business deal as well as considerations of 20th century history. "The Dam Busters! Sink the Bismarck! Where Eagles Dare! Surely no child can be allowed to grow up without – "

"I have a better idea," said Clara. "Do you have that sort of punchbag effigy German you made at the time you were really very cross with them indeed?" she asked Jeremiah excitedly.

He chuckled. "It's in the attic somewhere. But you took the Nazi hat, remember? You said you were going to sexually role-play The Sound of Music with Miles and trick him into goose-stepping past Harriet's house."

Miles stared at her. "What?"

Clara waved a hand. "Save it for our marriage counsellor."

"We agreed that kind of thing would be private!"

"Oh relax, I haven't told him about the elf ears or the St. Bernard. Anyway, my excellent idea – "

"Man on Wire!" cried Miles desperately. "Matthew has a print of Man on Wire! The human spirit, Clara! Art for art's sake! Bastard cops, Jeremiah! What could be better for a growing boy than seeing someone walking on a wire between the Twin Towers?"

"Miles, you are a genius!" Her eyes grew ecstatic as with some holy vision. His relief was short-lived. "We will *teach* him to tightrope-walk!"

Perhaps fortunately a croney of Jeremiah's entered just then, a hale, towering, ruddy-cheeked, white-haired old atavism named Joe, who could be found roaming the landscape in all weathers like a lost Titan. He sat and admired Ivor and when he heard the story chuckled and said that he had kept coming across Dolna moodily wandering the lanes and fields during his ramble. Miles instantly stood up, seeing a ray of hope.

"I *knew* she would still be wandering lost," said Clara. "Hungarians are used to galloping across big wide-open plains and so have no sense of direction in little twisty winding countries, I think. Miles go and find her."

"The last I saw her she was sitting by the Long Pond looking sad," said Joe.

"Hurry, Miles! That is very bad. She will be weighting herself with stones as we speak. She is probably an impoverished Countess and would rather die than live with the shame of being shouted at by a creature like Harriet. Hurry, man! Apart from anything else Hungarians can't swim, because they are landlocked."

Miles drove and then walked to the Long Pond, which was more of a lake in an abandoned quarry, and found Dolna sitting by it, looking sad. She was picking up stones, but skimming them moodily across the water rather than weighting her body with them. Still Miles approached cautiously, partly because he had noted that Clara's spur-of-the-moment national characterisations had an uncanny and at times quite annoying way of being proved true-ish: the lucky guess about the Italian home-wrecker when they were playing detectives being only a mild example of this. (Once before becoming rich Miles had worked with a Belgian he found it hard to get along with, and Clara had surprisingly said, "Talk to him about Elvis, all Belgians are mad about Elvis," and when one day he had seen the inside of the man's flat it had been covered with posters of Mr. E. Presley.) When Dolna looked round he smiled inanely and said, "Hello. I gather you've had a set-to with Harriet." Although they had seen her in the pub and had a friend in common neither he nor Clara had really talked to her.

She muttered something vicious-sounding in her mother tongue.

"It'll all blow over," said Miles. "She really regrets it already. She got my wife and me to look after Ivor but you can come and take over now."

She rose and gave him a look that was almost ridiculously like Clara playing an imperious and moody Slav, Young Mother Theresa perhaps, in one of their games.

"I will die first!" she cried.

"Right," said Miles.

"I will leave this place," she declared impressively, "never to return. Only I have forgotten my things," she added less impressively in an undertone. "Can you help me get my things?"

They drove to Harriet's house, which was locked up. Dolna didn't have her key. Miles reasoned that Harriet would have left one for her sister somewhere fairly prominent. He saw the edge of it gleaming under an ornament in the yard. He kicked this aside and then stood on the key so Dolna wouldn't see it. Dolna stamped around a bit and then heaved a rock through a window. A burglar alarm went off.

"You will help me break in," she said to Miles.

"I won't," said Miles.

Dolna looked irresolute. The window she had chosen was too small to crawl through and the alarm was spectacular.

"Then we will run away," she decided.

He drove her, silent and scowling, to Jeremiah's. Jeremiah's pert young dolly-bird assistant Jennifer emerged before Miles stopped the engine and said they had gone to the pub.

Miles's heart sank with foreboding. The Pub as an entity would only encourage Clara's schemes with regard to saving Ivor. They had a bad effect on each other. Recently she had handed some of the regular gang laminated passes constituting them members of the St. Mary's Star Chamber and said that she was their leader. They had no hoods or horses yet, still less a Giant Wicker Penis to burn malefactors in, and had lynched no-one to date, but it could only be a matter of time. It was quite clearly the germ of the Death Squad he had firmly forbidden her to organise and there were times when Miles started to fear he was a mute witness to history, an impotent onlooker to the rise of bad things like some helpless floozy in the Weimar Republic. He scraped the side of his car in his haste to get out of Jeremiah's yard.

He saw nothing he could immediately object to upon entering the Walpole's Head, or at least none of the things he had feared most: no infant tightrope-walking, for example, or juggling with clubs or flaming brands. It was Friday afternoon and there were a few of the regulars already in. Clara and Ivor were sitting at the bar sharing a Britvic and a packet of crisps; that the child had a dart clutched in his chubby fist was really nothing to fret about, Miles told himself.

"Well, here's Dolna now," he said jovially and hopefully as they entered, "come to take care of Ivor."

"Monster," spat Dolna, stalking past her erstwhile charge to sit further along the bar. "Spawn of a monster!" She crooked her hands in the air. "I will strangle her childs! I will drown her childs!"

"On the other hand, perhaps not," admitted Miles.

"She is so passionate," breathed Clara ecstatically. "Dolna is my new role model."

Miles got drinks in. Dolna lit a long foreign cigarette and indifferently heard commiserations and congratulations from some of the regulars on having quit Harriet.

"I am not to feed them goulash!" she suddenly cried. "I am not to feed them meats! I am not to tell them frightening stories. I am not to tell them stories of brave, and dragons, and fighting against invader. I know good stories of this, from when I am child, but she hear and say no, I am not to tell them such. If they are bad, I am to *reason* with her darlings, not slap. I must not shout, I must talk *niiiice, like thiiis*." She bared her teeth and spoke in a voice that was not nice but would have made Miles fear a shiv in his side had he heard it in a dark alley. Clara drank her in wide-eyed and worshipping. "I am to *smiiile* when I reason, even when little monster kick me, and to make friendly happy face, not anger. If I make smile face when bad, they think is good!" She started to enumerate on fingers. "I am not to let them play in woods without, I think, I stand behind and keep on lead, like dogs. Not to climb trees. I am not to smoke!" She held up her cigarette indignantly. "I am not to smoke within one hundred metres of house. She measure! I am behind wall, in field, ten feets behind wall, because the smoke, it will fly to their darling throats, like arrow! It's magic child-seeking smoke."

June the normally jolly barmaid at this point said, apologetically and blushing with shame, that actually they weren't allowed to smoke in here at the moment.

Dolna tossed her head back and laughed richly as if June had just made a good joke and nodded as if her point was proved. "Yes!" she cried, pointing with two fingers and the cig clamped between them. "Like that! She shout, she say that I have said I do not smoke. I do not smoke! Thirty a day! That is not to smoke." Scowling, she extracted another from her packet in readiness and resumed ticking off on fingers. "I am not to say man. Is this from England? Tell me. When I am learn English, you have … it is genders? He she it. No! If I am hear milkman is come or postman, I say, 'Oh *loook* little darling, is milkman, let's go wave.' She say, No! I must not say that. I must say, 'Oh! Milkman *or woman* is come.' " There were laughs and groans. "Yes! Or I may say Milkperson or postal employee." She ticked. "I cannot have car. Cooking – don't start me. Is not childs, is," she resorted to Hungarian, " … is Michelin, you know? No! No! Is monks! They are monks. And pardon me my English is better than this but I am angry. I am to ring home three times a week, no more. And – wait! – she try to ration my electric!"

"See!" said Clara to Miles. "My story!"

"Yes! She measure! She say, I am not to go above this much in one week! She dare say this to me! She thinks I am her slave!" She struck herself. "Me, the granddaughter of a countess! A slave to that ... " There was no word in English but the Hungarian sounded awful.

"*See*," said Clara to Miles. "What are you staring at me like that for? There is magic and romance in the world and I am always right about everything."

"So, this morning, she start again, before they go, to tell me what I must not do. She speaks to me as if I am dog. I will do this, won't I, I won't do that, will I? I explode! I tell her, when she has gone, we have smoking school! Cigars! I will give them cigars! We will put all the lights on, and dance! I will teach childs properly! When darling monster kick me, I will kick back! I will throw them into trees, I say! I will make them climb trees, by whip with belt, and then chop down trees with axe! I say I will chop her childs with axe! I say I will strangle and drown her childs, and then set fire to house, and then listen to stereo and leave stereo on standby! Then I lose patience and walk off."

"This is the second greatest woman who has ever lived," murmured Clara, rapt.

"Now I have no job, no reference," Dolna concluded indifferently, with a shrug.

"Don't worry, darling, I'm sure someone here will give you a job," said Clara eagerly. "Won't you?" She looked around appealingly. A man who actually was looking for a nanny avoided her gaze and slunk off to the toilets. "Anyway, I will forge you a reference! Miles give me a pen. June fetch some paper."

"Aha!" Dolna nodded approval and then stalked off to the payphone.

"Where's the cow gone anyway?" asked Jeremiah.

"They have flown to Barbados for the Global Warming conference," said Clara not quite neutrally. Jeremiah laughed bitterly.

"They won't let us feed it fucking tomatoes," said Miles.

"Fuckin!" said the forgotten child.

"*Miles!*"

"Whoops, sorry."

"That is a bad word, little one. By the way she rang the gallery looking for us just after you left. Jeremiah hung up on her. It rang again immediately so naturally we ran away to here. Oops, no, we don't eat darts, do we? Oh, dear, this is the cat all over again. Miles get that would you."

"I really think we should angle towards giving him back to Dolna now," said Miles as he and Ivor struggled for possession of the dart.

"I thought you liked the child, Miles," said Clara, who was nevertheless writing on a sheet of paper, 'Dolna is the greatest childminder who has ever lived, a lioness toward her adopted cubs, and has raised my seven backward children into sturdy upstanding pillars of the community or as near to it as their heritage permits, with a song in her heart, a smile on her lips, and a pithy Hungarian epithet for every occasion. She is a delightful cross between Mary Poppins and Elizabeth Bathory. Signed, Harriet Gilquist, girl reporter.' She scrumpled it and started to do a more plausible but more laudatory one. "He is now the legitimate target of an implacable Slavic blood-feud. She is my new heroine but I would not let her within ten feet of him, twenty if she had a throwing dagger."

"Tell me you knew about the countess bit already."

"Not at all, Miles. Hungarians are invariably countesses, in my experience, when they aren't pianists or violinists."

"Your experience being 1930s paperbacks and your imagination."

"Which lie to me less than the Big Bland Tranzi Book of the World they obviously had at your grotty comprehensive, where everyone is depicted in a national costume of jeans and T-shirt and listed as, 'Distinguishing National Characteristics: None.'"

Impulsively she added to the new reference, 'She is an accomplished pianist, violinist, bareback horse-rider and swordswoman, a mistress of intrigue and espionage, and can reduce a man to jelly with a single proud tilt of her lovely head.' She supposed this might make Dolna sound like a bit of a husband-risk, so she thought a moment and continued, 'However she is utterly frigid due to watching the Habsburgs execute her one true love.' Then she got annoyed at herself and started again properly once more.

Arthur the landlord emerged with a steaming plate of sausages and mash which he placed on the bar. "Here you go! And look what I found!" He produced a miniature plastic Union Jack flag, which he waved and placed in the infant's grasping fist.

"Union Jack – hooray!" cried Clara, cuddling Ivor as he laughed and waved it. "Remember," she whispered in his ear, "*remember*."

"I got hold of Sam," said Arthur, "but his quad bike's in the shop."

"Pity. Oh Arthur – maybe you could take him angling?"

"Ah, he's too young. There's a shoot in the woods, he might like that."

"Mmm – what's *this*?" Clara cut off a small piece of sausage and held it for Ivor to gobble. "*Flesh!* Flesh – hooray! Well, skin and earlobes, hooray."

"No," cried Miles belatedly. "No, no, no!" In a panic he lunged towards the child's mouth with his fingers, trying to pull the sausage out, and was bitten.

"See, he has the taste for it now," said Clara.

"Clara, stop!" He yanked the plate away, too late to stop her popping another cross-section of sausage into Ivor's maw. "I can't believe you! They are vegetarians – we should respect – "

"Oh it's only a little taste. It might be the only chance he gets, they will be banned by the time he grows up."

"I suppose if you were babysitting a muslim child you'd slip it a toasted bacon and tomato – no, don't bother to answer that."

"Miles, don't be so – " She suddenly looked towards the door in horror. "Christ, *Harriet!*"

Miles whirled in terror. The door was empty. When he looked back the rest of the sausage was disappearing into Ivor's eager mouth.

"Stop it! Don't encourage her, you bastards!" he said to the sniggering Arthur and Jeremiah, shoving the food further out of reach. "Vegetarianism is an entirely respectable – "

"It's just a taste, Miles. I want to give him one shining day of freedom to remember on some deep level throughout the rest of his miserable, grey, joyless, push-button, powder-and-water, regimented, metricated, sterilized life. Somewhere in his heart he will retain a memory of what freedom feels and tastes like and know that what has been done to him is wrong. Years from now when he is a member of the new oligarchy he will suddenly remember us and kill his parents and become the last man, like the Savage in Brave New World. Get him a pork pie and a beer, Arthur, and a map of the Empire, and a picture of Churchill."

"No, no, no! I forbid this!"

"I have Churchill's speeches on record," said Arthur excitedly.

"*Yes*," said Clara, eyes lighting up.

"Clara – this is what your own children will be for. They have a perfect right to – "

"It's only what They do to our kids, isn't it?" said Arthur aggrievedly. "I mean isn't it? Isn't it?" He looked around for support. "Warmist propaganda all the time, and, and be ashamed of your country, and look at things from Napoleon's point of view, if they even teach – "

"And sex," put in June, who was quite partial to it. "Teaching them about sex as soon as they can walk."

"You're right," said Clara. "We must Not, we must anti-, teach him about sex. We must deter him from sex. Penises – booo! No, but we must teach him romance, and chivalry, and protecting women. Look, one of you attack me, and Ivor will defend me, and I will reward him with a kiss." She pointed at Miles pouting. "Uncle Miles! Uncle Miles is bullying me, Ivor! Defend me! Kick him! Kick!" She demonstrated.

"Stop it!" said Miles. The child laughed and swung its hoof speculatively.

"Don't even think about it, child, I will knock shite out of you," he muttered rubbing his shin and scowling.

"*Shite*," laughed the child delightedly.

"*Miles!*" said everyone.

"Oh, sorry."

Dolna had returned to her stool further down the bar. "Ah – no – sorry – this is not permitted," she called, pointing with a cigarette towards the patriotic flag the child still clutched. "No-no. Ah-ah. This is trouble. Once, the husband has let the childs watch the football, they shout for England. The she-monster makes the face of sorrow at them, and say, 'But the other side are try their hardest, and they come from poor country. Perhaps one of you shout for them, and swap at half time?' Of course the England lose anyway, and she clap and smile, and tut at husband for texting friends that he is gutted, and say is bad role model." She leaned back and exhaled smoke. "I am well out of madhouse. I should demolish it stone by stone."

"So this is what lesbian crushes are like," sighed Clara dreamily. "I almost feel sorry for my own hapless victims. God I love to watch Eastern Europeans smoke," she murmured to Miles. "They know no guilt or fear. Dolna lives intensely in every moment. Hungarians have to because they know Tartars or Austrians could come sweeping across the plains at any time and kill them. Do you think *I* might have Slav blood, Miles? I have decided to start pretending I do anyway."

As abashed and ashamed as June had been, Arthur was trying to explain to Dolna that she wasn't actually allowed to smoke in there at the moment. She threw her head back and laughed voluptuously again.

"Stop, you will kill me," she said. "If you had a wig and lemon face, perfect. It is a shame, I will miss the English humour when I leave."

"You are not leaving!" cried Clara. "You aren't ever leaving! You can come and stay with us. We have a double bed. My husband can sleep on a couch. I want you to! I insist on it! You can look after our children!"

"You have children?"

"Not yet," Clara admitted or, Miles actually feared for a moment, remembered. "They are still somewhere in the eternally-optimistic twinkle in my husband's eye. But we will do. We will keep you on retainer. Someone here will want you! I have written you a reference, look!"

They passed it along to her.

"This is good," said Dolna. "But you exaggerate. My horse-riding is little more than excellent, my piano-playing average."

"*See.*"

The au pair frowned. "And what is this, 'adept at blowing up troop-trains'?"

"I feel sure you would be, if the need arose."

"And she does not have eleven children, only two."

"That's right," said Arthur, "she does have two, doesn't she? Where's the other one now, then?"

Clara and Miles, both of whom had completely forgotten the existence of the second child, looked at each other blankly and then in growing alarm. Miles whirled to look at the clock. Harriet had said the other one came back from school at four, and it was half past now.

"Miles, how could you?" cried Clara hitting him.

"Oh, fuck," cried Miles, appalled.

"Fuck," cried the first child.

"*Miles!*" Miles hastened into his jacket. "Hurry, man! The kid will be on his own!"

"Let him die," said Dolna contemptuously.

Clara sighed. "Go, Miles, hurry, and leave me to lez off with Dolna if I possibly can."

Miles drove fast. He saw the forgotten child impaled on a shard of glass having attempted to climb in through Dolna's broken window, successfully in the house but busily pouring itself a cup of poison, knotting a noose out of loneliness, flattened on the road, hitching a lift with a nice man with rabbits. In the event it – Struan? – was sitting on Harriet's gate kicking its feet, apparently talking to itself but not looking too sad. The burglar alarm had stopped.

This child was five or six or so and could talk properly, was even precocious at it, Miles thought.

"Gosh, is that an E-type?" he cried, jumping off the gate as Miles drove in.

"It sure the hell is," said Miles proudly, getting out and laying a hand on it. He loved it almost as much as he did Clara and it was far less trouble. "Do you like E-types?"

Struan nodded wide-eyed. "*I* think it's brilliant. Of course Clarkson says old cars are rubbish compared to new ones, but in engineering *not* in terms of soul."

Miles laughed. "You like Jeremy Clarkson?" he said in surprise.

"Oh yes. Doug brings the DVDs into school." For all Harriet's principles Struan went to a rather posh school with some very rich pupils. "Really even my dad's is probably better than this, technologically," he said as if trying to convince himself, still staring at Miles's E-type with wistful eyes.

"I bloody doubt it," said Miles, irked, "and anyway his is much gayer."

"Yes, that's what Doug and everyone says," said Struan sadly.

"Anyway, get in, and we'll go for a ride."

"OK." Brightening, Struan grabbed his satchel and piled in eagerly. He was a nice-looking, well-spoken, tow-headed boy.

"Wait!" Miles cried as he got back behind the wheel, struck by a thought, "what the hell are you doing? You don't know who the hell I am! You can't just get into a car with a stranger! Is that what you do?" He was outraged at Struan's behaviour and appalled at himself for having encouraged it.

"Oh. Oh yes." Struan looked guilty, slightly alarmed and more than a little confused. "Shall I get out again then?"

"No, it's all right. I'm Miles from down the road. We're looking after you until your aunty comes. I'm taking you to Dolna."

"OK then."

Miles wasn't satisfied with this complacency somehow. "But I could be lying, you know," he pointed out.

Struan was now very confused and alarmed. "Are you?" he asked in a small voice.

"No. But you have no proof. You should have asked me to prove it to you."

Struan nodded thoughtfully. "Go on then. Prove it."

Miles was nonplussed. "Um. I don't think I can. Oh! When your mum came round to see us she was wearing like a headband thing and a ... dress of some kind. And Dolna's wearing jeans and something and boots."

"*That* doesn't prove anything. You could have just seen them. Anyway they were both in dressing-gowns when I went to school so I don't know."

Miles thought unsuccessfully a bit more. "Look, you'll just have to take my word for it," he said starting the engine.

"OK."

"But another time be more careful. Especially while I'm looking after you."

Clara was right, he was a fusspot. Now he had probably given the kid a neurosis and a needless fear of strangers that would afflict him his whole life and prevent him ever attaining intimacy and blah blah blah. God everything was so complicated. Things were better in the days when you had eighteen children and let them fend for themselves and didn't fuss too much and some lived and some died and that was it.

Struan didn't bounce as much as Ivor but was wide-eyed with excitement during the ride. Miles drove fast and revved the engine and went by a long and roundabout route to give him a treat and impress him.

"Gosh it's like a fighter cockpit."

Miles grinned.

"Of course all cars are wrong really you know," the child added frowning.

"Put your seatbelt on," Miles remembered suddenly as they pulled into the pub car park. Struan looked very confused again but obediently put it on and then took it off again.

In the pub Struan went running eagerly over to Dolna, still perched on her stool at the far end of the bar. She didn't quite regard him with the murderous hatred with which she had the younger child, but swivelled away from him and tilted her head in the air scornfully. He ignored this and started to tell her about his day, including the ride in the E-type with the strange, the very strange man.

The pub had filled up more and there was something of a hubbub now. Also one of Churchill's war speeches was coming over the sound system; Arthur and some of the regulars were reciting along at points. Clara was sitting on a banquette against the far wall with Ivor on her knee.

"Churchill – hooray!" she cried, smiling and bouncing him and rubbing his arm. "Remember," she whispered in his ear, "*remember*." She turned the child to face the room and pointed. "*Look* at them all," she murmured. "Look at their shining jolly English faces. Noble. Free. Pissed. You will not see their like again." She picked up a huge fatty wodge of beef from a plate at her side and dangled it in front of Ivor's mouth. He made approving gargling noises and pulled at it with his teeth like a lion cub.

"Oi!" cried Miles. "Stop that."

Clara pouted and looked reproachful. "The honest roast beef of old England, Miles. Just one slice."

"The older one is here now and he talks like a trooper, which means he can grass us up."

"Hmm. It may also mean he is more susceptible to reason and easier to deprogram." Churchill reached his peroration. Everyone clapped and cheered. "Churchill – hooray!" Clara bounced Ivor and rubbed his arm.

Something had been bothering Miles for a while now. Agitatedly he said, "Look, I'm going to have to ask you – could you – stop rubbing his arm."

Clara stared at him. "What? Why?"

"It – you rub my arm. You rub my arm to cajole me when you want to make me do things."

Clara laughed. "You're jealous!"

"No, but – it's a form of positive reinforcement, and, I think it's wrong. You're – using your feminine wiles to – "

Clara's mouth hung open. She looked disbelieving and then very, very angry. "Are you implying – " She was speechless with outrage. The problem with physically attacking Miles for things like, say, telling her where jelly came from was that she had nowhere left to go, short of stabbing, when she was genuinely cross with him. She shook her head. "Miles, you're disgusting. Truly, truly disgusting. You're sick. I feel sorry for you. You're one of Them! I don't know you any more. We have never been closer to divorce than we are now."

"I just – "

"You're just implying that I am sexually titillating the child for purposes of – "

"No! I wasn't saying *that*, exactly. I just think that the smiles and the physical contact constitute positive reinforcement amounting to a form of brainwashing."

"It's how you rear a child, Miles!"

"It isn't your child to rear!"

"You meant something more than that."

"I swear I didn't, but since you raised it – don't you think you should be careful of – our primary sexual images come to us at an early age – "

"You are disgusting and Freud is disgusting." She smiled at Ivor fondly and mussed his hair. "Although naturally the poor kid is now in love with me and will spend the rest of his life hopelessly trying to find a woman who reminds him of me. That simply can't be helped and is far better than his being morbidly drawn to women like Harriet."

Miles laughed and pointed at a nearby speaker, from which growling poetic defiance was now again emerging. "I'm just worried he'll associate femininity with *this* and spend the rest of his life looking for a woman who reminds him of Churchill."

"He could do worse. Honestly, you – neurotics like you are poisoning the most basic, innocent, healthy relationships, and, and raising a generation deprived of physical affection, with results than can clearly be seen all around – "

"No, I just – I would prefer – the Hoorays are naughty enough but – "

"You are talking out of your – "

While they were distracted Ivor seized his chance to make an experiment he had resolved on for some time but which he knew from the other women in his life was discouraged. Nonchalantly, staring about the room as though he had many other interests and this was something that was happening casually and almost of its own accord, he insinuated his hand inside Clara's top and onto her right breast. He held the nonchalance and indeed the tit for several seconds, and then looked at her and laughed in delight.

Clara looked shocked and astonished and gave Ivor the coldly quelling raised eyebrow that many similar experiments of Miles's had met with. Then she smiled brilliantly and warmly and rubbed his arm.

"*Churchill*," she murmured cooingly.

Miles threw his hands in the air and then grabbed his head. While he was dancing round like that Clara pulled her tongue at him, inserted more roast beef into Ivor, and slapped his hand when he made a play for the other breast. Arthur came up with a Britvic for Clara and a half of beer in a plastic beaker that clearly wasn't. Miles stormed out.

He kept walking through the village and a short way down a lane leading off from it. His object was Matthew the fairly sober and sensible film critic, who was also vegetarian and might at least discourage the unethical flesh-feeding part of things if he could rope him in to give moral support. But there was no answer at his door. Miles walked further down the lane and along the field at the back of the house but was unable to hear any sounds from the cinema in the garden. He gave up and returned to the pub.

Now Jeremiah was declaiming a poem from a book he'd brought to a politely attentive Struan. Ivor was nowhere to be seen. Clara and Dolna were sitting on stools at the bar laughing together. When she saw Miles Clara swivelled away and tilted her head in the air as Dolna had done to Struan, then thought better of it and leapt off her stool and came dashing over to him.

"Miles, Miles." She drew him aside and lowered her voice. "I don't have time to be cross with you. You have to help me. I've done something stupid."

His heart sank. "Oh God, what? Where's Ivor?"

She waved a hand. "Having a go in someone's Aston Martin, as far as I know. Not that. I've invited everyone back to ours for a barbecue."

Clara frequently invited people back to their place on a sudden impulse of warmth and magnanimity and always immediately regretted it. They might see her Death Lists and Walpole fiction, unless she tidied them away quickly, which she was loath to as they made a home a home. They might want to use her bathroom, and there were only so many times you could pretend not to hear when people asked where it was. She supposed she had a slight neurosis about this, but the thought of other people using her bathroom distressed her somewhat, especially men. She had once told Miles that she wouldn't have married him if it hadn't been for his commendable, almost ninja-like bathroom stealth skills. They might find the full-blown costume and make-up room that had replaced the dressing-up box, and laugh, sneer or raise eyebrows at it. Worst of all they might not go away again when she wanted them to. Clara had been erratically but extensively and at times expensively educated, including two terms at a finishing school, but she had realised to her dismay that she had never been taught how to politely but firmly make people go away when she had done with them. Simply saying, "I want you all to go away now," was often considered rude, and when you faked the symptoms of a sudden illness people had an irritating tendency to want to call a doctor, she had found, rather than taking the hint. And they might develop lesbian crushes on her and try to come again another day when she wasn't in the mood, or in the case of the men start inviting Miles to come and do dreary man things with them instead of playing nicely with her.

So Clara's invitations to her house were invariably swiftly rescinded. She would always suddenly remember some domestic disaster or safety hazard that precluded it: the discovery of toxic wallpaper such as had killed Napoleon had been the last one. Since moving to their House of Love and Sanity and Go Away World very nearly no-one else at all had seen the inside of it, almost the sole exception being a workman who had been allowed into the kitchen, with Clara watching him morbidly from the doorway, but not permitted to use the bathroom, whose existence she had flatly denied.

"Clara! You know you don't – "

"I know, I know, it was a sudden impulse of love at all their shining pissed English faces, and now I hate them all and want them to go home already."

"Never mind that, we don't have enough meat."

"Oh, the Singing Butcher is bringing some."

"Also we don't have a barbecue."

"Oh, someone else is bringing one, or possibly building one. Maybe it won't be too bad if we can keep them all in the garden. Miles what exactly are death-watch beetles? Are they in fact deadly? I thought an infestation might – "

"No, Clara. You have to – "

"Please, Miles, think of some excuse to put them all off, except for Dolna, and possibly Jeremiah, if he will agree to wee in the bushes."

"No, I won't."

"At the very least you have to make sure they all go to the toilet before they come, especially the labouring types. Just sort of jauntily – 'Come on, lads, don't want to be wearing out my flush, ballcocks cost money, don't you know.' Or merrily propose a weeing contest before you leave."

"No!"

She bit a nail. "Oh God, what have I done?"

"Clara, you really have to learn to – "

"Miles Miles Miles, never mind that." She pushed him back and out into the porch. "Much more important, you have to go and get Shy James."

"James? Why?"

"For Dolna, you idiot! She's hellbent on leaving tomorrow. Don't you see? It's his last chance."

Shy James – to differentiate him from a boisterous James, and because it fitted him – was a diffident, stammering, but charming young man, a painter who had a cottage further down the road from Clara and Miles and Harriet and Richard. When drunk he would become eloquent and would pour out his hopeless, despairing, poetic love for Dolna and confess his seemingly unconquerable terror in her presence; Clara and Miles had been present at the last such unburdening and had also watched discreetly along with the rest of the pub the night Dolna had been at a table with another au pair and James had limped over (he was handsome but had various Byronic defects), stammered out a couple of sentences, drunk half his pint looming silently over them, and then gone away again. The whole village loved him and wished him success in his pursuit and the latest hesitant developments in the saga were an almost nightly source of gossip. Now it seemed he had blown his chance.

"Everyone's been ringing him but he doesn't answer. He doesn't when he's working. Go and tell him to come quick."

"It's not our business."

"Miles! You are an enemy of romance! He will be devastated forever if she goes. And Dolna must not be lost to the village. She is my new best friend and a dedicated foe of Communism and will be able to teach our children swordplay, the piano, and how to kill vampires."

"That is Rumania."

"Vampirism knows no borders. Go."

Grumbling, Miles got back in his car once more. Just after setting off he passed a speeding Aston Martin which beeped and flashed its lights and contained a local couple and a gleeful Ivor.

Shy James wasn't in. His brother who was staying with him answered the door and said James was sketching by the Old Mill. Miles explained his mission, which his brother grasped the urgency of, and left. He couldn't find James by the Mill. He drove fruitlessly by another couple of likely sketching spots and then went back to the Walpole.

It was emptier now and he found it devoid of Clara, Dolna and the two children. The owners of the Aston informed him they'd gone home; also that Harriet had just rung the pub looking for them and Arthur had hung up on her.

At home meanwhile the two women were curled up on the couch together in the former TV room, throwing Maltesers towards the two children. Struan stood at attention before Clara like the child in the painting 'When Did You Last See Your Father?' and Ivor was sprawled on the floor. When they had first come back Clara had neglected the two youngsters in her excitement at having a new friend and eagerness to make sure Dolna liked her in return, impulsively lavishing her with presents of jewellery, clothes, books, ornaments, board games and anything else she happened to look at, until at one point the bemused au pair stood loaded with a tottering pile of booty like a *Crackerjack* contestant. Clara now regretted much of her largesse and was tactfully taking some of it back. At length she had relaxed and had returned to the children's education while Dolna looked on in amusement.

"Dates of the Second World War?" Clara asked Struan again.

"1939 to 1945," he said promptly.

"Who won?"

"We did!"

"Thanks to?"

"Winston Churchill."

"Well done! You have won a sweet." She tossed a Malteser towards his mouth, to develop his reflexes, and he successfully caught it. "You," she said to Ivor, "say 'Churchill.' "

"Chu-chu."

"Close enough. Churchill hooray! A sweet for Ivor, please, Dolna."

Dolna flicked a Malteser off the couch; it bounced off Ivor's forehead and he chased after it.

"Of course we shouldn't have sweets *really*," said Struan frowning.

"Why not?" said Clara.

"Harriet doesn't allow it."

"Do you always do what people tell you?"

"Yes."

"Well you oughtn't. Now when I was young I was very good, but then they changed what being good meant, so now I go out of my way to be bad. Do you understand?"

"Not really," said Struan unhappily.

"Well, have another sweet and think about it." Dolna bounced one off his head too. "There's nothing wrong with sweets as long as your mother doesn't find out," Clara told him. "You're not going to tell her, are you?" Struan frowned and considered it. "That's a very important part of growing up, never to tell on people."

"Once I told on a boy at school and he punched me."

"Good. You deserved it. There's nothing worse than a snitch. That's going to be very important in the next few years, not telling on people. Even your parents. If ever a nice teacher at school asks if you are happy at home, you must smile and reply, 'Perfectly, thank you,' even if you aren't or you are cross with your mummy or something. Do you understand? Otherwise you may be taken away and sent to live with someone even worse." She tried to think of an example of someone worse but found she couldn't, really. "A murderer, perhaps. And you must especially never ever tell your parents or teachers anything that goes on at your friends' houses, anything their parents say or do. Do you promise? Promise me."

"I promise."

"Good boy. Have a sweet."

"Ask me more questions or give me more things to learn. Shall I recite the speech again?"

"No, wait for Uncle Miles. What is the best country?"

"Britain!"

"How big was our empire?"

"A quarter of the globe."

"Was that a bad thing?"

"Not necessarily," he recited, looking upwards to remember. "We spread civilisation as the Romans did and it was a ... bold and splendid enterprise, and we were better at it than the Europeans and kinder than them too. However empires per ... per say? are not always good things, and we should fight tooth and claw to be free of the one in Brussels."

"Correct, have a sweet. Who is the greatest man ever?"

"Winston Churchill!"

"Chu-chu," said Ivor eagerly.

She threw them both sweets. "Who is the second?"

"William Shakespeare."

"Shay-spar."

"Third?"

"George Orwell."

"What do you know about him?"

"He was a patriot, a fogey, and a lover of freedom." He looked upwards. "His masterpiece Nineteen Eighty-Four was *not* about the Tories or President Bush and he is currently turning in his grave."

"Sweet. Who is fourth?"

"You didn't tell us."

"Oh." She thought for a moment and then grinned. "I know! The fourth greatest man ever is Steve McIntyre. Say it."

"Steve McIntyre."

"Kin-tyyyr."

"He is a Canadian but that is almost as good as being British. Most of the best countries were born out of Britain. Oh, sorry Dolna. Hungary is a great country too. You can teach them some Hungarian songs and stories later, the bloodier the better."

"I teach them good," muttered Dolna.

"Uncle Jeremiah is bringing some books explaining why Steve McIntyre is a hero. There was a thing called the hockey-stick that made a lot of people panic and he showed that it was nonsense. He thought for himself, and worked very hard and very patiently to find out the truth. That is always an effort, but responsible adults must make it. You must always think for yourself, and remember that most of the people who tell you to think for yourself just want you to think like them. Trust no-one, not even me." Struan looked confused and unhappy. She threw him another sweet on general principles. "Do you know about the Medieval Warm Period?" He shook his head. "Well you should. It was so warm then that Greenland, which is now largely ice, was a green fruitful country. Before that again, in Roman times, it was possible to grow wine grapes near Scotland. Never forget that. After the Medieval Warm Period there was something called the Little Ice Age and it got very cold. The River Thames would often freeze over in winter, sometimes for months at a time, and people would ice-skate on it and there would be Frost Fairs with stalls and roast oxen. In 1536 Henry VIII travelled along it on a sleigh, and in 1814 an elephant walked right across the river. What year?"

"1814."

"Have a sweet. Since then it has mostly been getting warmer again, but just lately it is cooling down and we may even be heading for another Little Ice Age. Uncle Jeremiah will tell you more, about sun-spots and things. Anyway Steve McIntyre is a god, and you may tell your parents *that*."

"Ah-ah," said Dolna shaking a finger. "No-no. This is forbidden. I am not allowed to say God, even as a curse. And I am forbidden to wear my silver crucifix chain. She make the lemon face when she see it and make me take it off. 'I cannot allow that in front of childrens,' " she squeaked in a prissy voice. " 'Or other people, it offend and oppress.' "

"Oh my God," sighed Clara.

"Ah-ah. No-no."

"You'd suit a crucifix chain too. I'm not sure that one I've put on you *does* suit you," she added thoughtfully. "Perhaps you'd better give it back and I'll find you something nicer. No, no, keep it, it works. Are we friends, Dolna?"

"Sisters, Clara." Both having put rocks through Harriet's windows, as they had discovered in the pub, had made for an instant bond.

"Ask me more questions or tell me more things," said Struan impatiently.

"It appears I must tell you about Jesus. He was born in a manger on

Christmas Day, and died at Easter for your sins. Your sins are things like when you are naughty to Dolna, or being impolite. You must always pray to God, for strength and grace, and give praise to him for the beauties of creation. God likes beauty best of all and wants you to help make everything beautiful. Everything good comes from God, including sweets." She tossed him another. "And fast cars. And Christmas presents. If you don't say your prayers you won't get any Christmas presents. Jesus is the one behind that, Father Christmas is merely the front man."

"Harriet says there is no Father Christmas."

"Well, technically she is right." Leaning forward, she looked around furtively and lowered her voice almost to a whisper. "*It is Churchill.*"

Miles entered at this point, having been in time to hear most of the last bit.

"Oh hello Miles. We are playing nicely with the children as you can see. Absolutely nothing is happening that you could possibly object to."

"Uncle Miles! Listen." Struan stepped forward smartly and recited, "The Second World War was from 1939 to 1945. We won. For two years Britain stood alone against the greatest military machine the world had ever known, thanks to the British spirit and Winston Churchill, while the Europeans surrendered, although Hungarians are good fighters too. Today the freedoms our forefathers defended and their forefathers invented are being steadily eroded and we are in effect ruled by a new German socialist reich."

"Miles stop sagging like that. Go and put the kettle on like a good provider and leave the women to rear the young. Oh what can you object to, man? The truth he will never otherwise hear? Have a sweet, Struan. Now I will tell you about Nelson. He defeated the forces of Napoleon, another strutting continental tyrant, and won us the freedom of the seas. Nelson's greatness and love of danger were apparent from an early age. If someone told him not to do something, he would infallibly do that thing – be it jump in a river, run and bang his head against a wall, fight a Polar bear, anything. You should endeavour to follow his example."

"Clara!"

"Get used to it, Miles, this is how our children will be raised, those who learn to forage well enough to survive this long. Dolna will help me. Miles don't you see – go and play in the garden a minute, children, do something strenuous and risky."

"May I watch the television instead?"

"It doesn't do much." She gestured towards the screenless box Ivor was currently sticking his head into. "Go on, go outside. Take your brother. There is treasure buried in the garden somewhere, a chest of gold left by a pirate, see if you can find it. You will find tools in the shed."

"A pirate! So far inland?"

"Well, a banker, then. Go on, bugger off for now, we'll play school again later. Wait. What year could an elephant walk across the Thames?"

"Um ... "

"1814, nitwit! No sweet. You disappoint me. Go away."

"Won't we need the lawn for the barbecue?" Miles asked as the children left.

She waved a hand. "Oh, that's all taken care of, Simon came to the rescue, we're all going to his place instead. He has some young nephews or something staying and all kinds of exciting things for them to play with. There are all his cars too, and Beastman's war memorabilia. Everyone's rallying round. It takes a village to raise a child, you know."

"Dearest, you really have to stop with the – "

"No, Miles, I won't. Don't you see? This is how we'll get them." She rose and paced, eyes alight with an excitement he had come to fear. She rubbed his arm cajolingly. "This is how we'll get them all – via their children. We'll turn them all against them. They brainwash ours at school? Fine, we'll get theirs earlier, via their nannies. I have thought it all out. We will stake Dolna to open an au pair agency and training school. We will recruit only Reliable nannies, exclusively from the former Eastern Bloc, those with first-hand knowledge and hatred of Communism, who don't want to see it come back."

"I have no first-hand knowledge of Communism," said Dolna in amusement. "I remember only one parade. But it was bad; my mother has told me. I think you should not call what happens here Communism, Clara. Real Communism was something scarier. These people are not Communists. They are just," she exhaled smoke thoughtfully as she searched for the *mot juste*, and waved a hand on which one of Clara's bracelets now reposed, "pigs. But it is a good plan. Better plan, you build me a school to teach the darling monster kiddies. I teach them good, oh yes," she said darkly, scowling.

"I am not sure that bracelet works with your skin-tone after all," said Clara biting her lip in a sudden access of Indian-giving.

Dolna laughed. "You are a silly. Your husband gave you this. Truly I do not want your jewellery, Clara. You are good and kind to try to make me happy. If it were not for you I would say this place should be burned to the ground. But trinkets cannot make me happy." She took them off and, fetching a tremendous sigh, subsided onto the couch horizontally, exactly the way Clara had when playing the gloomy Swedish detective.

Clara nudged Miles discreetly and then, her back to Dolna, made an 'Ooh!' face and then a 'Where the hell is James, you incompetent' face, and Miles responded with 'I don't know, I tried, he was supposed to be at the Mill but he wasn't, I left a message with his brother' hands and eyebrows. While Clara was still glaring and trying to decipher these there was the sound of a motorcycle in the drive. James owned a motorbike. Dolna's eyes seemed to widen and then become studiously uninterested.

Clara studied her nails. "I wonder who that can be? I expect it is just a courier. I had better go and see." She dashed off as the doorbell rang.

"Why it is James, Dolna," she said returning. "You know, the painter fellow. He wants to talk to you. I have put him in the lounge."

Dolna had straightened herself, straightened her hair, slipped Clara's bracelet back on and was scowling moodily.

"That man! What does he want of me?"

"I think he wants to talk."

"Talk? Talk? Now he can talk!" She laughed bitterly and strode out.

Clara danced around and clutched Miles. "Ooh, ooh, ooh, how romantic."

"It's far too late. And she looked annoyed. What makes you even think she fancies him? All he's done in effect is stalk her. She looked positively irritated in the pub that night."

"Miles, you dolt! Do you think people heave tragic sighs like that because of leaving Harriet? Didn't I look as irritated at you almost constantly throughout our courtship?" That did ring a bell. Clara tiptoed to the doorway and put her head round to listen. "Hmm," she said. "It might not be going so well."

"What? Why?"

"She appears to be imitating his stammer."

"Hmm. Affectionately?"

"No, Miles. With such hideous cruelty that any man with an ounce of spirit would go away and hang himself."

"Hmm."

Now there were clearly audible shouts and then the sound of something smashing. Clara abruptly withdrew her head. There were limping bootsteps in the hall, the front door slammed, the motorbike roared off.

Clara rushed across into the lounge, followed gingerly by Miles.

"What happened?" she asked.

Dolna was stalking up and down looking thunderous.

"That man!" she cried, and with another, wordless cry swept a vase off a table to shatter on the floor. There were already the remnants of another lying against a wall. "How dare he!"

"What did he do?"

"He ask me to marry him!"

"Gosh." Clara widened her eyes. "Quick worker. But isn't that ... a good thing?"

"Good? Good? He never talked to me! He never talked to me before! I do not know this man! Now, now I am outcast, without home or job, have nowhere to go, he thinks he can take advantage!" She tossed her head proudly. "Ha!"

"It isn't *like* that!" Clara protested. "He has loved you from afar."

"Afar? Afar? Yes afar! Three months, Clara! Three months I have been here lonely, and sad, and bored, and crushed. He say nothing! Just hang back and stare at me like puppy dog."

"He adores you!"

" 'G-g-g-good m-morning, D-Dolna, l-l-lovely d-d-day.' Over and over! Now, suddenly, 'I l-l-love you D-d-d-Dolna, w-will you m-m-marry me?' I do not believe it!"

"He must have thought there was … an understanding between you."

"Understanding? From psychic?"

"From looks, and … "

"Looks! Looks! Is this all he can do, look?"

"He is awfully shy. His stammer doesn't help. But he walked you home from the village in the rain. He waited around for an hour to offer you his umbrella."

"Walk, yes. Talk, no."

"He painted you, Dolna!"

"Painted me! Yes! He painted me! Three weeks! Three weeks I sit there, night after night, expect talk, expect something, I think this might be interesting man. All he do is look! Look! Constantly looking at me! It makes me mad!"

"Well … he needed to see where your eyes and things were, I expect. It is an awfully good painting. He is obsessed with you."

"Look and paint, look and paint! Do you know what he say to me? Tea! Would I like some tea! Every five minutes, am I ready for more tea? Is this English courtship, tea?"

"Oh yes," said Clara. "It was Miles's constantly plying me with tea that–"

"I am supposed to fall at his feet? Throw myself into his arms? This is an arrogant, arrogant man. Well, I too am proud!"

"It isn't arrogance, it's shyness! I think it's sweet! He adores you! He didn't dare! He adores you so much he didn't dare approach you."

Dolna brooded upon this.

"Then he is a weakling," she pronounced contemptuously, turning her back and folding her arms.

"Well," Clara ventured after a moment, "weak and pliant men make very satisfactory husbands." Miles cleared his throat in annoyance. "Not that I would know, being married to such a domineering brute. Really, if it had been left to Miles, we would never – "

"It is English? This is English courtship, to constantly run away?"

"Some of them, yes! It was because Miles kept fleeing from me that I knew he cared. Of course, in retrospect, it may well have been genuine fear, but it is too late now."

"Then I say to hell with English men!" yelled Dolna, and stalked off through the French windows and across the lawn. Ivor tottered up and flung a trowel of earth at her and she clipped him round the head with enough force to knock him on his arse.

Clara meanwhile kicked Miles on the shin.

"What was that for?"

"She's right, you're useless. I had to practically throw myself at you and you have held me cheap ever since."

"That isn't true! I may have waited for certain signs of encouragement, and all I had to go on was pouting."

She kicked him again. "You liked the pouting."

"I liked the occasional smiling better."

"Well, I very much liked making you suffer." She sighed and sank down on the couch. "Poor James. He's blown it. Dolna is used to being carried off on horseback by the light of a burning village."

Miles laughed and sat too. "I think I might object to your cliches less if they at least pertained to the century we live in."

"She is used to texted innuendo and macho avatars, then, if you want to drain the colour out of everything."

Dolna came back. "I am sorry about the vase," she mumbled.

"It's all right, it was only one Miles's mother gave us. She has a kiln. She makes them compulsively and sends them to break my spirit. There are half a dozen others around equally dull and misshapen if you'd care to smash them too." She watched as Dolna fumbled out a cigarette then said: "James isn't a wimp, you know, far from it."

Dolna made a gesture of holding her hands over her ears. "Do not speak more of him. I ask this of you."

"Really, though. He was in the army, I think. And, and he has a motorbike."

Dolna snorted. "That does not impress me. When you have been carried away from a burning house, *then* you know what a real man is."

Miles stared at her. Even Clara had the grace to look rather scared.

"On ... horseback?" she asked timidly.

Dolna frowned. "Down a ladder. Although this fireman, his family had a stable. But he, too, could not speak. Men!"

"Yes," said Clara, slapping Miles round the head. "But James is terribly eloquent when drunk, he goes into lyrical raptures about you, like, like an Irishman with a prize-winning pig. Or an award-winning IT firm, if you prefer," she added for the benefit of Miles, rolling her eyes.

Dolna tilted her head disdainfully. "I despise drunks! I despise weakness of all kinds."

She stormed out again and could be heard shouting at the kids.

Clara looked thoughtful. "I wonder if I am merely psychic or if I am actually able to re-write space-time with my words? Let's try this: 'Hungarians always travel with gold and jewels concealed about their person and give them to those who have befriended them.' "

Dolna came back in, said, "I forgot to give you this back," tossed Clara's gold bracelet at her and went out again.

Clara blinked. "A childhood dream comes true. Let us begin, then. Me be invulnerable now. This house be a palace now. All world leaders be here now. My husband's penis turn into a pretty bunch of flowers now. No? Let's try: 'Imitating stammers is a sign of affection among Magyars and often heralds a betrothal.' "

"You should leave it alone. I think she genuinely doesn't want to know."

"Nonsense, Miles! She is passionately in love with him. She better bloody had be, I liked that other vase. They were made for each other. Deep down she wants to hold, cherish and protect her little bashful puppy."

Miles laughed. "Clara, you heard her, she despises weakness. James has a limp, a stammer, a scar, and a couple of fingers missing off his left hand. All she wants is to put him to sleep."

"It is the icy wind off the River Vltava that makes them Nietzscheans."

"River Vltava is Czechoslovakia."

"Your constant fact-checking is having a chilling effect on my right to free expression."

Dolna came back, paced around scowling a bit, went out again, came back again.

Clara said, "Proposing marriage may have been a bit precipitate, but why don't you give him a chance to woo you? Stay here with us for the rest of the summer – you can index my Walpole biography or something if you want to pay your way, or simply help me browbeat Miles – and just try going out with James a few times."

"So he can stare at me and say, 'D-d-d-d-Dolna'? So he can give me tea? He will take me to a tea shop and pour tea into me until I burst. Enough, Clara, or we quarrel. He has had his chance. This is not a man, it is a lost puppy. Me, I drown lost puppies!"

"*See*," said Miles.

"You have it all wrong," said Clara. "James is dangerous, a wild animal. It is only you who make him tame. Oh, you should have been there when – a man came into the pub one night and started talking lewdly about you, Dolna – remember, Miles? – and James, he went berserk. This strange, terrible light came into his eyes and he just kept beating and beating the man until he was nearly a pulp. It took six of us to pull him off."

Dolna tossed her head. "Who was lewd man? Him I like."

"Oh, nobody knew who he was, he was just – a passing tinker, a real low character, he was all unshaven, and wore this grubby neckerchief, you wouldn't have liked him at all. After James had beaten him up the rogue spat out a tooth and wiped the blood off his mouth with the back of his hand and looked all menacing and growled, 'I'll be even for this, my fine young gentleman, watch your back.' James just sneered and drawled, 'I'm scared, real scared,' because he was so angry he forgot to stammer, and he told the man where his cottage was and said he'd leave the front door open that night. The man slunk out like a whipped cur and cried, 'I'll be avenged on you, aye, and on your bonny Dolna too!' as he fled into the night. James went all pale and silent, terribly silent, and finished his drink and left." She saw it all clearly. Miles meanwhile saw his own hand held despairingly over his face. "No-one knows for sure what happened afterwards, but the tinker has never been seen from that night on, and the next day there was a strange mound of earth six feet long in the field behind James's cottage. No-one has ever dared ask him about it."

Dolna made a lip-noise. "Most like, he gave this man tea, and stared at him with his big sad eyes, and painted him, and painted, and stared, and offered tea, until he ran away screaming."

Clara sighed. "Miles you try."

"He has no real genetic weakness," said Miles brightly. "Most of his defects are the result of injuries. You wouldn't have to drown many of your children."

Clara backhanded him negligently. "He does come of a good family, though, a worthy match for the daughter of a countess."

"Great-granddaughter," said Dolna.

"Not that it should matter; *I* have married a semi-prole and have no real complaints apart from the hamster in the tumble-dryer. And, not that *that* should matter, but I think James is fairly rich and only slumming in his little cottage."

"Rich! Rich! What is that to me? I cannot be bought! Does he think he can buy me?" She destroyed another of Clara's ornaments to illustrate her absence of materialism. "I spit on his money!"

Clara sighed, dreamily. "Have you ever had any lesbian urges? If you stay here Miles need not necessarily be with us."

"The fine English milord thinks, perhaps, to take pity on the poor little nanny? I am, yes, descended of noble. I may not, now, have family silver or home, but I have a proud heart and red blood, not a tea-drinking coward's!"

She stormed out again, scattering the panicked children into the bushes before her.

"Spirited filly," said Miles.

"Oh, dear."

He touched her on the knee and quite quietly said, "Do we need to have the conversation about lying again?"

"What?" Clara looked indignant. "I'm fairly sure Jeremiah *did* tell me James is well off."

"He didn't beat a tinker to death!" Miles said, not quietly at all.

"Poetic licence, Miles! Adjusting the raw data! He unquestionably *would* beat a tinker to death if – "

"Apart from anything else she may not go for men who leave tinkers in shallow graves. All right, I retract that."

"It's such a shame. She's crazy about him."

"If she was he's blown it. Give it up."

"No, Miles. We'll get them to this do at Simon's and I will work the Clara magic on them. At university as I was renowned as a matchmaker. I gave no less than half a dozen of my friends a nudge in the right direction."

"With what result?"

She looked thoughtful. "At least one couple are still on speaking terms. Another are still on restraining order terms, so there is some kind of spark left. One of the girls is still speaking to me, when her Mother Superior permits it. That is irrelevant. The point is I brought them together. After that I make no guarantees. I cannot live people's lives for them, and nor should I be required to. I have quite enough difficulty managing yours."

"Clara – "

"Imagine if *we* had never got together, Miles. I wonder which would be worse, regretting it or never realising we ought to regret it?"

"Awww!" Miles suddenly felt close to tears. "How sweet! You soppy thing. I would have thought about you every day for the rest of my life if we'd only met once."

They gazed at each other dopily until Clara spoiled it by making an idiot face and going, "Ha, tricked you, I really don't like you at all." The doorbell went.

It was Jeremiah, with an armful of books and print-offs on Global Warming facts, World War Two battles, and art, plus news of James: he had turned up at the gallery, already drunk enough to be coherent, wanting the portrait of Dolna back so he could burn it.

"How wonderful!" Clara cried. "See, Miles? You must go and find him and straighten him out. Bring him to Simon's, fairly sober but not *too* sober."

"Clara – "

"Hurry, man! He is probably driving his motorbike off the bridge as we speak. Artists are worse than Slavs in that regard."

"If you will promise to stop experimenting on the kids," Miles said trying to snatch the print-offs from Jeremiah.

"Of course, Miles, go. Jeremiah listen. I will be giving them a quick grounding in both Burkean conservatism and John Stuart Mill. I think that is fairly balanced but I will let you tell them a bit about the Austrian School if you can avoid poor-mouthing the nation state too much. And none of your seditious anti-monarchist shit. Anyway, Dunkirk and El Alamein first, I think. Go, Miles!"

Miles went. He first checked the pubs but James wasn't in them. Neither James or his brother were at the cottage, but there was a bonfire in the back garden which proved to be composed of sketches of Dolna. Miles rescued some of these, out of sentimentality and feeling for art, and burned his fingers in the process, causing him to become cross with the world. James was not at the Mill or the Long Pond and didn't seem to have driven his bike off the bridge. Miles drove around aimlessly looking for him for a bit, feeling only irritation now at all the lovely summer lanes of England he was seeing for the umpteenth time that day. Then he saw James's bike outside the Dog and Duck, but he had just missed him there. He found him in the almost empty Walpole, alone at a table in a back corner, drinking determinedly and already not too sober at all.

"All my own fault," he said as Miles joined him. "Had every opportunity."

"Well, yeah. Still – "

"To hell with her. Mocked my stammer. Hurts. Should have painted her as a Magdalene, not the madonna. My Dolna madonna, my doll and my dolour."

Miles counted glasses and winced. James was already entering his telegraphic free-association stage, which succeeded the lyrically eloquent one and narrowly preceded the carried-home-on-a-table one.

"I think it was intended affectionately," Miles told him. "In Hungary, I think, stammering is considered lucky, and – "

"Oh? Like holy idiots. Unholy idiot. Rub 'em for luck. Love a lame duck. Never got a fuck. Never won fair lady. Never won fair lady. Quite right too. My fair unfair long dark lady of the soul. *Jast you wait, 'Enry 'Iggins, jast you wait*," he suddenly sang loudly, grabbing at Miles, eyes manic.

Miles got coffee and food but James managed little of either.

"I'm supposed to take you to Simon's. Dolna will be there. Clara's going to try to … bring you together."

"Super," said James. "Far too late. Ship has sailed. Ships that pass in the night. Exchanging glances. Bird has flown. Norwegian wood. The Christmas tree in Trafalgar Square. Tall, proud, pitiless, destroying men's lives and laughing."

"Have some more coffee," said Miles.

"Super," said James.

Miles helped him outside.

"You wouldn't throw up in my car, would you?"

"Capable of anything," said James. "Anything except action."

"Put your head out the window."

"Super."

This was stupid, Miles realised as they reached Simon's. The Super stage came right before the table one. James would win no haughty Hungarian hearts in this condition.

"Look, stay here and have a nap for a while," he said as he turned off the engine. "I'll send some more coffee and food later."

James, still lolling out of the window, nodded his head and heaved a long sigh.

Everyone was gathered in the front paddock of the farm some distance behind the splendid stately mansion. (As always, Clara had counted its windows greedily upon arriving, and thought how many playrooms she and Miles could have when they were rich enough to have a house like Simon's. They could have one done up as a throne room; one as the Vatican; one as a Transylvanian castle; one as a law court; one as a laboratory; one as a Fleet Street girl reporter's office; one as the control room of a nuclear submarine lying in wait off the coast of Belgium; one as the bridge of a spaceship; one as a Wild West saloon; one as an Egyptian temple; one as an igloo; one as 10 Downing Street for when they were playing Walpole; one as the office of a jaded 1950s Walsall solicitor for when they were playing the Walsall solicitor game; and so on. Clara didn't know how she and Miles were to become rich enough to afford a house like Simon's when they were so rubbish at working, but she lived in hope. It had been her experience that people sometimes just gave you money because they liked you, as her grandmother had done, or to annoy other people, as Miles's unexpectedly wealthy great-uncle had so unexpectedly but so nicely done, and she supposed this might happen again. She would like to keep their House of Love and Madness too, and one day have an island, just a small, easily defensible one, and also a castle in high mountains somewhere; so she was always especially nice to any rich people she met, just in case they were looking for someone to give money to. Like a well-brought-up child she didn't begrudge wealth in anyone else, especially when they had done nothing useful to earn it, but rather imagined being them. Simon had thrown splendidly decadent parties in this house before he had settled down and become a respectable squire. He had kept baboons behind one of those windows, and floating inflatable furniture filled with helium behind another, and a shrine to a rare toad with supposedly hallucinogenic secretions behind a third, and a thoroughbred racehorse in its own bedroom behind a fourth, on which he had ridden about the corridors, sometimes in a suit of armour, holding his first cocktail of the day. But that was nothing, she thought, compared to the real glamour those windows had let light in on back when the house was first built and for generations after, the balls, the ballgowns, the elegance and wit, the gaiety and grace, the uniforms, the whiskers, the weskits, the jewels, the furniture, the music, the civilisation, sanity, duty, beauty and fun; the managers and improvers, she thought, if they weren't kept safely foaming in asylums, kept safely managing and improving farms and animals instead of countries and people; she a society beauty, a salon hostess, a male-impersonating major, a saucy young maid seducing young master Miles, a pert young heiress riding to hounds, a flighty gypsy girl rescuing the fox; and all taking place in an eternal unselfconscious morning before the world became a bore. Oh those windows! Just look at them all. Imagine being able to look out of them all. She lost count, as always, but sighed happily.)

Everyone was gathered in the paddock of the manor farm in the evening summer sun. Even before Simon the reformed rock star Lord of the Manor had come to Clara's rescue in the matter of the party from the Walpole (after she had suddenly remembered Miles had burned down their kitchen and bathroom) he had already invited some neighbouring landowners round, and his cousin and her young children were staying with him. Trestle tables had been set up and food ferried out from the kitchens of the farm-office building. A clay-pigeon shoot was in progress. Miles got there in time to see Clara crouching behind Ivor, a shooting cap over his head, holding a double-barrelled shotgun in front of him.

"Help me, Ivor. Put your finger on the trigger. That's right. Now say 'Pull.' "

"Puuuull."

The clay target flew. Belatedly but very loudly the gun went off. There were cheers and claps. Ivor screamed and commenced to sob his heart out in terror.

"This child has French blood, Miles, take it from me," said Clara handing him over. She turned back to have a shot herself.

"Uncle Miles! Uncle Miles!" Struan came dancing up to him waving a half-eaten hot-dog. "Aunty Clara said I nearly hit mine."

"Tremendous."

"Uncle Miles, listen. According to Roger Scruton, Edmund Burke holds that revolutionaries' self-righteous contempt for ancestors is also a disinheriting of the unborn. The social contract includes the dead and the not-yet-born as well as the living." He took a breath and looked upwards. "Moreover our most necessary beliefs may be both unjustified and unjustifiable rationally, and attempts to justify them will merely lead to their loss. Aunty Clara said you'd give me some money now."

Miles gave him some money. "Perhaps we could find you some vegetarian food."

Struan shook his head. "I have seen where the pigs are killed and I didn't cry at all. Also Simon has a Ferrari. And I have had a go on a horse. Me and Jack have been on the rope swing in the big barn, it's brilliant. Aunty Clara says I am very manly. I'm going to play with Jack again now. Bye." He went haring off.

Clara gazed after him fondly and patted and fed sweets to the now only slightly crying Ivor and then languished against Miles. "Miles fill me full of babies," she sighed.

"Here?"

"We will clear that table. Wait, though, you unutterable dolt, where is James? Tell me he is here."

"Comatose in my car."

"Miles! I said only slightly oiled."

"I was too late, he'd already gone all David Helfgott when I found him."

"Damn it." She nodded over at where a sullen Dolna, nursing a flute of wine, was surrounded by three young country gents. "Dolna's making a splash with the squirearchy but she just keeps looking at them as though she'd ordered steak and been brought a badger."

"Evening, Miles." Simon came over grinning affably, gun crooked over his arm, dressed in tweeds and shooting cap. "Sorry to hear about your kitchen mishap, tends to happen when I try to cook too." Miles nodded intelligently. "Got a drink? Beastman!" he called.

Simon's quite scary-looking long-haired bearded butler was already approaching bearing a tray. Although Simon pronounced it 'Beastm'n', to rhyme with Eastman, as though it was a surname, his name had originally, or anyway more recently, been Beast-Man, for a number of very good reasons, and he was Simon's former chief roadie. Their relationship was and had long been more reminiscent of a mutually-devoted military officer and his batman than mere master and servant. Simon had been known to say that Beastman had saved his life once in Arkansas; Beastman that Simon had carried him half a mile on his back from a fracas in the Philippines when he should have left him behind to die; both were tight-lipped about the details. Beastman played the butler solemnly and conscientiously, according to his lights, processing with awful dignity, his hairy head tilted back from the stiff starched collar of a traditional butling uniform.

"Madam's Britvic," his gravelly voice intoned gravely as he proffered the tray to Clara, "and," he held it out meticulously between white-gloved fingers, "a straw."

"Thank you, Beastman," said Clara sipping. "Chilled to a nicety. How are the Mrs. Beastmans?" He shared his quarters with two Finnish teenagers he had picked up on their last tour.

"I regret to say they have mutually discovered sapphism, Ma'am, and have left me."

"Oh dear," said Clara. "The temptation comes to all of us eventually. Really it may be rectifying an evolutionary mistake."

"I brought it on myself, Ma'am."

Simon ordered Miles's drink. Beastman inclined his head fractionally in acknowledgement. Lowering his voice and gazing woodenly into the middle-distance, he said, "Will any of sir's guests be requiring," he laid a finger against his nose, "less liquid refreshments?"

Simon looked somewhat pained. "No, Beastm'n. We don't have that kind of guest now and I have told you you needn't trouble to cater for it any more."

"Oh, I would have had to send out, sir," Beastman assured him. He cleared his throat and continued, "However, one is informed by some riff-raff of the village that there is a certain crop of fungi in the lower meadow which will liven up any party, or indeed religious ceremony."

"No, Beastm'n. Wouldn't really mix with guns, what?"

"Sir did not always think so," said Beastman sadly. He moved majestically off.

"I'm afraid Beastman still misses the old days sometimes," said Simon with a cheery grin.

Simon on his side had reinvented himself as a huntin', shootin', fishin' gent as thoroughly and successfully as he had at different stages of his career created and inhabited the roles of hippy flower child, alien sex-tourist, schizoid demagogue, androgynous leather-boy, hammy Vegas lounge-crooner, cyborg synth-wizard and, in a rare and regrettable misreading of the zeitgeist, Formbyesque ukulele-strummer. He was now the ur-country-squire, of a Platonic purity rarely found outside literature. While he had fond memories of the old days, the fact was that this was his favourite incarnation, the one that was closest to his heart. He felt and exercised a noblesse oblige towards his tenants and dependants, had become a thorn in the side of government in helping his neighbours fight wanton destruction of the countryside and its way of life. When he had first seen the village it had felt like coming home. Growing up in the nation's dreariest, rainiest, dourest suburb he had acquired an almost mystical, fairytale image of England from Thomas Malory, E. Nesbit, Kipling's *Puck of Pook's Hill*, Betjeman, Blake, black-and-white films. It was xenophilia rather than patriotism, the disinterested love of an eternal outsider; England was always elsewhere, and possibly even elsewhen, but he knew it existed, the magical realm of Avalon to which he would one day find the key. Here, now, he had come as close to finding it as he could. It was within himself as much as without. He would will it to be as he had always wanted it to be, as he would will himself to be what he wanted to be. You became your masks; it was better to choose a pleasant one. On a more mundane level, as he aged he found he preferred waking up to birdsong and the scent of mown hay rather than dead bassists and vomit.

"Beastman must show the children his war memorabilia, especially his guns," said Clara.

Simon smiled indulgently and nodded. There was a boring maturity and even-handedness about Squire Simon at times, Clara found, and she had instinctively not pitched her scheme to him as 'Help me deprogram or if you prefer brainwash Harriet's children' but rather in terms of 'We have to give these poor kids the most fun day ever' and with that aim at least he was in harmony.

"Where's James?" he asked, still smiling. He was fully involved in this plot and a good friend of the young painter. "If he doesn't move fast he'll find Dolna has been elevated to the peerage."

"Drowned his sorrows a bit too thoroughly," said Miles. "He's being completely Super in my car. Not really the maiden's prayer at this point."

"Ah! Not to worry." Beastman was bringing Miles's drink. "One of your patent Revivers for the chap in the E-type, Beastman, full-strength," Simon directed. The butler nodded gravely and left. "That ought to do it. Beastman knows recipes Jeeves could only dream of. Used to claim this one was used by voodoo priests to reanimate zombies."

He moved on to other guests. Miles stood and watched Struan tearing round happily with the slightly older Jack, Simon's nephew/cousin-thing, and chatting to and being petted by the villagers, and thought what a shame it was that kids had to get caught up in adults' shit. Clara played the entirely uncoordinated Ivor at swingball, beating him mercilessly and laughing when he tangled himself up in it. The child threw his bat down and tottered over to Jeremiah, sitting at a nearby table, who showed him some pictures from an art book.

Presently Beastman returned. He gave a discreet cough – actually a throaty growl that made Miles jump – and said:

"The relaxed gentleman will shortly be able to put in an appearance, sir."

"Thanks, Beastman."

"I am having sir's car cleaned; with luck the upholstery will not stain." The butler paced off.

"Oh, fuck," said Miles.

"Fuck!" laughed Ivor. "Fuck!"

"*Miles!*"

"Sorry."

"We've only just got him to stop," said Jeremiah.

"Yes, it's quite worrying, he knows it's naughty so it's become his favourite word. I'm afraid Jeremiah and I suddenly developed Tourette's earlier, not realising he was there."

"A global warming conversation, was it?"

"Well you've been saying it all day. Let's face it, we are awful foul-mouthed bastards."

"Bastards," laughed Ivor.

"Oh shut up, you half-witted bloody parrot, or I will throttle you. I mean how do you know which one? You do it on purpose and are impressing no-one."

"Bastards. Bloody. Fuck."

"We can't return it to Harriet in this condition," said Clara unhappily.

"I'm more worried about young Edmund Burke, frankly," said Miles.

"That is something to be proud of, this is just embarrassing. Listen here, Ivor – "

"Fuck?" said Ivor.

"Stop saying Fuck, you little brat!" she cried.

"Fuck!" agreed Ivor.

"*You* stop saying it," said Miles.

"Oh fuck," said Clara wearily, then belatedly covered her mouth. "Arse."

"Fuck. Arse."

"Shit! I mean – shush, damn you!"

"Damn."

"That's an improvement, anyway," said Miles.

"Damn. Damn. Damn! Fuck," said Ivor.

"Listen, darling," said Clara sweetly, "that is a very bad word. Can't you say 'Fluff' instead?" Ivor looked scornful. "Go on, say 'Fluff.' "

"Wait, wait, you have to make him think 'Fluff' is the worst word ever. Fluff!" said Miles, and then gasped and covered his mouth.

"*Ahhh!* Naughty Uncle Miles! He said Fluff."

"*You* just said Fluff," cried Miles. The child stared at the pair of them with utter contempt.

"Stop saying Fluff!" cried Clara, slapping Miles round the head.
"Fuck!" exclaimed Miles in genuine pain and annoyance.
"Fuck," said the child.
"I think you mean, Fluff, Uncle Miles," said Clara through gritted teeth.
"Fluff off, Aunty Clara," said Miles, rubbing his head, through equally gritted teeth.
"Fluff you."
"Fluff! Fluff! Fluff!" said the child.
"Hooray! I mean, booo. *Bad* word."
"Fluff," said the child experimentally. "Fluff."
They exhaled.
"Fuck the Fluff," muttered Ivor disgustedly.
They sucked their breath in sharply again.
"Fuck shite bastard Tranzi leftard brat," added Ivor. "Throttle you."
They exchanged glances.
"Uh oh," said Miles.
"What a rotten ungrateful kid," said Clara indignantly. "They have probably trained it to spy on people. This is not a child, it is some perverted dictaphone machine."
"Dick," said the child.
Clara drew Miles aside. "We will blame Jeremiah," she murmured.
"Two hearts with but a single thought, my vixen."
"That appalling old man."
"He ought to be locked up."
"And doubtless will be."
Arm in arm they strolled off.

The relaxed gentleman made his appearance. James was first seen walking slowly along past the farm buildings like an automaton, looking somewhat dazed, staring at his surroundings with a thoughtful frown. He filled a pail with water, upended it over his head, shook himself like a dog and pushed his hair back. When he came over to them he looked more or less human, if a trifle unsteady, even resolute and manly, and managed a thin smile.

"James she's over there," hissed Clara. "Don't propose marriage again but go and plead your cause."

"I fully intend to," he said calmly, even confidently, and strode across. Clara squeezed Miles's arm.

It did not go well. At James's first approach Dolna's wine was flung into his face, to be followed swiftly by any other alcohol he could lay his hands on when he came back.

Dolna stormed off leaving her three admirers gaping. Clara hurried to intercept her on the edge of the paddock.

"Can't you give the poor man another chance?" she implored.

"This poor man, this very poor man, has had one hundred chances," Dolna declared. "Now he shames me with his drunkenness. I detest him," she said tossing her head.

"Miles found him trying to ride his bike off the bridge," Clara poetically adjusted the raw data. "If you don't at least give him leave to hope – "

"Let him die! It is no more than he deserves." She started to stride away then came back and held up a finger. "Again, he is weak. If I tried to ride a bike off a bridge, I would succeed. Probably, he stood on bridge, looking, and looking, and looking, and did not dare to jump in, and then decided to paint the river instead. Leave me alone, Clara, this is finish."

She went. Clara returned to James.

"What did she say?" he asked draining a glass.

"She has come to see you merely as a brother and cannot yet regard you in any other light."

"She despises me, doesn't she?"

"Yes. However I have found that borderline contempt can be a sound basis for a marriage." Miles cleared his throat and raised his eyebrows. "Of course so too is the husband being a world-bestriding colossus of a man."

"I'm not giving up," said James. He walked back towards Dolna but stopped twenty feet from her and regarded her with an expression they couldn't make out. Upon seeing him Dolna immediately commenced to flirt unsubtly with one of her country gent admirers, laughing loudly, touching him, flicking her hair, casting poisonous parenthetic glances at James the while. After a while James turned and headed to a table of drinks. With another scowl in his direction Dolna detached herself from her gallants and stalked off towards the farm buildings, opening her cig packet.

Clara sighed. "Oh dear."

"You tried," said Miles.

"And I will try again. We will get them both back to ours and contrive to lock them in a room together." She thought for a moment. "The one where I hide your mother's vases. Go and stop James drinking, and I will slander Dolna to the Hoorays to forestall competition from that direction."

At Miles's approach James muttered that he would rather be alone and wandered off, leaving the drinks but also several empty glasses behind, so Miles shrugged and decided to mingle, enjoying the paling of the three young Nimrods' faces as he sauntered by. " ... remarkable what they can do nowadays ... gather they turn the neck right round so the Adam's apple is at the back ... do with the willy afterwards, *I* should like to know, perhaps the surgeons take it home for the dog to play with," he heard Clara saying. He found he lacked the energy to mingle just now and skirted several groups with a smile of amiable benevolence, drinking in the evening summer sun, the hubbub, the happy or arguing faces of his neighbours, the dance of light on glasses, the sound of laughter, the scent of the grass, the drone of a bumble-bee, the thwack of the air-rifles and their targets which had replaced the shotguns, the trees and parkland in the distance, the breeze in his face, his drink. For the first time that day since Harriet's appearance Miles started properly to relax. It hadn't been that bad after all; even idyllic.

He wandered to the fence at the end of the paddock and then back. He was later to estimate that this interlude of peace could have lasted at the most about ten minutes, maybe even only five, but while it did last it was delightful. He serenely listened to a boring car conversation, an esoteric farming discussion, a heated sporting argument and a far more heated political agreement. He had lost track of, and did not particularly notice the absence of, James, Dolna, the children and now Clara. He got himself another drink. He ate some food. He idly took Jeremiah's part in a historical debate. Beastman juggled wine-glasses for a cooing county matron. Farmers complained of hard times but did not particularly show it. His host vied with an ancient, ramrod-straight former Desert Rat to produce the verses and refrains of even more ancient music-hall songs. All was good with the world.

The uneasiness started then. It could not be classed as premonition in any psychic sense. Cattle were lowing, a dog was barking. Where *were* those kids he was meant to be looking after? What was Clara up to? It was usually better to know for sure than to worry himself guessing, although as it happened this was not one of those occasions. There was a sound of shouts not far off. The crowd itself rippled with brief unease, faltered a little in its conviviality, but went on with its conversations.

It was when Clara reappeared around the corner of the dairy that his blood froze. It was during the micro-second she glanced his way, and due to the glare of guilty defiance she gave him. And by this point clouds of smoke were visible over the back of the dairy behind her.

"My palms sweat," murmured Miles to himself. "I wish to wake up."

Clara was not running but walking very quickly, her head erect, her eyes straight ahead of her, apart from that one brief shifty glance at Miles, and her arms swinging briskly at her sides, almost as though she was marching. She was, in fact, marching herself, as, although Miles didn't know it, she had once resolutely marched herself to the office of a headteacher to own up to something upon an almost equally awkward occasion in her girlhood. Her object was their genial host, not five feet from Miles at this point. Simon turned to look at her as she approached.

When she had reached him she stopped and in a clear calm voice said:

"Simon I have set fire to your barn with various children inside. I honestly meant well."

There was one role that Simon Smith had played almost all his life; a role that fit perfectly well with his current Lord of the Manor incarnation; that had sat more uneasily with some of the other guises he had worn in the course of his long, varied, strange, wonderful life, but had perhaps underpinned them, allowed him to play them, and into which he had invariably slipped as soon as he came offstage; that had always been with him in the most unlikely situations; one that went to the very core of his concept of Englishness; a role that Miles had understudied all unknowing when he had played Jimmy Badger Faversham; a role that he was only half-conscious of, and had never dared name to himself. It was the role of the unflappable British war hero.

The Dam Busters; *Reach for the Sky*; *The Great Escape*; these and a dozen others, in Pan paperback or celluloid apotheosis, had also been part of his childhood imagination; and out of them he had created himself, had distilled a tribute to those eternally cheery gods that had once walked or flown the Earth: ever-smiling, cucumber-cool, superhumanly calm and unfailingly polite. That, he had decided, was what a man was, and what he had moulded himself to be.

As a willowy teenage dandy menaced by dull suburban thugs; as the object of thoughtful, inventive and surprising sexual offers at the most unusual times and places from groupies, film stars and on one occasion a Bishop of the Church of England; trapped in a ruined limousine, rocked and pelted with rocks by an incensed mob in a quaintly antiquated backwater of the U.S.; nursing friends, colleagues, himself through the pangs of drug withdrawal; metaphysically wrestling with the devil – urbane, Dostoyevskian, reptilian, five-dimensional, wearing a row of screaming heads at his belt and hideously mismatched spats – during a hallucinogenic bout; waking up to find zoo animals in his room and no memory of how they had got there; jeered and jostled by anti-hunt activists, sneered at by parliamentary select committees, dealt non-sequiturs, obsequiousness, obsessiveness or inane questions about breakfast cereals or onanism by representatives of the media – at all times he had kept his breezy imperturbability, courteous good manners and unflappable, affable smile in place.

This smiling-on-regardless business had helped him cope with Clara before.

It failed him now, for a second, his unflappable smile; it flickered, faltered and faded.

But only for a second. There was a real war hero nearby; and Clara herself was calm; might even, save for her astonishing, startling words, and the hint of schoolgirl self-exculpation, have been some cool, capable WAAF girl or Wren out of his childhood Odeon dreams, briskly reporting some regrettable but not insurmountable reversal to her commanding officer. Almost he expected her to salute.

He hoisted his smile back into place.

"Right-o," he said. "Let's take a look, shall we?"

The thing was, Miles theorised afterwards, trying to rationalise the debacle, that Clara had had a remarkable run of success in recent months in imposing the products of her imagination on the real world, in a way that even genius rarely achieved: the Walpole's Head sign, the Stoic Endurance shop, the artist known as Pingu, perhaps even Dolna herself appearing to emerge full-blown from her psyche. She could almost be excused one folie de grandeur, one brief delusion of omnipotence, one moment of overreaching, one terrible faux pas such as setting fire to a barn with various children inside.

Clara said nothing of that. In days to come she would maintain, periodically, that it had been a brilliant idea gone sadly awry in the execution due to the lamentable intractability of the physical world; that really she had been inspired; that all things had pointed to it and she had probably been an agent of God. But deep down she knew it had not been one of her best hours, and on the whole she tended to keep quiet about it, except for sometimes when she would take it into her head to tease Miles about The Time He Had Been So Grumpy At Simon's.

It happened like this:

After she had finished dismaying the three young landowners with the idea that, having had a former life as a lumberjack named Otto, Dolna was probably not the ideal candidate to help carry on their family names, Clara had noticed James drifting off behind the farm buildings, in which direction Dolna had disappeared some minutes before, and decided she had better follow him. He might be intending to go home, in which case she must head him off; or he might be intending to offer himself to Dolna again, in which case she must be on hand to discreetly watch and sigh if all went well, or lend the putative lovebirds a gentle helping hand if not – causing a stampede of dairy cattle from which James could then rescue Dolna was one image that flashed across her mind, trapping them together between the prongs of a fork-lift truck another.

She tiptoed round the corner of the dairy. The farmyard contained a few sleepy hens, a wistful James, now somewhat doddery and glazed-looking again, but no Dolna.

"Bird has flown," he said as she approached. "Run away home. Entirely my fault. Tongue-tied and bashful. Tongue-tied and Bashful, the amazing performing SM dwarves. Limited period only. Limited period only; this offer has now expired," he concluded sadly.

"Oh knock that off. She must be around here somewhere."

She peered inside the Small Barn, which he had been wobbling uncertainly in front of. She thought she heard a noise; it was half filled with hay bales and half with junk, and there were plenty of places for Dolna to hide. She ventured stealthily in, trailed unsteadily by James.

Clara paced and gazed around. Dust-motes danced; a mingled smell of straw and oil; no Dolna unless she was crouching behind the sacking and crates in the far corner or conceivably the straw-bale ziggurat in the near.

"Gone to earth," said James. "Gone to ground. Can't be found. Little fox, come darn my socks, I will polish your clocks. Improve the shining hour. Time's winged, springed ... only pretty ring time ... "

"Shush! All right, let's try the others." Definitely a noise though. She stopped. "James!" she hissed, and pointed.

Half of one of Dolna's long exotic cigarettes was lying discarded, blackened at the end, atop a lone straw bale in the middle of the barn.

"Aha! Observe, Watson. Her spoor."

Not far from the bale was a rickety wooden ladder, nailed to a hole in the ceiling, leading to the loft.

Above them the wooden beams of the ceiling were creaking, they could hear now, regularly. Someone was pacing up there.

"She is up there brooding, James," Clara breathed delightedly, eyes wide, pointing upwards. "Pacing like a caged panther, trying to escape from thoughts of you. Go up and appear to her suddenly, like a manifestation of her denied desires."

James brightened and took a step, then hesitated. "She'll just hit me."

"Some of the happiest moments in my life have involved hitting Miles. Go, man! – Wait!" She held up a hand and listened. "Time it so you emerge while she is at the far end, gazing out of the window and sighing. Then she will turn and see you. Go to her and take her in your arms."

James nodded.

"I will try if I can to pull the ladder away after you're up, so she's trapped, unless she jumps dramatically from the loft window."

James looked doubtful. Clara herself bit her lip in sudden second thought. Dolna might well be capable of something as splendidly impetuous as leaping from the upper story window if trapped. Pile some straw outside in case? After all look at the heedless way she had flung her cigarette aside, doubtless in some sudden splendid gesture of moodiness, and in a barn of all places. Clara mentally tsked as she looked at it – how easily that bale could have gone up – but then was rather thrilled. It was quite wonderful really. What did Dolna care if she burned down a barn? It would be a perfect backdrop to her mood. Clara empathized with the large-mindedness of this attitude instinctively. She pictured Dolna stalking magnificently through an apocalyptic landscape of a hundred burning barns, a flaming brand in her hand, torching each one moodily as she passed with no more compunction than if she was lighting candles for a lost love. She loved Dolna for being capable of that and loved life for still being capable of smuggling the occasional Dolna past the barriers. Of course in this case Dolna would not have been picturesquely framed by a burning barn but trapped within it, for she had gone straight up the ladder after tossing aside her cigarette. James would have come upon her leaning from the top storey window crying for help, surrounded by smoke and fire ... he would have manfully fought his way through the flames to carry her to safety ... she would have sighed in his arms ... How wonderful! Clara came back to reality. She tutted in annoyance at life as she gazed at the blackened cigarette. It could so *easily* have happened ...

Clara's eyes went very wide and very bright.

"James," she breathed ecstatically, "I have had a much better idea."

Yes, yes! She saw it all. It was perfect. It was artistically *right*. It all fit. A rescuing fireman was Dolna's ideal of masculinity. James would never redeem himself otherwise.

"I will start a fire in the barn," Clara told James excitedly, "and you will save her."

James reeled somewhat for reasons other than drunkenness. "Not quite the thing, surely?" he suggested.

Clara could half see that. Practicalities rushed in on her. "Just a little fire," she said eagerly. "This bale." She dragged it closer to the ladder. "And perhaps some wood. Just the start of one. Don't you see? You will come in and discover it and raise the alarm and save her. It could so easily have happened from her cigarette. It positively *ought* to have. You will climb up the ladder – there will be smoke and flames from below – it will look as though the whole place is going up – you will hold her and comfort her, she will cling to you – and then, and then – carry her back down the ladder? But there'll be smoke, and one of you might really get burned – it might catch fire – better if it *does*, I will set fire to that a bit too, you have climbed up a burning ladder, you see? So then, so then – you lower her out of the window? I could pile straw, it wouldn't be much of a drop. No, you must carry her. Could you climb down the face of the – a rope! I saw a rope!" She looked around and located a big old tow rope in the corner. She coiled it around his head and shoulder. "Make it fast around one of the roof-beams or something, or there are usually pulleys, and then abseil out of the window holding her in your arms! Yes, yes!"

James frowned drunkenly as he strained to follow this.

"Won't do it," he said mulishly. "Won't do."

Clara didn't believe in slapping any man apart from her husband, mostly out of a quite mistaken belief that Miles must have come to find it an endearing expression of marital affection by now and would be jealous. But she grabbed James by the collar and shook him.

"Are you a man or a mouse? Don't you want to take action for once? Do you want to win Dolna or live without her for the rest of your life? Firemen are her ideal of manliness, she was rescued by one before. It needs something dramatic like this to break down her pride. She thinks you're a wimp! She thinks you're a weakling! Are you?"

He shook his head. "But Dolna in danger ... Simon's barn."

"It will only be a *little* fire," she explained patiently. "A tiny baby one. You will have *saved* Simon's barn. As soon as there's a good lot of smoke and flames and you're up the ladder, I – ostensibly alerted by your shouts, but really waiting here – will put it out again, you see? There's a hosepipe! I saw a hosepipe!" She dashed to the entrance and put her head round for a second. "Yes, look, right outside, it's all perfect. There will be plenty of smoke and flames and drama but no real danger. This will work. It's the only way. Trust me! At university they used to call me Cupid's Little Helper."

They had had other names for her, by the end, but she chose to forget about those.

James was still unpersuaded. He was not quite in the realm of infinite amenability where everything suggested was Super. He shook his head again. "Lady's not for burning," he muttered. "Or for turning."

"Trust me she will! Or she won't, and she will." She shook him again. "Do you want to lose her?" He shook his head vehemently. "Then will you do as I say?" He made a noise. "Give me matches or a lighter. Hurry, man!"

This might still have been a stumbling block to her great plan. James didn't smoke either. But he had started carrying a lighter after falling in love, and the opportunity of lighting Dolna's cigarettes a couple of times had afforded him a joy the memory of which had kept him warm at night. Automatically he patted himself and produced a Zippo.

"Right. Get ready."

"Dolna. Save Dolna."

"Yes, James, and most of all from a loveless life. You don't want her to go off with one of those shooting sticks out there, do you?"

"My doll and my dolour."

Now Clara was doubtful. Was he actually in any condition to perform the rescue? She bit her lip.

"Don't tell Miles about this," she said, and slapped him across the face several times.

"Ouch!" he cried resentfully. He seemed somewhat more focussed now. There had been a pail half-filled with water near the hose too. She nipped to fetch it and flung it in his face. He shivered and sneezed.

"Oh that is much better. You have emptied it over you to damp the flames, you see? Steam will rise off your shirt, it'll be great. Are you ready, James? Are you able to do this?"

"Capable of anything," said James.

"Good boy."

Clara listened. The ceiling was still creaking. Her excitement and certainty returning, she stooped to the straw bale and flicked the Zippo.

The results were disappointing. The close-packed straw was not as highly combustible as she had envisaged. It smouldered and smoked as she plied the flame but didn't quite crackle and whoosh as she had expected. It seemed to be dampish on top. It would take ages to catch. She burned her hand on the lighter. Maybe if she unpacked it a bit. She looked around for an implement with which to attack the bale. In a corner there was a petrol can next to a lawnmower. Now that was more the ticket. She went and got it.

"Shouldn't," said James.

"Stand back."

Clara uncapped the half-full petrol can and upended it over the smouldering bale. There were sparks enough there for it go up almost instantly in a splendid whoosh of orange flame. She gave a cry and danced back. She bit her lip in indecision a moment and then poured out the rest of the petrol in a trail leading from the blazing bale to the bottom of one of the legs of the ladder. That caught fire too.

"Go, James!" she cried.

"Oh, Christ, *Dolna!*" cried James in alarm, seeming fully alive to the situation for the first time, and unhesitatingly and quite nimbly leapt onto the already-burning ladder and shot up it into the loft.

It needed more smoke. Clara dropped a piece of sacking onto the burning bale. That smouldered for an instant but was consumed in flame in virtually the next.

It was the hell of a blaze. Clara watched it for a second, mesmerised and, although she did not admit it to herself, already quite alarmed. Now she had better put it out.

She rushed to get the hosepipe and dragged it in quickly. She pointed it at the roaring flames and waited expectantly, frowning and glaring in annoyance when nothing happened. She had forgotten to turn the tap on. She rushed back out again and remedied this.

When she dashed back in once more a quite feeble trickle of water was emerging from the end of the pipe. She stared at it appalled, already foreseeing the ruination of her plans. There were kinks and loops and snarls along the length of the pipe. Frantically she untangled and straightened out the worst ones. It didn't help much. The water splashed sluggishly out as from some piece of dental equipment. Anxiously, optimistically and entirely ineffectually she directed it towards the conflagration.

"Come on, boy," she urged the trickling hosepipe. She wondered if she ought to whistle as men did in toilets. Thanks to the intense heat she found she couldn't even get close enough to direct the small slow arc of water onto the flame and was reduced to pouring it onto the floor some distance from the fire in the hope the slowly spreading puddle would eventually do some good.

This, she thought later, was the big disappointment, the thing that constituted the tragic difference between visualization and reality. The fine, strong Platonic hose she had envisaged in her moment of inspiration had been another creature entirely. Clara had clear childhood memories of there being splendidly powerful hoses on farms, torrential handheld geysers for hosing down dairies and stables and animals' bums. They could clear out Augean muck within minutes and would have put out a burning bale in seconds. And indeed she hadn't imagined these. Such hoses existed. She had merely been mistaken in fondly imagining this was one of them. They required high-pressure equipment. This, it dawned on her belatedly, was just an ordinary common or garden hose attached to a tap in a wall, and a rubbish tap at that.

"Arse," said Clara.

Sadly she let the hosepipe droop. She saw the pail she had emptied over James and in sudden hope dropped the end of the pipe into that for it to fill. Then she caught sight of a watering can and inserted the hose into that instead. A sort of nice steady downpour like a sprinkler system might be better than one big splash, she thought. She could water the flames like flowers, she was good at watering flowers. A second later she changed her mind again and put the pipe back in the bucket. It started to fill very slowly. She idiotically glanced at her watch in impatience and then calmly started to note the progress of the fire while she waited. She might have been in shock at this point, although she later maintained to herself that the cool slowness with which her thoughts had moved were indicative of nerves of steel. Certainly, when her thoughts moved more quickly, they didn't arrive anywhere very helpful, so it was all one really.

The ladder was blazing merrily and the flames at the top of it were licking at the beams of the floor above. Firing the ladder had been a mistake, in retrospect. Meanwhile the fire crept outwards along the floor of the barn, inching a trail across scattered straw and stray bits of wood, flaring up like molten gold where it encountered petrol splashes or long-ago spills of oil, and was airborne in the form of pretty dancing sparks. She watched interestedly as one of these alighted in the midst of the ziggurat of bales mounting to the ceiling in the corner.

"Piss," said Clara.

She glanced stupidly at her watch again and then into the bucket. It was three-quarters full. The hose had stopped even its derisory trickle. One coil of it had passed over one of the now-lit splashes of petrol from her can and was bubbling and melting. She grabbed the pail and, in panic-stricken indecision, flung more than half the water at the blazing bale – it did nothing but cause a brief hiss – rushed over and cast slightly less than half towards where she had seen a spark land amid the Tetris-battlements of bales in the corner, and then tossed the last futile dribbles towards the burning skeleton of the ladder. Not too intently she wondered how James and Dolna were getting on. Noises from above had been coming to her over the roar of the flames but she could give them little attention. She cast the bucket away. The important thing was to keep calm and not panic. She grabbed a rake and started to hack at the burning bale in a frenzy. It tangled in the remnants of the sack; the end of the wooden handle went alight. She dropped it. Flinching from the heat she dashed to the back of the barn and dragged out six or eight more empty hessian sacks. She dipped and trod them into the puddle of water she had made on the floor and then flung them strategically over the bale. It seemed to do some good; a great cloud of smoke roiled out from under the last. She pulled it off again and started to beat with it at the burning straw round about, kicking and stamping too, starting to cough with the smoke but enjoying some success. Pleased with her work, she was just wondering what she ought to do about the ladder and the flames creeping across the ceiling from the top of it when she noticed that the lower slopes of the bale pyramid in the corner were now alight too.

"Oh, Fluff," said Clara.

She decided she had better abandon the barn. It was, she admitted, probably beyond salvation. She told herself Simon was rich and had plenty of other barns. Indeed, some right next door to this one. The important thing was still not to panic. There was a clutching round her heart she recognised as the first importunate knocking of guilt to be let in, but she didn't have time now to indulge it or, preferably, make it go away. This would at least make a splendidly realistic backdrop for James's cathartic rescue of Dolna, she reflected as she retreated wide-eyed and coughing before the heat and light and smoke.

Only where the hell *was* James? Distracted though she had been she thought she would have noticed a pair of cooing lovebirds rappelling down the side of the building. Irrationally she glanced at her watch again as she ran outside, then looked up the side of the barn. There *was* a pulley tackle, right above the loft window, she had been right about that anyway. He should have secured his rope to it by now and be descending manfully with Dolna in his arms. But there was no sign of him. Instead she saw two pale young faces, Struan and Jack, craning out of the window.

"Aunty Clara! There's a fire! The ladder's burning and there's all smoke coming up!"

"What the hell are *you* doing there?" she exclaimed in irritation.

"We were playing."

"Where's Dolna?"

"She isn't here but a man is, the man from the cottage, he came up the ladder shouting."

"Well what's he doing? Put him on. I mean let me talk to him."

"You can't, he's unconscious. He came rushing and stumbled and banged his head on one of the roof-beams. Jack checked and he isn't dead but he doesn't move, we can't wake him up."

Clara folded her arms and compressed and then wiggled her lips. She tapped her foot on the ground several times in annoyance. She counted to ten in her head.

"Aunty Clara, really, the barn's on fire! What shall we do?"

Clara sighed with vexation.

"Stay there," she told the children, turning her back on them and smartly marching herself off to make her surprising report to Simon, eyes straight ahead of her apart from one uneasy glance at Miles.

In imitation of Clara, Simon walked very briskly indeed, rather than ran, towards the scene of the disaster, and most of his guests did the same in imitation of him. However the farmhands present had no truck with this and sprinted past them.

"There, you see," said Clara conversationally as they entered the yard, pointing, as if to indicate a particularly interesting view, "they are completely trapped."

"Right-o," said Simon and, grabbing one of his men, ran to the other barn.

Dolna appeared from the dairy, yanking a cowshit-covered Ivor after her angrily, and scowled in confusion at the commotion.

"What are you doing up there?" she snapped at Struan. "Come down."

"We would like to," said Struan.

She looked in surprise at the smoking, blazing interior of the barn. "Is fire?"

"Yes, Dolna, and you have missed it," Clara told her in slight annoyance.

The fire was not yet quite as bad as it looked, and within the apparent chaos of the shouting crowd in front of the barn there was swift work and decisive organisation going forward. A grain-loader, a mobile conveyor-belt raised at a steep angle, was quickly dragged from the bigger barn and positioned in front of the loft window.

"Slide down it," Simon called.

Struan and Jack hesitated.

"Come on, Struan, be brave," called Clara. "Aunty Clara is here, nothing bad can happen to you."

The two boys slid down. Simon tousled their hair and grinned. "Wasn't that fun?"

Struan nodded breathless. "But what about the man from the cottage?"

"James is up there unconscious," said Clara.

Several men started forward. Dolna beat them all. Crying, "James, my James," she clawed her way past them and shot up the conveyor belt like a cat.

She vanished into the smoking loft to reappear moments later dragging the comatose James over her shoulder. Her three former admirers exchanged significant glances. But her upper body strength gave out at the window; she collapsed as she heaved him over and the pair of them tumbled, rolled and slid down the loader. At the bottom she clutched him sobbing while he groaned groggily in her arms.

All this time other men had been attacking the fire. Armed with tools they had ventured dauntlessly and efficiently into the smoke-filled barn to separate burning bales from unburnt and then overturn the former and smother them with sacks. Meanwhile one of the proper high-pressure hoses was brought from the dairy and quickly put into action. Everywhere its jet played the flames were doused like candles squirted by a soda-siphon. By the time people brought fire-extinguishers the battle was already over.

They surveyed the smoking ruins. The ladder was charcoal. The floor above was blackened and scorched in a dozen places and would have to be pulled down. Most of the straw was waterlogged rather than burned. A lawnmower and some other machines were twisted wrecks and some fencing had been reduced to ashes.

A mercy was that Jack's mother had been up at the house bathing and changing a younger child. Her mouth hung open when she arrived and was told some of the story; she hugged her son and then illogically clipped him round the ear. She thanked James, by this point standing upright and looking dazed but happy, for trying to save them, which was what everyone assumed. Dolna hugged his arm proudly, then clipped him round the ear too.

Simon clapped his hands. "Enough excitement for one evening," he called. "Everyone back to the lawn, there are drinks getting warm." And he shepherded everyone firmly back to the party.

The butler Beastman, skulking down a little alley between the dairy and an equipment shed, recruiting himself after the drama by indulging in a habit Simon no longer approved of, was privileged to be the sole audience to a singular tête-à-tête between a lone couple who had contrived to remain behind in the yard after everyone else had left.

The scene was underplayed, Beastman thought appreciatively, as he stubbed out a smoking curl of cardboard and eased closer to the corner, deciding against alerting them to his presence; their voices started off, at any rate, fairly quiet and subdued; the husband in particular struck him as sounding eerily, preternaturally calm.

"I let you out of my sight for five minutes," said Miles.

"Don't reproach yourself, Miles," said Clara generously. "The fault was almost entirely mine. There, I admit it, you see."

Miles nodded, thoughtfully. Clara thought there was something inhuman, even cruel, or at least downright irritating, about this calm quiet thoughtfulness.

"Miles give Simon some money," she suggested.

"Obviously. But – Simon has money. What he *doesn't* have is a barn."

"It won't help matters to exaggerate, Miles. It is standing right there, look. A little the worse for wear, but – essentially only the wooden bits were burned. And he has several other barns, completely healthy."

"Thankfully! Are you – are you familiar with the magical spreading properties of fire?"

"It has lately been borne in on me."

Miles nodded again. He cleared his throat and said:

"There were children in the barn."

"Yes, Miles," said Clara patiently. "And you can imagine how awful I feel about that. As I have tried to explain, I thought it was Dolna."

"Your new best friend."

"Yes."

Miles nodded.

He said, "Clara, look at me. I need to see some – no, no, not the sad face. And no pouty sexy tricks. I need to know you realise – this is far beyond – "

"I *do*, Miles, honestly." She honestly did.

"There's a place, you know, that naughty wives get sent to," he told her.

"I know, Miles." Clara nodded, biting a nail contritely.

"A place with rubber walls."

She nodded again.

"Naughty wives who set fire to neighbours' barns," he persisted.

"It was the bale, Miles," she said unhappily. "It spoke to me."

"See, that is *exactly* the kind of talk that leads to the Naughty Wives' Home."

Clara nodded once more. "I know, Miles, I do know. But it was all so *perfect*. And look how it has worked out. Perhaps God – "

"No, Clara! That, too."

She nodded rapidly and bit at her nail. This was awful.

There was a pause.

"I mean … is it just me?" Miles tried again.

"No, Miles. I can see I have let us both down in this case. I have Fluffed up badly." She cleared her throat and ventured, "However, remember the time you – "

"What? What? What? The time I did what?" Miles's voice was not so quiet now.

Clara had been vaguely thinking of the time on their honeymoon when Miles had let a bath overflow; on reflection she could see it didn't quite compare. She waved it away.

There was another pause.

"I owned up," she pointed out. "And I have said sorry to Simon, and given him a hug."

"Yes. Yes, you did," allowed Miles. "If *Hitler* had owned up – if *Hitler* had said sorry – "

"Oh, now you are picking on my heroes."

"It isn't funny! Do you – do you comprehend – "

"I *do*, Miles, honestly," she repeated.

They fell silent again. Clara decided to venture a sad face.

"You wouldn't *really* put me in the Naughty Wives' Home, would you, Miles?" she asked with wobbly lip and batting eyelashes.

"I – I would much prefer not to," he cried. "But I start to worry, you know, sometimes, that the climax of our marriage will be like the ending of 'Of Mice and Men'."

That hurt. That was too much. Clara's mouth hung open in outrage. "Are you saying that *I* – YOU are the Lenny of the marriage!" she cried indignantly. "I am sure anyone would agree!"

"Because I am stolid and responsible and boring and don't burn down barns?"

Clara shook her head, creasing her forehead, and held up a finger.

"No plural, Miles. *One* barn. I burned down one barn – just the wooden bits – as a good deed. When was the last time *you* did a good deed, Miles? When was the last time you thought about anything except your own peace and quiet? *You* would have left those poor kids out in the street. *I* took them in. I fed them and sheltered them and kept them warm."

"Warm? *Warm?*" The words would not come. He pointed spluttering towards the blackened facade of the barn.

"I do think you might have the good taste not to pounce on an unfortunate verbal slip like that. I try, Miles. My only problem is I care too much. *You* could stand to take a leaf out of *my* book. You are cold-hearted, Miles. I am warm and impulsive. I think I have the quick blood of the impetuous south flowing in my veins. You are too English for me. I made my friends happy. I would burn down a *thousand* barns to make my friends happy. *That's* the difference between us."

Miles was speechless for a moment. "Are you – are you seriously trying to claim the moral high ground?"

Clara shook her head again.

"No, Miles. I, unlike you, have no interest in occupying the moral high ground. I am maturer than you. I – forgive you."

She turned on her heel; Beastman, emerging from his place of eavesdropping, was in time to see her stalk superbly off, head at a haughty angle.

The butler cleared his gravelly throat as Miles stared after her.

"If sir will forgive my saying so," he intoned, "sir's woman is the craziest bitch I have ever come across; and my experience in these matters is not small."

He laid an arm around Miles and patted him on the shoulder.

"Would sir care to know the secret of a happy relationship?" he asked. "Booze. Lots and lots of booze."

"You have been a very brave boy, Struan."

"I was hardly scared at all, Aunty Clara."

"However, *much* the greater part of bravery is not talking about how brave one has been. Do you understand? It is far more manly to keep utterly shtumm as though nothing had happened at all. Miles teach him about stoicism and the stiff upper lip."

"Um – "

"*Especially* with your mother," Clara thought it best to spell out. "She might not understand, you know, the splendid adventure we have had. She might not let you play on the farm again, and you like playing on the farm, don't you?"

"Oh, yes, it's brilliant."

"Then maintain an aloof and becoming reticence about all that has passed here today."

"OK." Struan bit into a hamburger and frowned. "There's just one thing I don't understand, Aunty Clara. Why did you set fire to the barn? Was it to test us?"

Clara started and looked around to check if Jack's mother, or indeed anyone else, was in earshot. Then she gave a peal of merry laughter.

"*Hark* at the child! Why, whatever has put such a strange idea into your head, my cherub?"

"I thought of it just now." Struan concentrated earnestly. "I looked down through the hatch and saw you playing with a lighter and some straw, and just after that the smoke and burning started."

Clara laughed again. "Heavens, you are hallucinating, child. Probably your brain was damaged by the smoke. Perhaps we had better let the nurse take a look at you."

"No, I remember it clearly, you had the man's lighter, and then you came out of the barn when it started."

Clara looked around and lowered her voice. "Well, it *was* a test, a test of manhood, and you passed with flying colours. But if you ever speak of it, the results will be invalidated. *Especially* to your mother, or Jack's mother, or," she looked around, "just *anyone*." Although she had owned up properly to Simon and done her best to explain it to him, she knew he was too much of a gentleman to repeat the story; everyone else who had been close enough to hear her initial confession assumed her arson had been purely accidental, an impression she had not corrected as after all it largely had been, and had commiserated with her; most of the others thought she had merely been the one to raise the alarm, the heroine of the piece really, and had congratulated her; she had not corrected this impression either. "Anyone at all," she repeated firmly. "Miles give him some money."

Miles gave him some money.

"Now you shall have the same as that again every month so long as you keep your mouth shut. Miles teach him about blackmail."

She waved a hand and walked off.

She would have to coach Struan properly, and wash the sort of sooty bits out of his shirt and hair. But really, she thought, things hadn't worked out too badly. James – having been checked for concussion by the Singing Butcher's wife, who was a nurse, and passed fit for action if not for any more drink – was walking hand in hand with Dolna, framed against sun-gilded trees. She had done good work here today, after all.

"This child is a credit to you, Clara," called someone who was playing with Ivor. She inclined her head in acknowledgement and smiled.

"Fuck!" agreed Ivor.

"In fairness Jeremiah has had him for most of the day," said Clara.

She *had* done well with them on the whole, and they were adorable children for the most part. Perhaps Harriet would let her borrow them again some time.

Simon took his fellow landowners off for a serious talk about a campaign on behalf of farmers. The rest of the party grew somewhat more unrestrained. Beastman set up an electric guitar and amplifier for a drunken farmhand to noodle on. Goalposts were brought out and set up in the paddock. Returning to her educational scheme, Clara insisted the men play the boys at football and run rings around them and laugh, and then laughed at Miles when Struan ran a ring around him and scored.

Struan became moderately proficient with an air-rifle. Beastman brought some of his war memorabilia out for Struan and Jack to coo over. Major Fitzsimmons's Gurkha manservant showed them the kukri Clara had instructed him to bring. Then Clara remembered a plan from earlier and bundled Jeremiah into the car, and they fetched his effigy German and the Nazi cap from Clara's.

They set up the grotesque dummy with the Nazi cap dangling from a noose attached to the crossbar of one of the goals. Struan and Jack stabbed it with Jeremiah's Masai spear and a bayonetted rifle of Beastman's while everyone clapped and cheered. Struan picked up the fallen SS cap and put it on and started to goose-step around. A silence fell. Miles went very still. Clara helped little Ivor hold the rifle and encouraged him to bayonet the dangling effigy in its vitals while the child gurgled with laughter.

"*Good* boy," she cooed. "Hooray! It is *good* to kill the enemies of your country."

"Mummy!" cried Ivor, dropping the weapon.

Clara laughed indulgently. "I'm not your mummy! Do you wish I was?"

Then she noticed the terrible silence, Miles's unnatural stillness, the faces all pointing in one direction. There was a long shadow across the grass.

'Of course at the airport the silly cow has been overcome by an irrational fear for her children,' thought Clara. 'I expect I will get the blame for this, too.'

She straightened and turned. Harriet had come back early.

"Fuck," said Ivor, for everyone.

Chapter Nineteen

"Attention tourists! Attention foreigners!"

Clara stood in the middle of Trafalgar Square, near the base of Nelson's Column, holding a sign and shouting.

She wore a busby or bearskin hat like the sentries at the palace and so on, a smart red uniform with abbreviated skirt, reminiscent of an air hostess's but with golden epaulettes and a beefeater-style coat of arms sewn on the back of the jacket, and smart white gloves. The sign was a painted-over lollipop-lady's Stop sign, with 'Free Tour of London' on one side and 'Join the Tour Here' on the other.

"Attention tourists," she shouted, "attention foreigners! Don't just mill around like headless chickens! Join the official Royal Tour of London here! It is free! Informative! Fast! Not for dawdlers or the weak. See all the sights! Hear all the history that's fit to mention! Full access everywhere! Roll up! Don't be shy! You there!" she barked. "Man with a camera! Are you a tourist?"

Miles looked around bemusedly and then respectfully doffed a golf cap to reveal a head of grey hair. He was also wearing a grey golf jacket, tartan pants, glasses, and a benevolent look, and carried a camera around his neck.

"I surely am, Ma'am," he said.

"Then come and join the London Tour. See all the sights. It is free for foreigners!"

"Wull I'll be darned," said Miles in a slow wondering voice. "You mean I don't have to pay a cent? I call that mighty hospitable."

"Well don't just stand there gawping, come and form a line. Stand behind me! Put your hat back on or people will throw coins in. Behind me! We are forming a crocodile for safety. I am the head of the crocodile, you are currently the arse. You there! Japanese man with camera! Tenko! Come and join the free Tour of London."

The Japanese man with a camera approached and smiled diffidently and said, "Speak Japanese?"

"Of course you can," said Clara, and shoved him into place behind Miles. "Free Tour of London, everyone! Guided Tour of London, see all the sights! Free to all foreign tourists. We will also take Northerners depending on availability of translators. Hurry, hurry! We are leaving in five minutes. The next one isn't for six hours! Come and join the Guided Tour!"

A couple of Scandinavians joined the line of their own volition. Clara grabbed and manhandled a Latin-looking pair and an Oriental couple and a Teuton into place behind them and then roamed around hectoring anyone else nearby who had a camera. "Join the tour! Free tour! Hurry!" When there were about a dozen assembled she snapped, "Orderly line! Form a crocodile! No queue-jumping by the Latin races! Keep your eyes on me or the things I point at. Unless I am scratching my bum. Dawdle at your own risk. We will maintain an average speed of 15 miles an hour. And *off* we go." She blew a whistle. She led them snakingly around the square a couple of times, shouting and hoovering up more tourists until there were twenty or so in tow, and then they were off.

From start to finish the tour maintained a breakneck speed and bewildering momentum. It ricocheted around central London like a pinball or reeled around it like a drunk. It crossed its own path repeatedly; it meandered haphazardly; several times Clara was really lost and twice she snatched an A to Z from Miles's pocket and consulted it as furtively as she could and in deep annoyance. For long stretches of the tour she disdained the main thoroughfares and obvious attractions and led her flock into unfrequented byways, along quiet residential streets, down dingy back alleys, up to dead-ends and once through a busy building site. When they were on the main drags she would attempt to clear a path by blowing her whistle and yelling, "Coming through! Tourists coming through! Make way! Step aside! Official Tour of London! Show some manners!" and clobbering people with the sign. When she wanted to cross the street, she would simply step out into the traffic, blow her whistle imperiously, glare and wave the sign at the oncoming cars and hold up her white-gloved palm commandingly until her charges had passed. No-one got killed, and when the drivers swore at them she informed the tourists these were traditional British expressions wishing them good luck. She rehearsed a couple of the more monolingual and obliging foreigners in how to pronounce these good luck words and encouraged them to shout them back. As they hurtled around several of the party dropped out, unable to maintain the helter-skelter pace or baffled by her commentary; but these losses were made good by their frequently picking up new recruits en route. Twice she was moved to lead them all to run to catch a departing double-decker, losing some stragglers in the process; she would show the conductors the sign and a laminated pass and inform them that her tourists were entitled to travel free of charge; they would get off again at the point when the ensuing argument became boring, Clara vowing that the London Tourist Board would be avenged for the indignity.

From start to finish she kept up a running monologue, bizarre and almost entirely unscripted, gloved finger darting rapidly in this direction or that as inspiration seized her.

"We are now leaving Trafalgar Square. Keep in line! And keep your arms by your sides in case of dangerous machinery. Behind you is Nelson's Column. Don't look back, you will be turned into salt. He was a sailor. Political correctness forbids me to name his victories but he kicked the living shit out of a certain nation not far to the south. *A la derriere, le bon Lord Nelson, Mesdames, Messieurs, une pioneering pan-European et homme de la paix.* On our left now is the National Cheese Museum. Over yonder is Walpole's Winter Palace. His skull is kept there covered in gold. His penis is buried in a crypt beneath Westminster Abbey. Legend says it will rise again if England needs it. Coming up on the right now, the world's first Cotton Exchange, you could bring all your worn-out nighties here and swap them for new ones. Oh there is the international headquarters of the Tufty Club. Ooh, let's go down this way, this looks interesting. Follow me! Keep up! Stay in a crocodile! It is for your protection. I don't want to have to write to your parents. Not again, not after last time. Oh, that is Walpole's birthplace, take your hats off as you pass." She demonstrated and Miles followed suit, causing a chain reaction among others who were wearing hats down the line. "Over there is the house where Jerry Sadowitz shacked up with the young Polly Toynbee. It is said the bricks still glow from the heat of their copulation. In 1743 Handel bumped into Doctor Johnson on this corner and their wigs got mixed up. Johnson's head and wig were much bigger so Handel looked like a poodle for the rest of the day. Everyone laughed at him so he went home and wrote his oratorio, 'Can't Buy Me Love'. Meanwhile Johnson thought *his* head was swelling up even larger because of the tiny wig and that his brain was about to burst with all his knowledge, so in a panic set about *un*learning all the really useless things he knew, such as how to guess the weight of a goat by feeling its balls or the German word for humility ... That is a very interesting building but I don't have time to tell you ... Roger Bacon lived in that house. Contrary to popular misconception he did not invent bacon but he *did* invent the Roger. Prior to that husbands and wives just used to have to sit in a jacuzzi together and wriggle a bit and hope for the best. Roger Bannister lived in *that* house. He did not invent the bannister. He invented the four-minute mile. Let us walk faster in his honour. Pick your feet up. There is a pigeon! They are protected. Please do not shoot them without obtaining a licence. Only the Queen is allowed to do that. However you can bite their heads off on Tuesdays in Lent, a tradition whose origins are lost in the mists of time. Over there is the lamp-post that George Formby stood beneath in the film 'Aguirre, Wrath of God'. It is made out of a melted-down cannon captured in the Mechanoid War. Don't look back! Regrets are useless. Keep in a straight line. If I look round and you're not, there will be what for. Now what's down here? Let us see. Surely adventure lurks down every alley." Some bin-bags and then fairly quickly a dead end lurked down this particular alley. Clara tutted slightly as she realised this, then beckoned for her tourists to gather round. Then she pointed impressively and said, "James Boswell caught the clap for the first time against that wall. There was a blue plaque marking the spot but it cleared up after a couple of trips to the doctor." Miles said, "Wull I'll be darned," and took a picture of the wall. The Japanese man followed suit, and then an uncomprehending Dutch man who was nudged by his wife. "Time up!" barked Clara. "Turn around! Retrace your steps! Use your initiative! Wait for me at the street! Do not attempt to escape! ... Now re-form an orderly crocodile like good tourists. That is more like a salamander. I should leave you to die. Now we will go this way. Hurry, hurry! Halt," she suddenly said just as they'd started hurrying after her again, stopping dead and causing everyone to bump into everyone else. "Does everyone have a clean handkerchief? You may use them now if you wish, there will be no time later." People looked at each other. "*Pardon*?" said a voice. "Too late," said Clara, setting off again, "time up. Follow me. Hurry, hurry! Pick your trotters up. Let's go this way. We are getting to the good bits now. Cameras ready. There are parts we normally hide from foreigners out of spite but you shall see them all, my bonnies. At a ball in that house Florence Nightingale was goosed by Alfred Lord Tennyson and Lily Langtry caused a sensation by showing off a steam-powered bra. Many were killed in the stampede. Boswell used to score with a lady in that house. De Quincey used to score in that house. Handel used to score in that house. Boswell caught crabs down that alley. Since we joined the EU only Spanish fishermen are allowed to trawl there now. That house was built by Jacob Rothschild out of the proceeds of his cream-cracker monopoly. Speaking of which I once had a hotel on this street and my dad kept landing on it. I ended up with all the money in the box *and* IOUs, which I then traded for *real sweets*. That is true. Try telling the youngsters today that, they don't want to know. Walpole built this house out of the ground-down skulls of dead foreigners, ha. *That* house is made entirely out of Lego. It was captured in Denmark during the Napoleonic wars and reassembled here brick by brick. ... That is the Leper Hospital, count your fingers before you leave. That is the Inland Revenue, count your fingers before you leave. This magnificent building on your right is the British Embassy. The foundations were laid around 1210 and it was completed by 1805, which I call a solid afternoon's work. Here is the Old Jokes Home. Coming up on your left the Home for Fallen Women. Also laid in 1210, quicker if you gave them sweets. The Home for Slightly Stooped Women on the other side, a good place to pick up a hunchback.

The Home for Wobbling Women coming up, if you have an inner ear disorder or your high heels are malfunctioning you can stay there for free. The London Mushroom Exchange. The Earwax Museum, where the aural secretions of some of our greatest men and women are preserved. Sir Joseph Banks kept a hippopotamus in that house, his wife never found out. The Royal Society of Zoophiles coming up now. The Pot-holing Society on our left. Enter via this manhole. The London Society of Sodomites, enter round the back. The National Domino Federation, we must knock as we pass." She knocked on the door as she passed and they all followed suit. "I could keep this up all day, Tourist No. 1, I hope we don't run out of buildings. The Charwoman Martyrs were shot in that square in 1830, complaining that their knees were playing up and they'd been on the go all day. A statue of Irene Handl, disguised as a man on a horse. She was Handel's mother twice removed. My dad met her once. This was *before* we played Monopoly. I will be testing you on this later. That is a British postbox. Gaze on it and weep. Robin Hood hid behind it once. His hat stuck out. James Boswell lurked behind that lamp-post once, scouting for whores. His willy stuck out. It is thought that when Boswell first approached Dr. Johnson he had mistaken him for a gigantic bad-tempered whore. Johnson for his part mistook Boswell for the parish pump ... This eminent building coming up now contains Walpole's shoe-horn collection, he bequeathed it to a grateful nation on his ... Nelson's Column! What the hell is that doing here? Arse. London is the city of many surprises. Nelson's Column again, ladies and gentlemen, Mesdames et Messieurs, Schweinhunden und Damen. See how the shadow has inched around the square since we left. It was designed like that by Isambard Kingdom Hospital. The tour is not over! We are merely passing through. Do not attempt to escape! There are snipers on the roof-tops." Some of the tourists did in fact sneak off but she picked up more in passing. "Keep to the crocodile! Now is the time of maximum danger. Over there is the Plinth of the Invisible Soldier. He is riding a Stealth Horse and probably has your grandfather impaled on a big sword. ...We are now proceeding down a street whose name is too famous for me to bother to tell you. You can read, can't you? Over there is Walpole's birth-place. Take your hats off!" she barked, and those with hats complied. "Put your hands on your hearts and sing or hum the Walpole song if you know it." She put her hand over her own heart and sang, *"O Walpole father of our nation, strike our foes with your mighty sword."* Miles and the Japanese man obligingly tried to pick up the awful tune and hum along. "Enough! Hats back on! Pick your feet up! If you aren't in a crocodile when I look round I will know the reason why. Hurry! Down this way. No, on second thoughts not that way, that is certain death. This way! You there, are you more tourists? Join on behind, quick. Faster, walk faster! And keep your ears open. On the left, Bleak House, as featured in Charles Dickens's novel 'Barnaby Rudge'. Looming up behind that is the prison where naughty tourists who violate the bylaws are sent. Gaze on it and quail. I will be putting in a report about you afterwards. Coming up on the right is Walpole's birthplace. So is the house behind it. The infant Walpole was born seven times out of seven different women to give him extra strength. Hats off! On again! Off again! *O Walpole, father of our nation ...*

"Cleopatra's Needle!" she barked presently on the Victoria Embankment, pausing a moment and allowing her flock to gather round. "It is seven cubits high if it is an inch. It was made by druids out of an unknown stone that is really tough and durable and easy to wipe down. Watch what happens when I try to bite it." She put her teeth on a corner. "Nothing. You try." Miles tried to bite Cleopatra's Needle too. "See? Your teeth will break first. At night it always points directly towards the third notch in Orion's belt. Dan Brown readers won't need me to point out the Masonic significance. In the 1947 film 'The Gusset Thieves' Diana Dors ties a little boy's shoelaces here. Incidentally if you ever need your own shoelaces tying and are weighed down by shopping you can ask any policeman and they'll be more than happy to oblige." This was something she had planned to say and she repeated translations she had memorized in five languages. "A tradition whose origins are lost in the mists of time. Tip them with silver and rub their hats for luck." She looked round and pointed at the river. "That is the Thames. It would win a fight against any of your foreign rivers. At the inauguration of the Shitfire Club Walpole swam the river on his back here, with a whore on his stomach and Boswell on the whore. They all woke up on a dike in Holland. Re-form the crocodile!" she suddenly snapped, instantly moving off again. "Onwards, onwards! Hurry! Vite! Schnell! Pacey-pacey! Shake the lead out, grandpa!"

A couple of winded and footsore tourists did not follow but stayed by the monument panting and loosening shoes.

"Some are left behind," ventured an anxious voice in the crocodile.

"Leave them! It is Darwinism in action. I am coddling you enough. The weak and slowcoach among you might be better off in a more boring city such as Brussels next year. Hurry! There is not enough time. The developers never sleep. Soon this will all be giant glass penises as far as the eye can see. Look! That concrete abortion there was Anne Boleyn's cottage until last week. Hurry, hurry! Faster! Halt!" Again the line banged into each other as she came to a sudden stop. "Are your shoelaces tied properly? I could get done by the Health and Safety. Check, check!

Regardez le trotters! Too late, you'll have to ask a policeman. Onwards, onwards! Hurry! Leave the weak! I have not the faintest clue where I am now thanks to your whining. This looks like a likely direction ... Walpole punched a bear in this street. It had looked at him funny. Kind of man he was ... Oh! Look! Shh!"

There was a long-haired, long-bearded tramp sitting on the pavement, staring unseeingly into vacancy. Clara signalled a halt, put her fingers to her lips, beckoned her charges to gather round.

"That is the holiest man in Britain," she whispered. "He has sat there rain and shine for as long as anyone can remember. He is the Queen's cousin and was a famous soldier, much decorated. He had palaces, concubines, motor cars, but he gave it all up to contemplate the mysteries of the universe. We should try not to disturb him out of respect; but he will not see us anyway. People leave him offerings of food and drink, but no-one has ever seen him take any. He has not moved or spoken a word for twenty years."

"Change," said the tramp as she started to tip-toe past.

"A miracle!" cried Clara. "A sign!" She knelt and bowed to him. Miles and then the Japanese man and then several others followed suit. "Give him an offering! Give him your money!" she instructed rising. Miles set an example and soon notes and coins were raining down on the tramp's groundsheet.

"You are blessed, blessed!" cried Clara as she led them onwards. "This is something to tell your grandchildren, assuming the world doesn't end now. A welcome word indeed. Change, change! We must all change! Change is coming! This may be the sign I have been waiting for. I would give up my job and make a start at once, if I didn't have to look after you and I knew how to make bombs. Walpole's Autumn Mansion. It can sink into the ground when attacked. Hurry, hurry! And stay in a line. We are a crocodile. You are the tail, I am the head. Look at my bitey teeth!" She bit the air several times. "Walk faster at the back there! Keep up! You will get lost without me. This is London. A man can lose himself in London. *Loo-hoo-hooose himself in Landon!* Oh, Christ, is that Nelson's Column again? How is that possible? Arse. Extremely fat arse. Slip me the A to Z, Tourist No. 1, for the love of God. *Mesdames, Messieurs, regardez le Column du Nelson encore temps. Damen und Herren, ich regret zu informen sie das wir sind in einem Rekursiv-Loop getrappt und werden getötet sein.* No-one panic. These streets are designed as a maze to fool invaders. I am in full control. Do not try to escape! We are just passing through. It is certain death to leave the crocodile. Look, there are some policemen, they will get you. Oh, British police! Quick, get your cameras. Be discreet, or they will feel shy and run back to the safety of their car. Observe, ladies and gentlemen, their traditional British uniforms of piss-yellow plastic visibility jackets. A team of modern artists laboured for fifteen years to make them look so hideous. The British police force is recruited exclusively from timorous wimps who are scared of being knocked over. We are now leaving Trafalgar Square. Don't look back! We will be around again shortly no doubt. It is said that all roads lead to Trafalgar Square …

" … Piccadilly Circus! Picture if you will the roaring crowds, the sun glinting on bronze, the lions, the quaking gladiators, the sudden splash of blood on sand. Now the chariot races are re-enacted daily. All hold hands as we cross the road! If one dies, we all die, you wouldn't want to live with the survivor guilt.

" … Ah! Observe these hooded youths. They are the Slouching Monks, a very holy sect who are regenerating Britain. See how they spit on the pavement to demonstrate their renunciation of the physical realm. Watch as they make their pilgrimage into the lofty temple of Gameworld … "

Sometimes Clara became excited enough by her favourite places or some chain of association to try to do things properly for a bit, thinking this was a job she might like for real; but it never lasted long.

"Soho! Greek Street! Soho Square! Max Beerbohm parted from Enoch Soames here! De Quincey met Ann here. That is true. She was a whore but a nice one. He fainted on *that step*, I think, and she revived him! We must play that some time, Tourist No. 1, it will be an excuse for you to wear your romantic poet shirt … There are still plenty of whores around these parts now if you keep your eyes peeled … That woman's a whore!" she cried presently, pointing at a woman standing in a doorway smoking a fag who might just conceivably have been a whore or might just have been someone smoking a fag. "That woman's a whore!" she cried pointing at someone who was quite definitely just a waitress. "That woman's a whore!" she cried pointing at a passer-by with a load of shopping. "*That* woman will show you her bum for ten pence. Any male tourists who are looking for a little extra-marital walalawoola, see me afterwards. Or you can just go into any restaurant around here and ask for the special and wink. If you are Japanese, schoolgirls with big eyes are ravished by octopuses in *that* house every night … *That* woman's a whore …

"Charing Cross Road! As featured in the film '11 Harrowhouse'. Charing Cross! Oh! Oh! I really really do know this one. Halt! Gather round! Pin your ears back. Listen and I will tell you why it is called Charing Cross. There was a Norman king, Edward the First if memory serves, and his beloved wife died, Eleanor of Castile I think, and he was grief-stricken. There was a big funeral procession and he erected crosses wherever her body rested on its route to Westminster Abbey. And the last one was here and they called it the Chère Reine Cross. Do you get it? Chère Reine," she said to a Frenchwoman.

"Chère Reine? Dear Queen?" said the Frenchwoman.

"Yes! Correct! You win! You are a – my stickers! I forgot my stickers!" Clara produced a large round yellow printed sticker from her pocket, peeled it and slapped it on the French woman's lapel. It read: 'I am a GOOD Tourist!' "Chère Reine Cross! In time it became Charing Cross because it is effeminate to pronounce foreign languages properly, but it is really Dear Queen Cross in honour of his beloved dead queen. And that is true. Isn't that sweet? Would you do that for me, Tourist No. 1, if we were married and I croaked?"

Miles removed his cap and drawled, "Wull Ma'am, I surely – "

"Oh *far* too late, the moment has passed. Onwards! Back in the crocodile! Hurry! Leave the weak! Obviously you would commemorate me by sleeping with a whore everywhere my body rested. That woman's a whore! So is *that* one! And all the bookshops in this street are secretly run by dominatrixes. Just go in and wink and say you want something difficult and uncompromising in a leather binding …

"Nelson's Column! Mother of Arse. Hold me, Tourist No. 1, I am scared. I have seen the wretched man's column more often than Lady Hamilton did. No-one panic! This is the *other* Nelson's Column. We are making progress."

They were not to make much more for a bit, however. As they hurtled across Trafalgar Square a man who had joined the back of the crocodile somewhere after their last visit there, a Frenchman Clara thought, came sprinting to overtake her and implored, "Please, we arrest one minute, I would like photographs," pointing to his camera and the Column and the buildings. Clara glared and was about to tear a strip off him when she saw that Tourist No. 2, the Japanese man, whom she had decided was a little treasure, was also nodding and smiling and pointing to his camera. Besides she supposed she wouldn't mind resting her feet and mouth for a minute too.

"Very well," she barked. "There will be a two minute pause to take pictures. Do not wander off. And don't use all your film. I can show you much better things than this. You haven't seen Walpole's Summer Gazebo yet. Tourist No. 1 is responsible for ensuring no-one gets away. If they do he will be punished."

Her tourists started to snap pictures. The Frenchman's camera was very professional-looking; he had three different long lenses about him and mounted it on a lightweight tripod he had had slung on his back. Clara rolled her eyes and tapped a foot. "I said two minutes," she reminded him. "We are losing momentum." She strolled off to glower warningly at someone she thought was trying to sneak away from the tour.

A nondescript middle-aged man appeared from somewhere dressed in some kind of uniform and cap and the inevitable yellow plastic high-visibility jacket. He bent to the French photographer and spoke interrogatively. The Frenchman looked blank and shrugged and pointed to Clara.

Clara went over. "What's the matter?"

"He say I need permission."

"He needs permission to take pictures in the Square," confirmed the official.

"What? Who are you? Where are you from? What the hell are you talking about?" she demanded. "Oh – because of the kiddies around, I suppose," she groaned. "You're disgusting!" she exploded. "You're a disgusting little – " An idea struck her. "Oh! Oh! I get it! Just because there are Japanese and Belgians in my tour group you assume they are paedophiles! You racist! You appalling racist bigot! I shall report you! Did you hear that, tourists? What's your name? What's your number? I shall report you, you dreadful little man! The London Tourist Board will get you!"

The man held up his hands to try and staunch the flow. "No, no, no. The fact is they *do* need parents' permission if there are any children in their pictures. You might remind them of that or they could be arrested or have their cameras confiscated. But that's nothing to do with me. *My* problem is him. Professional photographers have to purchase a permit to take commercial photos in the Square. I was just making sure that – "

Clara gaped. "You are jesting, of course. It's a public square! It's a national landmark! Are you trying to license reality?"

He did the blocking gesture with his hands again. "I'm just doing my job."

"The 'I was only obeying orders' of the 21st century," said Clara with contempt. "You don't *have* to do your job. You *enjoy* doing your job, you ghastly jumped-up little nothing. Anyway he isn't a bleeding commercial photographer, he's a tourist, he is in my crocodile and under my protection."

She put a hand on the Frenchman and glared.

"And who are you?" asked the jobsworth. "I've never seen you before."

Clara banged her sign on the ground angrily and briefly flashed her laminated pass.

"What's that? Let me see." The man tried to inspect the pass more closely, and she suspected it would not bear closer inspection.

"It is laminated," she pointed out sulkily, snatching it away, and turned her back on him. "This is all nonsense. I don't believe you about the permit. That would not go on in a civilised country. You have clearly made it up as an excuse." Her tourists had gathered round curiously. She pointed at the jobsworth. "Did you hear that, tourists? This man won't let you take pictures. He thinks just because you are foreigners you must be paedophiles or terrorists. *Lui pense vous est le kiddy-fiddlers. Diese kleine Adolf gethinken sie sind kinderschtuppenlieben. Il bastardo animale pensa tu fungula la bambino*. What do you think of that?"

"Wull I guess I oughta slug him in the jaw," drawled Miles squaring up to the man.

"We *all* ought to slug him in the jaw, my simple-minded Columbian friend!" said Clara. "The world would be a much happier place if we all slugged these little parasites in the jaw whenever they annoy useful people with their inane yap."

"Calm down. You've got hold of the wrong end of the stick," protested the official, retreating a step before the muttering outraged tourists. "Now let me see your – "

"*Que pasa*?" asked a monolingual Spanish woman of her husband. He explained for her, or at least he told her what Clara had told them, with hand-gestures and indignation. The woman sucked her breath in and then shrieked and took a shoe off and started to beat the official over the head with the heel of it.

Clara watched wide-eyed a moment, then joined in, kicking the man in the arse as he cringed away from the Spanish woman's blows. Miles meanwhile shadow-boxed around him slowly and drawled, "Come on then, son, let's you and me go a few rounds, whaddaya say." Other tourists jeered and barracked the man multilingually and shook their fists.

"Attack!" cried Clara, bashing him with her sign. "Attack, my valiant globetrotters! Kick him! Kill him! Take his magic yellow jacket and render him powerless!" Miles started to grow nervous and to look around for policemen. The official fled properly. He had his head crooked trying to talk into a walkie-talkie at his shoulder but an early blow of Clara's had broken it. She held the Spanish woman's arm in the air like a boxing referee proclaiming a winner and, as the other tourists cheered, slapped a 'GOOD Tourist' sticker on her. Then she cried, "Flee!" and set an example by running like hell.

"Flee! Schnell! Run for your lives! Save yourselves! Leave the weak! If they catch you you will be sent to the Naughty Tourists' Home and then deported. It will be certain death to return to Trafalgar Square ever in our lives. The photo police never forget! ... Re-form the crocodile!" she barked when they were some way out of the Square. "That is what happens when you leave the crocodile or slow down for a moment, predators strike. Hurry. Onwards. Pick your feet up. You all did very well, however. I am proud of you. Really, ladies and gentlemen, I do apologise. I am truly embarrassed. It's all right for you, I have to *live* here. What you have to bear in mind is that we invented freedom. It is only natural we should get tired of the thing before you lesser breeds. Really you ought to quarantine us like lepers lest we infect you with our madness. Only for a few years. An uprising is coming soon and we will hang them all. I will show you some of the lamp-posts I have picked out. And perhaps, if we have time, Wembley Stadium, one day to be the site of a great national cleansing. But it is not all our own fault. There are enemies without who must be dealt with as well. Those of you with the misfortune to live in Brussels should move or start digging holes. Really, what has happened to us? I am so ashamed. Why have you even come to this wretched place? We should ban tourists for very shame until we have got our house in order. Really, you ought to invade us. We are rubbish now. You will never have a better chance to avenge all the total arse-kickings we've handed you over the years. Of course the EU *is* your revenge. That isn't your fault, you are good tourists. We all ought to get together against all of the parasites and institutional bullies like we did just now. I've had it up to here! I've had enough! I've had enough!" Suddenly she stopped and hurled her bearskin hat to the ground and started to jump up and down on it. "To hell with this country and to hell with the London Tourist Board!"

The tourists exchanged glances.

"Now slow down there, sister," drawled Miles.

"Fuck off! I'm emigrating! Jeremiah's right, why doesn't the bloody Queen do something? She has abandoned her children. What we need is a War Queen, and I know just the girl ... " She punted her hat along the pavement. "Let's start! Let's start now! Let's really, really do it!" She pointed to the nearest building and addressed her startled, uncomprehending or half-comprehending tourists. "Let's smash some windows! Most fun part of the tour! Anyone who smashes a window shall have a Good Tourist sticker and a free pass to Tussaud's! Smashez la Fenêtre! *Smashez la Fenêtre*," she sang to the tune of the Marseillaise. There was no response. She could see nothing convenient to hurl through a window by way of demonstration. She sighed and subsided. "Never mind. Re-form the crocodile! Schnell, schnell! Give us me hat back, Tourist No. 2, chuck. I have had a better idea than armed insurrection. I will take you all for ice-cream! Tourist No. 1 will pay as he is a moneybags American." She fitted her battered busby back on and led them off.

Some of the ungrateful bastards escaped while she was treating them to ice-cream, and just as she was growing fond of them too, but she managed to capture some new ones near the van. The crocodile reformed and rocketed off again.

"Hurry, hurry! History waits for no man! Revisionists never sleep! Everything will be dull and bland by the time we get there. That is the Russell Hotel!" she cried pointing. It wasn't, that was bloody miles away. "*Up, up, up past the Russell Hotel*," she sang, smiling at them over her shoulder, "as featured in T.S. Eliot's poem 'Burnt Norton'. Over there is where they burnt Norton, in the Badminton Trials of the 16th century, for his heretical proposition that Liz the First should come back to his place. That is the oldest manhole cover in London. It dates from 1976. All the previous ones were torn up and used as frisbees during the Lipton Tea Riots of 1975. Walk faster! Stay in a line! ... "

"Oh!" she cried, suddenly screeching to a halt in front of a very august-looking building not far from Buckingham Palace, which she had waved at dismissively from a distance but not visited because she was currently annoyed with the Queen for not leading a revolution and it was too famous to tell lies about. "Oh! Look, look! Halt! Careful where you stand! You are in luck!" With her white-gloved hand she pointed at half a dozen or so nuggets of dog poo on the pavement and then at the building behind them. "This is the Queen's corgi barracks! The Royal Corgis are kept here! *Les Corgis, mesdames, messieurs! Das Kleineschweinebeine-zeinehunden.* Breakfast," she called to a Korean couple. "The Queen's famous corgis. This is their royal spoor. It is considered extremely fortunate to see it."

"Wull I'll be darned," said Miles taking a picture of the turds. The Japanese man followed suit and then a couple of others.

"It is rare to find them before the collectors do. People scour these streets three times a day. On the open markets these stools will fetch anything up to £50 each. If anyone wants to take one I don't want to know about it but cut me in later. Who can tell me the names of the Queen's corgis?"

"Wull let me see now," said Miles amiably. "Isn't it Dasher, Prancer... "

"Quite right, the important ones are named Dasher, Prancer, Terry, Beulah, Gripper, Ziggy and Norman. They have their own cartoon show and patriotic citizens will often name their children after them. You are a good tourist," she said giving Miles a sticker. "The rest of you should have been turned back at Heathrow," she added with a glare. "But there are hundreds of spare ones too, and they all live in there. There are rumours of terrible orgies involving French poodles. The corgis have sacred status in London and they take advantage sometimes. They swagger around the streets stealing sausages from people's shopping baskets and no-one can stop them. You just have to smile at them and pray it ends there. They are a lot like the government really. But I mustn't start that again. Enough! Time up! Re-form the crocodile. If you wanted to stare at turds all day you should have gone to Brussels.

" … This is St. James's Park, where the Queen lays her eggs."

Silent for once and frowning, Clara led her crocodile unusually slowly through St. James's Park by a meandering route for a while. She stopped near the lake and tapped a finger meditatively on her lips for a moment. "It was here," she said at last. "Exactly here." She blew her whistle and glared. "Attention! Gather round." When they had assembled about her in a semi-circle she said, "We came here on a school trip to London when I was ten. It was on this spot," she pointed to the ground, "that I saw a pelican swallow a duck. I have never really recovered. I doubt the duck did either, and it can't have done the pelican much good. The duck – exactly like the one you see there – " she pointed to a duck and they all swivelled their heads to look, "had done absolutely *nothing* to the pelican – that is a pelican there – " they swivelled their heads again as she pointed at a pelican, "in fact for all I know that may well be the culprit. The pelican was just being greedy. It kept the duck in its crop for about ten minutes before swallowing it. The duck twitched but was silent, but that was worse in its way than if we had heard some lonely echoing quack. We could see a foot and some feathers sticking out. It was as if two birds had been horribly melded together, a thing beyond our infant imagining. The pelican kept making sort of sneezing sounds before it finally got it down. We ate our sandwiches and watched. I do not remember that anyone spoke. What could words possibly say?"

She strode off a few paces, beckoning them with her white-gloved finger. They followed. She pointed at a bin. "When we had finished our packed lunches we disposed of our rubbish in that bin. Jason Wild dropped his mum's camera in too by mistake. Whether his wits had been disordered by the duck-pelican incident I do not presume to say. There was at all times a magnificent carefree quality about Jason Wild and he had a gift for doing the unexpected. He only discovered his error when we had reached Westminster Abbey. Miss O'Neill detached Mr. Rose from the main body of our expedition and ordered him to accompany Jason to retrace our steps and retrieve the camera. They found it quickly, but then Mr. Rose also took the opportunity to go to the pub. He bought Jason a lemonade and gave him 50p and a cake not to tell Miss O'Neill. And that is true."

Miles stepped forward and took a picture of the bin. The Japanese man joined him. Clara posed for them solemnly pointing into it, and then with one foot on it and her chin on her hand, looking thoughtful. Then she made poses pointing at a duck and then a pelican and they photographed those too. "I would arrange a tableau with duck *and* pelican but that would be asking for trouble," she said. A few other people photographed the birds. Others looked frankly baffled. One Dutch man took a picture of the bin just in case, then riffled through an English-Dutch dictionary and then a London guide book, frowning.

"I could stay here all day musing, but I suppose we should move on," said Clara pensively. She waved a hand at the water. "That is Lake Jennifer. It is said that whoever dips his shoe in the waters will surely return to London one day."

Miles amiably slipped a shoe off, hobbled to the lake, scooped up some water with it, emptied it out and put the shoe back on again. "Wull I guess I'm coming back," he said. Grinning, the Japanese man followed suit, and then one other man. A few others gingerly dipped toes or heels in without taking their shoes off.

Clara, who had been staring at a pelican in an intense reverie, suddenly snapped out of it and looked at them in surprise. "Of course in reality it more often leads to ringworm and a species of foot-rot," she said. "The London Tourist Board will refund any medical bills." She blew her whistle. "Crocodile! Onwards!"

Momentum! Momentum! Impetus! She knew this was the key. Now she had to build it up again before they could get to some of the good bits they had planned. The tourists must be pulled along irresistibly and unstoppably in her wake like the tail of a comet. When the momentum was built up, when the Stockholm Syndrome had set in, when they were half-stunned and hypnotised by her litany of half-comprehended nonsense, when they had ceased to question her or blink at anything, then, then …

" … This is London's famous Welshtown. It is currently Welsh New Year. They celebrate by running through the streets naked firing arrows at helium balloons to which kittens have been tied. Come back tonight if you wish to be traumatized.

" … prior to the Restoration Charles II hid behind that hedge, playing peek-a-boo with an entirely unresponsive child … "

" … During the Gordon's Gin Riots Walpole pulled a man's head off and threw it," she raised on tiptoe and pointed, "all the way over that wall." Miles and the Japanese man raised on tiptoe to try and see over the wall and snap photos.

"We are now entering the notorious Midget Ghetto," she announced as they entered a quiet residential street, slowing her pace and lowering her voice and looking round conspiratorially. She indicated a short height off the ground with a flattened hand. "*Les Dwarfs. Das Diddymen.* Keep your voices down so as not to attract attention. Shh!" She laid a finger on her lips and then indicated the houses warningly. "And we must crouch down in case they stone us. Ladies, *Mesdames*, *Damen*, please take your high heels off." She demonstrated with her own shoes. "Quick, quick! They will think we are taunting them." Most of the high-heel wearers had already dropped out due to the unrelenting pace but those remaining puzzledly complied. Clara led her tourists along the street, tip-toeing stealthily and barefoot and bent almost double. "Shh! Quiet! And crouch, crouch, stoop! Heads down! Like that man!" She pointed at Miles who was practically waddling along the pavement. "He is the best tourist yet again! And he is the second best," she said of the Japanese man who was again imitating Miles. "Do what they do! And keep your voices down. They are grumpy if woken in the daytime. They have been up all night at the circus, or making toys." The entire crocodile proceeded along the street hunched down and with cautious silence.

Fortuitously a very short man came around the corner at the end of the street just before they reached it: not a midget, but a little, wizened, bad-tempered-looking old man, well-dressed, carrying a silver-topped cane and wearing a coat with an astrakhan collar. Perhaps not unnaturally he stopped in surprise at the spectacle before him and glared his displeasure.

"It is the King of the Midgets!" cried Clara in terror. "Forgive us, Your Majesty!" she begged, bowing so deeply as to touch the ground with her hat. "Flee!" she told her charges, running helter-skelter into a little park on the other side of the road.

Not long after on the other side of it, having reassembled the crocodile, still navigating a backwater warren of leafy, spacious residential streets, she halted as they reached a little street with gates on the end of it, standing open.

"There is a £20 supplement for this part of the tour," she announced.

Miles amiably and quickly handed over a note. She held it up to the light, bit it, and stowed it in the wrist of a glove. "No-one else?" The other tourists were still frowning at each other dubiously or consulting wallets in indecision. "Very well," said Clara instantly, taking Miles by the hand and pulling him along the street. "Wait there. Do not move."

They waited. They saw Clara and Miles disappear around a corner.

Two minutes later they appeared again, emerging out of a different side-street not far behind the group, walking as briskly as ever to rejoin them. Clara was buttoning up her blouse and Miles was buttoning up his trousers. He had a thoughtful, faraway look in his eye.

"Wull I'll be darned," he said.

Clara patted her hair and slapped another 'I am a GOOD Tourist!' sticker on his chest.

"Onwards! Re-form the crocodile! You will never know what happened down *that* street," she told them smugly.

They passed through a little square with a rather stunted apple-tree in it.

"That is the Tree of Knowledge! It was brought back by Crusaders from the Garden of Eden in the 12th century. It produces fruit once every hundred years. On the last occasion there was a big debate on what to do with the apple. It was finally decided that celebrity chef Delia Smith would bake it on live television and then serve slices to a panel consisting of three well-known personalities and three members of the public who had won a competition in which they had to complete the line 'I would like to know everything because … ' in twelve words or less." Clara led them to circle the tree while she improvised. "In the event they all agreed that knowledge tasted bitter. Delia apologised but was obviously hurt. She served tangerine and prosciutto on crackers to take the taste away. It was too late. The celebrities were consumed by awareness of their own mediocrity and destroyed utterly. One of the ordinary Joes realised he had never truly loved and subsequently entered a monastery or a whorehouse or something. Another just sat there grinning manically at the screen going, 'Go on then, ask me any capital city in the world.' The third attained total comprehension of the universe and died of ennui live on camera. There were letters of complaint to the BBC. His final words were, 'The only thing I *don't* understand now is the ticket pricing on British railways.' Onwards! Out! Hurry!"

She called a halt again at the head of another pleasant but unexceptional-looking side-street.

"There is a £20 supplement for going down this street too," she said.

Miles and half a dozen other male tourists instantly produced money.

"Come along then," she said snatching it, eyes lighting up. "Cheapskates remain there until we return."

She led the seven who had paid the surcharge along the street, around a corner, and down the next street. It was utterly ordinary and she led the expectant group along it in complete silence until, just before turning a final corner and rejoining the rest of the group, she waved negligently at the last house in the terrace and said, "That is Walpole's Easter Pavilion."

Momentum, momentum! King Alfred punched a bear here. George Orwell punched a Buddhist there. Virginia Woolf felt a bit sad on this corner. Emily Pankhurst chained herself to those railings and was rogered silly by King Edward. Karl Marx died in that house although his brain is thought to still live in a bunker beneath the BBC. A boy ripped his T-shirt on *this* bush and Vivienne Westwood saw it and went, 'Wow!' Jack the Ripper used to entertain urchins by making newspaper ladders here.

Handel lived there. Holst lived there. Holst wanted to be friends with Handel and sent him some of his work but he rejected his overtures. Boswell caught his willy in that letter-box one night when the whores had gone on strike. Bernard Shaw lived in that house. He once slid down the bannister and went flying off and got his head stuck through the transom. Oscar Wilde was passing by and annoyed Shaw by cutting off a bit of his beard while he was stuck there and wearing it as a buttonhole. It started a fashion among dandies and Shaw had to have his beard fenced off to protect it. Whistler's Mother lived in that house. Gainsborough's Blue Boy lived in that house. Bacon's Screaming Pope lived in *that* house. Dame Edith Sitwell lived next door and used to knock and complain about the noise. 'Could you not scream at all hours?' she would say. 'But Francis Bacon keeps looking at me,' the Pope replied. Ironically given her name Edith was unable to sit well as she was born with only one buttock. She had to have a specially made bicycle and was unable to slide down bannisters. Nor was she able to shit well. Roger Bannister performed his four-minute mile here, pursued by a bear. Edith Sitwell punched it. Hurry, hurry! Much more to see ...

When both she and the tourists had got into a rhythm she marched them up the steps of a house picked at random, rang the bell and rapped smartly on the knocker. While they waited a few moments she kept up a fluent stream of knowledgeable nonsense about the houses across the street.

"Ah, at last," she said when the door was opened, pushing past the man who had answered it and going in, followed by Miles and then the Japanese man and then the rest of the line. "Follow me! Hurry, hurry! Keep to the crocodile! This is the most famous house in London."

"What the hell's going on?" yelled the homeowner, barged and jostled aside and trying to squeeze past an interminable stream of tourists in the hall to get to Clara.

"London Tourist Board, official tour coming through," Clara told him airily, leading the way into the living room.

"This is my house!" he shouted, fighting his way after her.

"Not any more it isn't, didn't you get the compulsory purchase order?" Clara glanced around the room with distaste. They were in rather a nice neighbourhood but she had to say this house was a bit of a pigsty. The owner himself was dressed in underpants, vest, and loosely-tied dressing gown even though it was the middle of the day, and his hair was tousled as though he had recently got up. She gestured around at what looked like the wreckage of a party or conceivably just evidence of prolonged bachelor living. "This room has been preserved exactly as it was since Jimi Hendrix overdosed here in 1970." The name Hendrix reverberated with recognition down the line. Miles and the Japanese man and several others started to photograph everything in sight. Clara elbowed past the expostulating owner and led the way into the kitchen. "However the building has many more claims to fame than that. The garden was planted by Capability Brown in 1768. The gazebo was the site of a ritual murder in which both Aphra Behn and John Wesley Harding were implicated." She tried the back door. It was locked. "As you see it is currently closed to visitors as the Royal Peacocks are nesting there. You can just make out the eggs in the far corner," she added as she glimpsed some croquet balls. Photos were taken through the window. "You can't just – " said the owner. Clara pushed past him and opened a pantry-cupboard door, gesturing with a gloved hand. "A simple serving maid, Kate Winslet, hid Bonnie Prince Neville in here while the Leavisites scoured the country looking for him. He would have crouched just where that vacuum cleaner stands. It was designed by Sir Alec Issigonis who also lived here. In the 1970s the three Blue Peter presenters kidnapped by the Animal Liberation Front were imprisoned in there. While negotiations proceeded the Blue Peter pets had to present the show, barking and mewing strident manifestos. The three hostages were brainwashed by their captors and helped to make bombs out of washing-up liquid bottles and sticky-back plastic." She closed the closet. She opened the fridge. "I would not like to say when that yoghurt dates from," she said severely. She turned and looked the owner up and down and waved a hand at him. "The house was originally built for one of Charles II's mistresses. The curator is wearing the authentic regalia in which the monarch would have appeared to her. The vest is an exact replica down to the tomato sauce stains we have Pepys's authority for. The Donald Duck underpants are the closest we can approximate to the king's embroidered swan-motif breeks. The ratty-looking dressing-gown is genuine and quite priceless. The fluffy slippers are just unfortunate." The hapless homeowner backed away and held up an arm as he was bombarded by camera flashes. Clara led her swarm into the hall. She pointed at the phone stand and said, "Sheraton," then led the way upstairs. She roamed around opening doors. She decided the main bedroom was too grim to show them but led them into a spare one and told them Johnson and Boswell had shot peas at passers-by from the window while out of their faces on laudanum. Then she opened the bathroom and showed them the bath where the tyrant Livingstone had been stabbed to death by Charlotte Church and from which Walpole had leapt crying 'Eureka!' after inventing the submarine while playing with himself. Then she opened an airing cupboard and commented, "Look at the state of his towels." Miles and the Japanese man ran amok photographing them. She led the front of the crocodile downstairs again, en route pushing past the tail of it still coming up and grabbing the speechless owner, who had been trying to fight his way past them.

"For God's sake tidy the place and smarten yourself up next time," she told him sotto voce in the hall. "I covered for you this time but in future I'll have to report you." She extracted the £160 she had collected earlier from her glove and shoved it into his hand. "There'll be another tour through tomorrow. Have jelly ready as per the letter or you'll lose the contract."

She patted him on the cheek and led the crocodile out.

Speed, speed! Speed and brazenness and looking as though it was the most natural thing in the world. A while later in a busier thoroughfare she led them unhesitatingly down the steps of a public urinal set under the street. "As you can see this dates from Victorian times," she said casually as she led the way past a trio of extremely startled urinators. "That man's a whore," she said pointing at them, "that man's a whore. That man's a horse." She led them along a row of toilet cubicles and into, as many of them as could crowd in, an empty one at the end. "This was Churchill's secret war-bog. The ceiling is reinforced ferro-concrete. A network of tunnels now blocked off led from Downing Street. If you look down the toilet you can just make out the steel mesh net that was put into place to protect against frogmen." She rapped on the partition of the adjoining, occupied cubicle, from which could be heard the sound of two low, nervous voices. "Alanbrooke used to sit in there and give him the daily situation reports and read him bits from Beachcomber. He was proud to record that no matter how bad the news was Churchill never stayed longer than usual and he heard only a slow, measured, sedate, stately plopping. Oh that is a penis," she said pointing at some graffiti. "Churchill almost certainly didn't draw it. The line of the hairs on the bollocks seem to suggest an early work by one of the Vorticist school." Miles and the Japanese man took pictures, the latter with a flash. The muttering in the next stall got more urgent.

In the next street she led them through revolving doors into an office lobby, pointed at an apparently blank and unremarkable ceiling, said, "I'm sure I don't have to tell you about this," and then led them out again. She led them into a big department store, up an escalator to the second floor, down the other and out, saying only, "The original site of Wimbledon. There's not much there now but you can say you've done it."

It was a dream of total power and freedom. Access all areas! "I am sure, Tourist No. 1," she murmured to Miles, "that with a sufficient head of steam I could lead some of them on a smash-and-grab raid telling them it is an old English custom." From time to time after a particularly improbable disquisition she would hear one of the less browbeaten, less mesmerised, more English-fluent tourists muttering things like 'C'est une blague?' or 'Some kind of street-theatre, I think.' This would annoy her and she would round on the offending parties glaring and blowing her whistle and order them to leave for talking in the line.

"St. Paul's Cathedral!" she cried pointing at where it loomed some distance away. "Its perfect proportions are a wonder of the world. If you took a skein of wool and tied one end round a pillar in the south-west corner of the nave, and then walked diagonally and looped it around another in the north-east, and then crossed to the north-west playing it out behind you, and then finally tied it to one in the south-east, you would almost certainly annoy the priest immensely." She had lots of St. Paul's bits worked out, especially for the Whispering Gallery – whispering intriguing spy-secrets to Miles, or telling him that she would have sex with him if he helped her kill and rob one of the other tourists, things like that – and couldn't wait to get there. But the thing was she somehow seemed as unable to get them to St. Paul's Cathedral as she had been to avoid Trafalgar Square earlier. She would see it bulking behind other buildings and point and say, "We are nearly there now! No-one panic," but in fact each time it would be further away. "St. Paul's has the miraculous property of seeming to get further away the closer you get to it," she eventually declared. "In order to cross the last few hundred yards you have to walk backwards with your eyes closed or it shrinks to nothing before you." In the end she admitted defeat and said it was rubbish anyway.

"The City of London! The greed, stupidity and arrogance of its inhabitants are renowned throughout the world." She led them into the foyer of the offices of a bank which had recently been bailed out with billions of pounds of taxpayers' money, and the upper echelons of which had shortly afterwards awarded themselves millions of pounds of bonuses for their achievements. "In order to work here one must undergo an initiation ritual involving a rubber pig-mask and fishing money out of a tank of human blood," she declared loudly. She expatiated equally loudly and unfavourably on a mural in the lobby and then got into a shouting match when they were asked to leave. "We own you!" she shouted. "You work for us! We subsidize you, you failures!" Thanks to the tourists and cameras more than to her sign and laminated pass no-one called the police. She delivered a short pithy lecture to her tourists on the institution's shortcomings, roamed around a bit glaring and sneering and wondering if she could lead them all to invade the high-ups' private offices, decided she didn't quite have the momentum and left.

She was flagging a bit when they reached the Tower of London. She told them some real history she could remember and let them pause a bit to take pictures. They watched Tower Bridge raise and close and then crossed the river. They ran for, caught, and managed to ride a bus most of the way to Lambeth. After they were thrown off she led them at random through side streets and high streets, spieling intermittently, tireder now.

"Hugh Grant's dad owns that newsagents," she said pointing across a busy street. "He – Oh my God! Oh my God! Oh my God! I think that's Hugh Grant just coming out now!" she cried as a man in a leather jacket and sunglasses emerged who was almost exactly as unlike the film star as it was genetically possible to me. She jumped up and down and waved. "Hugh Grant!" she told them. "'Oo Grant! Hugh Glant! Look!" The tourists exchanged baffled glances. The man caught sight of her and waved uncertainly back. "Oh my God it *is* him! I knew it! He often roams the streets without his toupee and in blackface to avoid the paparazzi." She dashed into traffic and across the street without waiting for the rest of them and accosted the man eagerly. "No it wasn't him," she announced sadly on her return. "But keep your eyes peeled."

She had a fresh burst of energy as they came in sight of Westminster Bridge and started to point to things and whip her charges into line again, building up the whirlwind momentum with which she wanted to hit the Houses of Parliament.

Partway across the bridge there was a loud hooting from some river traffic beneath and sudden inspiration struck. "Oh my God!" she cried, giving a start and looking around wildly. She stared at her watch in disbelief and terror. "I'm afraid I have timed this badly," she announced. "The bridge is about to raise! Please walk faster, ladies and gentlemen! The bridge is about to be raised! Is the ground tilting?" she muttered. "I think it is tilting already. Oh God, I have doomed us all." She increased her pace to a very fast walk indeed, looking back and making urgent hurry-up gestures at the alarmed tourists, then moaned suddenly and broke into a full-on run. "Run! Run! Run for your lives! The bridge is about to raise! We will all be killed! Flee! Every man for himself! Leave the weak! Women and World War Two allies first!" The tour group bolted in a panic the rest of the way across the bridge.

"Phew," she said when they reached the other side. "That wouldn't have been good. Not after the last lot I lost. They'd have taken my hat for sure this time." She gestured. "Behold! The Mother of Parliaments! 'Mother' in the Black American abbreviation sense, of course. Those with crucifixes or garlic should deploy them now. Hurry, hurry! Follow me! Get back in the crocodile! Even there we are barely safe. Button all wallets in an inner pocket, hide watches and gold teeth. Those of a weak or nervous disposition should drop out now. Pacemakers should be set for stun. Abandon hope all ye who enter … The London Castrati School, there," she waved at the House of Lords. Momentum and her sign and simply not stopping carried them up to the Visitors' Gallery over the Commons. "The House of Commons, ladies and gentlemen! The greed, stupidity and arrogance of its inhabitants are renowned throughout the world. Those with fruit may pelt them. If you throw coins they will scramble for them. In order to work here one must undergo an initiation ritual involving a rubber pig-mask and fishing money out of a tank of human blood. That man's a whore! *That* man's a whore! That woman's a certifiable lunatic! That woman made taxpayers pay for her husband's porn! That man made us pay for his duck-house! That man ... "

They did not last long in the House of Commons Visitors' Gallery. "They work for us!" yelled Clara as they were bundled out. "We own them! We subsidize those failures! You don't *have* to do your jobs! The London Tourist Board will get you for this! Look at my sign! I have a laminated pass! Flee! Flee for your lives!" she told the tourists. "Don't stop until you reach the border or you will go to jail forever! Save yourselves! Warn the civilised world of what you have seen here!"

Miles was never afterwards quite sure how they managed to avoid being detained and arrested. It had to do with the unstoppable impetus of a twenty-strong crocodile of panicked tourists with an enraged Clara at their head stampeding past, through and over security guards and other jobsworths, with others being clobbered over the head or jabbed in the goolies with Clara's tour-sign, with her sense of direction functioning for the first time that day and a previously reconnoitred back-corridor escape route paying off, with a high-handed wave of her laminated pass unexpectedly working for once at a crucial moment, resulting in them being nodded through a barrier that would otherwise have been fatal, and with the sheer good fortune of running into and quickly mingling with a more legitimate tour group, just leaving, in the main lobby.

"Head count," called Clara briskly outside in the sunshine Miles had not expected to see again for months. "All assemble around me. Oi! Don't steal my tourists!" she yelled at the leader of the bigger tour. "Miles she is stealing my tourists! The ingrates are trying to escape! After all I've done for them! Get back here, you! The tour isn't over until I say it is!" By means of some rough manhandling she managed to get her flock back together long enough to at least perform a head count and check they had all escaped the heart of darkness. But after that many of them sloped off to join the proper tour that had facilitated their escape, while others simply ran to escape from her or the possibility of arrest.

She had had enough now anyway. She led the remaining captives along the Victoria Embankment at a casual strolling pace. When they were sure she was no longer paying attention several more drifted off. As they reached Northumberland Avenue she told the rest of them the tour was over and pointed the way back to Trafalgar Square.

"Not you," she said to the Japanese man as he smiled and bowed his thanks and prepared to depart. He was the only one remaining from the original group she'd started with and had been as good as gold all day. She pulled him back and put an 'I am a GOOD Tourist!' sticker on him and he beamed.

She put her arms around him and Miles and started to stroll contentedly with them up towards Cleopatra's Needle again, sighing happily as she watched the eternal dance of light on the Thames.

"We are going to dinner and then the theatre," she announced. "It is free for Good Tourists! Yes? Like to see show?"

"See bloody good show already," grinned the Japanese man.

"Why you wily yellow weasel," said Clara in delight.

Chapter Twenty

There was uproar in the back room of the Walpole's Head. A stay-behind was in progress and a council of war was in session. Voices were raised and counter-raised; empty glasses vibrated as tables were thumped. There was argument, lamentation and execration couched in such terms as to remind the listener that this was the country of both the King James Bible and Billingsgate fish market. Insurrection was in the air. Unwelcome news had just been sprung.

"If it goes through, it will be out of my hands," came the quiet patient voice of Simon Smith, the former Lucifer Mars, the quondam rock star Lord of the Manor, repeating himself for the severalth time. "It will be compulsory purchase."

"There must be something we can do!" cried Arthur the firebrand landlord.

"There is nothing you can do," quietly but firmly said a grey-haired little man named Ransome, the only recent newcomer present, sitting slumped at a table with his head in his hands, staring despondently at a puddle of beer.

"We have to object and keep objecting," said Miles.

"Don't you think we did?" snapped Ransome.

"I for one am not standing for it," cried Muriel the tweedy colonel's daughter. She directed a stream of clipped, soldierly, blistering swears at the forces of authority and concluded, "We must fight the bastards. The things are eyesores."

"To say nothing of what they do to birds," said an ornithologist.

"They don't even *work*," cried Miles.

Joe the titanic old roving landmark shook his shaggy silver head in puzzlement. "They'll have to devastate the woods getting the things up there. And it isn't even windy on top."

"They don't care," snarled Jeremiah. "It's the new religion, innit? Giant silver crucifixes plastered across the skyline, letting us know whose power we live under. I almost don't care that they're hideous and destructive. I'm just not waking up every morning in their shadow to be reminded that those lying sanctimonious thieving [chaps] have power over me."

"We have to *fight* it!"

Only Clara was unusually and unexpectedly silent, sitting at a table at the back, meditatively, and with arguably unladylike noises, sucking the dregs from the bottom of her orange-juice bottle through a straw.

They were talking, of course, about a wind farm, which was to be erected atop the local landmark of Hobson's Hill.

"They must see that it's an unsuitable location for any number of reasons," said Miles.

"There are no roads and it's covered in trees."

"They don't *care*."

"Pissing off country-dwellers is probably regarded as a distinct bonus, if it isn't the whole point of the exercise," drawled Major Fitzsimmons, the tanned hawklike army veteran and explorer.

"It's stupid."

"I have expressed my incredulity," said Simon when he had a chance. "I gather, unofficially, from those with connections to the local authorities, that the point is it is the least unsuitable location for many miles around, and one of comparatively few possible sites in the county. They have to show willing. There are central government edicts. Targets have been imposed." There was a general groan. "It seems there are now minions of authority driving round saying, 'I can't see one from here, that must be corrected, *there*'s a rise higher than sea-level, that will have to do.' "

There were shouts, curses, and elaborate, vehement insults. When these had fallen off and only Clara's sucking noises could be heard, the little newcomer Ransome, who now had his head slumped on his arms on his table, groaned, "I *came* here to get away from the things."

There were murmurs of commiseration. His tumble-down cottage was off a footpath halfway up the hill and would doubtless be in range of the wind turbines' noise.

"It's my favourite walk," said someone else.

"It's my favourite place to stand and see the view."

"It *is* the view."

"Come on," said Miles, "we're all talking as though legal objections are pointless."

"Aren't they?" said Ransome bitterly.

"Tell us," Miles appealed to Thomas, the village's resident lawyer. "We can fight it through the courts, right?"

"Of course," shrugged Thomas, the pugilistic enthusiasm that normally lit up his eyes at any prospect of a legal scrap noticeably lacking. "At worst we'll be able to postpone it, or looking at it another way keep it hanging over our heads, for a couple of years, if we spend a lot of time and money. Occasionally people have even won their case, although I can't see any rhyme or reason in why some have and some haven't. But the possibility has been growing more remote. The powers that be are becoming more intransigent. The government has made international commitments. There have been political pledges about 'green enterprise' initiatives. The wind-power corporations have been complaining about the uncertainty of getting permission and lobbying intensively for the process to be simplified. There have been a string of startling and high-handed decisions in the teeth of quite sensible objections. Frankly at the moment ... " He sighed and shrugged again. "Of course I can try."

Ransome raised his head to shake it wearily. "We tried *everything* back home."

"There is of course to be a consultation exercise," said Squire Simon with a smile, to the groans of everyone. "With the emphasis, naturally, on the exercise. Three of our lords and masters will deign to appear in the village hall two weeks from now to take whatever we can throw at them, poor buggers, and nod their heads understandingly – "

"And go off and do it anyway," Ransome nodded.

"And you have to bear in mind we won't even be able to show unanimous opposition. Harriet and the vicar and anyone they can guilt will be all for it." There were groans of assent.

"Makes no difference," said Ransome. "Every one of us were against it."

"Hopeless or not I'll be fighting it through every court, but ... "

"We did," said Ransome hollowly.

"We will form a human chain!" cried Muriel.

"Did it," said Ransome.

"This is an area of outstanding beauty," said Miles.

"So was our place!" cried Ransome aggrievedly.

"If there was a popular outcry," said Miles to Simon. "If you staged a protest concert – not just for here, for the wind turbine issue in general – "

Simon laughed. "Come on. I'm already known as the crusty reactionary singing farmer. Who else would take part?"

Miles vainly looked for help from Clara, who continued to gaze into her Britvic bottle and ply her straw around. He clicked his fingers. "If we can say it's the natural habitat of – some sort of mating ground for – "

"It is," cried Joe. He proceeded to list, from first-hand observation, the animals and birds who made their home in the woods, and was cut short before he'd barely got started.

"They don't care."

"There were brown hares and some sort of rare newt where they built ours," said the lugubrious Ransome. "Endangered and protected species. We had a celebrity naturalist to say as much and talk about the impact. Papers, petitions. Result? They built the things anyway, and the naturalist, he don't get invited on TV as much nowadays."

"They don't [jolly well] *care*," repeated Jeremiah. "They already *know* the things kill birds, they just don't give a [tuppenny damn]. Why should they? It's big business. Do you know how much the manufacturers donate to those [fearful rotters] in the government?"

He told them, and about the lobbyists and hospitality and directorships and other links, and then competed with several others in giving statistics about the whole vast 'global warming' industry and their tame politicians, the huge profits, the vast amounts spent on propaganda, the unholy alliance of banks and big corporations with blind fanatics, and about the pointlessness and counterproductiveness of wind turbines even if you granted the mistaken or deliberately falsified initial premise, and then the whole lot of them started to bitterly swap examples of the objections of residents being over-ridden by the blind imperatives of a fancied Progress that was anything but, and of precious and irreplaceable swathes of nature being destroyed in the name of a fashionable abstraction called the Environment.

Clara remained strangely silent, continuing to hoover optimistically at the bottom of her Britvic 55 bottle, her cheeks quite concave now.

"However bad you think it's going to be, it'll be worse," said Ransome in a lull. "They were stakes through our village, gravestones over the place. Now *I* couldn't settle for the noise, and I was half a mile off. There was a farm right under one, who couldn't sell up, and the wife went off her head with it. She's still in a home, poor cow. But it was the movement that got me, the constant distraction, as though there was a row of idiot children standing there eternally waving their arms at you. When they're still, which admittedly is a lot of the time, you just growl at the thought that *you've* been taken for an idiot child and want to cry at the sheer bloody wanton vandalism and wicked disfigurement of something you love." He sighed. "I suppose I'd better emigrate."

Muriel slammed her table with her palm. "We will *not* put up with it! If legal avenues fail, we will blockade the roads – sap the approaches – attack the bulldozers – " Several rowdy young farm labourers and other hot-heads indicated approval.

"We could write to our MP," said a wag, getting a cheap but widespread laugh.

Miles, pacing and gesticulating, said, "Look, if we all throw in and commission some proper hoity-toity impact report, dead professional, talk their language – tourism – there's the tea-room and the tat-shops and the bed-and-breakfasts – wildlife – "

He was jeered down.

"Dynamite." Arthur the excitable landlord slammed his meaty fist on the bar. "Simple as that. Dynamite! I say, let them build them, we'll knock them down again. My brother-in-law's in demolition – "

"So was I, come to think of it," drawled Major Fitzsimmons. "And if you're serious, I'm up for it, and I know some other hooligans who will be for the fun of the thing."

Jeremiah and two of the farm labourers said they could be counted in as well, and Simon's troll-like ex-roadie butler Beastman volunteered his own pyrotechnical expertise.

"Oh come on," said Simon, pained, and a couple of other somewhat more sensitive souls murmured their demurral.

"I'm telling you it's that time!" cried Arthur, wild-eyed, pounding the bar again. "We've got to stand up for ourselves. Dynamite! Dynamite! Tell them, Clara!" He looked around for her. "Clara! Oi!" She was still peering into the depths of her bottle making sucking noises through her straw. He rang the bell to gain her attention. "Clara!" She raised her eyebrows and looked up quizzically, raising the straw from the bottle in the process but continuing to suck through it. "Tell them! Tell them it's time for dynamite!"

"Yes, come on, Clara!" came other cries.

"Tell us what you think!"

Clara swivelled her head and straw around at the various expectant faces. She rose, removed the straw from her mouth, and quietly and sadly said:

"What I think? I think I am ashamed for my country and for my village. It appears there is not one gentleman remaining. When I was a girl, and it was not so very long ago, it was accepted in polite society that when you could hear a lady sucking dregs through her straw, it was the signal she was ready for another bottle of Britvic 55, and everyone present with any pretence to manhood would fight their way to the bar to be the first to obtain one for her. I am becoming sadly resigned to my husband having deep pockets and short arms, but I had expected better of some of the rest of you."

Arthur put a fresh bottle of orange juice on the counter and Miles conveyed it to her. "Thank you," she said ironically, eyes still wide with reproach. "And a fresh straw?"

They gave her a fresh straw.

Still looking put out and pettish, she took a sip and said, "Now. In order to punish you all for your lack of attention, I have decided to only tell you how our problem may be solved in return for a reward. That is, I will only tell you how we may do away with this threatened fart-farm *if* it is agreed that, when my solution is proved to work, each and every man here will buy me a crate of Britvic 55 for my private cellar."

"Yes, yes," cried Arthur. "Tell us, tell us!"

She raised an eyebrow and looked around. "Is the agreement general?"

"Yes," came a general cry, groan or laugh.

She inclined her head. "Very well. Then I will tell you."

Daintily she stepped onto a chair and from thence onto a table. By luck or more likely design she was now framed by the huge Union Jack hanging on the back wall behind her.

"My fellow Britons," she cried, flinging her arms wide, splashing her Britvic into Miles's face. "Arse. Sorry, darling. Another bottle, please, Arthur, and a cloth. I will start again. My fellow Britons! The rule of law has ended, the day of reason is over. We must fight fire with fire and madness with madness." She shook her head as Arthur slammed the bar triumphantly. "No, Arthur, it is not yet time for dynamite, but I promise you you will be at My right hand when that day comes. I talk of fighting Correctness with Correctness, setting one piety to catch another. But it will demand sacrifice, daring, and getting off your arses. I offer you nothing but blood, sweat, toil, and embarrassment. Will you follow me?" she cried.

"We will!" cried Arthur and half a dozen other of her most dedicated thralls.

"Will you give yourselves to me heart and soul?"

"We will!"

"Am I your leader?"

"You are!"

She wondered how far she could push it. "Am I your ... War Queen?"

"You are the new Boadicea, Clara," cried Arthur fervently.

She lowered her eyes humbly. "It is you who say it. Then listen, and I will tell you how it may be done. I only ask that before you laugh you pause to think if it is possible and to remember what kind of country we are living in. Listen."

In a couple of sentences she told them her plan.

There were laughs, but appreciative ones. "That's rather an amusing thought," drawled the Major.

Then there was an awestruck silence for a time as they considered it.

"That could actually bloody work," exclaimed Miles and three other people suddenly and more or less together; and among them was Thomas the lawyer.

"I know." Clara sipped Britvic modestly and then impishly curved her lips. "And won't it be fun to try?"

Of course resolutions taken in drunken back rooms are not always considered as binding. Even that night a couple of people gracefully declined to take part in the actual execution of the scheme Clara proceeded to sketch out and increasingly elaborate; they wished the enterprise luck but it was not quite their style. But the idea caught on among others in the village who were opposed to the advent of the ugly, pointless turbines. The question, Clara said, was whether they were the kind of people who had the balls to not merely admire an idea but actually put it into action. It turned out they were. There were a lot of people in the village who were at the end of their tethers with one thing and another being imposed on their country and on their homes without their consent, and a lot of them had reached a point where if they didn't try to push back in some way they would no longer keep their self-respect. Besides, and perhaps more importantly, and as Clara wisely emphasised, the whole thing would be rather a lark.

It was when they got the local Women's Institute types enthusiastically on board that she started to believe they were going to make it happen.

Preparation, organisation, rehearsal were required, and were forthcoming. There were excited confabulations at coffee mornings, confidential messages passed on to the trustworthy via the village grapevine. The whole place lit up with secret excitement as their minds lit up with ideas.

"I think we have to forge the parish records, insert references going back centuries. Perhaps have a guide-book printed?"

"No, Miles, well thought of but counterproductive. Anything demonstrably traditional will just incur the enemy's hate. In fact it would be much better to make it very clear that this is something utterly contrived and bogus that has just sprung up in the past few years, as an alternative to going to church or perhaps just because our set-top-box reception isn't very good."

"Seriously, though."

"Seriously. Get the phone, darling, I'm at a crucial stage in sewing this."

"Bialystock und Bloo-hoom."

"Miles? Simon. I sent Beastm'n up to the attics, he's rooted out all kinds of things from our old tours that are going to be very useful, everything I mentioned and more."

"Ace."

"Shall I send them over or keep them here?"

"There, I think, for now, the vicar sometimes tries to come round here. Bye. ... That was the Squire, he found them."

"We didn't really need them, though, you should see some of the ones the ladies are making. They're really throwing their hearts in. I'm quite worried by their enthusiasm at times, I may have unleashed something quite surprising here. Pass me the phone. ... Verity dear, it's Clara. That woman who made the furniture in your conservatory, what was her name again? ... Do you think she'd be interested in a commission for something bigger, much bigger, and ... more sinister?"

Miles looked at her. "Oh no. You're surely not thinking ... ?"

"Yes, Miles," she said gleefully as she put the phone down. "It might not be time for dynamite yet, but it is certainly time for *that*."

William Penge was a middle-aged, medium-ranking local government apparatchik with a six-figure salary, prodigal expenses package, and gold-plated, ring-fenced, index-linked pension. He had a shower in his office, a gym down the corridor, worked a flexible four and a half days out of seven, forty weeks out of the year, six of which might be spent on seminars, and was almost certainly underpaid.

His task it was, among others less arduous, to act as the sympathetic ear of authority in fatuous Consultation Exercises such as the one being staged in the village today. He had made his name in, and been swiftly elevated from, a role as a leader of focus groups and citizens' panels, and had proved himself masterly at steering these into saying exactly what it was hoped and needed they would say. Now, to his secret sorrow, he was the go-to man to be despatched to the front lines to be barracked by the refractory, the unsatisfactory, the perpetually unreasonable public, and to vow solemnly to Take Their Concerns On Board. Was there a destructive bypass, a greenbelt development, a demolition of a heritage site required? Phone-masts, wind turbines, landfill where none should be? Send for William to canvass the yokels, and you could claim that the public had been Fully Consulted at every step of the way. His official job title was long and meaningless, but to his department, and perhaps to his own conscience, he was the designated Disguiser of Foregone Conclusions.

He was a master of the intent frown; of the Earnest Assurance; of the 'We're all reasonable people' tone; of that particular sickly, nauseating, patronising, patient, tolerant, understanding, benevolent, unnatural, indescribable but instantly recognisable grin which Clara, in the days before she had shot her television, had once shudderingly dubbed the Smile of Consensus: the cult-member-like beam that flourished on a thousand loathsome, powerful faces throughout the country and the continent, the smile that loved and forgave you for doubting its owner's good intentions, that reproved you like a child, that sugar-coated a pill, that good-humouredly made light of your objections, that was intended to burn up your hatred with the force of its wattage like an electric insect-trap zapping flies; a master also of the pedantic clarification; above all of the misleading restatement and disingenuous summing-up.

His eyebrows alone could make you feel that not even your own mother had ever understood you as well. The most intransigent local Demosthenes would find themselves feeling grateful to him for re-phrasing their words in a way that almost exactly reversed their meaning and not notice the knotting in their stomachs until twenty minutes after the meeting had ended. Bile, bluster and bloodlust were all absorbed and dissolved harmlessly in the warm syrup of his concern.

It was a mystery to some that William had never been summoned to display his talents on a national stage or at a higher echelon of power. There was a slight old-worldliness about him that was out of keeping with the current style in loftier spheres of government, that certain something that had kept him a William rather than a Will or Bill. For all his communication-seminar finish he had something of the air of an old-fashioned local solicitor, and while this played well in many of the backwater arenas he was sent to it did not endear him to his looser-laced superiors. Like many great actors he was actually a rather shy man off-stage; and he was one of nature's bachelors or male old-maids; all in all he was rather unclubbable, especially now that the clubs in question were more likely to be night-clubs than gentleman's ones. This had certainly played a part in his lack of further promotion, and so too the fact that he was very valuable where he was. But sometimes William thought it was just that people could sense his growing inner mutiny.

He hated his job. He hated lying to the public, he hated the superiors who sent him to lie, and he very acutely hated the public he lied to, the flushed, sweaty, shouty, unruly, unreasonable public.

Above all he hated the countryside to which he was so regularly despatched at the moment. City-bred and personally fastidious, he had a purely instinctive rather than ideological aversion to farms, mud, cows, dogs, horses, manure, tractors, ditches, hedgerows and wide-open spaces, an almost Panic fear of forests, a dislike of being cut off from the amenities of urban civilisation, and a quite irrational prejudice, which he knew for irrational and actually endeavoured to overcome, against rural types whom, even before he had naturally come to associate them with sullen or shouting faces, he had associated from youth with incest, rickets, witch-hunts, sty eyes, slurred words, irritating idiosyncrasies of dialect, unnatural practices with animals and general backwardness and uncouthness. This did not mean that he prosecuted his task of helping upset their immemorial way of life with any great malice, zeal or enthusiasm; he would just rather not have been there.

The two colleagues who were to sit with him on the Consultation Panel today, who he was now greeting in the car park of the Dog and Duck, happened to share this aversion, one on similarly instinctive, the other on more ideological grounds.

Kate Plyne was a bright, pretty 30-ish woman who was a flack for the power company responsible for the electrical grid in this part of the country and others. This company was currently known as *lydia*, like that, in lower case, and italics, with an asterisk, for the privilege of changing its name to which from a more dourly utilitarian and descriptive monicker it had paid a consultancy firm upwards of £500,000. The logo on the car door she had just slammed shut, which might have been half of a flower, or a suggestion of a musical clef sign, or neither, had earned its creators another cool half million. The car's livery and the colour of her jacket had recently been changed from pale green to a particular shade of turquoise which was felt to be both less on-the-nose and easier to 'own', after eight months of consultancy but at a relatively bargain-basement price of £350,000, not including the cost of resprays, re-wardrobing, redecorating the corporate headquarters and launching a media campaign alerting the public to this fact. Six months from now they would be bought by Spaniards and renamed *Arriba!* and the logo and livery would be ditched in favour of a manic cartoon mole giving a thumbs-up.

The third member of the trio was a more exalted figure than would ordinarily have been present on such an occasion. Clementina Batt was a minister at the Department of Energy and Climate Change. She had risen from student activism and a stint as a council Equality and Diversity officer to be imposed on a safe seat and immediately translated into the corridors of power. Before her current post she had completed a successful term at the Ministry of Defence, success being defined in terms of doing away with old regiments, ceding powers to Europe, refusing requests for materiel, and above all making a landmark ruling on the status of transsexual soldiers in the event of their being taking prisoner. Her presence here today was partly due to the involvement of Simon Smith, the erstwhile Lucifer Mars: although he had deprecated his PR value to Miles, others did not, and in the event of a successful stink being raised about this case she wanted to be in a position to say that she personally had been involved in Free, Full and Frank consultations with the locals. But that was not all, William thought: protests about a similarly dubiously-located wind farm at a site on the other side of the county had recently got so far out of hand that questions had been asked in the House and his superiors rocketed by Whitehall. Miss Batt had stressed this was to be William's show and she would not interfere unduly, which made him suspect all the more that she was also there to assess his handling.

They held a murmured, last-minute discussion of tactics and exchange of information sheets at the back of the village Tea Rooms.

"No lattes, and you could choke up with cholesterol just looking at the menu," sighed Kate. "This is just like the place Harriet Pridgett writes about."

The other two smiled. None of them knew or, as they would fail to recognise her at the meeting, would ever know that this was, in fact, the village that Harriet, with a bit of help from her imagination and Clara's, wrote about, and nor would it have made much difference to their expectations and assumptions if they had.

"I suppose it has to be here?" said William leafing through a file. "It does seem a rather ... borderline case to say the least."

Clementina shrugged. "It's the principle. None of these types want the things at any cost. We can't let them dictate to us. They have to go somewhere. There's got to be a big push if we're to meet our targets."

They left the cafe.

"It's so ----ing cute," Kate complained as they went out and strolled along towards where people were drifting into the village hall. "If it gets any prettier I will scream. And they're all so ----ing friendly, and live in each other's pockets, I bet. I couldn't live here if you paid me."

"The phrase 'hideously white' springs to mind," said Clementina, who was both hideous and white.

Thomas the lawyer, who was neither, greeted them in front of the hall.

"Our three Aunt Sallies," he said smiling as he shook hands. The two women looked blank, although the phrase 'straw man' had been so much a part of their vocabulary since university debating days that it was now on a sort of automatic speed-dial button in their minds; and Batt, later, would come to think of the term 'Uncle Tom' in connection with the lawyer. "I'll be introducing you and helping deflect the brickbats."

"I'd really rather prefer to chair myself," said William quickly.

"Naturally, naturally." He ushered them in.

A long table with water and a gavel had been set up on the dais at the back of the hall. Painted flats and props from such things as the Harvest Festival celebrations and the children's Nativity Play, already disowned by the vicar but maintained by the villagers, stood against the walls behind it. Clementina curled her lip at the former and tutted audibly at the latter.

They sat and watched the last of the locals file into the bright airy hall and take seats on rows of folding chairs. There was a smattering of muttered talk, little open hostility yet. Thomas, sitting at one end of the table, found himself next to Clementina.

"How do you stand it here, with your background?" she asked in a murmur.

Thomas felt his shoulders sag slightly. He fought hard and, he thought, successfully, to keep the boredom, hatred and revulsion out of his face.

He raised an eyebrow. "My … ? Winchester and Cambridge?"

"No, I meant … "

"Oh, my Sri Lankan genes? Well, the monsoon season is longer here but they have rather a good cricket team," he said with a smile.

"I mean I bet you can't find a decent curry-house for miles."

Thomas stared at her, trying and failing to keep the sheer disbelief out of his face. He felt his toes curl on her behalf. To save from answering he clumsily knocked his briefcase onto the floor and stooped to retrieve it. A fairly kindly and laid-back man with a gift for ignoring things that bored him, he had nevertheless once, drunkenly, to a sympathetic friend, declared that if through some catastrophic and improbable concatenation of circumstances the BNP or similar ever came to power he hoped they would spare him long enough to watch the white liberals get theirs.

The hall was fairly full; the trickle of latecomers had stopped. Thomas glanced at his watch, gestured for a loiterer at the back to close the doors, rose and banged the gavel and made a short speech of introduction and looked forward to a cordial and informative exchange. He handed over to William and sat again.

Not rising but commandeering the gavel, William gave an almost equally short speech in which he expressed a hope that he and his colleagues would be able to set the locals' minds at rest on certain points, and a Firm Commitment to fully Take on Board their views. He emphasised that nothing was set in stone yet and if the project went ahead it would only be with Full Consultation with the inhabitants at every step of the way. He promptly invited contributions from the floor.

It was an unusual meeting from the first. William was not to deploy his weasel summing-up, all-adults-together tone, earnest assurance, consensus smile or even his eyebrows much. They were used to, and prepared for, angry barracking, impassioned if untutored rhetoric, pointing fingers, boos, jeers, insults and even tears of frustration. What they were not prepared for was a display of cowed submission and mulish silence. Hostility and resentment they could see in the serried glowering faces; but of a curiously abashed and even guilty kind, which ought to have pleased them but soon came to make them feel uneasy.

It began in a sprightly enough fashion. After a lengthy silent pause in which she, like the panel, waited in vain for the retrograde elements of the area to make themselves heard, Harriet (although they did not recognise her) sprang to her feet and chirpily said that she for one welcomed the proposed development, and went on to deliver a sententious, platitudinous speech about the need to save the planet, meet the national obligation to cut carbon emissions, and so on.

"Ah," said William delightedly. A small handful of people scattered about the audience clapped, half-heartedly, once or twice. These were cronies of the vicar's, and the sort of people who would have been cronies of Harriet's if she had made an effort to get to know anyone, and in theory they agreed with her. Privately they were all appalled at what the wind turbines would do to the view, to say nothing of property values, and found themselves guiltily hoping to hell that the neanderthal element of the community would shortly start raising spirited objections.

"Anyway *I* always think they look rather beautiful," Harriet concluded virtuously.

"*I* do," said the two women on the panel eagerly.

After Harriet sat the vicar rose and introduced himself and said that he would like to second that.

"Well, he would," muttered Thomas with a chuckle, loud enough for the visitors to glance at him.

Earnestly the vicar struggled for command of his fluctuating rhetorical skills. "This ... this is a long overdue development," he said. "This would be a victory for the forces of light over those of darkness."

Thomas snorted. "*Listen* to the man," he muttered in amusement, with a visible sneer. "What century are we living in?"

"Press ahead with it," urged the vicar. "Every socially mature and morally evolved person here will cheer on the project. When it is completed, I will finally feel that this parish has been fully civilised. I urge you not to even listen to the foot-draggers and the revellers in selfish backwardness." Adam's apple working, he glanced around the hall as if in defiance, for rehearsing this speech he had expected to be shouted down by protests and catcalls by now. "Our world must be cleansed, and I say shame on any who would oppose it!"

With a final defiant look he sat. There was an outbreak of sullen mutters but many of the villagers appeared to hang their heads as if rebuked.

Thomas sighed. "Oh, dear," he said sadly, shaking his head. "This is exactly what I was afraid of." The panel turned to look at him quizzically. "Look at them now," he muttered, gazing across the rows of surly hangdog faces.

William thanked the vicar and looked around expectantly for more. After a short pause Squire Simon's business manager got to his feet and asked for some clarification about the extent of the compulsory purchase and the route of the road through the woods that would be needed for construction and maintenance. William consulted his notes and volunteered this information, subject to change, and the business manager thanked him and said that, subject to certain guarantees about the wildlife, the landowner would not be objecting to the development. The panel exchanged glances and studiously suppressed incredulity and delight. There were disappointed mutters from one or two parts of the hall. Although he had materially aided Clara's scheme, Simon did not care to be implicated in its ultimate execution.

After another pause someone they had not known well enough to invite into the plot rose and nervously cleared his throat and asked, Yes what about the wildlife? "Ah," said William, quite pleased to start to earn his pay by this time, and bombarded him with fluent talk about Full and Comprehensive Impact Reports, assessments of irreplaceability, the possibility of relocation, gradual insertion of machinery, and so on, along with a full blast of his 'I am sure you are an intelligent listener' look, for several minutes, until his interlocutor, finding himself nodding repeatedly every time William seemed to expect it, was finally relieved to be able to sit down again.

After that silence fell save for coughing and the shuffling of feet. William and the other panellists glanced around but found only averted or drooping heads like a room full of dull schoolchildren hoping not to be picked for a question. They were almost relieved when someone else Clara hadn't instructed rose and apologetically asked about the noise.

Glad to be finally able to use some of her preparation, Kate leaned forward and earnestly said, "Lydia takes your concerns very seriously," causing several people who had forgotten their names and didn't know that of the company to stare at Clementina or her in confusion, wondering either why the government minister didn't speak on her own behalf or the

PR woman referred to herself in the Caesarish third person. She went on to droningly recite some meaningless-to-the-layman statistics about decibel levels at various distances, and concluded brightly by referring to a survey, largely conducted among new, town-escaping inhabitants of areas with nearby wind turbine developments who had moved there after the original, despairing inhabitants had moved out, and largely doctored anyway, which she said showed that a significant percentage of people came to find the constant noise oddly comforting.

After that there was silence and sullenness again. It lengthened to a point where the panellists individually began wondering if they ought to start doing both parts themselves, suggesting objections that people usually raised in order to then demolish them.

"Anyone else?" urged William in surprise. "Anyone at all?" he added pleadingly.

Coughs, shuffles, mute animal glowers.

"Well ... " began William.

Suddenly a shambolic figure sitting at the end of a middle row lurched to its feet.

"It bain't roight!" it cried. "It bain't roight, I tells ye!"

Everyone turned to look.

Miles stared back at them, wild-eyed and cowering but defiant. He was wearing a smock and a tow-headed fright-wig and had his mouth deformed by an acting prosthetic inside his cheek which caused him to slobber and slur somewhat. Finding every eye upon him he swallowed and tugged nervously at a neckerchief he wore, but imploringly addressed the wide-eyed panel in a spluttering explosion:

"We loikes to play, your honours! We loikes to play and frolic in the woods!"

"That's enough, Seth Bowman!" thundered Jeremiah, who had risen in the middle of the room and was pointing a commanding finger at Miles. "Not in front of outzidurs!"

Miles goggled at him in terror and cringed. He backed away, knocking over his chair, and held an arm up to shield his face like a frightened hen trying to conceal itself under its wing. He giggled shrilly in fear and fled shambolically from the hall making a high-pitched keening noise, knocking another chair over en route, hobbling in such a way as to indicate a club foot and a hunched back.

("You appalling ham," muttered Clara in the little vestibule, where she had been watching through a crack in the door awaiting her own entrance.)

The panel watched in amazement and alarm. Just as their mouths had finally started to close there was another contribution from the floor.

"Puritans!" bellowed the windswept old titan Joe, rising and towering. "Purse-lipped puritans!" He pointed at the startled vicar and Harriet, then turned to shake his fist at the bench. "Deniers of the life-force! Is my sister's nakedness shameful?" he demanded. "When the sap rises in the greensward, may not a man's do the same?" There was a pause. Clara had coached him in various bits from DH Lawrence but he had forgotten them. "Birds do it," he floundered. "Bees do it – "

"Still thy tongue, Joe Dunnock, or I will still it for thee," Jeremiah growled warningly. "Do not bring shame and the wrath of the Lunnoners upon us."

Joe glowered but sat grumbling.

Jeremiah bowed slightly to the bench. "My apologies, your worships, there will be no further interruptions," he said stiffly.

But then up popped Miriam, a mountainous mainstay of the W.I., who matched his glare defiantly until he sat shaking his head. She turned to the panel wringing her hands.

"What about the effect on the birthrate?" she pleaded. "What about all the little babies who won't be born?"

There were cries of agreement from several other women.

There was helpless startled laughter, eye-rolling, and a relieved letting out of breath from the panel. Here was something they could grasp and deal with.

"Who the hell's been telling you that?" the minister tittered pityingly. However it was Kate who leaned forward with a face of earnest concern to authoritatively assure them that there were no studies whatever to show the turbines had any effect at all on the fertility rate.

"Savages," muttered the minister contemptuously to Thomas. She suddenly went very still and blushed. "Oh, sorry, I didn't mean that in any … I didn't mean *you*," she said. Thomas busied himself inside his briefcase.

On a roll, and feeling they had better take control again, Kate and then William and then Clementina went on to raise and dismiss various other safety concerns or related misapprehensions the populace might have been harbouring but had hesitated to raise. Their spirits lifted to get it all off their chests. There were politely interested nods from those they picked out to pin with their eyes, and a general fidgetiness from the rest of the hall, as though in hope that this must be ending soon, as they ploughed eagerly on. Presently they felt that they had given their money's worth and done enough to decently declare the meeting over.

"Well," sighed William at length, shuffling papers and looking happily at his fellow panellists. "If there are no other points or queries from the floor … ?"

There were not.

"It seems we have reached a consensus that the Hobson's Hill wind farm will be a very good thing indeed. Thank you all for your attendance."

There was a scattering of disgruntled mutters but the crowd rose promptly and started to file from the hall like children let out of school.

"Well that was a pleasant relief," said William. "Much smoother than I expected."

"Inarticulate bunch," said the minister scornfully. "And infertility! That's a new one."

Thomas shook his head and drummed his fingers on his briefcase. "Exactly as I feared," he said sorrowfully. "I suppose, now, there is no option but ... Naturally after the reactionary elements such as the vicar intimidated them they all clammed up. He would be happy if the whole hill was bulldozed to the ground."

"Reactionary?" frowned Clementina in puzzlement. "But he – "

"In backward, superstitious places like this the heavy hand of the church still represses many of the villagers," he said bitterly.

"What do you mean?"

He glanced up, startled, as though he had been talking in a reverie. He looked away and bit a knuckle, exactly as Clara, in full Cecil B. DeMille mode, had coached him in rehearsals and exactly as he had vowed he would not do. "Perhaps I have said too much already," he murmured.

"Tell us," she urged.

He seemed to hesitate but shook his head. "I'm not sure I can. You're outsiders. You do not understand our ways. You might judge us. You seem enlightened and sympathetic but I can't – " He broke off.

William frowned. "What on Earth did that chap mean about – "

Suddenly there was a commotion from near the entrance of the still half-filled hall. The crowd backed away from the doors with cries and mutters and one door was flung back against the wall with a dramatic bang. A startling figure stood framed in the entrance pointing at the dais. It was a tall long-haired woman in a flowing white dress with dangly bits at the wrists. Her face was hidden behind a skull-mask. In one hand she carried a thing resembling a hybrid of an iron-bound oak staff and a voodoo wand, topped with a small animal skull. With this she struck the floor, raising another dramatic bang, and pointing at the panellists accusingly, cried:

"Woe! Woe! Woe and bloody vengeance upon you who would desecrate thee sacred groves!"

For reasons best known to herself Clara had adopted a voodoo priest's voice, although it was reminiscent, at many points, of the strange Welsh-Slav-Pakistani one that came out when she tried to do Scandinavian. It was, at any rate, the strangest, eeriest voice any of the panel had ever heard.

Clara danced, cavorted, capered, shimmied, gyrated and merrily skipped her way up the hall. She scattered handfuls of a sparkling powder from a pouch at her belt and the crowd fell back at her approach. Her wand rattled as she waved it.

The visitors watched mesmerised. She danced right around them once counter-clockwise flinging the powder over them – it made them sneeze – then capered halfway back up the hall along the centre aisle. Then she approached them again with a very horrible sort of writhing, jerking, spasmodic limbo-ing motion, while hissing and flicking her tongue at them through a gap in the mask. She straightened and shook her wand at them in a fey kind of jester-bladder-shaking way and then flung a strange bracelet-type object down on the table.

She pointed at the visitors in turn. "Thee Walpole's curse is upon you," she hissed venomously. "Leave this place and do not return!"

She whirled her hair around her head and then skipped gaily off down the hall. "Woe, woe!" she pronounced a couple more times, waving her arms in the air, then, pausing only to rattle her wand admonishingly in the petrified Harriet's face, skipped out.

The panel let out their breaths.

"Who the hell was that?"

"No-one," said Thomas woodenly, wiping his brow. He had been a pillar of a dramatic society at school; and of course he was used to performing in court. "Pay no heed." He summoned a smile. "Mama Clara, a local character, a madwoman who lives in the woods. Did she startle you? We've grown used to it."

"But what was that about sacred groves?"

He laughed and waved a hand. "Think nothing of it. A care-in-the-community case, I assure you."

William poked at the thing she had dropped with a pencil. It appeared to be a pet collar about which twigs, the skulls of small rodents and nettles had been twined. "Curious thing. It looks like – "

"*Don't touch it!*" Thomas cried in horror. "It is the Collar of the Suicided Cat! It's unclean!" They stared at him. "That is, you don't know where it's been," he said more calmly. "Could be rather unhygienic. Forgive me, I'm rather a fusspot. May I?" He took the pencil and flicked the thing off the table with a shudder. "Come, you've earned some refreshments, and I suppose you'll want to celebrate. Let's go and have a drink and you can tell me what the next stage will be."

The minister glanced at her watch. "Actually, I'd better be going."

"Me too," said Kate assembling her papers. "Thanks anyway."

Thomas grimaced. "Already? The thing is I was supposed to detain you for a few minutes. A small entertainment is to take place in your honour on the village green."

"Oh."

He waved at the now almost empty hall. "You will have seen that half the crowd rushed out quickly, they went to set it up. It won't take too long, really."

"Perhaps we'd better show willing," said William. "More tactful."

"It's really nothing, a miniature fete, just a few stalls and a traditional local dance. They wanted to make sure you saw the village at its best."

"In the hope we might spare it?" asked William. Thomas smiled wryly and made a gesture.

Clementina, in whom the prospect of a traditional local dance induced thoughts of arranging to wipe out the village with a bypass, snorted. "But, apart from the obvious inbreds, there didn't seem to *be* any objections to the development."

"I can assure you there are deep and heartfelt objections," said Thomas. "They simply weren't much vocalized because of fear of – I myself would rather – I assure you that if you build the turbines you will be destroying something precious here. Is there really no alternative?"

"I'm sorry," said Clementina saccharinely, and she and William started in reasonable voices to reasonably run through some of the reasonable reasons they hadn't had a chance to use at the meeting.

When presently they walked out into the late afternoon sunlight the green had already been set up for the impromptu fete. The diversion was as modest as Thomas had said (its point in the grand scheme being merely to help to keep the visitors around until nightfall): stalls decked with bunting had been set up around the sides of the green, a few offering hoop-la and similar games, most displaying tat from the tat shops and various comestibles the Women's Institute ladies had put together. The visitors put on patient smiles and strolled around like gracious royals.

They were plied with food and refreshments.

"Try my mandrake jam," said mountainous Miriam of the W.I. to William with a wink.

She pushed a piece of bread smeared with jam towards his reluctantly yielding mouth.

"Ah – mm – "

"Put a bit of lead in your pencil," said Miriam roguishly. "Not that I'll wager a game gent like you needs it."

"Ah – it's rather – it's got something – mandrake jam? Isn't that a rather unusual – "

"We are a rather unusual village," said Thomas blandly.

"Three quid a jar or two for a fiver," said Miriam. She winked again. "Treat for your missus."

"I'm not – ah – blessed that way."

"Go on, a bly chap like you? You must play havoc. In that case," Miriam looked sly, "a jar's my gift, provided you'll accept my otterwurzel into the bargain." She held up a sprig of parsley.

"Ah – thank you – it would be my honour," said William, baffled and bemused.

"No sir," breathed Miriam, strangely smouldering, "it is mine." She pressed the jam-jar into his hand and, to his large surprise, attached the parsley to his lapel with a pin.

"Really, Miriam," tutted Thomas. "You know Mr. Penge doesn't – he isn't – he won't be – "

Miriam pulled her tongue at him and kissed the flinching William on the cheek. "We shall see what we shall see," she said gnomically, passing back behind her stall with a flounce and a sidelong glance at the civil servant.

"What is – ah – an otterwurzel?" asked William as they strolled on, puzzled and somewhat demoralized to find himself with a sprig of parsley prominently attached to his jacket.

Thomas creased his forehead. "It's, it's, a symbolic token connected to, er, a local festivity. It performs the function of – well, to put it no more crudely, a love pledge."

The next stall featured a display of ginger biscuits of a curiously phallic shape.

Further on they were plied with offerings from a punch bowl full of a dark red liquid they were told was called Goat's Blood.

Abruptly pipes and flutes started to play. There was a jingle of bells, a tramp of feet, and morris dancers appeared on the green and started to trot back and forth. Clementina, glumly eating a strange home-made jam sponge she had been handed which was in the shape of a baby, didn't quite succeed in suppressing a heartfelt groan.

There was, however, something out of the ordinary about these particular dancers. William's polite smile quickly turned to a frown. For one thing, they all wore goatskin leggings. For another, they all sported long manipulable leather phalluses in front of their groins like actors in an ancient Greek comedy.

"The morris dance, of course, is thought to have derived from a fertility rite," Thomas told William. "We may well be unique here, however, in, er, pointing that up somewhat."

As the visitors watched the dancers formed two lines and extended their phalluses to right angles. These appeared to have pins attached to the end.

Various village girls and women with balloons tied around their waists took it in turns to dash along this gauntlet, shrieking as the phalluses thrust and jabbed and prodded at them and burst the balloons, which proved to be filled with water and in some cases what looked like blood.

William stared open-mouthed. This, and some of the strangeness he had already seen, and much of the much worse he had yet to see, was, as it happened, pretty much exactly the sort of thing he had always secretly feared secretly went on in the country.

Suddenly the music changed to a faster tempo and there were shrieks and excited claps and an eddy at the farthest edge of the crowd. Out of it burst a capering, wobbling, rather fearsome-looking medieval hobby-horse, a fabric-covered framework surmounted by a monstrous semi-equine head, snapping dragon-like iron jaws.

"Aha!" cried Thomas delightedly, "the Hobby! This also has a fascinating sexual significance. Watch." The Hobby raced around the green, clashing its teeth and tossing its head, the scurrying feet of the man within occasionally visible under its trailing skirts. It chased after girls, who fled from it shrieking. As William watched it caught one who seemed not to run so fast, rearing up over her and covering her so that she was trapped beneath. There were further shrieks from inside. Finally the girl crawled out laughing hysterically. There were black patches on her face and clothing. "A bucket of warm pitch or tar is slung within the frame. Actually ours is mostly just paint. The operator symbolically daubs the girls with it. Traditionally a kiss and cuddle is exacted as forfeit. You will note some of the girls don't run very fast."

Clementina looked completely horrified at this. Both she and Kate looked more so when the Hobby suddenly veered in their direction. They backed away and finally turned to flee but found themselves up against a jam-tart stall. Kate nimbly and unhesitatingly vaulted over it and escaped at the cost of a sticky hand. The government minister dithered fatally, backed up against it and stared in immobile terror as the sinister creature bore down on her. It reared up and engulfed her.

Many of the onlookers had the sense to look uneasy at this, including Miles, huddled watching with an ice-cream-licking Clara behind the flap of a fortune-telling tent no-one had entered.

From inside the horse clearly came the sound of a ringing slap, a panicked male shout of, "Christ!" and then a scream. The hobby-horse moved on, leaving behind it a discarded brush, an empty bucket, and a government minister lying on the ground covered from head to toe in black paint. The thing was that Jeremiah's visibility was poor from inside the Hobby, depending on a small hole near the neck, and his glasses had steamed up somewhat in his previous exertions. He had been fully convinced he was on target for the pretty PR girl, with whom he quite fancied a bit of opportunistic slap and tickle, and indeed he had been until her resourceful vault to safety, and no-one had been more surprised or appalled than him when he found the detested and conventional-beauty-paradigm-eschewing Miss Batt in his goatish clutches. He had thrown half the bucket of paint at her in instinctive panic; and then thoughtfully, slowly, cacklingly, reckoning the damage was done anyway, poured the rest of it over her out of inborn hatred of everything she stood for.

"Ooh," said Miles.

"Oh, dear," said Clara, not terribly sadly, imperturbably licking ice cream.

"It will be a nuclear power plant now."

"It is almost worth it."

A light, drive-by daubing of the female visitors had actually been part of the plan. Thomas could then apologetically invite them back to his place to see if his wife could lend them something to change into or at least help them clean up, and they would thus be kept around until the main festivities after dark. But this wholesale pantomime-horse-rape and terrible besmirching of a member of the government was far from part of the programme and, indeed, promptly put an end to the jamboree.

The musicians fell silent. Apart from a single cackling laugh from the disappearing hobby-horse so too did everyone else, staring morbidly at the tarred figure that raised itself slowly from the ground and stood there dripping, hands held in front of her curled into claws of revulsion, a mass of treacly black from head to toe. A spin-doctor in her head told her to gamely grin. She managed this, once, but Miles blinked and missed it.

Thomas the lawyer was at her side, urbane and concerned, gallantly holding out a futile handkerchief. "Terribly sorry ... slight mishap ... fun of the fair ..."

She pushed past him and stalked off.

"Come and let my wife clean you up," he implored hurrying after her.

"No thanks."

"At least wait till you dry, you'll get it all over your car."

"I don't care."

"You can't miss the rest of the festivities."

She stopped as they reached the high street, turned and at the top of her lungs shouted, "*Look* at me! I am *covered* in bla – "

Clementina Batt stopped. A small patch of cheek that *wasn't* covered in black paint went unusually pallid at the thought of the solecism she had just nearly committed. In her splendidly successful career of self-righteous, taxpayer-funded Applied Surrealism she had had seven fellow students, three lecturers, seventeen council employees, colleagues or superiors, two of them black, five Whitehall civil servants and counting, one of them blind, two serving army officers, a journalist and three waitresses reprimanded, investigated, retrained, disciplined or sacked for using words like blackboard, black coffee, blacklist, blackball, black market, black marker, black mark, black cab, black cloud, black mood, black day, black-avised (a lecturer), black hash (a student), black-hearted, black books, black box, black sheep and black pudding, and had issued countless edicts against the use of such phrases, and had, incidentally, lobbied for the name of Whitehall to be changed. Her mind raced frantically.

" ... in *non-light-reflecting* paint," she eventually finished feebly. "Not that that isn't lovely," she hastily added.

Thomas had loved England once, he remembered; possibly only yesterday. He found he was able to stop himself laughing fit to split the sky or shaking her by the throat. He had a better idea. He really couldn't help himself.

He stared at her aghast, letting his jaw drop a little.

"You fucking racist pig," he said.

Clementina burst out sobbing and ran off.

"You heard her, everyone!" he cried. "You heard her! I can't believe it! She was going to say *that word* right in my face! And she doesn't *care* for paint of colour! *White* paint would be fine, oh yes! Someone get some white paint for the racist imperialist bigot!"

He laughed hysterically to himself and then suddenly stopped, cleared his throat and adjusted his tie, feeling a bit ashamed. Really, he had been playing with Clara too much lately. Also, the plan was going to hell. While he had been standing in the road shouting like a lunatic about paint after a fleeing black-painted lunatic, a car had driven past him which was painted in a particular shade of just-so turquoise that other lunatics were currently trying to trademark or patent: Kate of the company currently known as Lydia had made her escape.

It didn't matter. As far as Thomas was concerned it was for the best. His instructions had been to keep all three around if possible but to keep hold of William at all costs, and really he felt that William was enough. Thomas was an old-fashionedly chivalrous man, the preceding unseemly outburst sorrily excepted, in fact somewhat prudish, and he was glad it had turned out like this: there were things that ladies ought not to have inflicted on them.

But where was William? Thomas stalked back towards the green. A confederate pointed and muttered, Thomas nodded and turned round. Behind him the mini-fete started to disassemble and its organisers stole off to ready themselves for the climactic phase.

William had sloped off to the Dog and Duck as soon as he had seen the blackened minister ejected from the Hobby, not keen to get caught in the explosion or be associated more than he already was with a horrible memory for an important superior. Poor Clementina. He was lucky to have got off with a parsley buttonhole and a bizarre dead-cat curse. What a day. What a place. The sooner he was out of here and surrounded by reassuring tarmac and pavement the better. He was resolved to resign rather than ever visit the countryside again. He sank a quiet half-pint and then, after he had seen the sorry tarry mess of Clementina get into her car and drive off, walked out into the car park to do the same.

The lawyer grabbed his arm. "So soon? Come and have one with me."

William smiled apologetically. "I'd really best be pushing off."

Thomas didn't let go. Equally apologetically he said, "I really can't let you leave before we've talked. There are things you ought to know about. I couldn't speak freely in front of the ladies. I'm afraid this process isn't going to be as straightforward as you imagine."

Torn between duty and the desire for escape from this terrible atavistic place, William sighed and led the way back into the pub.

They sat in a small cosy side-room they had to themselves. Over the drinks Thomas's polished voice led them through small talk, sport, the weather, the news, William's job. The lawyer suggested they eat, and William, who had been looking forward to a defrosted pie at home, reluctantly acceded. Over dinner Thomas again led them over neutral subjects, keeping up an easy flow of reminiscences of celebrated or interesting legal cases he had been involved with; several times William saw an opening to steer the conversation back to the matter of the wind farm but was never quite allowed to get there. The plates were cleared and they sat with coffee, and again the talk ranged over everything but the topic at hand. William grew restless. It was growing dark outside. Already he was doomed to drive home at night through meandering country roads where trees loomed sinisterly and things scurried across the road or threw themselves at your headlights.

"Look here," he said at last. "You said you wanted to talk to me. About the development."

"Yes," said Thomas. He frowned. "I find it isn't that easy." Abruptly he rose and stalked off, returning with two large brandies.

"Not for me," said William firmly. "I have to drive. I really ought to be getting home soon."

"Perhaps you ought to stay here for the night. Although ... on the other hand ... perhaps you might not care to, when ... " Thomas drained his glass in two long swallows and then took and nursed the one he had brought for William. He hunched forward on his chair, frowning intently and spinning the brandy in the glass.

Suddenly William was amused rather than impatient. "For God's sake, man! Out with it! I promise you won't ... hurt my feelings or provoke my anger or whatever it is you're afraid of. I am used to overcoming obstacles and so far I have had a very easy ride. What is it? Are you leading up to offering me a bribe? A threat? The mandrake jam and the woman who made it probably constituted both."

Thomas laughed and sat back. "If only it was that simple." He laid his briefcase across his knee and tapped his fingers on it for several moments. "Mr. Penge," he said at length. "The development on Hobson's Hill must not go ahead. It *will* not go ahead. A group of local residents have retained me to put their case and if necessary pursue it though legal channels. We would much rather not, but ... There are several quite wealthy men hereabouts, some of whom are prepared to back me anonymously if need be."

He paused.

"Go on."

Thomas shifted forward slightly and massaged his wrist. "Mr. Penge. Has it struck you that this village, some of its inhabitants, are somewhat unusual compared to other country villages?"

"No," said William truthfully.

"Well, the fact is we have ... an unusual secret. It is somewhat embarrassing to talk about it in front of outsiders. There is a reason the vicar and other reactionary elements are keen to see the hill razed and tarmacked over. The hill is vital to the wellbeing of the rest of us. It ... You probably look at it and see an empty eminence like any other. But ... it is being used."

"As?"

"It is the mating-grounds."

William groaned. "Is that all? I *dealt* ad nauseam with the ecological – "

Thomas waved a hand. "No, no, no. You don't understand."

"*Make* me understand. If you think you have a case, make it."

"Words," sighed Thomas. "How can words evoke what is so beautiful, so joyous? If I told you, you wouldn't understand. You wouldn't even believe. You'd laugh at me."

For all his refinement and obvious legal experience William was starting to think the lawyer was some kind of simpleton. Perhaps he had been living in the country too long. "I promise you – " he began.

"I can't tell you. I may not tell you. I can only show you." Thomas leaned forward smiling. "Mr. Penge. William. Will you humour me? Will you trust me? Will you have one more drink with me and then let me show you why the hill is so precious to us?"

"Very well," groaned William, not ill-humouredly. "If it will get this over with."

"Thank you."

At the bar Thomas found Mr. Ransome, who nodded significantly at him. Thomas nodded back and the latter went out. A few minutes later he and the civil servant left too.

For ever afterwards William was to regret his weak-mindedness in humouring the eccentric lawyer. Over and over he would tell himself he should have said no and gone home at the start. Sitting at his desk in his office with its en suite shower, and then sitting at home rocking back and forth on the edge of his chair while on extended sick-leave, and then later standing at the window in high-rise hotel rooms looking out over the sprawling neon spacescapes of Shanghai, Tokyo, Hong Kong or Dubai during the worldwide tour of megalopolises he treated himself to after winning his compensation claim, and after that sitting at his desk in his more modest office at the defoliant-manufacturing company he went to work for, he would fall prey to reveries in which the innocent frozen pie that had been waiting for him at home would appear very clearly and seem to reproach him for passing it up, as if he had *chosen* his terrible odyssey into the heart of rural darkness, as if some part of him had welcomed it. For years he would have nightmares in which he and the lawyer repeated their arduous journey through the night to *that place*. Often, just before they started to see the awful figures through the trees, he would seem to wake up – and there, before him, would be his pie, inviting on a plate, and nearby the solid reassurance of the TV remote, and it was *that night*, but he had chosen rightly, and none of it had happened, he had merely dozed off in front of the telly, and it had all been a horrible dream, he was safe and sound and surrounded by bricks and pavement and lamp-posts as far as the eye could see, and he would sob with relief and thankfulness. Then, however, he would flick round the TV channels, and a history programme would come on, and a voice would say, "Tonight, the career of Robert Walpole", and a capering figure in a white dress would appear on the screen, and behind that another figure that smiled at him with a terrible invitation, and the Thing he had trained himself never to think about, and he would really wake up, shaking and screaming and covered in icy sweat.

They drove as far as they could. William was mildly fearful for his car as they negotiated a twisting, rutted, unlit track, but the last drink Thomas had given him had been a strong one – as has been said, Thomas was a kindly man outside a courtroom – and he was already mentally engaged in crafting this strange jaunt into an amusing anecdote of rural idiocy and the ardours of his job for the benefit of certain colleagues at work. He had realised that the object must be to take him up Hobson's Hill, and at this point imagined that the lawyer intended to impart some loamy folk-wisdom there, or teach him some sentimental lesson, or dramatically and futilely bring home to him what he was destroying. "Look," Thomas would say at last, pointing and flashing a torch, after a lengthy and annoying schlep through the undergrowth, "some rabbits," or as it might be badgers, or elks, or a nesting turkey, or jackal cubs, or a family of lizards, or something, and expect William to fall to his knees crying. Or he would hunker down and pick up a handful of earth and solemnly ask William to smell it, and then to eat it to see how good and rich it tasted. Or he would show him the view, or it being night the stars, or a tree he had carved his wife's name on, or say, "You can see my house from here." Or it would be Caesar's initials, or King Arthur's throne, or an interestingly-shaped rock the locals came from miles around to admire and muse over when the sheep weren't in season. He chuckled to himself as he reviewed the possibilities, and then swore and stamped the brakes as the track, which had been rising for a while, turned a corner and then abruptly came to an end at a cutting of rocks, earth and tree-roots.

"We must walk from here."

William was sobered and annoyed as he emerged. Looking about in the moonlight it became clear that there was not space to turn the car round, and nor had there been for some time, and on the return journey he would be required to reverse a considerable distance down this intricate lane in the dark. He cursed this absurd fool's errand and the enigmatic idiot by his side.

"This way." Thomas strode up a steepish mossy grade at the side of the track and held out his hand to help William. At the top they stood in a forest, which rose before and descended behind them.

"So you want to take me up the bloody hill," said William in exasperation. "What's the point? It won't do any good. Especially as it's pitch-black. I won't be able to see anything."

"You will see enough. And," Thomas added dramatically, "that you may wish you didn't."

William groaned. A vole. It would be a little newborn vole, three days old, with a pink snout. The maniac would make him rub noses with it.

"Come." The lawyer led the way up the incline. William stumbled over a tree-root at his first step and sprawled full-length.

"Don't you at least have a torch?" he demanded as he picked himself up.

"I don't need one. My very soul knows the way, like a bird to its nest or a salmon to its spawning grounds." Actually Thomas had spent the past three nights learning the route, grumbling and cursing and ruining his clothes.

"Christ Almighty," said William with feeling.

"Do not speak those words here," said Thomas sharply, and set off uphill again at a brisk pace, leaving William no option but to follow or be left alone in the dark.

It was not quite pitch-black. The moon was almost full and it was so clear a night the twinkling stars alone could have defined the shapes of the trees and the looming bulk of the hill. As William's eyes became accustomed to the gloom he gradually found he could pick his way with only a minimum of stumbling, tripping, sprawling, slipping, sliding, caroming off trunks, walking headfirst into trunks, snagging clothes or skin on brambles, whippings in the face by branches, and jarrings of ankles in sudden pot-holes. Under his panting breath he cursed Thomas, his department, the government, the village, the trees, the darkness, the countryside or his own folly with every laboured step. Apart from anything else this madman's hike was the first sustained exercise he had taken for months: his lifestyle was sedentary and he used the office gym only in brief occasional bursts. He tried telling himself he was there now, on the treadmill, with the lights inexplicably out, and would shortly be able to step into his warm office shower and then pop downstairs for fifteen soothing minutes with the department masseuse, but he was fooling no-one. It was a relatively balmy night, and he considered taking his jacket off, what was left of it, but that would have encumbered a hand he needed for scraping on bark and impaling on thorns. Five minutes after setting off the right-hand hip pocket had impacted heavily with a tree-trunk and it was while he was feeling to check he still had his car-keys after a later tumble that he discovered it was now sticky with the contents of a shattered jar of mandrake jam.

Gradually the way became somewhat easier. The trees were more spaced out and Thomas appeared to be following a fairly well-defined, well-trodden path which William himself was able to pick out in a sudden moon-bright clearing. By degrees he ceased to feel irritation, self-pity and hatred of the relentlessly plodding silhouette ahead. What he now felt was fear. Intense, growing, all-encompassing, general and specific fear. He had never liked woods, even in the daytime. He associated them mainly with horror films on the television; it was asking for trouble to set foot in one. When people did, in horror films on television, he felt they had only themselves to blame for what happened next. He jumped at every owl-hoot, flinched at every scampering from the bushes. Once they started a pheasant, an explosion of outraged noise, and his trousers nearly became as mulchy as his jacket pocket. He feared the very ground they walked on. Were there man-traps? There would probably be man-traps, great rusty iron-hinged Victorian jaws that would bite into his bone above the knee and trap him there while the lawyer trudged heedlessly on. He would have watched every step except he was afraid to take his eyes off the menacing darkness ahead and all the known and unknown things that could be lurking in that. Once, far to his right and quite some way down the hill, there came a howling, Mr. Ransome's dog tied up at his cottage did he but know it, and he thought of wolves. Were there wolves out here? He thought there were. How about bears? He decided he feared bears above all things. He was fairly sure, on second thoughts, that there were no bears in the woods in England at this date. Ah, but some idiot might have reintroduced them. He was fairly sure they had. He had handled correspondence from, had chaired a meeting intended to soothe, outraged rurals, farmers, ornithologists and so on, protesting about the fashion for reintroducing extinct or rare predators, creatures red in tooth and claw that were now cutting swathes though gentler animals and birds; and any one of those gentler animals and birds would be faster, cannier, better attuned to their environment and harder to catch than a wounded, winded civil servant would be. Wolves. Not perhaps bears, but they *had* done it with wolves. Wolves had gone from Britain but, he remembered reading now, they had or were about to or wanted to reintroduce them to the island. Somewhere up north, he thought, possibly Scotland, but the point was you couldn't expect wolves to stay put, or to content themselves with a diet of fast and savvy animals for long when there were helpless humans blundering around. Idiots. Stupid bastards. Why couldn't they leave well alone? These people here were right, these despised shambling thorp-dwellers he spent his life placating and bamboozling: leave the natural world the hell alone. Far better and far safer, stay the hell out of it ...

But this phase passed. And then even more than any specific thing, he found he simply feared the woods, the dark dark lonely woods, the way that ancient man had feared them. Ancient man had been onto something. There were *things* here. There were forces. Spirits, entities, or *an* entity, the woods themselves perhaps, things that could reach out and tap you on your shoulder, physically or psychically, and destroy your sanity with a single glimpse of them, beings or a being older and more powerful than and inimical or indifferent to man, that might at best sport with you as an amusing plaything, at worst destroy you for trespassing on their realm ... William shivered and hurried to catch up to the lawyer.

And then, after a time, that phase passed too, or at least faded into a background part of his mind in favour of a more specific and pressing fear. Namely, of the lawyer. He allowed himself to lag behind again. What did he know of the man, beyond the fact that he was obviously unbalanced in some way? What were they doing here? What did he intend to do with him? And behind him the villagers. What the hell was going on there? He reviewed some of the events of the day. He had to admit that there was more at work here than ordinary and expected rural inbredness. The secrecy, the strangeness. This riddling lawyer with his literally unspeakable obsession with the hill. The determination to keep him here. Precious ... vital ... sacred groves. Dear God, had he lured him up here to kill him in an attempt to protect the blasted forest? He started to think again of horror films. That's enough ... mandrake ... a hobby-horse ... No. Nonsense. Pull yourself together. You are a grown man. You are a middle-aged civil-servant strolling with a Cambridge-educated lawyer.

He suddenly laughed aloud at himself and ran to catch up with Thomas. Thomas turned and smiled.

"We are almost there."

"Ah."

The ground was levelling off; they seemed to be reaching the summit. They walked on for a while in companionable silence.

"Do you know the local name for the hill?" Thomas asked conversationally.

"No?"

"We call it Hobgoblin Hill." His words seemed to come out unnaturally loudly and ring through the woods.

"Ah!" went William with professionally polite delight. "Is there a reason for that?"

"You will see now."

Ahead of them through the trees there were figures; figures and flickering flames.

William had forgotten his fear for a few moments. Now it came back to him. Within a few moments more, he was unable to remember a time when he hadn't felt fear. It seemed to him that he had feared what he beheld there forever, that there hadn't been a single moment all his life when he hadn't feared this, exactly and specifically this, even in childhood.

As the pair walked through the trees the terrible scene ahead resolved from a horrible suggestive vagueness to an even more appalling clarity. They entered the clearing on the crown of the hill and William was upon it, was in it.

Flaming torches of burning pitch mounted on poles had been set up around the edge of the clearing and at strategic points within. By their light he saw dancers; other things too, but the dancers were what first drew his eye and were what had mesmerised him, casting contorted shadows through the trees, at a distance. They were within a couple of yards of him now, the impact of their bare feet felt by his own as they trod the turf in front of him. The women skipped and leapt as they circled around the middle of the clearing, flinging their arms in the air ecstatically, chanting and shrieking, their faces exalted. Their ages ranged from youth to later middle age, and they were naked, or nearly so. That is, the primary and overwhelming impression was one of nakedness. Clara had encouraged, demanded nakedness from everyone apart from herself. "Think of the eventual film!" she had cajoled the ladies of the Women's Institute. "Think Calendar Girls with goat's blood!" But some were more naked than others. Jeremiah's buxom, rather exhibitionist young assistant Jennifer, for example, was completely and gloriously so, seeming to favour William with a frank delighted grin and a knowing look as she cavorted past him. The mammoth amazon Miriam of the W.I., following, vibrating all over as she pranced, wore only a flesh-coloured bikini thong, and also seemed to favour William with a bold and knowing stare. Others had followed their lead, some had been more bashful. Body-paint had been much resorted to by the more inhibited. Some who were nude or nearly so had daubed themselves in woad, or a blue paint that was intended for it. There were bodystockings or bikini tops elaborately painted to pass for unclothed bodies in the firelight. There were fig-leaves of cloth or actual leaf, several strategically-placed garlands of flowers, a painted corset worn by one blushing matron. But the abiding picture was one of bared and untrammelled flesh, ripe or more than ripe.

The men were slightly less nude. That is, from the waist up they proudly revealed brawn, flab or bone, but below that they almost uniformly wore jockstraps of fur or loincloths of goatskin or leather, the sole exceptions being a couple of smart-alec young farm workers who had obtained impressive prosthetic cinema body-pieces. Several wore goat-fur leggings on their shins, a few had riding boots. They all wore masks of one sort or another: bought masks, elaborate, costly and spectacular masks left over from the Lord of the Manor's rock concerts, or masks that their womenfolk had lovingly sewed, painted or even carved. They were mainly divided between demon masks and goat masks and there was a profusion of curved or twisting and often quite magnificent horns. There was a stray domino mask, one horned Viking helmet, and a striking wolfskin headpiece that became a fur cloak over shoulders and upper back. Some of the men were woad-daubed, to varying aesthetic effect. They stood in a circle around the edge of the clearing, blowing pipes or flutes, banging bongos or goatskin drums, rhythmically bashing sticks together, or simply clapping and chanting wordlessly as the women danced.

There were worse things than these in the centre of the clearing. There was a rock, a small boulder, and on it stood the madwoman Mama Clara. (Clara had insisted on having a rock to stand on, had spent two days scouting for the right one, and it had taken eight strong men marshalled by a landscape gardener to drag it into place and arrange it to her satisfaction.) She wore the same white dress but had removed the skull-mask. She span round and round, she raised her arms to the night sky, she shrieked and cackled. She hopped on one leg, she rattled her wand-staff, she banged it on the rock. Posing leaning back with one leg bent and her hair dangling down, she threw it twirling up into the air like a drum majorette's baton. She flinched and covered her head with her hands as she fumbled the catch and it came clattering down on her, causing her to fall off the rock. She recovered quickly and started to swing her hair and arms and perform a sort of horrible Maori war-stomp in time to the music. There was another, flat, almost rectangular stone, perhaps eight feet long and six wide, lying on or set into the ground some distance to the right; presently she started to gyrate around this, yipping and ululating and making strange horse-like whinnying noises. William could clearly see a couple of headless chickens lying against or near this flat stone. After a while the deranged priestess skipped to the very centre of the clearing and started to dance around and tap her wand against the thing that stood there, the centrepiece of the festivities, the Giant Wicker Penis.

Clara was not *quite* happy with the Giant Wicker Penis. It was slightly too artsy-craftsy, more like an oversize laundry basket or gargantuan raffia bottle-holder than a sinister pagan idol, she thought. She ought to have set the women of the village onto it rather than commissioning it from her friend's furniture-maker. For one thing she had chickened out of saying penis or even phallus over the phone, and instead had talked of 'a tall free-standing dome-topped erection', and even the design-sketch she had sent had been unusually modest. It would have looked far better flanked by a pair of giant wicker bollocks, for example. But William was impressed, was appalled, was rivetted with horror by the sight of it. It was well over twenty feet tall and, if it did not quite remind him of his own equipment, clearly something primal and earthy in intent. It had hinged doors, standing slightly open now, to admit of an occupant. And it was standing on a wooden platform, surrounded by heaped firewood and kindling, quite obviously an unlit bonfire.

And just as he had taken in this detail, the priestess stopped her cavorting, screamed and pointed at him.

The music and the dancing stopped; every face turned to him.

"Thee outsider!" cried Clara in her would-be voodoo accent, rattling her wand and undulating towards him with horrible writhing steps. "Thee man of wrath! Thee unbeeleevah! He who would foul Thee Walpole's sacred groves! He dares violate our circle!"

The civil servant swallowed, petrified, almost unable to breathe as the eerie madwoman advanced towards him. Her face was painted ghostly white, with streaks of dark make-up around the eyes. She had blackened or yellowed several of her teeth and made her tongue a strange colour with sweets. She flickered this at William now and prowled around him, sniffing at him.

"A sacrifice for our feast!" she shrieked, raising her arms and head to the sky, then pointing at William again. "He must burn! He must be burned in Thee Giant Wicker Penis!" Her voice fluctuated between Eartha Kitt, Mexican bandit and a demented Peter Lorre.

There was a shout of joy and the drums started up again. Two masked horned men seized one of William's arms apiece and started to drag him, struggling, forward.

"No," he whimpered in terror, "please, no."

"Burn," cried the priestess and the crowd, "burn, burn, burn, burn!"

"Wait!" said Thomas loudly, stepping forward. "He is no threat. I will stand sponsor to this man. He comes not to mock our circle but to join it."

The priestess scowled and hissed but made a curt gesture, silencing the drums and chant and halting the men tugging at William's arms.

"So," she said, "a fresh soul for Thee Walpole. Even bettah!"

She cackled and shook her wand and gyrated, skipped, pranced away behind the wicker phallus.

The horned men stepped aside and Thomas drew William gently back towards the circumference of the circle. The civil servant was trembling all over.

Thomas chuckled easily and said, "They wouldn't really have done it. It is merely an initiation ritual that must be gone through. Sort of formal call-and-response. We don't really have human sacrifices, we only burn effigies. Oh, perhaps some chickens, the occasional sheep, but we usually cut their throats first. You mustn't mind. I was the same when they pulled it on me. It's just like ... were you ever in the boy scouts, or ... "

He burbled on, filled with pity and guilt. He had not approved of the preceding part of the entertainment, but could see it would be useful psychologically. His chuckle might have been slightly less easy had he been present the night before when Clara had idly floated a last-minute modification to the plan. "We're missing a trick here," she had said. "It's such a waste. Why don't we really, *really* kill them and eat them?" But only Arthur the landlord had backed her up.

The civil servant was so silent and still that Thomas started to fear he had gone catatonic, perhaps permanently, with the terror. He had just been reassured by a dry swallow, a small noise in the throat, a tiny nod, when Clara returned.

She came tripping gaily across the firelit greensward, a large sloshing metal milk-pail in one hand, for all the world like some rustic milkmaid. She stopped before William and held it out to him. He looked down. The liquid inside was by no means milk. It was deep red.

"Blood!" she cried. "Blood to anoint thee new chosen of thee Walpole!" There was a metal ladle in the pail; she spooned some of the contents out and let it trickle thickly back, eyes lighting up. "Mmm!" she said happily. "Rich! Full of babies!"

"It is not really full of babies," Thomas reassured him.

"Baby goats," said Clara. "What is thee initiant's name?"

"William Penge," said Thomas.

"*William Penge?*" She made a face. "He is now named Salamander Goatchild."

She dipped up a ladle full of blood and poured it over William's forehead. He felt it trickle, warmish, all over his face.

He thought no thoughts and made no movement save to wipe his eyes clean. When he had done so he saw she was now holding another glistening ladleful before him.

"Now you must dreenk of thee blod," she said invitingly. "Mmm! Tastee!"

He looked at her. She held the ladle up towards his lips. Beside him he could see Thomas frowning and nodding at him warningly. He opened his mouth and sipped, then involuntarily swallowed and spluttered a little as the rest was poured in after.

The blood wasn't really blood, or not completely. But at least some of it was; this was a farming community and Clara had insisted. It had to taste authentic, she had said. The others, revolted, had asked how he would know what blood tasted like. He might, she retorted, at least have eaten his scabs as a child. Future civil servants didn't do that, said Miles. They filed them. But he would at least know what tomato juice or something tasted like, she had pointed out. And it had to *look* authentic too. It had to be all nice and red and glisteny. The others pointed out that even in films they didn't use real blood as blood; the fake stuff looked better. A compromise had been proposed: they could use the red 'goatsblood' punch they would be serving at the fete. Those who were growing uncomfortable at the more sadistic elements of Clara's program had seized on this: the poor man would need a drink by this point, and it wouldn't hurt the rest of them. It would make sense for intoxicants to be served at the orgy. Clara had muttered about bleeding hearts and insisted he had to *think* it was blood. She had presided over the final concocting, in concert with more experienced cooks, including someone who had once been an expert on artificial flavouring for a convenience-food company. The orgy blood they had ended up with was based on the powerful punch, with the taste of the booze disguised, and with various thickening agents added, and notable amounts of salt, and finally, when no-one else was looking, for her own artistic satisfaction, just a tiny little pint or so of animal blood, carefully pasteurized and sterilized, procured from a farmer. Anyway, it tasted bloody awful.

But it went down rather well. After he overcame the urge to throw up William found he felt somewhat warm and reassured after swallowing. Perhaps he was now possessed.

"There's a good choild," said Clara in a rural accent. She scooped up and proffered another ladleful. "One more for Nanny, now."

Reluctantly he took another small gulp.

"That'll put hairs on your chest." She winked and moved along to offer the ladle to Thomas, who took a token sip, and then the woman next to him, for the dancers had moved to mingle in the outer circle, and so on along the line, dipping and pouring gleefully. There was a humming, a swaying, a couple of drums started up.

"Blood!" she cried in her priestess voice as she passed along and her acolytes drank. "Blood! Blood to bind thee servants of thee Walpole! Fresh! Tastee! Eeh, it's a luvly drop of blud, that," she suddenly added in a northern accent as she moved on, "like we used to have in the owld days. The Blood Man would come round, tuppence a pint, we'd say, Mam, Mam, can we have some blood? She'd say, Naww, you must mek your own, you'll have fort awpen a vein in t'whippets … "

Thomas, like Miles, had feared from early on that, for all her tactical brilliance and powers of generalship, Clara's penchant for ad libbing would turn out to be the weak link in her own scheme. To cover her out-of-character chuntering he turned to William and genially said, "Of course, I'm sure I don't have to point out the significance of the blood-sharing … tribal bonding ritual similar to that found in many and varied cultures throughout … " and on and on, fairly randomly but with his voice raised.

He need not have bothered. William was still in shock, from the proposed burning, and from having been made to drink blood. Anything the madwoman said was no more surprising than anything else that was happening to him.

" … so we ended up wi t'Coalman 'ung up in t'larder, and he's blud was the thickest Ah'd ever seen, we said, Mam, Mam … "

Clara was approaching again round the other side of the circle, dipping and ladling to eager mouths. Thomas noted that, after she had passed, those who had foolishly taken too much would often discreetly step towards the darkness to spit out or throw up.

"Blood! Blood! Blood for Thee Walpole! ... And one more for babba," she concluded as she came round to William again. Mechanically he once more sipped from the upraised ladle. "Ooh, he loves his blood," she said chucking him on the cheek. She gambolled off and started to skip about dipping the ladle into the almost empty bucket and then whirling it around her head so that the last drops were scattered over her congregation, singing, "Blood! Blood! Glorious blood!"

The whole circle started to sway from side to side and hum along to this tune, holding hands, which William found was one of the most horrible things that had happened yet.

Worse was to come.

The priestess threw her empty bucket of blood away with a clatter and cried, "Now, the unveiling of the lesser mystery! Prepare yourselves!"

The naked women ran forward and danced round the wicker monolith in an inner circle again as they had at the start, performing one complete circuit and then stopping. The priestess disappeared behind the giant cock. Drums started up, low, slow, expectant.

When Mama Clara emerged again she was walking slowly and reverently and carrying something before and above her, a tall plank of wood with a cross-beam attached and on it, as she stepped closer to the torchlight, Dear God, thought William, that looked like ...

"Beehold!" cried Clara triumphantly. "Thee Crucified Otter!"

The Crucified Otter was a detail that was to haunt William long after much of the rest of the night had been successfully repressed. The original Crucified Otter, of course, had been sold, and now resided in an alarmed, dust-free, humidity-controlled room in a townhouse on the Upper East Side of Manhattan, and Clara had never been satisfied with her work on it. She had leapt at the chance to try again with this, Crucified Otter No. 2, as it in its turn was eventually sold as, and had succeeded in nailing the thing on straight this time. However, *this* otter was crucified upside-down, as was more fitting.

"*Kneel* to thee Crucified Otter!" she cried, glaring.

All the men in the outer circle, including William under Thomas's guiding hand, dutifully knelt. The women bowed their heads briefly but reverently and then assembled into a group.

Clara planted the strange standard in a mound of earth.

"Now we do thee Dance of thee Crucified Otter!" she cried.

The Dance of the Crucified Otter was terrible to behold, something reminiscent of 80s music-television backing-dancers on a bad day, with a few intendedly otter-like movements and mass crucifixion stances thrown in. Clara would have been hurt if you had told her this, for she had choreographed it herself, the W.I. ladies in leotards flinging their heads from side to side in synchronicity night after night, treading nimbly or lumbering heavily around the village hall after hours.

At the end of the dance the men, who during it had been sitting playing their instruments, applauded politely. Clara took a bow and most of the women returned to the outer circle. She flung out an arm and said, "The Crucified Otter Dancers, everyone! Fly back to your fauns, my nymphs!" she added as Miriam lumberingly passed her. "And now!" she cried, "thee revelation of thee greater mystery! Thee manifestation of Thee Walpole!"

They were all standing again now. There was a drumming, a swaying, a rhythmic chanting, starting as a whisper and slowly building up: "Wal ... pole, *Wal*-pole, Wal-pole ... "

Clara had retrieved her magic wand and, from behind the rock, produced and put on a top hat. She started to dance, caper, skip and gambol from one part of the clearing to the next. This was her big solo number and she made the most of it. The dance was an interpretive one, she had told Miles while rehearsing it in the back garden, intended to convey: O where is my lover? O where can he be? Oh, there he is, over there. Come to me, my lover, come! Wait, stay there, I will come to you. Run run run run run. At last we are together! How happy I am. Embrace me! Wait though, stop! I am terrified. What is that repulsive Beast in your pants? I am shocked at the sight. Are they all like that? Mother never warned me. Spare me, spare me! Look at my scared face. I am going to run away now. And yet I am strangely curious about the thing. Does it do any tricks? Hmm. I have nothing better on today so I may yield to you this once, but don't count on it happening again, laddie boy. It was a bloody awful dance and she hammed up every move. But Miles watched laughing from his hiding place and was glad that she was his girl.

The drums and the chant grew louder: *Walpole, Walpole, Walpole*.

She started to spin more shamanistically, and laugh and yelp and throw her head back and rattle the wand. She sprinkled the pepper-golden-sparkly magic dust from the pouch at her waist. At last she closed in on the flat horizontal rectangular rock. She danced around it, scattering dust at every corner and banging it with her wand. She had retained four naked backing dancers, who orbited her in their turn with balletic leaps and melodramatic arm-flinging movements.

"*Walpole ... Walpole ... Walpole...* "

Finally Clara banged on the centre of the stone and leapt nimbly aside. The four nude votaries danced behind the wicker phallus and came back with blankets. They stood one at each corner of the slab, holding up the edge of one blanket in each hand, so that these were suspended between them and thus concealed the slab. Looking like a magician or his assistant in her top hat, Clara prowled around the rectangle lifting each blanket in turn with her wand to show there was still nothing behind them. Then she pranced over to her posing-rock, and standing atop it raised her head to the sky and shrieked, "Walpole, I summon you! Come to mee, my daemon lover!"

The drums went mental. The crowd was stamping as well as everything else now. Women were shrieking and pulling at their hair.

Clara slammed her wand-staff down on the rock once, twice. As she hit it a third time the concealed pyrotechnics provided by Beastman the ex-roadie went off a yard from the rectangle on each side, and a great cloud of smoke rose up behind the blankets.

The drums and the chanting reached a frenzied climax with a great unified shout of, "WALPOLE!"

There was a silence.

Then the four nude caryatids shrieked and fainted to the ground, dropping the blankets, and when the smoke had cleared somewhat Miles could be seen stood there on the slab, dressed as The Walpole, coughing a bit.

Clara stood in her top hat with her hands on her hips, regarding the crowd smugly.

There came shrieks and cries from the crowd ad lib.

"The Walpole!"

"I see him!"

"He has come to us!"

"Show us the Beast, Walpole!"

"Walk among us, master!"

"Unusual character," remarked Thomas to William conversationally. "Quite fascinating. Purely local invention; I don't believe it occurs anywhere else. The Walpole, of course, is the local Devil-Pan-Dionysus figure, with perhaps a hint of Baron Samedi. You may have seen he is celebrated in the name of a local pub. He is thought to have been based on the 18th century prime minister Sir Robert Walpole, although how or why derived from him is anyone's guess."

For William this was perhaps the most surreal part of the whole experience, these blithe, casual, pedantic commentaries from the urbane lawyer, as if they were anthropologists calmly gathering notes rather than foolhardy gatecrashers of a convocation of frightening lunatics.

Miles was dressed in a Regency tailcoat, a shirt that came halfway down his thigh, polished riding boots, and no trousers. He wore the skull-mask Clara had worn earlier, and protruding from the side of it were a pair of florid sideburns. He wore gloves and carried a silver-handled cane. He was also supposed to have the top hat, but Clara had grown jealous of this in rehearsals and decided to commandeer it for her magic routine, so the first part of their performance was that he now strode across to her, to screams and shrieks from the circle, and held out his hand for it. Fearfully she handed it to him and he smartly fitted it on.

"Have pity on me, Walpole!" she implored. "Have mercy!"

The Walpole shook his top-hatted head no, and reached out his hand to her again, commandingly.

Clara atop her rock turned to face the audience wringing her hands. "Thee Walpole will ravish me!" she cried piteously.

The Walpole clambered onto the rock, Clara jumped down shrieking, and he commenced to chase her round and round it. "Oh no! Help! Help! Hayy-ulp!" cried Clara as Miles finally caught her and threw her over his shoulder. He spanked her with the cane a bit while she wriggled and then carried her to the rectangular slab and put her down on it.

"Pure pantomime," muttered Thomas.

Stick-clicking and a steady drum-beating broke out again.

Miles stood before Clara, his back to where Thomas and William were, fumbling at the bottom of his shirtfront.

"Thee Walpole is unleashing Thee Beast!" she wailed, cowering and writhing on the slab, averting her face and holding her hands up in front of it. "I have no choice but to submit! Avert your eyes if you would spare your sanity! None may gaze on thee nakedness of thee Walpole and live! Arise, sluts, and guard the awful nuptials of thee Walpole from human eyes!"

The four handmaids at the corners of the slab writhed and shimmied upwards, grasping the blankets between them, so that they were again forming a screen around it, but this time facing outwards so as not to see the terrible consummation going on within. They wriggled and shook their heads from side to side as if in pain or ecstasy. Miles's shoulders and top hat were still visible for a moment until he sank down towards the gasping Clara.

From inside the nuptial bower terrible shrieks, groans and cries started to give forth. The blankets billowed, shook and trembled as if at some great commotion within.

"Thee Walpole!" cried Clara. "Thee Walpole ees ravishing me! Thee Beast! He has put thee Beast upon me! Thee Walpole is riding me! ... Now he has fallen off. Never mind, try again ... You are right on target, Walpole ... Thee Walpole possesses me! Take some weight on your elbows like a gentleman, Walpole ... Thee Walpole consumes me! Never, never have I known such terrible ecstasy! Did you remember to put thee bins out, Walpole? ... Urg ... ak ... I theenk I weel get my hair done tomorrow ... Slow down, my daemon lover, eet ees not a race ... aii ... Promise you will sleep on thee fiery patch, Walpole ... eek ... gosh ... You are the greatest, Walpole ... he is showing me thee whole cosmos ... Take your hat off, man, for God's sake, look like you're staying ... and your socks ... ooga ... oh Walpole ... ahh ... that was not a yawn, it was a gasp ... "

"Do it properly!" muttered Miles within the tent, lying on the slab shaking a blanket. "Realistically!"

"This *is* realistically," muttered Clara, lying next to him kicking at another.

"The point is to save the village, not for you to show off," he hissed.

She glared. "We can do both. (Eek! Walpole! More!) I don't think it matters much, we have frozen the poor bloke's brain already anyway. (Woo! Yikes! Splendid!)" She frowned down at herself and tutted. "I have got blood on my lovely witch dress. (Cor! Smashing! Super!)"

"How come we are the only two not naked, by the way?" he asked.

"I am ashamed of your body. (Multi-faboso!)"

Outside Thomas had started talking loudly to William again to cover for Clara's self-indulgence, and others had instinctively started playing their instruments louder or chanting.

"It is a common mistake, you know, to think that this sort of thing only takes place on Solstices and so on. It is generally once a week but pretty much whenever the villagers feel like it. This was largely for your benefit, but it's also a poor night for television."

William managed a nod.

Thomas paused, stuck, and some particularly loud shrieks cut across the music.

"Walpole! Walpole you are super-bad! Oh ... ah ... ferme la fenêtre ... Ou est la salle a manger ... Mein Hund hat keine Nase ... tu madre es una paella ... veni, vidi, vici ... tora, tora ... lente, lente, dolce far niente ... "

"Aha! I believe now the Vessel of the Walpole is speaking in tongues," said Thomas.

"Thee Walpole's sexing has made me speak in tongues!" Clara's shriek confirmed.

Inside the shelter Miles speculatively touched Clara's hair and murmured:

"Um. You know, we could always ... perhaps we could ... I mean seeing as we're here together ... "

Clara bridled and stared at him in disbelief.

"It was just a thought."

She snorted and then rolled back a sleeve to glance at her watch. "Some hope! That's enough, anyway. Go on, piss off."

Miles crawled out under a blanket at the opposite side to the civil servant.

The over-the-top moans and cries of ecstasy from inside the shelter rose and peaked and finished with a hearty, "Ayiyiyi*yi*!" and then fell silent. So too did the drums and other sounds. The blanket caryatids sighed and collapsed to the ground as if spent.

Clara was revealed sitting on the slab, her hair in disarray, smoking a cigarette.

"Well that was the best two minutes of my loife," she said in rural.

At length she sighed and stood and, seeming to hobble somewhat and clutching the small of her back, started to make her way back towards her rock.

"Thee Walpole has departed," she announced sadly. "I hope he calls me. Such power, such ecstasy, such visions he has granted me!" Gradually she recovered her animation, recovered her wand, started to whirl and gesture and raise her voice again. "I was drawn across the universe by five fiery salamanders ... "

"She now relates her ecstatic visions," said Thomas. "She will testify and prophesy."

" ... and there I was introduced to five elementals, an elemental of fire, an elemental of water, an elemental of stone, an elemental of air and an elemental of cheese ... "

Thomas decided he had better keep talking. "Mama Clara, of course, spends all day out in the woods alone, indulging in strange reveries and living off mushrooms," he muttered confidentially.

William nodded and tried to look intelligently interested. He had decided to focus on Thomas. He was a solid plank to grasp at in a river of insanity. He was like some civilised subcontinental explorer come to be genially amused at the antics of these white barbarians. He had decided he liked his learned footnotes. It was like watching a horror DVD with the director's matter-of-fact voice-over commentary instead of the soundtrack. His voice was soothing. It was precise, refined. He wore a three-piece suit. He still, incongruously, carried his leather briefcase. He represented the Law. William would cling to the law.

" ... and the Moon spoke to me and said, Mama Clara, because we are on first-name terms, me and the Moon, you know, Mama Clara, dry your tears! Sheathe your anger! What you fear will *not* come to pass! Thee men of wrath will *not* violate thee sacred hill of thee Walpole, for they will be caught by their own snares ... "

Thomas chuckled. "Well, she's right about that, at least."

" ... and then I plunged into the earth, I was in a shimmering cavern of quartz, and there were five dwarves named Ignorance, Prudery, Prejudice, Blindness and Roger ... "

"Astonishing as it may seem I have unearthed references to this ritual dating all the way back to 1997," Thomas told William. "I would not have you think this is some Johnny-come-lately cult."

William nodded.

" ... and the spirit said, but the one you must most fear is Roger ... "

Thomas tapped his briefcase. "I can show you documents. We are officially affiliated with the various national councils of Satanists, Pagans, Druids, and also with a voodoo church. You have probably also recognised certain Sufi elements; I assume you know what that means."

William nodded. The thing was to keep nodding.

" ... and then I flew on the back of an eagle, in fact I flew in the stomach of an eagle, and we flew high over mountains and deserts, and I grew nervous and cried, You wouldn't ... "

Clara sensed her audience growing restless. There were a few coughs around the circle, shuffling feet, drooping heads. The ingrates wanted to get to their part again and the big fun climax. Next she had planned to put on half-moon glasses and, looking down her nose over them as the old vicar had done, intone, 'If you will all turn to page 15 in your missals,' and lead them in a made-up satanic prayer or hymn. Miles had vetoed this but she had the glasses concealed behind the rock. However she supposed she had better cut to the chase.

" ... and they all lived happily ever after," she hastily concluded. "And now," she leapt onto her rock, and writhed and rattled and shrieked, "thee dance of praise to thee Walpole, and thee Burning of thee Cock, and thee sexy sexy sexing!" She ground her hips obscenely.

There was a general cheer.

Pandemonium broke out. Semi-naked men and women alike rushed forward, everyone except the horrified civil servant and the indulgently-smiling lawyer, and commenced to stamp, dance and whirl in a circle around the Giant Wicker Penis. The drums slung around their necks were played faster and madder and louder, their frenzied shouts and cries rang out through the forest. The madwoman cackled and shrieked and writhed. She pointed with her wand and as William watched dry-mouthed in terror two stuffed guys were dragged forward, effigies he dimly recognised as being of the local vicar and the woman who had spoken in favour of the development at the meeting, the latter clearly made out of a grotesque inflatable sex doll. They were held aloft and then stuffed into the terrible wicker phallus, the female doll wrapped obscenely around the caricature vicar. The headless chicken corpses were tossed in after them before the contraption was closed. Flaming torches were brought down from their poles, touched to the faggots at the base of the pyre ...

Floodlights. There would have to be floodlights, and searchlights.

William would have great tall powerful banks of searchlights installed here, cutting through the night like knives, sweeping the countryside for miles around with their bright strong clean electric light, pushing back the sea of darkness without relent. He clung to that. The whole hill would be deforested, tamed, tarmacked. The road was not enough. It would be a vulnerable thread of civilisation that would snap. There must be maintenance depots, car parks, perhaps a research station. And arrays of floodlights, and probing searchlights. He would insist upon that. It would be necessary, for protection. They would, of course, require much more power than the sluggish inefficient intermittently-working wind turbines could even produce, but it couldn't be helped. There would have to be a petrol generator, or if he could arrange it a power station where the village had once stood. And barbed wire, acres and acres of barbed wire, and electrified fences, and automated machine-guns programmed to shoot at the slightest movement from the dark beyond. He would write a report insisting, apologetically but firmly and with all the authority of one who had experienced conditions on the ground, on the necessity of floodlights, and searchlights, and automated machine-guns, and an erasure of all vegetation in a five mile radius.

The barbaric wicker monolith took flame. The fire snaked, writhed, jumped, became a roaring, crackling pillar of light leaping at the night sky. Most of the remaining torches were now carried by the circling chanting dancers. They whirled before William like figures in a zoetrope. Horned heads were silhouetted against the bonfire, bare breasts limned with gold by torchlight. The madwoman capered on her rock, raised her hands to the sky with the wand clutched between them. "Thee sexing!" she cried. "Commence thee sexing for thee Walpole!" At that the drums and the chants took on an even more urgent tempo, the shrieks grew more hysterical and frenzied. A hunting horn blew. Faster, faster, faster they revolved around the fire. All at once the spinning circle flew apart, as if its constituent parts were flung out into the night by centrifugal force. Streamers of flame shot out into the woods and laughing, shrieking, whooping figures ran past William. Some ran hand in hand, some ran alone and then blundered about the forest searching for partners, more often laughing women pulled men after them or ran giggling from men who chased them, casting teasing glances behind. The splendidly voluptuous Jennifer flashed past into the trees, hair streaming, breasts bouncing, laughing giddily, pursued by a spear-brandishing figure in a Masai loincloth with torchlight reflected in its spectacles. The priestess had vanished. All around were shrieks, giggles, cries and moans, sounds of pursuit and capture in the surrounding undergrowth. The clearing was empty now save for the civil servant and the lawyer and the steadily burning giant cock.

"The traditional climax," said Thomas imperturbably. "You are privileged to have witnessed it. Perhaps our prudish reticence is foolish but I am sure you can understand it."

He looked around smilingly, hands behind his back, swinging the briefcase gently. From the eaves of the forest all around came sounds of what he hoped was, but in many cases feared wasn't, simulated sex. Across the clearing a bare-breasted figure carrying a torch lurked half behind a tree, beckoning. He frowned at it uncertainly.

This place would be devastated. William clung to that. He would devastate this hill and the village if he could.

"Why?" he asked shakily, and it was a question he would repeat to the lawyer, plaintively, in dreams. "*Why* did you show me this?" He still had his job, his role in society, the machinery of the department and the weight and majesty of government behind him. He clung to them too and allowed his anger to overcome his unmanning fear. "Do you imagine you can intimidate me? Do you think you can blackmail me?"

Thomas laughed loudly but genially, with genuine amusement. "My dear fellow! You really do take us for savages." He opened his briefcase, took something out, then closed it again and thrust it into William's hands. "Take this and examine the contents at your leisure. Developing the hill would be in clear breach of our Human Right to free religious observance, as laid out in the Act of 1998, and may well contravene sundry religious hatred and equality laws. In there you'll find copies of the restraining orders and multi-million-pound lawsuits I intend to file against the local authority, the government and the power company unless you very quickly back down."

William stared open-mouthed, clutching the case to his chest shivering. The thing the lawyer had taken out was a fearsome goat mask. Thomas fitted it over his head carefully, staring across the clearing. That *was* his wife behind the tree. He stooped and removed his shoes.

"I'll leave you to make your own way back," he said. He removed his trousers, folded them neatly, and hung them over a tree-branch. "Now if you'll excuse me ... "

With an echoing, primal shout he sprinted across the clearing and vanished into the woods.

William stood, silent and wide-eyed. Suddenly he heard the demented priestess cackling from behind the burning idol. He shuddered and ran.

He crashed blindly through the forest. He didn't know which way the car was. He didn't know where he was going. All he wanted was to be away from here. Cries echoed through the trees. All around him in the darkness were the sounds of copulation. His heart pounded and his breath came in sobs. Suddenly he went flying headlong over a tree-root, or it might have been a pair of horizontal legs. He crashed heavily through a bush and knocked his head against bark.

Powerful but tender arms raised him and pinned him against a tree-trunk.

"Where are you going in such a hurry?" The voice was purring, caressing, amused.

A hand stroked his cheek; fingers plucked the forgotten sprig of parsley from his jacket. Marble in the moonlight, a mighty edifice like the Taj Mahal, Miriam of the W.I. had come to redeem her love-pledge.

In a mere three days the machinery of government had ground to a halt and it was announced that, following a closer inspection of the situation on the ground, the planned wind turbine development on Hobson's Hill would not be going ahead after all.

"Beautiful." Jeremiah jetted smoke and sighed. "Purely beautiful." He settled back in a deep leather armchair contentedly.

When the final confirmation had come through Simon had summoned the original conspirators, those who had gathered in the back room of the Walpole's Head that night, to the manor house to hear it, and they were now sitting around his elegant smoking-room with drinks and celebratory cigars.

"Beautiful," said Jeremiah again. "Defeat one faddish, made-up, legally-recognised religion with another."

"Or two, if you count human rights as one," said Thomas.

"And play on what they expected us to be like," said Major Fitzsimmons. "We became what they always thought we were."

"It was great," said Arthur the landlord. "We should do it every year. We should do it every month. Make it a regular festival."

Clara raised an eyebrow and made her scared face at Miles.

"Call it Walpolgisnacht," suggested the Major.

Thomas cleared his throat and knitted his eyebrows. "Actually," he mumbled hesitantly, "I – I was thinking perhaps we *ought* to do it regularly – just, just, you know, solstices and so on, just to be on the safe side, in case they come and check."

"Thomas got lucky," said Clara.

Thomas looked down, abashed.

"Half the *village* got lucky," said Miles.

(Miles hadn't been among them. When, while they were trudging home, he had tentatively tried to get mildly amorous in a moonlit clearing about half a mile from the main action, Clara had looked him up and down coldly and said, "Mother was right about you."

But then a little later on, in another glade, they had danced a triumphant waltz in the moonlight, and then a slow tango, humming the music, and afterwards paddled in a stream; and that was much better than sex against a tree.)

"Penge got lucky, from what I heard – or Miriam did," chortled someone else.

"*We* got lucky," opined a farmer. "Probably the poor bastard just didn't want to ever have to come back here again. You should have seen the state of him when I pulled his car out of the ditch the next morning. Gibbering wreck. It was that and the Batt's fear of repercussions for her faux pas with Tom, you ask me. They would never have let us win in court."

"Balderdash and piffle," said Clara, glaring. "The principle was sound."

"She's right," said Thomas. "They wouldn't have had a leg to stand on."

"Of course I am right."

"I could have won it, if they'd called the bluff. Almost a shame not to have the chance to prove it. Tie them up with their own laws and rhetoric."

"Organise a march of angry phallus-worshippers on Parliament," suggested Miles.

"They'd find plenty to worship there," said Major Fitzsimmons.

"Really, I'm fairly sure I could have won it with a simple deposition, without all the shenanigans," said Thomas.

"Then what the hell did we all traipse round in the nak for?" demanded the farmer.

"Shock and awe, old darling," said Fitzsimmons.

"To prove it definitively before court," said Thomas.

"And because it was fun," said Clara.

"It *was* fun," said Arthur eagerly. He had got lucky too. "I vote we do it every year. Walpolgisnacht, that sounds good to me."

Clara reached out to take Miles's hand for reassurance. "Please take me back to God's own city, darling, these people are degenerates," she murmured.

"I didn't even hit them with half the things I could have done," Thomas persisted. "I can think of dozens more of their laws that would have applied. We could have had them on right to a family, for example, if we'd maintained we *only* conceived on the hill."

"The principle is sound," Clara repeated, sitting back and blowing smoke-rings. "And I bet widely applicable. We can use the same principles to defeat the bastards in any number of other ways. For example, if we lose the Smoking Theatre case, you, Arthur, must set up as a shaman or medicine man, and we must obtain affiliation with a Red Indian tribe, and erect a wigwam in the parlour bar; for tobacco use is a recognised part of *their* religion."

"Genius," cried Arthur, eyes alight. "We'll do it! Genius!" Clara inclined her head regally.

"It's a shame that *our* tribe isn't a recognised one with our own religion," said June the barmaid sadly. "The tribe that just wants to have a pint, and a fag, and some fun, and to be left alone."

"We should start such a religion; take Sid James or Andy Capp or Sir John Falstaff or someone as *our* deity," said Clara.

"Yes!" said Arthur. "Let's do it!"

"Another thought," she continued. "I understand you don't have *that* much trouble circumventing the hunting laws if you feel like it, but – it occurs that a few shrines and temples to Diana or Artemis or for that matter Herne strategically scattered around could end all difficulties in *that* direction." Muriel and Simon and the other hunters laughed and exchanged thoughtful glances. "The possibilities are endless."

"Well, I'm just glad it paid off this time," sighed Ransome. "Although I suppose now they'll erect the things on top of some other poor buggers somewhere else."

"I suppose we are terrible Nimbys," said someone.

"I have never understood," said Clara, "why that appellation has been allowed to become a term of abuse, rather than seized on proudly as a badge of honour."

"Yes!" cried Muriel eagerly. "Yes! *I've* thought that! Not In My Back Yard ought to be everyone's slogan. If we all looked after our own back yards – kept them nice and right and free of bad things, and said not jolly well here you don't when they tried to impose them – then eventually it would be Not In Anyone's Back Yard, and, and," she grew embarrassed at her speech and tailed off in a mumbled, "world'd be a much better place, my opinion."

There were calls of Hear, hear. Miles smiled at her and thought again how not the least cruel feature of modern times was some of the English being forced to speak up for themselves and indulge in blush-making rhetoric.

"The main thing is we all came together and stood up for ourselves for once," said the farmer.

"I must beg to differ," said Clara sharply. "The main thing is that everyone here owes me a crate of lovely Britvic. I believe Arthur will take your money and arrange delivery. And," she leaned back and puffed on her cigar, "for what little use they are, Walpole now owns all of your souls."

Chapter Twenty-one

The culture-shock started as soon as they got out of their space-car.
"It is so drab and unlovely. Concrete has not yet been outlawed."
"Adjust your eye-settings, my mated one, so as to filter out the ugliness."
"That would be contrary to the nature of our mission. Instead squeeze my hand-analogue as a token of support."
Miles did so.
"That will suffice. You may disengage now. I will be brave."
Two cars drove past, each in turn slowing to look at them. They were worth looking at.
Clara said, "Perceive, space-husband, how their primitive ancient cars cling nervously to the ground like so many scurrying insects."
"I am loftily amused, space-wife," said Miles.
"Observe with disdain how the pathway is quaintly two-dimensional, and may not be walked on upside-down."
"Already I miss the vertiginous helixes and mobius-strip walkways of our shimmering city in the clouds."
"I miss our nuclear star-cat. I hope you remembered to turn it off."
Some people walked down the street towards them.
"Behold," said Clara flinging out a hand towards them, "our first natives."
The people walked by, looking them up and down, turning their heads to look some more as they passed.
Clara tracked her head to scan them in her turn. "Their clothing is so drab. Implement disdain-concealment."
"Silver and PVC appear unknown here," intoned Miles. They key to doing a space-voice was to intone rather than say. "I feel like a dick," he added in his own voice.
"I do not judge your polymorphous sexual hankerings, space-spouse. Perhaps we can initiate orgy." An open-mouthed middle-aged man was walking past, again craning his head to look. "Will you orgy?" she asked him. There was no response. "Perhaps we are unattractive here. Although we seem to be the objects of unusual interest," she added as another passer-by bumped into a lamp-post while distracted by them.
The unusual interest was not surprising. They were dressed as future-utopian space-people and were quite eye-catching. Clara was dressed in a black PVC catsuit and latex thigh-boots and had a great deal of silver make-up around her eyes, and a silver-sprayed digital watch with lots of buttons on her wrist, and a silver utility belt hung with various gadgets,

and her hair pulled back in a pony-tail which was wrapped in tinfoil and terminated in a scart plug, and had tinfoil-wrapped eggbox bumps sellotaped over her nipple area. Miles was even more striking, largely resembling a 70s glam rock star. He wore a silver wig and silver platform boots and silver spandex pants, and a black plastic jacket with shoulder-pads and diagonal buttons, and over his groin a space-jockstrap Clara had made, which featured flashing lights made out of Christmas-tree decorations, and a radiation-warning sign, and, most prominently of all, a hoover suction-nozzle attachment, which dangled down his leg and then looped back to fit in a socket.

The space-people had been born or evolved out of one of their dressing-up games, and lingered to the point that they had found themselves doing them, sans costumes, for hours at a time while going about their normal daily idleness. They had received their public premiere at a fancy-dress party thrown by a friend, one of their few remaining friends from the time before they had moved to the country and gone mad, whom they had thoroughly pissed off by their refusal to ever step out of character and their tendency to insult his furnishings, music and opinions while in it.

Clara said, and Miles agreed, that being the future space-people really did help you see the world through fresh eyes, and realise that, as they sort of already knew, the modern era wasn't the pinnacle of anything, and would look backward, primitive, savage and supremely ridiculous to everyone one day, as in many ways it did to them already. They had both been excited about the prospect of taking them to town. But not in the costumes, Miles thought; the costumes were a distraction, it was the attitude that was the point. The costumes were a mistake, he thought looking down at the hoover-attachment dangling from his groin. Coming here – *not* the local market town where people might know them, it was the bigger, more distant, slightly knackered town where they had previously masqueraded as policemen – coming here in the full regalia today had been the result of a sudden mutual 'I bet you wouldn't' dare neither had been brave enough to back down from in time.

There was a bottle of space-nutrients on Clara's utility belt in case they needed its help or solace: a tinfoil-wrapped plastic bottle of what had once been Ribena but was now mostly vodka, but so far neither had had recourse to it, partly because a mutual bout of 'I bet you'll just get drunk before you're brave enough' had put it off limits, partly because going to the toilet was a rather involved process with the space-outfits.

As the latest passer-by caromed off the lamp-post now Miles said, "Attracting attention may impair the success of our mission to observe and record."

"Agreed," said Space-Clara. "Activating invisibilo-shield." She pressed a button on her space-belt and made a sound like 'Vooop' with her lips closed. "Testing invisibilo-shield," she announced as more passers-by approached, walking up to them and starting to skip, caper and gyrate in front of them, waving her arms about and pulling faces. They flinched and walked into the road to avoid her. "Invisibilo-shield malfunctioning," she reported flatly. "We will have to try to blend in."

"Indeed," said Miles, his eye drawn involuntarily to the flask of space-nutrients. "To minimize impact we must adopt local customs."

"Optimum," said Clara cocking her head robotically. "Let us affect contemporary speech patterns. Adopt conversation template omega-five. Did you see the match last night? One side put the ball into the net more times than the other side."

"It was a bleeding travesty," said Miles tonelessly. "The ref was a female sexual organ."

"Strange how they reviled female sexual organs in this era," mused Clara. "Looking back it is clear their pitiful 21st-century Earth-penises were much more displeasing. I am glad they were abolished and replaced by the much more user-friendly mk-II space-penis. Now we are linguistically camouflaged, shall we ambulate into the urban centre?"

"One nanosec, space-wife. I wish to investigate this strange metal idol." Miles approached the parking-meter next to their car and placed his hand upon it. "It appears to be a primitive robotic life-form. It requires metal currency-tokens for sustenance."

"I will manufacture some." Clara made a noise and opened a coin-dispenser on her belt. "Eat, my little friend."

"That will not appease it for long."

"We must return before it grows angry."

They turned in unison and headed along the side-street towards the centre of town. The heels of Clara's fetish-boots were higher than she was used to and once she swayed and stumbled against Miles.

"My cyber-knees are not yet adjusted to the primitive gravity," she explained. "Also, my bleeding space-thighs are starting to chafe already."

"Well, my atomic space-bollocks feel unusually warm. I hope you got the wiring right."

Just before they reached the high street an old man standing on a Segway electric scooter turned off it and hummed slowly past them with a solemn dignity.

"A space-chariot!" exclaimed Clara as he appeared.

"I feel homesick."

"We must hail him!"

As he passed they stepped back and extended their right arms in a sort of space-fascist salute.

"Hail, fellow space-person!"

"Hail, brave pioneer of the shining future!"

"We must ride around on those next time," said Clara as herself. "Or get Sinclair C5s."

"What next time?" asked Miles as they strode out into the middle of town.

There was no glory and not much embarrassment in just walking around like that. They attracted stares and comments, but could be and were taken for students, advertisers, street theatre, something to do with the television. The fun was in serenely and unselfconsciously *being* the future-perfect space-people. Clara was a natural at it and even Miles soon forgot his, he felt, far more awful costume. To keep moving would be cheating. They strolled unhurriedly around and paused to take in the sights, frequently stopping just to strike space-postures together, which often resembled the sort of poses held by couples in a C&A catalogue, if they had sold fetish-wear and embarrassing silver shiteness. Or they would turn and point or gaze at things in unison like figures in Soviet propaganda posters. They would scan around robotically; when people came close to stare at them they would stare analytically back. They drew each other's attention to points of interest and commented on what they beheld in clear untroubled space-voices, neither seeking to be overheard nor caring if they were.

"Observe, space-husband, the primitive environment."

"There is much food for study here."

Someone wolf-whistled.

"He wishes to mate with you, space-husband," said Clara raising an eyebrow. "I told you not to wear that jock-strap. The holo-teach cannot prepare one for the smells," she added as an overweight undeodorized man munching a hamburger passed nearby staring at her appreciatively. "Are you looking at my space-nipples?" she called. "Do not unless I invite you to orgy."

"He is a candidate for orgy. He appears hermaphrodite. He at least has dress-sense. Observe his silver running shoes. It is a conundrum that many of those who wear such shoes appear utterly unadapted for running."

"Few of the past-people dress in such a way as to give pleasure to their fellow citizens or to themselves. Many seem to dress to avoid being seen. Observe those youths who dress in hoods to conceal their faces."

"That may be a kindness to their fellow citizens. Regard this pallid glutinous substance with which the paving is speckled," said Miles. "It is a characteristic architectural feature of the civic spaces of the time. It is theorised it was a form of communal art. It is created by ejecting a masticated chicle-based substance from the mouth. Take care lest it adhere to your space-boots."

"See! That juvenile there, who dresses to conceal himself, has just ejected some from his mouth. He took no care or thought about the process. It cannot be artistic in function. Perhaps he marks his territory. See the distaste with which the older mated pair regard his action. See the loathing they feel for him. Yet they do not upbraid him. They mutter mutinously to themselves yet seek to avoid attracting his attention."

"It is theorised that such young unattractive males formed a higher caste at this period, and must be deferred to at all costs. They had baronial rights to maim and steal with impunity, and exercised a sort of droit de seigneur over the females of their estates, the offspring being raised by a levy on the public purse. They would duel with each other thrillingly in these very streets."

"Yet it is a conundrum. The older mated pair bore all the marks of wealth and status and the youth did not. Furthermore they are elders, whom all advanced societies respect. Surely the city watch would support them if they reprehended the youth."

"You will note there is no city watch to be seen in this backward era. Moreover if they were summoned they would be more likely to take the youth's side and punish the elders for attempting to restrain his free expression. What you perceive as the marks of status are the marks of shame here. There is a religion of guilt, the high priests of whom live cloistered lives of privilege and the serene contemplation of abstract theory and their own virtue."

"And yet, space-husband, it strikes me that the youths seem to walk in fear themselves. They have no pride in their bearing. They display the nervous aggression of the insecure. Those hoods, in effect, are wombs. They peep timidly out at the world from the safety of their mother's vaginas."

"How should they have pride or confidence? They have no function. A replacement population has been drafted in to perform the jobs their forefathers performed, or the jobs themselves have been exported overseas. And they have been taught no pride in their culture, among many other things they have not been taught."

"We behold a great civilisation in decline, perhaps terminal."

"These people have a history of sleepwalking to the edge of disaster and waking up when it is almost too late. Their salvation is in their own hands."

"And eventually," said Space-Clara piously, "comes the benevolent rise of the nanobots and gene-spinners, and there is free PVC for all."

"Yes."

They held hands for a moment and thought of the shining future.

They continued their tour.

"Strange to think that these streets will shortly run with blood."

"The Rationality Wars. This is the very square where twelve Warmists are pelted to death with snowballs."

"A great day."

Clara examined the gadgets on her utility belt. "I have not yet impressed the natives by playing with my tachyon-phased flux-enabled cigarette-holder." This was a bendy drinking-straw painted silver. It enabled the denizens of the future utopia to smoke around corners. "I require a packet of star-fags or their laughable third millennium equivalent if I am to do so. Let us venture into yonder commercial establishment and engage in barter. It will be something amusing to tell our clone-children at the next family orgy."

"This is a grumpy shopkeeper, if you remember," said Miles.

"Accessing data-banks," said Space-Clara, cocking her head and making a whirring noise. "You are accurate, my genetically-engineered consort. I see from my race-memory that my beauteous ancestress the legendary Clara, later known as the Lady Protector of England or the Butcher of Brussels, had an unpleasant encounter with the shopkeeper here while trying to impart joy to him with her frolicsome ways." Clara had taken it into her head to try to ask for things by way of mime and interpretive dance in this shop once. "We will certainly enter his rude hut, and perhaps disintegrate him if his manners have not improved. In fact we should make a point of visiting all known grumpy shopkeepers in our data-banks and attempting to cheer them with our lofty space-philosophy."

They entered the dingy newsagents. Clara peered around with keen interest, hands behind her back.

"Pictures of vaginas on the top shelf, but prurient murder magazines on the bottom shelf," she noted. "This was why dwarves were not to be trusted."

A cheery man standing at the counter buying something turned and grinned at them. "Are you Martians?"

Clara stared at him coldly.

"We are genetically-perfect future fascists," she said in slight annoyance. "Silver-plated supermen from Goldfrapp's Utopia or William Gibson's Gernsback Continuum, Trevor Goodchild's darling children, beautiful silicon-enhanced butterflies from a city that knows no tears."

He held his grin and winked at Miles. "Oh. Only I thought you were Martians."

"If a more highly evolved life-form said that to me I would dissolve it."

"Oh? Well. Have fun. You look silicon-enhanced in that outfit, I'll say that much," he said cheerily, nudging Miles as he passed.

"Certainly not! It is all me, with a bit of egg-box." She took out her ray-gun, a plastic one that lit up and crackled when you pulled the trigger, and shot at him in irritation as he left. "Get out."

The man behind the counter was not cheery. He was unsmiling and unshaven and looked weighed down by some intolerable grievance.

"We wish to engage in a commercial transaction," Clara told him, sheathing her side-arm and approaching. "However there will first be a pause for polite small-talk, as is proper. Engaging banter protocol 7-B. It is a nice day, is it not? Health-giving solar rays are freely available to all irrespective of social class or gene group."

There was no response beyond a sullen stare.

"Non-responsive. I will try again. Are you going anywhere nice this year? You look as though you have just returned from two weeks in the Rad-Mines of Zarg. Cheer up, mate, it may never happen. In fact in your case it does, horribly, but you are not to know that at this point in your history. The use of the term 'mate' is not an invitation to orgy."

There was still silence and a pouch-eyed stare.

"He perceives friendliness as weakness," intoned Miles.

"His life-task may have been erroneously assigned," opined Clara. "Nevertheless I will try again. How is the wife? No, don't answer that, I think I can guess."

"What do you *want*?" the shopkeeper almost shouted.

"A packet of Orgazmo pills, a flux capacitor, a portable gene-writer, a neutron grenade and, oh, what the hell, twenty Silk Cut."

"Purple or silver?" he snarled.

"Observe the redundant complexity of the simplest transaction. Purple."

"Silver would be more in character," said Miles.

"I would implode my space-cheeks trying to get a hit off them." The man slammed the cigarettes down on the counter, with hatred, and Clara created some more Earth-coins, taking a long time about it and whirring and beeping in between each one. The shopkeeper scattered some change across the counter and onto the floor, which they disdained to pick up.

"We would destroy you, but we may not interfere with the timeline," Clara told him. "One of your remote descendants may do something useful or aesthetically pleasing, although it seems improbable."

They rotated smartly and left.

"Miles, I think we must be the most annoying people ever to have lived," said Clara outside, not without a certain degree of satisfaction. "But also the winsomest."

She gingerly turned over the cig pack, steeling herself in case it was a really horrible picture on the back. It was only something moderately awful and shouty, not one of the ones that threatened to make her cry with anger and hate. She vowed, again, to make the effort to cultivate a twenty-a-day habit, at least, in spite of the fact they made her cough after a while, and post all the empty boxes to the government and tell them why, and then took refuge in being detached Space-Clara again.

"Note, my mind-linked clone-golem, how the clean lines of the packaging are disfigured by strident warnings and ugly images of death."

"The New Puritan era was at its height, my shiny-limbed meteor of delight. They took a malicious glee in curbing and spoiling each other's enjoyment. Ugliness was preferred to beauty at every turn. Moreover their leaders nursed a sadistic power-urge that manifested itself in an impulse to herd, upbraid and gratuitously demonstrate the citizens were in their power at every moment of their lives."

"I am glad not to have lived now," said Clara as she deposited the cigarettes into a tin at her belt and disposed of the ugly box. "Their psyches are malformed by the bars of their cage, left stunted by their being kept on reins like children. I can feel the tension and frustration. I do not think I can stand it here for long."

"Reflect that this era will not last, and that their leaders perish horribly."

"You comfort me somewhat, my hairless-bodied ubermensch. Let us further solace one another and express our lofty superiority by fusing nasally for a moment."

"At once, my quantum-vagina'd star-minx."

They rubbed noses in a space way then strolled on.

"Their very doors are plastered with orders, warnings and instructions," noted Space-Clara gesturing at the plate-glass entrance of a department store, half obscured by signs, symbols and interdictions. "One must almost negotiate a contract at every step."

"They had not yet learned the art of reducing things to their simplest essence, and letting objects approach their Platonic forms."

"Observe the cameras," pointing to a CCTV device up a lamp-post.

"Yes. Actually," said Miles as himself, "our characters probably wouldn't object to cameras."

"Indeed we do not," said Space-Clara, and leaned her head on his shoulder. "Do you remember how we first met, space-husband?" she asked kittenishly. "You were a sentinel in the Surveillance Unit, I was a terminatrix for the Gene Police."

"I spied on you for weeks."

"I busted you for thoughtcrime and found tapes of my bedroom."

"I had hacked the Grand Computer and made it order you to exercise nude every day."

"I whipped you with my electro-prod and sought to humiliate you by rubbing my forbidden mammalian orbs against your face."

"You couldn't work out why I kept re-offending."

"I sentenced you to the Rad Mines of Zarg and laughed as you grew and shed surplus limbs like an organ-tree in bloom."

"I travelled back in time and became your grandfather and groomed you all through childhood."

"The Grand Computer had both our personalities erased. This was an improvement of yours."

"We have never looked back."

"Hold my hand-analogue."

They held hands. Clara glared at the camera and then in her own voice muttered, "Let's give the bastards something to watch."

They snogged.

They entered the big shopping centre. The space-people approved of its megalomaniac gigantism. They rode up and down the escalators several times because they reminded them of home. Clara noted they were laughably short and straight, however, and said she missed conveyor-walks and anti-grav stairs.

The music they had suppressed as fake policemen was back on. They cocked their heads and listened.

"I theorize this is a converted penal facility," said Miles, "or that the shoppers are being punished for not having yet bought their daily quota of consumer products."

"They have not yet discovered psi-harps or ether-chimes, or the haunting death-song of the star-grampus."

"They have a primitive form of synth, however."

"Yes. While we are in this chrono-zone we must make pilgrimage to the birthplace of the great Bontempi."

Simultaneously they struck their left shoulders with a fist in salute and chorused, "Bontempi."

"This ancient songstress complains of the inconveniences of being celebrated and required to perform to great crowds," said Clara listening. "Perhaps my emotion-analogues are malfunctioning but I find I am unable to fake empathy."

"And yet I have seen historical footage of such performances to great crowds," said Miles. "Young devotees assigned to tasks of menial labour would sing along with such complaints as if they were able to fully identify with her problem. It is a conundrum."

"Perceive now," said Clara cocking her head in a different direction. "I believe the man now talking was known as a dick-jockey. He displays symptoms of mania. It is not infectious."

"I am unable to locate the source of his accent in my database. It does not emanate from any region of the planet."

"The specimen now exercising his vocal chords is making great display of sullen aggression."

"The primitives would pay to witness such displays. It was considered both more entertaining and more worthy of critical kudos than displays of cheeriness and bonhomie. This specimen was hailed as a great poet by those who did not share his inferior social status but, according to their downwardly-aspirational values, envied it. Note how he boasts of his toughness and ability to provide sexual satisfaction. It was not realised that verbal assurances of such qualities were reliably counter-indicative of, indeed inversely related to their presence."

"Indeed. I have eradicated several alien species and innumerable mutants and can regenerate after being squashed flat by a ten-ton weight, and yet I do not feel the need to boast about it."

"It was what first drew me to you."

"However the bass-line is primitively stimulating. Shall we perform a space-dance?"

"As you wish, pump of my silicon heart."

They remained perfectly immobile and blank but simultaneously rocked their heads from side to side several times.

"That was exhilarating," said Space-Clara tonelessly. "There is a place for the indulgence of atavism. Now let us activate digital over-ride until we have escaped the zone of sonic cruelty."

"Agreed." They placed their fingers in their space-ears as they continued on their way.

They ventured into a department store.

"Sentenoid sex-dolls," said Clara, approvingly, of some mannequins. "I am agreeably surprised. Will you orgy?" she asked one. "It is malfunctioning," she concluded when there was no reply, "or playing hard to get." She leaned forward and licked an unclothed plastic breast experimentally. "I do not like the flavour anyway." They moved on. "Who is that man?" she asked pointing at an advertising poster of a film star. "Why is he advising the citizens to buy consumer products? Surely they do not require such advice."

"He is a 'celebrity', my pneumatic space-possum. Due to the past-people largely interacting with screens rather than their neighbours it was necessary to have a caste of people who were known to all. Their doings could be discussed by all, facilitating small-talk at workplaces and acting as emotion-substitute for those with empty lives."

"As always I feel superior to the past-people. We orgy with our neighbours whenever we meet them on the slide-walks and diligently fake an interest in their doings," said Clara. "Also the past-people were laughably fond of small-talk, not having realised that mutual genital stimulation is far more effective for social bonding. But why is his advice to shop considered worthy of mention? Is he like Benevolent Uncle Argus, all-seeing, all-wise avatar of the Grand Computer, who watches and guides us and must be obeyed on pain of retroactive erasure?"

They slapped their foreheads in unison and chorused, "All hail Benevolent Uncle Argus, our Benefactor and Guide, Discoverer of Nano-Vibrators, Inventor of Silver Make-Up." They were used to the attention by now.

"No, he was not quite like Benevolent Uncle Argus," said Miles, and they slapped their foreheads and said it all again.

"Although it is theorized," Miles continued, "that the celebrity caste had similar status to our lofty-browed Lifeguard of the Gene Pool."

"You mean Benevolent Uncle Argus," Clara observed, and they had to do the salute and chant a third time.

"Yes," said Miles. "Him. The celebrities were similarly guides and benefactors. Their advice was prized. Their opinions were sought and offered on all important matters of the day. Not a topic was debated without consulting them. I personally theorize that the prevalence of this cult of fame was mainly a substitute for religious belief at a time before the invention of the life-extending Rejuvenation Jelly and Regeneration Custard we now take for granted."

"More great gifts for which we have to thank Benevol – "

"Yes," said Miles quickly. "By attaining to celebrity one was granted an electronic afterlife; even after they had died there was no escape from them. Those who hated them came to mourn their deaths even more than their followers did, knowing that now they would be canonized and banged on about more than ever. Osiris-myths of resurrection were frequent." He gestured at the poster. "In the case of advertising it was believed that the demi-gods' attributes of telegenic regularity of feature and sexual desirability could be magically passed on to the product and thence to the consumer."

"Even the past-people cannot have been so stupid."

"There is evidence to the contrary but I think I agree, my tinfoil-titted temptress. I theorize that only their upper echelons were that stupid, in stupidly believing the public at large were that stupid. While many were undoubtedly obsessed with these figures, few were of an IQ low enough to let it affect their shopping habits or political opinions, and a far greater number viewed the celebrity culture with increasing disdain, boredom and revulsion. Eventually consumers, trade unions and shareholders ceased to sanction the giving of huge sums of money to the celebrity caste for commercial endorsement, realising it was coming from them. And in the Great Disgust of 2016, newspaper editors who canvassed celebrities' opinions on current affairs or devoted undue space to their antics were put to the sword."

"You cheer me, space-husband. I am accessing image-banks to fondly envisage such scenes of righteous slaughter."

"In 2017 the Screaming Boredom Statutes made it law that no-one's picture could appear in a newspaper more than six times; after a seventh offence the celebrity's face would be surgically erased."

"Such perspective is uplifting."

"And the man in this picture loses his status next year after being caught fucking baby polar bears."

"The poor man. They were so repressed and uptight. Think how lonely and rejected Little Shako would feel if we were forbidden to caress him."

"Polar-bear-fucking was the last taboo to crumble." He gestured at the poster again. "The whole question of the past-people's reliance on advertising is an intriguing one. The practice spread banality, ugliness and annoyance throughout the media and intruded it into public spaces. Furthermore looking back it is clear that much of the advertising caste, the 'PR gurus', were parasitic shamen and witch-doctors, would-be alchemists who generated no real wealth. Billions of currency units were poured into absurd quests to find lucky colours, mind-manipulating typefaces, enchanting slogans, idiotic logos that were thought to act as magical talismen ensuring commercial success."

"They would sell a lot more schmatter if they just thought to paint it silver," opined Clara.

They wandered through the shopping centre again until they came to an Argos catalogue shop.

"Space-husband!"

"My augmented photo-receptors are functioning, space-wife."

"The name of the shop is reminiscent of – "

"Yes, him."

" – Benevolent Uncle Argus."

Miles sighed and they did the Benevolent Uncle Argus ritual again.

"His name is so mighty it has reached back through time to give these unwitting savages a glimpse of the silvery future," said Space-Clara. "Let us enter this emporium with the reverence we would accord one of his shrines."

They entered and looked around and concluded that Benevolent Uncle Argus (they hailed his name once more) would approve of the set-up. Clara sneered at some of the primitive gadgets and mistook others for robots and tried to talk to them or invite them to orgy.

As they left she fitted a cigarette to her silver-painted space-cigarette-holder made out of a bendy straw and lit it.

"See how the primitives watch me," she noted in satisfaction as they strolled unconcernedly around. "They are jealous of the way my superior futuristic cigarette-holder is able to bend at a right angle. We could set ourselves up as gods here."

"I suggest you are in error, my adjustable-nippled pinnacle of evolution," said Miles. "You attract their attention for violating one of their great taboos in emitting smoke within the confines of this vaulted, echoing but ridiculously puny ten-acre space. They feared it above all things."

"Except for carbon dioxide. Let us loftily amuse ourselves by breathing upon them and watching them scream in primitive terror." She discarded her space-cig into a concrete plant-pot, put the silver straw back in her mouth and commenced to blow through it at passers-by. "That was pure CO2," she informed them. "I have poisoned you."

People started to give them a wide berth as Miles too breathed at people.

"See how they flee from us! Let us express our scorn in lofty space-laughter."

"Ha-ha, ha-ha, ha-ha, ha-ha," they went together, monotone and robotically.

"Enough."

They deactivated laughter and strode on.

"And yet it is not enough, my bionic star-stud," said Clara. "I wish to make these smug and complacent people see that they are not a pinnacle of evolution but rude and superstitious barbarians with ridiculous taboos and fetishes. They must be forced to re-evaluate their culture and see that their values are not universal truths and that many of their cherished advances are dead-ends or steps backward."

"But the timeline, my parabolic paramour. We may not interfere, only observe with disdain and indulge our Olympian scorn."

"Yet it is hard to remain uninvolved. One pities them. They are people just like us, even though their limbs are not detachable and they have pubic hair instead of genital velcro."

"A disquieting thought has occurred, space-wife. Is it possible that one day a civilisation will arise which will look back on *ours* with scorn?"

Space-Clara swivelled to regard him with horror. "I have logged your subversive remark and must report you upon our return to Silver City Alpha. A few sessions with the mind-vortex and some corrective surgery will convince you of your simple error. Perfection cannot be improved upon."

"I thank you for your intervention, space-wife. I am proud you put loyalty to the Great Harmony above our personal bond. And yet now you have pointed it out, my error is so simple it seems a shame to involve the Guardians. Perhaps ... you yourself could correct me, with your ... forbidden mammalian orbs ... the way you used to?"

"Space-husband," cooed Clara, thawing. "You engage my blush-capacitors. It shall be as you wish. Let us nestle." They nestled. "Enough."

Miles had become aware of a security guard shadowing them and talking into a radio.

"Perhaps we should leave this zone and investigate others," he suggested. "Though I applaud the gigantism of this edifice, it is but a sickly parody of our own well-ordered plazas and the endless barter and vulgar injunctions to consume become wearying."

"Do not worry about the primitive Guardian, my lily-livered star-warrior. I am jamming his signal and will dissolve him if he becomes a threat. Though our eerie space-beauty is doubtless a source of confusion we have violated no local laws, that he has seen. I wish to study this place further."

They walked into a shoe-shop and sneered at some pitiful Earth-shoes, so sadly lacking in hover-jets or wall-walking functions, and mused on the way the past-people liked to wear logos identifying themselves with big corporations.

They went into a chain chemist's and laughed at the primitive toothbrushes.

"See how they boast of their flexible heads!" said Space-Clara scornfully. "What would they make of our mighty mimetic stealth self-regenerating Star Toothbrushes, with the new neutron-flux head that can destroy galaxies?"

"Let us not mock them, my all-purpose self-cleaning space-floozy. Let us see this rather as the first faltering steps towards the Neutron Toothbrush. They have at least discovered that constant innovation and techno-fetishry is the path to happiness."

"I take your point and am engaging self-correction. Let us also salute the till operatives," said Clara as they left. "Half organic and half machine, the whole process automated so as to minimize inefficient human interaction."

"It is a conundrum, space-wife, that while their culture revolved around purchase, they wished to hurry through the experience as quickly and unmemorably as possible."

They continued their regal progress. At times they were mobbed by schoolkids, wolf-whistled at by both sexes, smiled at by grannies, had their pictures taken. They remained serene and sometimes consented to enact space-poses for this last.

"Is it for the telly?" a granny asked.

"Is it for Doctor Who?" asked her friend.

"Yes," said Miles. He turned to Clara. "Come with me and I will take you on amazing journeys through space and time, show you sights you have never seen. Come with me ... to Cardiff."

"I don't mind if I do, luv," said Clara in a drudgey Mrs. Mauberley voice. "Only you'll have to get me back for the weekend 'coz it's me mum's hysterectomy."

The shopping centre security man was now openly following them, consulting with the security people of the various shops they entered. At last he walked briskly up to them.

"Can I ask what you're doing?"

Space-Clara stared at him as if at an insect. "Observing and recording, neutrally but with an unavoidable hint of lofty mockery."

"For what?"

"For the Primitive Anthropology Institute of Silver City Alpha," Space-Miles told him.

"Are you students?"

"We are in eternal quest of knowledge and new physical sensation," said Space-Clara. "But be informed that our IQs are already several hundred times greater than yours."

"Do you have a permit for ... whatever it is you're doing?"

"Of course," she said. "We are licensed by the Guardians, the Chrono-Police and the Order of Zeth."

He nodded. "Well could I see it?"

"Certainly," said Clara. "If you will lower shields I will project copies into your mind. – I will take the opportunity to mind-control the primitive," she informed Space-Miles aside but not quietly.

"An amusing stratagem, my cosmic tart," said Miles striking a foppish-looking space-pose against her.

Clara widened her eyes and stared intently and quite strangely at the guard. "Submit," she ordered. "Kneel and kiss my space-boots and pronounce 'I am an inferior life-form' and then bark like a Rigellian star-dog."

"Stop that," said the guard. "Talk properly."

"Mind-control inoperative," she reported. "There is nothing to take hold of."

"Talk to me properly," repeated the guard angrily. "Explain yourselves or I'll throw you out."

Miles looked quizzical. "Have we violated local law?"

"We have committed deviation," Space-Clara told him. "Perhaps we have violated the dress-code." She suddenly threw her head back and laughed her own laugh, loudly.

"This is private property," said the guard, agitated.

Space-Clara raised an eyebrow. "We understood this was a commercial zone. It straddles what were once public thoroughfares."

"It is private property," he repeated. "We have the right to refuse access. If we don't want you here you are committing trespass. Now I'm trying to talk to you calmly. I just want to find out what's going on. What are you doing in the shops?"

"Observing their primitive purchasing patterns."

"Well, shops aren't for observing, they're for buying. I've had reports that you've been ... laughing at things."

Miles laughed now. "Is laughter in violation of contemporary mores? Oh no, I have done it again."

"I am tempted to dissolve this specimen," said Clara.

"Talk properly. Why are you wearing those outfits?"

"Because my silvery star-breasts would startle you with their magnificence, were I to parade around naked, and my quantum vagina would violate local by-laws on the use of atomic energy and the harnessing of black holes. The effect of my husband's space-penis on unshielded eyes would be too terrible to speak of. It is a triumph of nano-technology."

"Oi," said Miles, "that doesn't sound very – "

"It has the power of a thousand suns. Better? Perhaps you ought to show it to the ape-man to subdue him with awe at its futuristic resplendence."

"Now that's enough of that talk," said the guard.

"See how he quails now! See how he is cowed by the threat of your mighty space-penis! Show it to him, star-husband. Show him your space-penis."

She unhooked the snaking hoover-attachment from Miles's groin and waved it towards the guard while Miles stood there with legs apart and his fists on his hips looking scornful.

"Stop that," said the guard. "Put it away." A tittering crowd was gathering.

"Wrap it around him, space-husband, and throw him through the air with it." She flung the suction-tube at the guard, who stepped back, and it clattered to the floor. "Ha!" she cried. "Watch as it throttles you."

Miles frowned and looked down at the unmoving space-penis. "I seem unable to attain prehensility. I am sorry, this has never happened before."

"Perhaps the batteries have run down," said Space-Clara sadly. "It is still under warranty." She kicked at and trod on it experimentally and Miles yelped.

"Look, I've had enough," said the guard. "If you're doing street theatre or something you need a permit. If you're just here to annoy people – "

"It is our raison d'etre," said Star-Clara.

"See how he is thwarted by your pretentious bilinguality," said Space-Miles, hands on hips, as the guard looked uncomprehending.

Clara too struck a space-pose with legs apart and arms akimbo. "By my silver space-knickers!" she cried. "This is the sorriest mutant outside the Rad Zones of Zarg!"

"You *are* annoying people," said the guard. "Now what was the thing where you were blowing and breathing at people?"

They both burst out laughing. "It's all right," Clara told him in her own voice, "we have a licence for that."

"Signed in triplicate by the Home Secretary," said Miles.

"All right, I've had enough, get out," said the guard. "If you won't tell me what you're playing at – "

"It's for the television, innit," Clara suddenly said in Estuary. "We're filming for a new series, Boys From Brazil: Britain's Silliest Little Hitlers. When Jobsworths Attack. Craps in Caps. What happens when uniforms fail to compensate for erectile dysfunction."

"Filming?" He looked around. "Where are your cameras?"

"All over us. Pinheads, aren't they, you pinhead. You're going to be famous, mate."

"Well where's your permit? There's no filming without permission."

"Public interest, innit?"

"I don't believe you. Where's your crew?"

"Back on our starship," she said reverting to Space Clara.

"I've had enough of this." The guard turned and walked off.

They put their hands back on their hips and laughed mightily.

"See how we have bested him!"

"See how he retreats in confusion before our winsome space-frolics!"

"Witness, browbeaten past-people, how simple it is to overturn the primitive authority system!" Clara told the crowd.

Miles stooped to gather and put away his space-penis. It took three goes and he got a knot in it.

"I would help you but I might unleash its power and annihilate the bystanders," Clara told him.

"Let us repel the dust of this place from our feet with forcefields and never return."

Clara was in no mood to leave, however. The crowd still lingered, muttering and smiling and taking pictures. "Presently, space-husband." She strode around with hands behind her back studying the bystanders interestedly.

"What was that about?" a woman asked.

"A minor altercation with a manifestation of the backwardness of your society."

"What are you?" someone else asked.

"Your genetic superior." She pointed at a snacking schoolboy. "I would sample your crisps." He offered them to her. She ate some and cocked her head. "Flavoursome and low in mutagens. I thank you. Crisps are the only thing we lack in our future paradise as potatoes evolved intelligence. I married my space-husband because he captured three in one day. You are a schoolchild?" He nodded. "Most of the things your teachers tell you will be proved wrong. You should learn independent reasoning and sucking up. And genetic engineering if available. Do you have genetic engineering lessons?" He shook his head. "You should request transfer to a better school. That was my favourite subject. I created a fire-breathing mouse that continues to wreak havoc in the eco-system. Would you like a timeline reading?"

Outlandish costumes or not the visit of the space-people had never been intended as a public performance, but since they had gathered a crowd she thought it was only polite to play to the audience for a bit rather than simply walk off and resume her private fun with Miles. She took a gadget off her belt she hadn't used yet, constructed out of a hand-held voltmeter with a radio aerial and an old-fashioned but shiny tin-opener attached to the end. It had velcro on the back for attaching it to a velcro patch on her belt. (The space-people believed Benevolent Uncle Argus had invented velcro too.)

She pointed the gadget at the boy and consulted it.

"What do you wish to be when you attain maturity?"

"A train driver."

"Your wish is fulfilled. You become a train driver and end by owning your own fleet of trains. Your grandson drives the first space-train to Mars. Who else wishes to know their future?" Hands went up. Clara scanned with her gadget. "You will become a billionairess and bury seven husbands," she told an old granny. She hit the gadget and frowned. "Or you *have* buried seven husbands, in your garden, and will shortly be arrested. ... Your grandson will discover the cure for bureaucrats," she told another woman. "You become a racing driver when you attain maturity," she told another schoolboy. "*You* never attain maturity but live to 103," she told his loud and lewd friend. "On your third regeneration you will become a Pirate Queen," she told a middle-aged woman, "and establish a brief but vivid slave-empire in the South Seas before going out in a blaze of glory in a zeppelin battle over Kuala Lumpur. ... He is the future prime minister of this country!" she cried pointing at a rather oafish young man. "You should all be nice to him and give him sweets now so he remembers you. He is the first to win leadership in the lottery after the Revolution. He fills Downing Street with floozies and attempts to pay off the national debt by gambling everyone's pensions on a single spin of the roulette wheel in Las Vegas. I will not tell you how it turns out. ... That man there is the greatest man of this age!" she suddenly cried pointing at a bemused swaying derelict on the outskirts of the crowd. "He is destined to save you all! Hail him! All hail him! Give him money! Give him money so he can continue his meditations in peace! He comes up with the answer to everything! All give him money or I will dissolve you!" People started to give the tramp money. "You will be happy," she told other people. "You will be rich ... You live to a ripe age ... You discover a new form of sex that takes the world by storm ... You will own a cat that saves the monarchy ... You marry the film star _____ _____," to another granny. "It ends badly but you get custody of the credit cards ... You have a sex-change, you know you want to ... You will live long and be happy ... Your lives will be filled with all the darkness and gloom you could possibly wish for," she told a couple of Goths. Clara approved of Goths, so she also told them, "And Siouxsie and the Banshees will re-form next year."

Meanwhile some flighty girls were playing with Miles's suction-attachment space-penis. "I do not advise that," Clara told them. "You are meddling with forces you cannot comprehend. It has the power to destroy us all." Miles at length wrestled it back off them. Clara supposed they had better start moving again. "We must leave you now. Enjoy your primitive lives. Remember you and everyone around you are supremely ridiculous. Pick your tackle up, man," she added as Miles tripped over his space-penis before managing to put it away again. They strode off; part of the crowd followed them but they affected to no longer notice. They sneered at some more things in shop windows. Miles tried to steer her towards an exit. "We should think of returning to our own time."

"Presently." They came to a bank, or at least a row of banking machines, and staff standing around to tell people to use the banking machines, and a single teller at a window hidden away in a corner, all unwalled and open directly onto the shopping centre to give customers that open-air part-of-the-crowd visible-to-everyone feeling that is so reassuring when handling large sums of money.

"Behold," said Clara, "one of the great temples of the age. Let us investigate." They strode in, or onto the unwalled flooring, there being no in, and peered around with keen interest, trailed by some of their followers. "In 2020 the current banking caste are exiled to an island, and given a currency of pebbles to play with. They could then speculate and deceive among themselves to their hearts' content without endangering people's livelihoods in the real world."

"See how the depositors have to be chivvied and shepherded to give their money to machines rather than real people," Miles observed. "They have a sentimental attachment to dealing with fellow humans and providing them with jobs."

"In my opinion they are wise, space-husband. Machines make great sex-slaves but are not to be trusted as masters. I except of course our own Grand Computer, more god than machine, more lover than leader."

"Is this a protest?" asked one of the people who had followed them.

"We are neutral observers. We may not interfere."

"Can I help you?" asked a female staff member coming over.

"We wish merely to observe and sneer," Clara told her.

The woman looked with unease from her to their trailing audience.

"Do you have an account here?"

"We will open one. Please wait while I manufacture money." Clara pressed her coin dispenser and made whirring noises. "Our loving government gives us all the money we need, just like yours does to you."

"It *is* a protest," said someone in the crowd who'd followed them.

"That's right, tell them!"

"Quite right! Pissing away everyone's money, and then getting hand-outs from us, and carrying on giving themselves huge bonuses."

"What are they going to do?"

"Are you anarchists?"

Clara turned and glared in annoyance. "We are genetically-perfect future fascists!" Her coin-dispenser was empty. "Manufacture some paper money, space-husband."

"I think you'd better leave," said the bank employee. She had been joined by a male colleague; and now by a security guard who was talking into a walkie-talkie.

"Let's go," Miles muttered.

"Not yet." She couldn't disappoint the expectant crowd behind her. This was the peril of assuming leadership, she supposed, you were sometimes at the mercy of your followers. She didn't have a clue what she was going to do though; at a rough guess carry on acting up until they were physically thrown out. She grabbed at the silvery purse Miles wore and extracted one of the notes he carried for emergencies. "We wish to feed your machines," she said holding it up. "Your bosses must not run short of bonuses when they are down to their last mansions," she added for the benefit of the crowd, who she decided were a pain in the arse and interfering with her art in their expectation of obvious protest. She didn't even have a clue if this was one of the offending banks. Still it was a ghastly place and they deserved to be annoyed on general principles. She strode over to one of the banking machines and started to push buttons at random and attempted to cram the note inside.

"Stop that. Please leave," said the woman.

"This is an attractive machine," said Space-Clara caressing it. "It reminds me of an early prototype of the Sexbot 5000. I wish to have sex with your machines," she declared, starting to writhe against and lick the console. To hell with the audience, she would go where her muse led her. Some of them were laughing anyway. She placed her hands on the screen. "I am fusing with your machine," she said, throwing her head back and moaning orgasmically.

"The timeline, space-wife," said Miles urgently grabbing at her. "We have attracted undue attention and must leave now."

"You are jealous of the machine," she told him pouting as he pulled her off and pushed her away, and waved at the cash dispenser heartbrokenly over his shoulder.

"I am asking you to leave," said the bank woman. "All of you."

"See how they resent the challenge to their primitive authority system," said Clara, escaping from Miles and stalking around. "See how they fear all that is deviant."

"Get out."

"You are uptight. Show her your space-penis, husband. No, that will traumatize her. I will give her a timeline reading." She pointed her gadget at the woman.

"What is that? Put that away."

"Come on, let's go," said Miles.

The security guard grabbed Clara's arm. Miles grabbed the security guard and made him let go of Clara. Clara unholstered her plastic crackling ray-gun and shot at the guard and then the bank staff. The shopping centre security guard who had quizzed them previously came in and grabbed Clara's arm.

"Oh, you!" she cried. "I will erase you and all of your ancestors from space-time." She broke free and ray-gunned him repeatedly. Miles interposed himself as he lunged for her again, and shoved him away. The bank security guard stepped forward; Miles unhooked his space-penis and used the long solid bit at the end to prod him in the chest and keep him at bay, then waved it at the two guards warningly.

"We are leaving now," he said.

All of a sudden the bank staff and security guards stepped away, continuing to watch them warily. "Your penis has intimidated them," said Clara. She covered them all with her toy ray-gun menacingly while Miles continued to wave his hoover attachment.

"Get back," she said. "Gene-scum like you are not allowed to touch us. We will depart now and leave you to your wretched degraded lives." They stepped backwards towards the muttering crowd and the shopping centre. "Do not attempt to follow us or you will be dissolved." She brandished her timeline device. "None of you ever does anything useful so we may slay you with impunity."

She continued to glare at them warningly for a second and then said, "Right, let's scram. Keep to a calm space-walk." They rotated smartly. "He made me do it," Clara said to the two policemen who had appeared behind them. "Anyway it's for television."

"We have failed in our mission," said Space-Clara in the police car. "Now our advanced technology will fall into the hands of the primitives and the timeline will be in jeopardy. They will probably dissect us to discover the secret of our eerie space-beauty."

Miles said nothing. He reached over and unclipped the bottle of vodka-based space-nutrients from her utility belt and took a healthy swig. Clara raised an eyebrow at him as he passed it back but took a little nip herself.

"I wonder what Benevolent Uncle Argus would do in this situation," she mused.

Miles gave her a dirty look. She raised an eyebrow again, mockingly.

"All hail Benevolent Uncle Argus," they chorused, Miles in a very flat monotone that had nothing to do with being a future space-person, "our Benefactor and Guide, discoverer of nano-vibrators, inventor of silver make-up."

The two policeman in the front, passenger and driver alike, swivelled their heads.

"I think he would keep his mouth shut so as not to make anything worse," said Miles.

"No," said Clara thoughtfully, "*I* think he would slay everyone involved and devastate an area of twenty or thirty square miles around with atomic weapons, would Benevolent Uncle Argus."

"All hail Benevolent Uncle Argus," and the rest, they recited again, Miles in a very quiet and sullen mumble.

" ... silver make-up, and immortality jelly-and-custard, and velcro, and spandex, and PVC, and thigh-boots, and hover-toilets, and neutron tooth-brushes, and silver space-knickers," Clara continued zealously, and to annoy Miles, who eventually laid a finger and then a hand over her mouth.

" ... and star-cats, and mimetic stealth-cheese, and tinfoil bras, and atomic cocktail-shakers, and everything that is good," she continued in a whisper when he removed it. "We should continue to observe and record, my teflon-testicled protector, until they deactivate us," she said more loudly.

There was no response from Miles.

"Behold, they wear the sacred yellow vest of power," said Clara, for both policemen wore the ridiculous plastic 'high-visibility' jackets affected by officialdom of the time. "It indicates high status in this age. It confers authority derived from its unique hideousness to a select elite of police, football stewards, roadsweepers, childminders, maître d's ... "

"Shut up now," said Miles quite urgently.

Clara blinked repeatedly and rapidly as if he had slapped her and she was fighting back tears, pouted and averted her face.

"May I touch your sacred yellow vest?" Miles asked the passenger policeman in a space-voice, leaning forward, several seconds later.

"No," said the policeman. "Don't even think about it."

"He is jealous of its power," declared Space-Clara. "You're so whipped," she murmured to Miles approvingly in her own voice, smiling proudly. "It's for a TV programme, you know," she suddenly told the policemen in her television-woman voice. "The whole thing was on camera. We're recording you now."

"We can talk about that at the station," said the policeman. "For now you'd be well advised to shut the hell up."

She smiled. "Take heart, space-husband. Remember that they do not believe in punishing crime in this era. In fact, the police's function is more often that of protecting criminals from the general public. Why do the police *wurrrrve* criminals?" she asked them in her own voice.

"That's ... enough of that, I think, dear," said Miles with a fixed grin.

"It is a well-established historical fact, space-husband, that in this epoch the nominal law-enforcement operatives felt an abiding admiration for and sexual attraction to criminals amounting to pure and all-consuming *wurrrrve*. When the law-abiding citizens defended themselves against them as the police neglected to do they would arrest the law-abiding citizens. Aren't you sick of it?" she suddenly snarled in her own voice, leaning forward, teeth gritted, to taunt them. "Aren't you sick of being on the side of the criminals? Don't you miss being on the side of the public? Don't you miss the days when we all looked up to you? You must do. Why don't you do something? Why don't you protest? Why don't you rebel? Why don't you just not enforce the stupid laws and bang up toe-rags like you're meant to? Why don't you frag your Communist superiors, and boo and throw things at the lectern every time you're sent on a sociology course? Why don't you burn your silly yellow jackets? You're a laughing stock."

"That's enough of that," said a policeman and Miles together.

She sat back and sighed. "Poor 'ickle policemen," she said in a frail quavering childish voice. "Dey get so scared out in the big wide world. Dey has to wear bwight yellow vests so people will notice them, in case they get wunned over by a car or knocked down by a big man who didn't see them. Dey do not have the force of personality to make themselves visible without it."

"Oh God," said Miles.

"Miles, I've had a great idea for a television series," she continued remorselessly. "It's about a man who is a policeman by day but fights crime by night. Obviously he is the last person anyone would suspect. He takes off his magic yellow visibility jacket," she added, bursting into laughter, "and instantly becomes completely invisible. He starts wearing this smart and dashing button-up uniform … he pulls all the birds … becomes a symbol of freedom and justice to the oppressed citizens … crime goes down, his Communist boss is outraged, in his day-job he is set to catch himself … What are you doing?" Miles was fumbling at her hips. "This is hardly the time or the place, husband. Help, I am being raped back here. I realise that is a low-priority crime compared to some but when you have a moment I'd be obliged if you could put a stop to it."

But Miles was only taking the vodka-spiked Ribena bottle once more.

She smiled at him. "Now probably isn't the time to break this to you, Miles," she said, "but I am actually your Tyler Durden. It's been you on your own doing this all along. They can't see anyone else back here but you, and you will be the one to take the beating."

"That would explain *so* much," said Miles. "In particular the way your voice is never out of my head day or night."

"Hear how is he oppressing me," she said to the police. "I wish to report a misogyny crime. Now you are in trouble."

Their outfits naturally caused a splash at the police station. Clara strolled around looking interestedly at everything in a space-fashion, hands behind her back, a bit like the Duke of Edinburgh inspecting something ex-colonial only not quite as wild-card. She played at being baffled or amused by Earth-objects and Miles, after another swig at the vodka-Ribena space-juice, started to join in. She didn't copper-bait at first and attracted an amused gathering of coppers.

They overheard a fairly friendly and cheery admissions sergeant consulting with one of the ones who had brought them in.

" … some kind of anarchists, I think … " the latter murmured.

"We are not anarchists!" Clara cried indignantly. "Do we look like anarchists? Where is the dog on a string? Where is the trust-fund? We are genetically-superior Utopian-future fascists! Why is that so hard to understand?"

"Describing ourselves as fascists, not going to help," Miles murmured.

"Hmm. You may have a point. *Tory* Anarchists, then!" she cried at the cops. "We are Tory Anarchists, like Beerbohm and Orwell and Swift. I insist you write that down. And I insist upon being treated as a political prisoner."

"Oh God," said Miles. "Please pass me the space-nutrients again."

She handed him the bottle. "Do not hog it all, I suddenly feel thirsty. Anyway it's for the television," she told the policemen. "We are a licensed television production company. Miles show them the paperwork."

"I don't have it."

"How could you not?"

"Because they don't have pockets in the future. All I have is a silver ladies' purse."

"Look, we are registered at Companies House and everything. Look up Albion TV and ring up and ask to speak to … well, us, it will leave a message at our house. We make that … Coppers Are Sexy programme. And … Miles name a famous television programme they will have heard of."

Miles randomly named a famous children's television programme.

"Yes, we make Blue Peter," said Clara.

Miles laughed. " 'Blue Peter producers arrested in kinky SM PVC transvestite … ' "

"I take your point. All right, we *don't* make Blue Peter. But this *is* for the telly … "

She carried on trying to persuade a changing audience of policemen of this. They were in some sort of central reception area with people going in and out and loitering idly. No-one seemed in a hurry to charge or question them; one of the policemen who had brought them in spent time on a phone behind the counter. Clara slipped gradually into her Estuarese TV-woman voice as if that would help make her case. She flirted mildly with some of the police.

"You're a tall one," she told one loitering at the counter by her and the sergeant. "You ever fancied being on the telly yourself? Only we've got this reality phone-vote thing coming up, Coppers Who Dance. Do you dance? Would you be willing to learn? Let me give you my number … "

Eventually they were shooed away and made to sit on a bench off to the side. They swapped the bottle of space-nutrients back and forth glumly.

"This is no longer fun," said Clara.

"Cheer up," said Miles. "It might come to court. Imagine all the fun you can have in court."

Clara's eyes lit up. "Bags I Spencer Tracy!"

"Bags I Gregory Peck."

"Rumpole!"

"Walpole."

"What the hell did we do, anyway?"

Neither of them were able to answer this.

"I suppose they could get us on the idiotic trespass thing," suggested Miles.

Clara looked at where one of the cops who'd nabbed them was on the phone again. "The bank people and the shopping-centre authorities are trying to decide whether to press charges," she speculated. "They could look silly, *if* we are just students, or *if* it really is something for the telly, and people really don't like banks at the moment and they're trying to make nice with PR."

But they knew that people were prosecuted all the time in Britain for not doing much of anything at all.

"We will have to pretend to be disadvantaged," said Clara. "Show them your penis, the real one."

"Listen to me, Clara," said Miles earnestly. "There's nothing they can do to us, just so long as we don't turn on each other."

"My husband made me do it," cried Clara loudly.

"She went to a public school," cried Miles more loudly.

"He wore a crucifix in front of an atheist once, I couldn't believe it."

"She punched a bat that flew into her hair, I will testify in return for immunity."

"He has a goldfish-selling ring, he hangs round outside schoolyards."

"She puts things into the wrong bins, I have seen her."

"I wish to report marital rape!" Clara cried. "Every alternate Thursday. Inept and all-too-brief marital rape, at that."

"She has a collection of Spike Milligan videos."

"He once said welsh on a bet, that is a hate crime."

And so on.

A policeman in a tank-top offered them a cup of tea.

Clara jumped and looked around puzzledly. "Who spoke? I cannot see you. Perhaps if you were to wear some kind of yellow plastic jacket you would be more visible."

So the policeman went away and they didn't get a cup of tea.

"Please don't milk that," said Miles.

"Is it a crime? Is it a crime to be appalled by the degraded aesthetic values of our age?"

Presently another policeman came up to them waving a sheet of paper.

"A red 1968 E-type with silver-painted egg boxes sellotaped to the bonnet. This anything to do with you?" He showed them the paper.

"They have towed our space-car," intoned Clara sadly.

Suddenly a number of shouting bleeding drunks were brought in, dragged by coppers some of whom were also bleeding. The reception area became loud and chaotic.

Clara rose. "All right, Miles, this is our chance," she murmured. "We're going to make a break for it. It's our only hope. Act casual. Try to blend in."

Miles got up and they started to saunter casually around the room, whistling for nonchalance, hands behind their backs, studying posters and notices with keen interest. "I have memorised the number of the keypad," Clara murmured. In the course of their amiable, ambling peregrinations, they presently came to the outer door. They studied that interestedly but casually too. Miles moved to try to cover Clara as she jabbed a combination into the digital keypad lock.

"Arse," said Clara as nothing happened, and tried again.

"Hurry up."

It was not the second combination either, or any of the next five she frantically tried.

"I thought you said you memorised it!" Miles hissed.

"Well it definitely had a three, and then something on the left."

"For Christ's sake, woman!"

Clara frantically punched numbers at random and rattled at the door handle. "Open, damn you!"

Hands fell on their shoulders.

"We just ... wanted some fresh air."

Heads were shaken. Hands were placed on their backs and they were propelled back towards the bench.

"Passively resist, Miles," said Clara, going limp and falling face-first onto the floor. "Make them drag us."

Miles helped the policemen drag Clara back to the bench.

The drunks had been taken to the cells now. The excitement died down. They passed the space-juice back and forth.

"Oh I have had enough Miles," said Clara at length. "Take me away from this. All of it. Let us move to an island and raise children. We will name them Winston, Clive, Sir Arthur Bomber Harris and Mabel. We will raise them to believe the British Empire still exists. We will send them forth in pith helmets to conquer new lands. Forth in pith helmets. That's quite hard to say. I believe I may be slightly drunk Miles. Our children will be brave and strong and clear-eyed, apart from the ones that are yours. I may have to reproduce by parthenogenesis. That's even harder. Oh to hell with this, what did we *do*?" she cried. "What did we bloody *do*? I demand to be charged," she yelled. "I demand that all you Communist policemen tell us what we did or let us go."

Just then the first two policemen came and took them to an interview room. They sat down across a table facing them.

"Would you like a lawyer?" asked one of the policemen.

"Certainly not," said Clara. "That is for scumbags. We have nothing to hide and have full confidence in the fairness of the British police."

The policeman laid Clara's timeline-reading gadget on the table. That and the raygun had been confiscated when they were nabbed.

"This constitutes an offensive weapon," the policeman said, pointing at the attachment on the end which, as has been said, was made out of a tin-opener, one of the pointy old-fashioned kind you just sort of hack at the tin with.

"Oh fuck off," yelled Miles angrily.

"Oh do fuck off," yelled Clara in disgust.

The policeman tapped the radio aerial bit. "And this looks like a radio-transmitter, something you were extremely ill-advised to brandish threateningly in a public area in the current climate."

Clara swore again. Miles was silent. He fumbled for and took the space-nutrients bottle from Clara and had a swig. She took it back at once and had a go as well.

"You also," said the other policeman laying the toy ray-gun on the table, "displayed a replica gun."

Miles burst out laughing. Clara swore hair-raisingly.

"Are you taking the piss?" Miles demanded. He studied the copper to see if this actually was the case but could discern no sign of it.

"This is very, very serious."

"No it isn't, it's ridiculous."

"You claim this was a stunt for a TV programme," said the first policeman. "Yet you were unable to produce a filming permit, and in fact clearly had no camera crew with you."

"We ... we make television programmes in our head," said Clara. "We ... are giddy frolicsome creatures left over from an age of frivolity and freedom."

"You admit you had no cameras?"

"Is it a crime?" she demanded. "Is it a crime to make a television programme without a camera? I'd like to see that one come to court."

The policeman consulted his notes.

"When the shopping centre authorities first approached you about your unusual behaviour, you were non-cooperative and abusive."

"We were derisive," said Clara. "He asked us why we were breathing. We are not yet admitting that we *were* breathing, mind."

"He says you abused him, and threatened to make an obscene display."

"My breasts," said Clara primly, "are not a threat. They are a promise of paradise."

"You offered to show your husband's penis."

"Oh, that," said Clara. "That *is* awful. Yes, that shouldn't be allowed."

"You admit that, then?"

"Is it a crime?" Clara demanded. "Is it a crime to offer to show a penis? Humble organ of our origin, taut one-eyed father to us all, wrathful Odin of the waistband, does it not inspire awe, pity, revulsion and piety in equal measure? Show them ours, Miles."

"Save it for court," advised Miles, head in his hands.

"Yes! A dramatic revelation in the last act, that would be much better."

The policeman sighed. "You also issued physical threats."

"We did not!"

He read from his notes. " 'We will erase you and all of your ancestors from space-time.' That sounds like a threat to me."

Miles burst out laughing again. Clara boggled in disbelief.

"It is only a threat if you can actually do it," she told him. "Several times my husband has threatened to throw me against a wall and pleasure me blue but I am still waiting."

The policeman flicked through his notes. "You were rambling and absurd in your responses, as you are being now."

"Is *that* a crime? Is it a crime to free-associate? Our only crime is to be too winsome for this world. Oh, and an unsolved murder on the A41."

"Oh God," said Miles.

"Oh and several unlicensed shotguns. And I *did* punch a bat that flew into my hair once, but it was in self-defence."

The policeman turned a page. "You claimed to be from the future?"

"Is it a crime? Is it a crime to masquerade as future persons?"

Miles laughed again. "Get us under the Witchcraft Act. Prophecies."

"You *did* tell fortunes, sir," put in the other policeman. "Did you accept any payment for that?"

Miles stared at him.

"You expressed your dissatisfaction with society," said the first policeman looking at his notes.

"That may well be a crime now," Clara conceded, "but we missed the announcement."

"Repeatedly described things as primitive ... You encouraged bystanders to 'overturn authority' and then you led a mob of them to the bank."

"We didn't lead them, they followed!" cried Clara. "In fact, they were silently egging us on. They pushed us! Their expectation drove me. I had a revelation. It is the crowd that is the motor of history. Consult the end of 'War and Peace', my good man. Personally I have always believed it is the great Hero and genius that shapes the world, but now I start to think it possible that I, for all my demagogic charisma, am merely the puppet of the urges of the crowd. For the first time I understand how Hitler must have felt. The poor man was merely a scapegoat."

Miles let his head fall onto the table with a groan.

The policemen exchanged glances. "You described yourselves as fascists on several occasions."

"Space-juice," said Miles clicking his fingers at Clara. "Immediately."

"*Future* fascists," Clara said witheringly. "Silvery utopian supermen! That's what we were playing. Look at how my husband is dressed. How far would he have got at Nuremberg? *You* are the fascists."

"In the car you described us as Communists."

"You should hear what I call you in private."

"Let's not antagonize the nice policemen," suggested Miles hopefully, briefly removing the bottle from his mouth.

"Don't be a wimp," said Clara. "For once I have them right where I want them."

"Oh God."

"This is all because they fancy a nice cup of tea and a sit down. Make a nice easy arrest towards their quota and then spend the rest of the day with their feet up filling in forms."

"Enough!" cried Miles. "You're being rude now. They're just doing their jobs. They – you saw that scene in reception. That's a daily thing for them. They still – put themselves on the line to protect us, sometimes. They can't help the rest of the madness."

"Yes they can! They revel in it."

"They don't know how to fight things any more than we do."

"I am distantly descended from Sir Robert Peel and am hence entitled to say he would be turning in his grave to see this lot of nanny-state bullies and criminal-coddlers in their silly piss-yellow safety-jackets. Look at what utter dicks they are being!"

"Hush now, dear." He smiled ingratiatingly at the policemen. "Pay her no heed – a giddy child – she – we men understand the ways of the world."

"Miles, you are a complete – "

The policemen's heads swivelled from side to side interestedly as Clara and Miles bickered.

"Personally," Miles told them earnestly, "I have a lot of respect and sympathy for the modern police force."

Clara burst out laughing at his solemn face. "Oh! Oh! You – you – look at that face! You suck-up! You Judas! You'll pay for that, my lad! Beastliness privileges are withdrawn for a month! You shall not see the inside of my boudoir, sir, until the other side of Michaelmas!"

"Well, come on, they have to do their job, and we did sort of – hold up a bank."

"Perhaps you might be advised to ask for a lawyer, sir," said a policeman in a monotone.

"We almost did, didn't we?" said Clara. "We easily could have done. I am impressed with us. We are desperadoes. This could be the beginning of a crime spree."

"Yes," said Miles, laughing again and gesturing at the table, "I mean look at our weapons, we're a walking militia."

"Would you like – " began a policeman.

"Shut up, however, we are talking," said Clara. "I am bored of this charade now." She adopted her space-voice. "We shall return to our own time. Farewell, retrograde policemen of the past. Do not come closer lest you be exploded by the vortex." She pushed her chair back, touched a button on her silver-painted digital watch and held Miles's hand. Then she sort of vibrated for a bit and made an eerie, 'Oooooooo,' sound. After that nothing happened. "Well what did you expect?" she asked in her own voice. The policemen had not reacted in any way at all but Miles burst out laughing. "Thank you, Miles, it's nice to have some response, sometimes I feel the need to wear a visibility jacket."

"It's the laughter of the damned," said Miles.

"I do not like these primitive chairs," said Space-Clara, trying to get comfortable. "They do not levitate and mould themselves to cup your buttocks like our futuristic space-chairs. No wonder the past policemen are so uptight, with their pitiful 21st-century buttocks uncupped."

"Perhaps a psychiatric appraisal is called for," the first policeman said to the second.

"Ooh! Yes!" cried Clara, eyes widening. "That could be fun!"

"No!" said Miles in alarm. "No, it wouldn't. That could – really, really be bad. We'll behave now, honestly."

"Miles don't panic," said Clara. "Just roll your trouser leg up – well, roll your space-boots down or something, and do what I do." She started making strange hand-gestures and winking. "There must be some freemasons left. We are strangers from the east! We serve the Great Architect, by the level and the square!"

"Knock it off. Just – have you considered," he asked the policemen, "that really our worst punishment is being married to each other?"

"Don't be disloyal, Miles." Clara left off making would-be masonic signals but continued to wink at the policemen. "Come on," she said to them. "Come on, let's talk honestly. Like humans. You must know this is horse-shit. You must much rather be out nicking villains like you joined up to do. You must hate everything as much as we do. You must hate the government and your Communist bosses. Why don't you join us? Why don't you be on the people's side again? This won't last. There's going to be a revolution, of one form or another, soon. But we all have to start making gestures. Gestures of defiance and humanity, so we know we're not alone. Talk to me! Tell me I'm right. Talk to me like humans."

The policemen just stared at her woodenly, arms folded.

"Talk to me like humans!" she cried, pounding the table. "Talk to me like fellow citizens!"

They continued to stare silently.

"Perhaps they think we are some kind of mystery prisoners, like mystery shoppers, sent by the government to test them," she said sadly. "Really we're not. Really it's going to happen, eventually. An uprising. Mass protests. A withdrawing of our consent to be governed in this way any longer. We will throw out all the bullies and lunatics and thieving parasites. We will be responsible for ourselves. We will all get our pride back."

They stared.

A terrible fear had been plucking at Miles; he had been brushing it off but suddenly acknowledged it fully now. This absurd palaver might or might not be terribly serious, depending on how prickish the people involved wanted to be. Again, there were prosecutions as silly every day. But this was also the town where they had impersonated policemen some months before. They had been idiots to come back. Who knew what cameras they had been caught on? Who knew what pictures had been blown up? What if the delay was because they had been recognised? What if they were preparing to spring that on them too? The policeman on the left, he thought, who was doing most of the talking, was boring his eyes into Miles's. He knew. They were letting them incriminate themselves further and Clara was doing it.

"Clara stop talking. Charge us with something or release us," he said.

"They are playing cat and mouse with us, Miles," said Clara.

"You consider yourselves rebels against a repressive system?" asked the left-hand copper at last.

Miles swore under his breath: with disgust, not fear. Something in the copper's voice or face had given away that he had nothing in particular up his sleeve. They *were* just being silly bastards. This *was* just because they had arsed around in the shopping centre.

"No," he said fairly calmly, "we are idle gadabouts amusing ourselves. We dress up and frolic like idiots because we damn well feel like it. Tell us what law we broke or let us go. If it's anything to do with the bloody tin-opener or the bloody ray-gun I will do my damnedest to make you a laughing stock."

Clara sighed. "It would just be one more little paragraph or so in the paper, that makes everyone swear, and wonder what they're meant to do about things, and then they turn the page. Meanwhile their pictures will probably be in the Police Gazette for apprehending genocidal terrorists from the future."

"You have potentially committed any number of serious crimes," said the first policeman.

"Potentially? Potentially?" Miles yelled.

"You were trespassing on – "

"Trespass? Trespass? It's a bloody public thoroughfare!"

"You staged an unlicensed demonstration in – "

Miles swore and swigged the space-juice again.

"And, yes, we do take very seriously the matter of dangerous and intimidating – "

Miles exploded. He swore and slapped the table and leapt to his feet and shouted.

"I've had it! I've had it with you people! You're lunatics! What's wrong with you? Do you enjoy it? Don't you have anything better to do? You're pathetic! Enough! It's over! I'm not letting you get away with it! I will fight you! I will fight you to the end!"

Clara looked at him wide-eyed. "Dear God, I have inadvertently married Spartacus."

"You're bastards! You're bastards! What's the matter, were you tired of being stuck in the car hiding from teenagers? You're right! They're just happy to fill their quota! They're despicable!"

"*Excuse* me!" cried Clara in outrage. "*I* am the loose-cannon one!"

"Fiona Pilkington!" yelled Miles. "Fiona Pilkington!" This was the name of a woman who had killed herself and her disabled daughter after the police had refused to do anything about the yobs who were terrorizing them. "Fiona Pilkington, you bloody bastards!"

"I would like separate lawyers, please," said Clara.

"Ooh, ooh!" said Miles. "Scary scary tin-opener! Scary scary voltmeter! Scary scary rich people acting the goat!"

"We are not *really* rich," said Clara judiciously. "Simon our neighbour is *much* richer than us, *he* is the one you ought to investigate. Miles had a terribly deprived upbringing, really, in fact I have never quite persuaded him to say lavatory instead of toilet."

"You're lunatics! You're lunatics! You're disgusting! Do you ever complain about the state of the world? You are no longer entitled to complain about the state of the world. You *are* the state of the world! I've had it! We've *all* had it! We're going to rise up and wipe you out!"

"I do not know this man," said Clara leaning forward to the second policeman confidentially. "Plainly he is some kind of right-wing sleeper agent. I demand you protect me."

"My wife is right! My wife is right! My wife has always been right all along! You're Communists! You're sadistic power-tripping lunatic Communist bastards who are taking glee in destroying this country!"

"I have never met his wife," said Clara. "I gather she is a frightful reactionary hag."

"You know what, Communist copper? You won't win. You won't win. We will beat you in the end. We will rise up! We will throw you out!" Miles paced, ranted, swigged the space-juice for inspiration.

"I would use your truncheons on him if I was you," said Clara. "Please let the record reflect that I am sitting quietly and behaving."

"If it takes fifty years of civil war the British people will be free again!"

"Oh dear," said Clara. "The poor man. We can only pity him. Perhaps his lavatory-training was inadequate."

"If it takes fifty years of fighting ... "

"And maiming," put in Clara eagerly. "Let's not forget that. Perhaps we *should* ask for a lawyer," she added thoughtfully.

"One day we'll be free again! The British lion will roar!"

"Surely this is the Second Coming of Churchill!" gasped Clara. "Why do you not kneel to him?"

"And then ... and then ... You know what? We will ... We'll help the rest of the world free itself from people like you. We were the first into the madness, we'll be the first out the other side. First again! And then you know what we'll do? We will, yes, go into Space! We'll fuck off Europe, and get together with our own people in the Commonwealth, and have a space programme! A new frontier! This planet isn't big enough for people like us! There will be a new British Space Empire stretching across the stars!"

"I hail thee *Space-Churchill*," cried Clara. "You are arousing me immensely."

"Shut up! I'm serious! It's what we need! It's what we all need! A goal! We will explore, and colonize, and spread civilisation across the galaxy, the civilisation you hate so much, Communist copper, the way we did all across the world, and if any little collectivist, ant-like green men object we will shoot them with lasers and plant the British flag on them and – "

"What's in the bottle, sir?" asked the policeman.

Miles pulled up short, shifty-eyed.

"Nothing," he said clutching the bottle to his chest. "Space-nutrients. Ribena."

"May I see it, sir?"

"No," said Miles. "Get your own."

The policeman got up and came round the table and took the bottle and sniffed at it and Miles.

"Don't breathe, Miles! Don't let him smell you! He is not allowed to smell us without a warrant!"

The copper poured some of the dregs on his little finger and sucked.

"Christ, that's almost pure vodka."

"Nonsense," said Clara. "It is God's own Ribena."

The second copper came and tried to sniff at Clara while she writhed away and held her breath like a child. Then he beckoned his colleague and they stepped out of the interview room.

"Quick, Miles, let's hang ourselves," said Clara as they closed the door.

Miles sat back down and put his head back in his hands.

The policemen came back in and announced they would be charging them with Drunk and Disorderly, with an option for an on-the-spot fine.

"We are *not* drunk!" cried Clara in outrage. "We are political prisoners! Miles don't give them any money! Miles stop!"

Miles counted out the money for the fine and gave it to them. "Sorry for … everything," he mumbled.

"Miles! No! I divorce thee! Give it back, you thieving bastards!" she cried trying to snatch the money from the policeman's hands. "We aren't drunk! Well we weren't drunk! You pussy! Make them arrest us properly or let us go! Obviously they had nothing to charge us with!"

"They do now."

The policemen closed the door on them and left them to it.

"Miles! How could you!"

"Shh! I think they were giving us a break! They were being human! Don't you see? It's a good sign! A joyous day! A new dawn!"

"No, Miles, they were being bastards! They had nothing on us! The bank must have declined to press charges! And we weren't drunk then! They bluffed you! We should have taken it to court! They – "

"Can we please just get out of here?"

She stamped her foot but subsided and they made their way out of the station.

"Oi, your receipt," called the second, quieter copper in the reception area. He handed it to them and let them out. "And I agreed with every word you said," he murmured. "You ever do that revolution thing, come and see me."

Just as they got outside another policeman came running after and thrust another bit of paper on them.

"I heard about the auditions for Coppers Who Dance," he said. "Here are my details. I'm good with a rhumba. Give me a ring."

They tottered across a dual carriageway and were back in the town centre. It was sunset. They had no car and no more money.

"Tonight will be a real adventure," said Clara. "We will have to fend for ourselves."

"In a strange and alien landscape."

"Indeed, space-husband."

They strolled through a park, observing.

"Poor past-people," sighed Clara wistfully. "All dead and gone now. All over and done with, long long ago. All the problems that seemed so big, forgotten. Were they happy? Did they laugh and dance as we do? Did they think it would last forever? Did they remember to take the time to be happy?" She looked at him. "Why are you smiling like that?"

"I'm married to you," said Miles. "Why are you?"

"I remembered something nice from my childhood," said Clara.

Extended Scenes

(Stormtrooper and nun)

"Miles, do stop showing off your secondary-school German. You know what happened when you actually tried to talk to one."

Miles blushed deeply. He said:

"I've told you, I *meant* to call him a ----. I find his conducting second-rate anyway."

Clara cackled at the memory. "You nearly made an old man cry. And a famous one too."

"We agreed not to talk about this. I'm entitled to one slight fuck-up after everything you've put me through."

"The difference is I do it deliberately. You want only to please everyone but, tragically, you were born to cause social mayhem. God knows what would have become of you if I hadn't decided I could put you to good use."

"Was that in fact why you married me?"

"Naturally. What other reason could there be?"

Miles pouted. "Are we playing Nazi stormtrooper or what?"

(Clara's desk: more correspondence)

Dear Sir or Madam or Transitional Entity,

I am writing to condemn you to eternal hellfire for disfiguring your otherwise pretty wine bottle with a pious admonition to 'Please Use This Product Responsibly.'

My good man or woman, I will pour your wine up my arse with a funnel or feed it to a yak if I so desire.

It is none of your damn business, you simpering pustule. Your business is to make good or cheap wine with beautiful, non-annoying and elegantly uncluttered labels.

I do not even drink; it is my husband who is the alcoholic. My boycott will not hurt. I just think you ought to know that for every puritan nanny-state government parasite or lobby-group lunatic you think you are impressing with such nauseating prissiness there are a hundred people who just want to be left alone to enjoy themselves without being treated like children, at least ten of whom, when they see a label like that, are consumed by an urge to run amok burning, stabbing, impaling and disembowelling. You are now on a list that I am compiling towards the day when we finally do. Rectify your mistake at once or I will cut your ears off.

Sincerely, and about to get smashed to the tits and break the bottle over a dwarf's head out of sheer spite,

a Lady

(Harriet arrives: Richard)

A preamble to a book review he had written once had inspired Clara to play a minor, briefly-amusing, not terribly satisfying prank by way of punishment. 'I have never,' he had blithely begun this review, 'read *War and Peace*. Tried, but I couldn't get into it. I managed to get as far as page fifty once when fate intervened. I was sitting on a bench at a train station, manfully trying to keep all the names and patronymics straight, when I became aware that next to me a rather attractive young female was also frowning over a copy of the good Count's long streak of misery. She, it turned out, had got significantly further than I but was having an equally hard time of it. Was it worth persevering, I asked? No, she replied, decisively shutting the book. "Let's both not read it," I said. With one accord we chucked the books into the nearest litter bin. That decisive young critic is now my significant other. Thus does literature bring us together.'

"And yet you forbid me to buy cluster-bombs," Clara said to Miles reproachfully when his attention had been drawn to this. She paced viciously. "The courtship rituals of the modern elite. Drawn together by their hatred of great literature Richard and Richardella go home and rut like baboons. [This was before she discovered that Harriet was in fact this significant other.] 'Let's not read Anna Karenina,' Richard shrieks ecstatically. 'Let's never read Dostoyevsky,' Richardella moans cretinously as they claw at each other's backs. Richardella wins Richard's heart by her winsome girlish habit of plucking the unread classics off his shelf and tossing them onto the fire. They build a bonfire of books in the garden and perform a naked bacchanalia in front of it. 'Let's not go to the theatre!' 'Let's never listen to opera!' Gradually they cut out everything apart from internet porn, gangster films, and watching reality TV in an ironic way. They shamble around the house like apes, revelling in their degradation, urinating on the carpet and smearing faeces on the walls. Gurgling moronically Richardella rubs snot on a leather-bound set of Dickens that Richard's grandfather, a former union leader who educated himself at nights and slowly worked his way out of the mines and regretted all his life never having a chance to go to university, left to him on his deathbed. Richard gurgles too and dribbles on her head as he mounts her roughly from behind … I see it quite clearly. And yet this man is allowed to write for a newspaper and I am not. Miles – I am displeased with Comrade Gilquist. I feel a punishment coming on."

It was a relatively simple matter for the Albion TV company to obtain a phone number for Richard from his paper. Two weeks later Miles rang him one evening adopting a generically manic radio-DJ voice and told him he was live on air and had been selected at random to take part in a quiz, and that if he could answer three general knowledge questions he would win £100,000 and two weeks' holiday in Bali.

"Wow," said Richard Gilquist.

The first question was on pop music, the second on television, and Richard answered both with ease.

"Now it gets more difficult," said Miles. "I don't know if you've been listening but this question has been stumping contestants for the past ten days."

"Gosh," said Richard Gilquist. "Fire away."

Looking at Clara listening in on the phone extension, Miles said, "Question number three then, for the hundred thousand pound rollover jackpot and the holiday in Bali. In Tolstoy's War and Peace, with whom does Pierre fight a duel?"

There was a silence. "I have no idea," said Richard Gilquist at length.

"Shame," said Miles. "Well, it's a toughie. I tell you what, I can hear someone else in the background there – would you like to quickly consult – would they have read it?"

"No."

"Oh well, never mind. You got the first two right anyway so we'll enter you into the draw for the second prize of the t-shirt and the CD voucher. Tell me a bit about yourself, Richard, what do you do for a living?" When

Richard said he was a journalist Miles went, "Uh-huh," and asked what kind of things he wrote, and when 'book reviews' at length appeared in Richard's rambling list screeched, "A literary critic! Oh no! And you've never read War and Peace! That's got to be embarrassing! I mean that's one of the biggies, right?"

"Missed the *point*," sighed Clara as soon as she had finished laughing. "Missed the point completely."

She tried to come up with a better punishment but instead just cancelled the papers for a while and pinned a caricature of Richard on their archery board.

(Art: at the exhibition)

"The basic thing with this rubbish," said Miles, "there's no scope for the artist to display skill. I think a precondition for art is the possibility for the artist to – not merely display skill, but to reach a state of grace. You can paint or sculpt out of your skin. You can," he looked around and nodded at an exhibit, "arrange a tray of buttons competently at best. You either chop a fish in half, or arrange bricks in a rectangle, or you don't. The 'idea' is nothing. The idea could be expressed by a writer in a sentence and would usually be utterly banal. The image is of minor importance. What sane people respond to in art, the thing that makes you go 'Fuck', is just the fact of the artist having been in The Zone, the state of grace. The artist surprising himself or God surprising the artist."

" 'The thing that makes you go "Fuck" '?" said Clara staring at him. "Did you get that from Walter Pater?"

"Entirely self-taught. Sorry, darl. Let's try, the feeling of 'How did a human do that?' The shock of newness by itself, if it's even possible now, is a masturbatory substitute for that at best. And temporary, it doesn't last. All Duchamp's urinal has going for it now is empty celebrity. Anything truly random or with too much mechanical element doesn't allow for it. Found art is bullshit. It needs to be the human hand and the human mind channeling something beyond or deep within. You need the opportunity for the artist to lose himself to find himself. The real thing is the product of a skilful man in the throes of the ecstasy of surpassing his skill. That's what electrifies you in great art, that's what lights us up in rapport, that's what makes the hair on the back of the neck stand."

Clara considered for a moment. "That *almost* satisfies me as a definition actually. It rules out all the things I hate but includes in the things I ought to hate but somehow don't; some of the early 20th century abstracts for example. They irritate me but there's occasionally something there. But it lacks something. Theoretically it might be possible for something utterly empty and banal or vile or ugly to be painted with outstanding virtuosity. I demand beauty. I demand something heartfelt. I think I would define great art as that supra-skill, that surpassing of self, wedded to vision. Ideally a vision of beauty and uplift, although of course bleakness can be cathartic. It needs … I won't say spirituality. I was going to say love of life but that rules out some good but unhappy people. Devotion to life, even in suffering? A livingness? Intensity? A *seeingness*. Heartfelt probably covers it, or passion. Ironic detachment kills it anyway. Not merely the artist but the audience must be lifted out of themselves. I think all I can say is that I know it when I see it and that what we see around us is the opposite. These people are collaborators with chaos and meaninglessness and banality. Art is where we prove that our lives aren't empty and meaningless, or failing that hold hands in the dark. An art gallery should be a temple to the human spirit, not a gilded recycling bin."

(Harriet's kitchen)

"My hus – that is my daemon lover Miles and I – wait, sorry, 'my' is wrong too, isn't it? I didn't mean to imply ownership. I mean, a person in his own right who happens to be my – argh! who happens to be a daemon lover in my vicinity – not that I own the vicinity, either – a man who has sex in my bed when I happen to be in it – and I *do* mean to imply that I own the bed – Miles – or would you prefer I say Kilometres? – he and I are very big fans of yours – and I do not say 'yours' to imply that we belong to you body and soul, although we would certainly join a fan club – and by saying 'we' I do not mean to imply that we have fused into some awful indivisible gestalt entity and that Miles has no will of his own – although to be honest – anyway, I and a person who lives in my house – arse, the house in which I also live – we *do* own the house come to think of it, although I do realise property is theft or at best a form of temporary borrowing from Gaia – what the hell was I saying? – a person to whom I do sex who is named Miles – and note that I am carefully *not* assuming that you will or s*hould* assume he is a man – a person of unspecified gender who sometimes inserts his penis – I think I am on safe ground saying 'his', no-one else would want it – wait, the person or persons unknown, to not discriminate against the polyamorous – the person or persons who sometimes inserts one or more penises into my vagina – am I allowed to own my vagina? – or is that too grasping? – the one or more persons one or more of whom may be named Miles who insert one or more penises into a vagina which happens to be located between my, oh dear, a vagina in which I happen to take a certain interest – I am going to drop this now, if it's all the same to you, and start talking like a human – Miles and I are very big fans of your writing. We laugh like hyenas at you sometimes."

(In bed)

Clara's Spitfire swooped down over the EU parliament, bombing and strafing. The modified targeting equipment showed a close-up of a fat bloated Eurocrat in lederhosen directly in her sights ... she depressed the triggers ... he exploded ...

" ... Orwell, in Goldstein's book," Miles was burbling, far away, "the history of the world is, is, the middle people using the bottom people to become the top people ... you've read The Leopard, right? That was a turning-point for me. I mean it's not a political book is it, it's resigned, world-weary, he has the weight of millennia of rising and falling civilisations on him, but the shock was ... "

"Yes," said Clara dreamily. "I expect you are right."

Returning to London she flew low over her cheering people, giving them a victory-roll, low enough to see the bastards and bureaucrats hanging from the lamp-posts.

" ... and these are, you know, Garibaldi's mob! Everybody loves Garibaldi! But they're these vulgar little nothings on the make, and it rang true immediately, I thought I know these bastards, these are the bastards who've assumed control over my life with the same self-aggrandising agenda, and they can deny themselves nothing, if just one of them was able to resist the ... like if you had a ... who was it, was there someone in the French revolution who was just, austere ... like the officer in The Power and the Glory, you know, self-denying, all right that's more worrying in a way but I would just feel less of a … "

"Mm … "

But what was this? A protest march coming over the bridge! Counter-counter-revolutionaries! Frowning, the Lady Protector of England zoomed her targeting system in on their placards. 'GIVE US BACK OUR EQUALITY OFFICERS' they were demanding. 'RESTORE SAFETY COMPLIANCE MANAGERS NOW.' Leading the mob, a familiar figure …

" … and every time that happens there is a reset to zero of these painfully accumulated intangibles of civilisation, you know, duty, nobility, grace … and, and, you know historically the barbarians often assumed the attributes of the over-ripe civilisations they conquered, so you can see it as they're essentially just injecting vigour, it's not so much overthrow of civilisation as *they* are being civilised, but what happens if your revolution is predicated on overturning all the values of your predecessors, so all you really take from them is the perquisites, the … fat living, without the responsibilities … "

"Yes, darling … absolutely … "

She was out of shells and bullets; her lasers were in danger of overheating. She would have to improvise. She threw the plane into a dive, levelled off and aimed at the leader. She hurtled towards the bridge almost at street level. Harriet's eyes widened in the targeting screen. Her face was visible now through the cockpit glass, beyond the whirling propellers … Clara's grin widened … The screen went red, the cockpit glass went red …

"Clara?" He was shaking her. "What were you … what are you thinking about?"

"Oh … something nice … Sorry Miles, I was just daydreaming."

"About what? You have such a … happy smile."

"Oh, it was lovely Miles, I was just remembering this rabbit I used to have … a lovely, lovely rabbit … "

"You … you said, 'Take that, Harriet.' "

"No, no, 'Take that carrot.' I was giving him a carrot … a lovely, lovely carrot … "

(Children: at the party)

"Uncle Miles!" cried Struan excitedly. "Listen. According to John Stuart Mill, the spirit of improvement is not always a spirit of liberty, for it may aim at forcing improvements on an unwilling people. The spirit of liberty in resisting such attempts may ally itself with the opponents of improvement. But the only unfailing and permanent source of improvement is liberty."

"Great," said Miles, looking around for another drink.

Struan took a breath and continued, "Furthermore the thing that preserved the European nations from Oriental stagnation and despotism was not any superior excellence in them which, when it exists, is an effect not a cause, but," he paused and protruded his tongue a moment, "their remarkable diversity of character and culture. Individuals, classes and nations were historically very unlike one another and struck out on a variety of paths, each leading to something valuable." He gasped again. "He says that William von Humboldt identified two things as necessary conditions of human development: freedom, and variety of situations. Aunty Clara said you would give me some more money."

Miles gave him some more money.

Gestation: 2000-2010 Birth: Feb-Apr 2010 Wandering homeless: 2010-2015

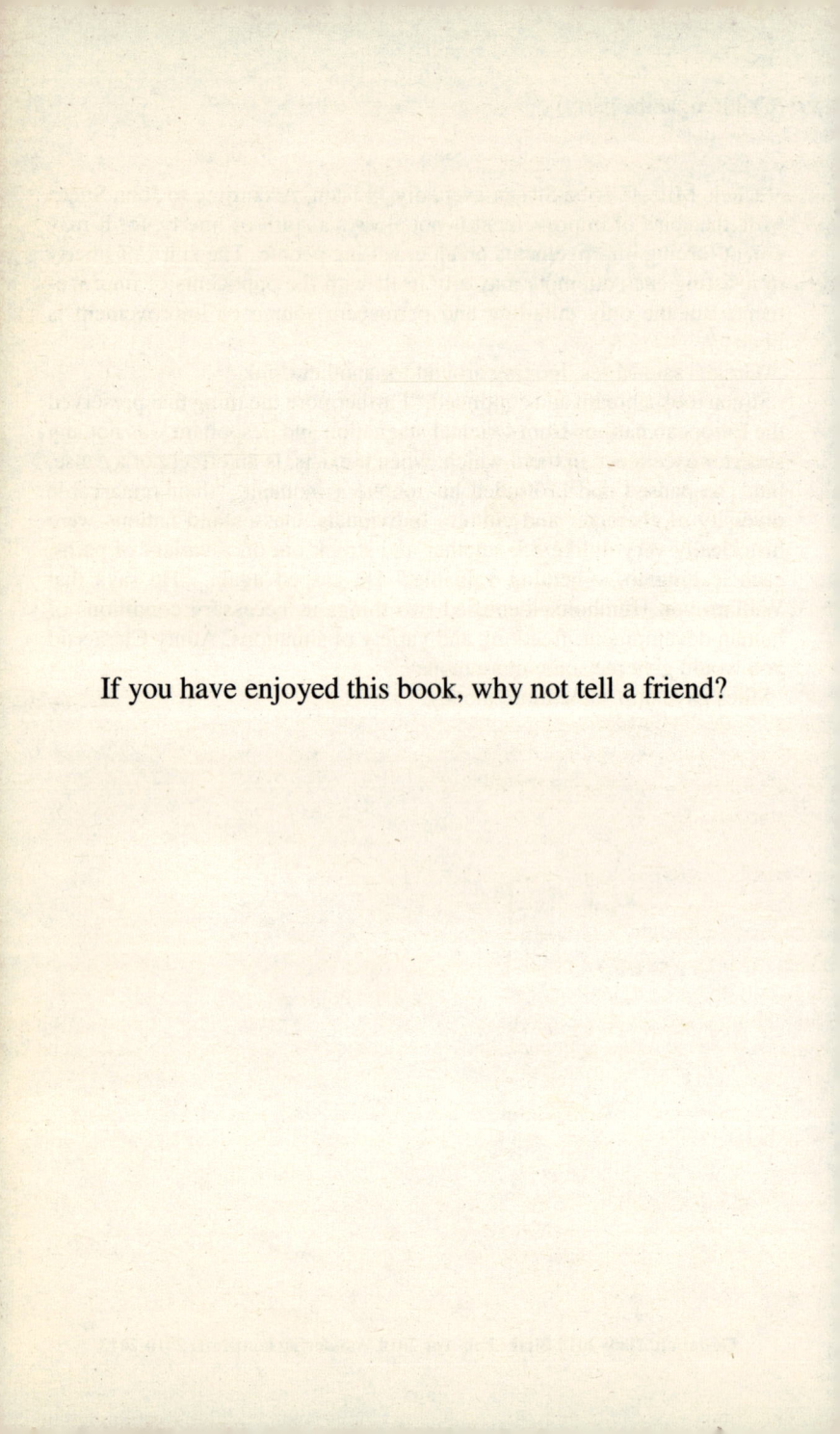

If you have enjoyed this book, why not tell a friend?